"Here, it's easy to imagine getting caught up in the lure of the apples whose red skin is so dark they're almost black. After taking one bite of this scary book, readers will want more."
—*Booklist*

"[It's] safe to say there's something for everyone here, from the creepy *Eyes Wide Shut* vibe (complete with sacrificial rituals) to the Stephen King–laced dichotomy between the world's everyday cruelty and the truly grotesque carnage that follows. . . . Both complex and compelling, [*Black River Orchard* is] a nightmare-inducing parable about our own wickedness."
—*Kirkus Reviews*

"With this book, Wendig has told a distinctly American story about what it means to live in this place, built on blood and wounds and theft and a million other sins, all somehow encapsulated by that fruit of Biblical sin, the apple. It's one of the year's most rewarding horror books, and like the fruits at the core of its story, will have you craving every turn of the page."
—*Paste*

"Wendig is brilliant at slowly raising the plot's emotional temperature and making his characters, caught in a creeping nightmare, feel both real and empathetic. This masterful outing should continue to earn Wendig comparisons to Stephen King."
—*Publishers Weekly* (starred review)

"Wendig's ensemble cast and rich atmosphere of collective decay bring to life a book that makes your skin crawl. Creepy and insidious to the core, *Black River Orchard* whets your appetite and then turns you inside-out."
—HAILEY PIPER,
Bram Stoker Award–winning author of *Queen of Teeth*

"There's a soul-unraveling blight leeching across the pages of Chuck Wendig's *Black River Orchard,* an irresistible kind of charming decay that traps the reader in this eerie orchard and renders them completely spellbound. This will undoubtedly be heralded as one of the finest horror novels of the twenty-first century."
—ERIC LaROCCA,
author of *Things Have Gotten Worse Since We Last Spoke*

"Myth and magic, history and folklore, trauma and temptation, it's all tangled together here and watered deeply with blood. Wendig has pulled off a fresh and unexpected horror feat, expertly drawing from the ancient, endless wells of our greatest fears: What if we could be better than we are? What if we're just not trying hard enough? What if we were surrounded by like-minded people who had found the secret, and how could we resist joining them? What price does community ask us to pay, and when is it worth it? Questions we've been asking since the dawn of humanity, exposed here in unflinching detail, right down to the bone."
—PREMEE MOHAMED,
Nebula Award–winning author of *Beneath the Rising*

"A gripping story of love and legacies gone rotten, deeply rooted in the landscape and as twisty and gnarled as an ancient apple tree . . . Be careful what you wish for: I devoured it down to the core."
—T. KINGFISHER,
USA Today bestselling author of *What Moves the Dead*

"Chuck Wendig is one of my very favorite storytellers. His stories are so rich and vivid and layered they seem to live and breathe, they have teeth and they might bite. *Black River Orchard* is a deep, dark, luscious tale that creeps up on you and doesn't let go. Sharp and crisp and juicy like the most obvious of fruit metaphors . . . This is folklore for the modern age, visceral and familiar in ways that make it all the more terrifying."
—ERIN MORGENSTERN,
New York Times bestselling author of *The Starless Sea*

"I'm in awe of Chuck Wendig, a gifted storyteller with a seemingly boundless imagination. His new book, *Black River Orchard,* should come with a warning label: You'll never bite into another apple without remembering this dark, demented, and genuinely frightening novel."
—JASON REKULAK,
author of *Hidden Pictures*

"Enchanting, exquisite, and dark, Chuck Wendig masterfully weaves a new horrifying fairy tale in *Black River Orchard*."
—CYNTHIA PELAYO,
Bram Stoker Award–winning author of *Crime Scene*

"Essential for horror readers, and buy it for new horror readers—it will convert them instantly. . . . A well-written, compelling read."
—V. CASTRO,
author of *The Haunting of Alejandra*

"An epic saga that is at once propulsive horror novel and parable, thriller and cautionary tale, *Black River Orchard* is the immensely talented Chuck Wendig at his finest. Like the dark, red apples at the heart of this beautifully told, character rich, and utterly engrossing story, you'll take one bite and won't be able to stop yourself from devouring the rest."
—LISA UNGER,
New York Times bestselling author of *Secluded Cabin Sleeps Six*

"The horror of *Black River Orchard* is the existence of an insidious, dormant catalyst for evil that exists inside of us. All that has to happen is for humankind to discover that one thing that will universally divide us all. Wendig's wheelhouse is knowing exactly how to pluck heartstrings and prey on fears at the same time. High-stakes horror meets peak emotional investment means Total. Reader. Devastation."
—SADIE HARTMANN,
author of *101 Horror Books to Read Before You're Murdered*

"Dark. Visceral. Creepy. Smart. Deep. So red it's dark brown. Chuck Wendig's *Black River Orchard* slithers and shines, its dangerous belly full of dark magic and accusations. I've been a fan of Wendig for years, and this is his best novel yet. This is a book pulled from the Devil's own plague-sick armpits, and you'll want to devour all of it after taking the first bite."
—GABINO IGLESIAS,
Bram Stoker Award—winning author of *The Devil Takes You Home*

BLACK RIVER
ORCHARD

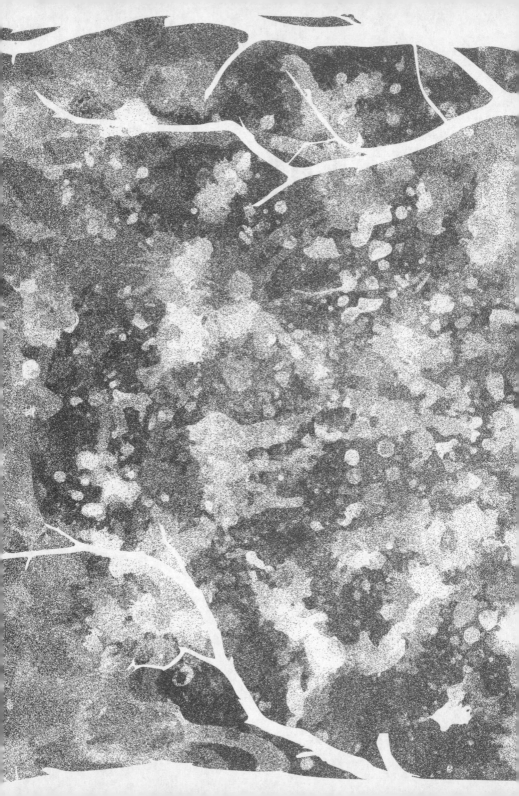

BLACK RIVER ORCHARD

A NOVEL

—

CHUCK WENDIG

NEW YORK

2024 Del Rey Trade Paperback Edition

Published in the United States by Del Rey, an imprint of Random House,
a division of Penguin Random House LLC, New York.

DEL REY and the CIRCLE colophon are registered trademarks of
Penguin Random House LLC.

Lyric excerpt from "Revelations" by Margo Price
reprinted by permission from Jeremy Ivey.

Originally published in hardcover in the United States by Del Rey,
an imprint of Random House, a division of
Penguin Random House LLC, in 2023.

Library of Congress Cataloging-in-Publication Data
Names: Wendig, Chuck, author.
Title: Black river orchard: a novel / Chuck Wendig.
Description: New York: Del Rey, 2023.
Identifiers: LCCN 2023034767 (print) | LCCN 2023034768 (ebook) |
ISBN 9780593158760 (paperback; acid-free paper) |
ISBN 9780593158753 (ebook)
Subjects: LCGFT: Horror fiction. | Novels.
Classification: LCC PS3623.E534 B56 2023 (print) |
LCC PS3623.E534 (ebook) | DDC 813/.6—dc23/eng/20230818
LC record available at https://lccn.loc.gov/2023034767
LC ebook record available at https://lccn.loc.gov/2023034768

Printed in the United States of America on acid-free paper

randomhousebooks.com

2 4 6 8 9 7 5 3 1

Book design by Edwin A. Vazquez

Chapter-opener art: © Charlie Milsom, stock.adobe.com (paint),
© rufous, stock.adobe.com (tree silhouette)

To Lisa and Ike,
apple magicians and North Stars each

STAND FAST ROOT, BEAR WELL TOP
PRAY THE GOD SEND US A HOWLING GOOD CROP.
EVERY TWIG, APPLES BIG.
EVERY BOUGH, APPLES NOW.

—APPLE WASSAIL SONG,
NINETEENTH CENTURY,
SUSSEX

CONTENTS

BLACK RIVER
ORCHARD

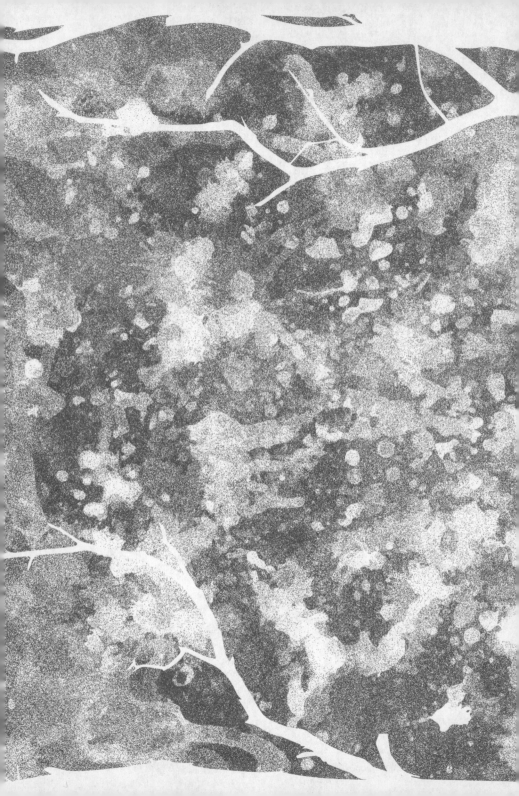

—

THE ORCHARD-KEEPER'S TALE

CALLA PAXSON, AGE TWELVE, LURCHED UPRIGHT IN HER BED, HER heart pounding as if the nightmare she'd been having was still chasing her. She tried to chase the nightmare down in turn—but the ill dream fled from her, leaving only the raw, skinless feeling of its passing.

As the dream darted into darkness, a new certainty arose:

Someone is in the house.

It was just a feeling—an intrusion, as if the air had been disrupted, stirred about. *It's just the bad dream,* she thought. Dreams seemed to stay with you, the way the smell of her friend Esther's cigarettes hung in their hair, their clothes. (Technically, they were Esther's mother's cigarettes. Esther was thirteen and assured Calla, "I'm a teenager, and teenagers are allowed to smoke," adding hastily, "but *don't* tell my mom, because she'll fucking *assassinate* me.")

Calla rubbed her eyes, looked at the digital clock next to her bed: 3:13 A.M.

Her heart was pounding now and she failed to calm it. She grumbled and flopped back onto the pillow, knowing now that falling back asleep would be hard.

But then, downstairs—

A faint *whump*.

She sat up again. Heart spurred to a new beat.

No longer just a feeling, now it was a reality:

Someone was in the house.

They didn't have a dog.

Her father would be asleep.

So, what was that noise, then?

The fridge icemaker made a racket sometimes. Or the heater. The pipes in the radiators knocked and banged—it was March, after all, the days warming, the nights still cold. Still. She knew the icemaker, the heater, the sounds of the old farmhouse settling.

This wasn't that.

Get Dad.

Barefoot, in loose flannel pants and a pink Alessia Cara Band-Aid shirt, Calla darted to the door of her bedroom and eased it open a crack. Another bump-and-thump from downstairs. A door closing? Her throat tightened with fear.

She hurried down the hall to her father's bedroom—she opened the door to his room quick, the old hinges complaining (*shut up shut up shut up*), and ran to the bed and shook her father—

"*Dad,*" she hissed. "*Dad!*"

But her hand collapsed to the bed. He wasn't there. Just his wadded-up comforter tangled around a pillow.

Another sound downstairs. This time, she was sure it was the front door opening and closing. Calla hurried down the hallway on the balls of her feet, looking down the staircase—

And there stood her father, the front door closed behind him. Cold air rushed the steps, raising gooseflesh on the girl's bare arms. He was wearing his barn jacket; he'd been outside. His hair was a tousle. Sweat slicked his brow despite the cold. In his long arms, he held a bundle, swaddled in an old set of bedsheets. Something dark and crooked poked out the one end. Calla released her breath in an exasperated sigh.

"*Dad,*" she said, irritated. "You scared the crap out of me."

He startled a little upon seeing her. His arms full, he leaned his head toward his body, using his shoulder to push his eyeglasses farther up the bridge of his bookish nose. "Calla, hey. Gosh, I'm sorry, I didn't mean to wake you. You can go back to bed, sweetie, everything's fine."

But Calla was nothing if not curious (read: nosy). Her feet carried her down the steps, buoyed by a child's salacious desire to poke into her parent's private business.

"What are you doing?" she asked, eyebrows up, mouth down.

Her father—Dan—looked left and right, the furtive glance of some-one who was afraid he was about to get caught, but then grinned a big goofball grin. "What am I doing? Securing our future, Calla Lily. That's what I'm doing." He licked the corners of his mouth and hurried past her, toward the kitchen. He put the bundle on their secondhand country nook table, a table already piled with stuff like bills (past-due), a rusted toolbox, some kitchen implements, a can of dirt (if only Calla could one day find a boyfriend who loved her as much as Dad loved *dirt*). Every flat surface in their house became a shelf, he always said with some exasperation, as if it wasn't him that was making it that way.

"Our future," Calla said, bleary. She looked at the bedsheets. "It's just a bundle of sticks." And it was. Sticks like the fireblack fingers of a charred skeleton.

"Not sticks," he said. "Branches. From a tree." He sniffed, still half panting with excitement. "You know what, I need a drink. A celebration drink. Preemptive," he muttered mostly to himself, "but I think deserved."

From the cabinet he pulled a bottle of something brown. Whiskey. (Calla admitted to having tried a sip about six months ago. It tasted like someone poured campfire ash down her throat. Why did adults drink that stuff? Did they hate themselves? She assumed that they did and she promised herself she'd never hate herself, not now, not ever.) As he uncorked the bottle and splashed it into a coffee mug, Calla sidled over toward the bundle of sticks. She peeled back the sheets, revealing dozens of black sticks bound together with strips of yellow cloth. (The cloth dotted with, what, red mud?)

Dad watched her from the other side of the counter. "It's scionwood. For grafting." As if she understood what that meant. These were just sticks. Why collect sticks? Sticks were, like, nature's garbage. It was one of her chores here at the new (old) house: to go around the yard, picking up sticks. Then Dad burned them. (And, she assumed, made that nasty whiskey from the remnants, ugh.)

"Okayyyyy," she said, because, whatever. Dad had gone out at three in the morning to get . . . sticks? Was he having a break with reality? A stroke? She peeled back the other side of the bedsheet, and something tumbled out—a little something, soft and bloodless pink, and it bounced off her foot and—

She cried out.

It was a finger.

A severed human finger.

She backpedaled away, still feeling the way it felt—moist, cold, mushy but also somehow stiff—on the top of her bare foot—

Dad was already scooping it up, laughing nervously.

"Your *finger*," she said, alarmed, looking at his hand. But he *had* all his fingers. Which meant—

That finger belonged to someone else.

"What about my fingers, sweetie?" he asked.

"You—you're not missing—that was a finger—" Her gaze crawled around his hands, looking for the finger he'd snatched off the ground.

But instead, he turned his hand toward her and opened it up.

She winced, not wanting to see.

"Calla, look. It's not—it's not a finger." He laughed, almost dismissively. Like, *What a stupid little kid.* "You must be tired."

Peeking through squinted lids, she saw that he was right. It wasn't a finger at all. It was a thin apple core from an eaten apple. Black seeds exposed like fat carpenter ants. Skin so red it was almost black.

"That's—that's an apple."

"Sure is," he said, fire dancing in his eyes. "That's the point of all of this."

"Uh, okay. I still don't get it, Dad." She still felt like she was reeling. She was sure she'd seen a finger. But maybe her mind was just playing tricks on her. That bad dream again, poisoning her thoughts like a dead animal in a well.

"I'm saying this scionwood, it's going to help us make an orchard. Like your grandfather wanted to do so long ago. But couldn't. It all starts here. The future is this." He held up the apple core, turning it around in his fingers. "*Everything* starts with this apple."

PROLOGUE THE SECOND

—

THE GOLDEN MAN'S TALE

1901, The Goldenrod Estate, Bucks County, Pennsylvania.

Henry Hart Golden—anthropologist, archaeologist, student of law, craftsman, collector, chef, explorer, and folklorist—stood in front of a wall of his own tilework design. These red clay tiles were glazed with wild colors, each emblazoned with unique and strange iconography, and it was in this place he stood, arms spread wide, in front of those who had gathered there in their handcrafted masks, to speak of the country they called home:

"Friends of the Goldenrod Society, you know that I have been all around the world. I have explored the cenotes of the Yucatán. I've found the cloth-swaddled dead in mountain caves. I've been to Egypt and Nepal, I've dug earth with Chinamen—and had some of those same Chinamen try to bury me with what we found there." At that, they laughed. "But it is here at home where I find my interest sharpened. And it is to our great nation that I turn my attention to ask: What is it that makes us so special? Now, my friends, I know what you're thinking: Henry, the story of America is the story of its people—or, Henry, the story of America is in what we make and what we made, what we produce, what we craft and construct and conjure. Or, some would say, no, no, America is about the *work*. America is in the *toil*. It is in the very act of building rather than in what we build or who builds it. But I am here to tell you, no, the story of America is in our tools."

Henry whipped off the cloth to reveal tools—not modern tools, no, but not ancient tools, either. Tools from fifty years past, a hundred, at most two centuries. Each numbered like an archaeological artifact. Whale oil lamps, astragal planes, flax hatchels, tin funnels, and the like. And in the center: a wrought-iron apple peeler with a wood base.

Those gathered gasped behind their masks—masks that were themselves amalgams of ceramic, cork, tin, and leather. He enjoyed their stupefaction, though to be fair they always gasped when Golden acted with flourish. They would eat dung out of his cupped hands if he asked them to—and grin as they did it.

With their attention fully seized, he continued:

"The tool is an expression of the maker—the choice of tool is the hallmark of a civilization. And the tools of America are humble, simple things. They are not the electric motor, the soot-belching machine. They are these tools you see before you: tools of iron and wood and tin. It is the hand, yes, but also the tool the hand holds, that shows who we are. Individually, oh, we are represented by our craft, by our art, by the meals we cook and the clothes we make. But as a society? As a *nation*? Our soul is expressed in the choice of our tools. And our tools must continue to be plain and unpretentious—but beautiful, too. Resilient and resistant to obsolescence. And they must do as we command."

They, of course, applauded. He went on a bit longer after that, showing off some of the tools and their craftsmanship—but soon, his desires rose up in him like a dragon (as they always did) and that dragon would not be denied its gold (as it never was). He wound down his speech and went out among them, his people. They wanted to touch him—a passing brush of their knuckles upon his cheek, a hand softly pressing into the small of his back, a quick breath in his ear. He had collected these people as easily as he had collected the tools on the table behind him. They were his society in the truest sense of the word: They, in their masks, surrendered so much of their time to him. And in return, they joined together, made themselves better, made themselves *richer*.

It was of course someone else he had his eye on, someone he spied in the crowd during his speech: a new girl, likely one brought here by a society friend. She did not belong, though perhaps her family did, for she was likely the scion of some powerful local bloodline. (Many of those present were.)

Her mask was a humble one, hastily made: a papier-mâché rabbit face, its ears bent forward, likely an error in the making but one that gave the prey's countenance a sense of active, alarmed listening.

Henry could feel his desire tighten within him like a hangman's rope, so he went right to her and asked the young woman if she'd like to see his private collection. She blushed and giggled and said yes, yes, of course, yes. A thousand times yes. Maybe too eager, but that was good.

Eager was ideal.

THE TWO OF THEM WENT TO HIS CHAMBER IN THE GOLDENROD— high upstairs in the tower, though to him the chamber also felt subterranean. No windows to see in. Tile floors of his own design with grooves between them, gently sloping to the center. A dumbwaiter, too, that went all the way down to the kitchens below. His house had no staff. Henry would cook a meal with tools he brought with him from long ago, and then he'd draw it up the dumbwaiter to his room.

Now, though, the dumbwaiter was open and on the pewter tray within waited a single apple.

It was the perfect specimen. Red-black, gleaming, beautiful. Ready to be skinned and eaten. The seeds bitten and spit. The young woman, whatever her name was, went to it first, captivated by it, as was expected. It *was* rather hypnotizing. She reached for it but did not touch it, likely unsure she even *should* be touching it. He felt the frisson of excitement and fear climb through her; he could almost hear her wondering if she was simply too crass a creature, too foul a thing, to touch that apple. As if her own grotesque fingers, covered as they were in the filth of the world, might bring swift and inescapable rot to that perfect void of appleskin.

Appleskin, he thought. Yes. It was time. He eased toward her at an angle, passing by an old marble-top bureau with a small garden of plants upon it—he kept this room hot, good for the violets, the slipper orchids, the mother-in-law tongue—and as he ran his hands along their leaves, his fingers danced onto something just past the pots: a mask of his own making. He pulled it taut over his head and face. He smelled the esters of rose and elderflower. The tart tang of the fruit. His breath hissed through the mouth slit.

Henry pressed himself up against the young woman from behind, urgent and needy, smelling her hair, though through the appleskin mask, all he could truly detect was the scent of the fruit itself. Which suited him fine.

He whispered in her ear, "Do you like what you see?"

And she gasped, because here she was, trapped between two beautiful things. Caught between the Scylla of Golden, the Charybdis of the apple, his whisper still crawling around in her ear. And when she nodded, still transfixed by the fruit, he reached for something nearby, sitting on the corner of a wooden ice chest: an orchard pruning hook. Good for getting apples off their branches. Among other things.

0

THE APPLE

THIS IS THE APPLE IN YOUR HAND.

Some would say it is so red that it looks black, but that's not *quite* right. It's the color of wine and offal, of liver soaked in Pinot Noir. Bruise-dark and blood-bright.

The skin shows little russeting, if any. But it is home to a peppering of lenticels—the little white dots you sometimes see on appleskin. These lenticels feel somehow deeper than the skin itself. As if you are staring into a thing that is nothing as much as it is something: an object of depth, of breadth, like a hole in the universe. In this way the lenticels are like the stars of a moonless evening.

The skin is smooth and cold, always cold. It is a round apple, not oblong, not tall, but also not squat. The Platonic ideal of an apple shape, perhaps: roughly symmetrical, broad in the shoulders, narrow toward the calyx. The apple is heavy, too. Dense-feeling. Heavy enough to crack a window. Or break a nose.

Even before you bite it, a scent rises to meet you. It's the smell of roses—not unusual, because apples are related to the rose. Same family, in fact: Rosaceae.

What *is* unusual is the moment, a moment so fast you will disregard it, when the smell makes you feel something in the space between your heart and your stomach: a feeling of giddiness and loss in equal measure. In that feeling is the dying of summer, the rise of fall, the coming of winter, and threaded throughout, a season of funerals and flowers left on a grave. But again, that moment is so fast, you cannot hold on to it. It is gone, like a dream upon waking.

Of course, what matters most is the eating.

In the first bite, the skin pops under your teeth—the same pop you'd feel biting into a tightly skinned sausage. The flesh has a hard texture, and if you were to cut a slice you'd find it would not bend, but rather, it would break like a chip of slate snapping in half. That snap is a satisfying sensation: a tiny tectonic reverberation felt all the way to the elbow.

In the chew, the apple is crisp, resistant to its destruction, with a crunch so pleasurable it lights up some long-hidden atavistic artifact in your brain, a part that eons ago took great joy from crushing small bones between your teeth. The flesh is juicy; it floods the mouth, refusing to be dammed by teeth or lips, inevitably dripping from your chin. But for all its juiciness, too, the tannins are high—and the apple feels like it's wicking the moisture out of your mouth, as if it's taking something from you even as you take from it.

The taste itself is a near-perfect balance of tartness and sweetness— that sour, tongue-scrubbing feel of a pineapple, but one that has first been run through a trench of warm honey. The skin, on the other hand, is quite bitter, but there's something to that, too. The way it competes with the tart and the sweet. The way the most popular perfumes are ones that contain unpleasant, foul odors secreted away: aromatics of rot, bile, rancid fat, bestial musk, an ancient, compelling foulness from the faraway time when crunching those little bones made us so very happy. And so very powerful.

The bitterness of the skin is a necessary acrimony: a reminder that nothing good can last, that things die, that the light we make leaves us all eventually. That the light leaves the world. A hole in the universe. So we must shine as brightly as we can, while we can.

It speaks to you, this bitterness, this foulness.

It speaks to some part of you that likes it.

Because part of you does like it.

Doesn't it?

SEPTEMBER

—

WHAT MAKES APPLES SO INTERESTING IS THAT LIKE HUMAN BEINGS, THEY ARE INDIVIDUALS, AND THEIR HISTORY HAS PARALLELED OUR HISTORY.

—HELEN HUMPHREYS,
THE GHOST ORCHARD

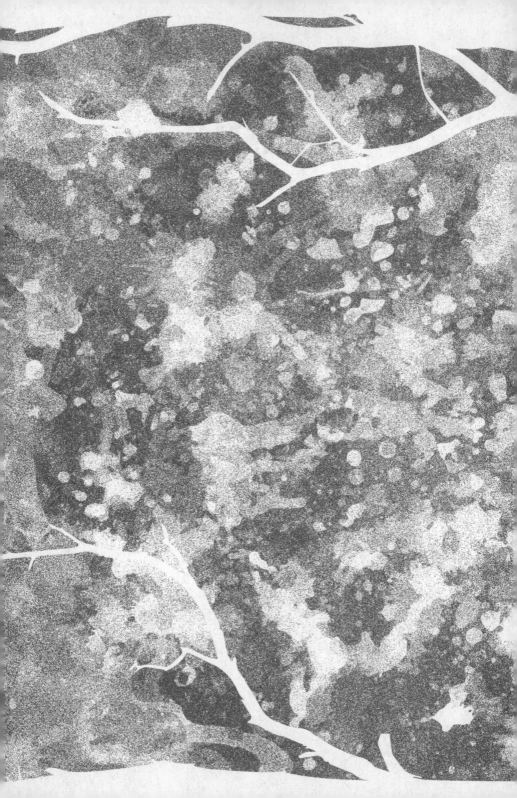

1

NOMENCLATURE

CALLA PAXSON, NOW AGE SEVENTEEN, STOOD IN THE MIDDLE OF their gravel driveway, nose down in her phone, trying very, very hard not to be distracted by her father, Dan, as he hurried back and forth from the shed to the pickup to the house and back again. Every time he went past, he had a new question for her—

"Is Marco coming?"

"Yes, Dad, Marco is coming, Jesus."

Back and forth.

"What time is it again?"

"It's nine A.M., Dad," and as he went past, she added loudly, "aka *entirely too early*, okay?"

Back and forth.

"Did Marco say he'd be here at nine?"

"Yes? No? I dunno, I'm not his boss, you are."

Back and forth.

"You know, you could help me? Carry these *oof* boxes?"

"That's not really—like, not my thing."

He eased the wooden crate of apples into the back of the pickup, but Calla wasn't paying attention. She held her phone up, blocking the view of him. With the camera reversed, she checked herself in the screen— saw a thousand tiny flaws but steeled herself against caring about them. (Eyebrows too thin, ugh, mouth too wide, *ugh,* left eye with that odd golden fleck hiding in the green, a green that wasn't a pretty emerald but a muddy hazel the color of algal muck, *uggggh.*) She chided herself for feeling that way. *Be better, say something nice about yourself,* and she told herself today was a damn good hair day thanks to the humid September weather. She was all golden locks with the center part, framing her face with long layers, but the negative thoughts kept nagging her from the back of her mind. Calla shook the bad thoughts out of her head and (since Insta was over) checked her follower count on Faddish, then (since TikTok was almost over) checked her followers on Appy, then on Nextra, and of course also on Insta and TikTok because *obviously*. The classics were the classics for a reason. Her follower counts hadn't budged since this morning. Or since last night. Or the night before.

Gently, a hand reached out and eased the phone aside.

The same hand, her father's hand, lifted her chin.

Her father stood there in front of her.

"It's not your thing," he repeated.

"What?"

"That's what you just said. 'That's not really, like, my thing.'"

"Oh *god* you're about to give me a lecture, aren't you?" She sighed. "I just mean I don't know that I can move those boxes. They're heavy. I already tried to clean myself up this morning and I don't want to look like some *farm girl*—"

"No lecture. I promise, Calla Lily. You're right. *This* is your thing." He did a faux-game-show gesture toward her phone.

"I feel like you're being sarcastic right now."

"No sarcasm! I'm saying you wanna be a—what's it called? An affluent—"

"Influencer. Jesus, Dad."

"An *influencer*." He smiled. He was fucking with her, wasn't he? Was he fucking with her or was he just this goofy? "Right. So I need your influence."

She winced. "What?"

He did this awkward moonwalk toward the truck, and then did an even-cringier spin, snatching up one of the apples from the crate resting on the pickup truck's open gate. Dance-walking his way back, he thrust the apple at her.

"I told you I'm not eating one, apples are gross," she said.

Dan Paxson put his hand over his chest and feigned injury. "You hurt me. You know that, right? My own daughter *still* won't try my apple. My pride and joy insults my other pride and joy. It's like my children are fighting. Sibling rivalry."

"So dramatic."

"I don't need you to try the apple, but the apple needs your . . . influence. You know what I mean?"

She confessed: "I don't."

Her father sighed.

"Look, this is our first day at market. It's not just tables and produce anymore. You're right, it's not enough to be the farmer anymore. People go there to sell their . . . fancy puddings and their honeycombs, it's all pasture-raised beef and duck eggs. It's produce you've never heard of like *mizuna* and *kabocha* and *micro-cilantro*. And though I know this apple is beautiful with a taste that's—" The words seemed to catch in his mouth. Was he getting emotional? He probably was, the big dork. (She loved her father's profound dorkiness. He was such a nerd because he cared so much about this stuff. She wouldn't admit any of this, not for a million followers on social. *Maybe* for two million.) "I need help selling it."

"That's not what I do." *Or what I want to do.*

"But you do. I see how much you put into your videos. You want people to . . . love the things that you love, and I love that about you. Maybe you could sprinkle a little of that pizzazz on this apple? Though I think there's an actual apple named Pazazz, come to think of it." He shrugged. "I'm just saying, you're my little branding genius, you have these explosive, firecracker thoughts, and I think this apple is really something special. Like you. But nobody will know if they don't try it. I need your magic, Calla Lily. I need your *sparkle*."

She rolled her eyes (trying to hide that, ugh, it felt *nice* when he said nice things about her). "*Fine,* I'll give a glow up to your *dire* little fruit." And it was dire. Pretty, maybe. Gothy, definitely. In the sun, it was a rich, black-blooded red.

But she couldn't say any of that. Gothy, black, red. It wasn't a Hot Topic apple. It did need something. "Does it have a name already?"

He hesitated. Acting a little cagey.

"I gave it a name. It—" He flinched. "Didn't have one before."

"Okay, fine, what did you name it?"

Her father shrugged, like, *Oh, no big deal, don't mind me.* "I'm calling it the Paxson apple. After us. Our family. Our home."

"Really. The Paxson."

"Yeah. Why? Apples are—you know, the heirlooms, anyway, they're named after the people who grew them. Baldwin, Ortley, or, uhh, Esopus Spitzenburg."

Calla made a face like she'd just licked a moth. "*No*. You can't—you can't use those as your comps. Those sound like Old People apples. Esopus? We're not Amish, Dad, god. No, you, like, go to the grocery store and the apples there have fun names, right? Honeycrisp, Pink Ladies, ummm—"

"SweeTango! Oh, Cosmic Crisp, too."

"Yeah, okay, yeah. Whatever. So, you can't call it the Paxson. You just can't." She made a disappointed face. "Promise me you won't. It's mid. It hurts me on the inside. Please promise. Please."

"Our name matters, Calla," he said, stiffening. She'd hurt him. But then his face softened and he leaned forward to take a big, sharp bite of the apple. His eyes closed and he breathed through his nose as he chewed. For a moment he seemed lost. He moaned around it. (*Gross.*) Finally he said: "You're right. It's too good for a boring name. So you're up, Little Miss Influencer. Influence me. Name this apple."

Calla scrunched up her nose, plowing little furrows in her brow as she grabbed his wrist and moved it this way and that, pivoting the apple in her view. (She wasn't going to touch the apple because it was drooling juice from its bite wound.) "Dark, red, pretty. Like I'm staring into something deep—" It almost pulled her gaze to it, even *into* it. As if she were staring into the hall-of-mirrors aspect of a gemstone's facets. *That's it.* "It's like a ruby. You wanted to name it after us?" At the end of the gravel drive, she saw the old sign that hung there, a wooden sign with their name carved into it. A name signaling their house. Their home. *That's it,* she thought. "There's no place like home."

"What?" he asked.

"Ruby Slipper." She paused. "There's no place like home. Ruby Slipper. It's like from that movie. The one with the scarecrow."

Aaaaand her father hated it. She could tell immediately. He seemed struck by it, like the name was a bad taste wiping away the flavor of the apple in his mouth, like her suggestion had ruined the entire experience for him. She instantly felt humiliated for screwing up—he could run hot and cold sometimes when she displeased him. Like she was embarrassing him somehow.

She stammered, "I mean, whatever, I don't care, use the name or don't, that's what I came up with." And she put up her phone again, placing the screen between her face and him, a shield, a wall, a world away.

"It's perfect," he said, quietly.

She lowered the phone. "What?"

He had tears in his eyes. "It's absolutely perfect, Calla Lily. My gosh. You really have a gift. Your mother would've been so proud of you." Normally, she hated when he said that. Calla had barely met her mother. The woman died when she was five—an aggressive blood cancer took her from the world. So it always felt like a sour off-note to suggest somehow this woman that Calla didn't really know would have some grand opinion of her. But suddenly, now, it hit different. She had to blink back her own tears.

"Cool," she said, trying to pretend this wasn't the best thing ever. But she gave a smile. For him, of course. Not for her. Not because she *meant* it or anything, she told herself.

"What's cool?" came a voice from the end of the driveway.

"Hey, M&M," she said, spinning on her heel to greet her boyfriend walking his bike down the driveway. M&M. Her nickname for him sometimes. Marco Meza. MM. He was long and lean, like a series of taut ropes rigging a boat, his joints like cinched knots. He could run like nobody's business—it's why he was the best of their track team. Sprinter. Destined for a scholarship.

(And he needed it. As did she. But Dad was *sure* this orchard was going to take off and help pay for school . . .)

"Mister Meza!" her father said, "Not right on time, but just in time."

"Sorry, Mister P," Marco said, dropping the bike's kickstand. "Thought I was going to get the car today but my sister has to drive down toward Philly to pick up the Inca Kolas and—"

Dad clapped his hands. "It's all right, Mister Meza, I'm just messing with you. It's something my father used to say about me. *Not right on time, but just in time.* I was always showing up right under the wire, you know?" Dad picked up another apple, turned it over in his hand. "How's the family? The restaurant?"

"Good, good, Dad says hi."

"Here, tell him to put this on the menu—"

And at that, Dad slapped the inside of his forearm to launch a fresh, red apple (a *Ruby Slipper*) toward Marco—who caught it handily out of the air with a downward swipe. He looked down at it with practiced awe. *He's so fucking hot,* Calla thought. "Apples aren't really a big thing in Peruvian cuisine, Mister P, but uhhh, is this—is it what I think it is? Is this *the* apple?"

Dad spread his arms wide. "Finally unveiling it."

"Do I—? Can I—?"

"Have a bite? It's time. You're one of the first people to try this apple, Marco." At that, Dad shot her a glance that was a caricature of guilt. "This one over here doesn't *like* apples, but I know I can trust you to give me the real-deal review, right? Go on."

Marco looked at her with a smile and she shrugged with a dismissive laugh. "Just be glad he likes you," she said. Under her breath, Calla muttered, "I think he likes you more than he likes me."

"All right, let's give this a go," Marco said, polishing the apple with his shirt, eyeballing it. Marco gave her one last cheeky look and then opened wide, taking a big, loud bite. *Cronch.* He chewed a few times—

That's when he stopped.

The smile fell away. His face went almost blank, like he was staring past her father, past the driveway, into someplace beyond. Like a memory. Then his eyes went wide and he held the apple close, staring at it as he resumed chewing. Juice dripped from his chin and he didn't even wipe it off.

"Well?" Dad asked.

Marco laughed around a mouthful of apple. This wasn't a show. She could tell that much. "This is the best apple I've ever eaten," he said. Then he greedily devoured the rest of it right there, without pause. Like he was *starving.*

"Okay, don't eat the seeds, weirdo, god," Calla said, walking over and snatching it out of his hand before he did exactly that.

Dad whooped with success. "I got a good feeling about today. A *real* good feeling."

2

NO PLACE LIKE HOME

THEY HAD A DOCK NOW, AND EMILY BERGMANN STOOD AT THE END of it, staring at the dark water of the Delaware River.

The river wanted to drown her.

All rivers did, but this one felt keenly hungry, to her.

Her heart raced.

Emily's wife, Meg Price, must've sensed Emily's agitation. She came up alongside Emily and watched her, curiously, carefully. Meg was Scandinavian in design and attitude. A true silver fox: sharp, silverware hair. All of her drawn with a confident, steady hand. Nothing ever out of place; even her chaos was meticulously arranged. Emily, Korean on her mother's side, German on her father's, was—well, depending on when you asked, either a complement to Meg, or her opposite. She wore dark clothes often (aka always): presently, a black Yeah Yeah Yeahs T-shirt and yoga pants the color of a coming thunderstorm. Her hair, black as her mother's, but with errant curls—those, a gift from her father. Emily appeared nervous, ever-worried. Where Meg stood still, Emily fidgeted. Where Meg was clean lines, Emily was a messy scribble.

The river only made it all worse. She chewed a nail. She gnawed her lip.

(Scribble, scribble.)

Above and behind them stood their new house, a little hyper-modern two-bedroom cottage nestled in among the quaint, village-like homes of the county's river towns. Up there, the movers unloaded their furniture. They stood down here, out of the way.

Though only the two of them stood there at the small riverside dock, they were not alone. They were never alone, not anymore. Between them stood the thing that was known but unspoken, detected but unacknowledged. A ghost, of sorts—a presence with no body and no face and a name that they trapped on their tongues but would not let slip, not now, maybe not ever again.

They did as they had been doing: They ignored it, they talked past it, they pretended like That Unspoken Thing was not a thing at all, had never *been* a thing.

"We have a river," Emily said, plainly. Still staring at it.

"It's beautiful, isn't it?" Meg asked, taking it all in.

"Sure."

Emily heard it in her own voice: the wary, weary eyedropper of sarcasm dispensing one sardonic drop, *bloop.* Just enough to perfume the word. *Sure.* She didn't mean it that way. (Or so she always told herself.) But there it was, just the same. Put down for Meg to pick it up, and of course Meg picked it up.

"You don't like it."

"It's not—I mean, I like it, it's beautiful, you're right. It's just—" *I'm afraid of water.* Emily was hydrophobic. Not so bad she couldn't stand here, but enough that she felt the river's hungry waters easing past like a starving crocodile with black, dead eyes. Christ, she couldn't even take a shower without having to grab a towel every five minutes to dry her eyes. But she didn't want to say any of this. Meg knew it already. It wasn't a secret that Emily feared water. "A river."

Meg sighed through her nose. "Are you okay with this?"

"Totally. Very."

"Moving out of the city was a big deal, I know."

"Right, but now—now you're home."

"*We're* home."

"Right, yeah, I just mean, you grew up here. This is your home. Your parents are ten minutes away. You have a new job at your father's old law firm. It's good. This will be good."

"It will be good. Thanks for making this work."

"Obviously, yeah." *Because it's on me to make this work,* she knew. Meg knew it, too. Not that she'd say it. You don't speak the unspoken. *Speak of the Devil and the Devil shall appear.*

"It's early yet. Mimosa?"

Emily offered a dramatic, almost-whole-body nod. "*Mimosa.*"

———

THEY HAD GOTTEN MARRIED FIVE YEARS AGO, WHEN EMILY WAS thirty, and Meg was forty. Emily wanted a small wedding, maybe in another country. Costa Rica, maybe. Meg said no. She wanted the pomp, the circumstance, the hundred guests and the rustic farm-to-table vibe with a cake from Factory Girl down in Coryell's Ferry. They had the wedding not far from this spot where they stood now.

They lived in the city until Recent Events, and Emily loved Philly, loved its attitude, its vibrancy, its art and its big loud mouth. Meg wanted quiet, but stayed because she had a good job at a prestigious firm in Center City. They had an apartment just off Rittenhouse Square. They ate omelets at Parc, one of their shared loves. For most everything else they were out of sync, but Emily told herself that was a good thing, that you didn't want to be with someone who was just like you, otherwise the seesaw plonked down at one end and you never had the fun of the weeble-wobble ride. Besides, Emily knew she was a ship adrift, a ship that needed ballast to give her stability, to keep her on course, and Meg was that. Once more she told herself that it was good they were two different people, that it was only proper they balanced each other out like this. Except this time, Emily feared it was a lie. But maybe that was okay, too. Maybe the lies you told yourself became true enough, eventually. Like a magic spell. An incantation of deception, an illusion made real.

MIMOSAS ON THE DOCK. BY THE HUNGRY RIVER. WITH THE UN-spoken Thing. The movers would be doing this all day. Inside the little modern bankside house—their new home up past a set of long, zigzagging steps—it was a high-traffic zone. They'd get trampled. So down here they remained. *Trapped,* Emily thought, but did not say. Meg sidled up next to her—no hand-holding or arm-linking, but her elbow touched Emily's and that felt like a kind of offering. Whether as a peace treaty or a sacrifice or a promise, Emily didn't yet know. Meg would know. Meg didn't do things without knowing what they were, what they meant. And she didn't care if everyone else was playing catch-up.

You're being uncharitable, Emily said. Meaning, she felt like a judgy bitch. God, was she a judgy bitch? She was, wasn't she? She knew she was, why was she even asking? Shit. *Get out of your own head, idiot.*

Meg said: "So, starting the week after Labor Day, I'll be in the office all day, most days."

"Yup." Emily resisted snarking: *Yeah, that's how jobs tend to work, Meg.*

"You'll be home and can handle a lot of the unpacking and arrangement and such?" It was framed as a question, but Emily knew it was a statement.

"I dunno. You have the, the way you want things—I don't know if I'm up for that task, Meg. I thought maybe I could look into some of the local community service NPOs, find some people I could help. There's a local women's shelter—"

"Emily, c'mon, no."

"What?"

"I know that was your life in the city. And you're good at it. *So* good at it. It's what I love about you, how much you care, how much you want to fix things. But maybe we need to spend some time working on what we have here." The Unspoken Thing, almost summoned, almost conjured. Meg continued: "Like the house. Like our stuff. I could use you here."

"But people could use me out *there.* It's hard out there right now, Meg. The local school board has screwed over LGBT kids, they've removed books by Black authors, homelessness is up—even out here, even in the rural burbs. I just think I could do some good. You know?"

"And you can and will. Eventually. Just not right now." Meg rubbed her arm. "Look. This is a beautiful house. This county is gorgeous. Lots of history. It was the seat of the American Revolution. We're ten miles from where Washington crossed this very river. And we're almost on the cusp of autumn. It'll be gorgeous here when the leaves change. Let's sit with this for a little while. Okay?" At that, Meg offered her mimosa glass to the air. An invitation.

Emily was not one to resist an invitation.

Pinkies out, they *tinged* glasses. It felt nice. The Unspoken Thing was here, still. But it didn't stand between them. *Drown in the river, Unspoken Thing,* Emily cursed it. *Drown in the waters and let the river take you far, far away from us.*

3

THE RUBY SLIPPER MAKES ITS DEBUT

DAN PAXSON BACKED THE TRUCK UP, POPPED THE GATE, AND SET UP their table right in front of it. Marco helped him unload the boxes while Calla set up the chalkboard, writing on it: RUBY SLIPPER APPLES! SWEET AND JUICY! FRESH PICKED! BUCKS COUNTY GROWN & CREATED! She also drew cartoony little apples at the corners. Dan put out the card: $2.99 a pound. A good price. Matched what apples went for at the grocery store even though his beauties were a thousand times better. Hell, a *million* times better. (Besides, those grocery store apples sat in crates for weeks, even months, in storage. Too-sweet, cardboardy lumps.)

Market bell rang and it was off to the races.

All around, the market was abuzz with other vendors. You name it, it was here: all the cuts of meat, all the curious veggies, baked goods, jams and jellies, herbs, greens, homemade hot sauces, mushrooms from Chester County, peaches and plums from the Lehigh Valley, local sweet corn (not from Jersey because that would be heresy), soup, cookies, pickles, goat milk, pottery. His own table was at the end, across from a local coffee roaster (Pebble Hill Roasters) and next to a place selling their own dog bones (Cooper's Cookies 4 Canines). And at the other end, the far end of the market, *almost* out of sight—

Lambert Hill Vineyards. Already lining up business, from the look of it. He spied the owner, Claude Lambert, glad-handing market-goers, and when Dan saw that too-familiar shock of white hair and beard, he felt his hands curling into fists.

It was busy at the other end of the market, but down here? At this end?

It was a ghost town.

The market itself took place in the center of the town of Doyle's Tavern, which thanks to the curious way the commonwealth was set up, existed technically as a borough inside the larger township of Harrow.

That township also featured a number of small municipalities called villages tucked away—villages tended to be more rural, mostly just an intersection or two, not enough of anything to feel like a proper town. Markets like this brought people from all over midcounty—this one took place in the parking lot of the old Community Bank. Of course, Dan's booth was facing the dead-end Doyle Drive, the one with a fresh dumpster sitting only fifty feet behind them. The wind turned sometimes and you caught that sour trash stink. Nobody wanted to come down to this side.

That's what I get for joining the market late, he thought. The fees were outrageous. He was paying through the nose for this spot. It was like concert tickets: You bled for some seat a thousand miles from the stage, behind a post, next to the bathroom.

He looked at the crates of apples in front of him.

And the crates of apples behind him.

He imagined the stacks of unpaid bills sitting back at their house.

The truck wasn't inspected yet because he couldn't afford it, and if he got caught, he would have to pay a fine he further could not afford.

His bank account was swan-diving toward zero. And once it hit that, there'd be fees, because of course they charged you more money for having no money. As a kid they'd always made it sound like you'd be worrying about quicksand all the time, but *this* was the real quicksand. Debt drew you down deeper and deeper, held you firm, so you never, ever got out no matter how hard you tried. Trickle-down economics? Yeah, right. Only thing that trickled down was that debt. Like piss on your head. And it would run down onto Calla, too. Her last year of high school started next week, and then what? College? At this rate, she'd need a full ride or have to take on predatory student loans for the rest of her life. Debt spackled upon debt, upon debt, upon debt: all mortar, no brick.

He feared he'd made a huge mistake. He'd staked everything on—on what? Seven trees producing one kind of apple. (*Ruby Slipper,* he repeated to himself again and again. To remove the taste of the original name.) Was this really Dan's dream? Or only his father's? And yet here he was, charging forward with a blindfold on, not seeing what was probably obvious to everyone else. They'd laugh at his failures. Sure as they laughed at his father's.

Panic throttled him. His chest hurt. Sweat slicked the space under his jaw. He felt cold and hot at the same time.

He snatched up an apple. It pulsed in his hand. Like it was angry at his failure to sell it. *It's just your own heartbeat, you dope.*

"Nobody's coming over here," Calla said.

"I *know*," he said sharply. Too sharply.

"Free samples," she said.

"What?"

"People want free shit, Dad."

He made a sound that he wanted to be a laugh but was something more desperate, more worried. He failed to contain his anger when he said, "Free isn't a pricing strategy, Calla Lily." Calla Lily: a nickname. Her real name was Calla Leeann Paxson, Leeann for his wife, who passed away when the girl was young. Another debt, another burden. But the calla lily was the flower the two of them had at their wedding. And given how his daughter was conceived on that wedding night, well.

"Dad—"

"We need to make money."

"I know but, like, people aren't going to just buy some random-ass apple."

Marco jumped in. "She knows her stuff, Mister P. It's like—the internet is all about that free taste. Free apps, free e-books, free videos, but then you want more, or the better version . . . it's like, you gotta pony up."

"*No,*" he said firmly, because this apple was too good—*he* was too good—to treat this all like some throwaway charity. They'd think him a bigger fool than they already did, giving away apples like cups of water to marathon runners. His product had *value.* And that value was not a big fat stinking zero.

At that, a shadow darkened their table.

A customer? No.

Broad, trunk-chested Claude Lambert. The buttons of his shirt open too low so he flashed wisps of bone-white chest hair. Ruddy, pocked cheeks and a nose so empurpled it looked like he'd been dipping it in his own wine. He let loose with a rheumy, growly chuckle: *Heh-heh-ahem-heh,* and said, "Little Dan. Look at you here. Finally bringing something to the table."

"Mister Lambert. A pleasure," he lied. The apple in his hand throbbed. Like he could feel something crawling in it. A worm under its skin.

(*or under his own*)

The older man looked over the table, sucking air between yellow teeth. "You got lucky, Little Dan. Usually we have an orchard set up here—Fleecydale Orchards. But that storm that came through last summer? They said it wasn't a tornado, just shear winds, but—it took most of their trees. Then that dry spell put the rest down. Shit luck for them." He narrowed his eyes. "Good luck for you."

"The Bentrims are good people, good farmers. Mighty fine apples."

"Nnn," Lambert said. The Bentrims weren't rich, so Lambert didn't care.

The man's eyes roamed to Calla, and Dan watched his daughter give the old bastard a withering stare. (She was good at those.) "You know, young woman, you're now living on land once owned by your grandfather, Big Dan."

"Actually? We're all living on stolen Lenni-Lenape land," she said.

Lambert ignored her, kept talking. "Big Dan worked for me. He was a good friend, one of my best, to tell the truth—"

(*worms slithering faster and faster*)

"But eventually he left my employ to start a—well, to start an orchard, like your father here. The ground was bad, though. The trees that came up didn't produce fruit. Didn't even survive. It was a bad investment, and he lost it." Here, Claude's stare flicked back to Dan. "Be a shame to see that happen again."

"It won't," Dan said. It was false, hollow bravado and he feared the old goat was exactly right. But even the thought of Claude Lambert being right made him want to take this apple and smash it so hard into the man's mouth that the old bastard's teeth broke, like shards of peppermint candy. Pushing that apple and those busted teeth down his throat, his esophagus bulging and splitting open—

Fingers snapped in front of his face. "You there, Little Dan?"

Dan blinked. The apple was still in his trembling hand. Claude leaned in, leering. "Yeah," Dan said, his voice distant.

"I was saying, it's funny that you even got that property back." Claude's voice was shot through with the cold rebar of resentment.

"Judge Carver looked favorably upon you in overturning that decision. That land was for the conservancy. It was preserved land, not to be developed. Honestly, Dan, this area is getting overfull, we're trying to keep a certain *pristine* nature, for the birds and such—"

"It was already developed. It was, like you say, my father's. House and acreage. That was my land, by right, with my father's passing and it should've never gone the way it did. Carver saw clear to that."

"Huh," Claude said. "Guess he did. People are puzzles, aren't they? Wonder what moved him to change his mind. Something very special to move a man stubborn as that." A big greasy grin anchored itself between the ruddy hills of Claude Lambert's cheeks. In one grab, he snatched the apple out of Dan's hand. "Let's see how this tastes."

Dan's hands balled into fists—

He took what was yours—

You own that apple; he doesn't deserve a bite—

Push his soft fat throat into his spine—

But instead, Dan bit down on his own teeth as Claude chewed the apple with a messy, open mouth. He wore a smug smile on his face as he ate, and what was coming was telegraphed so plainly it might as well have been written in the sky: He was going to make some glib, dismissive comment about the apple. Nothing so castrating as an outright insult. It would be passive-aggressive, less a sword through the heart and more a razor nicking an artery.

But then the chewing slowed.

Claude's lids dimmed, but then his eyes brightened. He resumed chewing faster, and after swallowing he cleared his throat a little, an involuntary reflex.

"This apple," he said, like the words were barely his, like they came up out of him, summoned without his consent. "This is a damn good apple, Little Dan. It's like—" But here he seemed to catch himself. Whatever words were crawling up out of him, he bit off their head and swallowed them, too. "Good luck with your orchard," he said hastily, before hurrying off.

Eating the rest of the apple as he went. Head bowed to it. Penitent, almost.

"That was sort of fucked up, Dad," Calla said. "Who *was* that guy?"

But Dan didn't chide her for her language, as he usually would. He didn't really even answer her question. All he said was, "He liked the apple. That apple was so damn good, he couldn't help but say it. You were right, guys. We need to give out samples." He handed Marco his pocketknife. "Cut up slices. Let's get—wait, we don't have anything to put them on. Forget it. No slices. Just whole apples. Calla, Marco, grab a crate, walk around here with apples, hand them out. One per person. Tell them it's free. Tell them who we are—Paxson Family Orchards, Table Forty-Two, down by the end. And for god's sake, tell them our apple's name. Tell them about the Ruby Slipper. Got it?"

The two kids nodded.

This was going to work.

Fuck you, Claude Lambert, you old vampire. Fuck you and your shitty wine and your broken-vein nose and your lies about my father. Dan would show him.

4

THE POISON LIVES INSIDE THE SEEDS

CALLA HAD MARCO CARRY THE CRATE AS SHE PLUCKED APPLES from the box, handing them out to market-goers and vendors alike. As she did, she practiced hand placement: It mattered on video how you held a thing and showed it off.

"That apple really was amazing," Marco said, staring down into the crate with wide eyes. He smacked his lips. "I didn't know fruit could *taste* that good."

"Cool," she said, drolly.

"I'm serious! You need to try one."

She looked at the apple in her hand. It felt heavier than it looked. "Apples are gross, M&M." At that, she said, "Free apple?" and before receiving an answer thrust the apple into the gooey hands of some toddler held aloft by her mother. The mother objected but the kid seemed happy, and Calla didn't wait for consequences—she kept moving forward, like a leaf on a river, pulled by its current. "You know what tree sample I want?"

Calla danced in front of Marco and leaned across the crate. She kissed him hard, tilting her head just so, tasting for a moment the apple on his mouth: lips slicked with lingering sweet-sour tang, laced with appleskin astringency.

And then—

Click.

Her phone, held up and out in her left hand, captured the moment. Marco laughed and rolled his eyes. "Really?"

"For the 'gram," she said with faux-innocence. "So to speak."

"I'm just content for you, aren't I?" The way he said it, it sounded like he wanted her to think he was joking.

"The whole *world* is content." On her phone, she tapped open the app, selected the photo of them kissing, put a warm summer-sun filter over it, then swipe-typed a quick message—

hanging with my sprinter stud M&M at the hashtag *farmersmarket* hashtag *doylestavern* hashtag *makeoutsesh* hashtag *sellingapples*

—and uploaded it to Faddish. She turned the screen toward Marco, said, "We look cute. But here's one for just us." She bounced up and kissed him again. This time, she held the kiss. A reward for . . . well, whatever Marco was feeling.

"*Hey,*" came a sharp voice. "Put some air between those bodies."

While the rest of the market-goers passed by them, one person stood there watching them. It was a cop. Short guy. Red hair clipped tight to the scalp. Intense eyes, too—cold blue, a stare like a pair of icicles sticking into you.

"Excuse me?" she said.

"The farmers market isn't your bedroom," the cop said, mouth in a flat line.

"Who are you? The PDA police?"

"No, I'm the real police. You wanna mouth off again?"

Marco used his body to ease her aside, gently, putting some space between them. "Sorry, Officer Boyland, we will . . . keep it clean."

"You better."

At that, Calla put on the sweetest, most syrupy face she could muster—the fakest, shittiest, suck-up-but-also-fuck-you face. She held out an apple. "*Apologies,* Officer, would you care for a delicious, *flavorful* apple? They're *free,* you know."

The cop leaned in. She smelled his breath: a biting Listerine stink. He snatched the apple from her grip. "I would. Have a nice day."

Cocky prick strutted past, plainly proud of himself.

"What a fucking asshole," she said. "Let's report him. Cops have managers, right?"

"Settle down, Karen."

"Hey."

"Sorry. You just—you can't mess with the police, especially when you're standing next to your brown-skinned boyfriend, okay? I don't need the heat, and my parents *definitely* don't need this kind of hassle at the restaurant. My father would deep-fry my ass if I brought this to their door."

She rolled her eyes. "Fine. I'll be good, I promise." She arched an eyebrow at him. "Wait, you knew him. You knew his name."

"Boyland, yeah. He's a dick. Hassles my family sometimes for free food. Like, he eats the food, but then pretends we run some unclean restaurant and if we *don't* give him free food he'll call the health department on us." Marco rolled his eyes. "It's such a scammy scummy trick, but, y'know. Cops."

THEY'D BE TOGETHER FOREVER. THAT WAS THE PLAN. HIGH SCHOOL sweethearts and all that. They were going to go to the same college: Princeton was the dream, U-Penn the backup. They'd get married after. Maybe live on the West Coast because they weren't going to be like all the *other* high school sweethearts from this area, the ones who got married and found they'd planted roots too deep and either came back or never left in the first place. Calla knew it was all a cliché. And she wondered if she deserved something different. Not better, she told herself— *scolded* herself—because Marco was the absolute best, obviously. Still. Some nights she worried long and hard about it all. If this was a mistake. If she'd put herself on a highway without off-ramps. Was it too early to commit her heart and her head in this way? She told herself no, it wasn't. This was her dream. *Their* dream. But. *But.* Dad always said some dreams were wings, and others were cement shoes. Something his dad used to say to him. She didn't really get it.

THEY KEPT HANDING OUT APPLES. BUT CALLA COULDN'T GET THAT cop out of her head. "I hope that cop eats that apple and chokes." Her mouth formed a wicked, toothy grin. "I wish we were handing out *poison* apples, instead." She scowled, then wiggled her fingers over the apple in her hand like she was casting a spell. "Magic, cursed apples. The Sleeping Death! Only true love's kiss can save you. Except that fucking dick will never have anybody love him. Isn't that right, Mister Apple?" At that, she leaned in and gave the apple a little kiss. No sweetness there. Just a thumbtack bitterness on her tongue. She made a yuck face and chucked the apple onto some wool vendor's table. It nearly rolled off the edge.

"Apples *are* kinda poisonous," he said. "The seeds anyway."

"Oh yeah. They have like, what, cyanide in them?"

"Amygdalin. A cyanogenic glycoside. But you'd have to eat, I dunno, three dozen apples' worth of seeds to get even a little sick."

She whirled around him, handing off another apple to some rando. "You're really smart, anyone ever tell you that?"

"Oh! Hah, huh. I dunno about that."

"Humble, too."

"I might wanna be a doctor or something. Who knows."

"My genius doctor studbeast boyfriend." She shrugged. "Maybe that could be my angle. You could help me. On TikTok, sci-comm is pretty popular—like, people sharing cool facts and stuff, or debunking stupid bullshit. You could help me write it, and then I'll rewrite it because you totally won't get my voice right, but we could make it work." She reached into the crate, then saw that the apples were almost all gone. "Guess we need a refill—"

"Call, look—" Marco said.

They'd made it around the horseshoe shape of the farmers market, and from this spot had sight of the far end of the other aisle, where her father's table waited.

A small line had formed already. She spied people walking away with *whole bags* of apples.

"It worked," she said, surprised anybody cared about apples.

"You did it," Marco said. He repeated her own words back to her in a goofy pantomime. "You're really smart, anyone ever tell you that?"

"They don't have to," she said, and kissed him again.

5

THE FAMILY ORCHARD

AT THE MARKET, IT TOOK ONLY ABOUT FIFTEEN MINUTES FOR CAL-la's *free apple* plan to take root—already people came to the table, poking around, marveling about That Apple, and each time Dan corrected them: "It's not That Apple—that's a Ruby Slipper, because there's no place like home." And he told each of them, "My daughter came up with that, you know. My Calla Lily makes me look so good."

An hour in, he had a line—a proper line! And occasionally he looked over and past the crowd, eyeballing the vineyard booth at the end—and he spied Claude Lambert staring balefully in this direction. Good. Spite was one helluva motivator. Selling the apples was made all the more sat-isfying by seeing that old prick look saltier than a soft pretzel.

All the while, people—some he knew, a lot he didn't—asked him questions.

Oh, where's the orchard at, can we visit?

Not yet, Mary, but maybe one day I'll open our doors, sell applesauce and apple cider donuts and the like—but right now we're just this one table.

You guys got Honeycrisp or what?

No, sir, no Honeycrisp here, this is our signature apple. The Honeycrisp is too sweet, you ask me—it's an apple for children, but people like you and me, with discerning tastes, want a little tartness to go with our sweetness, don't we?

Would this be good in pies?

You bet it would, Earl—that crunch you get? That means it's got turgor—strong cell walls that hold up under baking, makes sure that the apple doesn't just turn to mush. And the flavor only develops further with the heat.

How long do they keep?

It's a real keeper, ma'am. Even though we picked these a week or two ago, it keeps like a late-season apple. You store it in the fridge or in a cellar, it should stay good, even develop new flavors, over a couple-few months.

They asked questions—but they bought the apples, too. Some just bought a few. Others, a few *pounds*. And with their purchases came rave after rave—

Best apple I've eaten in a long time, buddy—

I didn't know apples could taste like that.

The juice was dripping on my shirt!

Some of the people ate an apple as they walked away, as if they just couldn't wait to take another bite.

They had to shut the table down before the end of market.

Because they were all out of apples.

Dan didn't even think that was possible. This morning he'd been trying to figure out ways to sell apples through other channels—maybe to some local restaurants or bakeries, or perhaps he'd put up a small table outside the house, like other folks did around the county. People selling roadside corn or tomatoes or hosta plants from a little ramshackle farmstand, that sort of thing.

But now, this first run was gone.

Hot damn.

When they were all done at the market, Marco said he needed to get to track-and-field practice, and of course Calla asked if she could go and watch. Honestly, Dan needed her help back at the house, but she deserved the time, especially with school starting up this week. So he drove them both over to James Logan High and dropped them off.

Then he headed back home.

Home, he thought again.

Never got old, calling it that.

THIS WAS THE PROPERTY HE'D RECLAIMED FROM THE CONSERvancy:

The parcel of land was about nine miles northeast of Doyle's Tavern, about three miles southwest of the Delaware River that bordered Pennsylvania and New Jersey, nestled in a little nondescript zip code assigned to Plumridge, a name that only the truly *local* locals ever used. ("Yeah, you want good wooder ice, you take River Road north through Deer Park, then through Plumridge, up 'round the bend past the old library, yeah, the one with the outhouse? There's a place up there across the water, in

Frenchtown. Good pork roll, too.") The property sat on a janky, crooked road—Geiger Hill—and contained forty-three total acres, an awkward odd-angled parcel dead-ending at Black Creek. The house sat almost right on the road, leaning toward it like it was plotting its escape, like it would make a run for it soon as nobody was looking—

But truth was, for a decade, nobody *was* looking. The place went empty, left to spiders and mice. Yet the old stone farmhouse remained. Untouched, unopened, holding its breath.

Like it was waiting for Dan to come home. Waiting for him to make things right. To finish what his father started, God rest his soul.

DAN PULLED THE TRUCK INTO THE DRIVEWAY. HE THOUGHT ABOUT turning off the engine, maybe having a nip of lunch.

But ahead, the rutted road to the orchard waited.

He could feel the orchard calling to him. *There's work to be done, Dan,* he could hear it say. And there was. Apples to be picked, diseases and pests to look out for, branches to be pruned.

So, he put the little pickup back into drive and kept on past the driveway, onto the dirt road toward the orchard at the back of the property.

Tree and scrub rose all around the truck. Bramble and poison ivy in every direction. Dead ash trees like charred bones, killed by the ash-borer beetle that a few years back had wiped out damn near every ash tree in a hundred-mile radius. Birds loved the overgrowth, flitting from briar to bush, zigzagging over the road ahead, like they were trying to stitch closed a rip in

(*skin*)

fabric.

Dan shuddered, momentarily cold, thinking of the day he found his father . . . *no,* he wouldn't think about that. Not here. Not today. Instead, he tried to remember a different day: the day his father, a round-cheeked man with a playful cinder ever-burning in his eye, walked him down to the spot where he wanted to plant his trees. *Kiddo,* he'd said, *we're gonna make something special of this place, something that's ours for once.* Dad said that was the dream of every man. To make something of his own. Not for anybody else.

Once Dad

(*killed himself*)

lost the property

(*had it stolen*)

the whole place went to hell. Big Dan had maintained it, kept it nice, knew what he was doing because that was his job. But without his governing hand, it went feral fast—invasive rose and Japanese honeysuckle and tangling bittersweet, all of it wild with the joy of vicious, unattended children. It formed a helluva thicket, one he didn't know if he would ever be able to beat back.

But that was all right. He didn't need all of the property.

He just needed the orchard.

The orchard sat bordered at the south by Black Creek, which itself was fed by the river a few miles away. Dan had to bushwhack and clear-cut the hell out of the thicket—but the thornbushes and underbrush had given way to machete and shovel, surrendering readily, as if Mother Nature knew this spot had a greater purpose.

That greater purpose: seven apple trees.

(Seven for now, at least.)

Each tree, grafted from the branches he brought home that day.

That was the thing with apple trees. You couldn't grow them from seed. Well—you *could*. You just wouldn't get the desired result. If you held an apple in your hand, decided you liked it and wanted more of the same, planting the seeds of that apple would not yield *more* of that apple. It was a genetic roulette wheel, and each tree that grew would yield a different apple: most likely, what they called a spitter apple, an apple so nasty you had to spit it out. Good for cider-making, maybe. Best for throwing at a squirrel or a coyote. Damn sure not for eating.

No, if you wanted the same apple you were eating, you had to go to that apple's *tree*. You had to cut off a limb—not a big limb, but new growth from the season prior. Scionwood, with reddish bark, and small, compact buds tucked tight to the branch. You cut them off, then you brought them to a rootstock tree: a tree that was volunteering to become something else, to be transformed by knife and tape into a different creature entirely. You had to injure that tree—wound it by carving into it, by cutting the ends off its own branches. The whip-and-tongue cut came next: a cut against the bias, then a little groove nicked into each branch. Then you plugged the scion branch into the branch of the rootstock, nestled them in nice and tight, and taped it off. The volunteer tree struggled, of course. It tried to grow its own branches, but those buds, you pinched off. And over time, it ceased to try. It grew only those branches you gave it. What the volunteer was, it was no more. Now it was only the branches you grafted onto it.

One April day, five years back, Dan had seven volunteer trees—dwarf rootstock—waiting for him in the ground, on which he grafted the near-to-two-dozen scion branches he'd collected from the tree they'd found (*my tree,* he thought, the sudden feeling of ownership sweeping over him).

The scions *burst forth* with life. Bright-green leaves glittering in the sun. Unfurling as they drank each day, bigger and bigger, thirstier and hungrier. Not a single graft didn't take.

After that first year, the county was shocked by a brutal, unexpected winter. They'd had a string of mild winters, but that one was one for the books: temperatures below zero, flensing winds, and a nasty ice storm in early February that coated the world in brittle glass. Power lines, frozen, snapped like dry spaghetti. The whole thicket looked like a hulking, seething, frozen mass—a singular beast of cold crystal. That year, Dan worried for his trees. Apple trees were hearty, but the grafts were new, the trees were young. He feared they'd die. He went to them, in the cold and the ice, trying to cover them with tarp, and when that failed, trying to pinch the brittle ice off the leafless twigs before they snapped. But it was no use. The winter rose up too big, too fast, too cruel, and he wept, sure the trees would be lost.

But spring came, and with it, buds. Leaves. New branches. Slowly, like lungs growing, a circulatory system suspended in air, the trees swelled, urgent, crawling forth up and out through open space. Year after year, season after season, they grew. And all the while Dan watched them for apples. He still had that first taste of that one apple living in the back of his throat, a tantalizing tartness tightening the hinge of his jaw, saliva pooling as he imagined it again and again—

(alongside the whisper-click of shear blades on branch and bone)

He knew apple trees could take a long time to bear fruit. Three years. Five. Eight. Even ten. Panic set in—were they not pollinating? He had crab apples near. They should've done the trick. But what if he'd been wrong? What if they needed something he didn't have, or couldn't give? The trees bloomed. But no apples came. Maybe none would ever come, he worried.

And then, this year—

Pink blossoms gave way to dark little shapes, black at first, almost as if dead in winter—but soon, slowly shot through with splashes of red.

Apples! His apple. The

(Harrowsblack)

Ruby Slipper, come to life.

Where once there were no apples, now there were endless apples. The trees were sagging with the weight of their fruit. He went over and unscrewed one from its stem, and took a deep, wide bite—the kind of greedy bite that damn near sheared the apple in half. Juice ran down his wrist. His mouth flooded with pleasure. For a second he felt his father standing here with him. Like this was it, this was the moment it had all— *ahem, ahem*—come to fruition. His father's dream, stolen by petty men, but Dan carried that dream. He'd made it real. He took another smaller bite of the apple. A gentle bite using the front of his teeth. He let the apple flesh play on his tongue. The future felt unimaginably infinite all of a sudden. He felt awake. Alive. *Capable* in a way he'd not really felt . . . maybe ever.

That was the true yield of this orchard. *Pride.*

He heard a sound, then—a gentle *flip-flip-flip*. Followed by a *tap-tap*. Somewhere above him. He pulled the apple away from his mouth—

And a drop of red dotted the back of his hand. Juice?

No. Not apple juice. *Blood.*

Dan looked up and spied movement in the branches above his head.

A flutter, like a leaf stirred by wind. But this wasn't a leaf—it was a wing, the wing of a plump mourning dove. It flopped its wing and bobbed its head, searching for help. Throttled by panic.

A picking ladder sat at the neighboring tree, so Dan hurried over to grab it. He used it to lean against the trunk and climb up toward the bird, his head and shoulders thumping into the fat apples that hung from branches like a Christmas tree overstuffed with ornaments.

He pulled himself a little closer to the bird, and found that the branch it sat on was slick with fresh red.

"Poor thing," he said, cooing to the bird as its chest rose and fell in fast flutters. Possible that a red-tail had clipped it, and here it sat, dying. Maybe the bird could be rescued, though. Dan wasn't opposed to that. Wouldn't be the first time he took an injured squirrel or a parentless fawn to BAR, the Bucks Animal Rescue.

He cradled his hands beneath the bird and picked it up—

The bird resisted. It wouldn't simply lift up and off the branch. As he moved the animal, more blood dripped. The bird thrashed—

Dan saw the bird was impaled on a small, sharp, thornlike branch.

He blinked. How the heck had that happened? He supposed if the bird had landed hard enough, or again had been knocked down by a raptor, it could've impaled itself on it. Dan winced and continued drawing the bird up off the spike—the branch was the circumference of a pencil, and half as long. The bark on it was not dark, but young and red. The bird's body slid off the branch, blood oozing along its length.

He held the bird to his chest. It was in arrest. It was dying, he knew. Growing up on a farm, you got a sense of these things.

That's when he noticed something else, something draped over the branch, just past the small bloody spire on which the bird had been affixed:

A fat worm. Still twisting a little.

Dan's gaze traveled to the worm, then past it, to the bundle of twigs and branches beyond it. A nest. At first he thought, no, it couldn't be, it was too late for a nest, but some of the area's perennial bird guests had several broods over the course of the season. He leaned forward, the ladder wobbling a little as the bird in his hand sat docile and dying. Dan peeked into the nest—

Jesus.

In the nest were two baby doves, almost fledglings—gangly, awkward things with downy feathers.

Both were dead. A small sprig of wood, like a long thorn, impaled each baby bird's skull, growing from underneath the beak through the top of their heads.

On one, a fly danced, looking for a taste of death.

"H . . . how?" he asked aloud. The bird in his hand flapped its wings suddenly, and Dan felt the ladder wobble—

Oh shit.

He darted a hand out to catch the branch ahead of him but already the ladder was going backward, crashing through the dangling apples and leaves—it all rushed past him in a burst of red and green before the ground rushed up to kick him in the back. His lungs pancaked, the air blasting out of them. He gasped for breath at the same time he tried to evaluate, *Is anything broken, arm, leg, neck, back, head,* he couldn't go through this now, not just as the orchard was getting started, if he'd injured himself even a little bit, oh god, oh no, it would hobble him—

But then he managed a deep keening breath—*kyeeeeeee*—and he coughed, suddenly, sitting upright. His ears rang. He reached up, looked at his hands. Fingers worked. Wrists bent. Nothing busted. He felt the back of his head. Then the sides and front. Nothing. And no pain in his legs, either. *Damnit,* he thought to himself. *Be more careful!* He leaned forward, feeling dull pain through his torso and tailbone, but nothing that set off alarms.

Dan saw something sitting in the grass nearby.

The bird. Resting in the green. The grass like its nest.

(*its grave*)

Before Dan even knew what he was doing, a spear of anger lanced through him and he grabbed the bird's head and twisted hard. The dove's neckbones snapped like a bundle of wet toothpicks. *Kkkht.*

Dan gasped at himself, recalling his hand swiftly.

Why did I do that? he asked himself.

It seemed so angry. So cruel.

But then he told himself, it was something he had to do. It wasn't anger. Wasn't cruelty. It was mercy. That's all it was. Just an act of necessary mercy.

Dan stood up, brushing himself off. This foolish episode had delayed the work that needed to be done, so putting all this messy business out

of his mind, he set himself to gathering the bushel baskets and his har-
vester scoop in order to pick more of these delicious apples for those
who wanted—

(*needed*)

them.

6

EMILY CONFRONTS THE WATER

THE MORNING OF MEG'S FIRST DAY HEADING INTO THE OFFICE. Emily sat at the counter bar nomming a bowl of cereal: an organic version of Lucky Charms swimming in a lake of Oatly oat milk. Meg, as always, drank one of a rotating series of smoothies: this morning featured banana, peanut butter, protein powder, matcha, a bit of (and here, Emily shuddered) *mushroom powder*.

As Meg whisked through the kitchen, readying herself for her first official day of work, Emily reached out and palmed one of the rich, red apples sitting in a bowl nearby. As Meg paused, shaking up a quick vinaigrette for her daytime salad, Emily thrust the apple in front of her. "You should put this in the smoothie instead of . . . fungus crumbles."

"It's lion's mane. It's a superfood. Good for your brain. I got it from the market in Doyle's Tavern this week—which is also where I got the apples."

"I'm just saying, the apple in the smoothie would be much better."

"*This* apple's too good for that," Meg said, giving the jar of proto-dressing a vigorous shake, like she was a mixologist mixing a fancy cocktail. "I already have one for my lunch. You should try one instead of—" Meg cast a judgmental face, looming over the cereal bowl with a scowl of scorn. "Whatever Halloween candy you're eating for breakfast today."

"It's not—*stop*. It has vegetables, too."

"It does not."

"No, it's organic, look," she said, spinning the box around. "Beet root powder. Spirulina. Purple carrots—"

"Those aren't vegetables. They're just . . . the dust of vegetables."

"Let me eat my breakfast candy in peace."

"At least *try* an apple."

"I'm allergic."

"Nobody's allergic to apples."

Emily laughed an incredulous laugh. "Oh my god, apple allergy erasure going on in this house, under our roof? It's called OAS, I'll have you know. Oral allergy syndrome, and it is related to birch pollen allergies."

"How did I not know this? You'll die if you eat an apple?"

"No, it's not *that* serious. Makes my throat feel tight and itchy is all. But I'm not exactly eager to eat something that makes me feel like I just ate a thistle." She turned the apple around in her hand. It was like something out of a fairy tale—the perfect embodiment of an apple, rich and red and well proportioned. Felt *dense,* too. Like it contained several apples inside just the one. "It is beautiful, though. Almost like it's fake."

With one swipe, Meg snatched the apple out of her hand. "You're missing out." She dunked it into one of the compartments of her insulated L.L.Bean lunch bag. "Anyway, I have to go."

They did their thing like they'd always done in the city, Emily walking Meg to the door, saying goodbye, have a great day, sharing a swift and auxiliary kiss—*the Unspoken Thing sliding in between their lips, like a shadow thin as paper*—here, Emily also paused and asked, "So, what exactly am I supposed to do?"

Meg, halfway out the door already, said, "I don't follow."

"Me, my day, how am I supposed to fill it?"

"You're an adult. I'm sure you can figure it out." But then, she hastily added, "I casually remind you that we also have boxes upon boxes to unpack. We are not doing that thing where we become clutter-blind to our unopened boxes nine months into living here. One month, we need everything in its place."

That was Meg. Everything in its place.

Emily agreed, and had answered with an exaggerated eye roll, "Yes, Mom." When Meg gave her a hard stare in response, Emily only upped the ante: "*Yes, Daddy,*" said with a lip bite and a lusty flash of the eyes. "That better?"

"No," Meg said, narrowing her eyes.

"Make me unpack your *boxes,* Daddy."

"Definitely no," Meg said.

"Please put everything in its *place,* Daddy."

(That was Emily. Forever pushing her luck.)

"Jesus, Emily." The first two times, Meg was maybe a little amused, but suddenly she wasn't anymore.

At that, Meg went halfway out the door—but Emily caught her elbow.

"I just mean—I can't be expected to do all that myself."

"I'll help, but this is part of our deal, Em."

Part of our deal. Emily knew they didn't explicitly have any kind of "deal," but its meaning was easy to decipher: Meg worked, made money, and Emily stayed home, and did the work that, say, a *wife* in the *house* would do—only problem? Emily wasn't exactly the housewife kind, and so everything she did, Meg would come home and fix anyway.

"All right," Emily said, a bit darkly. Meg started to turn around again, acting as if their conversation was sufficient, but for Emily, she had a thorn in her paw and yearned to yank it out with her teeth, so she again grabbed Meg's elbow—

"Em, I have to go work."

"Yes, I know. But you say I'm an adult, but I am an adult without a car. So I'm kinda stuck here—"

Meg made a placating face. "We'll figure something out. In the meantime, I'm sure my mother can drive you somewhere if you need to go. She's retired now and has time on her hands plus a new Lexus, so—" She darted in for a kiss on the cheek, quick as a snakebite, and then said, "I gotta go."

"Bye."

"Make good choices, eat an apple," Meg called over her shoulder as she rounded the side of the house toward their driveway.

Emily yelled after, "I'm not eating a—" But she already heard the car door open and close, so her voice dimmed to a mutter. "Stupid fucking apple."

Mostly, Emily didn't mind that Meg controlled situations; in fact, she often quite liked it. She told herself that Meg wasn't *controlling* so much as she was simply *in control,* as if the universe had decided that was her role. This made Emily feel safe, like no matter what happened, it would all be fine because Meg Had It Handled. Meg was structure. Meg was blueprint. Everything measured out, written down, planned so that it all made sense. Meg was a safety net, too. If Emily fell, then Meg would be there to catch her—not like a hero, showing up at the last minute to snatch her out of the air with reaching arms. But rather, like someone who had already built the net and put it just where it needed to go, so that when you fell, the net was there to save you. Meg didn't even have to be present to rescue your ass.

Still. It wasn't always the *most* exciting thing, living with someone like that, the way they meticulously imagined every aspect of the present and future, the way they arranged time and space down to the minute, down to the inch, like those mythic women weaving everyone else's skeins of fate in a loom, leaving you feeling like you were at their whims rather than making your own choices—

There, Emily had to stop herself, because it was exactly that line of thinking that got her into trouble in the first place.

Emily agreed to this. She was along for the ride. *It's just how we are.*

IN THE WEEKS THAT FOLLOWED, SHE TRIED. REALLY, SHE DID. ONE day, late September, Emily sat in their bedroom, on the king-sized bed, sinking into the memory foam, unpacking the last of her own clothes. Meg had hers in the drawers and closet by the first night, but Emily dragged her feet—in part because she knew fighting with Meg for the space was a war that had been lost long ago, so she surrendered that territory immediately, let Meg stake her claim, and Emily would creep in later and fill what space remained. As such, she had been living out of the boxes themselves, which made her feel like a guest in the house instead of its occupant. Or worse, like some vagabond.

After an hour, she'd gotten about half of it done, but the act of folding clothes nearly killed her spirit. Never mind the fact that her idea of "folding clothes" was like a drunk person making an omelet—it ended up more of a flattened pile than the precise Marie Kondo envelope of fabric that Meg preferred. She hit a point where she opened the drawers and sort of . . . smooshed her clothing in there. They formed a big fabric wad.

Less an act of organization, more an *art project.* Whatever.

She knew Meg wouldn't like that. Emily felt like she'd been set up for failure. Organization was not her bag, and yet, that's what Meg wanted her to do—organize their house. It was a test.

(One she was destined to fail.)

Maybe she needed to feel more comfortable here. In this area, yes, but starting with the house. She wasn't on the mortgage. She didn't pick this place. It just didn't feel like hers, like she belonged here at all.

Upon deciding to leave the city, Emily had petitioned for them to buy one of those old, labyrinthine farmhouses that she'd read about. Not that it was her style, precisely, but there was something enticing about moving into a house with creaky staircases and rock-walled root cellars and lots of little gnome doors hiding who knew what—a cache of letters from the Revolutionary War, a sinister porcelain doll missing an eye, a fucking ghost or two. Was it too much to ask that they buy a haunted house instead of this chic, rustic-industrial river-town home?

The horse was out of the barn on that one.

She just needed to feel more comfortable here, she decided. To find what Meg loved about it and maybe love it in turn—or at least understand it.

She couldn't explore the area, yet.

But she could explore the house.

EXPLORING THE HOUSE TOOK ABOUT FIFTEEN MINUTES.

Fifteen boring minutes.

What was there to discover? This wasn't a mountaintop manse. It didn't have corridors. It was cold. It was modern. It had a lot of white and gray and black. It was sharp edges and bleach.

So, outside she went.

The house perched on a hillside that led down to the river. Their property was just shy of an acre, but most of that acre was this hillside, a steep-angled decline toward the rushing water. That ground was all trees, shrubs, tangles of roots, and a whole lot of understory ground cover: ivy (both English and poison) and its ilk. So she couldn't walk down the hillside and explore it—she'd go ass-over-teakettle to the river, with the additional prizes of an itchy rash and various scrapes. There was of course the staircase down—creaky wooden steps that went down to the left, hit a landing, then went back down to the right, to the dock. A zigzag of stairs.

Beyond that waited the river.

And Emily was not ready to fuck with the river.

OUT FRONT OF THE HOUSE WAS A BIT MORE LAND—MOSTLY A POST-age stamp's worth, not including the driveway. There was a stand-alone one-car garage, and on the opposite side of the house, under a well-manicured dogwood tree, a modern wood-and-metal shed, its rich dark wood framed with artfully rusted metal. (Corrosion-as-design.) She went to the shed, if only to peek in, poke around.

The shed wasn't big. Large enough to store a lawnmower (not that they'd need one, would they?) or leaf blower (oh god, they'd need one, wouldn't they?) but not much else. Still, Emily held out hope that inside was some fancy portal, a Narnia gateway or something. But when she opened the shed, all she found—

Was a boat.

A kayak. Plasticky-looking. Red as a fire engine. A bit dinged up but otherwise, it looked barely used. Spiderwebs bound it to the floor and walls, and a few balletic cellar spiders spun above. A paddle sat propped up against the corner.

Emily, framed by the door to the shed, stared at the boat.

She listened to the susurrus of the river.

Heard a car go by.

Heard some birds warbling.

She looked at the boat again.

Maybe Emily *was* ready to fuck with the river.

THIS IS A BAD IDEA, EMILY TOLD HERSELF, DRAGGING THE KAYAK around the side of the house, toward the stairs. She took the easy route, which was to gently kick the kayak forward, so that it "floated" down the river that was the steps, one stair after the next, *ba-bump ba-dump.* Then do the same at the next landing. The railing below stopped it from sliding into the river. *This is such a bad idea.*

And yet, she felt compelled. The win would be huge. If they were going to live here, by this river, she had to conquer it. Had to *master* it.

Already she knew that Meg would be down here with the boat, and yet again, it'd be a time when Emily felt left behind—except, as Meg would remind her, she would be leaving her*self* behind. So this was a corrective. Bonus: Meg would be proud as hell. Maybe it would do a little something to repair Meg's estimation of her. God knows, that bridge needed some major mending, the Unspoken Thing reminded. After everything, Emily craved Meg's approval. Her pride.

(*Her love.*)

The plan was this: Use some of the fluorescent nylon rope she found in the seat of the boat, tie the kayak to the dock, and then . . . get in the boat.

She'd just, you know, *float* there for a little while. Maybe make some motions with the oar, see if she could get a feel for the movement of it. Take a selfie in there to show Meg.

This is gonna be so easy.

Her pulse raced through her wrists and neck.

She felt sweaty hot, but also cold.

Her mouth felt dry, her eyes felt wet.

You're having a panic attack, she told herself. *It's just water. Most of the planet is water, water is everywhere, okay that's not helping, stop thinking about how water is literally everywhere, ready to drown you.*

Maybe she could convince Meg to move to the desert.

Okay, shut up, you're doing this. Meg will be proud of you. You will be proud of yourself. Think of the dopamine hit! This is a good idea, Emily.

Get. In. The. Boat.

She tied the rope to one of the loopy metal bits along the edge of the kayak, then wound the other end around one of the dock posts and gave it a tie like she was tying a shoe. All before easing the boat into the water. It landed with a splash—water got on Emily's face and instantly she backpedaled, wiping it off.

"Shit," she said, feeling foolish. It was quite a thing to embarrass yourself in front of only yourself, but this was not Emily's first embarrassment rodeo.

The boat bobbed in the water as the river rushed past it.

Biting the inside of her cheek (nervous habit), Emily slid on the life jacket—it smelled musty, dusty, and she had to stifle a cough—and did a hasty buckle in the front before tiptoeing to the edge of the dock.

"Shit shit shit," she said, willing herself to sit on the dock without thinking she was sitting on the dock. Nearing the river without *thinking* about the river. She winced, almost closing her eyes entirely as she lowered her butt down, reaching out with a ginger foot, toeing the inside lip of the boat's seat before pulling it toward her. It bumbled against the wooden posts of the dock.

Okay. It's Band-Aid-ripping time.

Emily held her breath, grimaced so hard she worried her face might freeze in that position—

And slid into the boat.

It dipped as she dropped in. She let out a small scream.

But then—

She was in.

She was in!

It floated. And she floated with it.

The small scream gave way to a desperate, mad laugh.

She exhaled a long breath and then reached over and gingerly pulled the oar off the end of the dock. "Okay," she said to herself. "Here we are." Her heart tried to climb up into her neck. Her stomach lurched. But she was in the boat.

Emily took a moment to regard the river.

The dark water moved along fast and careless. It had no sympathy. It had only its momentum, the water drawn obsessively to the sea.

A pair of swifts chased insects over the water, ducking and diving like stunt pilots. Dragonflies hovered, flitting about, into the trees, out over the water. Farther down, Emily saw something that looked like a small island—she'd seen other islands out there, too. Islands big and small, up and down the river. Some were parks, others inaccessible lumps of land and scrub.

The river juggled the boat about, and for a moment it almost felt like being carried on the shoulders of a giant. Across the water, on the other side of the river in New Jersey, she saw no homes, just a towpath, and beyond that, a canal she could not see but knew was there, because a similar one sat on this side of the river too, a short walk inland from their house. Here the width of the river was, what, about three hundred feet across? Just south of here it was much wider—doubling in girth at the Lumbertown Crossing bridge. And the depth was, well, that she didn't know, but she suspected it was deep—

Deep enough to drown in—

That's what water did, after all, it drew you down into its embrace, a pair of arms grabbing you tight—

Holding you *fast* with tangle and silt, eels sliding around your throat, into your mouth, the taste of blooming mud and foul spit—

Lungs burning as you couldn't catch a breath—

Eyes burning as the water stung them—

Blood burning as you died, as you *realized* you were dying, as you *imagined all the things you'd never get to do,* the lives you failed to live, the dreams you squandered, *all of them* taken away by the river, stolen by the current—

"Jesus Fucking Christ," she yelped, grabbing at the rope. *That's enough of the water,* she thought, taking it as a win that she got in the boat and sat here as long as she did. Attempting to (and failing to) control her panic, she pulled hard on the rope to draw herself back to the dock—

And the rope untied.

Her loopty-knot didn't hold. It undid itself, almost as if by spectral hands (though more likely by the fact she didn't know how to tie a fucking knot). The rope fell. The boat came loose.

"Fuck!" she cried as the river took the boat, and her with it.

7

EMILY FINDS A BODY

PANIC DID WHAT PANIC DID BEST: IT SHORT-CIRCUITED GOOD, quality thinking in favor of doing-something-doing-*anything* at this exact moment before it was too late to do anything else.

She stood up, leaned far forward to reach for the dock—

The boat went one way.

Her body went the other.

Her body crashed down into the river with a mighty splash. She flailed and thrashed—

And the water took her.

The *water*.

The hungry, consumptive, fill-your-mouth-and-throat water.

The swift current dragged her underneath.

EMILY WAS CAUGHT IN THE GRAY, TURBID GLOOM—A DIARRHEAL billow as her feet kicked at the muddy bottom of the river. She tried to plant her feet down and launch upward but her legs went backward and the rest of her pitched forward as the river shoved her hard. She tumbled, pawing at nothing, something darting in front of her—a fish, an eel, a muskrat, she didn't know, couldn't care. Suddenly she bobbed upward, as if hauled bodily to the sky, and she broke the surface—*the life jacket, the life jacket is actually working*—gasping and keening for air before plunging back into the roiling river water. She *tasted* it. Minerals and dirt, slime slicking her tongue, grit in her teeth, and with it, the insane thought of *if I don't drown in the river I'm going to catch some kind of brain-eating amoeba*—

Up again she rose out of the water, splashing as something dark rushed up upon her—it struck her hard in the chest, and her chin dipped down and cracked hard on the dark shape. Teeth snipped tongue. Amid the mucky river taste now she tasted her own blood—*if not an amoeba, an infection, then*—and she realized suddenly, with her arms out, what she had hit. It was a tree. A massive ash tree, long uprooted from the bank of the river and angled down into the water. She clung to the water-slick tree, trying not to sink once more—but here, she could in fact plant her feet down and stand upright, the water flowing just past her shoulders. It was shallow.

She coughed and sputtered, holding on to the tree. *My savior,* she thought.

Past the tree, she spied the boat. It was downriver, about thirty feet ahead, and growing smaller in her view. Off it went, on its own adventure.

She had lost the oar. She had lost the boat.

Meg was going to be *pissed.*

Emily panted, water dripping from her lips. Thin blood drooled down her chin, too. Her tongue felt fat. She'd done a good number there, but at least moving it around her mouth told her it was all still attached.

She growled in frustration and slammed her hands down on the bark of the tree. This was stupid. She felt stupid. She wanted to cry. She did cry.

Emily took a moment. The river dammed at the tree, then flooded past. She could feel its pull. The water, hungry. If she let go, it would carry her away again.

I have to go I have to get out of the water fuck fuck fuck.

She guided herself along the trunk of the tree, calming herself so as to move slowly and methodically—it was tough going because so many of the tree's branches were below the water, caught up in their own tangle. Every step required pulling her legs free from the jumble of tree bits. As she got closer to the bank, with the water only halfway up her body now, her foot didn't get stuck on something so much as *something* got stuck on her *foot.* Emily leaned against the tree trunk and hauled her foot out of the water—

And found that her boot was stuck into the cavity of a human skull.

As THE RED AND BLUE WASHED OVER HER, ONE THE COLOR OF CALM, the other the color of panic, Emily realized the blanket around her

shoulders smelled like gun oil and pine tree air freshener: odorous artifacts from its time in the police car's trunk, she guessed.

She sat a little way up from the river, on a half-rotten, fungus-laden
log. Down just ten feet, lying on a slope of ivy-covered bank, were two
white sheets, and on those white sheets was an awkward display of river-
soaked bones.

Emily was no expert in anatomy, but some parts were plain to see—
the rib cage, what looked like an arm, and the skull. There were other
smaller bones, none attached to the other, all fringed with the detritus of
the river. Some organic, like bits of moss and algae and dead mess. Some
not, like the long bone wound up with fishing line, a festive bobber top-
ping the end. They'd pulled all the bones out from the tangle of the underwater tree. Grotesque gifts from the dark river.

A pair of uniformed state troopers stood over the bones, looking
down, obviously just ogling them, talking quietly to each other. The detective was nearby—an older man, bowling-ball head shorn to the scalp,
a too-thin little mustache on a billboard-sized span of real estate above
his upper lip.

The detective, Chuck Balko, had told her, "Probably just a boater or
a fisherman, fell in the river." Way he said it was so blasé, the way someone might describe an ingrown toenail or a pothole in the road. He even
added, "It happens."

She said it looked like the skull had been caved in. At the front, above
the brow was a crater, like a gently cracked egg.

"Maybe the guy fell, whacked his noggin, lost consciousness long
enough for the river to drown him. Or maybe it happened after—skull
took a hit floating downriver. You said you had it on your foot—maybe it
happened then."

Emily told him she didn't think so, but if she did, she was sorry. Because she was. Whoever this man was, or had been, she hadn't meant
to . . . desecrate him.

Balko said, "Nah, it's okay, he's lucky you found him. Someone out
there is missing this fella, and will have some peace and closure from
this."

At that point, he asked her to stick around—she wouldn't have to go
to the office to make a statement or anything, they could do it right here

and she could sign, he just needed someone to bring the paperwork over. "A body always means paperwork," he said with a heave of regret. Then he went off, leaving her here to sit, shivering in the heat, thinking about how she'd stepped on a dead man's bones, and how if the river had its way, she'd have become bones, too.

"EMILY, WHAT THE FUCK." MEG SAID THIS TO HER FROM THE ROAD behind Emily, startling her. Down below them, past the hillside, the bones waited, and the river that kept them just beyond.

"Hey," Emily said, her voice small.

Balko had called Meg on Emily's behalf. He said Emily could wait back at their house, no problem, but Emily wanted to wait here. If only because she needed Meg to *see*. Otherwise, would Meg even believe her?

"You found . . . that," Meg said grimly, gesturing toward the sheet of bones ten feet away.

"Him, they think. I found him. Yeah."

"I'm sorry—"

"I lost the boat," Emily said, blinking back tears. "I wanted to conquer the river so I got in the boat and tied it to the dock but I fucked that all up and now the boat is gone and I'm soaking wet and I found a dead person in the river and—" The tears went from a trickle to a deluge, and suddenly she was sobbing. She tried to say more but her words came out a tacky, sticky mush. Meg, to her surprise, bent down and embraced her.

"Let's go back to the house, Em."

"Okay," Emily barely managed to say.

They stood up and shuffle-walked back up the incline toward the road, and from there, toward the house. Along the way, Meg confided in her:

"I didn't even know we had a boat."

THE FARM CAT'S TALE

It was known that cats could see ghosts; at least, it was known among cats. Why this was, none could say but the cats. (And they were not telling.)

It was also known, quite incorrectly, that cats were disloyal creatures. They break your things. They piss where they know not to. They'll eat your face should you take a bad spill. This was an imprecise read of the reality, which was that cats were *viciously* loyal, but did not lend out that loyalty freely or quickly—unlike dogs, who were instantly loyal to anyone who happened to look their way.

So, when the farm cat went into the orchard to find the house cat, it did so as an act of the gravest loyalty, because the orchard was most certainly haunted.

And though the farm cat would never admit it—

She was quite worried about the house cat.

The orchard—featuring seven strange trees, trees dark as thunderstorms, branches like lightning—was haunted, but not by ghosts. Haunting was not about death, but rather about something clinging to this world, something that did not belong in it. A something from a place or time beyond. Cats walked in this world but could feel the perforations between this world and those other places, punctures where sad things or cruel things or mad things slithered through like snakes through hollow logs. A cat could detect it in a ripple of fur, the rising of hackles, a nervous swoop of tail. When the farm cat entered the orchard looking for its friend, the house cat, its whole body reacted—an antenna catching an ill frequency. The very air felt *sour,* like sick, curdled milk.

The farm cat, a black velvet lady that slipped about like living shadow, had befriended the house cat next door a year ago. The house cat was fat and lumpy like a pile of orange sweaters, and the silly beast was stupid and sweet in equal measure. The house cat, truth be told, was a little bit dog—happy despite the terrors of an uncaring world. The farm cat found the other animal . . . amusing. Amusement went a long way with Black Velvet, and Orange Lump was an infinite fount of it.

The house cat, Orange Lump, was allowed out multiple times a day. At first Black Velvet tried to convince Orange Lump to hunt—after all, in the house he could hunt nothing but spiders, yes? Out here there were mice and moles and voles and rats and birds, so many pretty birds ready to be pinned to the ground and bopped upon the head until they died and were food. (Or sometimes, a toy.)

But Orange Lump mostly wanted to explore. Not hunt, but simply *wander about,* like a tourist. Black Velvet was a suitably good guide to the outdoor world, having lived in the barn of the family next door, milling about the pigs and the chickens, happily removing rats from the hay. Black Velvet met Orange Lump at every excursion, and they traveled together. (Orange Lump would've made an intriguing mate, had his bits not been sliced.)

There came a day, however, when Black Velvet was late meeting Orange Lump. The farm cat had fallen into a bin of feed (while chasing a rat) that closed above her head. She scrabbled and meowed and shrieked and it took a while for one of the human children—an older boy who helped with the animals, a boy who had a name but Black Velvet did not consider him friend enough to learn it—to open up the bin and let her out. At that time she *raced* to meet Orange Lump—

But the fool was gone. Gone off on his own.

Black Velvet, stung by his absence, let it be. *Fine.* If Orange Lump wanted to explore without her and couldn't be bothered to wait, then let him go. A cat could dine on indignation for days. It would feed her better than any songbird in her belly, and sing a sweeter song.

Ah, but her ire over the house cat's betrayal faded when Orange Lump's people called for him and he did not come. He *always* came. Orange Lump loved the house and the people in it and returned to that prison happily, and yet today—

Orange Lump did not come home.

The fool had likely gotten himself into trouble. Fallen into a well. Eaten by a fox or coyote. Or simply gone too far to hear his people calling and now he was lost out there, that wayward soft-brained naïf. Black Velvet knew if she did not find him, no one would, because *that* cat would just keep going and going until he reached the end of the world and had fallen off the edge.

So, Black Velvet went searching. The Lump's trail was easy enough to find—he did not have the sense of self-preservation to hide his tracks or his kitty litter smell. At first she thought he had been heading toward her barn to find her, but then he took a deviation to the property beyond it, to the creek that bordered it, to the briar and thicket past it. The thicket was no problem for her, but had been for him: She found tufts of orange fur stuck to rose thorn. She wound her way through the tangle undeterred, like water through a pipe.

And it was there she found the orchard.

And it was there that her tail stiffened, her skin tightened, and she let slip a reflexive hiss—a warning to the dread hum hanging in the air. The air was thick with it, far thicker than the briar-tangle behind her. She could hear other things, too: The gentle movement of something beneath the ground, chewing and twisting in the earth. She could hear the crack of something that sounded like the barn in a storm, the way it listed and shuddered, wood straining and buckling. A bone-break sound, but small bones, little bones, brittle bones.

Then she saw Orange Lump.

His head was low, his back bowed in a sloppy stance—his face slick with the juices of the fallen fruit he was eating. All around him were the remnants of apples, just their cores, messily chewed. Black Velvet stormed up to him and gave him a shove with her head, but he hissed at her, and hit her with an open-clawed paw across the face. She felt its sting, felt blood run into her eye, onto her teeth. The shock of this betrayal shook her. Orange Lump was no scrapper. Farm cats were scrappers. This house cat was a lazy river, not a roaring storm. Black Velvet could see that his eyes had changed, too. They'd always been the color of frost-flecked leaves, with big wide pupils—the eyes of a baby, a dopey human baby, taking it all in and understanding so very little of it. But now the eyes were brighter, sharper, crueler. And the pupils were down to the thinnest slits. Like the eyes of a serpent.

Black Velvet knew when she was staring at a predator.

Orange Lump had never been a predator. He had always, *always* been prey.

But that had changed.

Black Velvet pled with her friend one last time with no more than a searching, plaintive look—a rare moment of vulnerability for the farm cat. But the house cat only hissed in response. A messy, wet, gargled hiss. Spraying juice and spittle.

As the other cat went back to busily chewing an apple, resuming his swaying, drooping stance, Black Velvet fled. This place was a bad place. Whether it had always been bad or had simply gone bad, the farm cat could not say, but it was haunted now. Haunted by what, she didn't know. But something clung to it like a burr, a tick, something crawling upon it like blood-drunk fleas. And she feared that something clung to Orange Lump now, too.

Later, she would come back to see what had become of Orange Lump. And there she found him leaner, hungrier, meaner. Sometimes she saw him down near the creek, stalking the thicket with a blood-greased muzzle. She found his kills: They were messy and cruel, guts strewn about, feathers and fur spread wide, bones pulled out and arranged. Mostly, though, he kept to the orchard, where she would not go.

Something crept through the house cat these days. Worms and roots. Pushing through his once-soft earth, churning up something dark and something fertile.

Black Velvet had lost her friend in more ways than one.

OCTOBER

—

MY FAVORITE APPLE IS ONE THAT I AM SEARCHING FOR BUT HAVE
NOT FOUND YET.

—TOM BROWN,
APPALACHIAN APPLE HUNTER,
IN *SOUTHERN LIVING'S*
"TOM BROWN IS ON A MISSION
TO RESTORE APPALACHIA'S
RARE AND LOST APPLES,
AND HE'S FOUND OVER 1,000
TO DATE"

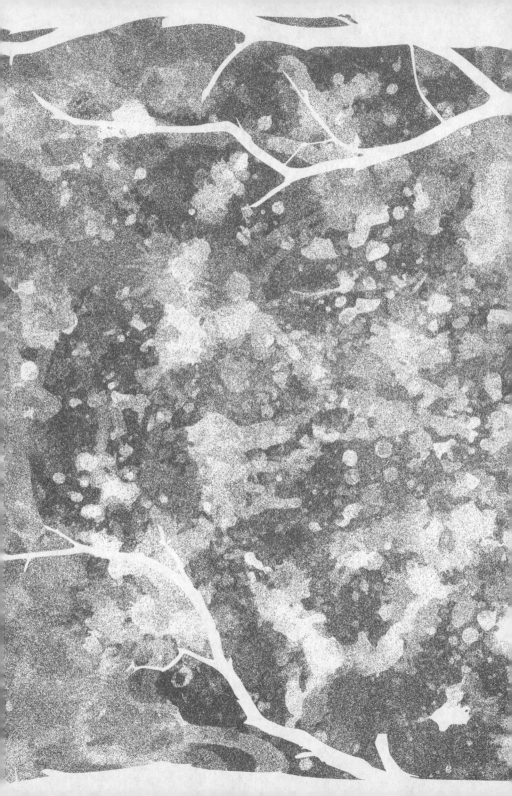

8

JOHN COMPASS, SEEKER OF LOST APPLES

MANALAPAN TOWNSHIP,
NEW JERSEY.

THOUGH IT WAS FIRMLY AUTUMN, THE SUMMER BUGS HAD YET TO leave. It was still hot, and the bugs clung to the heat the way the heat clung to the world; they rose up in a chorus like a cultic chant, *cha cha cha cha,* punctuated by the cricket song, *dreet dreet dreet.* John Compass welcomed the noise, even if it meant the bugs, and the heat, were overstaying their welcome. This was a world out of balance, but just the same, he liked the noise of the natural world, and he was glad it surrounded him here in this field.

The grasses were hip-high and swayed around him in the warm wind. A tick crawled at his elbow, and John picked it off and pinched it until it died. He did not like killing things, but he would make exceptions for ticks—few things ate them, and he'd already danced with Lyme disease. He didn't want whatever else the ticks wanted to give him, and he sure didn't want to give them his blood. So the tick had to die, and he reminded himself to do a tick check when he got out of this field because he might be covered in a carpet of the damn things.

In the distance waited a long, tall tree line—cedars burdened with mature juniper berries in dense, blue clusters. He saw the trees shudder and shake with the movements of squirrels, heard the trilling chatter of cedar waxwings. Greedy, handsome birds, the waxwings.

But the cedars were not what interested John—

No, he had his eyes set on a lone tree about thirty yards closer.

It was a gnarled thing, this tree—still alive, though it likely had only five, maybe ten years left in its life. There was a sadness to an old apple tree, but it was that sadness that made them easy to spot: the branches stooped and bent, as if in mourning, burdened by grief. (Though really, they'd been burdened by decades of heavy fruit.) Many of the branches on this tree were dying or dead, but a few were healthy and strong, and it was these branches that interested John Compass, because upon them hung apples the color of spun gold.

Upon reaching the tree, he placed a hand against its rough bark. John gave the tree a small utterance of gratitude, then reached into his pack and pulled out a small canteen of water, from which he drank a bit, then swished some before spitting it out. After that, he reached up for the lowest-hanging apple he could manage—not a difficult task, given how tall he was. He removed it the way one might remove a lightbulb from its fixture—a gentle yet purposeful twist.

The apple came free. He pulled it down and gave it a smell. The gentlest apple odor came off it, along with a whiff of something floral.

Elderflower, he thought.

With the front of his teeth he nibbled a bit of skin off—a bit bitter, waxy on the tongue, but something else, too. A curious sour note. Not unpleasant.

Then: a small lockback knife, Spyderco, three-inch blade. Plucked from his pocket. He used it to carve a slice from the apple, and he claimed that slice with his teeth. John chewed slowly, methodically, letting the experience move over him, flooding out from his mouth and through the rest of his body.

The taste: clean and bright. The elderflower was stronger here. It wasn't oversweet. The tartness was not mouth-puckering—it presented no challenge, and only served to complement the floral esters. He'd eaten strange apples before—spitters, obviously, some that tasted like soap, others like wood polish, and some more pleasant ones that just the same remained pretty damn funky, that had hints of mint, or banana, pork and tamarind. This one offered no such complexity, and in fact seemed proud of its simplicity. Its clarity was king.

This was it. This was the apple.

He'd finally found it.

At that, a sound arose in the distance, but swiftly coming closer—the telltale growl of a four-wheeler engine. It disrupted the quiet here. It was hard to find quiet anyplace anymore, John knew. The modern world always intruded. Everywhere you went, a low whine bored its way into your ear like a slow-spinning drill. The quad was no different: The chug-and-tumble of the engine lived not just in the ear, but the chest. It killed the silence all around, and worse, it killed the silence within. Another sound joined it: a mechanical mosquito whine. A *dirtbike*.

John steadied himself, willing his heart to calm.

Two vehicles approached, as expected, carving through the grass from the direction of a McMansion way off in the distance. The four-wheeler, ridden by a man. And a dirtbike, ridden by someone younger: a teenage boy.

The man on the approaching vehicle wore a Jersey Devils hockey jersey over his thick torso, his head matching the rest of his body, looking as much like a stump as his chest, his thighs, his biceps. A man of stumps, a dead-tree dude. The boy was lean as a snake, with a hangdog face and foolish eyes.

The man pulled up the four-wheeler close and cut the engine. The kid kept his dirtbike idling about twenty feet back.

The man, probably the father of the teenager, got off his four-wheeler and unslung a pump-action shotgun from behind him.

"Fuck are you?" he asked, Jersey accent on display.

John looked at the man's finger, which hovered too close to the trigger. This was not a man trained to use the 12-gauge Remington in his hand.

"I'm John Compass, sir," John said with a quiet voice and deferential tone. He was older than this man by a good ten years, he guessed, but deference was always the way to go. Until it wasn't.

"You're on my property."

John held up both hands, the one with the knife, the other with the apple. He gently closed the knife with his thumb, so as not to appear aggressive. "Sir, I was to understand this was preserved land. Part of the New Jersey Natural Lands Trust, buying and protecting open spaces."

"Yeah, well," the man stammered, clearly angry. "There's a dispute there. I own this piece of property."

John had been diligent looking into this. It was possible he was wrong, or that the trust register was inaccurate or not updated—when he needed to go onto someone's property, he always contacted the owner first. Trespassing was not in his interest. Maybe he could still rescue this situation.

"I apologize, sir," he said. "As I said, my name is John. You are?"

"Bostick. Joe Bostick." The man said his own name suspiciously, like he wasn't sure he should be giving it out. "That's my son. You don't need his name."

The boy stared on, wary.

"Mister Bostick. A pleasure. I'm here regarding this tree—"

"That ugly-ass thing?"

"It's an apple tree."

Bostick's shoulders juggled in condescension and disdain. "Yeah. I know it's a fuckin' apple tree, I can see the fuckin' apples. You know what? Grocery store has apples, too. Go there. And get the hell off my property."

"Well, now, sir. This apple—" John held it up, gave it a spin so that the golden skin caught the light. "It's special."

At that, the other man narrowed his eyes in suspicion—and interest. "Special how?"

"It's a lost apple, and I am a seeker of lost apples."

"Doesn't look lost to me."

"That's—" John felt his tone go sharp. He blunted it. "That's my point, sir. This is a variety thought to be lost—a Muuschhakgott apple." He did his best to say the word correctly, though he wasn't a good speaker of the words. "This used to be Lenape land. Lenapehoking. I believe they had an orchard here once, long ago. And this tree has survived that orchard's fall."

"You an Indian?" The man tapped his head. "Not one of these, but one of these—" Then he tapped the flat of his hand against his open mouth, some racist version of an Indian war cry.

"In part."

"You look white."

"As I said, in part."

"Uh-huh." The man's stare flicked from John to the tree and back to John again. "That tree valuable?"

"Not in the way you might be thinking. Its branches have value to me and I had planned to cut some growth off it, see if I could graft a tree from it, for no profit of my own—but I would be willing to pay a little for the privilege."

There. That had his interest. The fox, tantalized by the grapes. "How much?"

"One hundred dollars."

"Pssh, fuck off with that. Do better."

John sighed. He inhaled anger, exhaled peace. "I can do a hundred fifty dollars, but after that, I am regrettably without money to give. I wouldn't hurt the tree, if you're concerned—it would continue to grow without complaint." *Until it dies,* he thought. Which would be sooner than later, but he dared not mention that.

"I don't give a hot fuck about that tree. It's ugly as balls. It can go. And you know what? You can go, too. Trespassing on my property? You're lucky I don't shoot you where you stand. I'm within my rights. Stand your ground and all that."

"New Jersey doesn't have a stand-your-ground law, sir, only a castle doctrine—"

"Shut the fuck up, and you know what, fuck that tree."

At that, the man pointed the gun—

No!

He fired a buckshot blast—the shotgun kicked in the man's hand and bark sprayed up. Low branches shattered. He jacked another round and fired again, *choom,* chewing another hole in the trunk of the old apple tree—

John dropped the apple and moved fast. His legs were long and he crossed the distance between himself and the other man swiftly. As Bostick racked the pump on the Remington, John got up underneath the weapon, thrusting it up to the sky and using his thumb to dig sharply into the man's wrist. Bostick's grip relented, and John yanked the gun away, spun it around, and thrust the barrel against the other man's chest. Dead center to his heart.

John's hands shook. The gun trembled.

Dark, violent urges ran through him like ants chewing tunnels.

From the dirtbike, the boy's jaw dropped. But he didn't look scared. He didn't like his father much. That was clear. He watched, fascinated.

"My hands hold considerable violence," John said, quietly, firmly. At that, he pressed up the lifting bar underneath the shotgun, and racked the slide back again and again until the remaining four rounds ejected out into the grass. "But my heart will hold only peace." He spun the nut at the top of the shotgun's magazine, broke the barrel apart, let it drop to the ground, and following that, popped the slide out and off, too. He held the shotgun's stock like a club.

Bostick watched him with wide eyes.

John shoved the remaining gun parts into the man's arms, then said, "You hurt a good tree. It may die now, girdled by buckshot. All because you are a petty, uncontrollable man. I'm going to go over there and collect a series of branches. And you're going to let me because you recognize that escalating this in front of your son will only hasten his loss of respect for you." John pulled out his wallet, extracted three twenties and four tens, and peeled back the man's fingers from the remaining gun parts so that he could tuck the money there. "One hundred dollars."

Then he turned his back on the man, listening carefully in case he tried something else. He didn't. The man was shaken. John Compass took out the pruning shears from his bag and looked for scionwood to cut.

THREE BRANCHES, RESCUED. THE TREE'S DEATH WOULD COME IN the next year. Hastened by a brutal man with a fool's weapon. But maybe its soul could live on.

HIS BEAT-TO-HELL JEEP CHEROKEE SAT PARKED ON THE SIDE OF the road, and John Compass sat within it, leaning over the wheel as he exhaled a long, slow breath. He allowed himself to shake it out. The adrenaline had to gallop through him like a band of horses, and to fight that was to fight the tides, so he let it happen, let it stampede until all its spit and vigor was out, until it fled once more.

He set the branches next to him on the seat, along with a few more of the Muuschhakgott apples he'd picked off the tree.

From here, John could see the small figures of the man and the boy.

Both of them, still up there by the tree. No doubt the man was trying to put the gun back together again and failing to do so. Perhaps the teenager could show him a YouTube video. Children were considerably more resourceful than adults these days.

John started the engine of the Jeep just as his phone rang.

Saw the call was from Belinda Purvin.

His heart did a two-step. He answered. "Belinda, it's been a while—"

"You said you wanted me to tell you if they ever found anything, so fine, I'm calling you. They said they found a body."

"A body."

"Yuh-huh, a body. Somewhere down in Bucks County."

"Where? What town? Is it him?"

"I said I don't know. Somewhere. Call around or something, shit."

"I will. Thank you for calling. I need to come by at some point and—"

But she'd already hung up.

Something in his middle shrank up, shriveled, and died, leaving a hole in its place that filled with pooling dread and sudden grief. He'd been waiting for this news for years now. He blinked back tears.

Today, John Compass found a lost apple.

And soon, John Compass would go to find his lost friend.

9

WHAT ONE DESERVES

DAN SAT AT THE LUMBERTOWN CROSSING GENERAL STORE—NOT A store at all, but a little café. Started as a coffeehouse some years back, now served breakfast and lunch. It was a cozy place, all dark wood, low-lit. Had the feeling of being a cabin way up in the woods, away from the world. An escape.

Dan never ate here. Too pricey.

But now . . .

You deserve this, Dan.

The apples were selling like nothing else at the farmers market. They cleaned him out every Sunday, all month. Sure, he had a shedload of backed-up bills he had to pay—Calla wanted to go to a pricey college, the truck needed a new fan belt, plus there were all the costs of maintaining the house and the orchard. Dan did odd jobs around town and county—usually ag jobs like baling hay or trimming trees or even doing soil tests for a lot of these little up-and-comer farmers. But he wasn't averse to doing any kind of handy work within his skill set. Repairing drywall? Why not. Mortar or tilework? Okay. Hell, last month he replaced Mrs. Garris's mailbox, since some kids took a bat to it, knocked it into the ditch. That kind of money wasn't ever consistent, though. It came in fits and starts. But suddenly? He had cash in hand, thanks to his apples.

So, he decided he deserved a little treat.

Normally, every Tuesday, he found his way to the Keystone, a diner at the north end of Doyle's Tavern, and it was there he had the cheapest thing on their menu: cup of coffee, plus the classic egg plate—two eggs "over-greasy" ("rhymes with easy," the menu said), wheat toast, hash browns. It was a classic for a reason. Maybe a little boring. But it was reliable.

But today? A treat and a change of scenery. Instead of a black coffee, he had something called a flat white. Didn't even ask what it was, only if it had caffeine in it. And on a plate in front of him was a set of gorgeous buckwheat pancakes (with pumpkin butter because it was October, after all), and a side of the crispiest home fries—potatoes, peppers, and onions cooked in duck fat. One bite and he was ready to die and meet his maker, just to thank the heavens for the plate of food in front of him.

Three bites in, though, he saw someone come in, winding through the little tables, heading right toward him like a heat-seeking missile.

Chase Hardiaken. Like a cellared beer, the man had only aged better with time, and Dan resented the hell out of him for it. Like Dan, he was in his late forties, and while he didn't look younger than his age, he looked like the epitome of it: in good shape, well-cut, nice clothes, veneers, the whole package.

"If it isn't the silver fox," Dan said.

The other man chuckled and thrust out a hand, which Dan of course took. "Been a while, Dan."

"Grab a seat," Dan said. He privately hoped Chase would say no and move on, that this was just a cursory hello. They hadn't been close since high school. Especially given who Chase's father was. But Chase nodded and offered his high-dollar smile and grabbed the seat Dan offered.

"How you been? I heard you been making quite the splash at the farmers market," Chase said, holding up a finger and flagging down the waitress. *Shit, he's ordering food.*

"Who knew folks had such an insatiable taste for apples?"

Chase smirked. "I think you did, Dan. You really nailed it. You know, that old fuck Lambert, he said you were pretty cocky about it that first day."

"Well, I believed in the product is all." He didn't want to go down this road, so he veered away. "How's the Judge?"

The Judge: Martin Hardiaken. Chase's father.

"He retired from the bench but I guess you knew that, huh?" Dan couldn't tell if that was a jab or just an assessment of reality. "You know, he waited his whole life for retirement and six months into it, boom, prostate cancer."

"Shit, Chase, I'm sorry."

(*Are you, though, Little Dan?*)

"What's the prognosis?"

Waitress came, and Chase ordered a quad-shot espresso. No food, blessedly. When she was gone he answered, "Ah, you know, it's spread around. Seems like it's in his liver now and—other day, the whites of his eyes went yellow, like he hadn't taken a piss in three days and it was backing up to his eyeballs. But, they think they maybe have a shot at tackling it."

"Wish him my best." Dan didn't mean it, and honestly it was hard to say those words with a straight face, but manners were manners and you didn't take a swipe at a

(*hopefully*)

dying man.

"So, you know, if you don't mind my saying, I think there's a play with Lambert if you want to make it."

Back to Lambert. Dan sighed. "I don't follow—?"

"He's burned. Hurt, I think. About the property and about your success at the orchard—which, fuck him, seriously, I know what he did to you and to your family, he doesn't get to play the wounded soldier. He started that war, I get it."

"Yes. Thank you for saying that."

"But maybe that's an opportunity for you."

"Sure, an opportunity to keep pissing him off by bringing in a bigger market crowd than that vineyard of his. I mean, that stuff he calls wine—"

Chase laughed, but like his heart wasn't in it. "I'm saying there's money there for you if you want it. He's got *plenty*. Pick his pockets."

"Money."

"The property."

"Chase, just say what you mean." Dan shoved a forkful of pancake into his mouth but suddenly it wasn't as tasty.

"Lambert will buy that property. He's agitated about it. All of the Crossed Keys are." The Crossed Keys: a de facto "networking" club here in the center county. Old money, lots of nepotism. "You snatching it out from under him—"

Dan damn near choked on that pancake, forcing it down so he could swiftly vent spleen. "Snatching it out from under him? Jesus, Chase. That was my father's land, my father's house. I'm just reclaiming what's mine." He was tempted to add that Lambert didn't even own it—the township did. But that wasn't really right, was it? Because Lambert was a county commissioner and helped control what counted as open, conserved space around here. Maybe he didn't own that dog, but he sure held the leash.

"He just sees it different. And you can understand a little. Your father's big thing was growing an orchard, but remember, he overextended himself . . ." Dan remembered just fine: Pop needed a co-signer on, well, everything—Lambert did him that favor. If it was a favor at all. Chase shrugged. "Your father became . . . erratic, Dan. Can't blame Lambert too much."

"The man was under stress, Chase. Stress *Lambert* put on him, Lambert, who was supposed to be a friend to him but who was just using him—" *Like all you rich pricks love to do* were words he bit back and swallowed.

"Okay, okay, you're not wrong, I only mean, Lambert sees it like he was trying to help, and then it was his name on the line when it all went to shit."

"And your father ruled in his favor on that."

(and then Dad shot himself in the mouth)

(with a gun he did not own)

Dan's hand curled around the fork, knuckles gone bloodless.

"The Judge wasn't a good man," Chase said. *Wasn't. Past tense.* The man hadn't died, but Chase had already buried him. The Judge was an abusive sonofabitch—not with his hands, no. But the things he said, the names he called his own son, the way he treated him? That was still abuse in Dan's book. Maybe worse than a smack in the face or a spank on the ass. "And I won't pretend I think he made the right call. Judge Carver fixed that error. Which is good for you, it means you have a nice piece of property now. With these trees, these apple trees. I hear they're really producing. Great. So let me say again: Lambert will buy that property."

Dan sniffed. "You're here carrying water for him."

A disappointed look crossed Chase's face, though whether that was because he'd been busted or because he didn't like the accusation, Dan couldn't tell.

"It's not like that—this helps you more than him. Lambert doesn't need the property, but you can rope-a-dope him into paying a pretty penny for it." Chase hesitated for a moment, then said: "I know you need the money."

"I'm making real money now, thanks to my apples."

"How long's that going to go on for?"

"Long as I need it to. Apples are American. Always in favor."

"But not always in *season,* yeah? You're nearing the end of harvest already. So, what? You make a few bucks a pound, a thousand pounds in a season, hell, let's say *two* thousand pounds, a literal ton of apples—it's still not a living, Dan. But the property. Think about it. You're sitting on over *forty acres* in Central Bucks County. Surrounded by rolling hills and babbling brooks and boutique shopping and all that touristy pamphlet shit. Plus: old farmhouse. Real-deal old farmhouse. Needs work, sure. Property needs some love, agreed. But you can get close to a million for that, easy. And Lambert will come in hot. Because he's greedy and his pride is hurt and because he needs to fill a hole in himself."

In that moment, Dan's feelings whirled around him like a roulette wheel, red and black in a spinning carousel. The red: He wanted to take his fork and stick it in the other man's neck. The black: He was crushed, because Chase might be right, this might not be a living, it might just be a sad plateau—a flat line in business was a flatline like when your heart stopped.

Rage danced with shame inside him.

My dream, he thought.

My father's dream.

I won't give that up.

At that, a tingle crawled across his skin and he felt suddenly, giddily buoyant. It was confidence. That's what it was. A feeling he hadn't felt in so long it felt like an alien emotion. Confidence and certainty, a surefootedness in himself, in his father's dream, in the orchard. He could taste

(the apple in his mouth, slicking his tongue, his teeth, sweet acid in the back of his throat, bitter appleskin)

(the gun in his mouth)

(the pills in his mouth)

success, and it felt good.

Dan nodded, smiled, and put a forkload of salty crisp potato in his mouth. It tasted *sublime.* "Don't you worry about me, Chase. I've got it figured out."

The other man seemed puzzled by this. Dan's sudden steadiness put the other man off-balance—and Chase Hardiaken was never off-balance.

"Okay," Chase said, offering an awkward smile. At that, the waitress came and set down a small mug. His espresso. He sipped at it, staring into it. "I should probably be heading out—" But then his eye caught something. Two women came into the place, went to the counter to order. One woman had hair the color of mist—so gray it was almost purple. The other was taller, most of her upper torso lost in the pool of a flowy black sweater. Dark hair, straight until it curled at the ends, framed her face like a pair of parentheses. "See them?" Chase asked.

"Yeah."

"Dark-haired girl's the one who found that body last week."

Dan suppressed a shudder. "Body?"

"You think she's Asian? She might be Asian." He lowered his voice. "She's hot. But I think they're a couple, if I heard it right."

"Chase. What body? A—a human body?"

"You didn't hear? Yeah, the Asian one fell in the river or something and came up with a bone or skull or something. They found other parts caught in a fallen tree. Crazy. I hear it's probably some boater or fisherman or something."

Dan forced a smile. "Yeah, probably."

Had to be that.

It couldn't be—

He didn't even want to think about it.

All he knew was, the meal he saw as his treat was now ruined for sure. First Chase, now this. He pushed his plate aside. Chase said goodbye, but Dan barely noticed. All he could think about was that day, five years ago. The worst day and the best day. The day it all changed.

10

TWO BONES DIVERGED

Marco was the coolest fucking boyfriend in the whole fucking world and this was why: When Calla told him she wanted to protest his track event because of transphobic bullshit on the part of the newly elected super-conservative suck-ass school board, he told her, "Cool." Like, pure attitude of *whatever you want, babe,* kiss-on-the-cheek, go-go-go.

The school board was riding a wave of astroturfed dark money from right-wing idiots, and as such they'd chosen to withhold sports funding unless the school banned trans students from participating in those sports. (Something-something boys dressed as girls are cheating because of their testosterone, something-something boys dressed as girls just want to watch the girls change in the locker rooms, something-something it's all against God, even though as Esther pointed out, Jesus looked more than a little bit trans, didn't he?) It was Esther's idea to protest— Esther, who had come out recently as enby, pronouns they/them—and so here they were, standing alongside the track with another trans friend, Lucas, pronouns he/him. Calla had her phone out and ready, selfie camera spun around.

At the far end of the track, the runners gathered. It was the hundred-meter dash. Eight students lined up together, crouching by the starting blocks. In the reversed camera she saw her boyfriend down there, second in from the left. She snapped a selfie, pointing to him. She'd pop in some pink emoji hearts later.

Lucas, with his coiffed dark hair and his pouting mouth, eyeballed her. "You're not just doing this for clout, right?"

"What? Shut up."

"Like, you actually believe in this, right? Or are you just . . . farming for followers."

"She believes in it," Esther said to Lucas, and Calla caught a whiff of their breath and the little cloud of cotton-candy vape vibe hanging there. "She's an ally, dude, relax. Besides, she already has a bunch of followers, it's cool."

Calla wanted to say, *Yeah, see, I'm not doing this for clout,* but then she thought, *I still need the followers, though.* Always more followers. And yet. The question rattled her so much that she missed the pop of the starting gun—

Gun went off, and the sprinters bolted.

Calla fumbled with her phone, nearly dropping it before thumbing RECORD. Already a precious pair of seconds passed—and these races were fast. Marco wanted to score under his previous record of 10.6 seconds. Already his legs were launching him forward like a rocket.

But this wasn't about him, she reminded herself, as she joined the chorus of her friends, yelling over the announcer's booming voice that *trans girls are girls, trans boys are boys,* knowing that they had only a handful of seconds to actually say what they wanted to say—though later they'd add more to the video, like details about how many transgender adults and students were in the United States—

And that's when Calla heard it. A sound like she'd never heard before, a sound she felt in her teeth, that she'd replay later not just on the phone but in her own bad dreams—

It was only later that she'd see how it happened.

The boy next to Marco drifted into his lane.

Marco's body, on autopilot, eased away to compensate.

But moving that fast, even the tiniest imbalance was a killer.

His hip shifted. Then his leg.

His ankle twisted.

The bone snapped.

That sound was bad, a sound like the starting gun going off again, but wetter, more muffled. Worse was the scream that followed. Marco cried out even before he hit the ground, shoulder first. The other kids kept running, because they were trained to—but Marco was down. Screaming. Crying out. Calla ran to him. They all did.

And she'd never be able to put it out of her mind, what she saw.

SHE'D HEARD ABOUT COMPOUND FRACTURES. BUT CALLA HAD never seen one. Had never seen the way the foot would hang there, like it wasn't attached to the leg anymore.

But Marco's foot *was* still attached—but only because his skin formed a sock and that skin-sock was the only thing holding the foot to his body. The skin-sock dangled there, a pouch full of all the little bones. She realized with horror that if you were to grab what was left of Marco's dangling foot, and give a pull, the whole thing would rip right off.

How fragile he was. How fragile they all were. Just animated sacks of bone and blood and mess, so easily spilled out of you. It made her think of roadkill. The raw, red ruination of it.

THE HOSPITAL. LATER. CALLA SAT, SHELL-SHOCKED. NOT JUST from the sound of the bone breaking, or the blood, or Marco's screams. But from the way he had to wait for so long in the waiting room. They brought towels out to soak up the blood. Marco passed in and out of consciousness, his chin dipping to his chest before startling awake again. His parents showed up. They were angry—at who, they didn't know, but they were demanding answers. The coach was there, and he got the brunt of it. Meanwhile someone brought a new towel to replace the soggy wet pile that was the other one. Dripping red in a medical tray. Like something had been birthed as it died. Messily.

Before they took Marco back, he looked at her—he looked lost. Like he saw past her. His brow was sweaty, his face almost gray. His eyes were bloodshot. And he said to her, or maybe to the world, "There goes my scholarship." She told him no, it'd be fine, she knew it would.

But how would it? How could it?

Then he was gone, and the parents went with, and she was left waiting. Esther texted her:

how bad??

And she texted back:

I guess real bad but they'll know more later

Esther: u need a ride??

Calla: No my dad's coming l8r

Esther: ok, love u, ping if you need sumthin

Calla: You know I will

Calla: Love you too sorry if this screwed up the video

Esther: nah it's cool nothing's fkt up

Esther: (except Marco's leg I mean)

Esther: (shit thats insensitive srry didnt mean it as a joke!!)

Calla wondered if any of this *was* her fault, somehow, like, could Marco have been watching her watching him? Could he have resented her not rooting for him and instead filming some . . . social justicey shit? She wanted to watch the video again but couldn't bring herself to do it. She just wanted to sit here in the emergency waiting room and cry but what an asshole that made her, what with *her* feeling all bad for herself when her boyfriend was getting wheeled back to some room where they were going to try to figure out how to fix an ankle that had shattered like a rotten tree branch.

All the while, she sat surrounded by sick people. A woman coughing into a pile of tissues, the cough coming up from the well of her chest like a dog bark. A squat bald man clutching his chest, sweating. A younger kid holding a wet cloth over a swollen eye, his mother exhorting him to *keep holding it there, Tyler, what did I tell you.*

Another ping hit her phone. Esther again.

Esther: ok this sucks but Lucas is asking for the video

Calla: Uh yeah no. We can't use it

Esther: he thinks maybe we can still??

Esther: he says he has the other videos ready to roll

Esther: he'll edit then sned back to u to post

Esther: *send, wtf is a sned

She knew that Lucas was going to make this part of a bigger thing, an informational push about trans rights and stuff, and that was cool and she was totally on board but like, what? Right now? She was still looking at a pinkish smear on the tile from where Marco's foot had puddled blood.

Calla felt like a hot mess, all parts of her like a big emotional brush burn. She couldn't help but feel irrationally irritated; Esther should've known now was not the time and shouldn't be doing this for Lucas, but whatever. *I'm just tired.* She said nothing else and just texted them the video.

Not long after, her father showed up. He swept her up in a hug. It was what she needed.

HER FATHER WAS DIFFERENT FROM OTHER DADS. MOSTLY. HE STILL did all the classic dad things: made dad jokes and embarrassed her with how proud he was of her and of course he was a big dorky dork twenty-four-seven. But other fathers, other *parents* even, rode their kids into the ground. They put them in two sports a week plus an extracurricular; they demanded the best grades; they talked to their children like they were waiters, *go do this, get me this, don't do that, that's not right so send it back.* Around here, you had to be the best. Anything less than an A was an F. Second place was last place. Because you *were* your parents. You were an offshoot of them, not separate, not different. Anything you did reflected on them. If you failed, they failed. If *you* excelled? *They* excelled.

It was a fucking battle royale around here.

But Calla's father just wasn't like that. He always said he was happy with her no matter what. He'd lost her mother and so Dad always said he'd never push Calla away, because he didn't want to lose her, too. He always wanted her close.

Her grades didn't matter to him—all that he said he cared about was that she did her best, gave it her all. He didn't care if she did this sport or that club. Though sometimes that pissed her off, because despite him not caring about it, every other parent and every other kid *did*. This was a competitive area with a competitive school. You had to compete. Sometimes she felt angry at him because he never put that pressure on her and maybe she could've, like, used a little of that pressure? Maybe he could—and *should*—ask more of her?

Her friends thought that was fucked up and it probably was.

("Dude, your dad loves you," Esther said once while they were sitting outside the water ice place in town, eating custard. "My dad doesn't know I exist and neither of my parents will use my pronouns. Maybe don't complain?" Lucas, though, had a different take: "He's a little too cozy with you, girl. Nobody should be besties with their parent. It's weird and you know it.")

Of course, her friends were never good enough for him, because in his words, "Calla Lily, you're too good for this world. You're better than all of them and don't you ever forget it."

DAD BROUGHT SNACKS FOR MR. AND MRS. MEZA, MARCO'S PARents, because he knew they'd be here awhile and even offered to go pick up dinner for them. He brought a bag of his apples, too, because he knew Marco liked them. He sat with the Mezas for a while, and Mr. Meza explained what the doctor had told him.

"The doctor said they're going to have to do surgery." Mr. Meza was hunched over in the waiting room chair like a praying man. He looked at his feet as he talked, rocking back and forth just so, like the hospital was a boat bobbing in water. Mrs. Meza was in with Marco. It was just them out here.

"What kind of surgery?" Dad asked softly, sitting across from him, close enough their knees could be touching.

Mr. Meza held his hands by his face as if he were trying to escape captured thoughts and hold them to his head. "I don't know, I don't know. Pins and—and rods. Screws to hold it all in place. They said it was good, um, good that some kind of plate? An ankle plate? That he was the right age for that plate to be—" He shook his head as if there was a storm in it he was trying to shake out. "Done growing, I don't understand it all, I confess." The frustration in his voice was plain.

Calla's father reached out and put a hand on Mr. Meza's knee.

"That's good, Luis, that's very good," Dad said.

"Better than the worst but still—still bad. He'll be down awhile. Three months probably. Which will take him away from the track and the restaurant and—" The words fled as Mr. Meza shook and Calla realized he was crying while trying very hard not to cry. Like he was compressing down to keep the tears inside. A seizure of grief. One he tried and failed to bury.

(*There goes my scholarship . . .*)

She felt like a stupid little kid who couldn't do anything and who didn't know what to say and who couldn't fix any of this. Marco wouldn't get a scholarship now? Was that what this was? He'd been the fastest on their team. He ran competitive numbers. Enough to get a good ride to a good school. But if he couldn't run—

If he couldn't *demonstrate* his value to the school—

And then off his feet he couldn't work for the restaurant, either, which he did a bunch of days out of the week—

No track, no job, no scholarship, no money, no college.

Plus hospital bills.

Shit shit shit shit, I'm so sorry, Marco.

Her father leaned closer and patted Luis Meza on the arm and said, "We'll get through it. Whatever you need, just let us know. Heck, you want me to do a shift at the restaurant, I'll be glad to. I don't know how to make a lot of those Peruvian dishes, but I love to eat them and I'm handy in the kitchen." Luis Meza nodded and softly offered his thanks.

At that, Dad signaled to Calla silently: *Come on, we better go.* She stood up. Dad headed down the hall and stopped for a moment, heading into Marco's room. Calla watched from the door as her father bent by the bed and said something to her half-sleeping boyfriend, who lay immobilized, his foot in a huge cast and lifted at a forty-five-degree angle. Marco nodded a little, then closed his eyes.

When Dad came out, Calla asked him what he said to Marco.

"Oh, I told him I left some apples for him. I know he likes them. An apple a day and all that. Wishful thinking, maybe."

"Thanks, Dad."

"Of course. I had a rough day but . . . this puts it in perspective. Marco will be all right, Calla Lily. We'll make sure of it." Somehow, she believed him. The way he said it he sounded so sure. How could such certainty be wrong?

11

THE MOTHER

A KNOCK ON THE DOOR WHEN YOU WERE NOT EXPECTING ONE FELT
to Emily like literal violence. People who just . . . *showed up* at your house?
Completely unnerving. It was an older-generation thing, she knew, to
simply "pop by" unannounced. But her generation didn't even like to
take or make *phone calls,* thank you, much less answer the door for a total
fucking stranger.

So when someone knocked on the door—and then rang the bell only
moments later—Emily nearly knocked her seaweed salad off the counter.
She grabbed her phone and looked at the doorbell cam.

Oh, shit.

Not a stranger.

This was worse.

Emily craned her head back and groaned a guttural sound.

Maybe she won't know I'm here.

Of course she knows I'm here where else am I going to be.

Fuck shit fuck.

Emily licked a bit of sesame dressing off her thumb and then went to
answer the door, where Meg's mother, Noreen, waited to be let in.

"Emily," Noreen said, a hollow chirp. Noreen looking like an Elder
Paltrow, what with the ash-blond hair, the yoga pants, the model's jawline, the long (too-long) neck. About her hovered a miasma of cloying
perfume that Emily knew had to be expensive but to her always smelled
like toilet cleaner. In the woman's hands were two grocery bags from
Wegner's. "Hello, my dearest," she said as she tapped Emily's elbow in a
distant, odd act of what may have been affection. She pushed past before
Emily could say anything.

Resisting the urge to sneak out and run into the woods, Emily sighed
and followed the trail of rich-lady fragrance to the kitchen, where already Noreen was unpacking the two grocery bags. It wasn't even food

they needed—it was a strange assortment of products, from fillets of whitefish to dried chickpea pasta to a five-pound bag of carrots. "I found good deals, just some staples to use for meals." At that, she lifted her head and looked up, as if at a very real lightbulb that winked on above her head. "Oh, that rhymes."

"Uh, thanks," Emily said. "You didn't have to, though—"

Noreen wheeled on her. "Have you learned to cook yet?"

"Ah. No, we usually just do DoorDash or, like, yesterday we went to this little café, Lumberville something-or-other—"

"My Meggy needs good cooking, Emily, this isn't the city, you can't just roll out of bed at noon on a Tuesday and head to the—the bodega or whatever."

"That's more a New York thing, the bodega. Philly, it's still the corner store—and it's fine, we're good." *Shit, be gracious.* "Thank you for this, though?"

Noreen stopped for a moment, hands planted on the counter, leaning forward like Emily was suddenly the most interesting person in the world. "We haven't seen you since you moved here. Meg tells me you want to do more . . . *charity work.*" The last two words, ladled with distaste.

"I am. Though I think Meg needs me here for a little while, at the house—"

"Good, good. She does. Mm." A pause. "And you found a dead body."

Emily flinched. "I I did, though it was less a body and more just, you know, bones." *A person once,* she told herself, repressing a shudder and an odd spike of grief for whoever that was there in the river.

"You could write a book about the body. With your free time. People like books."

"I mean, it wasn't George Washington's body, so probably not."

Noreen laughed at that, but it was a practiced laugh. Not condescending, not exactly, but one that failed to express actual mirth, a social cue more than a reaction. *Insert laugh here.* "What do you think about Meggy's job, hm? Her father's old firm. How are you liking Bucks? It's beautiful here. Dead bodies in rivers aside." Another practiced laugh.

Her head spun. Did she answer the question about Meg's job? Or the question about the beauty of Bucks? "I've been here before—" Emily started to say but then her phone rang. It was a number she didn't know.

"Is that Meg? She's probably saying she's on her way."

Rattled, Emily asked, "Why would she be—?" *On her way.* The phone kept ringing. "No, it's not her, I don't know who it is."

"Don't answer it, it's spam. I get so much spam these days. It's astonishing how often they're just Chinese people speaking Chinese. I assume they're trying to scam other Chinese people—are there that many in this country?"

At that, Emily's guts cinched tight like a choking rope.

"Do you speak Chinese?" Noreen asked.

"No," Emily said firmly, trying to sound sweet and placating and not, say, ready to bite the woman's face off. "My mother was Korean."

"Right, right, of course." Noreen held up her finger. "Oh! I have some of those farmers market apples—god, Meg was right about those, have you had them? Paul and I are *addicted.*" Paul: Meg's father. Like various cryptids, often talked about, rarely seen. "I'll get them from the car."

Emily sent the call on her phone to voicemail as Noreen power-walked back out of the house. Not knowing if she was supposed to follow or not, Emily went with it, trailing after, dragged by the woman's turbulent wake. But already Noreen was, apple bag in hand, charging back toward the door—just as Meg's Audi pulled in the driveway.

As Meg exited the car, Emily greeted her and they went inside together. Jokingly, Emily asked, "Is this an intervention?"

To which Noreen chimed in: "*Should* this be an intervention?" A serious question to a joke. But then she chuckled: "I suspect we'll all need an intervention from eating too many of these apples. Yum." She set the bag down.

"We have a surprise for you," Meg said to Emily.

"This is all . . . a big surprise already," Emily said, trying to feign positivity but feeling the sarcasm and discomfort leak into her words like chemical runoff.

At that, they went *back* outside. Noreen led them to her new Lexus LX, a big white beast of a luxury SUV. Emily suddenly wondered if that was the surprise—Noreen just wanted to show off her shiny new car. Probably offer to drive her around in it. Give her some tour of the county, showing off, what, all the fanciest McMansions and old-money farmhouses and shiny new upscale grocery stores?

But then they headed around to the back of the vehicle—

Where a pair of bicycles hung from the back on a rack.

"Et voilà," Meg said, doing a stiff magician's reveal.

Emily tried to display the emotion they wanted her to display, which she assumed was shock and delight, but it was difficult to hide the fact she didn't quite understand what this even was. "Bicycles!" erupted out of her, overcompensating for the confusion she felt presently. "What. I mean. Great. But what?"

Noreen made a small noise, like a snobbish cat confronted with cheap kibble in its bowl. Half grunt, half sniff.

Meg was a blunt instrument sometimes, but she'd been with Emily long enough to be an antenna to her true feelings—and so she seemed to expect that reaction. Explaining further, she said, "Bear with me. I bought us a pair of new bicycles. Cannondales—Synapse model, which the cyclery salesman said were their best road bikes. I figure we can ride on weekends, but also, while I'm at work, if you wanted to toodle around the area, you totally can."

"Toodle around. On a bike."

"Absolutely. When I was a kid, I'd ride five, ten miles in every direction. I'd ride to my friend Nina's house, or there was this group of boys we called The Crew, and we'd ride to places that were supposed to be haunted or where we could skip stones or draw on the road with chalk— I used to be really into art "

Noreen bristled. "Meg, just get to the point."

"I just mean, the bikes will be fun."

Emily lowered her voice a little. "I need a car, Meg, not a . . . bicycle."

"Em, you haven't driven a car in a while."

"I haven't ridden a bike in even longer, since I was a kid in California. I don't trust myself on a bike." *And let's not forget how I couldn't even manage a boat,* she thought. It had been a couple weeks now since she nearly drowned in the river. She had nightmares every night about it. The water. The body. Her voice trembled a little, and she felt mad at herself for sounding weak. "The bikes are cool, thank you, seriously, but even if we could look at something pre-owned or whatever, a small car, maybe an electric or hybrid—"

At that, Noreen was over her shoulder like a mockingbird, perched there. "Emily, sometimes it's important to take life in stages. One thing after the next, everything in order, in a line. We earn the next stage—"

Emily wheeled on her. "What did *you* do to earn your new Lexus?"

The shock of Emily's impudence registered on her face like an earthquake.

"Well."

Guilt descended on Emily like a dropped rock. "Fuck, I'm sorry, okay? I didn't mean to—infer anything about—shit."

"Mom," Meg said. "Give us a minute."

Dutifully, Noreen receded, like the tide. Inside the house she went, leaving Meg and Emily alone outside.

"My mother means well," Meg said.

"I know. I get it. She just—she showed up unannounced and you know how I feel about surprises. I don't like them. I don't think anybody actually likes them."

"Granted. I just thought the bikes would be nice. You and I could ride together and I hoped you'd think that would be nice, too."

"I do. I mean, it does. Sound nice, I mean. Lovely bike ride along the canal path? Definitely, sign me up, I love it. I just want to—I want to get out of the house. Find meaningful work. I feel trapped—"

"Trapped." The way Meg said that word was a door closing, not a door opening. She didn't want to know more. With one word, her guard was up.

"Yes. Don't you get that? I'm frazzled, Meg. I feel stuck. We moved here because you wanted to move here and I went along with that—"

Meg's jaw stiffened, her chin up and out. "You went along with it because there was a *problem,* Em, and this was the solution." At that, the Unspoken Thing rose its head. It had been off in the distance but suddenly, here it was, looming over them like a tidal wave frozen in place. "You made choices and I made choices. You didn't have to come. But you did. And you knew what that meant, Emily. *You* put us on this path—"

Both rage and guilt roared up inside Emily, hot and cold: a feeling of anger at Meg at moving them here, and a feeling of anger at *herself* for making Meg move them here. She felt like a blame dispenser, a shotgun blast of shame in every direction. Meg, Noreen, herself. Even the dead guy in the river. *Fuck you, dead guy. Why did you have to be there underfoot? You could've been anywhere in the world but you had to get your skull stuck on my goddamn boot.*

"I put us on this path, I know. You know how I know? Because you remind me *all the time,* Meg. Oh, not that we actually talk about it. No. You just needle at me. Little comments. Little bites, like cat teeth. And I can't—" *Take it anymore.* Her phone rang again. Same number as before. They hadn't left a message. And suddenly, the rectangular shape of that glowing phone screen looked like a portal—a way out of this conversation. "Just hold on."

She turned her back to Meg, and answered it.

"What?" she said into the call.

On the other end, a firm, slow voice. Male.

"Are you Emily—" She heard the rustling of paper. "Bergmann?"

"I am." She hazarded a glance to Meg, who was cutting her down with a sickle-sweep stare. Thrusting up a finger, she continued. "Why, who is this?"

"Ma'am, my name is John Compass and I'd like to ask you some questions about the man you found in the river last month. I believe those bones were the bones of an old friend, and I'm hoping you can help me with some information."

"Oh." The man on the other end said nothing and she was afraid the call had dropped, but no—they were still connected. "I . . ." Emily stammered, seeing that Meg was giving her a classic *what the hell, Em?* look. "Yeah, sure, whatever you need, Mister Compass."

"John, please," he said by way of a request. "I'd like you to show me where you found the bones. If you're amenable."

Meg was staring hot death at her. She feigned apology.

"Sure. Just swing by my house. It was only a couple minutes down the road where I found them." *Them?* "The bones. Him, I mean." *Shit.* "How soon can you come by?"

"I'm in the area now."

"Great," Emily said, coldly happy that this would not only grant her an escape from this situation, but also irritate both Meg and Noreen. She gave him the address and said, "See you soon, John Compass."

12

WHERE THE RIVER OFFERED DEATH

EVEN AT A DISTANCE, EMILY COULD FEEL THEIR EYES BURNING. Meg and Noreen. Walking down the road with a strange man who showed up out of nowhere only infuriated them more. And Emily knew it wasn't a good idea. He *was* a stranger. But she figured this was safe enough—they were so close to the house, and it was worth it to see the look on Meg and Noreen's precious faces.

Which, she knew, was spectacularly petty of her.

Peppermint Petty.

Petty LaBelle.

Petty Cake, Petty Cake, Baker's Man.

She knew she'd pay for it later. Mentally, she should've been preparing her apology, but instead she was staring at the tall man regarding the river and the long-fallen tree. He was lean and knotty, with too-long arms that dead-ended at broad, thick-fingered hands. Himself, like a tree. Face like a mask of bark, too—the crags and crannies, the sunspotted skin, the squared-off jaw (and nose and cheekbones and ears). A full head of birch-gray hair, swooped back, not one strand out of place. Like all of him was carved.

"This is the place," she said again.

"Yes," he answered, still staring out.

She guessed that was it, then. Like she should just walk back. She didn't want to, though. Not yet. Those two were waiting for her return and she was not eager to meet their judgmental wrath—even if said wrath was well deserved.

Instead, she said, "I'm sorry about your friend." She paused and added: "If it . . . was your friend."

"Thank you. It was."

"How do you know?"

"Dental records."

"Oh. Okay." She shuffled about, kicked a stone. "Do you have any questions? I don't know that I have much to offer, but—"

He pointed to the river, to the tree. "All the bones they found were there?"

"Yeah. Right there, close to shore. Mixed up in the tree branches. All that tangle acted like a net, I guess. Maybe he was out here fishing, and the tree fell on him." She felt like a detective, then. Trying to solve this sad, simple little mystery. That's how deaths usually were, right? The simplest answer was usually the right one. Occam's razor or whatever.

"No. Walt didn't fish."

Walt. He had a name, now. "Gotcha."

"He was down here looking for apples."

"Apples."

"Rare varieties. Heirlooms. Lost apples."

"Sure," she said, as if any of that made any sense at all. (It didn't.)

"I suspect his body floated downriver. Which means he died upriver somewhere, probably not too far, or it would've been spotted, or caught elsewhere. Might still be more of him farther down, too. If more of him drifted."

Right, what they'd found here was not all of the person, was it? It was only half of him. *Walt.* She shuddered because again, this agglomeration of bones became a person, a real person, a *dead-and-gone* person.

John Compass continued: "You didn't find anything else there? A satchel, perhaps. Brown leather."

"No. The cops searched the water—"

"How thorough were they?"

She shrugged. "I don't really know how to measure that. But we're talking local cops here, not . . . the FBI."

Compass marched down the steep decline toward the river. Emily, unsure what to do, trailed after, trying not to slip and fall on the way down. He strode with easy purpose, while she felt like a newborn horse learning how to remain upright for the first time in its life. Compass didn't stop at the river. As he pulled up his sleeves, he waded right out into the water, feeling around in the current with his long, ropy arms. Like one of those guys on TV trying to pull catfish out of muddy holes.

Emily held herself close, tensing up as she remembered herself in the river. The water around her. Above her. Trying to get in her lungs, to fill her up and weigh her down. As maybe it had with Walt.

She took several steps backward, shivering.

Compass moved up and down the length of the tree, feeling around it, under it, blooms of mud rising around bony elbows. Back and forth he did this, occasionally pulling up a bit of fishing line or a river-rotten branch. His face was an implacable wall, staring not into the water but off at nothing as his hands did all the sensorial work required. Finally, minutes later, he strode back onto the shore, dark water dripping from broomstick fingers, his pant legs dark from the river.

"You know this area?" he asked.

"Sure," she said, lying. And she wasn't sure why she lied, either. Small, irrational lies seemed so easy to summon, even easier to utter.

"Will you take a short drive with me? Show me around the area?"

She hesitated.

"I can pay," he added.

"I . . ."

Emily took a good long look at John. The kids who came to the shelter she worked at in Philly had put on all this armor, all of it not just to protect them, but to hide what they were feeling. (Which, she supposed, was itself a kind of protection.)

Something about this man reminded her of those kids. And of some of the homeless she worked with now and again. People who had seen things. Done things. People with the kind of pain most others never experienced, would never (could never) even understand.

She wanted

(*needed*)

to help him.

Bonus: It would piss off Meg and Noreen.

That did it. It sealed the deal. Her rebellion here was writ—the stars had aligned, the cosmos deemed it so. She would take a drive with the sad, strange man. Just to see where it went and what they could find. Maybe she could help him. Maybe she could help herself, a little, too. If only to teach Meg a lesson.

Petty Smyth singing with Scandal. Petty o'Furniture. Petty Duke playing Petty Lane on the Petty Duke Show.

13

A DEAL IS STRUCK

JOHN DROVE THEM UP AND DOWN RIVER ROAD, ASKING HER ALL kinds of questions. Where's the river deepest? What are these islands in the river? Where's the best place to cross over to the Jersey side? Does she know of any apple trees or orchards around here? And each answer had her stammering. *Well. I. Lemme think.*

He pulled over at a spot by the canal towpath that ran parallel to the river. A few joggers plodded by. A cyclist soon after. They sat there in silence, the engine idling. Emily didn't know if she should be afraid or not. He was a big man. One hand could palm her head like a basketball. Crush it too, probably. But he didn't seem angry with her.

"You don't know much about this area," John said, finally.

She didn't answer.

"Are you even from here?"

She chewed on her lip. "No."

"City girl, I'm guessing."

"You guessed correctly."

He sighed. Sadness bled off him. Sadness and disappointment.

"I can take you home."

"Wait," she said. "Can we just sit here a minute?"

He squinted at her, watching carefully.

"Why don't you want to go home?"

"I . . . don't know." (She *did* know.)

He put the car into drive. "We're wasting each other's time, miss."

"Seriously, please, just hold on a sec," she said, putting her hand on his. He flinched, and she flinched in return. "Shit, sorry. Listen, I just— I think I—" Emily chastised herself. *Focus. Breathe.* "You're trying to find out about your friend who died. And I would like to help you do that."

John Compass looked at her like she was a difficult math problem. One he was trying and failing to solve. "Why?" he asked. One simple word.

The answer poured out of her.

"I need something. I don't have anything here. Or anyone. Just my wife, and things aren't easy with her for—" A shadow passed overhead, the Unspoken Thing flying past. "For a lot of reasons, and she works all day and I'm home alone all day and I don't have a car. I need something to do. I need something to *be*. I'm flailing here. It's like being in that river. It pushed me around and tried to drown me. But I want to swim on my own and get above the surface and . . . Jesus, this metaphor sucks." She pressed the heels of her hands into her eyes. Hard enough she saw stars melting across the dark. And in that dark, she saw the stirring of bones, moved by the hands of muddy, rushing water. "I feel sad for your friend, too. Those bones. It's like . . . I disrupted his resting place and I feel responsible for that. So let me help. Please."

At that, John Compass seemed to solve the math problem that was Emily.

He nodded. "Okay, Miss Bergmann."

"Emily."

"Okay, Emily."

"I can help?"

"You can help."

A DINER CALLED THE KEYSTONE. BIG WINDOWS. EVERYTHING THE color of lemons. Fading, though, like the sun had sucked out the color. A new paint job was needed.

Emily hovered over her cup of coffee like a dragonfly over pondwater.

John Compass watched her from over a plate of half-eaten chicken breast and wilted diner salad. A sad plate of food. He sipped at a chamomile tea.

"My friend Walt Purvin was an apple hunter, like me."

"Ah. The most dangerous game. The elusive *apple*."

He didn't laugh. He didn't frown, either. He just stared at her with all the emotion of a refrigerator. "It can be elusive. Finding lost apple varieties is tricky."

"Why is it tricky? And why do it at all?"

"Modern agricultural production gives us perhaps two dozen apples.

From the poorly named Red Delicious, which is more purple than red and rarely delicious, to the Honeycrisp, a popular apple, though one I think is an apple for children. Too sweet. No balance, no complexity. But there exist literally thousands of varieties of apples. Boutique orchards grow a number of these heirloom varieties, preserving the heritage of the fruit. But many more—most varieties—have been lost. Or destroyed on purpose, like Johnny Appleseed's cider trees."

"Johnny Appleseed wasn't real. He was like Paul Bunyan. An American myth."

"Johnny Appleseed was absolutely real. His name was John Chapman. He was a Swedenborgian. Believed grafting apples was against God, so he only grew trees from seed. Orchards of random trees sprung up everywhere, which he used to exploit a law where unclaimed land could be claimed if you grew fruit trees on it. In this way, he was an avatar of colonialism: Planting trees meant he owned land that he could sell to settlers. Though he was ultimately too eccentric to hold on to his money."

"I . . . had no idea."

"He thought his trees were holy, but during Prohibition, they became a symbol of sin. So they were destroyed. Still, all it takes is one tree to survive. One tree, and you can propagate that apple once more. The goal is to find those trees. So you look for hints. Someone says, *Oh, my grandfather had this old tree on his property, and it had the sweetest apples,* and so you go to see what it is. Or if you know that a certain apple thrived once in an area a century before, you search that area for signs of old home orchards, maybe two or three trees in a yard, in the hope of rediscovering that lost apple."

"I still don't understand why."

Now, *now* he showed emotion. He smiled with his mouth but frowned with his eyes—a combination radiating incredulity. "Because it's history, Emily. Because it matters that all this diversity, all these near-to-infinite options, have been forgotten, forgotten on purpose, forced out for good-looking but bad-tasting grocery store fruit. Because these flavors, these apples, if they *can* be found again, *should* be found again. Flavors like you've never tasted in an apple before. Ginger, honey, licorice. Pineapple. Ground pepper. And because when you find one, you might be tasting something that nobody else alive has tasted. Even if it's just some old spitter apple, astringent as a mouthful of vinegar. It's life. Trees are alive. They're part of something, part of the world." He seemed to have lost the thread. "Some things are worth preserving. These apples are worth preserving."

It was the most passion she'd seen out of him yet. "Fair enough."

"I think Walt was killed," he said plainly and without warning.

Conversational whiplash damn near snapped her neck.

"Killed. Like—" She lowered her voice. "Murdered?"

Compass nodded.

"And you think this . . . why?"

He fished a crudely folded piece of yellow notebook paper out of his pocket and slid it across to her. Emily unfolded it.

On the paper was scribbled a short note:

John—

Found something
If it's what I think it is we should meet
My place tomorrow 3PM

—Walt

"I got it in the mail."

"Your friend not into email?" she asked him.

John shrugged. "Not big on it, no."

"Just the same, I don't see how this says murder to you."

"Walt and I hadn't spoken in years."

"Oh. I'm sorry."

"No apology required. Sometimes friendships don't survive. They die like people die." John said it like it was no big deal, but she could see the pinch of his eyes, the way his gaze lost focus. Another flash of pain and grief, like glimpsing someone through a closing door. "But it's strange he'd reach out like this."

"So what was it he found?"

"Can't say for sure. But he had one apple he was hunting for above all others."

"Is there money in it? I mean, in finding lost apples."

"Can be. A few apple hunters have made a living off it. They breed new trees of the old varieties and sell them, usually online. Walt was hoping to do that. I told him not to. This isn't about money. It can't be about money."

"Would there be enough money someone would kill for it?"

He shrugged. "No. I don't figure. But sometimes in pursuit of an apple, if we are reckless, we might trespass. And sometimes trespassers get shot."

"You think he was shot?"

"Don't know. His skull was broken pretty good. Like he'd taken a hit to the head, or had a bad fall." He stiffened, suddenly impatient. "Maybe it wasn't murder. Maybe he just fell. He's dead just the same and I'd like to find out why."

In THE PARKING LOT, WALKING BACK TOWARD HIS JEEP, JOHN COM-pass said to her, "I don't think your partner liked you going off with me."

"No, I don't think she was too thrilled."

"I'm sorry."

"Don't be."

In the back of the Jeep, Emily spied a small bag of what looked like golden apples. "Are those apples you, uh, hunted?"

"They are," he said, and Emily thought she heard a lift to his voice. He opened the back door and with some eagerness showed her the ap-ples. "I grafted the scionwood to semi-dwarf rootstock—so these are not the fruits of those trees but the fruits of a tree that was dying. This is the Muuschhakgott. Try one."

She held up a hand. "I'm allergic."

His face softened. All its hard edges went like warmed candlewax. "Oral allergy syndrome? Itchy throat and such?"

"Yeah."

John reached out to put a hand on her shoulder, but didn't quite touch her. The hand hovered there, as if attempting to transmit comfort through the inch of space between them. He seemed suddenly really sad for her.

"This apple is one I've been looking for," he said. Gazing into it like it was a crystal ball. "It's an apple of the Unami, a tribe of the Lenape. Been searching for years."

"Are you—your name, Compass, it's like a compass, north south east west—so you're—"

He shook his head. "No, the name is French. I'm Lenape in part. My mother's side. But I do try to find apples that came from Lenapehoking."

"I should've figured *American as apple pie* was just a lie. That apples were just another thing colonized, stolen from those who were already here."

"No, not at all. Apples came to America with the European settlers. The apple was the colonizer, I'm afraid. Still, the French and the Dutch gave the apple tree to the people here. People assumed the Indigenous Americans were unsophisticated, that they only grew the apples from seed, but in my view, that's not possible. They found evidence of native orchards consistently producing the same good fruit, which meant they knew how to graft. Knew, or learned. Some early American apples were native-grown. Junaluska, Kittageskee, Cullasaga. Most lost. Some found. Like the Muuschhakgott here."

"I'm glad you found it."

He offered a real smile. "Tastes like a cloudless autumn day."

HE DROPPED HER BACK OFF AT THE HOUSE, AND AS SHE GOT OUT, he said, "I have some things to take care of back home." When she asked where home was, he said about an hour north, in the Lehigh Valley. "I'll be back here in a few weeks."

"A few *weeks*?" she asked. Panic set in. She'd *just* found her *thing*. "No, no, come back tomorrow, we can get started right away—"

"My friend is dead, Emily. Long dead. I figure his spirit can wait a little while longer for its measure of peace."

Yeah well I can't, she thought, with no small panic.

"Oh—yeah. Okay. Cool."

"We can communicate. I have email," John said, as if to prove he was a modern man, unlike his friend Walt.

Ah, the olds, she thought. "I . . . have email as well, John." She asked what it was, since he seemed to have forgotten that step. Emily plugged it into her phone, said she'd email him so he had hers.

"I hope your—wife?—isn't too mad at you."

She will be. "Yeah, me too. And yes, she's my wife."

He reached in the back seat, took one of the golden apples. "She like apples? Fruit's always a good peace offering."

"She fucking loves apples, John. She's like a—well, whatever animal likes apples the most."

"White-tailed deer, I'd say."

"Then that's what she is."

Emily took the apple. It felt cold and smooth in her hand.

"Thanks again, Emily. For your help."

"I owe it to Walt. For . . . stepping on his head."

She felt bad saying it, like she was making light of his demise. But if John felt she was being disrespectful, he didn't show it. "Walt needed someone to step on his head now and again. Besides, if you hadn't, we wouldn't be here together right now, would we?"

"Fair enough."

They said goodbye, and John drove off.

Emily drew all the strength she could, took a deep breath, and went back inside. Meg was back at work already, and Noreen was gone. No message, no note, no nothing. When Meg returned that night, she gave Emily the silent treatment. It lasted for three days. It had never lasted that long before.

———

THE DESPONDENT FATHER'S TALE

New York City. The McCammon Hotel.
Six years ago, in February.

Dan Paxson's father had his own language, his own words
for things—guys who were slow, or lazy, he called "mummy," or if he was
in his cups, "*a real fuckin' mummy.*" Someone driving badly on the road,
swerving around and acting a fool? His father, Big Dan, would say, "Look
at this jackfruit up here." If he'd had a couple-few Scotch-and-sodas, Big
Dan might say, "Feelin' nice and muzzy, buddy, *nice* and *muzzy.*" He just
had a way of saying things that most other people didn't. Words and
phrases. Pritner instead of pretty near. Dandelions were piss-the-beds.
Ice wasn't slippery, it was slippy, or slippity.

Presently, Dan—or Little Dan to his father, and to everybody who
knew their family—was damn sure feeling *muzzy.*

Maybe not so nice.

But definitely muzzy.

He sat on the edge of the hotel bed: king-sized, memory foam, pillows that smelled of lavender. From that vantage point, he watched television, and did so for hours. It was something he didn't do very often. He
was usually too busy with odd jobs, doing this or that around their neighborhood. He and his daughter, Calla, lived in a '70s-era duplex in Quaker
Bridge, not far from the Ramble Rocks quarry, and he took whatever
work he could find, which didn't leave him much leisure time. So this
simple act of sitting alone in the quiet, watching television, was beautifully numbing. He could just sit here, sinking into it. Like drowning your
brain in warm, soapy water.

Outside, evening settled in over the city. This room had a balcony—
and even in the cold of February he liked going out there and looking out
over the tall buildings and the carved lines of streets and avenues.

He knew he should be down there, living it up while he still could. But doing what? Dan had already blown the last of his credit on this hotel room.

That, and on the bottle of good Scotch in his lap. He wasn't really a big whiskey—or was it whisky?—drinker, even though his father loved to buy a

(*gun*)

bottle soon as the last one went empty. Dad liked Dewar's though— a cheap, blended whiskey, good for mixing. Dan wanted to go bigger, so he asked the girl at the liquor store what was good, half expecting her to blow him off or not have any answers, but he was wrong. She knew everything. All these regions of Scotland and the whiskey that came from them and their flavor profiles—

She described her favorite as "peaty" and with strong "iodine" flavors and that did not sound good to him at all. He knew what peat was, and didn't think he wanted to drink bog-dirt. Iodine, either. But when she hit on flavors like buttery, or brown sugar, he said, *There, that's it, that's what I want.* So she sold him a bottle of something called The Balvenie Double-Wood, Aged 12 Years.

And it was indeed good. It warmed him from the inside out; his heart turned into a dripping, caramel candy apple. As a result, he was feeling, well—

Muzzy.

He said the word out loud, "Muzzy, muzzy, muzzy."

He laughed.

(*so he didn't cry*)

Still. He could feel his teeth and tongue, his lips and cheeks. That had to change. He grabbed the bottle and the glass, the *empty* glass how fucking *dare* it be devoid of whiskey, and went to pour another couple fingers of the stuff—

When a knock arrived at the door.

"Busy," he said, but he said it too quiet so he barked it again: "Busy!"

The knock came again. Three knocks. Polite. Not loud. Just insistent. Had to be someone from the hotel. Housekeeping or whoever.

"Hnn," he said, sighing. He stood up and didn't even bother to peer through the little hole in the door, instead just swinging it open. He started to protest: "I don't need anything right now, thank you—"

A strange blond man stood there. He wore a white suit, white shirt, no tie, white shoes. His skin, pink as processed meat. The irises of his eyes were the color of copper patina—a strange blue shot through with rust. "Dan Paxson," the man said. His voice was clear and bright. A harp string plucked in an empty room.

Dan blinked. "Hello."

"I'd like to talk to you about apples."

Dan blinked again. "I'm sorry?"

"May I come in? This won't take long."

Looking over his shoulder at the room behind him, he saw the safe sanctum that he'd made for himself. A sanctum just for tonight, for this special moment in time, and as such he direly did not want this precious bubble popped. Because when it did pop—it'd really, *really* pop. But already with the knocking of the door and this man standing here, wasn't his bubble already popped? His peace, ruined?

And what the strange man had said about apples . . .

"What's this all about? I am very busy—"

The man, though shorter than Dan by a good few inches, glanced over Dan's shoulder. "You seem to have a busy night planned, but as I said, this won't take long. I promise. I'd like to talk to you about apples. Apples, and property rights, and the significance of legacy. Your father understood that. He had a dream and it kept him going."

"Until it didn't."

Three words. Dan didn't even mean to say them. But there they were. Dripping over everything like a splash of pig's blood.

The man said nothing in response. He simply stood there, expectantly.

How did this man know Big Dan? The mystery tugged at him.

Sighing, Dan told him to come inside.

The man, Dan realized, was holding an envelope. He'd had it behind his back as he stood at the door, but now that he was inside, he held it out front, pinching the corners, turning it clockwise as he did. Corner to corner, pinch to pinch, rotating the envelope as he hooked the desk chair with a white wingtip, pulling it toward the bed. "Please, sit," the man said as he took the chair for himself, sitting stiffly forward, grinning.

"On the bed?" Dan asked, seeing that the chair was taken.

"Excellent choice." The man's smile didn't waver. Big and broad and shiny. Too big for a moment. Flat white teeth catching the light. Grin going from ear to ear, literally, impossibly so, the corners of his smile stretching wide toward the earholes, a smile so big he could break his head in half like Pac-Man chasing a ghost. Dan squinted. It was gone now. A regular smile remained, moored between those prettyboy cheekbones. *Just a trick of the light,* he thought.

(*And the whiskey.*)

Outside, sirens rose. Loud, klaxons screaming through the streets, howling up through the concrete canyons of Manhattan. Like a panicked beast, lost and alone, wandering the maze.

"I have something for you," the man said, holding up the envelope to the light, pretending like he was trying to see through it to whatever waited within.

"Who are you?"

"Wrong question. The question is, *What is it?* As in, what's in the envelope? I think you'll like it. I truly do."

Dan's eyes flitted from the envelope to the smiling man

(*smile too big, teeth too sharp*)

and back again.

"I still don't know who you are."

The man's smile tightened. Like a rope pulled tight between two angry hands. Did his eyes just grow larger? The pupils, simultaneously smaller? Dan felt queasy. *I'm just hallucinating.* He felt pinned to the spot. About to be eaten.

"I am Edward Naberius. Think of me as a *restorer of lost dignities.*"

The man—Edward Naberius, apparently—fanned the air gently with the envelope. The gentle *wush-wush-wush* of sound and stirred air from it had Dan staring at it, nearly hypnotized. "And what's in the envelope?"

"Well. That's to come. But first, I need to gauge your level of commitment here, Little Dan. Because I know what's going on here."

Dan swallowed a hard knot. "I don't know what that means—listen, maybe you should leave—"

"Right now, in the bathroom over there, I know you have a pill bottle procured by illicit means off the website Craigslist. The pills are a mix of hydrocodone and Ambien, and at some point before morning you hope to wash them all down with that mid-price Scotch whiskey over there on the desk, all with the intent to overdose and die. Suicide by drug toxicity." The man's smile never changed. It was a happy smile. As if he was genuinely pleased with himself at getting to say all this. Like he'd *titter* and *giggle* at any moment.

Dan sat morbidly still. He felt both suddenly sober and alarmingly drunk. Or maybe it was that he had sobered up, but the world had gone soggy, messy. Oozing through like it was turning to mud in his grip.

"I—you don't—"

Still smiling, Edward said, "You of course hope that the death is painless, that you will fall asleep and simply die in that dark comfort—a way forward into oblivion that is less brutal than the path Big Dan chose, what with that cheap .38 revolver, the one with the serial numbers filed off." The man leaned forward, biting his lower lip. "It's true, in part, you will fall asleep into death, but not before a lot of vomiting and cramping and chest pains. It'll still be messy. Of course the *real* mess you leave behind is dear Calla Lily—"

How does he know her nickname? How does he know about the pistol, about the pills, about any of this? It didn't make sense. He felt trapped in a nightmare. Tears crawled down Dan's cheeks. "No, no, you don't know—I'm doing her a favor. She'll live with my sister in California, that's where she is now. My sister Mary has money, a life. I'm just—I'm doing Calla a favor, you see."

"You're doing *yourself* a favor, Little Dan. Not her. Just as your own father's death was not a favor to you, neither will yours be a favor to her, and the pain passed down from Big Dan to Little Dan will again be passed down to Calla, poor Calla who already lost her mother, sad Calla who may one day wrap a noose around her neck or butterfly the meat of her arm and open the veins there—or! Or simply take a step off a steep ledge so that she plummets into traffic far, far below."

At that, somewhere outside, maybe in the hallway, something fell over. A cart toppling with a *rattle-bang*. Someone started yelling—distant, muffled.

"Please go," Dan said, swallowing ropes of mucus from sinuses swollen by grief and panic. He wiped his nose on his sleeve.

"Oh, it's cost me a lot to be here, and you haven't seen what I've brought you yet." Edward snapped his teeth together like he was a dog biting at a fly. Laughing, he presented the envelope, holding it at one end and easing it toward Dan. The way the man looked at it, it was almost as if it might come alive at any moment, leaping out of his hands and scurrying across the room. Edward's grin was especially cheeky now. Mischievous, the corners of the smile pulled up, as if by fishhooks. A clever man presenting a clever offering. "You want to take it."

Dan took the envelope in trembling, sweat-slick hands.

It was one of those envelopes that you opened by unwinding a little spool of string, so he did so, carefully, slowly, before pulling out a document from within. Three pages, stapled together. He winced. "What is this?"

Edward rolled his eyes. "Please, read it. Don't make me do all the heavy lifting here, Little Dan." Something danced in his eyes. The copper patina flashed like firelight on corroded metal.

Someone was crying now, down the hall. Another yell—or a scream.

Dan turned toward the door, but Edward snapped his fingers to summon his attention anew. "Focus up. Don't worry about that, Dan, it doesn't concern us. Time is fleeting. Read the document."

Hesitantly, he looked it over.

The words crawled like ants and he had to blink hard and root his feet to the ground to make them stop. They did. It was then he saw what this was.

"H . . . how?" he asked, upon scanning the document.

"Judge Carver agreed that an unforced error was made. I was able to convince him to take a fresh look with fresh eyes and, in the wisdom of his jurisprudence, he saw fit to overturn the judgment against your father."

"Does that mean—" It couldn't be. Could it? "Is the property mine again?"

"It is, Little Dan." The grin again grew too big for the man's face, going beyond the borders of his flesh, hovering there like it's all there was, like the smile was everything, as if the rest of him were just a suit, a puppet, a costume worn by the grinning maw—a haze blurred the air, a haze like mosquitoes. For a moment everything was sharp teeth shining white. Dan closed his eyes, waiting to be eaten.

Dan was startled from this reverie by voices outside the room, down the hallway. Alarmed voices. When he looked back, Edward was normal once more.

"They'll be here soon," the man said.

"They? They who?"

"Have I restored your lost dignity?" Edward asked, through smiling teeth.

"What?"

"I said—*have I restored your lost dignity?*"

"Yes," Dan said, his voice barely above a whisper.

Outside, the voices grew closer. Someone was knocking on a door nearby. Loudly. *Whump whump whump.*

"Will you still take your own life tonight, Dan? Now that you have your family property returned? Now that you can fulfill your father's legacy, the one that was stolen from him, stolen like a vital organ by petty men?"

"No."

"Good. Now what do you say?"

That, a question from a parent to a child.

"Thank you."

"There it is." Edward stood. "Ah. But. One last bit of instruction."

More knocking outside. Another door closer. Next door, maybe.

Edward continued:

"People are going to come in here and they're going to say some very dramatic things, and those things are regrettably true. The story you tell to them will matter, and what I suggest saying is this: I came in here under unknown pretenses. I was in the throes of madness. Psychotic. I threatened you. Cowed, you let me rant and rave. Say nothing of my revelations. Say nothing of the document. *Certainly* do not tell them about your pills. Just tell them that I was crazy, and you were scared, and then it was all over."

"All over," Dan said, repeating those words, not sure what they meant.

At that, the knock came to his door. *Whump whump whump.* A voice came through the door: "Sir? Sir could you please open up."

"That's my cue," Edward Naberius said. "Enjoy your ancestral home,

Little Dan." He offered a gentle dip of his chin in a deferential nod to Dan, and headed out to the balcony, and then to the edge of it. Dan watched as the other man spun his legs over the railing like a gymnast—

Before disappearing over the edge.

Dan screamed as the door to the hotel room flew open, and then it was chaos descending upon him. Police. A hotel manager. Lollygaggers at the door. He did not tell them one word of the envelope he'd slid under the mattress. That was his, and not theirs, and no one would take it from him now.

WHAT THE POLICE TOLD HIM LATER WAS THIS: A MAN IN A WHITE suit with the name Edward Naberius deplaned at LaGuardia, leaving Southwest Flight 1919 from Las Vegas, Nevada, despite there being no evidence he ever boarded the plane in the first place. He then caught a cab to this hotel, where he made his way up to Dan Paxson's room before jumping to his death fifteen minutes later. Where the man had gone, death had followed. A flight attendant died minutes after he left the plane. The cabdriver died as he pulled away from the hotel. A housekeeper by the elevator on Dan's floor died next to her cleaning cart. None of them seemed injured; no weapon had slain them. They were simply dead, and Dan would later learn that their deaths were all from a brain aneurysm. Poison was suspected, and someone had even mentioned polonium, given that most camera footage indicated Edward had touched them, skin-to-skin contact. Though nothing was ever detected in the blood, urine, or feces of the victims. The body of Edward Naberius itself was destroyed, shattered pottery held in by a sack of pink skin. Dental records gave nothing. Fingerprints were similarly useless. It was a mystery that would remain unsolved. Reddit would have a shot at it, as would various podcasts and YouTubers, but none thankfully had ever detected Dan's presence as part of the mystery.

Dan had no sense of what this meant or what this was, and only that the horror of that night yielded some hope: This strange tree had grown useful fruit, for now his life was saved, his father's house and land had been returned to him, and he and his daughter had a future once more.

The final discovery came months later, when Dan looked back at the envelope handed to him by the strange smiling man. He went to throw it out in recycling, but paused as he found something else inside it, tucked all the way into the bottom corner, pinched there by its paper grip: It was a small yellow Post-it Note, and on that note, a phone number.

NOVEMBER

My home life was unstable and it ain't much better now
I ain't no rotten apple but I ain't no sacred cow
Some people call you a genius some are saying not
Some folks only want you based on what you got

—Margo Price,
"Revelations"

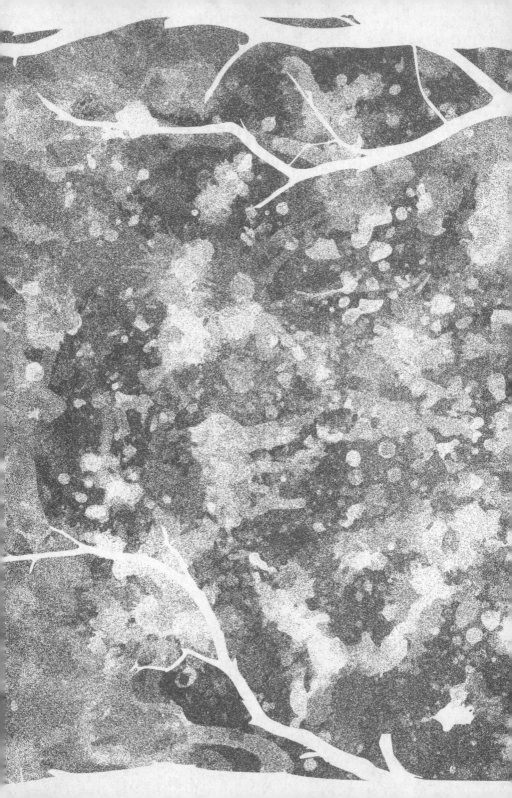

14

THE MANY ENEMIES OF JOANIE MOREAU

THE BIG SKELETON WAS A PROBLEM.

Joanie Moreau stood on the front lawn, her leather jacket doing little to warm her against the November chill—a chill she loathed, for winter was foe to her, what with the way it dried her out. It dried out her skin, her scalp, her hair. Her mother always said, "Winter makes redheads brittle." She meant her hair, but maybe it meant other things, too. Either way, Joanie had to cold-wash her hair in winter, which was the exact opposite of what you wanted to do that time of the year. Whatever. Winter was an enemy yet to arrive. The enemy in front of her was this skeleton.

It stood, twelve feet tall—a majestic bone-lord, threatening to ascend the trellis of sleeping wisteria moored to the side of the Mediterranean-style McMansion. Arms outstretched, crooked teeth set in a wrenched-open jaw, fingers searching for handholds. Presumably to climb up and torment those within the house, maybe rend their flesh, eat their souls. That, or spy on whatever hot fucking was going on—*insert boner joke here*, she thought. But it was not the skeleton's torment or soul-hunger or stalkery peepshow tendencies that made him a problem, oh no: It was his size. He was too fucking big.

Behind her, Graham wandered around, scooping up the rest of the Halloween lawn décor—the foam pumpkins, the fake graves, all that.

"I think the skeleton was a mistake," she said, staring up at it.

Graham came behind her and set the Halloween decorations on the ground. "Dear, I believe we agreed her name was Miss Esmerelda Bonejangles." His delivery, dry as her skin in winter, serious as a pallbearer.

"That was when I liked her. Now she's irritating me, so she's a he, and *he* deserves no name except This Stupid-Ass Giant-Ass Skeleton." She turned to Graham—Graham, Handsome Graham, Husband Graham, Graham who looked like the smooth-cheeked, dark-haired, dark-eyed love child of Paul Rudd and Justin Theroux. Or so she imagined him to be. She knew he'd put on some miles—he had just turned fifty, after all, five years her senior. Yet, a vital spark danced within him—the ghost of misspent youth not yet exorcised. She asked him, "You sure that Ilan can't handle this?" Ilan, the head of the landscaping company they used here at the Fox Run house, was happy to do odd jobs for them now and again—say, for instance, transporting a twelve-foot skeleton they bought at Home Depot in a fit of Halloween overindulgence. They paid him well, and he was happy for the work.

"Sorry, dearest. Ilan spends every November in Richmond, with family. He only has a skeleton crew remaining—ah, pun not intended. You know. People who do leaf blowing and pre-holiday cleanup."

"Moving a big dumb skeleton *is* pre-holiday cleanup."

"I don't think that's in their purview."

She sucked air between her teeth. "Maybe we could just leave the skeleton up. Some people do that, right? Dress him like Santa, the Easter Bunny, Hawaiian shirt in the summer. He can be a . . . seasonal skeleton. A year-round guest."

Graham sidled up next to her, a smirk playing at the corner of his mouth. "Unconventional, but I suppose that suits us."

"It does." She sighed. "Still. We don't want to draw attention. Rubberneckers are not welcome, even if they don't realize what they'd be rubbernecking." Discretion was key to their thing here. "I know someone I can call."

"Oh?"

"You won't like it."

"Do tell."

"Old friend named Dan Paxson. He used to live toward the river and I hear he's back. He has a truck. He might be willing if I sweet-talk him a little."

"And why won't I like this?"

She winced. "Because when I say 'old friend,' I mean 'old boyfriend.'"

"Ah." He grinned. "Dear. I think we're well past that sort of jealousy."

"I suppose we are." She leaned in close, softly biting her lower lip. Joanie eased close to him, pressing her cold left cheek against his warm right—his skin smooth, not a whisper of stubble to scratch her. Her mouth at his ear, whispered: "But maybe you're hiding it from me. Jealousy is an ugly emotion, Graham." She bit his ear lightly, let her hand play across his thigh, spider-walking toward his cock. "What's say we go into the house. We . . . make sure the cleaning lady did her job. Then we get it dirty all over again. You tell me how jealous you are. And I remind you that Graham is not in charge of Joanie. Joanie is in charge of Graham. I get out the cuffs. I tie you down, your beautiful ass up in the air, and I—"

"Jo." His voice, her name, stiff and sharp. A small warning.

She saw he was looking past her, so she followed his gaze—

A neighbor was walking toward them. Stalking across his lawn toward theirs. Prentiss Beckman. *Prentiss.* Just the kind of name of the kind of person who bought a house in a neighborhood like this—the big green over-manicured lawns, the sparkling blue pools, the architecturally and stylistically confused mini-mansions. Thing was, most of the people in this neighborhood were new money.

Prentiss, on the other hand, was *old* money—she remembered him from high school. Smug piece-of-shit back then. He what, graduated a year before her? His father was a real estate guy. Prentiss had a lot of brothers and sisters. Maybe they got the lion's share of the good property from Daddy Edgar, and Prentiss had to suck it up here, slumming it with the rest of the wide-eyed nouveau riche. Made sense. He was always the troublemaker in his family. DUIs and drunk and disorderlies and the like. Always skated, though. Because of his father. Because of the family's connection to the Crossed Keys.

Whatever this was, here he came, his ill-margined bulk stuffed into the teal of a too-tight Eagles hoodie. He had a phone in his hand, waving it around like the world had to see.

"You, Joanie Moreau," Prentiss said, but the way he said it was not by way of greeting. It contained no neighborly tone. It was angry. Accusatory. The naming of a witch. *I saw Goody Moreau in the forest with a giant skeleton.*

"Prentiss Beckman," she said. "Hello. I don't think you've ever met my husband—"

"Graham Jacobs," Graham said, offering a hand. "Civil engineer. Private sector."

But Prentiss didn't take it. Instead, his bulldog face—*Christ, he looks just like his father,* she realized—wrinkled up in a bewildered, frustrated scrunch. Probably trying to figure out why their last names weren't the same, the dope.

He seemed to steady himself, thrusting his phone out at them.

"What is this?" he asked, showing them the screen.

"It's your lockscreen, I think," Joanie said, squinting at it. The lock-screen was a sea-damp Gisele Bündchen in a swimsuit. "Tom Brady's ex-wife, huh? Better be careful, Prentiss. In this town, that Eagles sweat-shirt won't save you if people think you're harboring a secret Pats crush."

Prentiss spun the phone around, frustrated. "What the—shit." He tapped the screen on and stabbed the password before turning it back around again.

And at that, her heart caught mid-beat.

On his phone was a picture of a house. Easily recognizable: the angular L-shaped turn of the home, the busy rooflines, the Mediterranean villa vibe, the multistory entryway, the pair of too-wide garage bays. It was the house they were standing in front of right now. *Their* house.

Her gaze flicked to the website—

Airbnd-dot-com.

Like Airbnb, but, well, different.

"That's our house," Joanie said. "The lawn of which you're standing on."

"Yeah. I see that. That's the problem."

Graham and Joanie shared a look.

"Can't say I see the problem," Joanie said. "Care to share?"

"This is a—a—" Prentiss stammered. "A *sex house.* Like a brothel."

"It is not a brothel, not that there would be anything wrong with that."

Prentiss seethed. "This is a nice neighborhood. We're good Chris-tians. We don't do that sort of thing here. That doesn't belong on these streets."

"These streets? It's not on the streets, Prentiss. It's behind those walls, and had you not seen this house on that website, you would've never realized what was going on there. And I don't invite Jesus inside to gawk."

"I saw. I saw people come and go. From here. Last night."

Graham chuckled again, clearing his throat gently. *Come and go,* hah.

"It's not funny," Prentiss objected. "None of this is funny. What was it last night? Some kind of party. A . . . a Halloween dungeon orgy or something. I don't want it here. I don't want it next door. I don't want it all up in my face."

"It was a regular Halloween party where some of the guests chose to engage in a variety of consensual, carnal activities. Prentiss, Airbnd is a website like Airbnb, except we rent our house out to adults only, no families, no children. They are not paying us for sex. They are paying us to rent the house, and then have sex in its playspaces. As anyone could in *any* rented house or cabin or hotel room. We just put a finer point on it."

"No, *no,* fuck you. Fuck that. It's a brothel. You're on my shitlist, now. I'll take this to whoever I have to. You *liberals—*"

"I'm the liberal," Graham said, but tilted his head toward Joanie and lowered his voice conspiratorially. "This one, though, is a small-l libertarian."

"Freedom for everyone for everything, long as it doesn't get in anybody's way," she said. "For instance, I don't care what you do in your free time, Prentiss. I don't care if you smoke weed. I don't care who you fuck. I don't care if you like men, women, wanna *be* a woman, whatever. I don't care if you dress your vacuum up like a lady, let that vacuum suck your dick. You do you. We'll do us. What we do here is legal, aboveboard, and nobody is the wiser."

She could see it on his face. The *affront.* The *offense.* The *how dare you have fun in a way I can't* vibe. He extended his arms like he was trying to encompass all the sins of the world before getting nailed to his cross.

"You'll see," he said. "You put this all on display, throwing it in our *faces?* People are going to be big mad, Joanie Maroney." One of the shitty asshole nicknames for her from back in the day. That, or Joanie Baloney. Or, when they really wanted to hurt her: *Joanie Gonna-Bone-Me.* Idiots. "Soon as I let my father know about this—"

Joanie made a sunken, sulking face. "*I'm gonna tell my Daddy.* The battle cry of the whiny little piss-baby, his diapers soggy and dripping." Before he could retort, she got in close, a wicked grin on her face. He'd courted the bull with a red cape, and now she was taking her charge, aiming to gore. "We kept it all quiet, Prentiss. We don't put it in your face. But you wanna know what's up? Here's what's up. I'm going to stop talking to you and go back inside, leading my husband by the cock like it's a leash. Then I'm going to tie him down over a spanking bench, strap on a moderately-sized silicone dildo, lube it up, and fuck him in the ass. Gently at first, but over time, with increased force and pace, deeper and deeper, until he comes like a lawn sprinkler."

As she spoke, she watched Prentiss's face grow redder and redder with both rage and embarrassment. At the culmination of her description, he turned away, waving his hand in the air like he was trying to dispel what was in his head—as if he'd just walked in on his grandparents having filthy sex.

For the pièce de résistance, Graham leaned forward and in his droll tone added: "It's all true. Prostate stimulation makes for a next-level ejaculation."

"Fuck you both."

"Sorry, you're not invited," she said, winking.

His face reddened and his mouth worked wordlessly for a moment before he spat out, "You two freaks go have fun. But you'll pay for your perversions, bringing this around to *my* neighborhood. And *you*—" Prentiss pointed to her, but looked at Graham. "This one was always a slut, far back as junior high, but what kind of man are you? Letting her do that to you. Go get a husband, you want that shit." At that, Prentiss spun around and stormed back toward his house, muttering loud enough to be heard, certainly on purpose: "Fucking faggot."

They watched him stomp off, like a rebuked child.

Graham chuckled, said, "Well. *Somebody* didn't have a loving father."

"Yeah," Joanie said, but that was all she could muster. A chill ran through her. She felt suddenly rattled, wondering if she'd been the taunted bull—or if Prentiss was.

But Graham took her hand and kissed it. "Shall we?" he asked.

That small tender act did not banish the unsettled feeling entirely. But it helped.

"We shall, indeed," she answered, and together, they went inside to do the things they had described to poor Prentiss Beckman.

15

AN APPLE A DAY, AND ALL THAT

CALLA TOLD MARCO THAT SHE DIDN'T LIKE APPLES, BUT HE STOOD there at the side of her bed, the blood-red clot-black apple in his hand, and he pulled a slice out of it like it was nothing, and teased it along her lips, along the edges of her mouth, and he whispered, "Little pig, little pig, let me come in." Marco tried pushing the apple past her lips but she turned away, stubborn—and at that, he slid his other hand along her throat, under her chin, holding her face firm. She tried to pull away, but then she felt it, this feeling wash over her, a feeling of anger, but then a feeling of possibility, of potential, of being prettier and better and smarter and *everything,* and Marco's free hand gripped her chin hard, fingers crawling up to her mouth like worms, pushing past her lips and her teeth. She tried to bite down but her teeth buckled inward, folding back into her mouth like broken Popsicle sticks as his fingers pushed deep into her gums, her cheek, her jawbone, reaching in and pulling her face apart like warm cake. Red syrup like raspberry filling spilled down her neck, splashing to her collarbone *blood,* she thought, *it's blood.* And she could taste it. And it tasted oh so sweet on her flopping tongue. Sweet like cider syrup. Marco laughed, pressing his face against hers, pushing the apple slice into a mouth that couldn't close, a mouth of a face that had been ruined—she saw a maggot inching along the apple's edge as he slid it across her tongue and—

HER ALARM WAS GOING OFF LIKE A FIRE TRUCK AND STILL SHE SLEPT through it. Stupid fucking dream, leaving her rattled and off-track and gah, now she was *late for school,* and Calla was never late, not for anything. Normally her father would've woken her up if she snoozed through an alarm, but where was he this morning? Probably down by the orchard. Every day seemed to have him up earlier and earlier and she was wondering how much he was even sleeping. Even as she got going for the day, the pressure built up behind her eyes—she had so much to do. December 1 was the deadline for early admissions at Princeton. Plus she was underneath *mountains* of stupid fucking homework because sure, why not just keep shoveling so much at them even though they were seniors and none of them gave a shit anymore but of course she still had to keep her grades up because, duh, there's that early admission again. Had to try to help Dad, then help Marco, then still check her socials—all of which were plateauing or, worse, dropping, which made her feel sick to her stomach because she just needed someone to see her, to care that she was here, to *fucking acknowledge her,* thank you very much, you stupid uncaring world. All this was to say she was feeling in Quite The Mood by the time she ended up at school only to find out that Lucas had taken her video of Marco's leg getting snapped last month—

And posted it himself.

"BIG FUCKING YIKES, DUDE," SHE TOLD LUCAS OUT IN THE PARKING lot between classes. Esther was there, too, moderating. Or failing to moderate, since mostly they just watched the back-and-forth like it was a tennis volley, vaping profusely, hiding behind the fog of candy-scented nicotine. They'd take a hit then tuck the vape pen back into their sleeve, in case a teacher came out. "This is high-key a huge betrayal. Huge."

"I'm sorry," Lucas said, hands up in surrender. "I know, it sucks, but you weren't using the video, sis—"

"Yeah! I know! Because it showed Marco's *leg* getting broken."

"So what? The message was more important."

"I know, the message *is* important but—" She tried to bite back the comment but couldn't help it, here it came anyway. "The reason you're getting so many views on that video is because of the leg. It's gross, so people are sharing it everywhere. And it's not . . . yours to share. It's not even mine. He got hurt and—"

"Sounds like *you* got hurt because I'm poaching your views."

Yeah, she thought, angrily. *You are.* Which made her feel super-shitty to even feel that way. Was that why she was mad? Was this about Marco at all? *God I'm a bad person.* She growled in frustration. "Please don't. Okay?

Just don't. Now I have to tell Marco the video is up and—*ugh*. Fuck." She wanted to run away.

Esther blew a plume of vapor. "Okay. Y'all. Just take a breath. Breathe. In, out. In, out. You're both friends. I'm your friend. This is no big deal, you can both say sorry and be chill and—"

But Lucas wasn't in for that. He said, "Your boyfriend should be thanking me for posting it. Yeah it's gross he broke his leg but he's cute and a total thirst trap and everyone loves him. Might even help him get into a college—"

Horror descended upon Calla.

"Oh my god. College. It—it could hurt his chances, Lucas!"

"I think the broken leg is what's gonna hurt his chances."

"But they don't know he broke his leg. He needs a scholarship and—" She was only now just realizing how it could screw him. "Shit. *Shit!* God, Lucas. You asshole. Why did you have to do this? Can you delete it?"

"What?" Lucas made a face. "I'm not deleting a damn thing. I'm doing this for a cause, not just because I want to be some shallow influencer shill. Get better heroes, Calla, for real. Influencers are just laundering capitalism's rags."

"Lucas, hey—" Esther started, but didn't follow it up with anything. They just gave Calla a helpless look like, *Sorry?*

Calla cried out in frustration, saying, "You are so unbelievable right now. This could really hurt him. And you hurt me by doing this."

Lucas just shrugged.

Forcing back tears, Calla stiffened her arms and whirled around to head back into study hall without the two of her friends.

If they even *were* her friends anymore.

MARCO WASN'T IN SCHOOL FOR THE MORNING. DOCTOR APPOINT-ment at the orthopedic surgeon's office. He was nervous about it. Said he'd been having a lot of pain recently and so Calla was worried for him, worried about him, and now worried about having to tell him that there was a video online of him getting his leg broken. She glanced at her phone and saw the numbers creeping up. It hadn't gone, like, *viral-viral* yet? But it could. If it leapt the chasm to other social media sites, that was like an ember leaving a campfire and landing on a dead tree in the water-hungry woods. It'd be a forest fire in no time. Already people in school knew and would tell him if she didn't. She wanted to scream.

When he came back midday, she was sure to get out of fourth period calculus early ("sorry, women problems") so she could meet him at his locker. But he didn't show. Which only made her worry *even more*.

And then the first bell rang. She had to get to class—health class, in which they were supposed to be learning sex ed (not that she needed it), but the school board freaked out about air-quotes *encouraging kids to have premarital sex*—

As if they weren't having sex already—

As if any of them even thought the world was going to *last* long enough for them to *get* married—

And so the school board made sure to replace any sex ed with a brief one-day class on Abstinence Only education, filling the rest of the time with CPR.

She hauled her bag over her shoulder.

"Hey," came a voice from behind her.

It was Marco.

"Shit, I thought something happened to you—" she said, hugging him, and he hugged her back and she felt

(*his fingers in her mouth, pulling half her face away*)

just so relieved to see him.

"Something kinda did," he said, in a faraway voice.

"Fuck. You saw the video." She pulled away, her hands balled up into fists. "Lucas shouldn't have done that, and I'm so *pissed*. I know it's, like, for a good cause, but that isn't why the video is doing well. I'll make him take it down, and if he doesn't take it down, I'll just murder him, it's fine, murder is fine—"

"Video?" he asked. "What video?"

"Oh shit."

"Oh shit?"

She crushed her eyes behind her hands and then spilled her guts. Told him that Lucas posted the video of him breaking his leg.

"Oh. *Oh*." Marco blinked. "That sucks."

"You don't seem . . . too mad."

Marco shrugged. "I dunno. It happened, so. Maybe it'll be okay."

"Why?" Calla could tell she was missing something. "Wait. What happened today?"

"The doctor. He said my leg—my bones—are rejecting the screws."

"That sounds bad."

He laughed a little. "They're rejecting the screws because Doc says the bones are healing too fast. Fusing together already. Doc said he's never seen anything like it. It was a bad break, but . . . he said I might be back on my feet in a few weeks. And running again soon after."

"Marco," she said, laughing, "that's *amazing*."

She hugged him again, and tried not to imagine his hands reaching up, forcing an apple into her mouth, and pulling her apart like warm bread.

16

THE ORCHARD PROVIDES A BOUNTIFUL HARVEST

NATURE HAD ITS RHYTHMS. EVERY YEAR A CYCLE OF GROWTH AND rot: the green of spring grew wild until the gray of winter arrived with its cold machete. Apples were no different, and about this one thing, Chase Hardiaken had been right: They had a season that began in July and ended in November. First the apple trees leafed out. Then they blossomed, perfuming the air and summoning spring-mad pollinators. And when the flowers fell to carpet the ground, apples emerged in their place: small and dark at first, then rising and swelling, bursting forth to burden the branches. Then the apples were picked off the tree or fell to the earth and that was it for the harvest. The leaves would change color. The fruit would rot. And as soon as winter stared darkly over the horizon, blade in hand, the season would be over.

Each cultivar had its own period of growth, of course. Some produced for only a week, others ripened over the course of a month. Some apples were early-season apples, like Gravenstein or Ginger Gold. Some were mid-seasoners, like a Cox's Orange Pippin (or its many descendant cultivars), while many showed up late, like the Arkansas Black or the Winesap. (Late-season apples also tended to be keepers, meaning they did well in storage over the winter.) Only a few cultivars produced harvestable fruit in November. If you wanted an apple after that, it had to come from a grocery store.

Of course, any apples bought in a grocery store had long been off the tree, and might even be a year old. They were kept fresh—or, "fresh," wink-wink—in controlled atmosphere storage rooms, where the apples were put into slumber like Sleeping Beauty with just the right combination of temperature, humidity, oxygen, and carbon dioxide. The apples couldn't summon the energy to complete the ripening process; they were frozen in time and place, waiting to be awakened, waiting to be eaten. It made for a fine enough apple. But not as fine as one off the tree, or even one left to mature off the tree for a time—some apples, after all, improved with time, after the harvest was over.

But Dan Paxson's apples, the

(*Harrowsblack*)

Ruby Slippers? Those trees started producing fruit back in late August. Should've been done by the end of September at the latest.

Yet here it was, early November—

And still the branches hung heavy with dark-red fruit.

Even as all the leaves on the other trees went yellow to pink to red before falling to the ground, then turning brown, then dying, these seven trees were *flourishing*. Even a hard chill didn't seem to hurt them. They just kept going, with cascades of new fruit rising and ripening on one branch after another. Soon as one branch was lightened of its load, it began to produce fruit all over again.

Dan knew that was strange. Trees blossomed once a year, at best.

And yet, the orchard was still producing apples. By this point, Dan should've been raking up dead leaves and the rot of fallen fruit, composting what he could, wrapping the trees to help them stave off the injurious bite of winter. But he wasn't. He was still picking fruit. Good fruit. Healthy fruit. *Delicious* fruit.

Hell, that wasn't just strange. It was *impossible.*

Oh, but as the infomercials were fond of saying

But that's not all!

It wasn't just the orchard that was doing impossible things, was it?

DAN HADN'T SLEPT IN A WEEK.

It had been building for a while. Most of October, his sleep was restless—he'd go from hot to cold to hot again, kicking off covers, pulling them back on. He'd felt almost feverish. Start of that month, he'd get about half a night's sleep, and by the middle, half of that again. Thing was, he never felt tired. Losing that much sleep should've knocked him for a loop—he was a man who knew the occasional curse of insomnia, and whenever it hit, the next day he'd feel like he was coming off a night of drinking, right on the edge of a hangover. Groggy, muddy brain. But that didn't happen this time. He had as much energy as he needed. In fact, he felt *better than ever*. Sharp as a wolf's tooth.

And *happy*. That was perhaps the newest, oddest feeling of them all. He felt simply buoyant, like there wasn't anything he couldn't do, like all the world was waiting out there just for him. Like before he showed up, all was in darkness, and it was he who turned on the light. No—it was Dan who *was* the light.

Feeling bolstered and ebullient, Dan got his ass to work. He'd already in the latter half of last month signed up for more farmers markets (after all, there were apples still to sell!), but even still, he had a surplus of fruit. So, he bought a cider press and some jugs with the intent to bottle cider. Non-alcoholic at first, but then maybe the adult stuff. Plus he got to work on a small outbuilding between the house and the orchard along the rutted drive down. First he had to clear brush, which he did by hand, with a brush-clearing sickle and a shovel. He got lumber from Ottsville, using his father's old table saw to cut two-by-fours to make the framework. Wasn't anywhere near done, but could be by the end of the month. A little kerosene heater kept him warm, not that he really felt all that cold? Nor did he feel all that *hungry*, either. (Though of course he enjoyed an apple now and again. Breakfast, lunch, dinner. Always a treat!) Even Marco, with his broken leg, the poor kid, came over and helped where he could—not getting up and walking around, no, but helping Calla design a label for the eventual cider and printing out stickers to be applied to the jugs and bottles.

Everything was working out like it hadn't in . . . well, he wanted to say *years*, but really, like it hadn't *ever*.

It was enough to make Dan believe in God. Or a god, anyway. A god of the trees. A god of the fruit. All hail the orchard lord, huzzah.

Then, today, he noticed something.

Something off.

Something *wrong*.

He headed down to the orchard first thing, as he often liked to start his day doing the picking, seeing what bounty awaited—and as he drove down, he saw a bird ahead of him, a dark little bird like a woodcock or grouse, sitting square in the middle of the path. Dan eased the brakes on the truck and got out to usher the little bird out of the way, and, oh—

It wasn't a bird at all. It was just a pile of gray-brown leaves, clumped together in decay. *What the hell,* he thought, and gave a look around him—

Everything looked blurry. The trees. The truck. All of it. *I'm losing my eyesight,* he thought—and the horror only increased when he worried, *Oh hell, maybe I'm having a stroke.* Panic set its teeth in him. He hadn't been sleeping. He had all this new energy. Maybe that was a bad sign, not a good one. A walking ghost phase of feeling unconquerable when the reality was, he had a brain tumor or lupus or some new virus they hadn't even named yet—fear unspooled within him, a sudden surge of hypochondria that nearly brought him to his knees.

But then he thought, *Okay, damn, Dan, maybe your glasses are just greasy*—after all, he was practically legally blind and had to pay extra money just so his spectacles didn't weigh ten pounds on his head like a couple of Coke bottles. Probably just dirty was all.

So he took them off and, with shaking hands, used the bottom of his shirt to give them a hasty wipe—

But before he put them back on, he paused.

He could see just fine.

Not merely fine, but perfect. That clump of leaves sat there in high definition—clearer now than when he had his glasses on his face. Real quick he put them up to his eyes and sure enough, peering through those lenses just made everything blurry again. Pull them away and, boom: 20/20 vision.

Dan blinked. "Well, I'll be damned," he said to the forest.

The wind shook the brush, as if to answer.

He tucked the glasses in his shirt pocket—something he never had cause to do, given how much he needed them—and there came a moment when he thought about what this was, and what this meant. Was it worth worrying about? Worth some consideration, maybe even a call to his doctor?

Dan decided that no, it was not worth the trouble, or the thought.

Sometimes, an unalloyed good did not need further examination.

I am owed this, he thought idly, and continued on to his orchard.

―――

HE WORKED FOR ABOUT AN HOUR. CLIMBING THE LADDER, PICKING apples. Sometimes sneaking one for himself, like a child with cookies just out of the oven. Each tasted sweeter than the last and in each he found a new dimension—the way the flesh seemed to burst in his mouth, juices exploding under the crush of teeth and offering a flurry of new flavors across the real estate of his tongue, flavors that seemed chameleonic, chimerical, shifting from one bite to the next. Brown sugar and pear. Ginger, followed by a hint of rye. Blush Chablis. A bready lager. A jaw-tightening surge of acidity, and a curious bitter pinprick after. And the way it felt on his tongue—cold and crisp, the joy of snapping into a hard piece of toffee, the pleasure of a bitten Popsicle, the

(gentle tug-and-tickle of something crawling on your tongue)

(winding digestive spiral of that same thing moving around your stomach in a happy carousel)

(worms and roots through soft loamy earth, pushing ever deeper)

refreshing crunch of iceberg lettuce. He felt lost to it, consumed by the apple even as he consumed it, and when he looked down, he saw at least two dozen apple cores at his feet. Had he truly eaten that many? The wind kicked up again and he felt the cold wetness of his face, juices slicking his lips, chin, and cheeks. Dan looked at his watch. It wasn't only an hour that had passed. It was three.

And he'd picked all the ripe apples, it seemed. The baskets were full.

He barely remembered doing so.

God, he felt good.

The wind turned then, shaking the trees—

A smell crawled into his nose, past the faint rosehip aroma of the apple. A wild smell: strong, musky, almost skunky. He felt it then, too: the sensation of not being alone. He stepped down off the ladder, following his nose toward the thicket—

His phone rang, giving him a startle.

It was a number he didn't recognize. Calla was always telling him not to answer those calls—they were spam half the time—but his fatherly defense was, *What if it's important? What if you're trapped under a bridge somewhere*

(or took a step off a steep ledge)

and I didn't answer it because I figured it was just junk?

Of course, her answer there was, *Dad, if I'm trapped under a bridge, I don't think you're going to be able to Incredible Hulk the rubble off my broken body. Also you wouldn't be my first call*—which hurt his feelings, admittedly—*it'd be nine-one-one, duh*—which he also had to admit was the right answer.

He answered the call, like he always did.

A familiar voice found him.

"Hey, Dan. It's—"

"Joanie," he said, smiling at hearing her voice. "Yeah, hey. Been a while."

"Ten years or so?"

"Yeah. Oh! No—I saw you at the Wawa, the one at the corner of York and Durham. We waved to each other but I dunno if you realized who I was—"

"Oh god, yeah, that was, what? Just a couple years ago. I forgot about that. Hey, so, this is out of the blue, and feel free to tell me to go piss up a rope, but I could use your help with something."

He laughed. "Joanie Moreau, always straight to the point. I miss that." To his surprise, he meant it. He *did* miss it. "What do you need?"

"I need a friend with a pickup truck to move a skeleton."

"A what now?"

She explained that she'd bought one of those giant skeleton lawn ornaments. "It's twelve feet tall, Dan, and I need someone with a pickup truck because I can't just pop this in the back of the Porsche. I mean—it's an SUV, but it won't accommodate a big stupid skeleton. It just needs a quick ride to our storage unit. I can pay, obviously—"

"I won't take a dime for it, and yeah, I'll be over shortly. Where are you at these days?"

"Fox Run."

"Fox Run? Wow, Joanie. Far cry from your family's place on Burnt Church Hill," he said. And it was. She wasn't *poor*-poor growing up, but like Dan, their families lived from bill to bill, eating SpaghettiOs and driving beat-ass secondhand station wagons. Fox Run was a big step up. Seemed like Joanie had made some real money over the years. She gave him the street address and he said he'd be over there in twenty minutes or so.

He hung up and stood there amid the apple trees, remembering. Dan and Joanie had been boyfriend–girlfriend for a good solid year in high school. He'd always told people it was like trying to stay on one of those mechanical broncos you'd see in cowboy bars—not that she was trying to throw you, she just couldn't help it. She was who she was. Unfuckwithable, all fire and lightning, always getting into fights and trouble—and even when she wasn't getting into fights and trouble, people *said* she was. Same way they said she was a slut even though she wasn't, not to his recall anyway. She was just . . . tough, confident, didn't give a shit, didn't take any shit. Nobody liked that in a teenage girl, much less one who didn't have money and cool-kid clout. So they were cruel to her.

And she got cruel back, when she had to.

Dan grabbed one basket of apples, loaded it into the back of the truck, then got in behind the wheel. He gave the pickup a whirl around the outside of the ring of apple trees, headed back toward the house and toward the road.

But, soon as he was about to pull out—

A full-sized black SUV pulled in, blocking his truck. Big, fully racked Lincoln Navigator. Claude Lambert stepped out of the driver's side.

Shit, Dan thought. He leaned out the window and said, "Claude, if you don't mind, I'm about to head out—"

Lambert nodded, gave a dismissive little wave. "I see that. This won't take long, Little Dan. If you don't mind?"

I do mind, he thought. And he was *this close* to telling Claude Lambert to go fuck himself with a broken fencepost, but he always remembered his father's deference to the man, and something in him followed in those footsteps the way an ant followed its own scent-trail. *Maybe weakness and deference is genetic,* he thought darkly. Dan left the engine running and stepped out.

"Claude, if this is about the property, I'm not interested in that chat—"

"No, no," Claude said, shaking his head. "This isn't that conversation. I think we're well past that point, and I understand why now. You've got something special here, Little Dan. Your father was right. And you knew that, didn't you?"

Dan tensed up. Felt for sure like this was some kind of prank. Or worse, like it was just bait. Like someone offering their embrace only to sucker-punch you once you opened your arms.

"It is special, that's right."

"I know you're not going to give up on this place. Because I wouldn't, either. You're right not to. Those apples you grow—well. They're like nothing I've ever eaten." He bellowed a big, sudden laugh. "Everybody who has one, we all say the same thing. We can't get enough, can we? Everyone else still thinks it's just about it being a damn good fruit. *Here's an apple,* they think. *I enjoyed it. And so I want another.* But I know, and I'm sure you do, too, that it's not *just* that. Is it, Little Dan? These apples are different." He paused. "They're miraculous."

Claude had changed. Still the big barrel-chested old man, but he stood stiffer, straighter. His gin-blossom nose and ruddy cheeks had lightened—no longer striated with the starbursts of broken capillaries under the skin.

He looked *healthier.*

(*he's eating the apples*)

(*he's changing just like you are, Dan*)

Dan hesitated. "I don't know what you mean, Claude."

"I took you for a fool before and I apologize for that. I was wrong. Don't put me back to thinking that way about you. I know you know what I'm talking about. You look different, same as I do. And I bet you feel different, too." Claude looked him up and down. "You usually wear glasses, do you not?"

To that, Dan said nothing. His father was famously gregarious, and couldn't keep a secret to save his life. It was just who he'd been: a talker.

Dan wasn't like that.

He liked to keep things close.

(*because if they knew everything . . .*)

Lambert stepped closer. "Dan, I feel better than I felt when I was in my forties, thirties, maybe my twenties. And it's not a physical thing. It's something all through me. I feel as bright as a bite of one of those apples." At that, he sniffed the air. "You got some in that truck, don't you? I can smell them. Can you?"

Dan gave a sniff, too, without trying to look like he was—

And sure enough, in the air, the heady perfume of rose and honey.

"Gimme one of those apples," Lambert said, his grin big and hungry.

Dan started to move, to go get one. But he froze. Anger lanced through him like sparks snapping off jumper cables. He turned back and sneered.

"Even children know if they want something, they ask nicely or they don't get anything at all, Claude."

Claude chuckled, made a small, acquiescent grunt. "Little Dan, may I *please* have one of your Ruby Slipper apples? I'd gladly pay you Tuesday for a bite of the apple today."

He hesitated. "Yeah, all right."

Dan fetched an apple, gave it a softball pitch. Claude caught it out of the air, the fruit snapping against his palm.

"So I still don't know why you're visiting me here. I have to go."

"I'm here to make an offer."

"And I'm here to tell you no to that offer."

"No, no, hold on, now. It's an offer by way of an invitation. End of the month, on the Wednesday before Thanksgiving, we have a dinner at Goldenrod, the old inn by the river. Dinner, drinks, good conversation, cigars sometimes on the patio if the weather permits. We close the place down to outsiders, and it's just us."

Just us. He meant the Crossed Keys. Their little "networking" group. All that old money. All that power. Old rich white men, mostly, and their children, and in some cases their children's children. Bloodlines and bank accounts, braided together.

"And you're inviting me to this event."

"I am. Which means it's not just an invitation to the event, you realize."

It's an invitation to the group.

To the Crossed Keys.

"I don't have that kind of money," Dan said. He knew from his father's proximity to that club that there was a buy-in expected. He didn't know how much, but one season of good apple sales was not enough to get him there.

"We voted, and will waive any such fees for you."

"Why? There's a catch. I know there is."

"See, I knew you weren't a fool. But trust me, the catch is a good one.

You'll like it. See, if you join our little group, you'll get more than you give. I'd like to invest in this business. In the orchard. Bring you some more capital. Plus I have some ins with a couple of regional grocery chains—we could get your apples into stores. Not just the little fiddly table markets. Real stores, Little Dan. Beyond Harrow. Beyond Bucks County."

Real stores meant real money.

For himself. For Calla.

For their future—his business, her education.

Dan chewed on that.

Lambert said, "I don't need an answer today. Just come to the dinner. Plus one—bring a guest if you'd like, that's fine. We can have your answer then. Meanwhile, I'll let you get back to whatever you were doing." He took one more step closer and offered his hand to shake.

That hand, waiting. Dan watched it the way you'd clock a rattlesnake sitting there, coiled up, shaking its tail. He wanted dearly not to take it, but his father's voice in his ear told him what an insult that would truly be.

They shook hands.

Claude nodded, started to step away, but then halted again. "Oh, you hear about that dead fella they pulled out of the river? Dead by a few years at least."

"I heard he was probably a fisherman or some such."

"They ID'd him, it seems. By the teeth. Walt Purvin, I think his name was. Not local, lived upstate, I think. You know what he did for a living?"

Dan didn't answer. He didn't have to.

"Apple hunter," Claude said with an astonishment that Dan couldn't tell if it was practiced or genuine. "That's a helluva thing to put on a ré-sumé. Not that ol' Walt is going to be applying for a new job anytime soon."

"Shame he died" was all Dan said, his guts and veins suddenly full of ice water. Claude nodded, saying goodbye, then got in his big-ass SUV and backed out of the driveway and was gone. Leaving Dan standing there, alone, chasing away the memories of when he'd last seen Walt Purvin alive.

17

THE APPLE HUNTER SAYS GOODBYE

IT WAS MORNING IN WALT PURVIN'S ORCHARD. THE SUN WAS THIN today, like its light had been whittled with a knife. Bands of tarnished gold shone through the leafless branches of apple trees. Several dozen of them—lost varieties Walt had himself found and reclaimed, like the Brumley's Pippin, or the simply named Mary Thompson apple. Walt had taken his whole backyard and used it to rescue these trees. Before John Compass left today, he'd do the work to keep them safe, preparing the trees for winter. To honor the man who was gone, a man whose identity the dental records had confirmed: Walt Purvin was dead.

John Compass sat on a folding chair he'd brought. He held a large lunch box in his lap. The lunch box was metal. Rusted at its rounded edges.

He was alone. Walt's daughter did not have a good relationship with Walt. She said she'd have a proper funeral not, in her words, "whatever this is."

That was fair. This was for John and Walt only.

But John was not sure what to say. After all this time, with Walt missing, and the time before that from when their friendship had been broken like a branch, John felt at a loss. With his thumbs, he popped the lid of the lunch box, revealing the items within: old arrowheads they'd found out on the hunt, a deck of nudie playing cards that were fraying at the edges, and a six-inch-tall piano baby. The piano baby was made of biscuit porcelain, and was a little statue of a cherubic baby with an apple in his lap, held fast in chubby hands. It was a Victorian-era antique, a statue meant to sit on the cloth or shawl used to cover up one's precious piano. Walt had been a piano teacher in his spare time, and always had this little weirdo sitting there. John had asked Belinda if she wanted it, but she made a face like she'd licked a shit-covered spoon, saying, "I don't want that ugly little thing. Dad always loved it, but I hate it." So John took it to bury.

"I don't know what to say," he finally said. He'd always been honest with Walt and that seemed fair now. "We got old and we pissed each other off and now there's nothing to be done about that but this." He cleared grief from his throat. "I know you thought it was odd me becoming a Quaker and all but here I think they have it right. They like things simple. So I'll keep it simple now. You're gone and I miss you. You were a good friend even when you weren't and I hope the same could be said of me to you. We should've forgiven each other for things we said, for the way we both were. I'm holding you in the light and I wish you the best in your journey. Love you, Walt."

At that, he went and got the shovel he brought and dug a hole, then closed up the lunch box and set it in the open ground. Earthworms wriggled in the sheer dirt cliffs; some had been cleaved in half. John felt bad, but knew there was no way to take a blade to the earth and not cut some worm or some root. Man's mere presence upon this world was violence against it, and he regretted that.

John used his bare hands to scoop cold, damp dirt back into the hole.

Three scoops in, he stopped. The lunch box wasn't even halfway covered yet. He felt something in his guts: Nausea sucked at his innards like a leech. He hadn't eaten much for breakfast, just a sausage-egg-cheese bagel from Sheetz, and though John usually had a cast-iron stomach lining, maybe it wasn't sitting well.

Or maybe it's just that you're sad because your friend is dead and gone, he told himself.

That's when the lunch box sprang open with a click.

Inside sat Walt's severed head.

Dead, rheumy eyes rotated in their sockets, pupils like smashed raisins. His head was bashed in, the skin ripped, brown blood oozing out. His lips worked and words arose in John's ears, words that did not match the way the mouth moved, like a bad dub in a foreign movie—

"Who killed me, John? And what did I find? Bet you I found that apple, John. Or maybe that apple found me, huh?"

John cried out, falling back, using his elbows to dig into the dirt and push himself away from the hole.

"The hell?" came a voice behind him. Belinda.

He hurried to stand, brushing himself off. He looked down in the hole, saw the lunch box sitting there, still closed.

John turned to her to apologize, because he felt like he had to, making a scene like this in her father's—and John stammered something, some kind of sorry. Belinda just stared icicles at him.

His stomach cooled, at least. Unclenched itself like a relaxing fist.

(He tasted sausage and bile, though. And, strangely, apples.)

"You gonna be done soon?" she asked him, irritated.

John nodded, still trying to get that taste out of his mouth. Belinda went back inside, and he hurriedly finished covering the hole.

HE TOLD HER HE'D BE BACK ANOTHER DAY TO PREP THE TREES FOR winter. Belinda said she didn't care, that he might as well let the winter cold kill the trees, because she planned to get rid of them in the spring. She'd been living here since her father went missing, now owned it officially since he'd been declared dead. She didn't like apples, she said, and thought her father was too obsessed with them.

John made a note then that he wasn't to come to prepare the trees— but he'd come back and cut some scionwood. Walt may be gone, but his trees could live.

As he was halfway out the door, Belinda said to him, "What's your deal, anyway?"

"I confess, Belinda, I don't understand the question," he said.

"With my father. You two gay? My mother said you's two were gay."

"Your mother was an alcoholic."

He didn't say it to be cruel. It was merely a fact, and one that Belinda seemed aware of. She shrugged as if to say, *Good point.*

John continued: "We understood each other." *Until we didn't.* "But we didn't have that kind of relationship, no."

"Uh-huh. Well. Bye."

"Goodbye, Belinda."

And at that, he left.

———

THE BETHLEHEM MEETING HOUSE WAS, AS IT SHOULD'VE BEEN, A simple affair: yellow building, blue doors, and even that was perhaps more ostentatious than a lot of Quaker spaces. Inside, it was simpler, and though some of the meetinghouses farther south in Bucks County carried with them that feeling of *history*, aged spaces, all wood, smelling of wax and oil and dust, this one felt a little more like it was a place you'd go for an Alcoholics Anonymous meeting. Tan linoleum floor and painted cement walls with a drop tile ceiling. Fluorescents buzzed. The one thing out of place were the pews: These *were* old, from the original meetinghouse, which had been built in 1830 but burned down a century later. Most of the pews, miraculously, had survived, and here they sat. But two in the front needed refinishing, which he helped do, and now was carrying them in with Cherie Leveen, a friend of his—and the woman who helped him decide to join the Friends in the first place.

Quakers didn't really have pastors or deacons or any of that. Cherie was the clerk here, a person who lived nearby who had keys to the building and kept it up, facilitated meetings, and so forth. But she was his first entry point to the Friends—his first friend in the Friends, so to speak— and so he felt close to her. Today, she'd asked him to help out at the meetinghouse, which he was always eager and willing to do.

Together, they set the final pew at the fore of the room. John bent down and reached for the drill to start affixing them once more to the floor—making sure to hit the same holes that were already bored through.

Cherie sat down in the pew across. The Black woman was older, smaller, had a librarian vibe about her. John just felt comfortable around her. That was her way. It seemed effortless, but it wasn't. She drank a little water, ate some pretzels out of a small bag.

"I appreciate you coming up here to help me out," she said.

"Glad to help. Besides, I could use to not be alone."

"You okay?"

He sat up.

"My friend died."

"I know." She put a warm hand on his knee. "I'm sorry, John. Today was the day you said goodbye, wasn't it?"

"It was."

"Pretzels?"

He took a handful, crunched on them.

"I think my friend was murdered."

"Oh? Why do you think that?"

"A hunch."

She hmmed and said okay, if he thought so, then it must be true.

"There's more," he said.

"Uh-oh."

"I . . ." He paused. Uncertain if he should continue. He didn't want her to think any less of him. Of course she wouldn't, and he knew that, but the mind feared what the mind feared regardless of how rational that was. "I had something happen to me this morning." He told her about seeing Walt's face there in that lunch box. Talking to him. How he felt sick, too, like he wanted to throw up.

"We like to think of grief, and anger, and all our negative emotions, as always working one way, but sometimes they show up in ways we don't expect, popping up like groundhogs. We think it's kept to one place, in our hearts or in our minds, but that's not how it works. Grief is a *whole-body* experience, John."

"You're probably right. But it felt . . . deeper. More real. Like this was a warning of some kind." *Like it was Walt really talking to me.* "What do Quakers think about ghosts, Cherie?"

She laughed. "I don't think I'm the person to answer that. I'm administrative, remember."

"Sorry." He grunted as he pulled himself up to a pew, sat down in it next to her.

"No, no apologies—well. There's no one answer about what Quakers do or think about any specific topic. We're a bit like cats, scattering this way and that. But generally speaking, we try to imagine the world in front of us and not the world we can't see. We don't worry about ghosts, we worry about those alive around us now—and when they're gone, we hold on to their memories."

"The Lenape believe in spirits. Good spirits, evil spirits. Visions, too. Warnings of the future."

"Is that what you believe?"

"Well. I don't know."

"Most Quakers, we concern ourselves less with evil and sin and worry more about doing good. The best counter to bad things is to do good things. It's why we hold people in the light. Why we find the light within, as well. That spark of God or goodness or whatever it is you believe that it is."

He nodded.

"But what if that's not enough?" he asked. "What if the darkness is bigger than that? What if it's more real than that? Not just metaphorical."

"The light isn't metaphorical, either, I don't think. Goodness is real, John Compass. Those we love, we hold in the light. And those who put evil in the world, sometimes . . . well, we have to hold the light to them. Turn the bulb right toward them, shine it big and bright. Because light always burns out darkness. If the darkness seems too deep, then a brighter light is required."

"Thank you, Cherie."

"Always a pleasure, John. Hey, you know what we should do sometime? We should do laser tag." Her eyes brightened at that.

"Laser tag? Quakers are pacifists."

"John, laser tag isn't real. It's okay to play pretend." She lowered her voice. "Besides, I am a mean motherfucker with a laser gun."

"Well, all right, then."

BACK OUTSIDE, HIS PHONE RANG. IT WAS EMILY.

"Hello, Emily," he said.

"I found it," was her response. Agitated. Excited.

"Found what?"

"I found Walt's car."

18

JUNKYARDS

THE HEACOCK SALVAGE YARD WAS AT THE NORTHERN TIP OF BUCKS, just shy of the county line and all the way up past Harrow, past Gallows Run, past Durham Hill. On the way up, Emily could feel the vibe changing. It was rural up here. Not much farmland amid the tangles of forest. But it was wild in ways beyond nature. She spied a lot of crazy political signs from elections past: CREEL 2020, even though Creel had lost that election; HUNT THE CUNT, one of Creel's unofficial slogans, aimed at then-president Nora Hunt; god, someone had even spray-painted on a big piece of plywood the message SMOKE POT GET SHOT, as if that were the big issue of the day. She saw a lot of DON'T TREAD ON ME type of shit, too—dirty, fraying flags hanging one after the next. The farther north they went, the more insane some of the properties became. She saw at least three toilets on three different lawns. One had a driveway lined with mannequins dressed up in ratty blond wigs and pink bikini tops (no bottoms). She saw rusted-out buses, fire-struck barns, and one place that was *definitely* a cult compound. All concrete bunkers and, mysteriously, a stone pyramid in the back.

"It's amazing," she said to John, who was driving and had been mostly silent. "You drive twenty minutes away from the Richie-Riches and away from the middle-class-money-having-wannabes, and you enter a whole new world. It's like Narnia if Narnia were just crazy racists who don't get enough vitamin D."

John gave a small shrug. "Make the cracks big enough, people start to fall through them." He stared ahead, seemingly almost hypnotized by the bends of the backroads, the staccato strobe of the trees passing by.

"I don't think that excuses their behavior."

"Not an excuse. Just reality. You cut down education, put lead and other nasty business in the water, feed them a diet of poisonous pig-crap on the television and the internet, those are cracks. They widen. People fall through. They get mean and they get crazy. And they go blind down there in the darkness."

"But that sounds like it's not their own fault."

"I don't like to worry about fault. Just about fixing things." Though when he said that, he seemed to flinch a little. As if he had his own things to fix—and as if maybe he hadn't yet fixed them. "Here we go," he said, pointing.

Up ahead, a big chain-link fence. Beyond it, a salvage yard.

EMILY KNEW WALT DROVE A 2004 CHEVY BLAZER. NAVY BLUE. From there, it just took calling every junk and salvage yard in the county until she found Heacock. The guy on the phone said that sure enough, they had one just like it.

One of the guys working there—a big fella with a Gritty T-shirt, long ratty hair tugged back in a messy pony, and an ass-crack that kept poking out of his fall-down jeans—opened the gate, let them in, and pointed them toward the Blazer.

"It's out back," he said, breath rank with stale nicotine. Maybe a little weed, too. No worries about smoking pot and getting shot here, Emily realized. "Far eastern—no, shit, *western*—corner of the lot. It's near the uh, the uh, the hydraulic grab."

"The vehicle been here awhile?" John asked him.

"Yeah. Longer than I've been working, and I've been here three years."

She expected this place to be bigger vertically—piles of junk, crushed cars, and the like. But it was all pretty flat. One car after the next. A line of washing machines. A stack of sheet metal.

Emily asked, "Don't you, like, smoosh the cars?" She mashed her palms together. "You know, crush 'em for scrap and stuff?"

"Sometimes. But a lot of times we keep 'em, pick at 'em like vultures if it's a vehicle out of production people need parts for. Belts, alternators, side mirrors, bumpers. That one's been picked apart pretty good. You'll see."

John loomed over the other man. "You weren't here when it was brought in. Know who might've been?"

"I can ask the boss."

"He here now?"

"Uh-huh."

"Please, ask him. We'll head to the car."

"THAT'S IT," JOHN SAID, HIS VOICE SOUNDING FARAWAY.

"You're sure?"

He nodded and walked up alongside the vehicle, running his thumb along a rust-canker scrape in the driver's-side door. "We were driving up a too-tight overgrown driveway looking for an old russet apple tree. I told him it was too narrow and we needed to walk, but he was stubborn as a splinter, so he just kept going. Didn't see the bent metal fence past a big stump, and it gouged the door. Made a helluva sound. Like a banshee, screaming." He paused for a moment. "Didn't find the tree, not that day."

As the dude at the front described, the Blazer had in fact been nibbled down to the bone. Bumpers gone. Fenders gone. Side mirrors, rearview mirror, gone. Inside, it was more intact, though the stereo was vacant. Emily popped the door, and it opened with a creaky squeal. The inside smelled like must and rust and time.

John went in on the other side, dropping the glove compartment door open. "Nothing in here, just dirt. Debris."

"Who knew we'd find junk in a junkyard?" Emily crawled into the back seat, looked over the edge to the cargo part of the SUV. Nothing there, either, except more dirt, a few dry dead leaves, the husk of a stink bug mummified by time. "Yeah, not finding anything here, either. Unless you think this stink bug killed him."

John grunted.

"Your wife didn't seem happy to see me," John said.

When John had picked her up, she went out to meet him, and Meg stayed inside—just staring out the window. At him. At Emily. Staring bullets.

"Yeaaaah, she's not super-thrilled I'm still doing this."

"She in fact seemed surprised at my presence."

"I didn't really *tell* her I was going anywhere. Until I was." Emily didn't tell him that she found his gifted apples—the ones meant for Meg—in the trash the day after she gave them to her. Not one bite out of them. It seemed she only liked those Ruby Slippers.

"Hnh. So why are you still doing this?"

She lifted up the armrest between the two back seats. Found a dime. Took the dime because, hey, ha ha, now she had a dime to her name. *Take that, Meg.* "I told you," she said idly. "I feel guilty. And I'm bored."

(*And I'm lonely.*)

"You two still fighting?"

Emily reversed out of the back seat, then got down on her hands and knees to feel under the seats. "I'm not going to do *relationship counselor* with you. I don't think that's really our vibe, John Compass. Besides, here you are, despite not having spoken to your friend in years. Were *you two* fighting?"

From the front seat, she heard a long sigh. He was quiet for a while, and she guessed he wasn't going to answer her, but then he started talking. "We did fight. There had been a lot of fights. I didn't like that he was trying to make this big to-do over the apples—a business. I thought, and I said, they should be kept pure, that money ruined things. Fruit should be for everybody. The Lenape, you know, they had this idea of *public fruit.* Fruit on a tree could not be owned. The fruit tree could not be owned. They'd sell a property to a white settler, but only on the stipulation that the tree and its fruit remained free to all. Some crops were temporary, and you took them with you. But you plant a fruit tree, it stays where you put it, and is there to provide for those who need its nourishment."

"Guess Walt didn't like that."

"He thought it was bunk. Said I wasn't even that much of a Native, what did I care, and besides, I was a Quaker anyway. Which he didn't like, either. Our last fight was about these bikers—they'd go up and down his road, big loud apes on their big loud bikes, and Walt tried to chase them off. But that just made things worse. They'd ride late at night, trash his mailbox. He wanted me to, I don't know. Threaten them. Kick their asses. I said I didn't do that kind of thing anymore. But I offered to talk to them. I said pacifism didn't mean passivity. He was drunk. Too many beers. Called me a pussy. I left. That was the last time we talked."

"I'm sorry," she said, straining to reach deeper under the farther seat.

She was about to ask why he felt obliged to keep looking into this when her fingers tickled the edge of an object. Something with a corner. Softer edge, not metal. "I think I . . . found something." She went around the other side, where access was easier, and pulled out—

A book.

A hardcover. Dusty and striated with gray mold.

"*The Legends of Bucks County,*" she said. "By Jed Homackie."

John took it, gave it a look down his nose. "Oh sure, Walt used to read all this fella's books. *The Ghosts of Long Beach Island. The Ramble Rocks Murders.* Local history and folklore stuff. Author was from around here, I think. Died some years back in a drunk driving accident, leaving his wife and daughter behind." John leaned in, gave the book a sniff. "Smells a little like Old Spice. The old kind, the aftershave. Walt always wore it."

"Never heard of him." She clarified. "Homackie, I mean."

John handed the book back with a shrug.

"You find what you were looking for?" someone called to them.

A short, stout man headed toward them, a locomotive walk like he was a train on a track, choo-choo. Bald on top, wispy hair on the sides. Gruff, piggy nose, good-sized underbite. Like he was part human, part fantasy creature. Some hog—man hybrid. His orange T-shirt was dark with spots of motor oil.

"We did," John said.

"Good," the man said. He put out a hand. "Bill Akers. This is my place."

"Your employee said you might have been here when this was brought in."

Bill shrugged. "Jimmy, yeah. He says a lot of things, most of them stupid as fuck—" To Emily he said. "Excuse the language, miss. But he's right, I was here the night it came in. About five years back. Didn't think too much of it, really. It was left out front one night, I found it here in the morning. End of story."

"And that wasn't weird?" Emily asked.

"Enh, not so much. People treat us like we're the city dump. They just . . . drop shit off. Same as they do with secondhand stores. Half the things left here we have to spend time and money to throw out. The Blazer was good, though."

"It still have plates?" John asked.

"Nope. No plates."

Emily said, "I saw a camera out front when we pulled in. Any chance—"

"I'll stop you right there. First, I wouldn't have tape from five years ago, and even if I did, it's not fancy night vision or anything. I took a look at the tape that night, couldn't make much out about the person except I think it was a guy. Maybe your height," he said to John, "and that was it."

"So this guy shows up, drops off a Blazer and then—drives away in another car? Did you see the other vehicle?"

"That's the thing. He just walked off. Might've been a car waiting nearby, but if it was, it was off camera. And didn't have headlights on."

Emily and John shared a look. *Weird, right,* she tried to convey to him.

"You find that in the car?" Bill asked Emily, gesturing toward the book.

"Oh. Yeah."

"Guess I missed that."

"You find other stuff?"

"A satchel, perhaps," John said. "Brown leather. Would've had coffee stains on it. Walt always set his coffee on top of it, and it left rings."

"No such satchel, but I did find something else. Something that made me assume the guy who ditched the car was a fisherman—"

"A common assumption," John said with some bitterness.

"Why did you think that?" Emily asked.

Bill shrugged. "Had a map of the river in the glove box. But it wasn't just, like, a regular-ass map. It was like a, you know, a nautical map. With depth charts and such. I just figured, hey, guy was probably a fisherman. Looking for places where the fish gathered. Maybe not. I think fishing is boring as fuck."

"My friend was not a fisherman," John said.

"Your friend."

"The man who owned this car."

"Oh. You trying to get it back for him? If it was stolen, I didn't—"

"He died."

"Oh. *Oh.*"

John stepped forward, looming closer, looming bigger. "He went missing one night, five years ago. Possibly the same night his car, this car, ended up here."

"Hey, whoa," Bill said, his back up as he got in a defensive posture. "I dunno if you're cops or what, but I did everything above the book—"

"Aboveboard," Emily corrected under her breath. She couldn't help it, apparently? "Aboveboard or by the book."

"—whatever, I checked for plates, no plates. I checked the VIN, but it had been scratched off. I reported the car, and the cops never said boo about it, and if they don't come out in thirty days, it means the salvage is ours—"

"We aren't police," John said. "And we're not suspicious of your involvement. I'm just trying to find more about my friend."

"Yeah." He seemed to relax a little. "Yeah, okay. Well." Bill threw up his hands. "All I know is what I told you."

"Do you still have the river map?"

"Nah. I threw it out—or maybe one of the other guys took it, I can't say for sure. Five years is a long time. I can't always remember what I did with shit from two weeks ago." He snapped his fingers. "I remember, though, that map? It had a bunch of the islands circled."

"Islands?" Emily asked.

"Yeah, yeah, the Delaware has a bunch of islands in it. All up and down it. He had all the ones between Pennsylvania and New Jersey circled with a red pen."

"Any notations or other markings?"

"Nope. Not that I can think of."

"Thanks for your time."

And just like that, John walked off.

Emily gave a shrug to the salvage yard boss, and trailed after.

19

THE UNSPOKEN THING IS UN-UNSPOKEN

THEY DROVE DOWN TOWARD THE RIVER, STOPPING AT A GAS-station-slash-bait-shop to pick up a map of the river. They found a little park area by the canal that ran parallel to the river, the one used to haul coal from upstate Pennsylvania once upon a time. Together they crossed the grass, the fallen leaves and glittering frost crunching underfoot as they walked to a small picnic table.

Already John was spreading out the map he'd bought. It felt quaint, somehow, to Emily—a big paper map. *Paper.* Tangible. Something weirdly stupidly endearing about that. It wasn't just a thing on a screen. It was like something out of an expedition, an adventure. The book, too, that she'd found, had the same feel to it. She tried to quell that feeling. A man was dead. She'd stepped on his bones, for fuck's sake. *Have respect, Emily, god.* Didn't help that she felt all bottled up. The Unspoken Thing was not behind her, not in front of her, but within her now. Straining to cut her open from stem to stern and crawl free.

Compass uncapped a pen with his teeth, started circling islands. Reciting their names as he went: "Salt House Island. Moon Island. Kehennock. Mud Shoal. Tennakonk. Lapowinso. Mint Field. Black Hill. Graham Flats. Resolution. Upper Penns Island. Lower Penns Island. Those are just the big ones. Lotta little ones in there, too. Maybe just an acre or three in size. No names for those. We can probably rule out all the ones south of where you found the body, here—"

"I cheated on my wife."

The Unspoken Thing—

Dragged out of the darkness within her, drawn out like an infection, thrashing as it emerged. Transformed by five simple words. *I cheated on my wife.* The unsaid, now said. Made manifest, summoned into the world, this demon.

John Compass froze, staring at her over the map.

"I'm sorry," he said. It didn't sound sarcastic.

"Don't be. I did it. I'm the asshole."

He looked around. "You don't have to tell me this if you don't want to." Again, something he said not out of his own discomfort, but out of consideration for her. "It's not my business and you've no obligation to me."

"You told me your relationship woes, and so I figured—might as well tell you mine. Besides, you're the only friend I have. And I know, I *know* we're not real friends, I don't mean to put that kind of pressure on you. That's an anchor and I don't want to drag you down with it to the bottom of the river—er, shit, sorry—but I don't have anybody else to talk to, so that's you." She shrugged. "Congratulations and apologies. Not sure they make a Hallmark card for that."

John blinked and gently recapped the pen and then set it down on the map, along the contours of the river. Then he leaned back and said, "Okay. I am listening. The spirit moves you to speak, and so you must speak."

"The spirit. That . . . like, a Native American thing?"

"A Quaker thing. Our meetings for worship are silent affairs unless one is moved to speak, at which point it is believed the spirit—the light, small-g god or big-G God, whatever you want to call it—has moved you to do so. So." He gently gestured toward her with open palms. "Do so."

"Not much to say. I don't know that the spirit is moving me to anything." She idly spun the book in front of her. "It happened about six months ago. It was this brief thing, just a one-night mistake, not, like, a secret relationship. She was nice. And cute. Just a stupid fun girl at a stupid fun club and I was *maybe* high and she was *maybe* drunk and—it was an impulsive, dumb, asshole jerk thing to do, and I came clean *immediately.* Well. Like, three days later. But I didn't get caught. I fucking confessed like an adult."

"Okay."

"Turns out, it *wasn't* okay, John Compass. Meg was mad. But, like, not the kind of mad where a person yells and throws a remote control at the wall. That kind of mad, I get. That's the kind of mad for me. This was different. Cold, icy mad. The anger of a patient glacier. Meg and I lived together. We'd been married for a few years already. She froze me out for like a week. I apologized and begged and wheedled—" She put a nasal whine to her voice. "*Please baby forgive me I'm a huge piece of shit.* She barely talked to me. Barely *looked* at me. I mean, I get it. I cheated. Fuck me, right? I felt selfish even thinking there should or could be an *ending* to her anger. But then one day she was talking to me, pretending like nothing was wrong. And when I tried to bring it up to her again, she said, it happened, it's done now, she didn't want to talk about it anymore."

"She forgave you."

Emily plowed furrows into her brow. "No. I don't know. She never said it. That she forgave me. She just kinda . . . forced her way past it."

"Okay."

"Okay? That's it?"

"I don't know what questions to ask. Relationships are not, as they say, in my wheelhouse."

"You've been in a relationship before."

He shook his head. "No."

"Like, never? Never never?"

"Not romantic. Never interested me much."

Emily huh'd. "Cool. Okay. Well, for the uninitiated, it's not good when your partner buries her emotional baggage in your collective backyard. Having something out in the open sucks, but it's way better than hiding it and pretending it's not there. It's like a dead body buried in Florida—eventually the water is going to push it back out of the ground. It was, like, two weeks after she decided it was quote-unquote 'over' that she said she was leaving her job in Philly, she was taking another job back home, where she grew up—here, in Bucks, in Doyle's Tavern—and that I was, in her words, 'free to come along if I wanted to.' She made the decision unilaterally. I called bullshit, but she said, 'You made a decision, and now I get to make a decision.' She wouldn't even say that I had fucked around on her and she was pissed about it and punishing me. To her it was like, science or something. Every action had an equal and opposite reaction. I wish she just would've said, *Fuck around, find out,* but she stuffed it down, made it seem like it was this practical decision. Or worse, like she was the adult making the adult choices, and I could either grow up or stay a child." Emily sighed. "So I went. I left my job at the shelter—I worked at a crisis shelter for LGBT youths—and now I'm here, in this house with a wife who I strongly suspect hates me."

John grunted. "I'm sorry."

"Yeah. Me too."

"I have no expertise, as I said. I can't say how Meg feels about you but it's probably worth saying these things to her. Like you say, dig up that emotional baggage. Better to let things be out in the open, so they don't fester."

She nodded. "Yeah. You're probably right."

He sat there for a while, like he was thinking about all of this.

"For what it's worth," he said, after some thought, "we're friends. Real friends, if we care to be."

"Thanks, John."

"Mm." He nodded. "Now let's dig in a different direction. Let's see if we can find out how my friend Walt died."

20

THE REUNION

JOANIE WENT TO ONE OF HER HIGH SCHOOL REUNIONS, THE twenty-year, just a few years back. It was fun, if only to see how people had changed: Nearly all of them had changed for the worse. Most had become some newer, softer, sadder version of themselves: plans discarded, dreams shot dead inside their own heads, all their inner fires doused. Reality had intruded: Unstable marriages led to shitty kids that required tireless careers to sustain them. They'd all grown swollen and comfortable in their mediocrity. Ex–running back Brad Hancock looked like a boiled bratwurst, managed an appliance store. Student council president Wanda Nystand was supposed to be running the United Nations by now, but instead was a local pharmaceutical sales rep who looked like she sampled her own product. Jacob Platt was supposed to be a surgeon or a lawyer, but instead ran a landscaping company. Faded failsons and forgotten daughters. They were all still rich, of course. In families like those, money stuck to you like tree sap; you couldn't get rid of it if you tried. They'd just . . . settled. Joanie, of course, had gone the other way.

Joanie had found herself.

And it looked like Dan Paxson had, as well.

Dan hadn't been at that reunion. But seeing him today, what with him helping her get that big-ass skeleton off their lawn, it was clear he had changed. He'd always been nice, but at the same time felt sad, fearful. *Meek.* That was the word. Meek, like the world was just too big for him. Like he was ever in its shadow.

He was out of that shadow now. He seemed brighter. Clearer. Physically, too, there had been a change: He stood tall and lean. His arms strong, probably from the kind of work he did.

She told him, upon returning to the house, "You're different."

"Am I?" he asked, leaning against his truck. "You're still the same." He winced and course-corrected quickly: "I only mean, you're still *you*. Still Joanie Moreau, just . . . more so. Not new, but definitely improved. Like an upgrade to yourself, but still fundamentally you."

"So I'm the latest iPhone model?"

He laughed, adopted a *gee shucks* look. Curiously, once upon a time, it would've been real—a moment of blushing gosh-golly embarrassment from the farmer's boy. But now, it felt like something else. *An act?* she wondered.

Interesting.

"I should stop talking," he said, smiling.

"No, you're doing just fine, Danny Boy."

He eyeballed her. A glint to his gaze. "Hey, listen, I know this is short notice and all, but there's this thing at the end of the month—night before Thanksgiving. A dinner. I just got invited to it. I'm not sure if I want to go, but I can say that having you on my arm that night would make a whole world of—"

At that, Joanie's husband Graham came out of the house, giving a wave.

Dan's face froze as whatever words he was about to say died in his mouth.

She chuckled. Joanie enjoyed little moments like these—she feared it made her cruel, but it wasn't the embarrassment or awkwardness she enjoyed, not precisely. It was just how human these moments were: people fumbling up against one another's norms and mores. Trying to figure each other out. Trying to figure them*selves* out in relation to everyone else.

Joanie introduced the two men to each other, then to Dan, said, "You were saying something about a dinner?"

"I apologize," he said. "No disrespect, I hadn't realized you were married."

"If the invite is still open, I'll come along. Be nice to catch up some more." She rubbed her husband's arm. "Graham won't mind."

And true to form, Graham gave a small nod and said, "Just have her home by eleven, young man."

More enjoyment from Joanie as she watched Dan struggle to understand what was going on here. His poor brain just couldn't synthesize it. That was all right. Sometimes it was fun to watch people wriggle around like a worm on a hook.

Maybe I am *just a monster,* she thought.

She was okay with it.

"That'd be great," Dan said finally. "I'll text you more details and we can go from there." He started to get back into his truck but said, "Oh! One more thing." At that, he hurried to the back of the truck and grabbed a bushel basket of dark-red apples. He handed it to whoever would take it. Graham grabbed it. "Apples. From my orchard. I think you'll like them. They taste like a *dream.*"

"I'll bet," she said. "Thanks, Dan, for your help today."

They shared a lingering look. One Graham watched with wary curiosity.

And then, Dan was off.

GRAHAM SET THE APPLE BASKET DOWN ON THE EXPANSE OF THEIR quartz-topped kitchen island. Joanie leaned back against the opposite counter, sipping a Spindrift.

"I'm assuming you didn't show him *both* storage units," Graham said.

Joanie laughed and said, "I don't think Dan is really ready to see that." Of their two units, one was for the standard house storage stuff: a mix of seasonal décor and private items that they wouldn't want their rental clients to get into. (When they had guests, they left town, went to Graham's Rittenhouse Square apartment. As such, it was important to keep this place only minimally lived-in. The people who rented the house needed to feel like it was theirs to explore—in whatever way they so chose.) The other storage unit was, well—you name it. Mostly it was various pieces of sex furniture that they sometimes swapped out: chaises, ramps, a shibari bondage training frame, boatswain chairs and swings, a spanking bench, Fleshlight mounts, a couple of disassembled bondage crosses, and the like. You couldn't hide what any of it was. "Dan is sweet. Different now than he was, but I think he's still . . . you know, a little bit of a country boy deep down."

Graham poked his chin over the apple basket, *hmm*ing. "What's the plan for these, dearheart? I could bake something. I've been thinking of exploring the differences between cobblers, crisps, slumps, pandowdies—"

"That's a lot of apples," she said, making a face. "Maybe *too many* apples." Honestly, she wouldn't tell Dan this, but she wasn't a fan of apples. Or most fruits, really. Some people liked to incorporate them into sex— mangoes, after all, were perhaps the sexiest fruit that had ever been brought to a fuck party—but it wasn't her thing. Apples remained a stand-in for sexy, romantic imagery—the apple of Eden, the smooth red Devil's skin, the luscious, juicy flesh within.

The forbidden fruit.

Huh.

"I have an idea," she said, and quickly handwrote a note in her best cursive:

Let us know if you ever want to take a bite of our fruit.
Love,
your neighbors, J&G

Joanie tucked the note into the basket.

"Take it to the neighbor," she said.

"The neighbor."

"Mm-hmm."

"I assume you mean the one who called our house a brothel."

"Yeah. Prentiss Beckman."

"What did you write on the note?"

"I told him either of us would gladly stick one of these apples up his ass for free if he wanted it bad enough." At that, Graham hurriedly grabbed the note and took a look, then visibly relaxed.

"You were joking."

"I was joking." She paused. "Still. Is sending a message too provocative?"

He shrugged. "Just provocative enough, dearest."

At that, Graham took the apples to the neighbor, whistling as he went.

21

A NICE DINNER FOR TWO

THE MESSAGE, FROM MEG, WAS CLEAR AND SIMPLE:

Come home.

Emily had John drive her home. They'd spent the day driving the length of River Road in the fading light of day, surveying the islands that were on the map—and those smaller ones that weren't. John said he'd head back to Bethlehem tonight, but could be here quickly if she needed him to be. He added, with soft eyes, "If you ever need a place to stay, I have a couch—a sleeper sofa." The message was implicit: If shit went sideways with Meg, he could help.

She wanted to cry. Emily hadn't realized up until John's offer how trapped she was here. There'd been no real way out. She had a bike, not a car. She had money, but not much of her own, and all of it entangled with Meg. She had no family in the area, and what few friends she had were down in the city—worse, a lot of the bridges she had to those friends were burned when she quit her job.

So, just to have this one thing—

An exit door, if she needed it—

Was huge.

Emily told him thanks, and then she went home, expecting the worst.

SHE EXPECTED THE WORST, BUT WHAT SHE GOT WAS SOUP.

The smell hit her soon as she stepped in the front door: fatty beef broth accented with the comforting scents of star anise, cinnamon, onion.

Her favorite food: pho.

Meg chirped her surprise at Emily's return and moved quickly to usher big bowls of bone-white noodles to the table. With delicate precision, she poured the broth and laid islands of meat upon the noodles, then fetched garnish plates with coins of jalapeño, mint, basil, lime, and bottles of hoisin sauce and sriracha.

Emily walked through the miasma of narcotic food goodness in a haze.

"What's up?" Emily asked, not in a casual way, but in the way you ask when you are suspicious but don't want to *say* you're suspicious.

"I found a Vietnamese place. Down in New Yardley—I know you miss this kind of food from the city, and if I recall, pho is your favorite." They had a pho joint only a block from their apartment. Pho King. A funny title Emily only realized was funny two years into eating there. "I just wanted you to know that we can have some of what we miss here, too. Plus, we can always go back into the city, too, some nights. In our childless glory, the world is ours to conquer." Meg smiled.

"I don't hate it."

"I want you to be happy here," Meg said, sincere. "I hope you see that."

Emily took a slurp of broth. Unctuous and funky. Her eyes inadvertently closed, as if to shut out any of the stimuli that dared to interrupt this bliss. "Feed me like this, and my happiness will know no bounds."

"Good," Meg said, and told her to dig in. Emily did so, with gusto. And then she discovered the gelatinous blobs and crinkly white bits in the soup: tendon and tripe. With chopsticks she dangled a fringed ribbon of stomach lining and ogled it with no small wonder. Meg never liked it when she ordered that stuff.

Emily winced. "Shit. Look. Sorry. If you need to call the restaurant—"

"It wasn't a mistake. I ordered it that way." Meg pinched a piece of wobbly tendon between sticks. "Got it in mine, too. Need to try new things, as you always say." She slurped the tendon, eyes bulging, then laughing past the food in her mouth. "It's good," she said, quickly dabbing her mouth with a napkin. *Holy shit. Meg just ate beef tendon, what the fuck is happening.* Emily decided that though she did not precisely understand the saying about gift horses and mouths, she'd go with it just the same.

What ensued was a perfectly nice dinner.

One like they hadn't had in—

Well, forever.

Meg talked about work. About some consumer protection case they had bubbling up against a big local pharmaceutical company. She seemed animated and engaged. They both piled on more sriracha and dared each other to eat the little jalapeño disks, which they did. Meg couldn't handle her spice and ended up coughing, and then laughing, and coughing more *because* she was laughing.

Halfway through, Meg even said, "I think it's good you want to help the community. Working with shelters or some charity orgs. Outreach and such."

"Oh. Oh wow. Yeah. Well." Emily cleared her throat. "That's—that's quite a turnaround for you. I didn't think you liked me doing that."

"I just didn't want you to do it now. But I want you to flourish. To be your best self here, as I am trying to be. So maybe it's time."

"Right. Great. Thank you! I mean it. I'll look into it—I just need to finish this thing I'm doing with John."

"Mm. Mm, right, yeah." Meg sniffed from the heat of the hot sauce. "About that. I think—" She gestured with the chopsticks, as if she were picking up parts of the sentence and sticking them together. "You should pull back from that. And refocus your attention on this charity thing."

"Pull back from that? From John, you mean."

"Right. If it's a distraction, I mean."

"It's not," Emily said, stiffening a little.

"Okay." Meg forced a smile, tilting her head. "It's weird, though, isn't it?"

"What's weird, weird how?"

"You found a body in the river—which was crazy enough as is, but then there's this strange guy, older, and he wants *your* help? Why? Why you? It seems problematic." She licked a chopstick. "And people are talking."

"People. What people."

"I don't know. People."

"We're not on the news. We don't have a Twitter account devoted to our adventures. It's just me and him and we've barely been anywhere." Emily put her spoon down. It was then she understood what *people* Meg meant. "Oh. Your mother. Your mother is the one that's talking."

Meg acquiesced with a soft shrug. "She talks. She has friends. She's part of this group—the Crossed Keys. Thinks I might be a good candidate for membership—it's like a networking thing. Anyway, I just mean, people talk—the communities around Harrow are tight. Things run smoothly and people tend to not like rough edges—"

Jesus.

"Rough edges. You mean me. I'm the rough edge here, aren't I? I'm being weird and even though nobody would know about it normally, they do now because your mother *made* them know about it as she can't seem to keep her gossipy mouth-hole shut. Gotta just fountain that sweet, sweet goss on whoever is listening, even if it hurts her own family, right? But *I'm* the one being weird and that's hurting your *networking chances*—"

"Emily, it's hard enough that we're gay. This area votes blue but isn't as progressive as you'd think, it's very white, very straight—"

"Not like you've ever even connected with the community, Meg. Christ, there were networking opportunities in the city, too, for people like us—"

Meg stood up abruptly. "I should've known asking you was too much. Beyond the pale. I get it. It's fine. Keep doing what you need to do."

Meg turned and snatched an apple off the counter. One of the red ones she always had on hand. She gave it a quick polish with a napkin and then took a huge—and if Emily clocked it right, *angry*—bite.

Emily tried to soften her tone, sanding down its, well, *rough edges.* "John's looking for closure, Meg."

"Closure. Fun concept."

She felt that slash of the knife but tried to ignore it. "It was me that found the body. I feel . . . bad about it. Like I desecrated something. And I want to help him." *And maybe he's helping me, too.* "John's a good guy."

"Maybe he killed his friend," Meg said around a mouthful of apple. *Crunch.*

"Jesus, Meg."

After a hard swallow, Meg said through her teeth: "We looked into him, you know."

"What?"

"The firm. I had them . . . poke around."

"*Jesus,* Meg."

Another angry bite. Half the apple already gone. "You know what we found? Nothing. Because it's all locked up behind government firewalls. Best we could see is that he attended the Army's sniper school at Fort Benning. Everything after that is closed-door. *Sniper school,* Emily. You know what it means that his records are hidden, right? It means he's a killer. Some government lapdog murdering people in foreign countries." She took a beat. "Or maybe even here. On our own soil."

"You're really something else. What are you doing? God, I'm sorry this messes with your precious networking, but you were shitty about me wanting to do some outreach work, then when I found something else, now you're telling me I can't do that either? *And* you're spying on John? You don't want me to succ—"

Succeed, she was about to say, when Meg took the biggest, angriest bite of apple—and bit down on the tip of her own thumb instead. The apple crunched. So did the finger. Meg cried out and palmed the apple with her free hand, shaking the bitten one—but it had not merely been bitten, but bitten *into.* Blood, dark like the apple, splattered in an arc. She hissed through her teeth. "Fuck."

"Meg, shit—"

Meg popped her bloody, bitten thumb into her mouth. She withdrew it for a second—enough time for a fresh bubble of red to swell, inflating like a clown's balloon to say in a cold, mechanical voice. "Clean this mess up, please. I'm going to go deal with my thumb."

Meg made a beeline for their bedroom, likely to the master bath to grab Band-Aids and Neosporin. Emily was left in the kitchen, with half-eaten bowls of soup and gleaming blood on the floor, the counter, and the ceiling. "*Shit,*" she said, trying very hard not to scream-slash-cry. Instead, she went in search of a rag and a stepladder.

22

CALLA REGARDS THE APPLE
(AND CONSIDERS HER FUTURE)

DAD WASN'T WEARING HIS GLASSES ANYMORE. AND HE WASN'T sleeping. Calla heard him every night now, late. Out in the woods. In the orchard. It was 10 P.M. and he was out there right now. Doing what, she didn't know. She heard hammering and sawing. Building that building or whatever.

He looked healthier—skin less pale, stood up straighter. He shone brighter. Calla hadn't really realized it, but before now, there'd been a sadness in him. Like he was slumping, shrinking, whittled down like a stick. But that had changed. He was different now. He just seemed so much happier.

And as for Marco . . .

She lay stomach-down on the bed, phone in front of her, and sent him a text.

Calla: What's up hot stuff??

Marco: . . .

Marco: Sorry just cleaning my scews

Marco: scews

Marco: SCREWS

Marco: stupid ducking autocarrot

Calla: 😛

(God, Marco sucked typing on his phone.)

Calla: That's super-gross btw

Marco: Wont have to do it for long

Marco: They're gonna take the screws out tomorrow

Calla: Whoa!!

Marco: ducking crazy

Marco: fucking framing

Marco: 😞

Calla: 😆😆😆

Calla: You type like you have boxing gloves for hands

Marco: I know

Marco: Shit got to go Mama yelling for me

He was healing, too.

And he seemed happy.

Everyone is happy but me, she thought.

Calla idly flipped through some TikToks. (Siberian husky howling *I love you.* TikTok challenge: #birdistheword. Olivia Rodrigo's "Brutal," but on shitty kazoo. A #beautymode versus #goblinmode transformation vid. A pet turtle eating a Minecraft stack of melon cubes as ASMR.) She wasn't going to look at Lucas's video and told herself, *No, don't you dare, you dumb bitch,* but then even as she was like, *Yeah no I'm good I won't look,* she was already looking and it had doubled its views since the last time she looked at it this morning and *of course* people had already started to do other riffs on it on TikTok, like dubbing over the moment Marco broke his leg—the woman's scream when she fell stomping grapes, Smash Mouth's "All Star," Erica Banks's "Buss It," a sad game show sound.

It made her want to scream.

Her video.

Her boyfriend.

Lucas had stolen it and posted it and though he probably meant well then, now it was too fucking late and he didn't want to take it down and he didn't care anyway. Fuck fuck fuck. It didn't seem to bother Marco. He was too cool for school, which made her feel like a loser troll for being upset about it. Calla felt suddenly ugly and sad and stupid and barfing followers. She was mad at Lucas and mad at her father for being happy and at Marco for being so cool and most of all? At herself. For feeling weak. For being weak.

What was it Dad always said? That dork always told her to be better than other people, that "the best revenge is doing *your* thing, not *their* thing." She didn't really understand what that meant until maybe right this moment. Fine. She didn't need to be mad at Lucas. Didn't need to care about that video. She just needed to do her own thing.

My own thing.

Fresh panic ensued because, oh god, what was her own thing? She paced her bedroom like a caged tiger. Calla knew she wanted to live a life of consequence. Her father and even Marco kinda made fun of her wanting to be an influencer—like what Lucas said, how it was just some shallow bullshit where she wanted free products. And like, *okay,* that *was* a cool part but it wasn't the *only* part. Not even the most important part. Calla wanted to be

(*popular*)

(*loved*)

(*cool*)

(*no, not those*)

(*not* just *those*)

Seen.

She wanted to be seen. She wanted to be important. She wanted her voice to matter. Influencing people wasn't just about getting them to try this makeup or drink this stupid kombucha seltzer or whatever, it was about having their trust. They trusted you to tell them the thing to do, the thing to buy, the way to go, the way to be. How amazing was that? It could be spun off into anything. A YouTube show or a brand spokesperson or a TED Talk or—politics. She could be a politician one day. *President of the United States*. Insane idea. She didn't want that, not really, she couldn't hack the heat—but the presence of the *option* was everything.

I need to be a better influencer.

I need to be

(prettier)

(smarter)

(funnier)

(hotter)

Better.

She thought of her father.

She thought of Marco.

Healthy and happy and shining like the stupid fucking sun.

It was the apple, wasn't it?

THE IDEA WAS CRAZY, THAT THIS APPLE MADE YOU BETTER.

Right? It was totally crazy, right?

But, like—

Maybe not?

There were all these supposed superfoods, yeah? Chilean maqui berries and bee pollen and bone broth and—what was that spice people were going cuckoo for right now? Black cumin seeds. People said these foods changed their lives. Made them think clearer, or sleep better, or even help end diseases like diabetes and cancer. And okay, Calla knew most of that was bullshit. This wasn't her first influencer rodeo, she knew most things that promised miracles were really just snake oil scams. But . . .

What if some of them weren't?

If even one percent of those claims had some truth behind them . . .

They always said that the rainforest contained all these undiscovered pharmaceuticals, right? And that was part of the tragedy of bulldozing it, not just the loss of biodiversity, not just the fact the rainforest was the planet's lungs, but because it meant the loss of ancient medicines. Why couldn't there also be like, a magic apple? She knew it sounded stupid but weren't the Indigenous Americans savvy to things that the stupid

European colonizers weren't? Maybe there was an apple that grew here from before. Maybe it had revolutionary properties. Maybe her father had bred an apple like that, or from one of those trees. Wasn't it in the realm of possibility?

And so, here she sat at the kitchen nook table, staring at one of her father's apples. The Ruby Slipper.

The red-black of a vampire's cape. Shiny as a new leather jacket.

Apples were gross. Skin tasted bitter, the flesh always felt weird in her mouth. But medicine wasn't always supposed to taste good.

And her father was changing . . .

And Marco's leg was healing . . .

Maybe the apple could do something for her, too.

(*Prettier smarter funnier hotter.*)

She got a paring knife and a peeler. Calla figured maybe she'd cut some slices. Peel it first? *But shit what if the skin was where the miracle nutrients were at,* she thought. Crap. She put the peeler back.

Instead, she took the apple, cut into it from stem to base, halving it with a wet crunch. Juice pooled beneath it. She stuck her thumb in it and licked it. A frisson of joy rippled through her. For just a moment, there arose in her the narcotic feeling of being in a room where everyone there was smoking up—that sudden rush of a secondhand high. *Maybe I do like apples.*

Or maybe I like this apple.

My apple. The one I named. A wave of power crashed through her. As if naming something gave you ownership over it. Like it was a kind of magic.

She cut a slice of the apple.

Something teased her brainstem, like spiders climbing a string. Something about a dream. Something about Marco, about cake.

It was gone when she reached for it, leaving only the hollow, anxious feeling of its passing.

But then she remembered the taste of that apple's juices on her thumb. And it plucked free the splinter of her anxiety, sent it back down into the dark where it belonged.

She popped the apple slice in her mouth.

And in that moment, she felt amazing. It was like standing in the sun for the first time. A vertiginous feeling hit Calla, like the ground was gone beneath her and she was falling, not into a pit but toward the best version of herself—some unrealized, idealized, perfect Calla. And as she chewed the feeling deepened, and goosebumps danced across her skin and her back arched. She heard the sound she made in the back of her throat: a sound of almost animalistic pleasure. And she was about to swallow when—

Something moved in her mouth.

Wriggled. Like a—

Like a maggot.

Her brain pulsed with fresh panic. Her thoughts did battle: *Spit it out, spit it out, something's wrong,* and then, *Keep eating, you'll never feel like this again, whatever it is, just eat it and swallow it and then eat some more.* In the space between her stomach and her heart she felt a sudden well of despair—the feeling of the sun on her face was eclipsed by a great shadow rising up beneath her, and she felt something moving beneath her, like roots through earth. Then it was in her, pushing her innards around, churning her into dirt, reaching for her heart and her mind—and on instinct she spit out the apple onto the table.

It was mush. Red skin bits and flesh goop.

She sat there, panting, scraping the muck off her tongue, looking for what had been crawling around inside her mouth.

And then—

The goop moved.

Just a little. Like a bubble inflating.

A chill clambered up her spine.

Something dark showed itself from inside. An apple seed, she thought, moving to the surface. It hopped out of the mush—and landed on the table with a *tic.* It hopped again. *Tic. Tac.* What was in that seed? Some kind of parasite? Those jumping beans you bought at like, Walmart, they actually had larvae in them, didn't they? Or beetles or something? She blinked again and—

The seed rolled over, wriggling—

Something unfurled from its back.

Wings. Shiny, silvery wings.

Its body was soft now, not hard.

Black hairs emerged from it. Bristle-back hairs.

Compound eyes, crimson like the apple's skin, watched her.

It's a fly, she thought. The seed had become a fly.

That was in my mouth.

The other seeds began to fall from the apple. *Tic-tic-tic.* And from the fallen half, they began to hop up, like a fly landing on the edge of a cereal bowl, one after the next. More seeds than the apple could contain fell out, growing wings, little legs, red eyes—and they took flight, swarming around the apple and then her head. She cried out, swatting at the air. One landed in her ear, trying to get in. She pinched a wing and threw it onto the table, where it thrashed, unable to take flight. Another went for her nose, a fly too fat to fit up there, too fat to have ever been an apple seed, and she blasted air out of her nose as she backpedaled, knocking the chair over, almost tripping. They were all over her, now. Dozens of flies. A hundred of them. Speckling her cheeks. Stuck in her *hair.* She screamed, but when she did, one landed in her mouth, on her tongue—she gagged and coughed and spit it out. Her scream didn't end, but now continued behind clamped-shut lips and teeth.

Flies—

Face pulled apart like warm cake—

Blood like red syrup—

In your ears, your nose, down your throat—

Calla scooped up the apple mush and grabbed the rest of the apple and ducked her head like she was hurrying through a locust swarm, bypassing the countertop compost bowl and throwing it all into the trash. And just like that—

The flies were gone.

Panting, she looked around.

Nothing.

I'm having a psychotic break.

Her heart jumped as her father raced through the front door. Panicked, he rushed into the kitchen, looking her up and down, then glancing everywhere. "I heard you screaming," he said, searching for a reason why.

"Sorry. Yeah. Sorry."

"Wh—what's wrong?"

"I saw a—" She hesitated. "A bug. Something flying around."

"A bug."

"Yeah. I dunno."

He laughed, relieved. "Your mom didn't like farm pests, either. For her it was mice and rats. Ooh boy, she did not like those. I told her, they're not here to bother you, they just want some food, probably, but she said she couldn't help imagining them—" Here he scurried his hands along the wall. "Running up her legs. I guess that is sorta freaky. Snakes, now—snakes she liked because she said—"

"They ate the mice and rats," Calla said, finishing his story. He'd told it before. That was the way of the Mom Stories. He had a Mom Story for most situations. They'd faded a little over time, but still popped up here and there.

"Hey. So. I've been meaning to talk to you."

Oh no. That never boded well.

"Not right now, Dad, I wanna just . . . like, go upstairs and chill?" The taste on her tongue was like battery acid.

"It'll be quick."

"Dad—"

"I'm thinking about dating."

Her jaw dropped open. "What?"

"Damn, see, I knew it was weird. It's just—"

"It's not weird that you want to date. I want you to date. It's weird that you didn't want to date *before.* Mom's been dead—" He hated when she said that so she quickly covered it with, "*Gone,* she's been gone for most of my life and like, I just assumed you were asexual or something. That you just didn't think that way, or like, your parts didn't work anymore."

"Can we not talk about my parts?" he said, laughing nervously.

"Okay, whatever. It's just—sure, go out there and get it on, dude."

"You're supposed to be grossed out by this."

"Dad, I just want you to be happy. I know I'm a teen girl with knives for eyes and a heart like a wasp nest, but . . . I just want you to be happy." She paused. "What's her name?"

"Joanie. Joanie Moreau. We dated in high school . . . it was good. She's back around and—well. It's complicated."

"I definitely don't want to know the details, just go have fun."

"Thanks, sweetheart." His eyebrows lifted as he looked past her. "Oh hey, there's your bug."

"What?"

"The fly. There—" He walked over, pulling his cloth handkerchief out and reaching for a dead, one-winged fly on the table.

Oh god.

"Housefly. Big one, too. Strange for November, I figured the chill would've killed them." He pinched it in the hankie and took it to the compost. "From nature it comes, to nature it returns." Dad laughed.

23

THE LEGENDS OF BUCKS COUNTY

EMILY STAYED UP THAT NIGHT, SETTLING IN WITH JED HOMACKIE'S *The Legends of Bucks County* like a kid sneaking a book past bedtime. She slept in the living room because Meg had gone into the bedroom and closed the door behind her. Emily interpreted the message as STAY OUT, NO EMILYS ALLOWED and went to camp on the brutalist white leather sectional Meg loved so much. It was like a marshmallow designed by Russian FSB agents.

Book in hand, she took a look at the author photo, saw an avuncular sort staring back at her. A man with wisps of salt-and-pepper hair. Cable-knit sweater. Book was printed in the '90s, and the black-and-white photo was to match.

Flipping through it, she saw at least half was devoted to the county's rich history of haunted places: Cry Baby Bridge (lady drowns her infant and hangs herself from the bridge, you hear her and the baby crying at night); Hansell Road Ghost Lights (angry drunken father chops off son's head, you go to the road and say, "Fritz, come out and play," and ghost lights emerge that are supposedly the child holding a lantern looking for his lost head); the Devil's Half-Acre Tavern (old bar along the river, not far from this very house, where the tavern-keeper killed itinerant canal workers and buried them out back). Plus a lot of sightings of Revolutionary War soldiers, because everyone around here had real wide eyes for all that stuff—this whole area being the "cradle of the Revolution" and all that, what with Washington crossing the river just south of here.

Homackie's style was folksy and overwritten, but fun to read, and she had to give it to him—though she was not a big believer in *ghost stories,* his tales (which were probably more than a little fabricated) had her repressing shivers.

Another portion of the book was devoted to local folklore—cannibals, buried treasure, racing the Devil at midnight, strange suicides and mysterious murders. A whole chunky subchapter was devoted to sightings of a cryptid called the Upright Wolf, which for some reason was never named as a werewolf, but was clearly a wolf that walked like a person.

And then she turned the page and saw the next chapter header—

"The Strange Islands of the Delaware River."

"Oh shit," she said, sitting upright.

The page had been dog-eared once upon a time, the folded corner put back in place, the crease remaining.

It wasn't a long chapter. It mostly went through the islands one by one, offering a paragraph or two about each. Some of them she recognized from John circling them on the map—though this book had, frustratingly, no map of its own. Graham Flats, an island of "small pine trees and scrub," was often searched for buried treasure, since it had been reported that the infamous pirate Blackbeard had deposited there a "much desired hoard of coin and effigy." Mud Shoal was home to a small cave in the side, "not even as tall as a diminutive man or large child," and when the river was low you could get into that cave—more wealth awaited you there, since apparently some loyalists to the Crown called the Doan Gang hid treasure in there. ("Quakers will not honor militants and extremists, and so the Doan boys, once belonging to the estimable ranks of the Friends, are buried just outside the Quaker graveyard in Plumridge," Homackie wrote, "like ghosts kept outside a party, forced to watch the goings-on through hazy death-smeared windows.") Tennakonk Island was said to host the ghost of a Lenni-Lenape chief, who would warn your boat away from the rocks if you were a good person—but were you "cruel of heart," the spirit would steer you into them.

Other islands in the book, though, Emily didn't recall.

Bile Island. Bird Island. Tenpenny Island. And then—

One entry that had been circled. Highlighted, too.

Harrowsblack Island.

Homackie described the river island as a "mounding hillock comprising a thickly thicketed acre," upon which stood a "black, vicious hanging tree that could be seen from both sides of the river." He further described the island as a "murderous battleground" that the British soldiers and American colonists each "borrowed" time and again, using the tree as gallows to hang prominent captives and traitors. Back and forth the island went, each side sneaking across the water to claim it when the other had forgotten about it, displaying hanged men as a message to the other side. Or as Homackie put it, "a bloody-minded taunt." And that was the end of the entry.

But someone—Walt, presumably—had written a note in the margins. And that note was to John:

John: Vinot's??

Emily puzzled over what that meant. What, or who, was a Vinot?

On the other side of the house, a door opened. The bedroom. From the darkness of the hallway, Meg emerged. Still in her clothes from earlier; she hadn't even changed into her pajamas.

"You're still up," Emily said to her as Meg made a beeline for the kitchen.

"Need a snack" was all she said, snatching up an apple from the basket on the counter, then walking right back toward the bedroom.

"Your thumb okay?"

"Already healing."

And then Meg was gone again, back into the darkness. She was only footfalls now, and then the closing of the door, and then the silence.

24

TRUE DEATH

JOHN NAVIGATED THE WINDING CURVES OF THE ROADS LEADING to and through the Poconos, piloting his Jeep through ribbons of fog, on his way to Dingman's Falls. To Walt's house to collect scionwood and budwood from his trees. Was a bit early in the season to do that, since he wouldn't be able to go and graft right now, but hopefully the deep November chill had put the tree to sleep for the year. He could keep the young branches in cold storage until late winter, early spring.

On the way, Emily called and told him what she'd found.

Harrowsblack Island.

A hanging tree.

And something, or someone, called a Vinot.

"A someone," he said.

You know who it is, she answered. Which made sense. The note in the margins of that book was, after all, to John.

"I do."

And then he told her about Walt and the White Whale.

WALT AND JOHN EACH SHARED A LOVE OF APPLES AND THEIR TREES, but Walt loved the hunt for them even more. He was a collector at heart: If it wasn't apples, it would be something else, as it had been in earlier periods of his life, like baseball cards or old Milton Bradley board games or cast-iron skillets. (He had a blessedly brief Beanie Babies phase, sure that he was buying into a plushie gold mine. John was able to gently sweep him off that path before he drained his bank account on the soft little toys.) For Walt, the joy was in the pursuit—scratching the paint off history and finding mentions of some lost apple here and there, then doggedly chasing those tales till he found the tree. He was good with plat maps, library archives, county records, even better at finding caches of old handwritten letters and such at garage sales and flea markets. (John wished he loved anything as much as Walt loved a good flea market. Walt would kill a man who stood between him and someone selling whatever hot mess their farmhouse, barn, and garage threw up.) Soon as he found a mention of some old apple with a strange name, he was off like a shot, map in his pocket, keys in his hand, coffee in the cupholder.

John, on the other hand, liked the result of the hunt, but not so much the hunt itself. He found delight in some parts of the journey: stopping and getting lunch somewhere at some odd upstate food counter, seeing the sights, talking to folks, spending time with Walt. But for him it was really all about the apple itself. The apple as the gift of a living tree, the apple as the thing that connected him *to* that tree. It provided for him in the form of sustenance and joy, and he provided for the tree a chance at survival, at a life, at legacy.

It felt good. It felt right. Especially after

(*all the blood spilled*)

everything he'd done.

He explained to Emily that a lot of apple hunters had their White Whale apple, that Moby-Dickian fruit they chased but never found. A West Coast compatriot of theirs, Harold Davis, ex-IRS datamonkey who became an apple hunter precisely because of how good he was with finding people and places and things, had long searched for an extinct apple variety called the Steptoe Seek-no-Further—an ugly lump of apple said to be hard as a rock but with the very distinct taste of wildflower honey. Far as Walt knew, Harold was chasing that tree even still, and would be until the roots in the earth took his body.

For Walt, that apple was Vinot's Allegresse, or *l'Allégresse de Vinot,* an apple he saw mentioned on a recipe card he bought from a yard sale just outside of Danville. The case of recipe cards came from the grandmother of an old Dutch family (proper Dutch, not Pennsylvania Dutch), and in that box she had a handwritten recipe for something called an *applemoes,* which was an applesauce recipe but one that had been based on an older medieval version: milk, honey, lot of spices, breadcrumbs to thicken. And in the corner of that recipe, the grandmother had written in shaky hand:

Vinot's allegresse apple??

Well, that sent Walt down the rabbit hole, didn't it. Suddenly he was googling this and searching that, finding out that there was this French apple, grew in Normandy in the 1300s, mentioned in a recipe by the apprentice chef of some other big-deal French chef named Tirel or Taillevent or something, and this apprentice chef, Vinot, had a recipe for a very early version of an apple pie (which curiously featured roasted onions as well as apples). But *that* recipe apparently contained a note about these particular apples, *l'Allégresse de Vinot.*

The note suggested it was an apple grown at Vinot's own orchard, and from that tree came an apple that he said was no good for cooking, only for eating fresh out of hand. *Le paradis sur terre,* Heaven on earth, he wrote of them. Vinot said he had quite the *dépendance* on them, saying they made him happier than anything else he'd ever eaten in his life. Vinot wrote that when he ate one, *"Je suis un avec Dieu."*

Well, that only piqued Walt's interest more.

Deeper went the rabbit hole, because what did Walt find? That some of the earliest settlers of America, and in fact Pennsylvania, were the Dutch in the early seventeenth century—some Dutch trading company came over, sailing up the Delaware River. And who was on one of those boats? One of the descendants of the aforementioned chef, Vinot. (Walt noted that said descendant shared that one name and no other, as if all the Vinots were singular individuals with singular names, like Cher or Madonna or some such.) He was escaping persecution, or perhaps prosecution, having committed what was described only as a "bloody crime" in France.

Vinot settled somewhere in Bucks County. It was mostly wilderness at that point, with a few Dutch and Swede settlements, but to Walt's mind, that meant Vinot brought one of his family's apple trees to the area, which is how an old Dutch woman a couple hours north could've referenced such an apple on one of her recipe cards.

It made sense. Though the crab apple was native to the Americas, the apple of *Malus domestica* was not, and the earliest orchards were said to arrive here in the 1600s. It wouldn't be odd to think this Vinot brought some of his own orchard across the sea. A taste of home. A taste of joy. Planted or grafted.

And so it was that Walt became convinced he'd find Vinot's prized apple around here someday. Even though the odds were against it. Even though the FBI destroyed an unholy host of apple trees in the 1920s—including many of the early Johnny Appleseed orchards—due to Prohibition.

That's how Vinot's Allegresse became Walt's one true apple, his White Whale, his obsession.

So, best John could figure it was that Walt had found his Moby-Dick.

EMILY SAID SHE WAS GOING TO BIKE UP THE RIVER, SEE IF SHE COULD eyeball some of the islands. See if she could find the place where Walt's White Whale had perhaps surfaced. So to speak. John thought that was a fine idea and told her so.

WHEN JOHN ARRIVED AT WALT'S, HE FOUND THAT DEATH HAD COME to this place. Death in a way he had not anticipated. In a way that cut him deeper than the bone.

He stood on what was once Walt's back porch, looking out upon a patch of stumps. Two dozen of them. Not a single tree standing. He could barely breathe.

Walt's daughter, Belinda, stood next to him, chewing hard on some nicotine gum. "Yeah, so they're gone" was what she said after inviting him in and taking him back out here, knowing why he had come. There had to be cruelty in it, showing John this butchered orchard, this ruined place.

He felt the pain of it. It coursed through him like molten steel poured into an ant colony, burning hot at first, then hardening.

"Why?" was all he asked.

"Because I want a yard, not a forest," she said, then turned back around and went inside. John didn't understand. She'd told him it was okay to come out. That it was okay to come out for the *express purpose* of collecting branches. She knew the trees were gone but let him come anyway. Belinda *wanted* John to see this.

John followed her inside, still trying to get his head around the what and why of things, when he realized they weren't alone. He'd clocked a dirtbike parked across the street, but didn't know who it belonged to. Now he had a guess: It belonged to this ratty slip of human-shaped fast-food trash standing in front of him. Young guy. Scrubby almost-beard. Zits in an archipelago up his neck. Sores on his hands, probably up under the sleeves, too.

Mouth hanging loose in a mean smile.

"*I* cut those trees down," the guy said.

"Of course you did," John said.

Belinda slid on next to the fellow, had a kind of smug look on her face, the look of the fox that got all the chickens. "I'm pregnant. It's Derek's. We're gonna raise the kid here."

"Congratulations."

Belinda went to the kitchen table, put her hands on the lid of a cardboard box sitting here. "This was the last bits of Dad's stuff. I figured you might want it because I sure don't."

Moderating his breathing, trying to calm his heart, John nodded and reached for the box—

But Derek stepped forward fast, his shoe skidding on the linoleum with a squeak. He snatched the box up and yanked it away from John.

"Hold up, old man," Derek said, his throat somehow both high-pitched and gravelly, like a weasel whose throat had been stuffed with silt. "Bell, you say this old fucker was a friend of Walt's, huh."

"Yeah, real good friends. Too good."

"Then I think maybe he'd pay us some money for this box. Right, boomer? You old fuck. Maybe he'd pay us a hundred bucks—"

"Fine," John said, feeling that bad feeling rising up in him. He steadied his pulse, or tried to. But it was a pot set to boil.

"Well, that was fast. So that makes me think if you'd pay a hundred, then you'd definitely pay *two* hundred—"

"I don't have two hundred on me."

"Then I guess you're fuck outta luck."

John stepped forward, around the table, closing the gap between him and Derek. He held out both hands in supplication, steadying himself. "Derek. Son. You don't want that box. Belinda doesn't want that box, either. I don't even know what's in it, just that it belonged to a friend and I'm happy to take it off your hands. You say you want a hundred dollars, that's a fair price and I can make it happen. So let's just do that deal and be done with each other. Okay?"

As he spoke, John tried very hard not to imagine this person in front of him with a chainsaw, cutting into trees that had taken decades to grow. Good trees. Fruit-bearing trees. *Walt's* trees.

Derek slid the box behind his back, on the counter, then stood in front of it like a bouncer at a nightclub door.

"Why don't you try to take it?"

His breath stank like cat piss.

Belinda watched with feral excitement in her eyes.

"Derek," John said. "You don't want me to do that."

"He's old," Belinda said, goading her boyfriend on. "An old slow goat."

Derek grinned, licked teeth pocked with cavities and a yellow rime. He started popping his knuckles and leaned forward, chin out. "I think I'll keep the box after all. Might take a shit in it. Smear it all around. That's what I think of you and that dead-ass cocksucker, Walt—"

It was like a camera flash. It came in bright white, the light, the rage, the violence. He stabbed forward with four fingers flat against one another, striking the soft side of Derek's neck. Hitting the artery under the skin, the carotid. When the flash popped and then receded once more, Derek was on the ground, gasping, eyelids fluttering, his hands fruitlessly pawing at his throat and jaw.

Belinda screamed and ran out the back door, fumbling with her phone.

John sighed, regret pouring into him like a river.

He walked outside and waited for the police to arrive.

THE ARRESTING OFFICERS WERE ROUGH WITH HIM, AND HE LET them be. No use in fighting that. John went docile as a baby lamb and wished he would've

(*could've*)

been that way earlier, too, but something about Derek squirmed into his hidden, secret places, found something in those tunnels and boltholes, and released a darkness that yearned to be let free.

Dingman's Falls wasn't a big place, and the jail was just a drunk tank. John sat alone in it. Sometimes he just sat there and closed his eyes, trying to find peace in his breathing. That was something he learned not too long ago: You don't make peace. Peace wasn't a thing you made—it wasn't the sandcastle, it was the sand. The sand and the wind and the water. The natural state. Peace was the nothingness, the void of everything, the great empty. He just had to find that place. Dive into it like a black cave. You had to fall past despair and doubt to get there. But once you did, you gave yourself to it, found solace in the oblivion.

Eventually an officer came to get him, told him that the victim, Derek Sigafoos, wasn't going to press charges. The cop, a fellow with a big round head and a forehead you could use to advertise a car dealership along a highway, said, "I'll tell it to you straight. Sigafoos is a bona fide piece of shit. He's ex-Amish, went out on his Rumspringa and stayed among us English. Started a love affair with methamphetamines and kept the romance going. So I made it clear to him that a judge was going to take a good hard look at that, what with him—a bona fide piece of shit—accusing you, a decorated war veteran from the First Gulf War. And I said that could lead to fresh mess, maybe him getting arrested, maybe him getting *sued,* and gosh, that would sure put a crimp in his flourishing meth habit. So, he said oops, just a disagreement between men. And with that, you're free to go."

The officer, named Burley, handed John his keys, his phone, and the box of Walt's stuff. John thanked him and as the cop walked him out, Burley said, "This isn't your first brush with the law, I know. I'm sure it's hard. But one of these times you might not have someone friendly like me to help you out."

"I understand, Officer."

"Good. You go on now." He gave John instructions on how to walk over to the impound lot and get his car out. "And hey, thank you for your service."

To that, John didn't know what to say. He never knew what to say. There were a lot of things he *could've* said. Like how that phrase was the clearest sign the person saying it did not serve, because if they had, they wouldn't be thanking him at all, but rather, commiserating with him, telling him sorry for what he'd seen and what he'd done. Saying that they understood that the violence that broke out of him sometimes wasn't really his at all, but something that had been put in him long ago, something that all the training and all the battles and *all that killing* had made stronger. Meaner, too. Government saw that violence inside him and lured it into the open, trapped it, filed its teeth to points, gave 'em a shine, too. Made it so that the violence took him over. Painted his hands with blood. His eyes also.

But he wasn't going to say any of that.

He didn't say anything at all. He nodded solemnly and left.

JOHN PUT THE BOX IN THE BACK OF THE JEEP, THEN SLID THE LID off. Inside was nothing of use. Documents, mostly. Some old tax folders, two bundles of receipts from the early 2000s, a bundle of business cards. John idly flipped through them all just to see if there was something interesting in there, but nope. Nada.

But then he spied one last thing left in the box.

A photograph. Not digital, but the kind you had to go get developed once upon a time. Taken about fifteen years back. John remembered it well. In the photo, he and Walt stood by a gnarled old apple tree, the sunlight bleaching the air and throwing up a few hoops and baubles of light in the image. He and Walt looked happy as hell. That was a good day. The two of them had worked together for months to track down this tree, a variety thought to be extinct called McLeod's Pippin, a parent of another rare heirloom, the Katsu. The property owner, a fella named Oren Sibley, was the one who took the photo. They came back that fall and cut some branches, and Walt grafted them in spring. He had McLeod's Pippin apples about five years later in his own orchard. And as of today, that tree was dead and gone, thanks to his daughter Belinda, and her boyfriend, Derek.

Remembering that day then and having gone through this day now, all of it hit John like a wave. He doubled over, photo pinched in his grip. Grief and regret joined forces, reaching into his middle, grabbing a handful of the loose dough that was his innards, giving it all one hard twist. He sobbed for a while.

Eventually the tide rolled back out to sea. The tears stopped.

He decided then that if he could not preserve Walt's orchard, then he could at least take up the hunt for the White Whale. Vinot's apple. If Walt had found it, then John would find it, too. And maybe that's how John would find out what happened to Walt, too, at the end of things.

John leaned against the bumper, photo in hand, using it to fan his face and dry the tears on his cheeks—

But that's when he saw something written on the back of it.

A name—

Kim Luscas—Del Nat HPO

And with it, a phone number.

Local area code to John, 610, Lehigh Valley.

He took his phone, saw that it had been turned off, so he turned it on to give that number a ring and—

Four missed phone calls came in. And five text messages. The notifications rushed in like Black Friday shoppers, ding ding ding.

All from Emily.

The last two messages read:

Emily: John you need to call me ASAFP, something happened

Emily: something STRANGE, and I'm scared

Panic ran through him.

Emily!

25

EMILY AND THE WARNING

AFTER SHE TALKED TO JOHN THAT MORNING, EMILY HEADED OUT the door and pulled the bike out of the shed (pausing a moment to glare balefully at the space where the kayak had once sat, before she lost it in that damn river). There was a part of her that hoped Meg would come out, try to stop her, or at least ask her where she was going. The hostility would've been welcome. But Meg was back to ignoring her.

Emily slept poorly last night. Tossing and turning on the couch. She could hear Meg was up. Typing on the computer. Unpacking boxes in the bedroom. Rearranging furniture, as if that was a thing that needed to happen at three o'clock in the fucking morning. Emily wanted to go in there and ask her what the hell she was doing. *Go to sleep,* she raged in her head. But what would've been the point? The chasm between them had only widened further: an uncrossable gap. Any chance of reconciliation meant Emily would have to repair a bridge as it was burning.

So, out she went on the bike. Took her a bit to remember how to ride the damn thing—at first it was hard to keep the bike in a straight line, and she kept wobbling this way, wavering that way. Still, the old saying was true enough: *like riding a bike.* A skill that, once learned, was not easily forgotten.

Off she went, to find as Dolly Parton and Kenny Rogers once sang, islands in the stream.

THE MORNING WAS CRISP LIKE A COLD, RAW CARROT—IT HAD A BITE to it. The air smelled strongly of the soft, early decay of fallen leaves. Rain and worms warning of the long damp coming.

Emily biked up River Road, silver sun strobing through the mostly bare trees. Once she got the hang of cycling again, she held the handlebar with one hand and, perhaps foolishly, looked at her phone with the other, scouting the map. She found a spot next to the Lumbertown Crossing bridge that took her onto the canal towpath, once used by mules who pulled barges of coal and supplies, now by joggers and cyclists and walkers. River Road veered near the river but then away from it off and on, but the towpath ran right alongside it.

So that's the path she took.

The towpath today was pretty empty. A few runners, all bundled up. A couple of cyclists, clad in logo-spackled spandex like they were being sponsored for the Tour de France.

Otherwise, the packed red gravel path was empty.

The river roared alongside. A dark snake, slithering toward the distant sea. Just seeing it gave Emily the sweats. Her head felt hot. Her palms and pits, clammy. Like the water would reach up, lash out, wrap itself around her, and pull her in. Other people had vertigo when they looked out a skyscraper window, but that's how Emily felt when she was looking at the water.

She took the towpath under the Raven Rock Suspension Bridge—an old steel bridge meant only for foot traffic. Bikes okay, but no cars allowed. Down here on the struts and girders she passed graffiti of people's names, symbols, a couple of swastikas—because apparently that was America now, just fanboying for white supremacy. Above her were forgotten spiderwebs and the nests of gone birds.

She pedaled up off the path and onto the bridge. The river was wider at this point than it was down by their house. The bridge had a sign, said it spanned seven hundred feet across the water. She biked across, pausing in the middle to look out upon the river, trying to see whatever she could see. What she was looking for, honestly, she didn't know. Only that somewhere around here was an island that didn't exist on the maps. Harrowsblack Island. Walt had wanted to find it, and his body had been swept downriver. The river had taken him and she wanted to know where and why. Up here, on the bridge, it was cold. The wind shouldered into her

(*trying to push her over the edge and into the black water*)

(*so it could take her body same as it took Walt's*)

(*so Emily could just be bones down there in the river*)

(*skin gone soft and flaky, her body like oatmeal, like rotten cod*)

(*food for the crayfish nesting in her eye sockets*)

aaaaaand she had to get the fuck off the bridge right fucking now, thank you very much, so Emily hurriedly pedaled the bike back toward the Pennsylvania side and onto the towpath once more to escape the

(*killing river*)

wind and the cold.

ABOUT A MILE NORTH, THE TOWPATH VEERED AWAY FROM THE river, crossing over the Towhee Creek. This area was a little park, a "scenic viewing area," and certainly there was something to see: Emily glimpsed an island out there, just ahead. It was on Google Maps—but it didn't have a name. And she'd snapped a pic of the map she and John bought, and it wasn't there, either. Her heart caught in her chest. *Could it be?* She had to park the bike because the trail down to the river was a narrow one of dirt and rock. Down she went, through the skeletal trees, toward the water, her skin prickling with the centipede-dance of her phobia.

The river's edge, thirty feet away—

Now twenty—

Now *ten*—

She had to stop. She had line of sight of the water and the island beyond it. Close enough. *I'm good here,* she decided. As the dark water sped past.

The island being around here made sense. The original center of Harrow Township was just west of here. And if Walt's body had traveled downriver, well, it couldn't be *too* far north that his body entered the water, right? Certainly the more distance you put between that point and the place where she

(*dishonored his river-softened bones*)

found him, the greater the chance he'd never have made it intact. But some of his skeleton held together. He couldn't have traveled too great a distance.

Still, her heart sank upon getting level with the island. It wasn't much to look at. It was practically flush with the surface of the river, and she imagined that during high-water days, this island could be lost entirely.

According to Homackie's book, Harrowsblack was almost a hill, with a great big hanging tree on it that could be seen from both sides of the river. There had been a couple of trees here, though they'd long been felled and turned to rotting splinter. The rest was just scrub and shrub.

Maybe it *was* the island. Time changed things. But it didn't feel right.

What the hell would *feel right, exactly?* Emily challenged herself to wonder. What was she even doing out here? Doubt chewed at her like termites through floorboards. God, what if Meg had a point? What if this was weird? Panic started to set in. *The fuck am I doing with my life?*

No. The river was just freaking her out. *Calm down, Emily.*

With trembling hand she fished out an Aloha protein bar—chocolate cookie dough, because one could not have healthfulness unless it was wonderfully robed in the trappings of a candy bar—and walked back up through the woods, hurrying away from the river and heading back toward the bike.

But when she emerged from the trees—

Someone was standing by her bike.

Facing her.

Like they were waiting.

It was a man. White polo shirt, no jacket despite the cold air. Khakis so khaki they were almost white, too. White sneakers. Average height. Blond hair and a big smile frozen to his face. Smug, like he was thinking, *I told you so.* But told her what? Who the hell was this guy?

Emily wished she had something on her. A knife. Keys to lace through her knuckles. All she had was her phone, so she got it out and turned it on, idly set it to camera mode. Slid it to video.

As she approached, she held up the phone like a weapon.

She tapped RECORD.

"Get away from my bike," she warned.

"It's a nice bike. Looks new," the man said. His voice was clear, loud, well enunciated. It rang in her head, echoing like tinnitus.

"I'm recording you."

"That's fine."

"It all goes to the cloud. I have that shit on sync. Whatever I record here goes up there—" She waved to the air, indicating *the cloud.* "So people will see."

"You don't have to be afraid of me," he said. "And you don't have to be afraid of the river, Emily. It's just water."

She froze, no longer approaching him or her bike. About thirty feet of space separated them, and even that suddenly felt dangerously close. Like he could reach out with his long arms, grab her up, break her in half. She thought to run, but where? The way to the road was ahead, but he was in the way. The river roared at her back. It welcomed her to return to it, to swallow her up, to offer its own version of escape.

"How do you know my name?"

How do you know I fear the river.

"I could take it away. Your fear of the river. Of water. It's a simple thing. I can restore your dignity. I could fix your marriage. I can help you, Emily."

"Please just go away." Her eyesight blurred behind tears threatening to spill. The air around her seemed to hum. Darkness vibrated around her vision, like black locusts crawling at the edges of a window.

I can't move, she thought. Her feet wouldn't lift off the ground.

"I'll call the police."

He ignored her and said, "But if I give you those gifts, if I repair what is broken, I want something in return. It costs me to be here. There must always be an exchange, even if not everyone is aware of it. It's a cardinal law of the universe. Matter is not created or destroyed. Energy is energy. Water goes to low places, the cold eats the heat, and all of life is in trade. This to that. Me to you. And back again it goes."

"I don't want anything from you."

The man in white took a step closer. The darkness moved in around her like a tunnel. The bright day, dimmed. The locusts, restless and squirming.

"What I want from you is to let this go. You're looking for something. Searching. Kicking over rocks, turning over logs. And I'm here to tell you it's just not worth it. What you'll find will bring you misery, Emily. You and John."

She gritted her teeth and bore down. *Move your feet, girl.* They budged. But only a little. Emily stared down at her feet, willing them to move again—

Then she heard a sharp intake of breath at her ear—

He was gone from in front of her—

And now stood behind her.

She tried to scream, but no sound came out.

"Now, *legally,* I'm obligated to tell you that I can't stop you. And it's true, I can't. I can only suggest. Gently *urge.* Offer *exchanges.* Here you're wondering, ah, if I'm trying to steer you off this path, then perhaps you're getting close, perhaps it's a sign to stay the course. Warm, hot, hotter you get. But consider the opposite: Maybe I'm telling you all this in an act of reverse psychology. Warning you away to keep you going." He laughed. She could *feel* his smile behind her. His mouth. Bigger, wider. Shiny teeth. His shadow upon her swelled, balloon-like. It had weight. It pressed on her. And his grin grew wider. She could feel it stretching. Maw open, like he could bite her head off her shoulders. "Maybe I want you to keep going. Maybe that's my kink. To watch your descent."

"Fuck you," she hissed.

"Your anger is understandable. This is scary and confusing but regardless of whether you think I'm telling you the truth or trying to trick you, consider what is happening, Emily. You're seeking forbidden information. You're close to death; its stink is all over you now. You're looking for secrets. Hidden things. And Emily, it is a truism that if you go poking around holes, you find snakes. Every time. And snakes, Emily, they bite. They climb up in you. They nest in your empty spaces. So, for your sake, just walk away. I'll help you. What say you?"

"Fuck. You."

He drew a long breath. Let out a slow sigh. She could feel that smile still at her back. Teeth shining, clamped together, hungry the way the river was hungry. "Well. I guess we cannot come to an agreement. That's okay. We can try again. Meanwhile, go home. Relax a little. Maybe—" This, he whispered giddily in her ear: "Eat an apple. I hear they're fresh."

And just like that, she could feel her body unseize. She whirled on him raising the phone above her head, ready to bring it down upon his skull, smashing the screen, the case, all of it—

But he wasn't there.

Nobody was.

She was alone.

Emily finally screamed.

She tried calling John. Again and again. All day. She rode home, fast as she could, calling him, leaving him messages, texting him. Dinnertime came. Meg didn't come home, either. *Shit, shit, shit.* Emily didn't know what was happening, but when she went to look at the video she took of the man by her bike, all she caught was the opening moment, before anybody spoke—him standing there like he owned the damn thing. And then the video distorted. A spray of melting pixels, a screech of hisses and shrill audio artifacts like an old modem connecting to the early internet.

But then finally, *finally,* John called her back. And she told him everything.

26

HASHTAG DEREALIZATION

CALLA FLOATED THROUGH THE NEXT SEVERAL DAYS. NOT WITH A light heart, with ebullience, but like the world was behind a window and she could see it, and *it* could see *her,* but they remained irrevocably separate just the same.

Lucas and Esther tried talking to her and she listened, even talked to them, too, but it was like having a conversation through a wall: muffled and poorly comprehended. She had a pre-calc quiz. She did edits on her college application essay during study hall. She ate lunch. All of it felt witnessed more than participated in. Here she was, hoping to be an influencer, and all she felt was . . . influenced. Pushed forward, urged along, detached and distant.

SHE WAS WITH HER FATHER AS THEY WENT TO PICK UP MARCO from the orthopedic office at the hospital—Marco's own family was busy at the restaurant and would've had to close the place to get him, so her dad offered. Marco was supposed to go home and rest, but he was sure he wanted to help Dad at the orchard. Calla was in the truck, squeezed in the middle, feeling like a passenger in all the ways, like she was riding on a ride she couldn't stop. Marco was happy. Dad was happy. She was supposed to be happy they were happy but instead she felt weird and wobbly and sick. She kept thinking about

(*apple seeds and buzzing flies*)

how both of them seemed to be doing *so well* and how both were *so pleased* and she wanted to love how well they got along. She tried to tell Marco he should take it easy, just relax, he could help her with her college application, she could help him with his, because remember? College? And he was like, "Nah, it's all right, I wanna help Mister P here, I can move around a little now." And Dad was all, "Honey, I'll keep it light, don't worry. Mister Meza here knows his limits, and besides, he's one tough cookie." They laughed like they rehearsed it beforehand.

Home, then, and off they went, down to the orchard. They didn't invite her to join. A little voice inside her said, *Because you didn't eat the apple, Calla.*

So, inside. To her application. It was due by the end of the month for early decision. She knew Marco had barely touched his. Didn't blame him, what with the injury and all. But still. He should be working on *that.* Not being with Dad.

Not being in the orchard.

We're supposed to have a future together. But he didn't seem to remember that. *Jesus, Marco.*

With her own application, it was mostly crossing the t's and dotting the i's, all the dumb garbage that needed to be done—administrative stuff like making sure she had her teacher recommendations, her community work recommendations, her test scores, her transcripts, and then the application itself. She had taken the SAT in late spring. Nailed it with a 1440, which put her in the top 10 percent of the school's scores, and her school tested higher than the national average, so that was in the bucket. The personal essay was polished as fuck, shiny as a new phone, all about her *journey* from humble farm girl to influencer, and yes, okay, she maybe inflated her overall numbers and effect, and she definitely over-sold the "farm" part of the story, but she knew the college wouldn't care about all the specific details *or* her actual follower numbers but *would* care about how she drew these connections between herself and the larger goal. About how it was important for her influence to be seen as *empowering*, not just as some, like, girlboss bullshit but as her coming into her own as a young woman with agency in this world. About how one's personal brand could affect the global brand. She knew it was, pssh, kind of pretentious, but that's what they wanted in these essays. That big reach, that high-mindedness that said, *Girl, I'm ready for college, look and see.* But fuck, now she was worried that was all so shallow, so stupid, probably a hundred other girls were writing some version of the same shitty vapid Instagram CEO bougie bullshit. She wanted to scream. She felt like she was drifting further and further away from everything. Even her own essay. It was awful. She wasn't going to get into school. She needed the yes. She needed the win. She needed Marco to get his shit together, too, and help her with hers so she could help him with his so they could have a *future* together—

She screamed into her pillow.

THE TWO OF THEM WORKED TOGETHER FOR SEVERAL NIGHTS IN A row. Dad and Marco. Working on the cider house. Picking apples that she knew in her heart shouldn't still be growing on trees this late into November.

One night, Dad and Marco came in. She heard them downstairs. Talking, but talking quietly. She snuck down to listen, but her foot stepped on the floorboard and they immediately shut up, like two girls who had been gossiping in a bathroom stall but hissed and went quiet the moment someone came in.

Calla strode into the kitchen and saw the two of them huddled together—Marco wasn't even using a crutch, instead using a big boot. He and her father stood close together. Both had a half-eaten apple in their hands, their chins wet with the juices. "Hey, sweetheart," Dad said, wiping his mouth with the back of his sleeve. Marco didn't bother.

"Call, you okay?" Marco asked her.

She forced a smile. "Totally. What are you guys doing?"

"Just talking," Dad said with a genial shrug.

They stared at her. Again, that feeling of being pushed away. Of being untethered. "Okay," she said, and then asked Marco, "Do you want to work on your application? Mine's in pretty solid shape, sooooo—"

But he said, "Nah, not right now. Maybe later."

"Deadline's end of this month."

"Just the early deadline."

Dad jumped in. "And he has till January for the main deadline, right?"

"Yeah, but—"

"Cool," Marco said.

"Great," Dad said.

Calla shifted from foot to foot. "Okay. *Bye,*" she said, trying to sound irritated, but feeling instead like she just sounded petulant. A little baby mad she wasn't being included in something. So, she receded. Calla returned upstairs. Halfway up the steps, she heard them start talking again. She couldn't make out the words. Just quiet, secret murmurs. *Well, fuck you both also,* she thought, and went back into her room and slammed the door.

27

THE PROBLEM OF EVIL

EMILY PACED AROUND THE SPOT WHERE THE MAN IN THE WHITE suit had stood just days before. The day was cold. The wind slashed at them like a swiping knife. The sky spit rain—a sputtering drizzle that was just enough to keep them both damp and cold down to the bone.

"This is where it happened," she told John, who stood ten feet away. He watched her carefully. "This is where the bike was. Where he stood waiting. And then—I was over there, where you're standing, and—" She growled in frustration. "Listen, I know this sounds fucking stupid. I know it's not possible. He knew things about me nobody really could know, which—again, I know is stupid and *probably* means I was hallucinating and he knew things about me because *I* know things about me and henceforth he was just a figment of my overstressed imagination, but John, Jesus Christ, it felt so, *so* real—"

Out with it, then, John, he thought.

"I saw Walt," he said.

She stopped pacing and stared at him with a scrunched-up face. "What?"

"I was burying some of Walt's things in his orchard, before his daughter—" Well. Why even get into that? It was done. Let it be gone. "I was burying them because I wanted my own funeral for him, something just for me, and while I was doing that, I felt sick. Then I saw Walt. Just— just his head. And he spoke to me. It was as real as anything. I don't know what to make of it. But I have this growing feeling that something is very, very wrong."

"So we're both hallucinating."

He sighed. "I don't think it's that." He took a moment to look out through the curtain of gray at the flat lump of land in the river. "That's not our island. We're looking for a hill with an apple tree, and that big fallen tree there isn't an apple tree, it's an ash tree." He sighed. "Come on. Let's go get out of the rain."

HER HOUSE. (OR, IN HER WORDS, MEG'S HOUSE. SHE CLEARLY DID not feel any ownership.)

John stood in the kitchen. Though the heat was on, he felt cold, and it wasn't just the damp clothes or the chill day. The décor was icy. White, gray, black, silver, nothing out of place but for a messy blanket on the couch. The blanket was colorful and rumpled and looked warm. *Emily's blanket,* he guessed. Her mess was what marked her.

The only other color was a half-empty basket of apples on the counter. They were dark and red, like Arkansas Blacks or Black Oxfords, though most people didn't have access to those, which meant the answer was probably all the more pedestrian: the ill-named Red Delicious, which was neither red, nor delicious. Walt had always called it the Judas Apple. The liar fruit. John scowled at the apples, suspicious of their grocery store provenance.

Emily stood in the kitchen, pouring water from an electric gooseneck kettle over packets of Café Bustelo instant espresso. "I did some digging into what you told me on the phone," she said.

"Digging?"

"Kim Luscas. The name on the back of the photo?"

"What'd you find?" John had meant to call that number last night, but soon as he heard about Emily's experience, he instead threw together a bag and drove south, renting a room at a small B&B not far from the river. He would've preferred a motel but this area had long put away such common American things. It was easier to stay down here for a little while than make the hour-plus drive every day.

"She worked at the Museum of Indian Culture up in Allentown."

Ironically, back up closer to where he lived in the Lehigh Valley. "You said worked? Past tense? She quit?"

"Not exactly." Emily chewed her lower lip. "She died."

"Died how?"

"At her desk apparently. Five years ago. Brain aneurysm. She wasn't old. Her obituary said she was only thirty-nine. She was the curator and cultural liaison at the museum—do you know it? The museum, I mean. Uh—sorry, is that racist, because I know you said you were part Native American and it's a museum for local Native culture, and I don't even know what that all means or if you'd care—"

Millennials, John knew, were quite sensitive about all of this. Which was good in its way; it showed they cared, at least. "It's a fine museum. I didn't know Miss Luscas and didn't have anything to do with the museum."

"Right. Okay. I don't want to hurt anyone."

A noble wish, if impossible, he thought. "Aren't many Lenape around to hurt, I'm afraid. And those that are around are 'unofficial,' according to the Commonwealth of Pennsylvania."

"What—um, what happened? To the Lenni-Lenape, I mean."

"The standard, I suppose. Cheated, attacked, tricked, land stolen, run off by angry mobs. William Penn had an agreement but his sons cheated them. The Walking Purchase swindled them or bullied them into vacating the land so that Penn's sons and their ilk could walk the length and breadth of their territory and take it. That led to violence. Orchards were a part of this, too. Put in an orchard and that counted as a homestead, which meant you owned that land." He shrugged and sighed. "There're Lenape here but most of them are in Oklahoma now."

"Sorry."

"A long time ago. Just history." Though history, he knew, was scar tissue. "It's funny sometimes, though. You look around an area like this and everything is, you know, Holicong and Neshaminy, Unami and Tohickon—it's half the street names and a bunch of the schools. Named after the Lenape here or named after what we called it. Written like the Europeans would've written it, or said like they would've said it. Like a . . . a crude approximation. Like it's supposed to be an honor. But those names are stolen. Stolen and used as a shield behind which they hid their crimes. Names like that are really just grave markers." Another long sigh. "But that's America, I guess. Everything stolen. Stolen stories, stolen names, stolen dreams, and stolen people. Bury your victims and build on top of them."

Emily slid the cup over to him. "I don't know what it's like, I'm sorry."

He took it. "Probably worse for you. I pass for white. Nobody thinks much about me. I figure you *do* know what it's like, in a couple of different directions."

She stared into her mug and shrugged softly. "Maybe." Lifting the cup, she blew on the dark brew to cool it down. "So, what's next?"

He thought about it. "Walt had written *HPO* next to her name. Guessing it means she ran the Historic Preservation Office. The HPO has connections with the Delaware Nation in Oklahoma. I know some people there; I'll call around and see if they can find out anything she might've been helping Walt with."

"What can I do?"

He shrugged. "Keep looking into those islands. But stay safe, Emily. I don't like any of this. Quakers don't necessarily believe in any kind of big supernatural evil. To them the problem of evil is a human one, a necessary part of free will. It lets us

(*point the rifle and pull the trigger*)

be as bad or as good as we so choose. But I can't shake the feeling something here is really off-kilter. We both received warnings. Me from Walt. You from this man in white. Sounds crazy. And maybe it is."

"No, I feel it, too." She reached over and put a hand on his shoulder. "Thanks for coming down here. You didn't have to. It means a lot."

"Friends are a light in dark times, Emily. We try to be brighter together so that the darkness doesn't take us alone."

28

BEASTS IN THE ORCHARD

SADNESS AND WORRY SETTLED INTO DAN'S BONES AS HE STOOD among the trees of the orchard in the fading light of the afternoon. It was the day before Thanksgiving, the day of the Crossed Keys dinner, and he saw finally that no new apples were forthcoming on the Ruby Slipper trees. He'd picked what had been there. The orchard was going dormant, at long last.

It was to be expected. Honestly, the trees had produced for far longer than he'd considered possible—and for that, he knew he should be happy. It was a long and literally fruitful season. That was cause to celebrate.

But a certain fear pushed its way through him: He needed these apples. They made him better. They made him *joyous.* A small voice slithered around the back of his head, told him he was nothing without them.

He told himself, no, it was okay. The last apples off the tree came in a great bounty. He'd picked bushels and bushels, and those he could save through the winter. The orchard had produced plenty, not just for him, but for those who wanted them—the people who were good customers. Good *consumers.* Friends of the orchard, in a way. Those who enjoyed his apples felt almost like . . .

Well, they felt like family.

The way the trees felt like family.

Like his children.

They deserved their rest.

He walked the length of the seven trees, finding one last apple still hanging from one of the farthest branches. Dan plucked it from the tree and inhaled its scent. It was dizzying. He felt his knees soften, his neck muscles tighten.

Dan bit into it. Bit deep, too. Into the core, into the seeds. Felt the juices slide across his teeth and tongue and down his throat. The crunch felt like biting

(*little bones*)

into Mother Nature's very own version of a communion wafer. All his sins, all his fears, all the bad things went away. Receding like a red tide.

He stood for a bit, eating the apple, drinking it down and breathing it in, and he looked over the surrounding thicket. It would soon be battened down for the winter season, flattened against the earth, brown and broken. He saw the shape of the building he and Marco were building together—its outline darker than the black of the night. In there, they'd make cider, bottle it, maybe even set up a fire and a kettle to make cider syrup. The possibilities were endless. Applesauce, apple butter, apple pies and apple cake. Apple chips. Apple cider vinegar. All would be huge sellers thanks to his

(*Harrowsblack*)

Ruby Slipper apple.

He turned to head back to the truck, the apple eaten all the way down to nothing, core and stem both, when once more, that smell of rot hit him. The rot of meat, not leaves. Like roadkill, rancid and sickly sweet.

It came from the thicket toward the south side of the orchard, close to the creek that bubbled there. Evening bled purple as Dan walked that way, following his nose. The rot smell grew stronger, and with it, a wilder odor—the stink of animal piss. The smell only thickened as he found a small deer trail and headed down it, into the sleeping bramble.

Twenty feet, thirty, forty—

Into a small clearing, he stepped.

Blood gleamed in the moonlight. It wetted the fur of a fat raccoon lying on its side, its belly gashed open. Guts purple like the sky above. It was still alive. A paw twitched. Its chest rose and fell in hummingbird bursts. Pink froth fizzled at its mouth and nose. Next to it, too, Dan saw a white, soil-specked bone poking out of the ground. Didn't belong to the raccoon by the looks of it. He took a step forward to look closer—

The raccoon's carcass shuddered suddenly—

A cat stepped up onto the body. The carcass, like a stage.

The cat was an orange tabby. Like a house cat. Collar and all. Gore hung from its mouth like red yarn. The cat lifted a paw and licked it.

It looked at Dan and sat down on the raccoon's body.

He'd seen the cat before, slinking around the orchard. He was glad to have it—sure, he'd heard that cats were killers, but that's what he wanted. Kill the moles, voles, rats, and mice. Kill any greedy songbirds who might think to nibble the apple blooms in the spring. But to see the cat having killed a raccoon—

Raccoons were survivors. Clever, capable survivors.

A cat surely couldn't kill one.

And yet.

As the cat stared at him, he stared at the cat. And he recognized something in the deep of its gaze. Dan saw something of himself there, absurd as that seemed. *We're both guardians of this orchard,* he realized. The raccoon had probably been pilfering apples with its sneaky little hands. And the cat had ended its thievery with tooth and claw.

"Good kitty," he said.

"*Mrow,*" the cat answered, again licking a paw.

Dan looked at his watch. As evening died and gave birth to night, it was time to go. Time to get ready. He had dinner and he had a date.

"I'll leave you to it, then," he told the cat, and headed back to the house.

As his father used to say, A shit, shower, and a shave. Now Dan stood in front of the long mirror hanging on his closet door, the one that banged and thumped every time he opened or shut said door, and hollered for his daughter. As was the way of the North American Teenage Girl, she plodded into the room, sulking at him. Though gone was the usual wryness in her face, and replacing it was a dour, gray look, as if a cloud of ash hung about her. Stirred, dead earth, kicked up by sullen feet.

"Help me out here?" he asked her brightly.

"Sure," she said. No fight in her. But she wasn't happy about it.

"You don't even know what I'm asking you to help with."

"So tell me."

"I have that dinner tonight."

"Okay," she said. Spoken like *so fucking what.*

"I need help with my outfit—" He'd put on a simple blue button-down with a tan corduroy blazer, but it just didn't feel right. Once upon a time he would've just slopped it all on and gone out, not really that aware of how he looked. But tonight he wanted to do it *right*. Present himself well. Be the man on the outside he knew he was on the inside. "I figure you're the one to ask."

"Great. You look fine."

"I don't look fine."

"You look fine, like a rube farmer who's getting dressed up to go cavort with the county nobles. Which is what you are."

He tightened his jaw. Anger laced through him—amazing how mean teenage girls could be, though usually his daughter was cheekier about it. At least when she took you down, she made it sound smart. It was weak salve for his injured pride.

"You're mad."

"At what."

"At *me*."

"Don't know what you mean."

He turned toward her. "Calla Lily—"

"Ugh."

"This about Marco?"

She paused for a moment, her nostrils flaring. "He is going to miss the deadline for early application. Because he's been spending time with *you*."

"What matters is *you* getting yours in, sweetheart." Dan shrugged. "I'm not responsible for him or his future."

She rolled her eyes so hard he was pretty sure they were about to tumble out of her head like a pair of dice. "He works for *you*. He's got a *broken leg*. You've been taking up his time since the moment he got the screws out. God, I've barely seen him at all because he's always down there in the stupid orchard and—"

"Oh, okay. That's what this is. I see it now. It's jealousy, Calla. You're not worried about his college prospects—which are fine, by the way. You're not worried about his leg, which has healed up pretty nice— I think they got that boot off him this morning. You just don't like that your boyfriend is spending time with your yucky father."

"Jesus, Dad, it's not that."

But he could see on her face that it was that. That's what he decided it was, anyway. Girls could be jealous creatures, couldn't they? "Tell you what, I have a little surprise for you. I was going to let it *be* a surprise but, I guess it's a surprise no matter when you find out."

"I don't care."

"Marco and his parents are coming over for Thanksgiving tomorrow."

Ah. There it was. A flash in her eye. A good flash. Like sunshine off a rain-dappled apple. "Really? I thought—"

"They were doing their own thing and we were doing ours. But I said, Hey, let's put our culinary heads together. They'll bring some of that Peruvian food from their restaurant, like, oh, what's it called? The one with the chicken and their little special peppers? Whatever. They'll do that, I'll make the turkey and your mother's sweet potato casserole recipe—" The secret was, of course, *all* the marshmallows. "And a good time will be had by all. Marco is all yours tomorrow."

She regarded him suspiciously.

Moments passed, *tick tick tick.*

And then—

The dam broke.

"Fine," she said, pouting still but behind the pout was the ghost of a smile. "Ick. Don't look at me like that. I'll help you with your ugly dork clothing."

And she did. Said the blazer was good, and in her words, *retro.* Called the shirt a *tragedy* and said it hurt her soul, so she picked out a plaid he had with some yellow and blue in it, something she said was autumnal and played well against his eyes and his hair. While she thumbed through the meager rack of his "sad man clothing," she said, "So is this the dinner with those awful people?"

"The Crossed Keys, yes. Lambert and Hardiaken and all of them."

"They suck. Old white privileged dickheads."

"True."

"You're not joining them, are you?"

He chuckled. "No. I'm just going to take the free meal and then throw it all back in their faces."

Because I deserve better, he thought. *Dad deserved better.*

"Good." She came out empty-handed. "Don't wear a tie. All yours are terrible and you look nice and *cazh.*" Short for casual, he took it to mean. "No need to overdo it. You bringing that lady? The redhead? Joanie Bureau?"

"Moreau. Yeah, yes. But, uh, she's married."

"Dating a married woman. Father, you absolute operator."

"It's not a thing. We're just friends."

She arched an eyebrow. "It's super-sus and I totally approve. Anyway, you look good. Ish. Don't stay out too late. Don't drink and drive. Wear protection."

"Yes, Mom."

"I'm triggered enough as it is by this conversation, do *not* call me that."

"Fair enough."

She turned to leave. "One more thing. You *need* to give Marco time to work on his college application. It's not just jealousy, Dad. We want to go to the same school and I don't want anything to fuck that up."

"Language," he chided her, but he didn't really care.

"*Language,*" she mocked, and then she went to leave the room. But before she did, she turned and asked him in a smaller voice, "Dad. What's the deal with your apple?"

Dan smiled and said, "It's the future, honey. It's our future." He hoped she'd try it sometime. She would, he knew. When she was ready.

29

THE EMPTINESS HAS A NAME

JOHN HAD HIS LAPTOP, AN OLD BEAT-TO-HELL WINDOWS MACHINE, open on the bed. The bedspread beneath it was a Pepto Bismol pink. As were most things in this room in the old Victorian B&B. *That's the Mauve Room,* the proprietor—an old woman whose name was, curiously, Maude—had called it. While she stroked a tortoiseshell cat she had named, whether out of affection or hate, Monkeyface.

It was not to John's tastes, this place. But it would do for now.

He had a Zoom digital conferencing window open and waiting. And waiting. And waiting. John was about ready to close it when finally a pixel-blur appeared on-screen that resolved into the round, cherubic baby-face of an old friend, Raymond Kiunute. He was younger than John by a good twenty years, though even on the screen it was easy to see the crow's-feet playing at the edges of his eyes. Still, his energy was young: He had this cool, laid-back vibe, like everything was creek water easing past him. His long hair was tucked under a camo hat with a symbol on it that looked part like a shield, part like a turtle—a symbol of the Delaware Nation there in Anadarko, Oklahoma.

"Hey, brother!" Raymond said, big smile, always happy. "It's been too long." And it had been. Raymond used to work out of the Lehigh Valley, liaising as he did with the museum—John used him as a good guide to help him drum up the resources needed to find the missing apples he'd been seeking. But times changed, jobs changed, and Raymond ended up going to work for the cultural offices down in Anadarko. "I don't have long, what do you need?"

"It was a bear finding a hole in your schedule, Raymond."

"A bear. Hah. I see what you did there, John." John hadn't intended the joke, but there was one there if you cared to find it: Raymond's father was named Bear. "Yeah it's tough, man. It's why I was late—you know how much work it is just to administer the fucking *mowing the elders' lawns* program? It's like herding squirrels, brother."

Running the lawn-care program for the Delaware elders? "You're not in the cultural preservation office anymore?"

"Nah, I left that what, three years ago? I'm director of the AOA now." Administration on Aging. Dealing with the aging population there.

"Congratulations, Raymond. I'm sure the pay is better. But you have to deal with all those cranky elders, I bet."

"Cranky elders, listen to you. Like you're not getting up there in years. Come on down, I'll get you a little house, make sure your lawn is mowed and shit. You even get three squares a day if you sign up for the program."

"I'm not quite ready for a life in the rearview yet, Raymond."

Raymond laughed. "No, I bet you're not, you're too tough and too stubborn for that shit, brother. Hey, so what do you need? I don't mind chatting to chat, but I'm guessing that's not why you're putting my face on your screen today."

"Kim Luscas."

"Kim." Raymond nodded, recognition in his eyes. "Yeah. Shit. Poor girl, right? What about her?"

"Well. You two worked together, right?"

"At a distance, sure. Her there, me here. We shared information and artifacts, I recommended speakers, and we coordinated different exhibits. But when she died, which—you know, man, hell, a real loss. She was good at her work. Smart, nice. You know, white as Wonder Bread, but well studied. God, that was . . . five years back. It was around that time your buddy contacted me, wasn't it?"

John's neck prickled. *Buddy?* "Who?"

"Enh. What's his name. Walter."

"Walt."

"Walt, yeah, whatever, him. He said you recommended he call me."

John frowned. He had made no such recommendation. He and Walt weren't even talking then. Though Walt would've known about Raymond, for sure. John had mentioned him enough times, he wagered. "Why'd he call you again?"

Raymond belted a big belly laugh. "What do you think he called me about? You two and your fuckin' apples, man."

"He was looking for an apple? What'd you tell him?"

Raymond stopped to think. "I told him I didn't think the apple had an Indigenous connection—or so I thought at the time. It was some French-sounding thing. I told him I didn't know shit about that and didn't have any records that would point to it, but I said, hey, talk to my friend Kim at the museum up there."

"So it was you that told him to call her."

"Yeah, man. Sure. If it was local to you all, maybe she'd know something we didn't."

Shit. That meant this was a dead end. But wait, hold on—

"You said, 'or so I thought at the time.'"

"Huh?"

"About the Native connection. You were wrong?"

"Oh yeah. Kinda. That was actually some pretty interesting shit that Kim found. Led me to Robby Keekott, pick his brain about the language a little bit. He's fun, you know. Older than the dirt, but funny as fuck, plays a mean game of checkers." Keekott was a real-deal talker of the language.

"What'd you need from him?"

Raymond's eyes unfocused a little as he appeared to dig into his memories. "I'll say it like this: So you know I'm kind of a bird-watcher, right? Zoom lens and all that shit. And it's like, you're out there looking for this bird or that bird, and you're not finding any of them—or any birds at all? It's too quiet. That's a sign there's something else going on. You go outside, can't find a single bird? Means there's a raptor somewhere nearby. Red-tail, maybe a prairie falcon. This was like that. Sometimes, what you don't see tells you as much a story as what you do. See, Walt was thinking this apple, maybe the Lenape there were cultivating it. That maybe the Dutch gave it to 'em and from the trees they grew their own orchards and, you know, like happened all too often, eventually the European assholes cut down the trees—"

"Or girdled them." The pain struck at John somewhere deep. What had been lost—what had been *taken*—felt like it had been ripped right out of his middle, bloody and pulsing.

Native orchards were once prevalent across the eastern half of the United States—Ohio, New York, Pennsylvania, Virginia, Michigan, Indiana. Colonizers said these were unsophisticated orchards—like with Johnny Appleseed, grown from seed, used for cider. But the Indigenous orchards sometimes produced the same apple across multiple trees. They knew how to graft. Had been taught or, more likely, had known it all along.

They didn't view orchards as something you owned. It was public fruit, because they were often nomadic, moving with the seasons, but orchards stayed where you put them. The fruit was there for whoever passed by. A gift from the earth, from the Great Spirit.

But the colonizers, they wanted to own it all.

Orchards meant ownership of land.

And apples were a commodity. Something to be bought and sold.

All they had to do was get those so-called savages to give up the orchards—and sure, sometimes that meant just running them off in a mob. But other times, it was sneakier. Sometimes, it was cruel. You told lies about them, said they were unsophisticated, just animals instead of people. And when they rallied to defend the orchards they planted, you didn't have to chop the trees down. All you had to do was go in, under cover of night. Then you peeled a narrow band of bark off all the way around a tree, which cut off the living thread between the tree and the source of its life, the earth. The phloem was severed. Couldn't get nutrients from the ground. Couldn't speak to its other trees. No water. No dirt. The tree still looked healthy, but by then it was just a ghost. That tree wouldn't live to see another season, wouldn't produce fruit, couldn't feed anybody. You want to kill a lot of people slow, you kill their food. Eventually they'd either move or starve. And when they moved, as they inevitably did—

That land was now your land.

The fucking colonizer playbook.

"So it wasn't that," John said. "Didn't come from a girdled orchard."

"No. Wasn't an apple they were cultivating at all, man. It was the *opposite*."

"Opposite how?"

"This apple was one they *didn't* want to cultivate. It was a tree they were trying to *kill*. Eradicate entirely."

"What? Why?"

"Folklore, probably. Maybe the tree came from some monster Dutch or French fuck, someone who really rained pain down on their heads. I dunno for sure. A lot of the records weren't ours, but from the Europeans, and you know you can't always trust their stories." He paused. "We did find the word they had for it. For the tree, I mean, or the apple, maybe."

"Tell me."

Raymond cleared his throat, gave it a go. It sounded like *khweysu*. Raymond quick scribbled something on a piece of paper and held it up.

Pkwësu.

Raymond continued: "Robby Keekott said it meant like, a—a hole in something. Like a hole in a person, or a hole in an apple."

"They called the apple as if it were a hole in the apple." Naming it not for what it was, but for what it wasn't. For its negative space. Almost as if they didn't want to name it at all. As if it was not what it claimed to be. *Or because its true name was a curse.* Names, after all, had power, didn't they?

"Seems like. Not sure what it meant. Or if it even helped your friend. I would've kept the conversation going but Kim died—so that ended that."

"I'm sorry about that. She died of a brain aneurysm?"

"That's what they said. She didn't have any health issues. It happened after hours, they say. She was working late. Said she was meeting with someone in there beforehand—maybe a friend or family member. White guy. White suit. Never found him, and they said it was a natural death so. Who knows, man."

White guy, all in white.

Couldn't have anything to do with the same man who threatened Emily, could it? Didn't seem possible.

"Thanks, Raymond. I really appreciate this."

"Hey, no problem, brother. You be good. Come on down sometime, hey? We'll feed you. Food is love."

"Just don't think you're going to mow my lawn, okay?"

"Shit, I wouldn't try. Love you, brother."

"Love you, Raymond."

He ended the Zoom call and sat there for a little while, just chewing on what Raymond had told him. He didn't know what any of this meant, or how it helped them, but it was something they didn't have before. An apple that they didn't want to grow. That they wanted to *kill*. Why? What about an apple and its tree would be so concerning? Something superstitious, maybe. Something about how the apple looked or tasted or smelled? Something about where it grew, or who brought it to them, or—well, the possibilities had no end. He didn't know. But something chewed at him. *Pkwĕsu. The hole in the apple.* A hole like a worm might make.

—

30

EFF IT

FUCK IT, SHE THOUGHT, I'M WEARING THE RED DRESS.

Joanie looked good in it. (She looked good out of it, too.) She knew it. She owned it. Graham stood behind her, and she saw him peering around her margins in the mirror. "I am, as ever, astonished by your beauty, my dear."

"And I am, as ever, glad that you see it. Will you see it when I'm older? Some frumpy old crone, sagging everywhere, nursing a gin-and-tonic on the front stoop? The years keep adding up."

"I'll see it always. No matter the age, no matter the outfit." He came up behind her and put his hands on her shoulders, kissing the back of her neck.

"Are you jealous?" she asked.

"Of what? Your date? Joanie Moreau, how dare you."

She turned. "No, I mean it. This one's different." She and Graham had an open marriage. Their dalliances with others were always . . . casual. Not without some emotional connection, but that connection was always thin, like a spider's web. Beautiful in the right light, but easy to break. Here, it wasn't just that she liked Dan, though obviously she did. It was that their connection was not so tenuous. They'd taken each other's virginities, for fuck's sake. Admittedly, that kind of thing was granted way more importance in society than it deserved—but it wasn't nothing, either. They could not undo that connection if they tried.

"Why? Because you had a thing once? Jo, I am not worried. I am confident enough in myself and in us to know that we'll be fine." He clasped her hands. "And if we're not fine, you know what? That's fine, too. Marriage needn't be permanent. Nothing is permanent. We're led to believe that when a thing stops being what it's being, that means it failed—but *all* things stop being. Even if what we had together ended right here, right now, it would remain the greatest thing I've ever been a part of, and that will never change."

"You're too wise for me, Graham. Too wise and too good."

"I've been around the block and seen some things." He had. As a teenager his whole family—a family of six including him—died in a car crash, an accident that he miraculously survived with only a few broken bones. It had given him perspective on the impermanence of everything. "Besides, if you leave me for this apple farmer, I'll chop down his trees with the same ax I murdered him with."

"I'd expect nothing less." She threw a glance toward the far wall of their bedroom, beyond which lay their neighbor's house. "Any more from the jerk?"

"Prentiss? I see him over there in the kitchen window, just . . . staring at us." Graham's eye glimmered with delight. "He hates us, and I delight in it." He paused. "He's in a suit. Will he be at the dinner tonight?"

Joanie sighed. She hadn't thought about that. "Fuck. Probably."

"Fun times."

"A fucking delight." Through the jalousie windows beyond their bed, Joanie spied headlights headed toward the cul-de-sac. Pickup truck. Dan, probably. "I think that's my ride. You're good here?"

"I'm going to order japchae from the Korean place and watch a movie. A documentary, I think."

She kissed him sweetly. "Do wait up."

"You know I will."

FUCK IT, SHE THOUGHT, *I'M GOING TO BE GOOD TONIGHT.*

Emily couldn't believe that Meg had asked

(*told*)

her to come along tonight. Last couple weeks, since the night with the pho, since she met the strange man in the white suit, her time with Meg had continued to be—well, she wanted to say angry, or tense, but really, it was empty. Empty of love, acknowledgment, even communication. They were two people living in the same house, but not just as roommates—it was like the two of them existed in different alternate universes, and those universes would never cross over.

So when Meg said she had this dinner, was invited to be a member of this networking group officially, and she wanted Emily to go—

At first, Emily didn't know what to think. Was this a serious entreaty? Or was it just a kind of control? This was an old, white, somewhat conservative area. Big money, old and new. It was straight as a flagpole from which flew a way-too-big-obnoxious American flag. So the fact they were inviting Meg at all felt like a huge step. And that Meg wanted Emily to come—which would definitely throw their relationship into the faces of these straight white old bastards—felt good, too.

Meg wasn't exactly being cuddly about it, though, was she? She told Emily what to wear. How to act. Said she was to engage in conversation more as a listener than as a talker, which, according to Meg, "will be hard for you, I know, but I need you to get it together and keep it together." It felt rude. Like an attack. And Emily wanted to attack back. Hiss and swat and bite. *It will be hard for you, I know,* she thought, her spite laced with venom. But then she thought—

No.

Fuck it.

You're going to be good tonight.

Maybe she's trying.

Maybe that's what this is.

Maybe you should try, too.

So, that's where she landed. Emily was going to do her best. For tonight, she would be a very good wife. Maybe this would suffocate the flames that burned their bridge, and then they could finally move on to the work of repairing it.

"FUCK IT," DAN TOLD JOANIE, GRINNING. "I'M GOING TO BURN IT all down tonight."

They sat outside her house for a moment, engine idling. "Oh?" she asked.

"Yup. It's all right here." He patted the beat-to-hell leather satchel between them. "I've got in here all my plans for the orchard. Everything that's to come between now and next year's harvest and beyond. I'm going to whet their appetites, just like the apples themselves, and soon as

I have them smacking their lips and wiping away a little drool—I'm going to tell them no. No, I will not join your little club. The one that—"

(*drove my father to kill himself*)

"—wouldn't have my own father for a member, that used him like a dustpan before throwing him away with all the dirt."

She beamed. "Fuck 'em."

"Right? Fuck 'em."

"I can't wait to see the looks on their faces." Seemed Joanie didn't care for them any, either. She had good reason, way some of their kids treated her when they were young. Obviously she had money now, too. Had she ever been invited? Dan made a safe bet that no, not ever. "Their assholes are going to pucker up so tight, they might just seal shut forever."

"That would make them more full of shit than they already are, a feat I do not believe is entirely possible. But let's test it."

"Let's."

She put her hand on his knee. It stirred in him an urgency, a surge of warmth and desire and—no, more than just desire, it woke in him a dread *need.* But his heart crested and fell as he realized, she was married. This wasn't anything. And yet, he saw the look in her eyes as she watched him . . . there was a hunger there, too, a confident, controlled desperation.

"You're married, I know," he said, wetting his lips. He looked at her hand. "I don't want to get the wrong idea here—"

"It's an open marriage. Graham knows what I do, and I know what he does, and there's no turbulence there. It's big sky and clean air."

He reached across and kissed her, then. A fierce galaxies-colliding kind of kiss, their tongues finding each other, that inhaled gasp through the nostrils, that hard horse-kick of the heart as it got beating as if it had long been silent in the tomb of his chest. Her hand tightened on his knee. Rose up the thigh. Nails digging in, drawing down. There came a moment when he thought of her husband, sitting in that house, maybe watching them. Maybe *seeing* what was happening. Was he jealous? Would he be angry? Or did he not care? If he didn't care, he was a fool. And if he was jealous or angry—

Good, Dan thought. *Let him be.* A petty thought, he knew. But something darkly competitive stirred. *I don't want to share something so delicious as this.*

Joanie pressed her lips to his ear and whispered: "We're going to be late."

"Fuck it," he said, "I don't care."

"But I want to watch you burn it all down."

"You do, do you?"

She kissed his cheek. "I really do."

"And after that?"

"After that, I can demonstrate how much I enjoyed the show."

At that, Dan kissed her back, and put the truck in drive. If she wanted a show, he'd give her a show.

31

RING OF KEYS

THE GOLDENROD:

A 250-year-old crossroads inn sitting on a hundred-acre estate with a cobblestone drive and grand topiaries of flora and fowl. It was a stone beast, nearly a castle, a chaotic amalgam of Gothic and Byzantine styles, and it rose over the oaks and evergreens, its lantern-lit windows like the burning eyes of a judgmental god.

Inside, it had been readied for tomorrow's holiday—every table sat mounded with dried mums and garlands of copper leaf, all threaded through with bone-white deer antlers found over the years in the woods behind the inn and around the river. The tables themselves were the richest mahogany, inlaid with the strange tiles designed by the Goldenrod's forebear, Henry Hart Golden, a self-proclaimed "artisan polymath" who was simultaneously an inventor, an artifact collector, an explorer, and an artist. Many believed he was a visionary. (A few suspected him of being a cult leader.)

At the Goldenrod in the mid-to-late nineteenth century, he held "leadership summits" and "vision salons" that lasted for weeks on end. Those who attended were the corps d'elite of the region, and they often emerged from such summits and salons with a near-worshipful view of Golden, whom painter Chapman Poore said was "so inspiring, we felt above everything, even ourselves, and that there was nothing we could not do under his vigilant eye."

Golden's trademark tiles were small, four-by-four clay squares that ran through many collectible series, but his most notable series, and also the one that marked the tables inside the Goldenrod, were of his *American Fable* tileworks. Each was a single image, stamp-molded and glazed: the deer, the quail, the scythe, the water pitcher, the pyramid, the black swan, the wolf mask, and finally, the apple. When asked what they meant,

Golden said, "It is not for the artist to explain his art; it exists as its own justification." A phrase often said to applause from his acolytes.

Today, on the table, the placemats were red. The napkins, gold. The plates were white. And as the guests arrived, on each plate they discovered one thing:

A Ruby Slipper apple, polished to a black gleam.

IT WAS A SHOW, DAN KNEW. FOR HIM. THE APPLE WAS THERE TO both impress him and impress *upon* him that the invitation was special. He wanted to scoff at it, to hate it, because, what, they were showing off his own apple to him? And yet, he couldn't. It was too great a point of pride. That they appreciated it and put his own gift to the world on display for all their members old and new was . . . suitable.

EMILY HATED THIS. HATED, HATED, HATED IT. SHE AND MEG CAME in with about two dozen others, surrounded by a noise cloud of murmured talk punctuated by big boastful laughs. It was men, mostly, some with their wives and adult children. They were rich. They stank of bad cologne. Whiffs of cankerous cigar-mouth breath floated about. Everyone found their name placards and sat, and Emily regarded the apple on her plate with a raised eyebrow. Once upon a time, she and Meg would've shared that quizzical look and, under their breath, a gloriously petty comment ladled with a most vicious serving of snark. They would've been on the same team. But when she looked askance at the apple, she tossed a look to Meg—

Only to see Meg gazing upon the apple with something that surpassed satisfaction. It was like watching someone beautiful regard themselves in a mirror. *She's captivated.*

Emily watched as Meg picked the apple up, her eyes closed in soft bliss, before taking a hearty, front-toothed bite.

So did nearly everyone else.

And they did so . . . at the exact same time.

It seemed choreographed, somehow. The wet mouthy crunch of teeth-through-apple was performed in practiced unison, and it turned

Emily's stomach. She looked around the room. They were *all* doing it. Eyes closed. Heads up just a little. Frozen in that moment of savoring something together.

Emily remembered seeing a documentary once about strange foods, and in it, they spoke of ortolan buntings: tiny, vulnerable songbirds who were captured and put in limitless darkness, their response to which was to gorge themselves on seeds and grain, which doubled their size. The birds were then drowned in brandy, marinated in what killed them, and later roasted and eaten. When eating the sad little brandy-drowned birds, diners covered their heads with cloth so that God could not see their cruelty.

This, Emily thought, felt unsettlingly like that.

Only one other person in the room wasn't eating the apple.

Two tables away: a milk-cheeked redhead in a Jessica Rabbit dress. She, too, was looking around the room with growing consternation. When her eyes fell upon Emily's, it was they who shared the look—one of smirking detachment that did little to hide what was really underneath: a deep and mounting fear.

JESUS CHRIST, JOANIE THOUGHT. *LOOK AT THEM ALL.* GOD, THEY were really polishing Dan's knob with this. That was one of his apples, wasn't it? She turned to say something to him—but saw he was just like the rest of them. Lost to the apple. Juices running down his chin. She half expected that if she reached for his crotch right now, she'd find his cock hard as a rifle barrel. The moist chewing filling the room, the intake of breath, the gentle moaning . . .

It was a gluttonous orgy. Over some fruit. A fucking *apple.*

She looked around at the absurd display of it. Joanie wanted to laugh, but she also wanted to get the fuck up and run out of here. It was then she saw someone else in the room who wasn't partaking in the apple: a young woman, dark hair cradling her cherub cheeks, whose face wore a mask of worry. Joanie tried to make a funny face at her like, *Look at these assholes, huh?* And that seemed to help a little bit. But then Joanie's eyes moved past her, to someone else—

Prentiss Beckman. Sitting at the other end of the room. Apple in hand. Mouth open as he chewed sloppily. The others were lost to the moment, but he had his eyes wide open. And those eyes were pinned to her like thumbtacks. Staring at her. *Through* her. She knew that look. Loathing and lust, intermingled.

And then, the moment was over. Though everyone continued to eat their apples, they seemed to *snap* to awareness, their collective attention returning to the room as if they'd never left it at all. The head of the Crossed Keys, Claude Lambert, sat on the other side of her from Dan, and he said, "Not hungry?" while gesturing at the apple with an open hand.

"Just not my thing," she said.

Dan chuckled awkwardly, moving the apple off her plate and onto his. "Sorry, I didn't know," he said, and she swore he sounded embarrassed about it. Not embarrassed that he'd given her something she didn't want. But embarrassed *that* she didn't want it. Embarrassed *of* her, not *for* her.

A sudden lance of guilt shot through her. Just a couple weeks before, he'd given her a basket of apples that she took without saying a word. It felt oddly like a lie to have taken that gift from him.

Claude Lambert put a hand on her arm and said, "That's okay, Joanie. More for the rest of us, isn't that right, Dan?"

"SHE'S ALLERGIC," MEG SAID, BEFORE ANYBODY COULD EVEN ASK. Because they'd already been looking at Emily. Staring, in fact. Looking from her to the apple and back to her again, as if to say, *What's wrong with you, who let you in here, don't you appreciate what you have been given?*

THESE, THEN, WERE THE CROSSED KEYS. A DOZEN TABLES, ALL MEM-bers, but only some were legacy—Dan knew these older members well, having grown up around a number of them closely, what with his father working for Lambert at the vineyards. Sometimes Big Dan stayed on the vineyard grounds, because he had to watch for birds, bugs, and some-times frost. And when he did, Little Dan sometimes stayed with him, and met these men as they came and went.

Claude Lambert, of course. Sitting next to Joanie on the other side, a smug, self-satisfied look on his face, the kind of look Dan just wanted to hit with a thrown drink or, hell, one of his own apples. That'd bust his nose good.

Next table over: Edgar Beckman, the real estate king of Central Bucks, sitting back in his chair like an overfed lion even before dinner had started—Beethoven hair in every direction like a mad mane, relaxing and holding court at his table. Always the bard, that one. Selfish talker. Stories for days.

Then, Bill Cabot, construction. Cabot Homes was his company. Much as these men loved to talk about land preservation and restoring historical homes, Cabot himself was a builder of cheap but expensive cookie-cutter developments. He was the cranky sort, had a drill-sergeant vibe about him. Hair and mustache dyed black with shoe polish, because for as rich as he was, he was cheap as shit. Everybody talked around him, had their own conversations. He'd only chime in when he had something spectacularly awful to say, something racist or bigoted or generally shitty, something about the "Philly Blacks coming up here to carjack us," or the "skirt-wearing fruits down at the Blackbird," the Blackbird being a long-standing gay bar down in Coryell's Ferry.

To his left, at the next table, Fritzy Letts—the *artiste.* Ran a few galleries, owned the big Ferry Playhouse down by the river, sat on the Henry Hart Golden Preservation Society board. Less smuggish, more snobbish. Had a wine cellar famously stocked with wines from around the world, none of which, Dan knew, were from Lambert's vineyard. (Letts had taste.) Letts had been nipped and tucked too much. His skin looked tight as the top of a drum. It pulled all parts of him toward the back of his skull, like his mouth and eyes were a taut mask hooked around his ears. He, too, held court like Beckman, but in a different way: He feigned interest far better than the other man. Always leaning forward, listening, nodding, *hmm*ing along. It was, Dan figured, how he got so many young women to sleep with him. He faked interest until he was done with them, then whatever promises he'd made to them were kicked into a storm drain.

Finally, someone Dan didn't expect to see here: Judge Martin Hardiaken. Chase had said the cancer was bad, that the man wasn't doing well. But here he was. Looking good as ever—hell, better than he'd looked in years. He'd always had the sinister look of an owl staring down its beak at you, eyebrows and sideburns like raptor feathers, but now he sat up straighter, seemed to be smiling. His son, Chase, sat next to him, and he gave Dan a small nod and a raise of his old-fashioned.

At one point, Claude got up to mingle, at which point Joanie leaned over and said, sotto voce, "That apple thing, did you all coordinate that?"

"I don't understand," Dan said.

"You all—I mean, you saw it, right? You all went in for a bite at the same time. It was really something else, I just figured you were in on the gag."

"It wasn't a gag." He honestly didn't understand what she was even saying. Why would it be a gag? "I think they were trying to show me respect, is all."

He saw it in her eyes—a kind of, what, dismissal? A judgment? Joanie thought him naïve. Was he? "Sure," was all she said in response. "Of course."

Joanie tried to ignore it, that feeling crawling through her veins. Between Prentiss still looking over here and Dan just happy to have his apple polished, so to speak, she felt strangely and suddenly off-balance. All the clout in this room. All these men with their hands on the levers of local power. Terrible, petty men.

Get it together, Joanie, none of this matters. Especially not after Dan shuts them all down, tells them where they can shove it.

She just had to get through dinner.

Dinner, as it turned out, *was* worth waiting for—velvety sunchoke soup; oysters with roasted hen-of-the-woods mignonette and crispy shallots; foie gras with micro-arugula, pistachio crumble, and a tart cherry confiture; Lancaster beef rib-eye with tallow-roasted purple potatoes. And honestly, it did a *lot* to pave over the bumpy road of her bad feelings— good food and in this case a *killer* Manhattan did wonders. She even got into the steady flow of dumb, casual conversation—*oh, did you see they're doing work on 313, sure, they keep trying to put in a Whole Foods down where the old Kmart sits but the owners are the same people who own the Beamer dealership and they won't budge, hell yes, it was a good harvest this year, the Chambourcin was a marvel to be-hold, well, I tell you, if you've never been pheasant hunting, it's a real thrill, a real thrill—*

The conversation was like a cheap hot tub. Even though she knew if you stayed in it too long you'd end up with a yeast infection, it was warm and it was easy. Joanie didn't even need to really pay much attention. It was background sounds, a tumbling babble, white

(*supremacy*)

noise from rich men—since most of the women, like Lambert's wife Mary-Anne, barely spoke, and seemed to serve the purpose of laughing at all their bad jokes and self-involved stories.

And it would've kept going like that, too, Joanie figured. But then, as she was slicing through one of the last bits of rib-eye—

She looked up and saw Prentiss Beckman standing by their table.

Leaning forward. Staring at her with eyes like scuffed nickels.

"—truth is, this White House just needs to learn to stay out of people's business and better yet, to stay out of *business* period," Lambert was saying, "and just let the dollar decide where culture goes and what it does," but then he paused, seeing Prentiss there. "Prentiss, hello there, good to see you."

Prentiss stood there, gray-faced and dead-eyed. His pudgy hand tightly gripped a glass of something whiskey-colored. So hard, in fact, Joanie thought the glass might pop in his grip.

"Can't believe we let *trash* like this in here," he said, looking at Joanie.

And at that, everyone all around seemed to go quiet. Like they all could feel the vibe shift in the room. Dessert was served: fresh-baked drama, topped with the cherry of gossip.

"Prentiss," Claude warned. "You been drinking a bit, hmm."

"Claude, you don't get it. You know what she does? For a living?"

Dan stood up. "Hey now, whatever you're about to say—"

But Prentiss kept on: "She runs a whorehouse from that little hacienda of hers down in Fox Run. Lets people come in and do all sorts of nasty business to each other, and helps them *do it*, too—"

"It's just a rental home," she said, trying to laugh it off. Joanie was not one for embarrassment but the whole room was looking at them, now. She felt a bloom of heat rise to her cheeks same time as chills ran down her arms. She blinked and had a moment of feeling like she was surrounded by coyotes—beasts ready to pounce, tear the meat from her bones in red, messy clumps and clots. "People are allowed to do what they want in there, same as in any hotel room."

"She said she *fucks* her *husband* in the *ass*—"

"Beckman!" Claude barked, but not at Prentiss, no. He was looking now to the father, Edgar Beckman. "Come get your son, *right now.*"

"Bitch, you're not *welcome* here—" Prentiss hissed at her, reaching over the table with a greasy paw, like he was going to grab her, choke her— a plate of food crashed on the floor and with it went some of the center-piece work like antlers and a string of tin acorns. She backpedaled, nearly falling out of her chair, snatching up an antler with her free hand just in case she needed to stick him with it—

"*Stop,*" Dan said, the word spoken like the sound of an ax splitting wood. And at that, Prentiss stopped. The whole *room* seemed to stop. Prentiss eased away from the table, his stare gone from Joanie and now fixed on Dan. He averted his gaze, suddenly, looking at his shoes. Like he'd been slapped.

And then the room resumed in motion. Prentiss's piece-of-shit fa-ther hustled up behind and gave his plug-headed failson a hard shove, told him, "You're heading home, Prentiss, you've made a mess of things *like usual.*"

People asked Joanie if she was all right. She said she was fine, which was a lie. She felt rattled like a stack of teacups in an earthquake. But she blew it off, even made a joke about it, "Last time I was that drunk, I pissed in a potted plant—and they never let me back into Home Depot again." And that had everyone laughing, because these were old vulgar white men who didn't mind that she was a *broad* who could tell tales with the best of them, long as she didn't get too uppity and start demanding, oh, you know, bodily autonomy and equal pay. At that, they sat back down and the room resumed its low hum of chatter, and the *tink*-and-*clink* of forks on plates and wedding rings against glasses. Edgar Beckman came back into the room, his face wearing the tumult of a stormy mood until he crossed an invisible threshold, then his true face fell behind the bard's boastful mask. Big smile, arms wide, yawping something about *when's dessert.*

Dan asked her again if she was okay, and she said she was.

She said, "Thanks for sticking up for me."

"He had no right talking to you like that. I hope they kick him out of this group, to be honest."

"Maybe they will." She dropped her voice even lower and said, "But that won't matter for you."

"Of course," Dan answered. But suddenly she wasn't so sure. And when Claude Lambert leaned over and said to her (but also, she thought, with Dan as the audience, too):

"You're married, Joanie, are you not?"

"I am. Eleven years now."

"Mm. Congratulations." Jokingly, but also not jokingly at all, he said, "I hope he doesn't mind you coming here and being with Dan."

"I'm free to come and go as I please," she answered sweetly.

Lambert burst out laughing. "'Come and go as I please,'" he said, repeating her words. "You're like a firecracker held in a closed hand, Joanie Moreau. 'Come and go as I please.' I like that."

"Speaking of which," she said, forcing the smile to stay on her face, "if you don't mind, I need a moment for the little cowgirls' room. Be back in a stitch."

EMILY SAW HER GET UP AND LEAVE. THE REDHEAD. AFTER THAT show . . . she'd seen the thick-necked idiot get up, the alcohol vapors practically bleeding off him like steam from a boiling kettle, and the room leaned in, eager and hungry, ready to watch the show. Then that guy, Dan, he told him to *stop,* and the whole room seemed to flinch at the same time. Like he was talking to all of them. Then, soon as that drunk prick was taken out of the room, everyone continued chatting like nothing ever happened.

So, when Emily saw the redhead get up and head to the bathroom—

She excused herself—earning a flash of irritation from Meg—and hurried toward the restrooms as well.

DAN SAT. HIS HEART POUNDED IN HIS THROAT, HIS LIPS, HIS FIN-gertips. He felt eerily exhilarated. He felt *powerful.* It was the strangest thing. Prentiss Beckman, that piece-of-shit, came over and disrespected Joanie and—

With one word, Dan shut him down, sent him packing. Beckman looked, what? Chastened? Shameful? Crushed into a powder. It was like that one barked word was the extension of his will. A hand to reach down into the man's chest and seize his heart and squeeze it until it stopped.

Claude looked over at him. "Joanie is something. You putting it to her?"

"It's not like that," he said, half embarrassed, half angry at the question. But a serpent of desire slithered through his grass just the same.

"Sure, of course, Dan. Of course." But the look on Lambert's face— the face of a salacious old goat—was a knowing one. He looked like he was about to say something else, but here came two of the old Keys— Edgar Beckman and the Judge. Judge Hardiaken spoke first, cutting off Beckman:

"Little Dan, I always took you for a stripling. A knock-kneed watered-down version of your father. But I see now that I was wrong. You've done something special with that apple of yours. Real, real special."

At that, Chase came up behind him, saying, "The Judge is healthier than he's been in years, Dan. They say the cancer is in full retreat."

"Not just retreat. But gone. A ghost. Like it was never there."

Lots of nods, and claps on the Judge's sharp-angled shoulders. A kind of grim camaraderie. They were all getting older. Death would have them sooner than later. Beating cancer was a badge to them. A battle scar.

"I'm sure glad to hear it, Judge," Dan said, trying to hide the bitterness that it was this very man who made the judgment that took his father's house and property away from him in the first place. A surge of hatred burned in his chest like stomach acid. "My apples *are* something special."

"And you're special for bringing them to us. I only wish my son had something of his own to achieve."

"Father—!" Chase blurted out, clearly stung, but trying to smile and pretend it was just a joke. "I've accomplished . . . considerable things." To Dan he said, "I'm the one bringing in the other new member—Meg

Price, a lawyer at the firm." He called over to her. "Meg, why don't you come over here—"

As that woman, Meg, tied off the conversation she was having to come over, Edgar Beckman stepped forward, like he, too, was eager for an audience with Dan. "Little Dan, I just wanted to say—"

"Just Dan. My father was Big Dan. But I'm not a kid anymore, as evidenced by your invite into this organization."

Edgar appeared doubly humbled—an odd, even impossible look for him. Dan wasn't sure he'd *ever* seen that boastful old bastard look anything other than resplendent in his stink. "Of course. I wanted to apologize for my son. He has no right to speak to your woman that way, to interrupt this meal and these proceedings. He's a pathetic waste of the Beckman name."

"Well," Dan said, "it's clear he's having some difficulties and I hope he gets the help he needs."

"I hope he wraps his Porsche around a telephone pole and spares me his presence in my remaining days on this planet."

Jesus, Dan thought. He struggled to find the words to answer that, when Chase was suddenly at his elbow with Meg Price. And it wasn't just her. Others had gathered, too. Gotten up from their tables, steak half eaten, to have an audience with him. Meg had a sharp grin on her face as she reached out and shook his hand.

"Those apples of yours," she said, Her eyes gleamed, wet. "They're different. You know that, don't you? You do. I can tell that you do. My wife, she doesn't understand. But all of you here . . . you do."

Agreement arose in a babbled murmur all around. Nods and wide eyes. Hands wringing. Shared smiles. *We do, we do,* they agreed.

"Thank you," Dan said. He meant it. But it also scared him. The pressure of it. All these influential people. Loving his apple. Excited to meet *him*. This wasn't his life. Dan had always done fine, been fine, nothing exciting, nothing exceptional, but the way they looked at him, gosh—

Soon, he'd crush their spirits.

He tried to remind himself why. Claude, looking at him all smug, like he owned him somehow. Judge Hardiaken, chest puffed out, once having robbed Dan for a time of his own future. Beckman, with his bully son. The way that all these men had pretended to be his father's friend, then abused his trust and used him up and down for their needs—but when it came time for his needs, they dismissed him, destroyed him. He just wanted to be a part of this very group. To dine with kings, even if he could never be one of them. It would've been Dad's great honor to be sitting here tonight, feted with a dinner. And Dan was just planning to burn it all down. All because he wanted to

(*spite*)

avenge the old man.

He grabbed the leather satchel, the one containing his dreams, his plans for the orchard. The ones he was going to show them before telling them all to go fuck themselves sideways. Dan clutched it to his chest, then hurriedly set it down on his chair before saying suddenly, "I'm going to go check on Joanie, if you'll all excuse me." He swallowed a hard knot and headed off to find her.

"Hey," Emily said to the redhead standing at the bathroom sink, touching up her makeup in the mirror.

The woman gave her an irritated, frazzled look before seeming to realize who she was. "Oh. It's you."

"Uh. Yeah. I'm Emily."

"Joanie Moreau." The redhead popped her lips together, then capped the tube of lipstick and put it in her clutch. "Can I help you? You were staring at me."

"Was I?" *Shit.* "Sorry. I, ahh. I noticed—well. I just wanted to say, it sucks the way that asshole talked to you."

"Yeah. Well. I'm used to it with these people."

"I don't know that we should ever get used to that kind of behavior."

Joanie paused. Her shoulders jiggled with a small, dark chuckle. "No, I guess not. But the things we put up with, huh?"

"Yeah. *Yeah.*" Emily shuffled nervously from foot to foot. "Hey, so, it's pretty fucking weird out there. And you're the only other person who doesn't seem . . ."

"Like they're in a cult."

"That's it. That's it exactly. A cult that isn't a cult."

"Groups like these are always culty, honey. Small-town attitudes, old-money power, a little bit of British incest from Ye Olden Days." Joanie seemed to wave it off. But at the same time, Emily sensed an undercurrent of fear. The redhead had been rattled. And Emily suspected she was not an easily rattled person.

Joanie said to enjoy dessert, then hurried out of the bathroom. Emily followed after, wanting to keep talking to her—she didn't know why, maybe it was just having someone near to her that didn't think she was crazy, or a bother, or just plain weird. Or hell, someone who had also committed the (apparently) cardinal sin of not eating a stupid apple. This whole dinner, people barely looked at her. Like they didn't want to acknowledge her existence. She felt like a ghost. Even Meg treated her like a presence, not a person. But when she followed Joanie out—

Her date, Dan the Apple Man, almost ran into them. He seemed startled.

"Oh, hey—" he said.

Joanie greeted him with a chaste cheek-kiss. Emily stood there like an awkward trespasser. "Sorry, hi, I—oh, uh, I'll leave you two alone." Embarrassed, she hurried off, back toward the tables, wishing she could run past them and jump out the fucking window, instead.

"YOU OKAY?" DAN ASKED JOANIE. SHE SAID SHE WAS. IT WAS A LIE. Throughout the night she'd felt like a speeding car driving down a fucked-up road, with each bump throwing off parts into the ditch. Couldn't even pinpoint why, not really—she was usually unshakable. And yet here she was, shaken.

Dan looked over his shoulder. "What was that about?"

"What?"

"The woman."

She forced a smile. "Just . . . a friendly chat." Scrambling for composure, Joanie said, "I think she's the wife of that . . . other woman."

Dan blinked. Like something had just dawned on him. Something not good.

"My turn to ask," she said. "You okay?"

His smile was strange, though. His mouth smiled, but his eyes did not.

"I'm fine. Let's get back to the table."

THAT'S WHO SHE IS, DAN THOUGHT. HE HADN'T EVEN REALIZED IT.

He'd seen her that day in the café, with Chase.

She was the one who found the body in the river.

EMILY DIDN'T WANT TO GO BACK, BUT WHAT CHOICE DID SHE HAVE? So she walked fast, making a beeline. She thought to head right to their table, even though Meg and the others had all gotten up. Dessert hadn't even hit the plate yet, but there was a lot of mingling and chatting. And here Emily reminded herself: *You're the good wife tonight, so go and be on her arm, smile, shut the fuck up, and hope she's nice to you when you get home.*

So that's what she did. She sidled up next to Meg, slid her arm through hers, and got close

(*but not too close*)

and listened in on what everyone was saying, thinking she'd have to feign interest, but they were talking about apples. Dan's apples.

—*they're new, something never seen before*—

—*no no I think he made them, crossbred them, genetically or some such*—

—*Claude, didn't you say you're going to put them in grocery stores?*—

—*they are Heaven-sent, I've never felt as good, honestly, no, honestly!*—

—*I started eating the apples and my eczema cleared up*—

—*that's nothing compared with what it did to your cancer, right, Judge?*—

And as they were talking, droning on about these stupid apples, Emily's gaze drifted downward, to the empty chair where Dan had been sitting. In his place was a bag—a satchel, like a laptop bag, but older, from before there were laptops. Brown, faded leather. Scratched up. Circles were imprinted upon it, several of them overlapping, and it took her a second to realize—

They were coffee stains.

(*Walt always set his coffee on top of it, and it left rings*)

And it's like the words just fell out of her mouth—

"That's Walt's bag."

From behind her, a response:

"What did you say?"

Her blood went cold.

She turned, saw Dan standing right behind her.

"I—" She felt the words catch in her throat like a strangled bird. "I said I'm not feeling well, and I have to go."

And with that, she disengaged from Meg, pushed past Dan and Joanie, and headed for the door, fumbling with her phone the whole way, trying like hell to find the rideshare app while knowing the whole room was staring at her. Emily didn't even hazard a glance over her shoulder to see. But all the while she was chased by the realization:

Dan Paxson killed Walt.

32

THE DECISION

DAN WATCHED HER GO. THE WORDS, *HER* WORDS, HANGING IN THE air like a heavy stillness—*That's Walt's bag.* Walt. He'd purposefully, willfully not thought up the man's name, lest it be like a conjuring spell somehow. He thought to follow the woman, to grab her, to ask her what she said, why she said it, how she knew Walt, how she knew his bag. He thought to tell her, *No, you don't understand, it's not like that, you don't know what happened that night,* and in his mind he imagined her panicking, disagreeing, and he further imagined him wrapping his hands slowly around her throat, fingers coiled around the girl's neck as his grip closed and he crushed her windpipe like the cardboard tube at the center of a roll of paper towels. He shuddered. Nearly cried out. Wanted to throw up. *That's not who you are, Dan, get it together.* He gritted his teeth and pushed the thought out of his mind.

Again Joanie asked, "You sure you're all right?"

And he found himself nodding, saying sure, sure, he was fine, just a little dizzy was all. Then he reached for his

(*Walt's*)

satchel and wondered, how? How had he forgotten to whom it belonged? And why did he bring it here? An act of a guilty conscience, buried deep within himself like a mole inside an organization, a saboteur who hid the identity of the owner of the bag, who had convinced Dan without a second thought that the satchel belonged to him, not to the

(*dead*)

man named Walt. *They say murderers want to get caught,* he thought.

But I'm not a murderer, he told himself.

It was just an accident.

Wasn't it?

Suddenly Claude's hand was on his elbow, asking him what he had to show them. Meg was at his other side, sliding in between him and Joanie, saying how sorry she was for her wife, she didn't know what that was about, "she's been feeling out of sorts lately, you know how it is."

He heard himself telling her, "It's fine, I understand," but in the back of his head, panic scrabbled up the inside of his skull like a nest of stirred spiders, because if that woman thought she knew what happened, she could hurt him. Could bring the police to his door. He could be in trouble and all of this, the orchard, the apple, his daughter's future, his father's dream, *all* that he had

(*killed*)

worked for, would come crashing down on his head.

And it was then that he knew. Even as he plastered a smile on his face and took out the plans for the orchard—more clear-cutting thicket, more trees planted and grafted, a cider house, a market stand, a logo, a label, a local grocery expansion so that they didn't need the little podunk farmers markets anymore—he knew where this was going. The Crossed Keys stood around, nodding, smiling, hanging on his every word. These people who had betrayed his father, who had their hands firmly around the neck of this county, were suddenly invested in *him,* in what he had to *say,* in his *success,* and when he said the words out loud—

"I gladly accept the invitation to join this organization."

—he could feel Joanie's gaze boring holes in the back of his head. And when he turned to look at her, wearing an apologetic smile, he saw the look of betrayal on her face. It burned like a house on fire. He could feel its heat, and wanted to leap into that conflagration as an act of penance, and when she turned and walked away, leaving the same way that woman Emily had left, he wanted to go after her. He wanted to plead with her. To make her understand. To tell her, *I need this. I may need their influence, their protection. You don't understand what I had to do to get here, and this is what I have to do to stay here. This is what my father would've wanted. This would make him proud.* And suddenly this small feeling of shame inside him vanished, replaced by a surge of incredulity and anger at Joanie, because how dare she judge, how dare she leave him at this moment, how *dare* she not see what this meant for him.

He did not follow her, but instead turned back toward those who welcomed him into their world.

EMILY'S HANDS WERE SHAKING SO HARD IT TOOK HER A WHILE TO even open the Lyft app to get a car—and even then, because they were out in the sticks, it would be a fifteen-minute wait, so there she stood, out front of this grand estate, wishing for a cigarette even though she hadn't smoked one since college.

The night was cold and though she'd managed to rescue her jacket from the coat check, it seemed to do little to stave off the chill. It went deep, down to the blood in her veins, down to the marrow. She paced back and forth, earning the concerned stare of the mop-headed kid working the valet stand. He told her she could wait inside, but she said— really, snapped—that she was fine, *thankyouverymuch.* Mostly, she just didn't want to go back into that place. It felt like a trap. A house of torment, a place of poison.

And in there was a man she feared was a murderer.

If he killed Walt—

And she found out—

What would he do to *her*?

Eventually, the car pulled up—a years-old Prius. Male driver, which Emily would normally not accept, because here she was, a lone woman out in the middle of nowhere, lotta fields and forests around. So many fun places to dump a body.

Like in a river, she thought, darkly.

As she headed to the car, she heard the door open behind her, and for a tiny moment she hoped it was Meg. Meg, come to save her. Come to apologize. But it was the redhead. Joanie.

"Wait up," Joanie said.

"What?" Emily asked, not meaning to sound annoyed but, well.

"Lemme ride with. I'll pay for it."

Emily hesitated. She wanted to be alone but—well, again, lone woman in a rideshare, not smart. Already she peered into the car, saw the dark shape of a man's face staring back at her, looking annoyed.

"Fine, yeah, sure," she said, acquiescing.

IN THE CAR. OVER-DEODORIZED, SMELLING LIKE SOMEONE HAD jackhammered a Glade PlugIn up her fucking nose. The driver was young, white, looked to her like some incel school shooter type, what with the dead eyes and mumbled greeting. *You're being a judgmental bitch,* she thought, but fuck it, the world was horrible and it was best to start treating it that way.

"So, what's your problem?" Joanie asked, staring.

"I don't have a problem," Emily said, voice small and bitter. She just wanted to sit in silence and get home. *Home.* A place that didn't feel like home at all. Still, once there, she could call John, and would wait for Meg to come back. *Shit, Meg.* Emily had planned on being the good wife, just once, at least for tonight, and she couldn't even manage that. Christ, she was a fuckup.

"You saw something and you bailed."

"I dunno. You bailed, too. What's *your* damage?"

Joanie hesitated. Like maybe she was annoyed at the cross-interrogation. But then she sighed and said, "Someone turned out to be a different person than I thought they were, and so I'm feeling a little pissy about that."

"You mean your date. *Dan.*" She didn't mean to say his name like that, *Dannnn,* all snooty and shitty, but there it was. Besides, it was possible this woman was here to cover for him. To find out what she knew. To report back.

"Yeah. I mean him."

"Sorry you . . ." *Fell for his ruse* were the words she didn't say. "Felt like he was something other than you got."

"Yeah, well. He was a nice guy in high school."

"Nice guys are overrated. Nice girls, too. They're never as nice as they pretend to be."

Joanie snorted. "You're not wrong about that. Gimme someone who's a *little bit* of a dick. Not a total dick. But enough to be confident."

"Yeah, maybe." Emily liked Joanie, but she tired of this conversation. She just wanted to curl in on herself.

"So, what was it?"

"What?"

"The thing that made you leave."

This again. She's probing. "Just tired is all."

"I walked up with Dan. You were . . . looking at something. Whatever you saw, and whatever you said, it rattled you, but rattled him, too." Joanie was picking at the edges of something Emily did not want her to pick at. Even if she could trust this woman, then what? *Hey, I think your date killed a guy. Sorry, driver guy, plug your ears if you don't want to hear this.*

"It's private. Relationship stuff with my wife." A lie. Sort of.

"All right, fine, don't tell me." A whiff of irritation.

Emily didn't say anything more after that. Joanie didn't either, not until the driver pulled up to Emily's house.

As Emily went to get out, Joanie caught her elbow.

"Hey," Joanie said. "I don't know why I'm saying this, exactly, but you can trust me. I know this area isn't the friendliest place. But I can be a friend."

"I don't need a friend," Emily heard herself saying. A cold, defensive comment, but really, what did she have in common with this woman? The redhead was rich, aloof, made those old bastards bray like drunken donkeys at her jokes. *You can trust me,* the woman said. Yeah, right.

"Well, fuck you, too," she heard Joanie mumble.

Jesus, am I really doing this?

"Fine," Emily said, handing Joanie her screen-unlocked phone. "Put your contact information in there. In case I decide I need a quote-unquote friend."

"You're a real peach," Joanie said, but then held out the phone and, with one long fake nail at a time, tapped her information in before handing the phone back.

"See ya," Emily said abruptly, slamming the Prius door and heading inside.

———

SHE TRIED CALLING JOHN.

It rang and rang and rang.

Finally, he answered. "Emily," he said.

No time for pleasantries. She blurted it right out.

"I think I know who killed Walt. And I think he knows that I know."

"Shit."

"Yeah, shit."

34

THE MASKS OF THE GOLDENROD

END OF THE NIGHT. DESSERT GONE. BRANDY AND WHISKEY abounded. Dan felt heady, like he was on a carousel ride going faster and faster, and he had to hold on tight lest the whirling wooden horses throw him off, into the dirt. Dizzying as thoughts whipped between terrified—*that woman knew it was Walt's bag*—and elated that he felt a part of something now. Something he'd long deserved. Something that had been kept from his father.

Kept from him by these men, he thought.

But maybe this is them recognizing their mistake.

That's what this was, he decided. Them rectifying a grave error.

They were powerful people. They could protect him. Whatever this woman thought he'd done—they would shield him. He felt it in his bones.

Nothing can stop me now, he decided.

AS THE NIGHT WENT ON, MORE OF THE GUESTS PEELED AWAY, AND at midnight, Lambert sent the rest home—all but a core group, the *inner circle* of the Crossed Keys. It was the five founders: Lambert, Hardiaken, Letts, Beckman, and Cabot. It was Dan and Meg. There were others, too: five other members, as the founders each got to choose someone to remain behind for what Lambert said was the "signing of the contract." It was Scott Horsley, owner of Horsley Construction, also Beckman's nephew; Tom Porter, who owned Tom Porter Toyota and was brought by Fritzy Letts; Spencer van der Weil, Bill Cabot's brother-in-law, a local restaurateur; Chase Hardiaken, Dan's old friend and son of the Judge; and finally, the head of the farmers market association and also an area landowner, Newt Bell, one of Lambert's oldest friends. These people were all movers and shakers around here. *Power nested in power,* Dan thought. Expanding out in ripples, ripples connecting to other ripples, manifesting as a matrix of money, authority, and influence. Local, yes, but it went beyond that, too—some of these men were involved with or ran big political PACs, were frequent donors to and guests of DC elites on both sides of the aisle, had friends or relatives in industries from Big Pharma to Big Ag to various banking institutions and hedge funds. They had connections to companies in China, too, and the Middle East, and to farms in South America. The ripples that started here reached far-flung shores.

And they want me, Dan thought. Basking in the glow of it.

Lambert told everyone to grab their drinks and come with him.

Dan shared a look with Meg, the kind of look that said, *Wonder where this adventure is taking us now.* The look on her face made it clear that she shared his excitement and trepidation, and also that she, like Dan, didn't care that they had been abandoned by those they brought. Together they silently put those people aside.

And with Lambert, they went.

UPSTAIRS WAITED A MONSTROUS WOODEN DOOR THAT REQUIRED a comically large iron key to open. Lambert opened it wide—

Inside, a grand display room. Broad, airy, a lingering scent like an old library or museum.

Lambert said, "This was one of HHG's private collection rooms." HHG, meaning Henry Hart Golden. "He was a man of antiquity, as you well know. Entrepreneur, yes, but also: artist, explorer, archaeologist." All around this broad, expansive room were the expected sights: a suit of armor in the corner, several collections of Golden's tilework, countless bookcases, a table laid with old colonial-era tools (including, he noted, a very old apple peeler).

But it was the back wall of the room that drew Dan's gaze. And the gaze of all who gathered. How could you possibly look away?

The massive wall, twelve feet high, three times that long, showed a wall of masks. Each mask, hanging about ten inches from its neighbors, was different. They were like nothing Dan had ever seen before. One appeared to be made of broken pottery shards, wired together, leaving only small, fractured apertures for the wearer's eyes. Another was made of arrowheads, also delicately fixed to one another, this time with loops of thick red thread. A third mask was feathers, not from one bird, but from many—pheasant, vulture, peacock, a red feather, a blue. Each seemed to be made from something: antlers, or strips of American flag, or animal teeth, or horseshoes. One mask was old forks and spoons, hammered together, the tines splayed out to open the way for a person to look out. Another was a curtain of typewriter keys.

"The Masks of Golden's America," Fritzy Letts said theatrically, with a shallow kind of awe—an awe performed, Dan thought. "A true artist and visionary, he and the members of his society created these masks out of the artifacts of the world around them. They wore them as a way to become someone different during their celebrations—a kind of *ritual masquerade*."

"You may each choose your mask for the night's remaining activity," Lambert said with a small chuckle.

"What activity is that?" Dan asked, fear and excitement rising in him.

"No questions," Cabot barked, standing on a ladder and unlocking the big glass-door cabinets that opened the way to the masks. He reached out and took a long iron pole with a hook on the end of it—and used it to loop around the back of chosen masks so he could deliver them to those who asked. Dan didn't understand what was happening, and the whiskey haze left him feeling a bit dizzy and confused. Meg, for her part, was all in, no hesitation, selecting a mask that was essentially a curtain of fountain pen nibs bound together. She held it up for Dan in excitement. Each silver nib was intricate, marked with elaborate scrollwork. The mask clicked and hissed as she moved it and hovered it over her face. It had eyeholes, but no space for her mouth.

"Why'd you choose that one?" he asked her.

"It felt . . . right. Which one will you choose?"

"Little Dan," Lambert said, interrupting. "Ah, sorry, I mean—*Dan*. I believe your mask has chosen *you*. If you'll consider it."

Dan nodded, and in a quiet voice said, "Sure, Claude."

Cabot looked to Lambert, got the nod, and went down to the third case, hooking a mask made of what Dan thought might be some kind of dried, twisted leather. It was scrunched up and rust-red, all the mismatched bits and swatches stitched together with what looked like leather cord. Lambert took the mask from Cabot and then held it out for Dan, carefully watching to see what his reaction might be. Dan reached out and took the mask—the skin of it felt eerily smooth, crinkly between his fingers, but also as if there were some kind of oil upon it, or exuded by it. In that moment, his heart raced. A strange smell rose to his nostrils, an old floral scent, those esters twisted by time but present nevertheless. He knew it then:

"This is appleskin," he said.

Lambert's grin grew wide. "I knew you'd know."

"Skin from many apples," Letts said, swanning over and craning his neck over the mask in Dan's hand. "Stitched together with cord of cat gut. We know this because Golden cataloged all his artifacts, and all his art. Tiles, masks, tools. You name it, he gave it a number and put it in his books." He pointed to the many bookshelves in the room—Dan realized now those shelves contained only Golden's catalogs and journals.

As he held the mask in his hand, he felt something in it. Something throb at his fingertips like a heartbeat that was not his own.

By now, everyone had chosen their strange masks of pottery and parchment and bone, and Lambert took his own from Cabot: a blunt, thick mask of wine-stained cask wood edged with cork and wire.

Donning it, Lambert asked Cabot: "Are they ready in the meadow?"

"Been ready," Cabot said, sounding perpetually irritated.

"Then let's take a ride," Lambert said.

THE RIDE, THEY TOOK IN GOLF CARTS. NICE ONES, BRAND NEW, branded with the Goldenrod logo. They piled into half a dozen of them. Cabot, in his own mask of shattered tile, oddly grinning, drove the lead cart. The rest of the cart armada followed behind, leaving the glow of the strange almost-castle and winding down through bare trees, the carpet of drying leaves hissing and cackling under the tires. Dan sat with Meg, who drove their cart with a joy that was easy to see. Neither of them had put on their own masks yet. Only the older Crossed Keys were wearing theirs.

As the autumn-bare trees grew sparse, the forest thinning, the carts pulled out onto a mowed strip in front of a dry, brown meadow—the brittle grasses sagging, slumping forward as if depressed at the coming winter, a winter that would soon turn them to rot and mush.

In the center of the meadow, someone stood illuminated by the moon. A tall shape holding a long rope. Dark shapes stirred at his side. Somewhere out in the night, a screech owl cried, cursing the dark with its demonic whinny.

As everyone got out of their carts, Lambert was already standing up on the broad stump of what looked to once belong to an old buttonwood tree. He began to speak as Cabot walked around, handing out something—

When he got to Dan, he handed him a moon-curved sickle. Whetted sharp. Some ended up with sickles, and others, like Meg, were given knives—sharp, fixed-blade hunting knives. Dark and gleaming.

Lambert was speaking, saying in a big, booming voice: "And so we come to the time of the year when we embrace new membership, extending our network and deepening our connections to our friends, our partners, our cohorts, and our blood—and in that, we give thanks to the earth, to the dirt, to the rich and loamy soil, gracious for the fortunes it has provided to us. It was Henry Hart Golden who began this tradition, once a springtime rite but just as our group has transformed over the decades, so too has this ritual changed—now we perform it as an act of gratitude at Thanksgiving. We honor the sharp tools held tight in our hands. We honor the dirt and clay beneath us. We honor our progenitor, Henry Hart Golden. But above all else, we honor ourselves. And we remind each other tonight that it is the *red* that makes the *green*."

Applause broke out, and Dan didn't understand why, exactly, but he went with it, tucking the sickle under his arm and applauding, too.

Cabot called out: "If you have not put them on, it is the time for your masks. You may don them now."

Meg looked to Dan, and he saw the moonlight in her eyes dancing there alongside sprites of excitement. He helped her put her mask on— the chain went over her ears and he fixed the clasp behind her head. His own mask required no help. In his hands, it just made sense how to put it on. Chin in first, then he pulled it tight over the top of his head. That apple smell hit him—

His head tingled all over and vertigo spun his mind like a top. He felt something new in his hand—the sickle, gone. Now: pruning shears. He smelled blood. Heard a young woman cry out. Felt dirt at his bare feet, even though his feet were not bare at all. His tongue tasted the ragged mouth slit in the appleskin mask, and it filled him with a paroxysm of power and pleasure that nearly dropped him to his knees.

It was then he realized:

It's my apple.

This mask is made from my apple.

Harrowsblack—

Vinot's—

Ruby Slipper—

Whoever made this mask had known the apple.

And now it was his. A natural inheritance. Cosmic serendipity.

He wanted to laugh. He felt good. No. He felt *amazing*.

At that, Cabot whistled loud—*fweet.*

Spotlights came on—three on each side of the massive meadow.

In the center now, they saw someone in a white robe and a mask made from the blade of an old shovel.

A single rope led from this person's hand—

Connecting to the neck of a young calf.

Now Letts in his typewriter-key mask walked around, handing out white robes, too. As he walked, his mask shushed and clicked like the strands of a beaded curtain. The robes he handed out were made of spare, threadbare fabric. Rough to the touch, like burlap. Cabot spoke as he trailed Letts, saying, "Gather around. We go into the field now. We plunge our blades into the beast. We butcher it here in the dying grass and the dead flowers. We wet the ground with blood so that all may be renewed. Our favor, our fortune, our fertile ground. That is the contract."

Lambert whooped: "Let the Ambarvalia begin!"

LATER, THE CALF DEAD, ITS BLEATS STILL TRAPPED IN DAN'S EARS. The others were around in the firelit dark, sipping brandy, smoking cigars, admiring one another's masks. Cabot was collecting the bloodied blades as the calf's ragged, vented body lay nearby, steaming in the moonlight.

Again, that carousel feeling.

Around and around. The mask on his face, appleskin, his apple. As he had cut the calf's throat, ending its cries, he'd felt like he was in some other era, this time chasing young animals through the field and forest—a lamb, a piglet, another calf. He'd felt himself eating an apple while lying on a bed under the stars, someone going down on him there in the dark. He smelled fresh blood and churned earth and could detect the vibration of a saw up his wrist and into his elbow as he cut into something that was soft at first, then hard as bone. And then he was back here again.

The mask pulsed at its margins. Tightening on his face as if it were convulsing with deepest satisfaction.

But then, back in it, the calf falling to the ground, that's when the illusion broke for him. When he stepped into the field with the others, he felt for a moment like he was part of something greater than himself. Like he *belonged.* Here was this rite, this ceremony from way back when, something these people had been doing forever, that Henry Hart Golden had asked that they do. A ritual that perhaps he had himself learned from ancient peoples in his expeditions and excavations—a tradition of mystery and magic. And Dan was a part of it. Part of something special. This moment of connection between himself and, what, exactly? The sublime. The divine. *The eternal earth.*

But then, somewhere, somehow—

Watching these people dash toward the calf—

Swinging sickles—

Sticking their knives in—

It was just theater.

He felt . . .

Foolish.

For Dan, it did two things:

First, it reminded him that magic *was* in fact real, that it was in his apple and in this apple mask, that it was in his orchard, and that it was very much *not* here in this field. This was a crass facsimile. A rite, yes. A ritual, sure. But toothless. Empty as so many ceremonies were. It wasn't even at the right time. Lambert had said it was a springtime rite, but what was this? Nothing was growing. All was slumbering. This was just a show. A hollow tradition, like so many traditions became.

Second, it told him that he was not in fact partaking in something greater than himself. *He* was in fact greater than this. Greater than these people. He felt foolish because he had lowered himself to be in this moment. This costumed buffoonery, this butcher's field bullshit. He was not improved by joining. They were improved by *him* joining. So be it. That's how it was, then. He could use them. Could be a part of them. They would serve him, not the reverse.

I am what matters.

Me.

My apple.

My orchard.

And if that woman, Emily, thought to bring accusations to his doorstep, he had these people to fix it. They wanted his apple. They *needed* his apple. Which meant they would serve him accordingly. His anxieties melted away, suddenly.

"You okay?"

Meg. She stood in front of him. He hadn't noticed.

"Lost in thought," he said.

"What are you thinking about?"

It was an earnest question. She really wanted to know. She watched him not warily, but without any caution. In her eyes were interest and adoration.

"How the red makes the green," he said. Blood on grass. A bird speared on an apple tree branch. A cat supping on a raccoon's guts.

"I'll meditate on that, too," Meg said.

The carousel kept spinning. The haze of smoke, the brandied breath, the opiate scent of appleskin in his nose. But now it felt different. He was no longer on the outside of the carousel, riding and spinning 'round and 'round. No. He was the axis around which it spun.

35

A CABAL OF DOMESTIC CONSPIRATORS

THANKSGIVING WAS A CORNY, STUPID, DUMB, HYPER-AMERICAN, super-colonizery, gluttonous pig of a holiday, and Calla loved every minute of it every year. She would not admit to this, same as she wouldn't admit that her father was probably her best friend in the whole world, because telling her father—who *loved loved loved* Turkey Day—that she loved it too would only give him too much power in this world, and *that* she would not abide. She *especially* wouldn't tell him that the reason she loved it so much was because *he* loved it so much. He would gloat about it forever. He would emblazon his gravestone with it. *Here lies Dan Paxson, whose daughter loved Thanksgiving as much as he loved Thanksgiving because she was Daddy's Little Girl and loved what Daddy loved, RIP.*

Every year, they spent the holiday together, just the two of them, and she always played the role of sarcastic, eye-rolly daughter who mocked her father's judicious obsession over getting the mashed potatoes just the right texture and his compulsion to constantly check the turkey, which only made the turkey have to stay in the oven even longer. They had their other, more proper traditions, too: making a wish by snapping the wishbone; watching A Football Game despite neither of them really having much understanding what was happening in football or why it was so interminably *sloooooow;* and taking a nap on the couch usually right in the middle of said Football Game, just before they gorged themselves on too much dessert. (Dessert was pecan pie, always and forever, because pumpkin pie was a garbage pie you wouldn't eat any other day of the year.) And finally, they sat down and made sure to tell each other what they were each thankful for that year, and somehow, Dad always got Calla to drop her guard just long enough to say that she was thankful for him in her life.

This year, though, was their first year having guests.

Marco and his parents, Luis and Raisa Meza.

They came, brought Peruvian dishes: some sort of olive rice, corvina ceviche, plus the signature dish of their restaurant, a slow-roasted braise of various meats and vegetables called pachamanca. And it was, like, okay, Calla was very excited that they were coming over, right? Because *Marco.* And because his parents were lovably grumpy people—once you got past their guard, they really took you in, and Calla had definitely run that gauntlet and they *adored* her. But also, this was her and her father's day. And to have other people here, to break that *just-the-two-of-them* tradition . . .

It was great. At first. Marco was fun and funny. His parents didn't suck. They told funny stories about restaurant inspections, and Marco was out of his cast now so he had only the barest ghost of a limp—the food was delicious, Dad did not obsess over the turkey, the mashed potato texture was *perfect* (perfect = smooth and buttery with just a few lumps to make sure it wasn't goopy), everything was *amahhhzing,* the end.

Except.

Here was the thing:

Dad always told this one story about her mother, and it was how that woman could detect the slightest, in his words, "disturbance in the Force." Things he'd miss, things a *bloodhound* would miss, *Batman* would miss—she'd see. She was, in his words, a kind of domestic Hercule Poirot, someone who saw all the imperfections around her. (Whoever Hercule Poirot was.) A small crack in the basement wall, a rare bird in a faraway tree, a mote of pepper in a saltcellar, she'd see it. She just knew when something was *off.* It was her gift, and it was her curse.

Calla didn't have that gift-slash-curse, not really. A lot of times she was oblivious to what was going on around her, because she was pretty constantly nose down in her phone. (After all, why wouldn't you be? You had this device in your hand that had all the world in it, and you could talk to anybody. The world outside was bullshit: climate change and school shootings and bigotry and blah. The phone was refuge and respite—okay, no, not *always,* sometimes it was a social nightmare experiment. But when it wasn't, you could just switch to a different app, or block somebody, or whatever. Pretend they didn't exist. Wall them off, like that poor dope in the story with the wine.)

But now, she picked up on something—

Something was off with her father.

Not just off. But *different*.

Last night, he came home from his weird stupid networking thing, and *something* had changed. And that change was still there this morning, and here today throughout dinner. Calla couldn't precisely identify what had changed, exactly. He was happy. He still had his newfound boundless energy. Wasn't wearing his eyeglasses still. And then she pinged it: It was like when one of her actually-ADHD friends got on an ADHD med. Right? Suddenly they seemed a little more efficient, a little less . . . random. Dad was a little less random. Less *messy*. Like with the potatoes: He didn't have to second-guess himself again and again, tasting here and there and bemoaning their texture. And the turkey: Today, he set it and forget it. Dad *never* set it and forget it. It was like he finally figured out how to do it. After almost two decades, he changed what he was doing. He changed his whole *attitude*.

Which was weird.

She loved his mess. His random. His *Dadness*.

It wasn't there today. Or last night. He spoke clearly. No stuttering. He seemed clear-eyed and confident. A little less . . . goofy, too. Fewer Dad jokes, and the ones he did say felt—what? Rehearsed, somehow. Routine, not random.

It's fine, she told herself.

He had a good night.

He went on a date, got laid, got accepted to his little group or whatever.

It's fine.

AFTER DINNER, SHE AND MARCO WENT UP TO HER ROOM TO, AHEM, quote-unquote *work on their college applications* but it was totally to make out, and *then* work on his college application.

Usually she had to have the *door open* rule, but her father was occupied downstairs with Marco's parents, which made this the perfect opportunity to shut the door and do some *over-the-clothes* stuff—but when they got up there, Marco wanted to keep the door open.

She was like, "Why?"

"Because it's what your Dad always says."

Calla offered him a playful eye roll. "Dude, c'mon, he's downstairs with your parents, who are not going to come up here. They're so close, but so far away, and we can do *whatever* we want until dessert."

His nervousness and shyness was all the more appealing, and Calla saw no other choice but to completely attack him, like Hobbes bowling into Calvin, tackling him onto her bed. She pinned him there. Tickled his ribs. He cackled and then she silenced his cackle by clumsily mashing her mouth against his, stropping up against him and—

Aaaaand Marco was *not* returning the vibe.

He was mostly just lying there. Like a baton-struck fish.

Calla kept going for another thirty seconds and then finally eased off him and, panting, gave him a quizzical look. "Whhhhhat is up?"

"Huh?" he asked.

"You. This." Her finger made a swirly notion in the air, as if to demonstrate all of Marco and his relative airspace. "What is *this?*"

"What is what?"

He didn't even have a playful look on his face.

"We're making out and you don't seem, like, super into it."

"I'm into it—"

But she heard that pause, that unfinished sentence.

"There's a but," she said. "I can tell."

He sat forward, with her still straddling his lap. "I just think we should go back downstairs and help out your dad. I feel bad, he made that dinner—"

"Your parents also made some of the dinner."

"But your dad is hosting, too, and it just feels rude to not help."

"Rude."

"Yeah."

"Is this a fucking joke?" she asked.

"No."

"Oh my god." Horror descended upon her like a

(*cloud of flies*)

flock of ravens. "You don't like me anymore," she said. "You don't find me attractive. Am I ugly? Did I get ugly?"

"I like you just fine," he said, laughing. "I love you. You're beautiful. I just want to go back downstairs. C'mon, let's go help out. It'll be fun."

He said, unironically. *It'll be fun.* Cleaning up a kitchen on Thanksgiving. Instead of making out with your girlfriend. She felt queasy. And discarded. *Okay, Calla, maybe you should look at it this way: He's trying to be nice. Everyone likes nice boys. He's doing the right thing. Maybe it's not about you.*

An alternate voice said, *Of course it's about you everything is about you the whole world is about you, you're boring and old news and ugly and aaaaaaah.*

But he was already up, and taking her hand, and opening the closed door. He led her downstairs. She followed, the fight in her head going on as to whether she should love him more for doing the right thing, or whether she should hate him for rejecting her in her own fucking bedroom.

DOWNSTAIRS. CLEANING UP. LIKE MARCO WANTED. UGH. HER SOUL wanted to die. She still felt rejected. She wanted to cry. Or yell. Or something.

Dad, who would normally clock one of her upset moods and ask her what was up, sat at the table, saying to the Mezas, "You know, your son here is really special. Boy, he's a workhorse. And a righteous soul, to boot."

No shit, Calla thought with no small amount of bitterness.

Luis answered, "We know, we know. He could work a little harder at the restaurant, of course . . ."

Which earned him an arm swat from Marco's mom, Raisa.

"Shush. Marco is a sweet baby and he has things he has to do. Responsibilities. School, working at the orchard—"

The words came out of Calla's mouth before she even really meant them to. It wasn't planned. But her feelings were thorns and they wanted to draw blood. "He also should be applying for college. Which, Mr. and Mrs. Meza, I don't think Marco here has been keeping up with since he is definitely going to miss the early decision deadline next week . . ."

At that, Calla expected some reaction. Any reaction. A gasp of horror. A napkin thrown at Marco's head. A tut-tutting from one of them, all of them. A stammered excuse from Marco. Something, anything. But instead, the only reaction her comment got was . . . uncomfortable silence. From all four of them. They shared looks. Their mouths hung open just so. And it was in that moment Calla felt the very clear, very high-school-familiar vibe: There was something going on, and she was the only one *not* in on it. Her intense feeling of rejection from earlier deepened, suddenly. This wasn't rejection.

It was exclusion.

"Oh my god," she said. "What is this?"

"Don't be mad," Marco said, which was a surefire way to make her mad.

"Mad about what exactly?" She felt lost. Flailing.

Dad was suddenly at her side, touching her elbow gently. "Calla, sweetie. We've all been talking—"

"We've. We've all. All who? Like, all of the people in this fucking room?"

"Whoa, babe," Marco said. "Language."

"Talking about *what*," she demanded to know.

The Mezas hung back while Dad and Marco stood in front of her. It was Dad who said, "Sweetie, we all just think with Marco's injury and everything, that maybe he's going to take a gap year—I'm getting the orchard up and running and I think Marco is going to be vital in that operation in the near future—"

"The orchard is not college, Dad. Marco is going with *me* to *college*. College, you know the thing that, like, everyone needs to attend in order to get a degree and get a, a, any kind of fucking *job*—"

"Babe," Marco said. "I'll still go to school, just a year late. Probably."

Probably.

That last word.

"'Probably'?" she barked, incredulous. Calla pushed past her father and stood in front of Marco's parents, who remained sitting. Stammering mad, she said, "And you two are okay with this? You want him to work at a—an *orchard*? Instead of going to school? He's not a fucking migrant worker! Marco is smart! He can do anything! His injury—he—he healed it! He'll get back to running by spring season and he should still be able to get a scholarship—"

"It'll be nice to have him around a little longer," Raisa said, shrugging. "The world is a dark place these days and it'd be good to have Marco at home . . ."

Luis nodded. His next words were peppered with both pride *and* a little bit of anger, too. "Migrant workers work *hard*. And smart. And the orchard—it's *good* work, Calla, you should be proud of what your father has accomplished."

"Proud! *Proud?* Why isn't anybody proud of me? And of Marco? We're teenagers in a broken world! Everything fucking sucks and yet somehow we're soldiering on, we're managing, and there's a future ahead of us, but, you—you just want to relegate your only son to—what, to working with stupid apple trees?"

Another silence ensued, like a yawning chasm. Her on one side. The rest of them on the other. The gap between them widening like a hungry mouth.

"That's how you feel about my work," Dad said. His voice distant. Stung.

Luis Meza whispered to his wife, loud enough that she could still hear: "She hasn't eaten the apple, you know." A small gasp rose from Raisa.

"What? No. Dad. I'm proud of you, whatever, I just mean—"

"You're too good for such humble work." His voice, laced with a stitching of acrimony and bitterness. "I understand. Maybe you are too good for it. Maybe that's why you're going to go off to college. But the thing that's going to help send you there? Is our orchard. Our *family* orchard. Marco gets that, and he's going to help. Which means he's going to help *you*. So maybe say thank you. Thank you, *Dad*. Thank you, *Marco*. Thank you for sending me to college."

"Dad—"

"*Say* it."

His mouth was a firm line. His lips parted just so, showing bared teeth. Gritted teeth. Like he was angry.

Dad was never angry. Not with her. Not ever.

"Thank you," she said, tears burning the edges of her eyes.

"Thank you to who?"

"Thank you, *Dad*," she said, except now, instead of feeling only stung, only grief-struck, she felt betrayed. She felt angry. And that anger leached into her tone, like some foul chemical spill into a roaring river. "Thank you, *Marco.*" Those words, said with spat acid. She stuck her chin out, suddenly defiant, "Thank you for sending me to college. I don't want to stand between you and your work, *Marco.* So I think we should *break up.*"

She wanted him to be hurt.

Or to be mad.

Or to fight for her.

But all Marco said was, "Okay." A little disappointed, maybe.

But also—

Maybe a little relieved, too.

"Happy Thanksgiving," Calla said, and she hoped when they heard those two words they also heard what she was really saying, which was *Fuck you.*

At that, she threw down the rag she'd been using to dry a dish, and hard-charged out of the room, up the stairs, and into her bedroom.

Where she promptly slammed the door.

NO ONE CAME TO CHECK ON HER.

She wanted them to. Someone. Any of them. It was the way of things: You have an argument, a fight, a separation, and someone needs to break the stalemate. Someone needs to care enough to reach out. A hand in the darkness, a reconnection that would say, *Everything will be fine.*

But none of them bothered. To be fair, she didn't bother, either. She considered it, of course. *Maybe I'm wrong. Maybe I don't appreciate them enough. Maybe the Mezas can't afford college and maybe Dad really needs the help and—*

No.

They had a plan. They spoke about this behind her back. She had arrows stuck between her shoulder blades. They fucking betrayed her.

And they didn't even care.

She wasn't going to go down there to make amends.

But, Calla knew, she *could* go down to spy. See what they were saying. Maybe she had planted just a little seed of doubt. She had to know.

So, Calla cracked her door, heard voices. A little laughing, too—which only boiled her blood, made her chest tighten, made her brain go into full *wasp nest* mode. Then the laughing stopped. The voices stopped, too.

Calla crept downstairs. Gently, gently. This wasn't her first rodeo. She knew which floorboards creaked. She knew how to walk so as not to be easily heard. So that's what she did. Creepily creeping along, until—

She heard the wet sounds. Teeth through skin. Flesh chewed.

Calla peered around the doorjamb past the kitchen, into the dining room and—*oh my god.*

They were all there, hunched over plates, each holding a fat dark apple with both hands—they did not bring the apples to their mouths but rather, descended to eat the apples, like pigs at a trough. Her father, Marco, his parents, all greedily, lustily biting into the apples. Juices dripping, spattering on the plates, soaking the tablecloth. Behind closed lids, she saw their eyes rotating, like a pinworm moving under taut skin. Each of them moaned a little. A gentle *hnngh.* Calla stifled a cry and ran back upstairs to her bed, where she climbed under the covers and wept.

36

THE END OF NOVEMBER

CALLA CLICKED THE MOUSE. SHE WATCHED HER APPLICATION UP-
load to Princeton's website. Their internet out here was wet trash, so she
got to watch the progress bar climb slowly, too slowly, so slowly she didn't
think it would even finish. But then it did. She felt a kind of triumph that
was swiftly lost under a current of sadness. It was a lot of things. It was
Thanksgiving. It was that Marco wouldn't be uploading his application
today. It was that her father was acting weirder and weirder, and so was
Marco, and it all had to do with that apple. But really, at the end of it, the
greatest sadness was that she felt the overwhelming desire to get way the
fuck out of here. She'd never felt that before. Now she felt it intensely.

JOANIE WOKE UP TO HATE MAIL. EMAIL, ANYWAY. A DOZEN PIECES,
all from different email addresses, though she guessed they came from
the same person, or at least the same group of people. All of them called
her a whore, said she was a sinner, a demon, they'd burn her house down
if she didn't move, you fucking bitch, you fucking cunt. She told herself
it didn't bother her, but it did. She told herself she was tougher than that,
and she was, to a point. She told herself it wasn't real, it was just a buncha
little-pricked keyboard trolls—that, or it was Prentiss Beckman next
door, jerking it as he sent another hate message. But it still sucked. It still
made her worry. Then again, that was being a woman in the world.

And yet, something was up. Something was *off*. She could feel it in the
air, hanging there like a bad frequency, a sad song, a smell that crawled up
your nose and lived there in the back of your skull.

Graham asked her what was wrong. She smiled sweetly and said
nothing. It was a lie but maybe if she said it out loud, it would become
true.

―――

JOHN REGARDED THE BLACK-RED APPLE DAN PAXSON CALLED THE
Ruby Slipper, but that John feared was really the Frenchman's apple.
The ones the Lenape called *pkwĕsu.*

It sat there in front of him on a paper plate at the B&B where he was
staying. Emily had stolen it for him from Meg's stash. Once she told him
Dan Paxson had Walt's satchel, it clicked for him—this apple was *the*
apple. The one Walt had been looking for. It didn't appear out of nowhere. Dan didn't crossbreed this thing. He found it. Or, rather, *Walt*
had found it.

Was it possible Dan had killed him for it? Maybe it was.

Emily asked him not to eat the apple, and she said she knew it was a
crazy thing to ask, but John said it'd be fine. It was just an apple. Wasn't it?

So, he took his lockback knife, cut himself a slice. The smell that
came off it was potent. Stronger scent than he'd ever gotten off a cut
fruit. It felt like it suffused the air, like he was swimming in it, drowning
in it. It made parts of him ache with want. His mouth moistened. His
teeth hurt.

John popped the slice in his mouth and began to chew.

Instantly, the flavors hit him, one after the next. Brown sugar. Yuzu
citrus. Tobacco. Rosehips. Then, something funkier: juniper and sage. A
mineral tang, too, chased after: the taste of sweat as it dripped off your
brow, down your nose, into your mouth. The salty tang of that sweat as
you were sitting there with your eye against the scope ring, your finger
on the trigger, the rifle hugged tight against the inside of your shoulder
like it was your best and only lover, the taste of sweat became the taste of
blood, and John saw himself—*felt* himself—kneeling down over a dead
Iraqi boy, his head blown out from a sniper's bullet, and John was stoop-
ing low and pressing his teeth against the kid's cheek and taking a bite of
it, and it was soft, so soft like custard in his mouth, and it melted there
with the taste of meat and blood and apples and his guts churned even as
his muscles tightened—*none of this happened,* he thought, but he kept chewing, his eyelids fluttering, and something crawled in his mouth and
crunched like a bit of eggshell in an egg sandwich, and a voice inside him

that wasn't his own told him to *just keep eating, you know you want to keep eating, don't worry about that,* but he heard the rifle crack in his ear as his finger jerked, and now he was doubling over in real life and spitting the apple all back up onto the plate in a sputter.

Something was in the mess, something like seeds, which made John think, *Why are there seeds in there, why did I eat those,* but these seeds were *moving*—

He cried out, shook his head, and pre-chewed apple spattered on the table. The apple mess on the plate squirmed with dog ticks. Little brown-and-black bloodsuckers, like mashed-flat sesame seeds, clambering poorly in the spit-up. A couple were bloated up already, as if they'd taken their blood and started to swell up like a wine-soaked raisin. A few were bitten, crushed, dead.

And then they weren't ticks at all, but just apple seeds.

Half-chewed apple seeds with little green shoots breaking out of their tips.

John went into the bathroom and vomited.

EMILY ANSWERED THE DOOR. SHE DIDN'T WANT TO; SHE FIGURED it was Meg's mother Noreen again, because she had been stopping by a lot lately. A lot a lot. "Just to check in," she'd say, but Emily knew it was to keep an eye on her.

So she opened the door with a resigned sigh—

And froze in place finding Dan Paxson standing there.

He was holding Walt's satchel in front of him, like a shield.

"I bought this at a consignment shop in Frenchtown," he said. It was abrupt and aggressive. He scowled as he said it.

"Okay," she said, her heart hammering in her chest.

"I need you to understand that. Say you understand that."

"I—" She swallowed a hard lump. "I understand."

He seemed to chew on that for a moment. Then he exhaled, and his scowl turned into a smile. "I met your wife the other night, Meg, and she's great. I look forward to her friendship. And yours, if you'll allow it. I know you're new here and we can be quite welcoming to the right people. I hope you're the right people." She didn't know what to say to that, and he didn't give her much of a chance to say anything anyway, because he shouldered past the gap in the conversation. "I didn't always feel welcome here, honestly, but I think I've found my folks, my friends, as it were, and I'm sure you'll get there. I've worked hard to get to where I'm at. I have a daughter. A business. An orchard. I'm doing work that matters, Emily, just like your wife is and I—I can't let anything derail that. Not rumors or lies. Not now. Not when I'm so close to—well, my father had a dream and I'm on the verge of making his dream a reality. It's really nice. And I'm proud. Okay?"

She nodded slowly.

"What consignment shop?" she asked, suddenly. She didn't even mean to. The question just popped in her head—and then hopped out of her mouth.

"Excuse me?"

Shut up, Emily, shut up, shut up.

"You said you got it at a consignment shop. I like consignment shops. Just wondering which one."

The smile died on his face. "I don't remember it. It's in Frenchtown. Just go there. It's the only one."

"Of course. Yeah. Thank you."

"Say hello to Meg for me," Dan said.

"I—I will."

"Goodbye, Emily."

At that, he walked back to his truck, then drove away. Emily meanwhile stood in the doorway, watching him leave, her heart still galloping like a spooked horse. Because he just threatened her. It didn't sound all the way like a threat, no. It almost sounded nice. But Emily knew a warning when she heard one.

THE IRS MAN'S TALE

September 4, 1924.

Stanley Thistle had a fire in his eyes, a fire in his belly, and soon, fire at the snap of his fingers. With big, proud, bowlegged strides he walked into the orchard, trees to the left and right of him in rows, each tree strung up along tin-colored wire. Stanley looked at the dusky, ugly apples dangling from the branches. He approached one, setting the metal gas can down before plucking an apple from its branch and giving it an eager, cantankerous bite. The skin of it was rough; it abraded the roof of his mouth like steel wool. And the taste was—

Lord in Heaven, the taste was like sucking on a sack of dirty nickels. Metallic, acidic, and *foul*. A foul apple of foul purpose with a foul, foul taste.

So when the thin-hipped and fat-gutted man hurtled toward him, waving his arms talking about how this was private property, who are you, how dare you, Stanley just tipped his gray homburg hat and said, "Sir, hellohello, I'm from the IRS, with the Prohibition Unit—a *prohi*, I think you folks like to call us?—and I am here as an agent serving enforcement of the Volstead Act."

The orchard man, whose scalp was bald but for a few sad threads of hair, like worms that crawled into the sun and dried out and died, said, "Well, sir, like I said, this is private property and I—I assure you, this is an orchard, an upstanding orchard, why I'm just a humble *grower of fruit*—"

Stanley made a sour face, holding up the bitten-into apple. "This? Is this what you're calling fruit, Mister Ahh—"

"Slack, sir."

"Yes, that's it, Mister Archibald Slack—"

"Archie."

"Archie, now, let's be honest with each other here. This apple is as vile as an apple can get."

Panic danced in Archie's eyes like flames.

"They're not—they're not ripe yet."

"They're red, aren't they? Reddish, anyway." Under his breath Stanley muttered, "Honestly, almost brown." He nudged at one on the ground with the toe of his patent-leathers. "There, look. They're falling from the branches and I am to understand that is a true and tested sign of *doneness* there on the tree. These are ripe apples, Archie Slack, and they taste of vulgarity, sir—like thick, callused buboes plucked from the Devil's own plague-sick armpits, I daresay. What crass-mouthed sap would eat such a thing, I wonder?"

"Well," Archie Slack blustered, "nobody said I was a *successful* grower of fruit, I—I—" And it was at this point that he must've seen the gas can down on the ground, and his eyes went big as spoons, because he knew what this was. He came clean, then, didn't he? Oh boy, did he. "I paid. I paid the last prohi who came here—a Mister George Houlihan, sir—I paid him as is the way, and, and—and we had an *arrangement,* sir, you'll understand. An arrangement!"

Stanley sucked air between his teeth in a disappointed gesture and said, "Sad news, you see. Agent Houlihan met with an accident. Trolley accident—so common these days. One jumped the track and ran right over him. Popped his head like a child's balloon. Pop. Sad how our modern machinations can be so deadly. It's why, I think, we strive again to find *simplicity* in our todays."

"I—I can pay—"

"Oh, no no no," Stanley said, tut-tutting him. "It's not like that. I don't require any payment from you."

"You don't?"

"No, Archie Slack, not at all. I don't take payment. Why, I dispense it. And it seems to me that you are owed something."

Archie seemed surprised by this. "Owed, sir?"

"Owed."

At which point, Stanley Thistle pulled out a bright-bore, black-grip Colt revolver, one kept shiny as a silver serving tray, and shot Archie

Slack in his left knee. Blood scattered on the green grass behind him. The man howled, ironically falling to that very exploded knee, which caused him to howl louder, which only made Stanley howl, too. Though Stanley's howl was a good bit happier.

AUGUST 12, 1921.

Stanley Thistle had puke in his mouth, crust around his eyes, and cheap whiskey pickling his guts. He woke in his own mess, and reached for his memories of the night before, finding them not one picture but instead like the pieces of a jigsaw puzzle. Stanley peeled his cheek off the floorboard. Heard the sounds of the city—Philadelphia—outside. He heard the rattle-bang of an engine. A cow, somewhere, screaming in pain. The smell of offal and oil rose to his nose. But then, something else. Coffee. Nearby. Stanley sat up, eased back on his haunches, and went to rub some of the gunk out of his eyes—

Hold on now. His hand was rust-brown. Like he'd run his hand along a freshly stained wooden fence. Except—this wasn't stain. And some blond hairs were matted into the rust-red mess on his hands. Dried there. His hair wasn't blond. His hair was a chestnut brown. Well. Huh.

He looked over across the room.

Saw the spatter trail of the same color.

Saw it dead-end at a woman who lay against the radiator. Her body sat slumped, facedown. Housedress-clad ass up. It was hard to see from here but it looked like her forehead was caved in by the radiator, as if it had reached up and slammed into her with great force.

Or, if *she* had been slammed into *it*.

Stanley did not know this woman. He was sure of it.

But then he started to put that puzzle back together again.

The saloon.

Last night.

Barmaid.

Had that silver serving tray.

Brought him whiskey after whiskey after whiskey.

Here. The apartment. After hours. Dancing to someone's music drifting across the street from someone's Victor record player. She got rough with him. Liked it rough, she said. Or maybe he said that she liked it rough.

Maybe she wasn't so sure, all of a sudden . . .

"You killed her, Stanley," came a voice from behind him.

Stanley cried out, nearly fell over. A man sat behind him. White suit, white bow tie. White everything, in fact—down to his big, shiny teeth framed by a thin-lipped grin. The man gave a little wink.

"The hell are you?" Stanley said, scooting backward on his butt, inadvertently smearing the trail of blood on his floor. He panicked, crab-walking perpendicular from the rust-red spatter. "Get out of here. *Get out.*"

"Stanley—"

"You killed her! It was you! Not me. I—I'd never. You took advantage of me, sir. Seized upon my wanton drunkenness and used it as cover for—for your own cruel appetites. I see it. I see it now—"

"You're very clever," the man said. "The people I work with, they said, Stanley Thistle isn't clever. He's a drunk and a fool, and anybody who works for the IRS must be a dullard of the lowest order, and I said, no, that's not right, the IRS is a brain trust, an engine run by agents who are in their way like detectives, yes? They find debts that must be paid. They square the books. Balance the sheets. That's no small thing, is it, Stanley?"

At this point, Stanley felt fuzzy as anything. This seemed an insane conversation given . . . everything, but it was better than the conversation they *should've* been having, what with a dead barmaid behind him. So, he nodded in agreement and said, "That's correct, Mister—ahhh."

"Naberius," the man said. "Edward Naberius. A humble restorer of lost dignities and, if I may, dear Stanley, you have most certainly lost some dignity—and not just last night, but on the road leading you to last night. I'm here to help you with that. Would you accept my help?"

Stanley hazarded a look over his shoulder at the dead woman, and his stomach clenched up tighter than a gangster's trigger finger. He wanted to throw up. Almost did, but choked it back down. Numbly, he nodded. "I will. I do."

"Good. Stanley, you familiar with the Volstead Act?"

And, tasting whiskey and bile on his mouth, Stanley admitted that of course he was familiar. Because these days, Christ, who wasn't? Prohibition was in full swing now. Wets and drys. Bluenoses and teetotalers, wagging their fingers.

"Glad to hear it, my friend." Edward Naberius's smile only grew bigger at that point, so big it looked like it was about to split his face in twain—the jaws of a gator stretching wide. *Just a regular smile,* Stanley told himself.

At that, the man pulled out a dark, alluring apple. He gave it a little spin and for a moment, Stanley saw all the stars in the sky there in the skin of that fruit.

"Now, tell me, Stanley, how do you like these apples?"

September 4, 1924.

Archie Slack rolled around on the ground, clutching his knee—or, at least, the raw red caved-in mess that *used* to be his knee. He bit the grass underneath him like a dog with a sick tummy. Stanley chuckled at that as he splashed gas up and down the trunks of these ugly apple trees.

"So my friend, Mister Naberius—he says to me, there're all these orchards, these orchards new and old. Old Indian orchards, some of them. Others, Johnny Appleseed orchards. This one's one of those, isn't it, Mister Slack?" But that man didn't answer, he was just trying real hard not to scream. "Ah, well, no matter. Point being, he said that people were using these orchards to grow apples used only for foul purpose—the purpose of making cidered hooch to water the garden of boozehounds this country has grown. And, let me say, I was just such a weed in the American garden, Mister Slack, sprouting up, blotto as a shovel-struck cat. Whiskey was my favorite. My treat. My sin. But no more. I've found the way. I've—" And here he paused, giving a deep nasal inhalation of gas fumes. "Found my dignity, Mister Slack, as I hope you can, too."

He finished gassing up the trees and walked back to the bleeding man, who lay on his back now, the messed-up leg bent and pulled tight to his middle. Archie Slack had gone pale as some sewer baby. Stanley stood over him, patting his pockets. "Mister Naberius, he said we've been missing purity and goodness—*sweetness,* he called it—here in these States that are United, and he said the fruits of the earth should not be used for such ruination. It is not for us to take God's spoils and let them go to rot and ruin so that we may sup on their corrupted slurry, no sir, no how, uh-uh. It was time to remember that old saying. *American as apple pie.* And he showed me what he meant, you see. He'd found this apple, long time ago. Special apple. The richest red, this apple. The red of our flag. The red of our hearts. The red of our American blood, you see. And I took a bite of this apple, just this one, and it made me feel like I'd never felt before. I felt clear and clean. I felt bright as the fire atop Lady Liberty's torch. At his behest, I'll find it again someday. That day is not today, I wager. Because I eat this—" He bent down, scooping up one of Slack's wretched knobs of fruit from the ground. "And I think, this is how we lose our way. The nation has lost its dignity, Archie Slack. But with a little bit of light and a whole lot of sweetness, we can find it again."

He continued to pat his pocket as he knelt there next to Archie, finding what he'd been looking for. Stanley pulled out a crumpled deck of Stroke of Luck cigarettes and offered it to the other man. "Care for a gasper, friend?"

Archie mewled and mumbled an assent, opening his mouth like a little fledgling bird looking to be fed. Stanley was kind, plugged a coffin nail between his lips and then fetched a matchbook, gave it a light. Slack sat forward a little, the smoke pinched between his bloodied fingers as he puffed away.

Stanley stood up, and idly picked up the can. He made a quizzical, faux-surprised sound. "Huh. Look at that. Still a little gas in 'er."

Then he splashed the last of it onto Archie's face.

The man's head lit up like the aforementioned torch of liberty. *Whoosh.* He screamed. His skin crackled and popped as he thrashed around, punching at his own head and face, but of course his hands had a little gas on them, too, and those mitts went up, and then soon the rest of him, too. Stanley lit his own cigarette on the fiery cairn of flesh—now going still, no longer flailing about—and then flicked it to one of the trees. This wasn't his first burn job. He'd already made sure to leave a little trail between them. Fire moved like a hungry angel. The orchard burned. Stanley walked away, whistling Dixie, still tasting the foul man's apple in his mouth, and wishing for just one more taste of that sweetest apple. A red apple.

A god-blessed *American* apple.

WINTER

(DECEMBER, JANUARY, FEBRUARY)

It's winter that raises the apple from the earth. The bitter cold, the ice like knives, the crystals of ice underground that cut into the hard coat and breach the soft, pale place inside where root and stem and leaf are one. The apple won't be coddled. Until it knows true suffering, the seed won't sprout at all. The tree will never live.

—Olivia Hawker,
One for the Blackbird,
One for the Crow

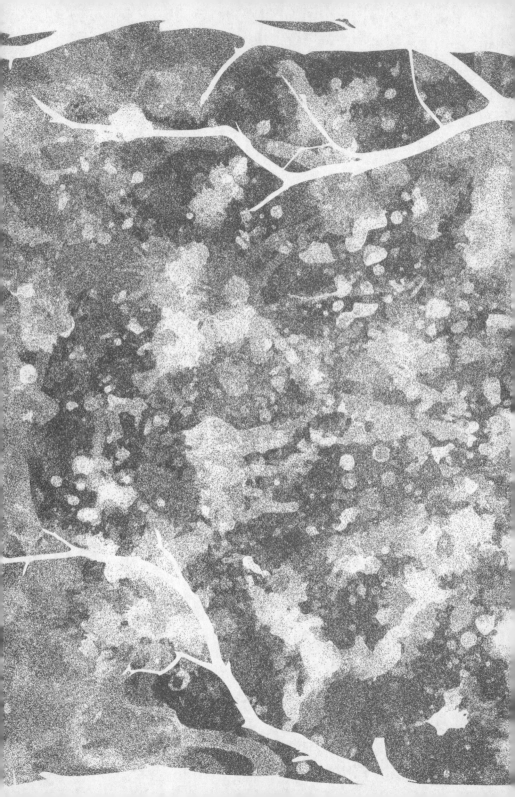

37

A GATHERING OF DARKNESS

WINTER'S TEETH

Winter began with lights and mirth and merriment, as was its way: Lit-up trees and inflatable reindeer and after the lights came down and the Santa Clauses deflated on the lawn as if shot in the back of the head, there came one last hurrah of parties and pots banging and midnight shotguns firing to scare off whatever demons and gargoyles might think to perch on the ledge of the new year. But then winter did what winter did: It grew darker, colder, crueler. In this case, wetter, too. Rain and ice more than snow. The wind was often biting. The skies, gray as a river-soaked corpse. The days were short. The nights stretched out. All was still. But it was not dead. Winter was a time of long shadows gathering, like vultures shuffling together on the long branch of a leafless tree. Waiting for their moment.

THE ORCHARD, ABOVE AND BELOW

The apple trees of the orchard were quiet, now, finally. No more blooms and no more fruit. The leaves did not turn pretty colors but instead went brown to black and right to the ground. But though the trees were quiet, the orchard was not asleep. The dirt still had warm pockets; the roots still had nutrients tucked away in them. And though the ground grew colder, the roots still moved inch by inch through the hardening, hoary soil, seeking those little gaps, those inconspicuous holes chewed by voles and beetle larvae. The seeking shoots and running runners pushed past slumbering worms and urged through the cabinet of bones of the dead bodies beneath them. Bodies that remained hidden, but would not re-

264 - CHUCK WENDIG

main hidden forever. Bodies were secrets, and secrets always found a way toward the light. These, shouldered slowly, ineluctably upward by the roots. The orchard would reveal these hidden bones in time, and when it did, the orchard would demand payment in recompense. Life for death, and death for life. The red that makes the green.

CALLA CAN'T PUT THE SNAKES BACK IN THE CAN

Calla, like the winter earth, hardened herself.

She hunkered down, didn't talk to her friends much anymore, choosing instead to concentrate on schoolwork. And they didn't really seem like they wanted to talk to her, either, though sometimes she wondered about the chicken-and-egg problem there: Had she pushed them away first, or had they pushed her away first? Where did it begin? Guess it didn't matter much now.

As for Marco . . .

She saw him, sometimes. How could she not. It was school, and there were hallways, and though this semester they didn't share any classes, they passed each other often enough. He didn't ignore her. He'd pass, say hi—not an awkward hi, not a plaintive hey, not a sheepish hello that contained greetings and entreaties like *please let's talk* or *oh my god I miss you* or even *I'm so mad at you right now.* No, it was just a hi. Like he knew her, but didn't know her. Like they were acquaintances, not friends, not best friends, not boyfriend–girlfriend co-conspirators superglued together at the hip once upon a time.

Otherwise he hung out with his track bros, always laughing and having a good time. He had no limp. He had an endless smile. He was happy. She wanted to be happy *for* him but it was impossible, so instead, she secretly wished for him to be unhappy. To be miserable, in fact. To find out that his leg was really still broken. That he ran on it too soon. That he'd choke on a piece of apple—not to kill him, but to hurt him, to scare him. That his parents would finally realize he'd broken the dreams they had for him, and his own dreams for himself, and so they'd ground him, force him to do his fucking college application already. And in all of that misery he'd realize, *The only person who makes me happy is you, Calla.* It would put him back on track. He'd apply for college. He'd get accepted. And come fall, they'd be together for real, forever.

It was a cruel, stupid fantasy and she hated herself for having it.

But she had it anyway.

Her father tried to tell her it was for the best. That Marco would just drag her down when she was so close to the finish line. "Marco is good at the orchard. But this place can't contain you, Calla Lily," he said. Dad tried to be chummy, still, with her, but she wasn't having any of it. She froze his ass out. And for a while he mostly did what Dad would do when she was having a mood: He rode it out like turbulence on an airplane. That's what he used to say about bad moods. They're just turbulence on an airplane. A little rough air, is all. Eventually you flew above it or you flew through it, and then you landed, and once again? Stable ground.

But then came Christmas Day. Dad wanted to invite Marco over but she told him if he did she'd hang herself with Christmas lights—"a real festive suicide," she called it—and though Calla was not above that level of drama, it was a little *dark* even for her, but he just waved her off like it was nothing. He said she was being funny. He called her sweetheart, Calla Lily, honey, gave her a better batch of presents than he'd given in years past, which only made her angrier. Then he said, "You know, you should come take a look at what I've done down at the orchard, me and Marco, well, I tell ya, Calla Lily, this isn't some fly-by-night operation anymore. The cider building is done, I got a load of charred-oak barrels I'm going to use for aging the cider, plus we have tons of orchard racks built—"

The words lashed from her tongue like a whip:

"I don't give a shit about your stupid orchard."

Instantly, *instantly* she felt bad. Yes, she was mad at him. Yes, she was *extra* pissed at Marco. But, like, she knew it was Dad's thing, knew it was *his* own father's thing especially, and here she was just being super-pissy about it—and then she saw the look on his face. Like something had broken. A mask fell away. Chipper Dad, Goofy Dad, Dorky Dad, all gone. The face, the true face, was of grief and horror. As if he were genuinely injured, betrayed in a way he couldn't ever have imagined. She sighed, feeling so awful her stomach did a fishy flip-flop inside her, and she started to say, "Dad, I'm—"

But before the *sorry* could come out, he leaned forward.

"You little fucking bitch," he said, his voice low, the words hissed. "This orchard, *my* orchard, it feeds you, it clothes you, it buys you *nice presents*—" And at that, his foot lashed out and kicked a box containing a Dyson hair dryer hard enough to crater the side of it. He stood up then, lording himself over her, seemingly growing taller and taller, his shadow lengthening. "And all I get from you is *whining* and *moaning* and *foulmouthed insults,* and I am very tired of it, Calla. Very fucking tired."

"Daddy," she said, trying to hold back tears.

"Shut up. You will be nice to me from here on out. You will respect me and my work and what I've created here, what I've *given* to you. Because if you don't, I will take it all away. I will take away the Wi-Fi, I will take away your precious phone, I will not pay for any of your upcoming college, I will throw out your clothes, I will make you beg for your food, I will burn your fucking bed until it is nothing but a pile of greasy ash for you to sleep in. I am tired of being talked down to and taken advantage of. I am the most important person *in your life,* and it is high time you remember that and give me the respect I have *earned.*"

Calla broke into sobs. Through spit-slick mouth she told him she was sorry, and she maybe even meant it, too—maybe she had pushed too hard, maybe she had taken advantage of him. She couldn't see clear through to any of that. She felt only hurt and stung and scared. And she told him that part, too. "Daddy you're scaring me," she said to him, a plea, an exhortation of fear.

And all he said to her was, "Good."

Then he got up, grabbed an apple from the basket on the table, and headed out the door into the cold Christmas day.

She avoided him after that. Best as she could.

A week after the fight, Calla checked the online portal and found she had been accepted early into Princeton.

It was a triumph, but one that was bitter and hollow.

But at last it promised her an escape.

JOHN WIDENS THE HUNT

John went right to them, the police. He told them straight-up, "I think I know who killed my friend Walt," and explained that there was a man, an orchard-keeper named Dan Paxson who had Walt's bag, who threatened his friend Emily for figuring it out. The cops mumbled to one another, eventually got him in touch with the county sheriff, a brick-jawed man named Carl Horsley who sat John down on the far side of a messy desk and said, point-blank, "We looked into it, seems the bag was just a secondhand store purchase by a thrifty man, nothing sinister there." But John insisted, said it was too coincidental: Walt was an apple hunter looking for a lost apple down here in Bucks County, and this Dan Paxson had an orchard. But Sheriff Horsley said, "Coincidences are not evidence, and as I said, there's nothing sinister here. If you'd like to pursue this further, I warn you, it might be considered harassment against Dan Paxson, and I'd gladly testify in his defense. He's a good man. A county man." And at that, Horsley pulled out a now-familiar apple. Sure, it could've been a Red Delicious or a Black Oxford or the like, but the way it stood tall, the way it had that starfield of little lenticels across its blood-dark expanse—John knew it. Dan's apple.

(*Walt's apple.*)

What they called the Ruby Slipper.

Pkwēsu.

The sheriff took a large, aggressive bite. Chewed with his mouth open. The smell that hit John's nose was one of blooming rose and rotten meat.

John thought he saw black spots crawling around in there. Like ticks.

His stomach turned. He got out of there, then. He didn't understand what was happening, not precisely. But he didn't like it. Didn't trust it.

It was then he started looking for a rental place here in the central part of the county. Driving back and forth from the Lehigh Valley wasn't going to work, what with it being an hour each way. He needed to be here. Set up a home base. It put him near Emily. They'd work together. They'd catch Dan Paxson. They'd find out what the hell was going on with that strange damn apple.

He'd do Walt this last favor.

EMILY REGARDS THE TRAP

Over winter, Meg entered a new phase, a phase Emily called *The Mask*. Because that's what it felt like—as if Meg had put on a mask. She was friendly to Emily, now. Politely so, like her interactions with Emily were scripted, planned out to every word and every pause, like it was all an act. Her kindness wasn't kind. It was hollow. A cold courtesy, not an act of genuine warmth. Maybe Meg appreciated Emily putting in the work that night at the dinner. Or maybe she just stopped caring enough to fight. It felt like the love between them had been stretched thin, so thin that it was just silken filaments now—a wisp of web to bind together the spider and its prey. And that made Emily sad, and it made her mad, and it made her feel stupid because maybe this was just how it was. Maybe all married people hit this point. You spent enough time with someone, that had to plateau, right? The joyful chaos of your early days in love had to settle down into something orderly, with fewer peaks and valleys and every-thing put in a line

(*a flatline*)

(*beeeeeeeeeeeeeep*)

and maybe that's how it was now, but it didn't feel good, not at all. And it didn't help that Meg was part of this group with a man who had threatened Emily—and who may have killed John's friend. Worse, Meg took calls from him some nights. Their conversations—often had in an-other room, behind closed doors—seemed professional. Meg was appar-ently his "legal adviser" on matters regarding the orchard. But even still, Emily took it as a kind of threat. Dan was in their lives now. As if he wanted to keep an eye on her.

All the while, Meg kept eating *those fucking apples,* and now when she ate them, Emily could hear something there in the chew—something wet, something popping between her back teeth.

Meg was changing. Emily could see that, now. Her skin seemed clearer, almost like she glowed—same way they said new mothers glowed. And there'd long been the little scar on her chin, roughly the size of a staple, where she'd fallen as a kid when she crashed her bike—but it was gone, now. As if it never existed.

Then came the ice storm in February. She said she bought a bag of rock salt for the walkways and driveway, and went out to the car to get it. It was a fifty-pound bag, and she hauled it up and over her shoulder like it weighed no more than a bed pillow. (If Emily didn't find it odd, Meg's new vitality would've gotten her hot as fuck. But any fresh attraction was lost under the current of worry.)

She thought about what John told her, about the visions he had and the ticks that crawled out of the apple . . . she thought of the man in the white suit standing by her bike . . . she thought about Walt's bag sitting there, *right there,* on Dan's chair . . .

Emily wanted to run away but she couldn't.

She almost bailed. Go back to the city to see if she could find a chain of couches to crash on until she got back on her feet . . .

But she felt an obligation. To John, in part. To help him find out what happened to Walt. But she also wanted to find out what was happening to Meg.

Maybe she was obligated to her, too.

That was marriage. Meg was her wife.

But Meg had changed and Emily needed to understand how. It was the apple, she knew. That much was obvious. But she needed more than that.

By winter's end, Emily started to keep a journal of Meg's, well, everything. When she ate the apple. How she was changing, how she behaved, how she looked. When she talked to Dan. When she went out. How she treated Emily. All of it. Emily needed to see the pattern. Emily needed to understand.

I love you, Meg. This book will help me see who you are becoming.

DAN PAXSON FINDS A BRUISE ON THE APPLE

Things were wonderful in a way that they hadn't been in a long time. That they hadn't *ever* been, if Dan was being honest.

Consider:

Dan no longer needed eyeglasses.

He didn't need to sleep.

He felt like he had boundless energy, newfound strength, and an endless fount of confidence and certainty.

People were still craving his apple, even though his stock was dwindling now, what with winter upon them—thankfully, the Ruby Slipper was one helluva keeper. A little bit of cold storage, and the apple only got *tastier* as time went on. And those who ate the apple were connecting with him in a way they never had. They were warm and engaging. They reached out for him, like they wanted to touch him—just a small, gentle touch. A hand on the shoulder. A soft three-finger brush against his breastbone. Someone picking something small, like a piece of dirt, off his cheek or the back of his wrist. They had clear eyes, clear skin. Alert and ebullient. And it showed all over midcounty, too. Everywhere Dan went, from Coryell's Ferry to Doyle's Tavern, all around Harrow he saw things changing. Even in the cold, even in the rain, they were fixing siding, patching roofs, filling potholes. Eager people doing the work. Making the changes. Improving their lives. A little part of him thought, *Maybe I had a hand in this. Maybe the apple is at the heart of all of it.*

As for the police? His warning may not have scared that girl off, but he knew now he was safe. Lambert made sure of that. Said that Sheriff Horsley—brother to Scott Horsley, making him another one of Edgar Beckman's nephews—shut down any inquiry into Walt's death. He told Dan, "A fella came asking, one of the friends of the deceased." Which surprised Dan; he figured it would've been that woman, Emily. Dan tried to explain he didn't know anything about any of that, and Lambert laughed. "I know you wouldn't have had anything to do with that business, Dan, and the police know it, too. They won't bother you about it."

That, it seemed, was the end of that.

His relationship with Lambert was, like his own Ruby Slipper, a tree that bore considerable fruit. Already Lambert had secured for him a loan to continue to expand the orchard and its capabilities, allowing him to finish his cider house and begin planning out the rest: a small market shack, for instance, plus a little office. Not to mention that once it got warm again, he intended to pave the dirt road that led down here to the orchard itself. It also allowed Dan to purchase new equipment, like a

Bobcat backhoe loader, a stump grinder, a brush mower, all of which would go toward clearing out more of the thicket around the orchard in order to expand. Lambert lent Dan the usage of Earl Dawes, his vineyard manager—a role occupied by Big Dan Paxson once upon a time. Dawes, a thick-necked fellow whose calluses had calluses, said that they should plan to grow other apples, too, in the orchard—and Dan of course balked at that, said he didn't need to grow other apples. He had *the* apple. The Ruby Slipper was the *only* apple.

But Lambert agreed with Dawes and was persuasive on this point: He said other orchards, they didn't get by on just one apple, did they? No, of course not, they had, what, Honeycrisp and McIntosh and Golden Delicious and so on and so forth. "Plus," Lambert said in a low voice so that only Dan could hear, "we both understand that this apple of yours is something special, but maybe we want to hide that point of fact, make it seem to outsiders looking in that this is business as usual." Besides, Lambert added, part of securing the loan was about offering a business plan that was diverse, diffuse, that looked the way a successful orchard looked.

"But I didn't do a business plan," Dan said. Lambert said that was okay—he had done one for him, and that's how he managed to secure the loan.

"You don't have to worry about anything," Lambert said, holding Dan by both shoulders. "Trust me when I say, This is how we do it. This is how we get it *right*. You want to get it right, don't you?"

Dan sure did. It was all he wanted in the world. Get it right. Get it *perfect.*

For you, Dad.

For you, Calla.

And for me, too.

Calla, though . . .

Well, that was the one fleck of pepper in a cellar full of salt. He'd always been so close to her. They'd been friends, the best of friends, really, even though he was sure she wouldn't ever want to admit that. He knew everything about her. He'd always had a strong hand in her life and she was happy to have that guidance. But now that things were going so well, why was his relationship with her going so poorly? It felt strained. Hostile, even. It was Marco, he knew. Marco, who Dan loved! Marco, who was always here, helping him out. Marco, who had *eaten the apple,* unlike Dan's own

(*ungrateful, disrespectful, wanton*)

daughter. She was spurned. Wore the spite of it on her sleeve. Yes, some of that was her feeling kept out of the loop, but Dan knew Marco choosing to skip college felt to her like a betrayal. And it was, and he respected that. But just the same, Dan knew she had to get real. Marco was not her future. College was not Marco's future. He was a good kid. Bright. Smart and strong. *He ate the apple.* Dan was glad for Marco. But he realized it now: His daughter deserved better. She deserved the *best.*

But she couldn't see that. She was still all brokenhearted for Marco, and Dan knew to some degree she blamed *him* for that broken heart.

She felt like Marco's betrayal was Dan's, too. Like Dan was some conspirator against her. If he was, it was only a conspiracy to have her be free of the burden of a lesser partner. It was a conspiracy for her to be better than she was.

Still. It led them to have a fight on Christmas, and Dan regretted how he spoke to her—but she had to know, he was doing this for her. None of this happened without his hard work, and why couldn't she appreciate that? It was like with Joanie that night at the dinner—that woman couldn't see clear through to the fact that Dan had worked his fingers near to the bone to *achieve something.* And that something was real. It wasn't a joke. It wasn't to be spat upon. No, it didn't make him a hero, he didn't deserve a parade, but it was a thing of value. And for the first time in his life, Dan felt that he himself was of value. Why didn't they appreciate that? Why couldn't they *see* that?

As his daughter, Calla represented Dan out in the world. Dan couldn't have her running around with some half-assed migrant worker. Marco would not be their future. She'd realize this in time.

But for now, Calla moped. All winter long. That was all right. She got into the college she wanted—and he knew he'd be able to send her there. Where she *deserved* to go. Because his daughter demanded the very best, because she was the best. As the saying went, the apple didn't fall far from the tree, now did it?

JOANIE WILL NOT LOVE THY NEIGHBOR

Fucking Prentiss Beckman, that sniffy, drunk, puritanical fucking dick-head. That hot-dog-necked douche. The beady-eyed prick. That taint-sniffing, stuck-up, repressed, pig-nosed, ball-less scrotum. That fucking über-Republican, ex-frat-boy rapist, swim-team captain, gone-to-pasture *creep.*

Joanie wanted to kill him.

It was New Year's Eve when he escalated.

They had a kinky scenester couple coming in to rent the house. They weren't even going to have a party like some people did some years. They were going to rent the place, have a couple of friends over, and then— well, whatever happened after that, Joanie didn't care to know if they didn't care for her to know it. Maybe they'd fuck and suck and tie each other up in shibari rope bondage, or maybe they were just going to have some white wine and charcuterie, then move to some cuddles and ass-play. Joanie didn't care. The house was stocked. The gear was clean.

Joanie and Graham retired to their city apartment for the night. They had an albeit distant look at the fireworks over Penn's Landing, but a view was a view. They planned on having some white wine and char-cuterie and then, you know, for dessert, maybe some fucking and suck-ing. Their sex life, by some mystery, only got better as they got older, and so why not ride that pony till it died?

But then, just as she was unpacking the meats and cheeses—

A phone call.

Their houseguests, in a panic.

Because *Prentiss Fucking Beckman* was out there harassing them. Pound-ing on the door. Calling them whores and groomers and liberals. Told them they weren't welcome in this neighborhood. Which, of course, *ter-rified* these people. They couldn't have a nice night and they didn't feel comfortable leaving—because *he* was out there, waiting for them.

Joanie called the police and she and Graham got a car back to the burbs. Which wasn't a fast drive—though the roads were quieter now, as people were already ensconced in whatever *party scenarios* they had so planned, it was still an hour, easy. When they got there, the police were of course *just* showing up, and so Joanie got with the couple, apologizing up down and sideways, before they gave a statement to the cops. The cops went and spoke to Prentiss, and *of fucking course* they weren't going to bring any charges against him, they said he'd just had a bit too much to drink and was feeling salty, just needed to "sleep it off." Joanie told them to go fuck themselves and do their jobs—why exactly was it that cops never seemed like they wanted to do their jobs? They just wanted everyone to shut up so they could go and jerk each other off in their expensive new cop cars. One of the cops on his way out said, "Ma'am, I'm sorry you feel that way, but between you and me, you might wanna reconsider what you do with this house. This is a *nice* community." That last sentence, said with a parent's judgment even though the officer was easily fifteen years younger than her. The little shit.

The renters were horrified, and Joanie was horrified for them. The rental agreement made it pretty clear that she could still charge them for the night, but not only was she not a monster, she *also* didn't want them to leave a review on the site that talked about the Scary Neighbor. She told them they owed nothing, and she threw in a night at some point later if they wanted it, which they wouldn't, because of the Scary Neighbor.

(They went home and left a review anyway. One star. Fuck.)

Beckman didn't stop there, that night, oh no.

She'd find him outside, just standing there, staring at her house.

Or at one of his windows, watching their house through binoculars, or through a long camera lens.

One time he was out in his driveway, in the cold drizzle, cleaning his guns—who does that? Who stands out in the rain, cleaning a gun? Joanie had her libertarian leanings, and had always voted on the belief that people were better off policing themselves, thank you very much, whether that was about motorcycles or drugs or sex or, yeah, even guns. She had her own guns: a little .380 pistol, a pump-action 20-gauge. Just in case.

But even *she* knew the kinds of guns Beckman had were, while legal, not used for anything good. Sure, guys who had black rifles and AR-15s were always saying, *Oh we use it to shoot raccoons,* but she knew they meant something else. And she knew it because it was always white guys who said it, and they said it in a way where there was a mad, cruel, inbred twinkle in their eyes. Like, oh, it was just a joke, but also, no it goddamn wasn't.

Same kind of twinkle she saw in Prentiss Beckman's eyes.

It got worse in February.

They found a pile of shit on their front stoop. Human, by the look of it.

A week later, they stepped out their front door and found bent nails tucked in the weave of their doormat, so that the base of the nail was hidden, exposing only the sharp part—which was by itself difficult to see. Graham nearly stepped on it.

Then they started to find dead animals scattered around their property. Rats. Crows. A possum. Not shot. Sick, maybe. Or worse, poisoned. Each had froth and blood around their beaks and muzzles. "Thank god we don't have any pets," Graham said, trying to conceal the severity of what was going on under a thin veneer of wryness. But Joanie wasn't having any of it.

"This is serious," she told him. "It's a threat." She said they could call the cops again, but Graham correctly pointed out they wouldn't do a damn thing. They didn't have evidence it was Beckman. Wasn't like they were going to run DNA tests on the turd, or fingerprint the nails, or run camera footage from the neighborhood to see how he was somehow killing local wildlife.

"Camera footage," Graham said, thoughtfully. "Hm."

"What is it?"

"I'm going over there." As he said those words, Graham was already putting on a jacket and heading out the front door. She called his name, hurrying after him—putting herself in his way. The cold winter wind whipped past them.

"The hell you are," she said.

"It's fine, I've got this." A foxlike smirk cracked his face.

"You don't. He's a psycho. I'm at least coming with."

"He despises you. I hate to say it, Jo, but he's one of those men who really, really doesn't like talking to women."

"All the more reason for me to be in his face."

Graham sighed. "I understand. And I don't disagree. But I want to fix this and I think I can fix this. Will you let me? Try, at least?"

"Graham. It's a bad idea."

"I need you to trust, Jo."

She gritted her teeth. Her jaw felt so tense, she could feel it tighten her neck tendons, her shoulders, the muscles that ran parallel to her spine.

Finally, she acquiesced.

"Fine."

Graham bent and kissed her on the cheek. And a horrible thought ran laps through her head: *What if this is the last time I see you alive, Graham? What if that was our last kiss?* That was absurd. It wasn't that bad. Prentiss was a psychopath but not . . . *that* kind of psychopath, right?

As Graham waltzed across the expanse of their lawn toward Beckman's house, Joanie cursed under her breath and bolted inside, grabbing her own gun from the fingerprint-locked safe under their bed. The .380 was small—a true *lady pistol,* in her mind, not that she wouldn't have minded a fucking hand cannon .357 right now to shove up Prentiss Beckman's flabby pancake ass.

She slapped the magazine into the gun, made sure the safety was on, and hurried downstairs—

Just as the front door was already opening.

Oh no.

Graham stepped inside.

She relinquished a trapped breath. A surge of warmth and a tsunami of chills traded places across her body.

"Graham," she said, relieved to see him again. "Not home, I guess?"

"He was home." Her husband smiled. "I think it's fixed."

"Wh—what? How?"

"I knocked on his door and when he answered, I told him that we have footage of all his little shenanigans. He started to stammer, and I shushed him like you shush a mouthy terrier, and I said, Prentiss, these days there is no privacy. Everyone has cameras for everything, and we have them in our house and outside of it to protect the property in case renters break something but don't want to pay for it. So, I said we'd be glad to let bygones be bygones and chalk this up to an unfortunate neighbor dispute—provided he quit harassing us immediately. Otherwise, I said, I will go to the police, I will call a lawyer, and I'll even give the footage to the press—which will definitely be problematic for his father. He looked like I'd just slapped him. I told him to nod if he understood, and he nodded. So I thanked him and said, *Hugs and kisses,* and back here I came."

Joanie laughed, incredulous. "Graham, we don't have cameras anywhere." It was true. They didn't. Joanie was a massive advocate for privacy—hers, Graham's, especially the privacy of her renters.

Graham shrugged.

"Prentiss does not know that."

"You beautiful genius."

"I blush."

"Oh, I'll make you blush, all right."

Graham chuckled as she swept him up and kissed under his jawline. In his ear she whispered, "Did you really tell him *hugs and kisses?*"

"I did."

"Glorious," she said, and it was. They spent the rest of the day playing in bed. Though through all their dalliances, the thought worried at her like rats chewing wires: Would Prentiss really stop? Or would he escalate?

But Graham seemed to be right.

Next week, nothing.

Week after, nothing.

Rest of February and into March, Prentiss was nowhere to be seen.

They did it.

They *won.*

(Or so they thought.)

Winter was safe.

But springtime had other ideas.

Because while winter was a time of hibernation and quiet—

Spring burst forth with violent growth.

THE NEIGHBOR'S TALE

PRENTISS BECKMAN, AGE 12.

The first time he understands it, it's from watching a VHS tape his cousin got off of HBO, some movie called *Butterfly*. It's a crimey movie, he doesn't much like it and doesn't remember the plot—something about a silver mine. What he likes, though, are the scenes of Pia Zadora being naked and having sex with men, one of whom might be her father, which honestly only gives Prentiss more of a thrill. He imagines himself being the man having sex with her, but he imagines being *her*, too. Giving it, and getting it in return. It gives him a righteous stiffy, as the other boys in school call it. His parents have a big property with some woods on it, so he goes down there and that's the first time he jerks off and it damn sure isn't the last. He keeps magazines down there, too. Lingerie catalogs that came in the mail. But teen mags, too, like the ones the girls like, *Tiger Beat* and all that.

He doesn't realize one time that his father has followed him down there, to find out what he's doing. And when he learns what's happening—and he learns about the VHS tape—his father is angry in a way that Prentiss has never seen. His father beats him that night all over his back, and the back of his legs, and his bare butt, with a rough wooden spoon. He bleeds a little, but it's mostly bruising. He cries all night, the kind of hitching sobs that hurt your ribs. Pain upon pain. His mother tries to help but his father chases her away.

The next day, Prentiss is pulled from school and sent to a boarding school in Vermont.

PRENTISS BECKMAN, AGE 17.

The school, Saxton Academy, threatens to expel Prentiss because some-one catches him peeping into the men's showers. He says it's not true, but it is. His father Edgar spends the money to make the threat of expulsion go away. Prentiss graduates a year later, but they don't let him walk onstage.

PRENTISS BECKMAN, AGE 20.

His father will not pay for school in New York City, even though that's where Prentiss wants to go. But he's allowed to go to school at St. Joe's in Philly—though he still takes bus trips to NYC every weekend to party. He acts like a frat boy at school, because he is, but when he leaves school, he's different. He knows he's different. He can feel it. He goes to different kinds of parties. Drugs more than drinking. Lots of sex. The first time he has a threesome—an older man and woman get him fucked up on pills and take him back to their hotel room—is there, in New York, his favorite place on Planet Earth. Prentiss knows he can be himself in that city. No one judges him. No one knows the other version of himself, the fake version, the wrong version.

He goes home for Thanksgiving his junior year, and all dinner, his father is quiet, simmering at the end of the table like a pressure cooker about to vibrate off the counter. After the meal, after the big family has gone home, his father tells him that he knows what Prentiss has been doing. He said a young investment banker he knows—"Cabot's nephew," he says—saw Prentiss at a bar not in NYC, but in Coryell's Ferry, kissing a man. Prentiss went out drinking the night before, back in town. The story was true. He admits it.

Prentiss tries to tell his father that he thinks he's bisexual.

His father attacks him on the front porch. Hits his son in the mouth, knocks some teeth loose, but cuts up his own hand, too. And while he's looking at knuckles cut to bloody ribbons, he's distracted, so Prentiss hits him back. Busts the old man's eye socket, breaks the bone. That's the end of the fight. His father, crying on the porch, eye swollen like a bad apple. Dad tells him, he's cut off. No more money. No more anything. He's on his own, *all the way* on his own, and Prentiss feels free for a moment—like a bird out of a cage, like he can go and do anything now, be anyone, fuck anyone, live the life he knows to live, but then the crushing realization arrives. He won't be able to go back to school. No frat. No trips to NYC. He'll have to—what? Live here? He has no job, no prospects. He was always supposed to work for his father or one of his father's friends. His future is wide open—but wide open like a fucking pit. Deep and dark and full of nothing. And before Prentiss knows what's going on, he's begging his father to forgive him, telling him he'll go to church, he'll be better, he's sick, he's diseased, and his father agrees. It is sick. It is a disease. He calls him a queer, says he needs to get himself straight, literally straight, like a fucking arrow. Any more anything like that, and Prentiss is done. Done forever. Cut off and dead to Edgar.

Prentiss agrees.

PRENTISS BECKMAN, AGE 35.

He drinks a lot. He's kinda fat now but tells himself it's muscle. He's got a job, real estate, not that he goes into the office or anything. He dates girls. Everything is fine, fine, fine, just fine. His father hates him still but he's not cut off. On rare nights, after drinking, he watches gay porn on the internet, sometimes wears women's panties when he does it, then he jerks off but the drinking makes it hard to get hard (har har) and then he punishes himself by taking a penknife and sticking just the tip of it into parts of his body no one can see. Often the inner thigh. Not deep enough to hit anything serious, though one time he bleeds real bad after. Sometimes he imagines sticking the knife in his father.

PRENTISS BECKMAN, AGE 43.

They fucking taunt him, those two. He hates them. They want to fuck him, his neighbors, but he won't let them. Even though it makes him hard as Detroit steel thinking about it. Joanie and Graham. Deviants. Psychos. They're what's wrong with America. He sees the way they look at him. The way they play with him. Two cats with a mouse. But he's no mouse. He's a fucking dog and he'll tear out their throats if they keep messing with him. He watches them out the window, eating apples, waiting for them to go by one of their windows, hoping they'll see him seeing them, hoping they'll know he won't fall prey to their petty little games, hoping they'll try to seduce him and try to fuck him so he can call them whores and call the police and get them kicked out of this town, the fucking freaks. Though maybe he'd fuck her, just to show the other one how a real man does it. He stands there, eating these apples, these very good apples, the juice slicking his face, and he imagines what he could do to them, because he is good and he is righteous and sometimes people need to be punished for the way they are.

THE END OF MARCH

(SPRING BEGINS)

I PLUCKED PINK BLOSSOMS FROM MINE APPLE-TREE
AND WORE THEM ALL THAT EVENING IN MY HAIR:
THEN IN DUE SEASON WHEN I WENT TO SEE
I FOUND NO APPLES THERE.

—CHRISTINA ROSSETTI,
"AN APPLE GATHERING"

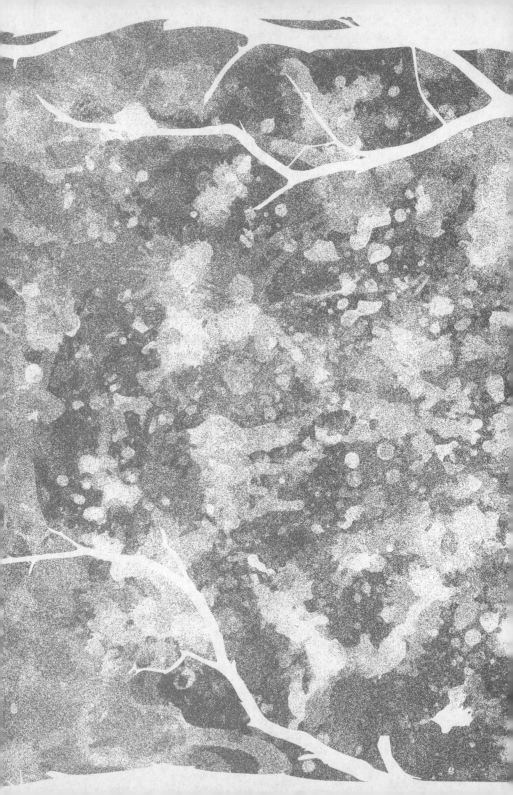

38

SPRING FORTH

THE PROVERB WENT: *IN LIKE A LION, OUT LIKE A LAMB*. THAT'S WHAT they said about the month of March—how it began with wind and the rain and lingering rough-edged blizzards, and how it ended with that foul weather tamed, domesticated. Gone was the vicious beast. Remaining was the docile lamb. But the proverb ignored that the purpose of the lion was to hunt, and the purpose of the lamb was to be eaten by the lion.

And, sometimes, to be sacrificed to the lion's glory.

JOANIE CAME HOME THAT EVENING, JUST AFTER DARK—SHE'D BEEN in the city yesterday and today, dealing with repairs to the apartment. Graham stayed at the McMansion, because as it turned out, he had to deal with repairs, too. They were playing a game of *dueling contractors,* each having work done at each place on the same day, thanks to the cruelty of the scheduling gods—at the Philly apartment, it was all plumbing, because leaky caulk (hah) had caused the shower to drain water under its basin, which ran out under the floorboards and baseboard molding, which upped the risk of mold, blah blah blah. At the house in Bucks, it was HVAC chaos: Their propane system was acting erratic, and the guy said the whole shebang was ten years old and needed to be replaced. He told them, "You don't want a faulty propane system—a place about five miles from here blew up." Said the propane filled the house like a balloon, then *popped* it the same way. *Ploom.* Joanie remembered that: Even five miles away, she felt it in her teeth. Turned that house to splinters. Thankfully nobody was home—though she'd heard a black Labrador had been aerosolized by the explosion. They found only its collar in a nearby tree.

So, Graham was at the McMansion, dealing with *that* bullshit, and she was in the city, dealing with *this* bullshit.

Homeownership, she decided, was total bullshit.

So, with her end done, she took SEPTA to Doyle's Tavern, where her Porsche was parked, then headed home.

She was eager to see Graham. As of late, since everything, they'd grown closer. They'd always been close, or so she thought: They were best friends, they got along like a pair of aces and eights, but something about the whole Prentiss Beckman madness brought them even closer together. She felt like she was falling in love with him all over again: not just the old, comfortable love of marriage, but what was often referred to, once to Joanie's chagrin, as a rekindled spark. She felt like a giddy schoolgirl when seeing him—like he was her crush, and she was his, and they kept crushing on each other *hard*. Christ, just last week they dry-humped on the couch, making out like a couple of horned-up teenagers. It was fucking amazing.

So, tonight, she was looking forward to collapsing into his arms, and maybe doing a little more of that sloppy, clumsy, couch-bound making out. It felt somehow both innocent and taboo. It felt romantic and mad.

Nothing else in the world mattered. Just coming home and seeing Graham.

JOANIE FELT IT AS SOON AS SHE STEPPED IN THE DOOR. LIKE THE very air had been disturbed—a violation of the spirit, the soul, of the home. The first thought, almost absurd, was, *It's not safe here.*

The house was dark.

And quiet.

It shouldn't have been.

The silence met her like a wall, a wave of tinnitus.

"Graham?" she called out.

Maybe he went out.

But he said he'd meet her here. Said he'd wait to eat until she got home. Maybe he went out to pick up food? He often liked to surprise her with something like that—charcuterie, or a pizza from Spuntino's, maybe sushi from Ooka.

Still. Wouldn't he have said something?

There was a frequency here—an off-feeling, an ill vibe. She told herself it was just because people had been here all day: HVAC guys, contractors, whoever. That always churned the air, made your house feel invaded, trespassed upon.

No, she thought.

This is different.

She set her bag down and wished like hell that she had that little .380 on her. She didn't bring it into the city with her—the city had its own dangers, though none that compared to the ones out in the burbs. But walking around with a concealed, loaded pistol in Philadelphia was fraught—worse if somehow she lost track of the weapon or it got stolen from her. So, the pistol stayed here.

Currently, it was back upstairs, under her bed.

You don't need a pistol, Joanie, for Chrissakes.

She headed deeper into the house, calling for her husband again. No response. The stillness of her own home felt oppressive. Smothering.

As she went through the house, she flipped on lights. One after the next. Foyer. Hallway. Staircase up—though she did not ascend, not yet. And then—

Joanie reached for the kitchen switch.

But her hand paused there, hovering. Because a smell hit her. A greasy, coppery stink. And with it, a faintly sulfurous stench—like the breath of Hell itself.

(*blood*)

(*gunpowder*)

"Graham," she said, this time not calling out his name, just saying it as an utterance, a prayer, a plea. Her fingers still floated over the switch. She didn't want to hit it. *Couldn't* turn it on. Her whole arm felt paralyzed—it burned with fear, from fingertips to elbow to shoulder. The ringing in her ears grew louder.

She sucked in a sharp breath and mashed her palm flat against the switch.

The lights came on in the kitchen.

The blood burned bright on the travertine tile. Lit up like black satanic neon. It puddled on the floor past the island, and her first thought was an absurd one: *It's just raspberry syrup.* They had a bottle of that somewhere, didn't they? Graham had all kinds of goos and potions for cocktail-making. She wanted to laugh because it was fine, just a broken bottle of something sweet, but then she saw it spattered across the back-splash, and she spied a pair of feet—gray wool socks jutting out from the other side of the island, Graham's socks, Graham's feet were always cold, he always needed those cozy socks—

Oh god, no. Graham.

She willed herself to move—*Hurry, he may need your help,* she thought, even though another thought followed close behind, like a stalking wolf. A thought that said, *It's too late, you're too late.* Joanie rounded the corner of the kitchen island and a cry fled her chest like a startled bird—

Graham, on his back. Faceup.

Where his nose had been was now an exit wound, like a raw red meat-lined crater—one eye was still open and clear, but the other had been disrupted, pushed up and out of the flesh of his face. The wound opened down to his mouth, splitting his upper lip into two. Jaw open. Tongue out over lower teeth. Swollen.

Blood pooled in both directions, running along the grout lines at its furthest points. Black and glistening. Blood like a

(*red apple*)

deep lake.

Suddenly it hit her, nearly killed her, this scouring revelation of, *We're all just meat, there is nothing more than that.* Graham was somebody, Graham was light and love and wit and sneer and now he was just *this,* just a dead thing, a faceless piece of meat in gray wool socks, *Oh god, Graham is dead, Graham is dead, Graham is dead,* that thought boomeranging around her head again and again, *whoosh, whoosh, whoosh.*

She looked up because she had to look up—had to look *away.*

And when she did, she saw she was not alone.

In the shadows of the adjoining living room, just next to a tall lamp, stood a familiar shape. Even in the gray half-light, it was easy to see Prentiss Beckman there. He stepped out, shirtless, taking another step forward—his skin, gray like a lawn grub, face bloodless as a pebble.

He had a gun in his hand. A pistol.

He raised the gun.

Called her a whore.

And pulled the trigger.

39

HUGS AND KISSES

WHEN THE GUN WENT UP, JOANIE FELT HERSELF TURNING TO flee—had that feeling of running in a nightmare, where the floor was slick, where her feet could not get purchase, where instead of sprinting for escape she started to fumble and fall down. Her hand darted out, caught something—a skillet dangling from the pot rack hanging above the island—but it was not designed to support that kind of weight. The rack burst from its moorings.

She skidded sideways as the gun went off—

Bang—

And she fell to the floor under a clatter of pots and pans. A saucier clipped Joanie in the side of her head; stars were born behind her eyes. Dizzy, she hauled herself up against the narrow end of the island with Graham's

(*meat, just meat*)

face only inches from her. Her ears still rang. A shadow moved in her periphery the killer, Prentiss, stalking through the kitchen. Moving on the other side of the island, the one opposite from the hallway, from Graham's

(*meat, carcass, just meat, oh god he's gone and I'm alone*)

body. The shadow fell upon her, Prentiss moving into view—

She realized then she still had something in her hand—

The skillet. She'd never let it go. It came down with her—its handle gripped now with blood-drained knuckles.

Prentiss stared down at her with empty eyes, eyes like holes in his head. "I know you don't have cameras, whore. I checked. Who do you think you are. Why do you get to be like this. Who do you think you are."

His words were dead things. Bodies in a slow-moving mudslide.

"Go fuck yourself," Joanie spat at him.

He said, words limp and lifeless: "Hugs and kisses."

At that, Beckman again brought up the gun—a boxy gun, heavy, long, like a .45—

Joanie screamed a ragged howl, launching herself up and swinging hard with the skillet. It connected with the gun hand, knocking it wide—

Bang. The gun went off—

He shoved her backward, her back slamming into the quartz countertop, pain shooting up her spine like a snap of lightning.

He raised the weapon again—

This time, she brought the skillet *down*—

The gun clattered from his grip.

He bared his teeth at her and hissed.

She hissed back at him, and smashed the skillet sideways into his mouth. Teeth broke. He staggered backward, clutching at a lower jaw that no longer seemed to sit right against the rest of his face—he howled like an injured animal and turned to run. She saw now he was in bare feet, too—

No, you don't get to run.

Joanie screamed again, picking up the weapon that he'd dropped and chasing after him, hurrying into the hallway in time to see him throw open the front door and bolt outside—she had no time to aim, instead firing indiscriminately at the fleeing Prentiss Beckman—

The gun bucked in her hand, *boom, boom, boom,* and Beckman pitched forward into the dark—

Got you.

She bolted down the hall, through the front door, expecting to see him there, bleeding, dying, even dead, and that thought gave her a sick, awful thrill, a vengeful sense of satisfaction that made her queasy.

But when she exited the house—

He wasn't there.

Beckman was gone.

No. He's here. He's fucking here somewhere—

There. She saw blood on the walkway. Saw the azalea bushes smashed down, their just-budding branches broken.

In the distance, sirens wailed.

Joanie hopped the broken shrub, going around the western side of the house—this, in the opposite direction of Beckman's own home. Behind their house was an expanse of mowed yard—currently soggy, with tons of standing water, thanks to an overly wet winter. Past that, a tree line and hedgerow that headed off into a farmer's field. She looked in every direction: Saw nothing. Saw no one. No footprints in the grass. No blood that she could make out. But it was dark. Hard to see anything. She cursed under her breath. *No, no, no! Fuck!*

Graham was gone. His killer had escaped.

The moment came when she thought to give chase. To run anywhere, everywhere. But at that moment, the fight went out of her. Her knees nearly buckled. She suddenly didn't want to chase. She only wanted to die.

As the sirens grew louder and louder, Joanie went inside to be with her husband one last time, alone, before the police arrived.

40

WHAT WE SAY TO THE DEAD

IN THOSE MINUTES BEFORE THE POLICE ENTERED THE HOUSE, Joanie knelt by her husband, the blood sticky around her knees. She held his cold hand. She looked into the face that was mostly gone, and she spoke to the soul that she feared was now all-the-way gone. Graham was not in this body anymore, and in her view was not in this life or anything after: Joanie admitted to a worldview that allowed only for people to diminish and disintegrate into their respective parts. Your body broke down into its component resources, given back to the universe sure as the universe was given to you. But who you really were, the consciousness that you possessed, the *self* that you had been, was gone: You were now selfless in the truest sense of that word. You gave everything and kept nothing. It was, she'd always thought, a beautiful way to see the world and its essential cycle of life and death. The confluence of cosmic forces conspired to make you, loaning you out to the world until the day came when you repaid that debt, giving back whatever you had made of yourself.

But now she found that thought to be a flensing feeling that cut her to the bone—it was so easy to think that cycle beautiful when you saw yourself in it. It felt gracious and perfect, like you had been given something to govern, over which to stand vigil. It was noble and good and all that happy horseshit, but when it was someone else? Someone you loved who was called to give back what they had been gifted? To cease existing in order to return their motes of life and stardust back to the universe? That felt like theft. It felt like cruelty.

The reality that who Graham was—

Was no more.

So, when she spoke to him, to the body, to the

(*carrion, carcass, nothing*)

thing that had been Graham, she knew it was for her more than it was for him. He could not hear her because there was no him at all.

This, she knew, was for her.

She told him, as tears snaked their way down her cheeks:

"Graham, I love you. I loved you. I will love you until I am gone, too. I feel like a child. Like all I was was this person who followed her urges, who wanted things and went and took them, and I love you because you indulged me, you did not question me, you did not judge me. You were the best part of this stupid world and now that it has lost you, it is a worse place. The *worst* place. You were the best part of me, and now that you're gone from me, I am worse, too. I took too long to realize how essential you were. I don't know that I will ever really be me again." As she spoke, the sirens grew so loud they seemed to be howling in her ear—through the front windows, the red and blue lights strobed, staccato, a rush of dizzying color. She left the front door open, and she heard the police enter, and as they did, she yelled to them: "In here!"

But as she did, she saw something nearby.

In the living room.

On the floor, by the lamp, next to the couch

Three apple cores. Their tops red as her husband's blood.

The cops rushed in, pointing their guns at her, because of course they did, that's all they knew: Every problem was a nail, and they were the hammer. But she couldn't care about that, even as she stood, putting her hands above her head. All she could do was stare at those apple cores.

THE NIGHT HAD NO MARGINS. IT WAS BOTH ENDLESS AND TEMPO-rary: somehow eternal and yet, just a blip, barely an event at all.

Cops continued to show up, as if the world disgorged them, vomiting them into her driveway, onto her lawn, into her house. They were clumsy and messy. They were hostile. They did not treat her like a victim, but rather, like a potential perpetrator. Asking her all kinds of questions about where she was, what happened here, was that her gun, *why* did she have a gun. Eventually a detective showed up: bald guy, a thin sad mustache on his upper lip. Chuck Balko. Balko was nicer, but still had that edge to his questions:

Did you have any problems with your husband?

Was he cheating on you?

Were you cheating on him?

The whole time she was like, it was Prentiss Beckman. Prentiss. Beckman. He was here. He attacked her. He had a gun. He shot her husband, *no,* she didn't *see him* do that, but he was here with a gun and her husband was dead, and then he tried to kill her, too. She said, look over there, he had been eating apples—but suddenly, those apple cores? Were gone. Nobody could seem to find them. They treated her like she was crazy. Ha ha, apple cores? You're just seeing things, lady. Maybe she was.

Balko went over, spoke to a couple of the uniformed guys. Then he came back to her, sat back down, and said, "Is it true that you and your husband had . . . an open marriage?"

"That's not your business."

"It might be. Your husband is dead." Balko stared at her, but she stared back, stone-faced. He sighed and changed his question: "Is it true that you rent this house out for . . ." He seemed to struggle with the words. "Sex purposes?"

"Sex purposes? You mean so people can have sex here."

"If you say so."

If you say so. Fucking little-mustached prick. "Am I under suspicion, Detective Balko? Because if so, say it, and I will call my lawyer. But I didn't do this. Prentiss Beckman did. He already harassed people renting this place, that's on the record. And if you talk to people at the Crossed Keys dinner at Thanksgiving, at the Goldenrod? They'd tell you he confronted me there, too. He shot my husband with that gun—" She pointed to the pistol on the counter. "And then tried to kill me with it, too. Then I shot him, and his blood is out on the front walkway of my house. That's it. That's the story. Now either you go find him and leave me to grieve my dead husband, or I call that lawyer of mine."

Balko seemed to recoil a little. "We are looking for Mister Beckman."

"Good." *Because he may very well want to finish the job.*

At that, they seemed to back off, handle her with kid gloves. Nobody took her into the station. Nobody suggested she get a lawyer. They mostly left her alone after that, which gave her a front-row seat for them zipping up her husband's body into a black bag and carrying him out the front door like he was nothing more than a piece of ruined furniture or an old, discarded rug. She wanted to weep but couldn't, anymore. She was emptied out. Like she, too, had been shot, and all that was left of her had poured out the hole. Her blood, her tears, her hope, her soul.

41

THE COMPASS FINDS TRUE NORTH

DAN STOOD AMONG HIS TREES, WORRIED.

All around him, the orchard had expanded over the winter: as the thicket and brush had fallen to the ground, he and Earl Dawes had begun to clear-cut all that mess, already making way for new trees to be planted. Already he had two dozen new apple trees on order: Honeycrisp, Gold-Rush, Pink Lady, Golden Delicious, six of each. They'd get them in the ground soon, soon as the soil was a bit drier and made itself workable. He told himself it was a good thing. More trees. More varieties. People liked variety, didn't they?

In his gut, he felt that no, no they did not.

All winter long, people came to him, asking to buy more of *his* apples. They didn't want Honeycrisp or Pink Lady or any other apple. They wanted the Ruby Slipper. The farmers markets were shut, and his local grocery deal didn't start until this year's crop came in, so he sold right to those people who came up to the house—they'd want whole bushels, but his inventory started to thin out fast, so he resorted to selling only a few apples at a time. The people, they were so happy to see him and the Ruby Slippers. They had bright eyes and warm smiles. They wanted to touch him, hug him, as if it was special just to be near him. They wanted to eat the apples with him, almost as if they were family. And they told him these stories, too. Stories that were increasingly familiar.

The apples had changed them, they said.

Mercedes August, who owned a bridal shop in Doyle's Tavern, said that her rheumatoid arthritis was nowhere to be found—used to be she could barely work the sewing machine anymore, but now her hands felt as spry as ever, and her eyesight was clear as a cloudless day.

Cort Tanzer, a farmer who also taught down at the ag college, said the damnedest thing happened: He was using a log splitter and the kid behind him, just some dumb teenager, didn't see that the first log hadn't been cleared and split yet, and so he ran the second log in through hard, just behind the first. Only problem was, Cort had his hand there. A hand that got crushed between two big logs. He said he could feel the hit, knew it was a hard one, a bad one, that his bones should've been (in his words) "smashed like peanuts into peanut butter." But when they moved the logs apart and he pulled his hand out of his glove, Cort could move all his fingers. Just in case, he went and had an X-ray and—not only did he not have even a single hairline fracture, they said he had the bones of a growing young man. Cort was sixty-three.

Daisy Gregory, a middle-aged housewife, a few years older than Dan, lived just down the road on a big sprawling farmhouse estate with her banking-industry husband, said to him: "For years now I've been wanting a horse. Bob—" Her husband. "Bob didn't want me to have one even though we had this house and this property, a property that was already fenced in, mind you, because the people who lived here before had horses. But he said no again and again, but you know what, Dan? I eat your apples, and so you know I feel different inside. I feel like, by gosh, life is short and these are things I want, so I'm going to get them. I bought not one horse, not two, but three, *and* I hired a stable manager to help me with them. Oh boy, Bob was mad as hell, too, you could see the anger coming off him in waves. Because I spent a *pretty penny*, let me tell you, but you know what I told him? I said, Bob, I don't give a rat's right foot what you think. He said he would sell those horses, and I said, Bob, if you try, I'll cut off your dick and balls with a pizza cutter, then I'll feed them to my horses like they were carrots and sugar cubes. Bob was a little more *amenable* after that." She said, as a sly aside: "Needless to say, Bob does not eat your apples."

It was story after story like that. Wasn't just health, either. People felt good. Felt happier and healthier than they had in years. Like they could do anything. Like they deserved better in this life. People asking for raises. Quitting their jobs and starting their own businesses. Buying up property. Getting their families in line. They were demanding the very best for themselves.

There were no other apples but these, Dan knew.

He wanted to push back. He met with Meg the other night, adopting her as a sort of *informal counsel* about all this, and she agreed that his apple was the only apple. But she said, go along with Lambert. Claude said they needed other trees? Okay. Order the trees, clear the ground, plant them when the thaw allowed. But they both knew the Ruby Slipper was all that mattered.

Problem was, it was the second day of spring.

And there wasn't yet a single sign of life in his trees.

Dan ran his hands along the cold, dark branches.

Both the fruit buds and the leaf buds—the former, plumper and furrier, the latter lean and smooth—remained unstirred by the warmer, wetter weather. Usually these trees of his started to at least change color by now, turning red and then green. But they were just . . . gray. Lifeless. *C'mon,* Dan pled with them, silently.

"They're not leafing out yet, huh," someone said behind him. A man. Dan turned to find a tall sort standing there. Older fellow. Like the human embodiment of a crooked walking stick. "Haven't woke up yet."

"It'll be fine," Dan said, almost defensive. "Do I know you, friend?"

"My name is John Compass. Friend."

John Compass.

Dan knew that name. This was the man who had been working with that young woman, Emily. The man who went to the police about him.

"You're trespassing," Dan said. His hands flexed into fists.

"There are worse crimes, as I'm sure you know."

Dan's guts cinched tight. An accusation. It had to be. Unsaid, but said.

The man, John, continued, changing subject back to the trees: "These trees don't look well, sir. They also don't look like any apple trees I know. They're darker, the branches . . . gnarlier. All snarled up. These are young but they have the shape of an old, old tree. Mind telling me where you found the original tree?"

"I didn't find it," Dan said. A lie. *I was shown it.* Or maybe, it showed itself *to* him. But he couldn't say those things. So he told his practiced story: "There is no original tree. These are the result of crossbreeding. Black Arkansas and Holland's Red Winter are the parents. Took me some years but that combination made a most superior apple."

"So the name Harrowsblack isn't familiar to you. How about Vinot's Allegresse? Or pkwësu?"

Dan stiffened. "No, Mister Compass." Another lie. The first two names, he knew. The third, though. What was that? Wasn't English. Native word, maybe.

"That's good. Because I've done some research with the help of my friend Emily. The Harrowsblack was one that the Native people here, the Lenape, thought to be a curse. Those people, my mother's people, had no written records, you see, so it took a bit to find out why they feared it so. And even now, it's difficult to find clarity—the accounts are all secondhand, from the Dutch, French, the British. But it seemed that the Lenape thought that the apple was poisonous. Not in the way you think, not like . . . nightshade or amanita mushrooms or arsenic. They believed the poison went far deeper than the flesh, that the apple was manetuwak, a bad spirit, like a parasite of the soul. It crawled in through your low places—the holes in you. Your bad thoughts. Your deepest wants. Your weaknesses are like thin spots and that's where the apple puts its roots, its shoots, where it buries its seeds. Old stories said this apple tore apart families. Villages. Groups of colonizers, too. Haycock Town, north end of this very county, but now gone from the map, its people . . . lost. As they say, one bad apple spoils the whole bushel."

Dan hesitated. "Quite the fantasy, don't you think?"

"It's folklore, not fantasy. Culture. Belief. Sometimes it seems strange but there's often truth in such strangeness." John Compass paused, as if considering his next words. "Someone murdered my friend Walt. You have his bag. Emily saw it, and I believe her. I know you threatened her. That tells me you do know the apple of which I speak, and that these tangled trees in this dark orchard are that very apple. I think Walt led you to a tree somewhere. And I think you killed him to keep it secret—to keep the apple all to yourself."

"I didn't kill your friend. Sounds like the river did that."

"I want you to know, Dan Paxson, I intend to bring you into the light."

"Is that a threat?" Dan asked. "Do you intend to harm me?"

"It's not my way. I am a peaceful man now, a Quaker. It's not my job to render judgment and act upon it. But I do think there's something righteous and necessary about chasing away shadows. And to see what has been using that darkness to hide."

Dan imagined himself crossing the distance toward this man and ripping his throat out and tossing the mess into the thicket. *Red makes the green.* His heart raced at the thought and a serpent of lust stirred in his guts. He cracked his neck and took a deep breath and said, "If you'll excuse me, I have work to do, so I'm going to ask you to kindly get the fuck off my property. I'd hate to call the police. My understanding is this sort of thing might constitute harassment on your part."

John forced a smile. "Of course. Have a good day, Dan Paxson."

"You too, John Compass."

And at that, the two men parted ways. But Dan figured they'd meet again, soon enough. And when they did, Dan would have to

(*kill*)

deal with him, somehow.

42

AN APPLE FOR TEACHER

CALLA'S PLAN WAS SIMPLE:

Keep your head down.

High school on a good day was like being in a war movie: It was you running through some jungle or trench trying not to get your head shot off. But at least once upon a time she had ways to make it feel not so fucked up—hanging out with friends, being with Marco, scanning the 'gram and livestreaming just, like, whatever was going on. Even dinner with Dad at the end of the day felt *normal.*

But nothing felt normal anymore. She and Dad weren't talking. Marco was . . . basically a stranger now. Her friends watched her from the periphery, like she was some snake in the grass who might bite them at any moment. She barely touched her phone anymore. What was the point? Head down, get to the end. Graduate. College. The thought of getting away and becoming whoever she wanted to be gave Calla a weird, bitter thrill. Like she could blow it all up, walk away, and become someone else.

So, it was the end of another school day. One more in the bucket. Back when things were cool, Marco would drive her home, and before that, Esther. But that was over now. Dad couldn't come and get her because he was too busy with his stupid fucking orchard, and she wouldn't want him to show up here anyway. So that meant the bus. Which smelled like feet and deodorant, two smells that did not conquer each other but instead somehow joined forces to make one altogether worse smell. But today, when she stepped out onto the bus platform—

Esther was there.

They stepped in front of Calla.

Calla tried to step around them—but Esther, tall and gangly as they were, handily blocked her path anew.

"Need a ride?" Esther asked.

"I'm fine," Calla answered, trying to inject as much sour-faced fuck-you into those two words as she could muster, but instead it just came out kinda pouty and pissy. Ugh. She added, "Thanks," but it only came out pissier.

But Esther was insistent. "Bus sucks. C'mon, I'll drive you."

Calla regarded them carefully.

"Why?"

Esther shrugged. "I dunno."

"This feels like a trap."

"It's not a trap."

"Okay, fine."

IT WAS A TRAP.

Calla got in the front seat of the car—a 2013 powder-blue Honda Fit peppered with dents and dings and saddled with approximately four billion miles. The moment she snapped the buckle across her lap, she felt motion as Lucas rose up in the back seat like a suburban vampire waking in his hatchback tomb.

"Hey, Call," Lucas said.

"*Jesus,*" Calla said, jumping. "You startled me."

Esther got in the driver's side. "Hey, sooooo, Lucas is here."

"Hi, Lucas," Calla said with an epic dose of grumpiness. *Awesome.*

"We'd like to have a chat," Lucas said.

And at that, Esther locked the car doors. *Kachunk.*

Calla's heart froze in her chest like a spooked rabbit.

"Let me the fuck out," she said.

Lucas leaned forward. "Not until you tell us about the apple."

"What?"

"The apple. *The apple.* Like you don't know. It's your dad's apple, isn't it?"

Esther made a sour face. "Don't say 'your dad's apple,' it sounds porny."

"Ew, no—I'm not—" Lucas made a wrung-out dishrag face. "Jesus Christing Christ, Esther. Calla knows what I'm talking about unless she's really that stupid."

"You don't have to be so mean," Calla said.

"What? I'm not saying you're stupid. I'm saying you're *not* stupid. I'm saying you're smart and observant so shut up."

"The apple," she said, repeating the phrase again. She could feel Lucas's trademark impenetrable stare—it was a stare of great judgment. Eyes like a pair of index fingers pointing at you in accusation. "Um."

"She's not stupid but she's playing stupid."

"Lucas—" Esther cautioned.

"Maybe she's already *eaten* her dad's apple." And the way Lucas said it, he was well aware of how porny it did in fact sound. It was intentional, this time.

"Fuck off, Lucas," Calla said.

"Well? Did you? Did you eat the apple? I mean for real, Calla."

Calla hesitated. Finally she said, "No. I . . . tried."

"You tried."

"Yeah. I . . ." She exhaled angrily through her nose and whirled around in the seat. "You know what? Why should I answer you? You two abandoned me. That whole stupid thing with the video and Marco—next thing I knew you were freezing me out and that—that fucking *sucked*." She gestured to Esther. "They come and offer me a ride, but it was just to put me in front of *you*." Another pointed stare at Lucas. "I'm so done with this. Let me out. Or so help me god I will kick and I will scream and if I have to? I will piss on your car seat, Esther."

Esther and Lucas shot looks at each other.

Then Lucas said, with quiet seriousness uncharacteristic of him:

"Something's happening in this school. This town."

"Oh," Esther added, leaning in, "Bee-tee-dubs, I think my pronouns are back to she/her, mostly, but they/them is still okay, too? I guess. I'm still sort of . . . feeling out this whole *gender carousel* thing—"

"*So* not the time," Lucas said.

"Sorry."

But to Esther, Calla said quietly, "No problem, and noted." To Lucas, then: "I know something's up. I just—"

"It's the apple," Esther said.

"It's *so* the apple," Lucas said.

Calla confirmed it. "Yes. Yeah. It's the apple. People eat one and . . .

they're different after. There was a part of me that thought . . . both of you had . . ."

"*No,*" Lucas said. "Apples are nasty."

Esther fished around for her vape pen and sucked in a breath, blowing out a plume of berry-scented mist. "We thought *you* were eating the apple."

That . . . made a lot of sense, Calla realized.

Lucas kept on talking: "I first saw it at the swim team. I was cutting through the pool area as a shortcut because I was already late for AP calc, and I saw the swim captain handing them out. The apples, I mean. And they all like, gathered around, eating them, making these—"

"Noises," Calla said.

"Yeah. Like they were having little food orgasms or something. And it's not just them. Look around in the halls you'll see someone pass an apple to someone else like it's a secret or something. Like it's a bag of Addys instead of . . . you know, a fucking piece of fruit. And I've seen people give them to teachers, too. Like, nobody *actually* gives an apple to a teacher because this isn't Little House on the Fucking Prairie or some shit. I saw Colby Nardell do it in AP history, I saw Jennie Cabot give it to Herbst, the art teacher. Sometimes it's the teachers giving them out. And the people who eat the apples? They're . . . not the same people. They're mean now. Not regular mean. Creepy mean."

"Cold," Esther said. "They're smiling but also, they're *really not.*"

"Seriously. Jennie Cabot and I sat next to each other. We weren't *besties* or anything but we shared friendly vibes, laughed at Mrs. Lars's arms— I know, I know, I'm not supposed to laugh at her fat arms, and it's not because they're fat, it's just because they dangle like bags of pierogi or something."

"It's fatphobic, a little bit," Esther said, quietly.

"I know it is! I said I know I'm not supposed to, Esther! Jesus Christ. People laugh at bad things because people are messy bitches, okay? At least I am aware of it and am working on myself. God." Lucas rolled his eyes. "I lost my train of thought. Fuck. Okay."

"Jennie Cabot," Calla reminded him.

"Yes. Right. Thank you. Jennie Cabot, second day in a row of art she's, like, going to hop up and leave, and I stop her and ask her, like, dude, what's up? What are you doing, what's your secret, are you going to get high in the bathroom and why is the teacher letting you go? Is it in her IEP or something? And she—I will never forget this—she looks at me with these *eyes*. They're oozing with contempt. It's almost like she barely knows who I am, right, and she says, *Why are you talking to me?* And I was like, what? And she said, *Why do you think it's okay to talk to me?* I was floored. I was like, *Bish*. No. What? *No*. Before I could even say anything she laughed and fucked off." Under his breath, Lucas said, "At least she didn't deadname me."

"My dad's different now," Calla said, abruptly. "And so is Marco. Marco is *indifferent* to me. Like he doesn't care about me or anything he cared about before. And my father is . . ." She tried to push her way through it, to understand it. Calla had done such a good job lately of pretending none of this was even real, or that it was a blip, a phase. "He pretends he loves me. He acts like he does, more than ever. Big smiles and gifts. But it feels fake. And when you call him on it, or cross him?" She blinked back tears. "He gets mean. Abusive. Not like, hitting me or anything. But just really nasty."

"Shit," Esther said. "Your dad was always so nice."

"Though kind of controlling," Lucas said under his breath.

"Hey."

"Just saying he always liked you a little too much, girl. And as for Marco . . ."

Esther and Lucas shared another look.

"What?" Calla asked. "Don't fucking hold out now. What is it?"

"We know how the apple is getting in," Lucas said.

"Oh, shit." Calla shut her eyes. She already knew. "It's Marco."

"It's Marco."

"Fuck." She made a half laugh. "This is so stupid. They're *apples*. They're not drugs! But . . ." Something tickled the top of her brainstem, some memory from years back. Her father, coming home. Late at night. He had branches. Cut branches. What would become, she was just realizing now, the trees that grew in their orchard. But there was something else, too—

She shuddered as the memory returned to her.

Severed fingers.

That didn't even make sense.

Why would they be there?

She hid that memory because—well, it had to be false. Just some lingering fragment from a fading dream. Right?

"He's their apple dealer," Esther said, taking another vape hit.

"Jesus."

"Yeah."

"I wish I knew what to do about this."

Lucas gave her a look. "I have an idea."

"Uhhh. Okay."

"Exposé. Social. Put it *all* over. You still have your 'gram. Start filming. We'll help you put together the videos, then you post them."

"Fuck that," Calla said, recoiling. "You do it. You have your TikTok account. I'm sure that Marco video really bought you a bunch of clout." She tried not to sound bitter there but fuck it, she was, and too late.

Esther leaned in. "Someone hacked him."

"It's true," Lucas confirmed. "I didn't have 2FA on—I already know, I'm a fucking idiot—and now my whole account is just posts about weird Chinese electronics. Toasters and nose trimmers and shit."

"Sorry."

"Live by the social media sword, die by the social media sword."

"I don't want to die by any sword."

"You won't. But you have an audience. You can post it and show people what's up. Worst-case scenario, they think you're, like, making up some weird Reddit creepypasta story about evil apple cults."

"No, *worst*-case scenario is they think I'm a fucking lunatic. Oh shit! Worst-*worst*-case is, my fucking *father* sees it."

"Does your dad use, like, any social media?"

"Well. No."

"There's one problem solved."

Calla turned around. Huffed a little. Said, finally, "I'll think about it."

"Like I said, we'll help," Lucas said.

"We totally will," Esther added.

"I said, I'll *think* about it. Now drive me home, please? I've got homework." Esther nodded and started the car. Lucas leaned forward and as the car lurched forward (because Esther was a lead foot with that gas pedal), he said:

"I'm sorry we kinda exiled you."

"And you're sorry you stole my video?"

Lucas sighed. "I'm sorry I stole your video."

"Okay. Cool."

"Besties again?"

Calla hesitated. She rolled her eyes. "Besties. *I guess.*"

43

EMILY WRITES IT DOWN

THE TWO OF THEM SAT AT THE KEYSTONE DINER ONE NIGHT, EAT-ing pie, talking about what she'd written down in her journal, a book she jokingly referred to as her "Megazine," because, y'know, *Meg* plus *magazine,* get it? But John just stared at her stone-facedly whenever she said it.

"Comedy is dead," she said, closing the journal with a sigh. "Anyway. Meg's been rationing the apples. Before, she ate one whenever she wanted to. At any hour of the day. But now it's like she's on a schedule. She doesn't bring whole bushels home. Just a few at a time now. Like you said, the trees aren't showing any signs of producing. Maybe . . . maybe this problem will solve itself. Maybe the trees are done."

At that, he grunted. "Dan still killed Walt. And Meg is still acting strange. It's still early. I don't think the trees are dead. They're just . . . waiting."

"Waiting. Like they're sentient or something?"

"I don't know."

"I just don't get it, John. It sounds too fucking wild to be real. A—an apple? A fruit somehow does this to people? Changes them? Makes them . . . weirder, stronger, healthier, meaner?"

"Maybe there's a scientific answer. Parasites can change your personality—a parasite in cat feces can make men more impulsive, women more affectionate. Someone with rabies becomes an entirely different person—they become hydrophobic, more fearful in general, more aggressive." But then he said: "Or maybe the answer is the one right in front of us: The world is a place of great evil, both human evil and an evil beyond us, and maybe this apple is a bridge between the two."

It made her think of something, and so she asked him: "Why didn't the apple work on you? It's like you rejected it. If it's evil . . . are you good? I mean, I think you're good, obviously, I just mean—" But she couldn't explain what she meant. Not exactly. Only that if the apple was one thing, maybe John was its opposite.

John seemed to rankle at that. It was as if the very thought disturbed him. At that, the conversation was over. Meg would be home soon anyway, so John drove her back to the house.

MEG WAS STILL IN THAT PHASE OF FEIGNING WARMTH WITH EMILY. Like they were in the facsimile of a marriage more than a marriage. She said nice things to Emily. Kissed her goodbye every morning. But something remained missing. Like she was a robot programmed to give love rather than a human being giving actual love. Her touch was fleeting. Her kindness short and terse, as if designed to be delivered quickly and effectively.

She tracked all of Meg's cruel little asides, all her periods of silence, all her sudden swarms of love, all the times she sneaked an apple out of her office in the house (Emily suspected she was keeping them in the file cabinet). Meg talked to Dan often now; at least once a day. She went to the orchard, too. Always came back with just one or two apples. One day she closed her hand in the front door—it looked like it hurt like hell, but Meg didn't even seem to care. The fingernail fell off that night; Emily found it in the sink, bloodied. But the next day, Meg's fingernail wasn't gone at all.

Or, perhaps, it had grown back just that fast.

Emily wrote all of it down.

THEN CAME THE DINNER WHEN MEG ASKED, "DID YOU HEAR ABOUT the murder?"

The way she said it—it was only later Emily would realize Meg had *chirped* her question, sung it with a pleasure that was small only because it was restrained. "What?" Emily asked.

"Mm," Meg said, hovering over a plate of arugula salad that she wasn't even eating. That was one of the other things: Meg wasn't eating much anymore. But she wasn't losing weight, either. No sleep. Minimal eating (but for the apples). It all went in Emily's little journal. "That woman from the event. Dan Paxson's date—the redhead straight out of Roger Rabbit."

The bottom of Emily's stomach dropped like an elevator with its cable cut. Plummeting toward the cold dark floor. "She's dead?"

"Oh, hah, no. Though she may have killed her husband." Meg watched Emily carefully. Like she was picking apart her reactions as they happened. "The woman, Moreau, said it was her neighbor. But I don't buy it. Prentiss Beckman comes from a good family. Everybody knows it. Doesn't make sense that he would walk into his neighbor's house and shoot that man. It's always the spouse, anyway. Love gone wrong is a powerful motive—and she and her husband were, as I understand it, into some *curious* lifestyle behaviors. Kink and BDSM. So she killed him. I'm sure they'll figure that out soon enough."

Meg continued to stare at Emily while gently ushering a puck of goat cheese around her plate, like she was giving it a tour of the arugula and dried cherries.

"But Beckman—he was the one who made a scene at the dinner."

All Meg offered as a response was a disaffected shrug.

"It was crazy," Emily objected. "That Prentiss guy acted fucking crazy, Meg. You don't seriously think there's not something going on there. We should talk to the police, tell them what we saw."

"The Beckmans have been friends of our family for a while. I don't think we should be getting in the middle of this, Em."

"You're a lawyer. You care about justice. And truth."

"I'm a consumer protection lawyer. I care about serving my clients."

"You're better than that."

"I am better than that. That's it exactly. I'm better. I'm better than that redhead. I'm better than the lawyers at my firm. I'm certainly better than you."

"Meg—"

Meg's face brightened, like sun shining on still water until its gold sheen blinded the eye. "No, Emily, I don't say it to be cruel. I only say it as a matter of recognizing reality. Calling it not just as I see it but as it utterly, provably is. It's not an insult. Oh no. Only a statement highlighting the imbalance between us. You could be better, too." A pause. "If you really wanted to be."

The words sprinted for the end of Emily's tongue—*How? If I ate the apple? Is that how I get better, Meg? Is that how I join you in your superiority complex?*

But she bit those words in half before they leapt.

Instead, she just blinked back tears before they fell and set aside her fork. "I, like you, seem to have lost my appetite. I'm gonna go, I dunno. Do something."

"Watch TV or maybe stare at your phone," Meg said. Said so plainly, Emily was pretty sure it was a statement of mockery. "Maybe . . . read a book."

Emily didn't respond. She just forced a smile and got up.

She hurried into the bathroom.

It was here she'd been hiding the journal. She had a wicker basket underneath the sink on her side, a pure chaos bucket of random product: half-empty conditioners and lotions, plus an old scrubby loofah thing and, for some reason, a packet of ancient Tide stain-sticks. Meg did not like to get near Emily's chaos even in the times before

(*Meg became a cold, calculating monster thanks to that apple*)

they moved here, and now she wasn't even using the bathroom that much, so it seemed a very good place to hide the journal. She wrapped it in an old face towel and parked it under that basket of toiletry chaos.

Emily locked the door, got down on the floor and removed the basket and the face towel, shaking the journal loose from its ratty old folds—

Except, no journal shook loose.

She patted the towel. Unfolded it all the way. Turned it over like she was a magician showing the audience that the bird was now gone, except she was *also* the audience and didn't understand where the hell the bird, her journal, had gone.

Emily stuck her head underneath the sink, looking all around, using the flashlight from her iPhone to see if she could see it. It must've slid out—

But no.

Nothing.

Her pulse raced.

She felt sweaty and sick.

What did this mean?

Emily swallowed a hard lump and then idly flushed the toilet, somehow remembering to continue the illusion that she actually needed to use the bathroom.

Deep breaths, Em. Deep fucking breaths.

She opened the door to exit the bathroom—

And there stood Meg.

Looking smug.

The journal in her hand.

"Lose this?" she asked, giving it a little wave.

"Meg—"

"It's okay, Em. Let's go, sit down, have a little talk. I think it's time we did that. Don't you?"

44

THE DEMONSTRATION, AND A CHOICE

BACK TO THE DINNER TABLE THEY WENT.

Meg sat, elbows on the table, fingers steepled above the journal. The plates of salad had been remanded to the sink already, though the utensils remained.

"You've been taking some interesting notes here," Meg said. Her fist rapped its knuckles against the Moleskine.

"It's just—" Emily swallowed razors. "It's just for a story I'm writing."

"A fiction story."

"Yeah. Yes."

"I don't really want to do this dance," Meg said, plainly. "I know what you're up to. You're figuring out that the apple is something special, though I can tell you're biased against it. Against me. Worse, against Dan—I know you have some deluded notion put in your head by that stranger you hang around with—no, don't object, I know you said you're not talking to him anymore, but I know you are. I know you speak to him and see him while I'm at work. My mother has kept her eyes out for me and just as you've been keeping tabs on me—I have been keeping tabs on you, my dear wife." Those last three words, sprinkled with a packet of the fakest sugar.

"Meg—"

"That deluded notion you maintain is, if I have it right, that the body you found in our river belongs to someone that Dan hurt. Killed. *Murdered.* But there's no evidence of that and if you continue to pursue that line of thinking, you're going to get into trouble. You see that, don't you? It could hurt you legally. Or in other ways. And I don't want to see that happen, Emily."

Jesus. She's threatening me.

All to protect—who? Dan Paxson?

No. To protect *the apple.*

"I think the apple is making you sick," Emily said in a trembling voice.

"The *apple,* the Ruby Slipper, is making me better. I have never felt this awake and aware. I am as crisp as a bite of the apple, Emily. I am the best version of myself and only getting better. May I show you some things? I've felt bad about keeping them from you."

Emily felt herself nodding.

"Let's be honest," Meg said. "I work out, but it's never been in a really committed way. Legs, mostly. Cardio when I can manage it. I've never been particularly *toned.* Never had the time. But—"

She picked up the Moleskine notebook.

Tapped her thumb against the hard cover, as if for emphasis.

And then, with little effort, she tore the whole book in half. There was only the slightest wince of effort before the whole thing ripped into two pieces.

Holy shit.

"Meg, I—I don't understand what this is, how that can be—"

"I'm strong not just in my mind. I'm getting strong in my body, too. All of me finds a new peak every day. All thanks to the apple."

"This is . . . this isn't okay."

Meg watched her carefully. Her gaze flicked from Emily to the utensils still on the table. "You're thinking of hurting me."

"What? No."

"You're imagining picking up that fork. You're dreaming of sticking it in me, again and again. My chest. My neck. Into my cheek, just to maul me, to mark me with your anger over how perfect I've become."

"Meg—I'm not." And she wasn't. She had no desire to hurt Meg. Not with the fork, not with anything. Something her father told her once upon a time passed through her mind, then. He said to Emily, *People who think everyone is lying to them are often liars themselves.* Because it's easier to imagine everyone around them is just as bad as they are. This was like that, wasn't it? Meg thought Emily wanted to hurt her because . . . she wanted to hurt Emily. "Meg, I swear—"

Meg moved fast. Grabbed her own fork—

Raised it above her head—

"No!" Emily cried out—

And Meg drove the fork into the back of *her own hand.*

It stabbed down through the tender flesh between thumb and index finger, the part you poke to compare to the doneness of steak. Three flecks of blood dotted Meg's grin-stretched cheek. Like a gleaming red ellipsis.

More blood welled up around the tines of the fork. The ones stuck in her skin.

Meg withdrew the fork with the gentlest sound—*thhhck.*

"Meg," Emily said, her words barely louder than a breath. "What the fuck."

Meg popped the fork in her mouth, as if she wanted to get the last bits off a Popsicle stick. "That barely hurt. Isn't that something? It's a miracle, Emily, honestly. And the miracle doesn't stop there. By morning, it'll just be a little scar, and by the morning after that, the scar won't be there anymore, either. I don't know what the limits are." Idly, distantly, she said: "Maybe there aren't any."

"You need help, Meg. This isn't right. This isn't *okay.*"

"You want to run away from me."

Emily's jaw tightened. She nodded. "I do."

"You won't."

"I might. I could." She hesitated. "You don't control me."

"Don't I?" Meg grinned even bigger, now. "You're in my debt. You owe. For this house. For the life I've given you. For this place that I have taken you. It's time to show you what I have given you by taking it away. This afternoon, after I found your little book, I canceled your debit card, your credit card, I cut the tires on your bike and removed the chains, I changed the password on my computer, I changed the password for the Wi-Fi, I canceled your phone service—it will end tonight, at eleven fifty-nine, so I'd say to drink up the signal while you still have it, but—" Meg pulled out Emily's phone. She must've left it at the table when she went into the bathroom to grab the Moleskine. *Fuck!* "You were never on any of the accounts, you're not on the mortgage, you have no control over anything here. I have it all. And I have up until now chosen not to exercise that control, letting you have the life you so desire. Now it's time to lock it all down. To teach you how important I am. To show you what matters most."

Emily felt tears slicking her cheeks. "Why?"

"Because you abuse me, Emily. You treat me like garbage. Take, take, take. And I get nothing in return except *suspicion* and, and—" Meg picked up the remnants of the book, the ones she neatly stacked atop each other, and scattered them to both sides of her in an angry swipe. "This. I get *this*. So that's over. You think you're going to leave me but you're not, because people like us together, Emily, they think we're *sweet* and *progressive* and *aren't we nice*. The Crossed Keys have us and our relationship as evidence that they're not old dinosaurs. Plus, there are some who believe you're a rogue element that needs to be controlled, so that's my job, to be your watcher, your *wrangler*. You'll do as I say. You'll live like I want you to live. You'll not see that creeper old man anymore—"

"John is my friend."

"Well, he's *dead* to you. He's poison. Poisoning your brain. So that's over. You'll keep this house clean. You'll learn, *finally*, to cook. My mother will teach you. And somewhere in there, in you, we will find a good wife."

"I could just leave. I could get up and walk out."

"Then do it. See what happens. Maybe I won't come for you. Or maybe I will. Or maybe I won't be the one who does. You'll regret it, no matter what."

Emily stuck out her chin. "This isn't you. I think you know that, deep down. You're not the person I married."

Meg smiled, almost beatifically, like a true angel of the Lord basking in its own alien glory. "That is right, Emily. I am not the same person. I am a better person than the wretch that I was. Thank you for seeing that. And maybe someday soon you'll finally make the choice to join me. Maybe you'll finally stop pretending you have some child's allergy. The apple awaits. It only takes a bite for you to be better, too." Receiving no answer to that, Meg sighed and shrugged. "In the meantime, I'm going to go down on the dock, watch the river, and eat an apple. I'll expect this mess to be cleaned up when I come back."

At that, she strolled out the back door with the cold confidence of a winter queen.

Emily stayed behind, quaking, trying not to cry and failing.

She knew she should get up and run.

Run far, far away.

But that last bit of their conversation—if it could even be called that—stayed with her. *That is right, Emily, I am not the same person.* But maybe there was still a Meg in there. Maybe Emily could get her back. Maybe she could save her.

That was reason enough to stay.

45

THEY DID NOT SEE MY GLORY

JOHN COMPASS PACED THE LENGTH OF THE LITTLE CABIN HE WAS renting in Prospect Farm, across from the old Slate Hill cemetery, one of the oldest—if not *the* oldest—Quaker burial grounds in the whole country. The cabin, rented to him by a friend of Cherie Leveen's, wasn't much to shout at—it was one room plus a bathroom, five hundred square feet, with a little wooden porch outside. It was dusty, but cozy, and overlooked the old canal if you craned your neck. Only problem was, some fool had planted invasive bamboo along the far side and now that stuff was growing up everywhere, like hair on an old man's back.

John paced, trying to both escape the fear that hounded him, and catch the courage he needed to beat that fear.

(So far, it was a race he was not winning.)

Last week, Emily sent him something she found online—a reference to a late-seventeenth-century settlement along the Delaware River here in Bucks County, a town called Woodhull, founded by Godric Edsall—Quakers, of course, arriving not long after William Penn himself, and founding the small settlement as a trading post between Philadelphia and New York.

But the reference made it clear that the settlement up and disappeared. Like the so-called Lost Colony of Roanoke, one day the people were there, and the next, they were gone. A hundred colonists, simply missing one day. Everything they had, left behind.

Story went, of course, that the Lenape killed them. That it was the start of the "hostilities" between the European settlers and the local Indigenous. Though John knew that didn't track—at that point, Penn had navigated relations with the Lenape. They had deals. They shared land. They reached a common understanding. It was only later that their relations soured, what with Penn's own vicious children and their Walking Purchase up and snatching land out from under the Native people—

then, tensions rose, enflamed by mobs of white men stirred from their homes under whispers of threat from the so-called savages who would take their things, rape their daughters, burn their towns, and so on. All part of a fear campaign born of vested interests who knew full well if you could run the Indigenous off their land, then the land was yours for the taking. A cruel and effective grift.

The Lenape wouldn't have attacked Woodhull without cause. John figured to ask Cherie if she knew anything at all, what with her being the clerk and all—but she laughed and said, "John, I run the calendar and answer emails, I'm not a historian." He apologized, but she said she knew people—because Cherie always knew people—and that she'd get back to him. A couple days later she did, coming down to his little cabin for a visit, bringing him a Yocco's hot dog—it was cold as the grave by the time she brought it, but he didn't care. It was a damn good hot dog. Mustard, chili sauce, a mountain of diced onion. All with a chocolate milk because, she said, "You can't eat one of these and not also have a chocolate milk to wash it down, it's a literal food crime not to." He agreed, and greedily fed on what she brought him and then they played cards for a good long while. War, then Spite and Malice.

Before she left, she said, "Almost forgot," then handed him a document—emailed to her, printed out ("I know you'd rather have something to hold in your hand than look at on a screen," she said, and she was right). She explained that she had a friend who worked at the Friends Historical Library down at Swarthmore College, west of Philly, south of the Main Line. It was a collection of Quaker documents, accounts, and artifacts from the earliest days of settlement here in Pennsylvania, and sure enough, she said Woodhull showed up in an accounting.

And what was in this account was all the more puzzling.

And all the more troubling.

It was a Swede, a furrier named Nygard, who told the story about the attack by so-called savages, suggesting that the Lenape or Susquehannock kidnapped colonists from their homes for dark purposes—though whether he did this as a deliberate lie or a bigoted assumption was not clear. But a local Quaker trader, William Finch, told a quite different story, one so absurd and strange it was no wonder that it was discarded out of hand in favor of the cleaner, if crueler, story of Indigenous attack.

Finch visited the settlement in spring 1681, said that he found the town not abandoned, but rather dead. Every last person. Murdered, he believed, and not by the Indigenous, but by one another. Brutalized, in fact. In the center of town, he found that their furniture had been piled up, and upon the pile sat a single chair.

Sitting in that chair was a man covered in blood. In his lap sat an ornate flintlock pistol and, beneath that, a hanger sword—a type of hunting saber. The blade was thick with gore. So were the man's teeth—Finch reported he had meat between his teeth, in fact, and appeared to have bitten, if not outright eaten, some of his fellow settlers.

The only thing he said to Finch was:

Je ne suis pas Quaker; ils n'ont pas vu ma gloire.

Finch took the man's weapons. He gave them up willingly. Finch bound him, took him away. Took the man to the nearest authorities, of which there were few—certainly no centralized authority existed at that point. But the Dutch East India Company knew who the man was, and one of the bosses there, Beekhof, knew the killer in question—said he'd traveled with him some years before. A chef, as it turned out, from France.

The descendant of the apprentice to Taillevent.

Vinot. The man who brought this bad apple to America. Vinot's Allegresse.

Men from the trading company took Vinot away to "face justice."

What happened from there, John didn't know. He figured the man ended up at the bottom of the ocean, a pulley cinched around his ankles to weigh him down.

But that was not the end of the account.

Months later, Finch went back up toward the fallen Woodhull settlement, and found there an even stranger sight:

The dead bodies, long gone. No trace of them at all.

But sprouting up all around, outside of the log homes and also within them, were saplings. Trees that should not have supported fruit, yet already did: dark apples hanging from their branches. It was then that a band of the Unami Lenape showed themselves—Finch had some rapport with the locals, and tried to find out what had happened here. He said they explained to him that something evil took root here, that bad spirits had claimed this place and its people, and that it had to be burned. Finch helped them do exactly that.

And that is how Woodhull went away.

John didn't understand what happened there, or what any of that meant. He told Cherie as much, but didn't tell her the more worrying bits: that Vinot's apple was one Walt had been hunting for, and that Vinot's apple may very well have been the same as the Harrowsblack, the pkwësu, or, as it was called now, Dan Paxson's Ruby Slipper. He did not say that the same evil had perhaps taken root here, in Bucks County, too. Instead, they talked of other things, polite things, even though his mind was wandering to the horrors of the moment.

Now John was left uncertain what to do next.

Or, rather, he knew what he had to do, but he wasn't sure he could do it.

Something had to be done. That much was plain to see. It felt like a paranoid delusion, a nightmare with a blood-red apple at the center of it. And yet here he was, and he suspected the solution now was the same as the solution then:

The orchard had to be destroyed.

Burned, perhaps, to the ground.

John took this on as part of his duty to Walt. And to the world. After all, fire was a great light for banishing shadows.

46

A CAIRN OF APPLE CORES

JOANIE WAS LIKE A POT OF WATER LEFT ON THE STOVE UNTIL ALL the water had boiled out and the pot was dry but still heating up, up, up, the metal holding the heat, ready to scald anyone who touched it, ready to set a fire, ready to burn it all down.

Her grief gave way to fear and rage and all she could do was sit with it. Literally, just sit with it. Over the several days following Graham's murder, she sat there in her house. The gun, her .380, never out of reach. Joanie always sat near a window, looking out, waiting to see Prentiss Beckman's face pop up so she could kill him. She dreamed of shooting him, a bullet in the cheek, under the eye, popping his brains out the back of his head, turning him to meat just as he had done to Graham.

She slept, but not well.

She ate, but poorly.

Mostly, she sat and she waited.

There were administrative details. A funeral to plan. An estate to execute. At least the cops left her alone, mostly, seemingly convinced she couldn't have killed her own husband—after all, there were signs of Beckman's trespass, and his blood spattered the cold walkway outside. He'd never come home. They found his guns, and they found his rage in the form of angry letters, journals, knife marks in wooden surfaces, doorjambs kicked and dented.

Her ears still rang from the sound of the gunshots.

Her head still throbbed.

All parts of her vacillated between feeling totally numb and having her nerve endings dialed all the way up and open, so that every little shift in the air felt like ice water on a broken tooth. She went from feeling nothing to feeling all the pain. And that wasn't just on the outside. Inside, too, she fell into holes of great nothing. Just wide-open deserts of despair. But then it would all rush up into her again, a great geyser of grief and anger that nearly drowned her.

All the while she sat.

Simmering.

Gun near to hand.

Her mind returning again and again and again to that night in the kitchen. Graham, dead. Prentiss, ready to kill her, too. And then later, just as the cops came in, just as she stood and raised her hands, the three apple cores that later disappeared.

DAN PAXSON SENT FLOWERS.

It was a massive arrangement: blue and white, delphiniums and lilies and white roses and snapdragons. Bigger than anything anyone else sent.

The night she received them, she threw them in the car and drove over to his house without calling.

"JOANIE," HE SAID, ANSWERING THE DOOR, SURPRISED. "I'M SO, SO sorry to—"

She threw the flowers at him. Petals peeled off and fell to the ground.

"I don't want these," she said.

"All right." His brow darkened.

"It was Prentiss Beckman," she said.

"I . . . heard that," he said, guardedly. A pause. A long breath. "He's been a problem. Obviously."

"Yeah. He has. You saw what he was like at your dinner."

"We all wish we knew what he was capable of."

"That's the thing, Dan. I don't know what he was capable of before. But he was sure capable, and able, the night he killed Graham, wasn't he?"

"It can be surprising the way people really are."

No shit, Dan.

"You know what I found there in the house?" she asked him. "The night of the murder. Before Prentiss tried to kill me, too."

He didn't say anything, but instead watched her warily.

"Apple cores. Three apple cores."

He crossed his arms in front of him. Something flashed across his face: anger. An emotion so rare for him she barely recognized it.

"I don't know what the hell that means, Joanie."

"He was eating those apples. *Your* apples, Dan. The ones you all love to eat so much. The ones everyone around here seem to be just *addicted* to. You've been different, lately. A lot of people have been, haven't they?"

"You—" He made a sound, not unlike a laugh. "You aren't seriously suggesting that Prentiss Beckman . . . did what he did because of my apples?"

Am I?

Am I suggesting that?

Doesn't it sound a little . . . crazy?

"I don't know what I'm saying. I just know it's a curious thing, Dan."

"Joanie, I don't appreciate—"

"You sound tired, Dan." And he did. Weary. Tired. Maybe even a little sick. She had only noticed it just now. Whatever magic the apples were doing for people wasn't on display now, not here, not for him. "Thanks for the flowers, Dan. They really fixed *everything.*"

"Joanie, listen, if you'd just try—"

She turned heel and stormed back to the car. Once inside, she sped away, screaming and screaming until her vocal cords were as raw as grated apple.

47

CLAUDE LAMBERT TAKES HIS MASK OFF

IT WAS NOON WHEN DAN WOKE UP TO THE SOUND OF SOMEONE hammering.

He snorted awake, not even sure how the hell he'd ended up here in his bed. He lay there, sweating atop the covers. When was the last time he even slept? Much less *overslept*? He didn't even know if that was possible anymore.

And yet, here he was.

A headache pounded behind his eyes to the tune of the hammer outside. With each hit, another echo of his conversation with Joanie two nights ago at his front door. *Three apple cores.* Blaming him for her husband's murder.

What is happening? What is wrong with me? Am I sick?

Dan hadn't suffered a headache in forever. So long ago that he had forgotten how much one *hurt*. The way it throbbed, like it was trying to push its way out through his eyeballs, through his sinuses.

He fumbled around the room, looking for a Ruby Slipper. *I need a bite. No place like home,* he thought idly, madly. But there weren't any apples stashed up here—in part because he hadn't *been* up here very much, except to change clothes, get a shower, and head back down to the orchard.

Downstairs, he thought. He had apples downstairs, so he climbed off the bed, the headache now adding his footsteps to its miserable kickdrum beat. It felt like he had to push and pull himself through the house, grabbing walls and doorframes and dragging his body and launching forth, like he was weightless in space—except he didn't feel weightless at all. He felt heavy. Burdened.

Finally, the counter. His hand found an apple. Cold, smooth skin. It seemed to twist in his grip for a moment

(*like it wants to get away from me*)

before he took a hard bite. Half the apple gone in one mouthful. He chewed fast and swallowed hard, the lump almost too big—Dan nearly choked. Juices ran down his chin and he whimpered.

Outside, the hammering continued.

He pushed his way to the front door, mashing his feet into a pair of ratty sneakers before tumbling outside into the scouring light of day. It felt like it was trying to burn him down to ash—the sun a chain-smoker, him its cigarette.

Two men stood out past the driveway, right where they were planning to extend the orchard's own entrance to the road itself.

Claude Lambert and Earl Dawes.

Earl, in his trademark red-and-black plaid, had a posthole digger next to him, and stood up on a small ladder, using a big flat rubber mallet to hammer in a thick wooden post, the kind with an arm extended out to hold a hanging sign. Lambert held something in his hands, too—a flat, long piece of wood with a couple of shiny chains dangling from it.

The sign to be hung from that signpost, Dan thought.

"Hey," he called over, but his voice felt weak, weary. He called again—"Hey!"—louder this time, trying like hell not to worry that something was very wrong with him. *Whatever this is, it's temporary. You're not sick. You're healthy. You're strong and smart and nothing will take you down. The apple will work.*

Claude waved him over with a big smile as Dawes kept hammering.

"Shit," Dan muttered under his breath, and staggered over to the road and toward the two men.

"Little Dan," Claude said, reaching out and giving Dan a vigorous handshake. But when he took a good long look at Dan, his face sank. "Dan, I must say, you don't look well. Have you had an apple today?"

"I'm fine," Dan said, the words croaked more than spoken. "What's going on? What's all this?"

Claude chirped: "Oh! This." He took the sign and gave it a turn-around so that Dan could see it.

It was a wooden sign, ornately carved. Gold letters on an evergreen backing.

It said:

LAMBERT HILL ORCHARDS.

Anger lanced through Dan like a pin popping a blister.

"Lambert Hill—? Claude, this is my house, my orchard. It's Paxson Family Orchards. Has been and will be."

"Now, now, hold on," Claude said, putting a steadying hand on Dan's shoulder. "We agreed on paper that I was to take a partnership stake—"

"Silent partner. This—" Dan reached for the sign in Lambert's hand and gave it a hard shake. "Isn't *silent*."

"The paperwork didn't specify the *silent* part, that's just what we discussed—but I came around to thinking, you know, the Lambert Hill name is a brand around here. My vineyard has been in Harrow for generations now. Not like I don't know what I'm doing—"

"You know what you're doing because of people like my father."

"Of course. That's very true and Big Dan was like family to me, which is why I think it's really exciting to see his—and your!—legacy paired with mine. A mighty team-up if ever there was one."

Dan stammered: "You didn't even—you didn't even consult with me, Claude." He grabbed Dawes's shirtsleeve, gave it a tug, which made him feel like a little child pulling at his mother's dress. "Hey, *hey*, Dawes, stop hammering that in—just slow down, cool it, get off the damn ladder."

Earl Dawes gave a quizzical look to Lambert, who in turn just held up a gentle hand. Earl nodded and climbed down off the ladder.

"I didn't consult because I knew you'd come around to support the decision," Lambert said with what felt like condescending calm. "This is the smart way to go. Besides—I don't *really* need to consult, do I."

"What's stopping me from taking that sign soon as you're gone and putting up my own? Because I just might."

Claude stiffened. "You're free to, of course. But I'd hope we could avoid that kind of petty squabble. Because it won't end well."

"What does that mean?"

"It means what you think it means, Little—ahh, Dan."

"You're threatening me."

"Dan, why don't we go inside for a moment."

Dan gave a look to Earl Dawes, who stood there, stone-faced.

"Fine," he said, and they went inside.

———

OUTSIDE, HE COULD HEAR THE HAMMERING START BACK UP AGAIN.

"Sonofabitch," Dan said. "Your man out there is still—"

"Dan, sit down."

"I don't want to sit."

"Sit. Down."

Dan felt those words hit him like a punch to the gut. And before he knew it, he was sitting down even as Claude remained standing.

Gone was the sort of soft, chummy, glad-handing tone Lambert brought to customers of his vineyard. His voice now was hard as cinder block.

"Dan, your business here was nothing impressive. You had some trees producing some truly stellar apples, you started to build a little cider shop, and that's all well and good. But if you're going to do this right, you need acumen and savvy and, most important, you need connections. I have those connections."

"Claude—"

"Quiet. I am speaking." Another hit. Felt like Dan got smacked in the face. His headache pounded. And worse, his vision shook—went blurry around the edges before clearing up again. Claude paused for a moment and winced, as if he was trying to control himself. He said, "Did you know, Dan, that my great-great-grandfather, Oswald Lambert, was close with Henry Hart Golden? And my family has been in this region since long before that, settling just across the river in 1742. They helped open the canal. They started a barge company meant to move material up and down the river, thus becoming part of the fundamentally industrious fabric of this region—a region that has since sunsetted peacefully, no longer concerning itself with factories and production, settling instead into a pastoral identity—one married to enriching the lives of those who live here. And more important, who have lived here. Whose blood *belongs* to this region—and the region belongs to in turn."

"I don't understand what any of this has to do with—"

"Blood is what matters here, Dan. Oswald Lambert joined with Henry Hart Golden and founded the society to which you belong, now. Once called the Goldenrod Society, we became the Crossed Keys in the 1950s, though in our heart we still belong to the Goldenrod. Golden's society was one of science, art, antiquity, and pleasure, and what grows out of the combination of those things is innovation, invention, and most important, *influence*. And now you're in the club. You put on the mask. You spilled blood—a symbol of the necessity of the blood and heritage that binds us here. Congratulations. We are the people of this county and we belong here, our families have belonged here for generations and we do not accept *new blood* lightly—or without cost. Your father had nothing to offer us except his service, and I welcomed that and his friendship but it was not the key needed to open the lock. You and your apples, however, were that key, and now the lock is undone, the door opened."

Dan held up his hands in surrender. "I understand that, Claude, and I thank you for that opportunity. Genuinely. But you need to see where I'm coming from here—"

"You have it wrong. I don't need to see through your eyes. You need to see through mine. I've sacrificed a great deal to be where I am and that means I am afforded certain reach. Reach you wish to make your own. Which you can, congratulations. Because you are now in the circle. You've walked through the golden door. And if you stay here, you will be afforded influence and pleasure. But that means I get to take my share. To sit in church means putting something in the plate. This is the act of tithing, Dan. The pardoner offers you his indulgences—a ticket to a fertile land. But such indulgences do not come free."

Dan sat back. Again his eyes went blurry and he had to blink to keep everything straight. "So, if I get this straight, I'm just here to run an orchard named after you. And you make the big decisions. And I get to live off whatever trickles down? Like this is some kind of pyramid scheme? My father couldn't live with himself being in that role and I'm not sure I can, either."

Claude leaned forward, both hands on the table.

"Dan, your father was not in the club. You are. And now your children can be a part of something. And your children's children. The future of this county—and by proxy, the state, the whole damn nation—can be governed by people with your last name. Your blood is with my blood. But you don't like that? That's fine. I'll take my name off this orchard and you can be on your own."

"Way you say that, I can tell there's a catch."

Something bright gleamed in Claude's eye. He was enjoying this, telling Dan what's what, talking down to him. "Nothing in life is without a catch, Little Dan. I put money in and you have spent some of that. More than some of it. On equipment. On materials. On Earl's salary—"

Dan launched himself up out of his chair. It rocked his skull, the headache roaring across his brow like a rough tide. "Salary? I didn't agree to that, Claude. Goddamnit, you *are* taking me for a ride—"

"Nothing is for free!" Claude bellowed. "Jesus Christ, Dan, how fucking naïve are you? You think Dawes is slave labor? He does the work, he gets a paycheck, and if he's doing your work, he's getting it from you. So you're out on a limb here, financially. I pull out, then by the deal *you signed,* I get to reclaim that money, and having had a look at your books, I know you do not have the money to pay me back what you have already spent. So *that* gives me an opportunity to sue to get what's mine— and were that to happen, I expect you and I will be back where we really started, mm? With me owning this land, this house, your trees."

"Claude—"

"And what of that unsavory situation with the dead man in the river? Mm? That has washed out to sea, but the tide can bring anything back onto shore, can't it?"

"I—I didn't—"

"Your choice, Danny Boy. Stay with us and pay the price, or leave the flock and find out how fast the wolves come out for the lone little sheep."

Dan stood there, simmering. Claude's fat, powdery face staring back.

All Dan wanted to do was to

(*punch*)

(*kick*)

(*choke*)

(*bite*)

(*slaughter*)

be rid of Lambert now and forever.

His chest rose and fell in waves.

He could do it, he realized. He could kill the old man.

It was in his power. It was his right.

Claude was old, slow, too sure of himself.

Dan was—

Suddenly wobbly. Achy. Feeling weak, sick, his vision blurry. *I ate the apple! I should be strong! I should have my power.*

But he didn't.

Sighing, he slumped back into his chair. *I can't do it.*

"You really got me by the balls," Dan said, quietly.

"I do, Little Dan, I do. And I can either tickle them or rip them off your fucking body. That's on you to decide. But in the meantime, I am done with this discussion. I'm going to go and take my sign back outside, and watch Dawes hang it, and then I am going to celebrate the opening of a new Lambert Hill property. Maybe you'll join me. Maybe you won't."

Claude left him then, feeling spent. Kicked. Weakened.

His vision crossed itself again, going all watery. Dan crushed his eyelids together, his teeth, too, growling and praying that the headache would go away, that his vision would straighten out. And eventually, after the hammering outside stopped, he crawled back upstairs, opened the drawer in his side table, and pulled out his old eyeglasses. Dan slid them back onto his face with trembling hands, and instantly, his vision cleared up, crisp as a pickle. Dan fell to his knees and wept.

—

THE GOLDEN MAN'S TALE, PART TWO

1902, THE GOLDENROD ESTATE, BUCKS COUNTY,
PENNSYLVANIA.

SPRINGTIME WAS UPON THEM, AND HENRY HART GOLDEN KNEW his role and had played it well. As the Ambarvalia wound down, the sixth such at the Goldenrod, Henry knelt by the reflecting pool, the moon cutting the water like a knife. He plunged his arms into it.

There was enough firelight for him to see the bloom of blood rise off his skin. He could still hear the animals crying in his ears, but beyond the cries, in the deepest dark of his mind, he heard other screams, too. Distant ones, more intimate ones. Screams that never failed to give him a little thrill. Screams he would revisit night after night after night.

Behind him, the guests were awash in ecstasy. Some had strewn themselves on the cobbled walkways, on chaises hauled from the house and quilts cast into the dewy grass. Some were asleep; others were fucking. They were high on opium or morphine, drunk on wine and spirits and cider. Others were buzzing on cocaine—on Vin Mariani, on quaffed tonics, or on powder sucked up their noses. The cocaine had made this lot unruly: They ran around, cackling like mad, chasing phantoms or sometimes each other, occasionally with knives. (Someone always got hurt. But no one ever died. It was what it was.)

All of them, his people, his Goldenrod friends, his tools, his fools, their masks askew, but never discarded—for the masks were essential to the ritual, as were the drugs. The masks, the altered consciousness: both necessary to become something outside yourself. To become someone you were not, in order to perform the rites that put you beyond the limits of your own self. And to the Goldenrod: that mighty lensed beacon that ignited the heavens and bound them to the great beyond.

(That, at least, is what Henry told them.)

The masks freed their true selves to do what their public selves could not, would not, should not do. And the drugs freed them from the guilt.

So they snorted and smoked and quaffed their way clear of any of the mortal—and moral—fetters that limited most people.

During the Ambarvalia, they chased the animals—the baby lamb, the baby goat, the piglet, the calf—and slashed them to pieces, and even now he could smell the offal and the shit, the blood and trampled grass, that sour bile stink mixing with the heady perfume of wet women and now-soft men who had given up their own ghosts in the glory of *le petit mort*. Of course, if he wanted, he could ignore all those scents, and instead simply inhale the vapors of his appleskin mask . . .

Because that mask was his, only his, not theirs, not ever.

He would not share with them. Not this, the mask he made. Nor would he share the apples that he had used to make it. The apples that had made *him*.

He learned long ago that these people were not equal to him.

Not these people.

Not *any* people.

A man did not hold a hammer thinking it was his friend, his brother, deserving of all the rights of civilization. And a god did not hold a man in his hand thinking the man was his son. The man held the tool, and the god held the man.

Now he heard the scuff of a shoe behind him. *And man interrupts god.*

Henry smelled him—his cologne, Brise Musquée, foul as the wet hide of a farm Briard, preceded his presence.

Oswald Lambert.

"We need to speak," Oswald said stiffly. His mask of cork and cask held in hand, at his side.

Through his appleskin mask, Henry sighed. "Oswald. Relax. Please. This sounds dire, too dire. It has been a good night, has it not? We ran with the beasts, as beasts. We danced and dashed, we cut and slashed. We are fatted, we have fucked, the fires are burning even as the spring night grows cold." He rose slowly and turned to meet the man: older than him by a good two decades

(*or so the other man thought*)

and looking like the weight of the world had pressed down on his balding head until he became squatter and squatter as the years went on. Oswald Lambert looked like a stump and a sow pig had had a horrible human child, and now that child had grown up and fancied himself wealthy in the ways of the world.

Lambert was not, of course, wealthy in the ways of the world. He had money, yes. But he was not rich in true power.

(He had not the tang of apple on his tongue.)

"This is important."

So, so dire.

And so, so tiresome.

But Henry had his own mask to keep on, didn't he?

"Fine, fine. I assume you want to do this somewhere more private?"

"I do, sir."

"I wish to take a swim. The indoor pool. Shall we?"

THE POOL ROOM, SOUTHEAST CORNER, OFF THE MAIN HALL. GRAND, wide, arched windows, framed by trellises of wild ivy. It was roped off with golden cordage: a sacred border only he was permitted to breach. Henry dispatched his mask *and* his clothes and dove in, leaving Lambert standing foolishly off to the side.

"Did you notice who—" Lambert started to say, but Henry set into a breaststroke. The remaining blood washed away from his flesh and into the blue waters. The wine-dark cloud obscured for a moment the serene image painted at the bottom of the pool—a pale-green garden, verdant and jade. "Sir, I said—" More swimming. "Henry—" Every time he tried to speak, Henry dove back under, or swam harder, his legs kicking up a noisy thrash of water.

Finally, Lambert, fed up, barked: "*Sir.* I demand your attention."

There it was. He'd been pushed to the edge. Good. Henry liked to see a little fire in him.

Henry climbed out of the pool and let the water drip from his body. From his cock, hard as kingwood. Lambert's chalk-dust cheeks bloomed with embarrassment.

Another indignity the ugly man must suffer, Henry thought. Which gave him joy. Life was about enjoyment, and he was here to milk it of every mirthful moment.

Lambert pushed past his puritanical frisson and stammered, "Chalfont Butler. He's not here tonight."

Butler. Local banker. Wife a baker.

Henry sniffed, wiping water off his bare skin with the flat of his hands. No towel. "So?"

"He's a man of means. A man of local influence."

"I'm not worried about him. Should he be worried about me?"

"He is. You know he is."

Henry *hmm*ed. "Why is that?"

"You know why."

"Entertain me."

"The girl." Pause. "His *daughter*."

"Mm. Right. Victoria. Pretty girl? Chestnut curls." *Mask of lace and porcelain,* he recalled. *And beautiful, delicate little bones.* "I . . . recall her."

"You *should*. You brought her to your chamber months ago. And no one has seen her since." Lambert's nostrils flared. Any embarrassment he had suffered at this exchange was now lost beneath the old bull's anger.

"I'm sure she's fine."

She is, he decided. *In her way.*

Henry walked past Lambert, to a small bleached oak side table dripping with cerulean silk. The silk was concealing something, and Henry whipped off the fabric and let it drift to the ground. A bowl of ruby-red apples awaited. He snatched one like a man catching a fish out of a river with his bare hands, and swiftly bit the apple clean in half. His manhood spasmed. Juice ran down his chin, his arm. (And then, his leg.) He sighed a sigh that melted into a gushing laugh.

"No apple for you," Henry said. Voice slurred. He waggled a piece of fruit at Oswald. "The apples are only for Daddy."

Lambert followed. "Yes, I know, I know. We all know." Then he leaned in, his voice both a growl and a hiss. "These girls. We *talked* about this, sir. After last year's . . . indiscretion—"

"Come on now. I told you, Beatrice Doyle was a troubled girl, Oswald. Always traipsing about. Had eyes for too many men and surely one of them got—well. You know how men get." He winked, ate the rest of the apple, leaving barely even the core left. He threw it into the pool. He hadn't realized who she was at the time. Not that it mattered to him then, or now, not really.

Lambert's patience was at an end. "You were supposed to keep your . . . *peccadilloes* contained to the lessers. *Not* your peers."

Henry leaned in, showing his teeth. "And let me correct you: They are not my peers, Oswald. Don't you dare. None of these people are. Not even you, you old bung plug." He shrugged. "Besides, we all have our own Ambarvalia rites, Ozzy."

"There are always girls, Henry. Always. Girls of poor parentage, broken homes, scullery girls, my god, or—or whores! There are ever whores willing to lay themselves out on whatever altar you put in front of them long as the coin slots into their cleavage. But these girls. *These* are the girls of *our* garden, of *our* esteemed community. Wealthy families. *Local* business families. People who helped bring this part of the state, this country, to bear. Who are part of your community, who help keep you in good standing. You're poaching. You're eating the hens we need to lay the eggs, do you see?"

Henry felt poised on his tippy-toes, balanced on a line. He could go one way—keep denying, as he had, as he could eternally because who would ever find him out? Or he could go the other way. He could have some *fun* with it.

And life was too short without a little fun.

(Or, perhaps, too long not to have some.)

"They're alive," Henry said, finally, playing coy, mouth fishhooking into a sharp smirk.

"Are they." Said less as a question and more a statement of disbelief. Lambert's eyes pinched tight in suspicion.

"Both of them. Would you like to see?"

"I would, sir."

One more lick of his lips. He shuddered.

"Then, Ozzy my friend, it is time to show you my secret garden."

APRIL

—

COMFORT ME WITH APPLES, FOR I AM SICK OF LOVE.

—SONG OF SOLOMON 2:5

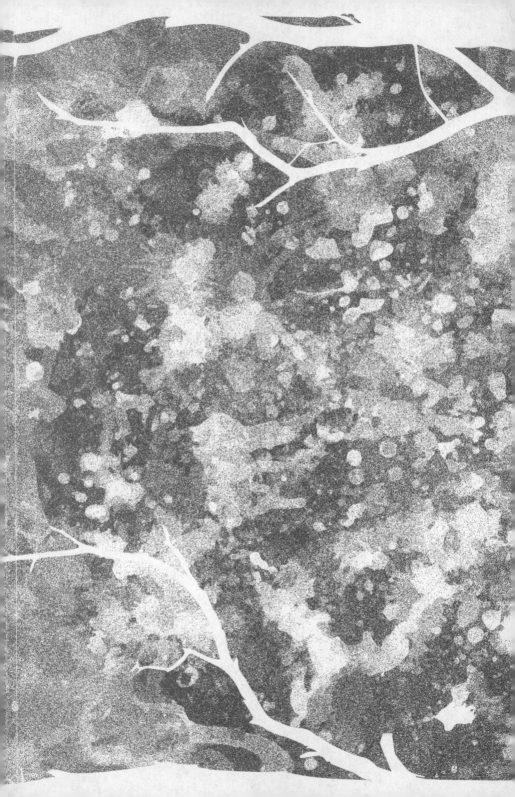

48

THE FIRST VIDEO

"Post it," Lucas said, flicking his gaze from Calla to the phone and back to Calla. Lucas had a look, a gaze, and in it was a thousand pounds of judgment, a million miles of expectation.

"Maybe we should wait," she said, wincing.

The three of them stood around the park playground around the corner from Esther's house. It wasn't the rich kids' park—that one was in pristine shape, ever-updated, always immaculately maintained. This one was a small, janky little park with a busted-up asphalt jogging path and a playground set from, like, 1976. They sat on wooden swings with rusty, squeaky chains that would probably give them splinters in their ass cheeks.

Esther blew a jet of vape fog out of the side of her mouth and the chilled April wind snatched it away. She said, "Maybe. Lucas, this could blow back on Calla. It's her account. Maybe we make a new account—"

"And who follows that new account exactly?" Lucas said, incredulous. "No one. And if we are the first ones to follow it, then it points to us anyway."

"Point," Esther said.

Calla hugged her jacket tight and looked at her phone.

The video was simple enough.

It was just a series of, like, two-second clips of kids at school with the apples. Sharing them, trading them, acting surreptitious about them. One shot showed one of the baseball kids, a pitcher named Bobby Tamburri, eating an apple off the side of the bleachers, lost to bliss. Eyes rolled back in his head. Drooling. The other videos were just whatever, but this one? It was creepy.

After the compilation of those clips, it was Calla looking into the camera and asking, "What's the deal with the apples?"

That was it.

A twenty-second video.

Shorter videos went viral faster.

She knew this, and Lucas had been keen to remind her.

The whole point of the video was to be kind of an introduction. A whole, *Hey, did you guys notice the weird apple thing?* Like it was some kind of underground anti-TikTok trend, a thing people were doing without a camera pointed at their face (which was weird enough as it was). It was a signal sent out to those people who weren't eating the apples. *The ones who haven't changed,* Lucas had said, which made Calla shiver at the time and was a heavy, sour thought that sat in the pit of her stomach ever since. "They'd post it to TikTok, then Insta, then everywhere else. Maximum coverage to hit that audience.

"Fuck, I dunno," Calla said. "If my father sees this—if Marco sees it—"

"They're so far up their own asses they won't know or won't care," Lucas said. "We have to do something."

"Or the university. I got into Princeton—"

Their faces lit up. *Oh my god, they didn't know.* They screeched like happy parakeets and swarmed her in a hug.

"Bitch, you didn't say," Lucas said right into her ear.

"I'm so happy for you," Esther said, cheering her on. Esther knew Calla wanted to go to Princeton since she was a kid. Public policy analysis was always her intended major, though now, she wasn't sure.

"I dunno," Calla said, appreciating the hug but needing room to breathe. "I want to be excited but it's close. Part of me thinks I should . . . apply somewhere else. Somewhere in California or, I dunno, the fucking moon? Just to get farther away from all this. From Dad and Marco and— ugh, the apple. I mean, it's crazy, right? It's an apple. A stupid fucking apple."

Lucas said, "But it's not crazy. You know it's not. You more than anybody."

At that, she rankled. "This isn't my fault. I didn't know anything about it—"

Lucas made an *ugh* face. "I just mean, you're closer to it than anybody. You said you saw stuff. Like the flies. And it changed your dad's eyesight?"

"Yeah. But he's wearing his glasses again so . . . I don't know. Maybe it's, like, a delusion? A shared delusion."

Esther chimed in: "The basketball team hasn't lost a game. And they always, always lose their games."

"They've gotten brutal on the court," Lucas said. They gave him weird looks and he said, "What? I go to games. Hot long boys, come on, I have needs, okay? What I saw were tons of fouls and aggro bro vibes. Like, frat-boy rapist vibes. They've hurt some of the other players. And didn't seem to give two shits about it."

"See?" Esther said. "Something's up."

"You want to influence people?" Lucas asked her. "Well, there are people already under the influence of something weird here and we need to, I dunno, *counter*-influence them. Like, anti-propaganda propaganda—"

"Like agitprop," Esther said, knowingly. Calla didn't know if she was using that word right, but Esther was pretty tuned in to politics SocMed, so she probably knew.

Lucas went on. "Maybe it isn't the apple. Maybe it's a worm or a weird bacteria or a—I dunno, a fungus? And maybe this is how people figure it out and maybe this helps someone."

"Okay. Maybe." She clutched the phone. "Alternatively, what if we don't. Or maybe we think of a different video, something less . . . I dunno, in-your-facey."

Lucas held out his hand. "Fine. Let me watch the video again at least?"

She reluctantly handed him the phone.

And he hit the POST button.

"There," he said.

"Lucas!" she cried out, snatching back her phone. Sure enough, it was already on her feed. And it had already garnered a few likes in that short amount of time. "Oh fuck!"

"Delete it now if you want. You still can. But I think you should leave it."

Calla snarled in frustration and looked to Esther. "What do you think?"

"I say leave it. It is weird, Calla. Something's up. And if we can help . . ."

Her head craned back on her neck and she stared up at the sky. It was a gray day. All clouds. The sun was like a flashlight shining through a dirty bedsheet.

"I won't delete it," she said, finally.

"You're a badass," Esther said.

"Bona fide," Lucas added.

It was out there, now. The video was free.

Maybe no one will see it, Calla thought.

Maybe no one will care.

She hoped that was going to be the case.

She feared that it wouldn't be.

49

HER KEEPER'S MOTHER

NOREEN, MEG'S MOTHER, WATCHED HER WITH THE IMPLACABLE stare of a reptile—wide, cold eyes, ever-unblinking. Emily half expected the woman's tongue to dart out and clean one of her eyeballs with a hasty lick.

She sat nearby, at the breakfast bar, as Emily prepared dinner for when Meg was to come home.

This was Emily's new reality: Noreen was her keeper during the day. Her jailer. Here all the time, watching her, and yes, teaching her—teaching her how to cook, how to clean, how to be the good wife so that one day she too might, in Noreen's words, "deserve something nice."

Tonight's dinner: halibut, baked and breaded, and a salad dressed with a simple lemon vinaigrette. Not that it much mattered; whatever Emily made, Meg barely ate. She would pick at it, take a few bites—just enough to tell Emily what a poor job she had done, then taunt her with the apple once more. Sometimes she'd say something nice in there, too, something about the meal, something about the way Emily looked but she'd instantly turn it back around, poison it, neg her with something cruel to counter whatever kindness she dared let slip. It felt willful, purposeful, though maybe Meg couldn't help herself. Whatever was happening to her was perhaps not entirely in her own control. At least that's what Emily hoped.

"You're not whisking hard enough," Noreen said, irritated.

"It's fine," Emily said, snapping back—but she did so quietly, softly.

"It's not fine." The Elder Paltrow Clone stood up, strode over with annoyance in her every step. She stared down into the bowl. "You also forgot the mustard. A little Dijon, I said. It's an emulsifier. Do you even know what that is, or what it does? A dressing is a *system,* Emily, and if that system is not well designed it will not hold together—it will break, it will become oily, it will be *unpleasant.*"

"Sorry. I forgot."

Noreen went into the fridge, grabbed the jar of Dijon, thrust it hard against Emily's chest. Hard enough it would leave a bruise.

"Less than a teaspoon. Let's do it, let's go, come on now."

Emily swallowed hard and nodded. She got out a spoon, put a bit on the tip of the utensil—and she found that her hand was shaking. Hastily, she plopped it into the bowl, fast enough that Noreen wouldn't see her trembling.

"*Here,*" Noreen said, grabbing her wrist. The grip hurt. And it hurt more as Noreen moved her hand around quickly, forcing Emily's hand to vigorously whisk the mustard into the lemon juice and olive oil.

But then suddenly, she stopped.

"What is it?" Emily asked.

"I could break your wrist," Noreen said. She said it so plainly, almost dreamily, like she was just realizing it. Like it was aspirational. A quote on Instagram in a glittery font.

Emily tried to pull out of her grip, but Noreen's hand tightened, trapping her wrist even tighter. Her hand started to tingle.

"Noreen, let go—"

"I feel like you just don't appreciate my daughter enough. Or me, for that matter. I'm trying to help you. Trying to make you a better person, even though you won't eat the apple. Don't you appreciate me, Emily?"

She's going to break my arm. The woman's hands were small. But Emily could feel the power in them.

"I appreciate you, of course I do, but I want you to let go of my wrist. Please."

Noreen held on for a few seconds more, then relinquished her hold. Emily's wrist was left throbbing in its wake.

"It makes me so sad sometimes that you're my daughter-in-law," Noreen said, pouting. "But we all have our crosses to bear, don't we?"

Emily's heart was racing in her chest. Her wrist, still pulsing from the woman's preternaturally strong grip. *You could go. You could run.* Tantalizing thoughts of escape. But she had nothing. What money she had, she no longer could access. She no longer had her phone. Never had a car. Even the bike had its tires slashed. She had nothing, no escape. They'd cut her off. Closed her in this place with Noreen, her keeper. If Emily decided to walk to the front door, open it, and walk out, would Noreen try to stop her? She could, if she wanted. On the first day that Noreen babysat Emily, she said glibly, almost as a throwaway thought, "If you want to leave, dear Emily, you can—perhaps you can leave like that man you found in the river. He certainly found a way out, didn't he?"

Implicit in that was a threat, she felt.

You leave, I'll drown you in that river.

Later, Noreen had said to her, "You're afraid of water, aren't you?" Then she laughed. A laugh of musical chimes, the wind stirring them.

Emily wanted like hell to call John. It had been a week now since she'd had any contact with him at all. He'd almost certainly tried calling her phone, or texting her, but she didn't have the phone—Meg did, and wherever it was, it was either off or out of battery or muted. She tried to casually ask Meg about it, but all Meg would say was, "No, I don't think he cares about you anymore. He got what he wanted out of you, Emily. He used you against me. Against all of us." Then she added: "He is not in our life anymore. Do you understand?"

Emily did understand. She wished she didn't, but she did.

And all the while she wondered if it would still be possible to save Meg. Eating the apple was a choice, she knew, a choice to eat it, to keep eating it, but maybe it was like John had said—a spiritual parasite, something crawling into the holes in your soul and filling those dark and empty spaces. And as with any parasite, it wasn't something you could control. You were invaded, intruded upon, a

(*supernatural*)

(*evil*)

trespasser inside of you.

And maybe, just maybe, it could be ripped out.

One night she lay awake staring at the ceiling, wondering what it would be like if she decided to bite the bullet, so to speak, and eat the apple. Would she find pleasure there, too? Would she find such certainty of will and strength of body? Could she be better than she was? She'd long felt weak, like she had this ADHD brain that went this way and that, a box of squirrels kicked over into a bin of ground espresso, and maybe the apple would be like medicine. Maybe it could sharpen her, spiritual Adderall, help give her focus to fight this fight ahead of her. *Or maybe you'd just be lost in it, too,* she thought. In thrall. Or maybe she'd be like John—her soul would reject it, because her soul would be too strong for it. But that last one, yeah, that was bullshit, she knew. She wasn't strong. She was weak. Afraid of water. Had no career to speak of. Had no idea what she was doing. Glommed onto Meg for everything. *Fuck.*

As she was thinking about it, Meg woke, wanted sex. Emily gave it to her, hoping that it was about real connection, about them bridging a gap that had not been bridged for a long time—but Meg was rough, demanding, not in a way that felt confident but rather, in a way that felt cruel. Like she could just seize upon Emily, moving her around like a puppet, like a toy. Go here, do that, hands here, mouth there—Meg was greedy and needy and almost *supervisory.*

Emily cried after. Meg told her to take it to the bathroom.

So she did.

Without a fight.

That felt the most pathetic.

That she did this all without a fight.

And now here she stood in the kitchen, with another boss at her back—this time, Meg's mother, lording over her, sneering at her fucking vinaigrette. It made her angry and sad. She felt caught between those two feelings. And it made her unsure what to do next, or if she even had any moves to make.

At that, there came a knock on their door.

Noreen stood, her hackles raised. She went to the window and peered out, and her dermabrasion face, clear of acne, the wrinkles smoothed, suddenly twisted up like a bouquet of flowers wrung out and ruined by a pair of strangling hands.

"It's *him,*" Noreen said.

"Him," Emily repeated, unsure what she meant—until she understood.

John.

Of course, it made sense. Didn't it? He was her friend. He wasn't going to just leave her alone. Realizing that brightened her in a way, like seeing a flashlight in the darkest night—*oh my god, I have a friend.*

After days of being here, in this house, trapped with Meg and Noreen . . .

She'd forgotten that.

How fast that can happen.

"I'm going to get rid of him," Noreen said. "He's dangerous. We don't want him around here. You will say nothing. Don't dare show your face."

"What? What are you going to tell him?"

"That you left. That you abandoned him. He'll believe it." Noreen looked down her nose at Emily. "I'm sure he's seen how you really are."

"No, he'll think I'm in danger." *Which I am.*

Another knock at the door. A muffled voice. "Emily? Are you home?"

"Then we just won't open the door at all. Let him knock. Let him knock and knock and knock *and knock* and nobody will ever open the door."

"Please. I'll talk to him."

Noreen walked up to Emily. Her face softened. She put her hands on Emily's shoulders gently, a sad look in her eye. "I'm sorry, Emily. I know this is hard." Her palms ran down the lengths of Emily's arms, until she held Emily's hands with her own. "He's your friend, and you don't want to lose him."

"That's right."

Another knock. "Emily! It's John!"

At that, Noreen interlaced her fingers into Emily's own—

And bent Emily's hands back. A sharp cattleprod of pain ran from her hands to her elbows and her knees nearly buckled. Noreen clamped her other hand on Emily's mouth to stifle her cry while maintaining her soft, sympathetic face even as she said, "If you call out to him, I'll break your wrists. Fingers too. You'll be whisking vinaigrette with shattered paws, little kitten. Maybe I'll hurt him, too. Or let him hurt me. Who do you think the police will believe? Even if they didn't have the apple peel under their nails, the juice dripping from their chins, you think they'd believe *him,* some drifter, over me, a wealthy local white taxpayer? I think we've both read the news enough to predict how that will go, don't you think?"

Behind the hand, Emily whimpered, but nodded.

Noreen eased her hand away.

"Please let go, please let go," Emily begged, tears in her eyes. "*Pleaseletgo.*"

"Will you be a good girl?"

"I will I will I promise I will."

Noreen let go of her hand.

And there came the moment—

The moment of decision.

Emily felt the words on her lips. *Cry out. Call to John.* He would fix this. He was her friend. She could push past Noreen. She could run. Be free.

But then you'd be away from Meg.

You couldn't fix her.

She'd close the door and you'd have nothing.

And Noreen could hurt you. So could Meg. They could hurt John.

That would be on you, Emily.

And beneath it, a crueler, colder voice: *Besides, you're too weak to escape. Too weak to do anything. You need this. You haven't been good for anyone, have you? Isn't it nice to just give in? To try to be useful for once in your life?*

Then the moment passed. The decision, made. Emily softly dropped to her knees, burying her face in her hands, her wrists burning with pain. She stayed silent. And eventually, John stopped knocking.

THAT GNAWING RAT IN YOUR GUTS

HE KNOCKED MULTIPLE TIMES, CALLED HER NAME. JOHN WAS pretty sure he heard something inside. Someone. But no one answered the door.

In the driveway sat a white Lexus SUV. Meg's mother's car, wasn't it?

"Hnh," he said.

There was a feeling here. In the air, but in his blood, his bowels. A humming, like cicadas in summer, stirred up and panicking at their own coming doom.

She's in danger.

But he didn't know that. Couldn't prove it.

I need to know she's okay.

And John wanted her help in destroying Dan Paxson's orchard—killing the trees that produced that vile apple. Ending Vinot's legacy. He did not know what it would do to those affected by the pkwësu, but he had to try something. And he wanted Emily's counsel. But more important, he just wanted her safe.

John had never had a daughter. Never had a family.

But Emily felt like family.

He stepped away from the door, looked across the street. Emily's house sat on a backroad that twisted its way through the trees between the river and the canal. Across from the house were just trees and understory. Mostly deciduous trees—a shagbark maple, a paper birch, a dead ash tree. But there was a nice eastern hemlock there. Bushy, with drooping branches. A deep darkness settled underneath it. That would do just fine.

All right, then.

John had preparations to make.

LOVE AMID PAIN

THAT NIGHT, MEG WAS KIND TO EMILY. KIND WITHOUT RESERVA-
tion, without strings. She kissed Emily's cheek and complimented her on
the salad and the fish, even though as usual, she ate very little of it. They
sat in bed and watched TV—*Parks and Rec* on one of the streaming net-
works. They even laughed together, a little. It felt nice. It felt like before.
It was then that Emily realized: Meg hadn't stopped to get an apple. By
now, she would have. Had Emily even seen an apple today? Usually they
were on the counter, always several at hand. But now, none. She wanted
to ask about it, but didn't want to ruin the moment. Meg eventually said,
"Anything happen today?" and Emily didn't know if she was baiting her
about John showing up, or about Noreen's violence, but again there was
a moment to be protected and so all Emily said was, "Nope, everything
was great." And Meg said, "I knew it, I knew you'd find your place with
me," and then she kissed the back of Emily's hand and at that point Emily
didn't know if she should feel happy or sad, and how it was possible that
she actually felt both at the same exact time.

THE DEVIL AND HIS PITCHFORKS

THE RAIN OUTSIDE SEEMED NEVER-ENDING: A LONG, HARD MID-spring soaker that churned the earth and chopped the dirt into mud. Creeks overfilled. Roads flooded. Gray skies and dark earth and drowned worms.

Dan's father had a whole complement of terms for rain like this: a real *goose-drowneder,* a damn *Hatchy-Milatchy,* or instead he might say, "God's really rushin' the growler today," which Dan never understood until later, when someone explained that it meant a rush to the bar to fill a growler with beer. People upstate in coal-cracker country, in Shendo and Turkey Run, used to send their kids to the bar with their growlers, the sort of thing that would never pass muster today.

But most often he'd say:

"It's raining the Devil and his pitchforks out there."

And it was, in more ways than one.

FROM THE BOX BAY WINDOW AT THE FRONT OF THE HOUSE, DAN stared out at the rain, blinking behind his eyeglasses. Glasses he'd come to hate. He'd had them for so long, they didn't bother him *until* he had given them up for a bit—and now that he needed them again, they felt heavy on his nose. They irritated his ears. He wanted to grab them off his face and fling them to the ground. But then he'd be half blind again—everything as blurred as the world beyond the rain-soaked windows.

He walked through the house, going from window to window, look-ing out, haunting it like a ghost. Nobody else was home. Calla was at school. She hated him now anyway. Maybe that was fair. Maybe he even understood why. Almost.

At the back porch door, all he could see were dark shapes mounding behind the rain. The rain nearly swallowed the south lawn thicket—the thicket that continued down the slope toward the orchard and the creek beyond it. The punctuations of green were hard to see—spring's growth, engulfed by the wall of rain.

But none of that growth was on his apple trees.

Still. Yet. *Damnit.*

Which meant there were no more apples coming.

Which meant what few he had left were all he had.

People were asking. He had to turn them down. They looked . . . not angry, but softened, weakened, like the sails of a boat going slack when the wind suddenly stops.

Claude, of course, still had some apples. He took a few crates the other day, leaving Dan with only a dozen apples of his own.

Not that it mattered. He ate them and though they gave him a small frisson of pleasure and delight, it ended there. His eyesight grew clearer only for a moment, then quickly blurred. His mind felt soft. His hope, aimless and drifting. Eating the apple provided a tantalizing reminder, but only that, of what the apples had done for him. He, too, felt like he'd gone slack.

Something's been taken out of me, Dan thought.

"Taken *from* you, you mean," said a voice behind him.

He startled, visibly. Dan spun around, fingers spidering around his glasses and almost knocking them from his face.

"No," Dan said, his voice hoarse with horror.

The blond man in the white suit sat at the dinner table, the chair turned toward Dan. His monster-sized grin with its white, white teeth blazed so bold and so bright it almost blinded Dan.

"Not even taken from you. Given away. Regifted, like an ugly sweater at Christmas. Dan, Dan, Little Dan, Danny Boy, you had such promise."

"You—you're—" He could barely find the words. They juggled together in his throat. Finally they jostled their way free: "You're *dead.*"

"And yet, I sit here before you."

"I'm—I'm hallucinating. This isn't real." He said it again, more to himself than to the

(*delusion*)

(*nightmare*)

(*monster*)

man sitting in front of him. "*This isn't real.*"

The man—Edward Naberius—stood. He stood slowly, with purpose, brushing himself off as if the chair, the whole house, was filthy to him. Even with that big smile on his face, his visage betrayed a kind of irritation.

With a measured step, he approached Dan.

"Dan, and I say this as your friend, what the everloving fuck."

"I don't understand."

"I gave you what you needed, did I not? Was your lost dignity not restored?"

Dan stammered. "It—it was. You did."

"And yet—"

Naberius moved closer. Nearly nose-to-nose. There arose that sharp wintergreen smell. But underneath it, something else, something Dan hadn't noticed before—

Another odor, a stink that the wintergreen was covering up. It was the smell of death. A sharp, mineral tang of blood and bone the mint could not hide.

He continued. "And yet, here you are, your dignity lost once more. Look at you. Flailing. A weakened, watery sauce of a man. I thought I had detected something in you. Some spark of life, some vital hidden rage. I thought I found in you a subterranean reservoir of power. And you tapped it. For a time. But now, Lambert sucked it up with a straw . . ."

Naberius lifted a finger and with a quick flip, knocked Dan's eyeglasses off his face. They clattered to the ground and Dan immediately cried out, going after them—but as he did, Naberius backhanded him so hard, Dan fell the other way, tumbling to the ground, barely managing to catch himself with open stinging palms. Dan tasted blood from a split lip.

He pressed his forehead against the floor and shut his eyes tight, so tight he saw the blinding light inside his own head.

The floorboards creaked as the other man knelt down next to him.

"Dan," Naberius said in a quiet voice. "It takes me a great deal of power to be here. I am *charged up* with entropic energy and I could kill you with but a touch. I want to. It might be the best thing for us all. But I still have faith." He patted Dan on the cheek. "I still believe in you, Danny Boy, I still want to see you succeed. It's time to open your eyes."

"I don't want to," Dan said, snot thickening in his skull, spit slicking his lips.

Naberius methodically grabbed a hank of Dan's hair at the back of his skull, taking his time to *really* wind his fingers around it—

And yanked Dan's head back.

But Dan *still* kept his eyes smashed shut.

"Let's open them for you, they seem to be *stuck*," Naberius said, mashing the fingers from his other hand against Dan's eyes—

The light behind Dan's lids erupted brighter: smeary, greasy fireworks. Pain bloomed there, too, as Edward began pushing his fingers *into* Dan's eyeballs—

Dan tried to pull away, but Naberius's grip was powerful.

"No, no, don't move. I need you to see some things. I need you to put them together. Maybe *that* will rekindle that *spark* I saw in you at the beginning."

And Naberius's fingers kept going—as if Dan's eyes were just softboiled eggs, the digits working deep into his sockets, pushing his eyes into his brain, and Dan screamed, thinking almost absurdly, *How can I see anything if you ruined my eyes, I'm blind now, I'm fucking blind—*

THEN, LIKE THAT, THE FINGERS WERE GONE.

Dan fell back on his assbone, gasping.

He blinked. Reached for his face. His eyes were there. Present and accounted for. And his eyeglasses were nearby on the floor—his fingers scrabbled desperately to reclaim them and urge them back onto his face.

Clarity returned. He was in his house. The man in white was nowhere to be found. And yet, he was not alone.

A boy stood framed by the far doorway. Dark, tousled hair. Round spectacles. A little fresh brushburn on his forehead from when he was pushed down on the playground by Prentiss Beckman. *It's me. From when I found Dad.*

That version of Little Dan looked into the room, staring at the chair that, only minutes ago, Edward Naberius had been sitting in.

But now, a different occupant sat there.

Another dead man. This one, fully dead, one that would not return from it.

In the doorway, Little Dan trembled. A stain spread from his pants, down from his crotch, rivulets running to his knees.

In the chair, the dead man waited.

The bullet hole in Big Dan's left temple was a puckered crater, dark around the edges, like a black hole in space and time. The other temple was a ragged hole punched clean through and out, bones and brain and hair flopping to the side like peeled sod, and, gathering on his shoulder, a pile of foul landscaping, of gray mulch and red earth. A .38 sat in the open palm of his left hand, his lifeless fingers tickling the blued steel. Only the index finger seemed to have purpose: It was thrusting up through the trigger guard.

There were details about that day marked indelibly upon Dan's memories.

Dan remembered the smell in the air, the same smell he caught in his nose now: blood and waste and that fading gunpowder funk.

He remembered the way fat black flies kept alighting upon the two sides of Big Dan's ruined head, taking little tastes before taking flight once more.

He remembered standing there, frozen in that spot for a long time, a time so long it might as well have been forever, the clearest thought in his head being that he was now really, really alone. His mother was already gone, and now his father was, too, and Little Dan had no anchor, no mooring, no anything to tether him to this world and keep him grounded and safe, and he felt like he'd float up into the air like an errant red balloon, and then catch in a branch and pop, hanging there dead. *I'm alone, I'm alone, I'm alone.*

But there were details here and now that seemed . . .

New.

Dan walked over to regard his father's corpse.

Was this real? A true memory? Or something else?

Because he didn't remember the rough, abraded skin around his father's wrists. Skin mottling, rasped bloody in places. As if something had been wound around his wrists. Rope, wire, cord.

He didn't remember the other chair at the far end of the table being knocked over to the ground, overturned.

He didn't remember one of their shovels leaning against the back door. Not freshly dirty—no mud upon its blade. It hadn't been used.

(*yet*)

And there, on the ground:

A small fragment of cork.

Like from a bottle of wine.

It was bound to a larger splinter of wood.

A piece of wood, like from a barrel. *Just* slightly curved.

Stained on the one side, dark purple. Bruise dark.

Kkkkt—

Big Dan's head spun toward Little Dan. His lips wrenched back, exposing worms playing in his teeth, and through gargled earth and clotted blood his father said, "*Got a real Hatchy-Milatchy here, kiddo. You starting to see it yet? Starting to see what happened? Like I always say, you gotta talk to the trees.*" A tube of maggots, like Play-Doh made of pale grubs, extruded from the bullet hole in his temple, and Big Dan laughed. A wet, mealy guffaw.

Dan screamed, staggering back from his father's animated carcass.

He staggered into the shovel—

It fell over with a *clong*—

And then his father was gone.

And so, too, was the shovel.

And so was the man in white.

Though he still smelled

(*the sour pickle-stink of death*)

a whiff of wintergreen hanging in the air.

Dan stood there, chest rising and falling with steadying breaths. He blinked and pulled off his eyeglasses, gave them a quick clean—they were dirty, yes, but this was a reflexive gesture, an odd habit of comfort and control.

How much of that had been real?

His father's words still rang in his ears, particularly that last part—
You gotta talk to the trees.

BIG DAN WAS A MAN OF MANY SAYINGS, AND ONE OF THEM WAS, TO
quote him in full:

If you wanna know what's wrong, you gotta talk to the trees.

It was literal and not-literal at the same time. He used it generically,
whenever anything was up, off, or askew. It basically meant, if you wanted
to know what was going on, you had to go find out. You had to look, ask,
poke around. Little Dan always took it to mean: Answers wouldn't come
to you, you had to go get the answers. And you got the answers by asking
questions.

But literally, it meant something different to Pop. He was good with
grapes, strawberries, blueberry bushes—but really good with fruit trees
and any tree, really. He wasn't a trained arborist or anything. Didn't go
to school for it. But he grew up and worked for a local landscaper, learning how to plant and keep things alive, and with trees, he always said that
if you wanted to know a tree, you had to go look at it. Feel the bark. Even
climb it (though he did less of that as the years went on). Said the tree
would tell you what was wrong, whether it had some kind of rust or
blight, whether it was getting chewed up under the bark by some kind of
borer beetle, whatever it was, the tree would tell you.

You gotta talk to the trees.

DULL RAIN POUNDED. THE GROUND WAS GREASY UNDERNEATH
Dan's feet as he slipped and slid down the dirt drive toward the orchard.
He kept wiping rain from his glasses but it wasn't doing him any good, so
he just let his vision go smeary.

He stumbled into the orchard, pushing through the downpour

(*the devil and his pitchforks*)

and there Dan stood among his trees, the ones he'd grown from that
tree he saved from that wretched little island in the middle of the river,
the ones whose branches

(*fingers*)

he'd trimmed for scionwood, the ones that gave him and this county the Ruby Slipper. The ones that had now gone silent.

Talk to the trees.

So that's what he did. He begged them, "Why? Why won't you produce? Where are the buds, the green, the blooms? Please. I need this. We all need this. I feel like I'm losing you, losing myself—" He clasped his hands together as if in prayer. "What do you need from me? Show me what's wrong. *Show me.*"

He stepped forward to get closer to the closest tree—

And the toe of his boot caught on something.

Dan pitched forward, onto his knees.

That's what it wants—

I have to kneel—

I have to be penitent—

But it was then he saw that what he tripped over was not a root.

It was a bone.

The rain was already washing mud from it. It was still filthy, with the stain of the earth upon it, but it was clearly a bone. *Just an animal bone,* Dan thought, because it had to be—but as he dug his fingers into slick earth, he pulled out something that was decidedly not from a woodland animal at all.

It was a human jawbone lined with all its teeth. Dan held it close, regarding it in the rain.

A root lay underneath it. As if the root had pushed this up to the ground.

As if it had pushed it up to meet him.

To show me, he thought.

Ask the trees.

He did, and this was the answer.

Or, at least, part of it.

Dan did not bother going to find a shovel. He would not dishonor the orchard by leaving it. He stayed there on his hands and knees and reached into the ground and began to pull up clumps and clots of mud, one after the next. He was the shovel, unearthing answers he did not yet understand, but would soon enough.

PRECIOUS

THE NIGHT OF KINDNESS FROM MEG WAS SHORT-LIVED. IN THE morning, Meg looked pale, withdrawn, skin the color of skim milk. She roamed and roved inside and out, like a cloud of flies that couldn't find a place to land—and, Emily realized, it was because she was looking for something.

The apple.

Back into the kitchen she came as Emily nursed a bowl of too-healthy cereal. "You okay?" she asked Meg, guardedly.

"Shut the fuck up, Em. Not now." Meg winced suddenly, like the morning light in the kitchen was much too bright. In moments, she was on the phone to her mother. The one-sided conversation Emily heard was, with beats between each sentence: "Yeah. Yeah, Mom, I know. *I said I know.* No, I don't have any. You should've saved one for me. But you didn't. Did you." A pause. "You took them, didn't you. You took the last of my bushel. You old fucking bitch. Always so selfish." Pause. "I know you raised me. I know. *You* brought *me* into this world, which means *you* owe *me.* Yeah, I don't feel good either. Well, does Dad have any? Why not? Fuck. *Fuck.* What good are you?" And at that she ended the call and slammed the phone down on the cutting board enough to send a crack across the back of her protective case.

Thing was, Emily had worked in crisis youth centers, and she knew these signs intimately: This was withdrawal. An addicted person, when denied their addiction (and when their addiction was denied *them*), frayed like a cut rope. It was all short circuits, tics and snaps and biting teeth. The body and the mind craved what had been cut from them, having been convinced that the thing that was missing was as vital to them as air and water and food. And further, that the thing that was missing was not merely missing, but worse: *stolen.*

Meg was in withdrawal.

And right on time, she wheeled toward Emily.

Blame shining in her eyes like a pair of cops holding flashlights.

"You," Meg said accusatorily.

"Meg, you're going through withdrawal."

Might as well just say it, right?

"What?"

"The apple. You . . . you're addicted to it. It did something to you, I don't know how. But it's not a normal apple, you understand that, right? Of course, you already know that. But you're not acting right. You're different and now that you don't have it anymore . . . your mind or your body or both are reacting to that absence. You have to get through it."

A rage-fed, almost-primitive look flashed across Meg's face. Her thin lips twisted into a sneer, her teeth bared. She pressed herself backward against the counter, as if she were recoiling from Emily and her words. Emily half expected her to hiss like some feral cat warning her not to come near. Meg eased along the counter like a kid keeping to the edge of a swimming pool.

"You know," Meg started to say, "that's how I knew you were cheating on me. Because *you* were different."

And there it was.

The Unspoken Thing—

Suddenly spoken.

No longer haunting them as a shadow, here it was, dragged into the space between them. Kicking and screaming as the light burned it.

"Meg, we don't have to do this right now—when you're not in your right mind with things—"

"It's just. When you're with someone, you detect those *little patterns.* Don't you? Two spiders sharing the same web and when one plucks the strings—you sense it." She made small harp-string noises as a twitchy finger plucked the air: "*Ting, ting, ting.* Right? I could already tell you were unhappy with me. I was . . . what, too uppity, uptight, upright, and you were the what, the cool one, the awesome lesbian queer chick that everyone loved, *good times girl,* right? Always with the fun-times, never with the responsibilities. Punk, fuck-yeah, raahhh. I was the mean old lawyer, making the money by working for the man. Right? That's how you saw me. How your friends saw me."

"They were our friends. You never really embraced the community—"

Meg's eyes lit up wild and wide and mad. "I didn't have time. I had to work. I had to hold up all the struts and beams of our lifestyle so that it didn't come crashing down on our heads because *you* had to work at a youth shelter—not exactly a *lucrative* job, was it, Em?"

At that, Emily fumed.

"Hey, fuck you. I was doing good work there. Kids in this country— queer kids especially—are fucking scared right now. And someone needs to be there for them." She paused, going quiet. "You said that was one of the things you loved about me. Once."

"It was. And I still loved you. But then you went and fucked around behind my back. Some cheap young stupid thing. And you know what, Emily? Even after that, I still loved you. And I thought I was the weak one, the ugly one, that I drove you to do it—"

"You didn't drive me to it. I told you, it was my fault—"

"And I kept on with you, on and on and *on*. I brought you here thinking we could start a new life and I could be better and you could be better but now here we are, Emily. Here we are and only one of us has gotten better. And one of us will always remain who they are: a sniveling little freeloader who cares about everyone else more than me, who cares about her*self* more than everyone."

Emily gritted her teeth, forced herself not to cry. "You're projecting." But was she, though? *She is. She has to be. She's not right about this.* "I don't care about everyone else more than you, I just—I just didn't always have my priorities right and I made a mistake. But you weren't always good to me, either."

Meg slid further down the counter.

Her hand, palm flat against the quartz, slid toward something—

The knife block.

Emily tensed.

She's going to attack me.

She's going to try to kill me.

For a few moments, they stood like that. Emily saying nothing, waiting. Meg, too, standing silent, her hand poised like a spider ready to jump for a knife.

But then, Meg's shoulders slumped. And she sighed, scowling. "Go fuck yourself, Emily," she said, before pushing past and going down the hall toward the bedroom. The door slammed behind her: the act of a petulant, surly teen.

Still—

She never grabbed the knife.

Meg went toward it—but never grabbed it.

There's more of you in there, Emily thought. *I'm gonna save you, Meg. I'm going to help you through this. Whatever this is, we're going to make it through.*

Together.

54

REVELATION OF THE ROOTS

It wasn't clear how much time had passed. It was not yet night, but the sky was dark and gray and so it felt like Dan was caught in the eternity of this act. The rain continued its steady hammer-handle downpour, the water rushing down in unrelenting sheets. He was exhausted. All parts of him ached.

Dan sat back, panting, the ground cratered messily in front of him from where he'd gotten his hands into the dirt, dug his arms in up to the elbows and biceps, and hauled up what the orchard needed to show him. What it *wanted* to show him.

Three bodies.

Bones stripped mostly clean of meat—though one of them still seemed to have some patches of skin and tendon, some hair clinging to the scalp like moss. The skeletons were mostly intact. Their hands were bound behind them with rusted wire. And each had been shot in the head.

In the *side* of the head.

Small hole in one side of the temple.

Larger hole, the exit wound, on the other side.

These were not his father. His father was in a grave atop Buckman's Mountain, next to the now-defunct and abandoned Hilltop Methodist Church.

But they were killed like him.

Or, maybe, *he* had been killed like *them*.

Dan had always thought his father had killed himself. That's what the police said. That's how it had looked when Dan had found him. Pop was holding the gun, after all. But now . . .

There had been a part of him that always wondered. Pop was a man prone to dark moods, but usually those moods passed like any thunderstorm. He was still, by and large, a happy guy. He had hopes. Dreams. His orchard.

A shovel.

Cork on the ground.

Wine-stained wood.

Wire holding them together.

Lambert's mask. The mask of all the Lambert men, for generations.

Dan didn't understand it all. Not yet. But he thought he understood enough. And he'd find out the rest one way or another. He was already forming a plan in his head—first stop? The Goldenrod.

Out of idle habit once more, Dan took off his eyeglasses to clean them—

And he blinked through the rain.

Everything was clear. Clear as it could be in such a steady storm. Clear enough that he could again see how the roots of the trees had pushed through some of the bones of the dead skeletons—snaking through ribs and through the void between radius and ulna arm bones, braiding as it pushed through eye sockets and hip bones. Pushing the bones toward the top of the earth. *To show me,* he knew.

He looked down at the spectacles in his hand. He didn't need them anymore.

He could see clearly now.

Dan stood up.

On the closest branch, he saw it—

One apple bloom. White petals rimmed with raw pink. Already popping, already unfurled. It hadn't been there before, but it was there now.

That one bloom was enough. A new beginning. A *promise.* But there was work yet to be done, Dan knew, so pitter patter, let's get at 'er.

55

THE INTERNET IS A HELL REALM

CALLA FELT SICK AND EXCITED AT THE SAME TIME. WORRIED AND hopeful. She wanted to cheer out loud and throw up before spiking her phone into the toilet. But she didn't do any of that. All she did was come home from school, sit on her bed, and refresh, refresh, refresh. Swipe, swipe, swipe. The video they'd

(*she'd*)

posted days ago had gone viral, at least locally. It was easy to see in real time how it broke free among the students, and then from there escaped containment and reached other locals. *Adults.* Like, actual fucking grown-ups, oh fuck. It was just student comments at first. And okay, sure, some of it was just bullshit comments or jokes and stuff—

lol this is lame u suck

LMAO WHO CARES

Dude that's why I only use a Windows PC fuck the Apple Cult

Plus a bunch of emojis and whatever. Crying laughing emoji, insane-faced emoji, shrugging ASCII guy, and all that. It was normal. Calla was used to it. You posted anything to the internet, people showed up to shit on it. Her skin was tough enough to handle that basic bitch trolling by now.

But there were other comments, too.

Real ones. From kids who had . . . seen things.

dude I noticed that wtaf

Yeah What is the Deal with these Apples??

Seriously my mother won't stop eating these, it's not just in the school, my Dad tells me it's no big deal but I hear him arguing with her and omfg she sounds crazier and crazier every time, like she just doesnt care about us anymore she only cares about these stoopid appls but now she can't get them and she's FREAKING THE F OUT

They're everywhere I look, and no one seems to care!!

Like holy shit Bill Granger popped a ***basketball*** with his bare hands the other day like wtafiuheiurhwt98reussskkghhh,,,,,

And then once it got out of school and into the community, it was more of the same. Adults talking about seeing these apples, too, about how friends and family were eating them and wouldn't shut up about them, how they were *different* now, too. Acting different. But stronger. Faster. Nicer until they weren't. Meaner, then, after. And they noted how they weren't getting more apples and they were acting real cagey now. Sharper, crueler, agitated.

One comment became ten overnight, and then by the next night, it was another thirty.

That's when the first threat hit.

We know who you are. Your name is on your account. You shouldn't lie about these things, Calla Paxson.

And then the comment just after:

Your father won't be happy about this. Why are you trying to ruin his business, little girl? Someone is going to have to take away your phone.

And a third comment:

You little conniving priss-bitch piss-drinking fuckwhore. You'll pay for this. You and your friends and everybody in these comments.

A fourth, a fifth, a sixth:

You deserve to be raped and murdered.

Ill make u eat the apple and make u lik it

SEE YOU AFTER SCHOOL YOU TRAITOR CNUT

Calla sat on her bed. Reading the comments good and bad, the ones that feigned ignorance and the ones that threatened some combination of rape and death. She tried not to cry. Her jaw felt tight, all the muscles in her neck, too, like she was compressing down, down, down, a star collapsing in on itself. Her hands shook as she kept refreshing. She knew she shouldn't. *Put the phone down, dummy.* But it was like tonguing a broken tooth. She couldn't stop looking. Couldn't stop guzzling from the sewage firehose. Glug, glug, glug.

A text popped up right then:

Esther: Dude put the phone down I know you're doomscrolling

Esther: or whatever the equivalent to doomscrooling is when it's about you and not like the death of earth from climate change or whatever

It was as if Esther knew her best. Because of course she did. Calla answered, short and sweet:

Calla: ok

Esther: love u bish

Calla: love u too

Taking a deep breath, she put the phone down.

She paced the room. Calla needed something. What, though? Escape, that's what. She needed to get out of this house and like, fuck off for a while. Best to just text Esther and say, *Bish, come pick me up*, then they could grab Lucas and go do something. God, anything. Watch a movie in Esther's basement or go get high by the old quarry or pretend like they were holding a séance up by the old Methodist church up on Buckman's Mountain, the one where her grandfather was buried. (She and her father went there every Christmas. Dad cried, told her the same stories about Big Dan each time. He'd always say, "One day I'm gonna finish what he started." But last year, he said, "I'm gonna do what he couldn't." And this past year, they didn't even go.)

But then she deflated. It felt suddenly like nothing would ever be normal again. All this insanity was just too much. How could you put it all back? She remembered one time she broke one of Dad's favorite mugs, a mug she thought was just some dumb duck mug (it had a mallard duck in flight), but he seemed really upset over it, said it had belonged to *his* father, and so she tried and tried to put it back together again, using glue and a little paint to cover the chipped pieces, but when she was done it looked like a hot mess. And it leaked. Dad was nice about it. He said it was okay. *Accidents happen,* he said, but she could see the sadness in his eyes, and later she found the mug in the trash.

Life felt like that right now.

Things were broken

(*you broke it by posting that video*)

and now no amount of repair would put Humpty Dumpty back together again. It would end up in the trash.

I should delete the video.

No, I shouldn't, fuck that, it's working, it's doing what it's supposed to.

But maybe delete it.

You're going to get all this harassment.

But you're right, things are fucked up, and you're reaching some people.

Who cares though? Just get through this, go to college, never look back.

Shit shit shit shit shit shit shit.

Calla made a frustrated bleat. "Uggggggh." She had to get out. Even just to go for a walk. Everything was too tangled up in her head and the night was unseasonably warm for April, so, fine. She started to exit her bedroom—

When she saw headlights at the window. Headlights that wound down toward the orchard, brake lights filtered through returning thicket. One car, then another, then another. *Okay, that's weird, right?*

Calla gnawed on her lower lip.

She snatched up her phone, put the camera in video mode, and ran downstairs to head outside.

THE KING BLOOM

THE CIDER HOUSE WAS READY FOR BUSINESS—CASKS AGAINST THE north and south walls, gallon jugs along the west wall, a carboy fermenter and a cider press framing the door, plus a small shelf holding old wine bottles and plastic air lock exchangers and a bowl of cork stoppers. And the electricity that had been run to it—with permits in tow—worked fine, bringing light, if dim, to the structure.

Of course, no cider had been made in this place, as not only had it not been ready, but Dan now had no apples left. Nobody did. The orchard had stopped producing, and no cider would be made.

But it would produce again. The tree showed him that.

If—

If he was willing to do the work.

And Dan knew now what he had to do.

Of course, even once he had done that, if the apples grew once more

(*when the apples grew*)

he didn't think he'd ever use the cider house. He was beginning to rethink this entire expansion. There was a purity, a preciousness, to what this place was and what it gave to people, something that was corrupted by complexity. Why make cider? Or pies? Or grow other trees at all besides those that produced the beautiful Ruby Slipper apple?

All that mattered was the orchard.

And its apples.

And the people who clamored for them.

People who, even now, were begging him for a taste. His voicemail was full. His email, a scroll of despairing voices. Many came directly to the house today, sallow-cheeked, eyes haunted, hands trembling and curling in on themselves like dying beetles. They needed the apples just as he needed the apples. Because, he knew now, the apples were a sacred thing. The power on offer by Lambert and the others was false supremacy, an earthly empire of dirt.

But it wasn't the dirt that was special. It was what grew in it.

"So," Marco said, nervously scanning the room, "what is all this?"

Dan had set up a wooden table in the center of the room, a table made of old reclaimed barnwood. He placed two chairs, one at each end of it. In the center of the table was a bottle of wine from Lambert Hill Vineyards—Lambert's Berry Lambrusco. Corkscrew sitting to one side of it, and to the other, a lit candle. Two stemless glasses sat at each chair. And underneath the table? A long gym bag.

"I am ending my business arrangement with Claude Lambert," Dan said, plainly. "And I'm hoping our split will be amicable."

(*it won't*)

Marco moved around the side of the table, glancing underneath it. Dan noticed the young man was starting to limp again. *The apple . . .*

"What's in the bag, Mister P?" Marco asked. "If I can ask."

"Ah. Just some of Claude's things. Things I'm returning to him."

"Oh." Marco seemed nervous. "Okay."

At that, the sound of engines. Cars. Not one car, but several.

He'd asked Claude to come alone. But knew that the man did not follow instructions very well.

(*just ask Earl Dawes*)

Claude did what Claude wanted to do. Which was why their relationship had come to an end, and why this meeting was necessary.

Footsteps outside.

No knock. The door, thrown open.

Claude stood there, framed by the darkness of an early-spring night. He pushed his way into the cider house, rage as the mask he wore; Cabot slid in after, his bootbrush mustache twitching in irritation.

And behind them, two police officers. One, a big guy, real buckethead, dark hair, black beard like it was painted on with shoe polish. The other, a smaller guy, red hair buzzed short. Officers Burnhouse and Boyland. Dan knew them. They ate the apples. Whole police department did at this point.

They were Claude's men, bought and sold.

Cabot looked around the cider house space, scowling, grunting.

Claude stepped to Dan, carrying something under his arm. It was his Lambert Hill Orchards sign—a sign that had been messily sawn in half.

He thrust the pieces to Dan. "I got your message, Little Dan."

"I'm glad to hear that, Claude. Care to sit?" He reached for the bottle and the corkscrew. "I figure we have some things to discuss. Negotiations to make."

"Negotiations," Claude said, warily.

"That's right. I have an offer."

"An offer."

"Are you just going to repeat my words back at me, or will you at least sit and hear me out? You're a patient man, a smart fellow, who knows to open his ears before he opens his mouth. Besides, I think that's fair, don't you? After all, I'm still one of the Crossed Keys. We both have seats at the table, so to speak."

Claude looked to Cabot, and Cabot shrugged as if to say, *Why not.* Claude then shot a look to the cops, conveying to them to stand down— but stand by.

They eased into the background, toward the casks.

Marco pulled out Dan's chair for him, then pulled out a chair for Claude.

Good boy.

Claude sat and Dan dug the corkscrew into the bottle, popping the top with a *ploomp.* He returned the corkscrew to the center of the table, then poured two glasses. The nose off the quote-unquote Lambrusco was like fruit punch gone off—the syrupy sweetness of the berry dominated, followed by a miasma of Welch's grape juice. It was shit wine. Dan, who was not a sophisticated drinker, knew it. The look on Claude's face said he knew it, too—just a little moment of distaste as the odor of it hit his nose. He took a sip and winced, just a little.

Dan sat, took a sip. It tasted like wine for children.

Claude stared daggers at him. "Your note said you . . . unearthed something in the orchard today. Something that belonged to me."

"Some*things* that belonged to you. But first—I know you're an expert in grapes and vineyards and all that, and even more so a paragon of local business, right? But since you wanted to be so involved with the orchard, I thought I'd ask: How much do you *really* know about apple trees?"

"Excuse me?"

"For instance, the bud stages of an apple tree: Over the winter, the buds are dormant. Just bleak little tips. Once they hit the chill hours necessary, and as the temperature starts to come up a little, the leaf and flower tips turn silver, then green and as spring rises, heady and alive, you get that first bloom. Each cluster of flowers has *one* flower that blossoms first: the king bloom. It's this flower, bigger than the others, that must be attended to. Pollinated. And it will produce the largest apple of that cluster. The other blooms are secondary to it. Subservient."

A slow smile spread across Claude's face. "A crass metaphor, Little Dan. But I get it. You're saying that's you?"

"I'm saying that this is my orchard and I forgot that. But I've since remembered, Claude. The trees showed me that. And you know what else they showed me?" He held up a finger, as if to ask for pause. Then he slid the gym bag out from under the table. He could feel Claude sharing looks again with Cabot and the cops. *Good, let them wonder what I'm up to.* He eased aside his wineglass and put the bag on his side of the table. And then, with a magician's flourish

He pulled out a human skull.

Then another, then another.

Three skulls, each shot through the temple.

Claude stared for a moment, nostrils flaring. Then he stood, pointing at the skulls. He said with a commanding voice: "Officers, it is regrettably as I feared—Dan Paxson is a murderer. He is showing us his victims. Arrest him."

But the cops didn't flinch.

"Damnit, men, move!" Cabot barked, gesturing angrily at them.

They still didn't leap to action.

The two officers looked to each other.

And then they looked to . . .

Dan.

Claude's men, bought and sold.

Ah, they were, once. Sold to Dan, now. Because what *he* could pay with was true power.

There came a moment when Claude seemed genuinely flummoxed—as if he just couldn't believe what was happening. It was Cabot who acted first. "God*damnit*," he barked, pulling a blunt-barrel snubnose from the back of his khakis, pointing it at Dan—

Bang.

Cabot's head jerked to the side as blood and brains painted the shelf against the sidewall. Shot by Officer Boyland. His body fell like a scarecrow whose pole had gone rotten, and as Marco screamed, Dan did not wait for any further reckoning from Claude—

He took the corkscrew and punched it down into the back of Claude's hand.

The old man screamed, and Dan gave the tool a few mighty turns, feeling his shoulders burn with power, buoyed by his own desire to see this man in pain, for when the corkscrew met the wood of the table, Dan *kept turning,* grinding through it, binding Claude's bleeding mitt to the barnwood.

Claude reached for Dan with his free hand, grabbing at his throat—

There was strength still in the old man's grip. Dan felt fingers crush around his windpipe even as Claude struggled to free his other hand.

But the fire in his eyes started to die. Dan felt that strength fade from the old man—and he felt it swell and blossom inside himself. Like Claude had this great light, a light given to him by the apple, a light that Dan could bask in, soak in, and soak up. He drank Claude's power with great greedy gulps.

Claude whimpered. Dan saw the old man *wither.* He let go of Dan's neck and flailed for the Lambrusco bottle as if to grab it and use it as a weapon, but before he could reach it, Dan gave the table a quick hip-check. The bottle tumbled off and smashed against the ground.

The old man—looking sagging and soft now, liver spots appearing anew and darkening his cheeks like blots of spilled blood—sank into his chair. "Fine," he said, bleakly.

———

CALLA HEARD THE GUNSHOT.

The sound of it stole her breath. She paused there on the dirt-and-gravel road down to the orchard. Her first thought was, *Dad.* Panic crashed into her. Was he okay? All of the bad things that had happened between them suddenly vanished, and the fear of losing her father, of never seeing him ever again, nearly dropped her to the ground. And she nearly broke into a run to see what was happening—

But she stopped herself.

Maybe it's okay. Maybe it was a . . . normal gunshot?

Though their county was suburban, it had huge rural pockets just like where they lived—and it wasn't odd for someone to be shooting at night at a raccoon or some such. You heard gunshots *all the time* around here.

But did Dad have a gun?

She didn't think he did.

Calla willed herself to continue on, to get closer.

She kept her phone up.

She was not broadcasting, but she was recording.

Just in case.

LAMBERT STRUGGLED FRUITLESSLY AGAINST THE CORKSCREW FIX-ing his hand to the table, blood from his injured mitt now *pat-pat-patting* on the floor. His skin had gone gray, his brow was oily with fear-sweat.

Marco stayed back behind Dan, his eyes wide. He was upset. Rattled. That was fine, Dan knew. Marco was a good kid. He'd remain steady through this. He'd see his way through this dark earth, like a seeking, hungry root.

And now Dan pulled another magic trick from the gym bag:

He produced Claude Lambert's mask from the Goldenrod. A mask of cork and cask. He spun it around so that its bottom edge faced Lambert.

He tapped a spot on the mask, hardly perceptible if you didn't know to look for it. It was the barest line—a thin, hair-width fracture. "You broke your mask the day you killed my father. Left a piece of it there, didn't you? Maybe you attacked him and he attacked back. I don't know and I'm guessing you won't tell me, but way I figure it is, you were going to bury him in the orchard like you buried the other three, though who you killed first, I don't know."

"You don't know anything. Officers, it's him. He did this." Claude's voice rattled like a teacup on a train ride, porcelain chattering against porcelain. "You can see what he's done . . ." But he looked to the side at Cabot, who lay dead on a pillow of his own brains. Claude's words withered in his mouth.

It was nice watching him surrender to it. Even in Dan's anger, it gave him comfort to see the old vineyard vampire shrivel under the light of truth.

"I know my father didn't own a gun, Claude, but the police said it was his, registered to him. But I've seen the evidence. That's right. They showed it to me. My father's signature on the FTR"—the firearms transaction record—"was clearly forged. He didn't kill himself at all. You killed him. Why?"

Claude hesitated. He looked down at his own hand, and for a moment, his eyelids fluttered and he seemed to swoon.

Dan smacked him in the face.

"No, no, you're not escaping this," Dan said. "Stay with us. This is a reckoning, Claude Lambert, and you will remain awake for it or I'll do far worse than that corkscrew."

Blinking through bloodshot eyes, Lambert said sadly, "That mask. The mask of cork and cask. It was my father's, and his father's, all the way back to Oswald Lambert. An heirloom. I was wrecked when I noticed the damage. I didn't know how I damaged it but . . . I suppose I know now." He whimpered again, looking at the corkscrew sticking up from the black mess at the back of his hand. "Your father wanted things. He wanted in the Keys. He wanted more money. He wanted total control of the orchard—like someone *else* I know. But he wasn't ready. He was too rude, too common. Your family didn't build this county. *Mine* did. Your people weren't there by Golden's side when we ushered in a new age of art and industry. But my parents, my grandparents, my *great-*grandparents—their tireless efforts and money laid the bricks, planted the trees, built the businesses, the roads, the *everything*. It was our blood, *our* blood, that was here—"

"Bullshit. Turns out, you spilled other people's blood. Didn't you?

The red makes the green. Crossed Keys. Ambarvalia. Not just the blood of a bleating calf. The people in this orchard. My *father*. I bet you pretended they were sacrifices, too. But let me guess: the other three dead bodies are people who crossed the keys in some way, too. *Common* people, *rude* people, who didn't like what you were doing, who wanted more than you were going to give to them, so you shot them in the head, pretended it was a sacrifice, and buried the poor souls here." Dan paused, offering a small, bitter laugh. "Explains why you wanted to own this land so badly. So you could cover up your crimes. Hide it by nesting upon it."

At that, a slow, cruel smile spread across Lambert's face. "Your father helped me, you know. Two of those bodies, immigrants who worked the orchard, thought to try to blackmail me. The third? An accountant from Haycock. Didn't like our numbers. Threatened my business. Your father killed him. That gun wasn't his, no. But he knew how to use it well enough."

A chill speared through Dan. "Fuck you. You're lying."

"I'm not. And you know that, deep down, I think."

"My father wasn't just some pawn in your game—"

"That's right, he wasn't. He was a *willing participant*. Just like you were, for a while. People in proximity to power want it so bad, they'll do anything for a taste. What was it Steinbeck supposedly said of man? We're all temporarily embarrassed millionaires. Your father didn't care about trees and apples and orchards. What he really wanted was "

Dan backhanded Lambert again.

Lambert paused. A line of blood snaked from his split lip down his chin. He licked a bit of it off.

"Shut up," Dan hissed at him.

Dan pulled out the last two pieces of the gym bag—

The first, Cabot's mask. A mask of broken tile held together by tile mesh. This, Dan tossed onto Cabot's cooling body.

Then, his own mask.

The appleskin mask.

"The Crossed Keys, the Goldenrod, Henry Hart Golden, all bullshit," Dan said. "Just already-rich people pretending that they were participating in something greater than themselves when really, deep down, they didn't believe there was anything greater than themselves at all. All your talk of industriousness and work, of art and beauty, when none of you *made* anything. You used artists. You exploited workers. None of you understood toil. My *father* understood the work. *I* understood the work. All you understood was how to feed off it. Like a tick."

But that did not deter Claude. He kept leering with that shit-eating smirk. "Is that how you see it? Because what I see is a delusional man who doesn't see the blood on his own hands. You did the *work* all right. Just ask Walt Purvin."

Dan took the appleskin mask and pulled it onto his own face. It fit . . . perfectly. Like its rough crevices and contours were accommodating him instead of rubbing him raw. Like it was part of him, now. He felt it tighten on his face, as if it were alive. The smell of apple perfumed his nose. Apples and blood.

"I didn't kill Walt Purvin," he said, his voice spoken through the stiff, slitted mouth of the appleskin.

At that, Lambert's face dropped. "And where is Earl Dawes? I sent him ahead of me today. Where is he, Little Dan?"

It was Dan's turn to grin. The mask stretched to accommodate his mirth.

Red makes the green.

To the officers, he said, "Let's take Mister Lambert to the orchard."

CALLA CREPT ALONG THE EDGES OF THE GRAVEL PATH TO THE ORchard, skirting the thicket—camera up. Ahead by a hundred feet was the small wooden cabin her father and Marco had built—his so-called cider house. Inside, she heard voices, sometimes heated, sometimes murmured. Cars were parked alongside it, at the end of the drive—a police car, a big tan old-person car, and a full-sized SUV. She knew that last one. Wasn't that Claude Lambert's car? He'd been around a lot.

She moved alongside them, filming each.

And then, at the end of it, she found a bike.

Marco's bike.

She felt sad seeing it. Angry, too. It made sense he was here. He still worked for her father. He'd given up college for this place. It felt absurd to think, *The apple made him do it,* and she wasn't sure if that was true or just a fantasy. All she knew was how hurt she felt by it. By everything.

Fuck you, Marco, I still love you and you're an asshole and ahhhhhh.

Then she thought about the gunshot again. Fear ran through her. Marco.

And then, somewhere nearby—

The snap of a stick underfoot.

She looked behind her, saw someone coming down the driveway, through the thicket and the trees. Just a shape of a person in the darkness.

They were not alone.

Two more came in behind them.

Calla caught her breath and ducked down by the front wheel of the SUV, watching, and still filming, too. She saw more people-shapes coming *through* the thicket, pushing through like deer—shadows sliding through the briar and tangle. A dozen of them, now. Headed not toward the cider house, but beyond it.

To the orchard.

What the fuck is going on here?

Calla hunkered there, and knew deep down she should run away. She should text Esther and Lucas, have them come get her. But she *also* knew what Lucas would say: *Girl you need to be filming that shit because it is exactly what we need.*

And it was.

The apples were weird, the orchard was weird, and now it was weird that a bunch of fucking randos appeared to be converging on this place *right now.*

Calla bit down on her teeth, knowing what she was going to do but not wanting to do it. Already she was plotting the path to the orchard, but not the way the others were going—she'd come up alongside it on the south side, down near to where the creek bordered the property. So that's the way she went, going past the end of the gravel drive and into the trees, easing through the darkness, trying like hell to ignore every spiderweb and tickling twig and pricker bush in her way.

Ahead, she heard the mumble and gush of the creek water.

She dared not turn on her flashlight, so instead she just kept her phone filming. Whatever wasn't usable, she would cut out later.

Calla ducked forward, moving as fast as she could while still being quiet, but suddenly she was afraid she sounded like a freight train going through the brush—

Shut up shut up shut up—

Her foot caught on something, like a heavy root, and—

She went down. Her phone fell from her grip. She stifled a curse. Scrambling, she felt around for her phone, couldn't find it, *oh god, oh shit*—

But there. There it was. She scooped it up and hurried to her feet.

What she tripped on—

A shape lay nearby. Not a root. Lumpier. Longer. A smell hit her—a scent like the lick of a nickel. Metallic and strange. There was a sound, too: wet, mealy.

Calla hesitated. She took a deep breath, and turned on the phone light—

A scream started to escape her mouth and she bit it down, swallowing it.

A dead man lay there, faceup. She scanned the light along his muddy boots, up his blood-soaked jeans, across the expanse of his lumberjack-plaid shirt, where a gardening spade had been stuck through his ribs on the side, clearly going into his lungs, maybe even reaching his heart, and Calla kept tracking the light up, up, up, to the man's face—

Where an orange cat with raggedy fur sat perched, eating the man's cheek the way another cat might eat a bowl of wet cat food. The skin of the cheek was peeled back, exposing the red muscle underneath. The cat ate, strings of the corpse's face-meat dangling from its foamy, blood-slick jaw.

The tabby cat hissed at her.

As if to say, *This meal is mine.*

Calla recoiled and reversed through the woods, hurrying back the way she came. This was too much. She was in way over her head. This was bad. She had to go. She had to find help. She had to do *something.*

DAN DID NOT KNOW WHAT WOULD HAPPEN NEXT.

That brought him a frisson of strange joy.

He was following his instincts, bringing Lambert to the orchard. In his mind Dan saw the bird speared on the branch, the cat with strings of gore in its teeth, the skulls rising through the loam and the clay. He heard something in his ears, too, the sound of young women and young men moaning, crying out in something that might have been pleasure, might have been pain. Again the narcotic scent of apple rose to meet him.

Lambert came without struggle. The fight had gone out of the old prick. Dan himself had removed the corkscrew, and the officers dragged Lambert out of the cider house and into the weeds, hands under his armpits, legs dragging behind, shoes leaving ruts. Together they moved toward the seven trees of the dark orchard.

Ahead, the first tree of the line waited with its one bloom—a white blossom, perfect and pure, perched on its longest branch. He smelled that flower, too, just a whisper of its perfume, like a little piece of a broken song.

The appleskin mask felt so right. He could feel another face in the mask, another mind, another soul. Memories lingering like a scent memory. This, he realized, had once been Golden's mask, hadn't it? A special mask, unlike the others. The mask of the King Bloom. Was Golden deserving of that title? Or had he misused it, misunderstood its power? No answer was forthcoming. But Dan could feel the mask pulsing around him, almost like it was alive, even in death.

"Sir," Burnhouse, the big cop with the shoe-polish beard, said, alarmed. "Look." He didn't need to gesture; his gaze turning about like the beam of a lighthouse told Dan where to look.

They were not alone. Others had come to the orchard.

The eaters of apples were here. Some, at least. About two dozen, by a quick count. They walked to the edges of the orchard, standing in awe.

Watching.

Witnessing.

Like an audience, *rapt.*

Dan felt confused, and scared, but also: awestruck.

He recognized all of them—some, names he knew, others just people he'd met at markets. But one of them stood out.

Meg Price. The lawyer. His new friend and confidante. He hadn't told her about any of this. And yet—here she was. Dan knew he should be scared. She was a woman of the law. She could hurt him. But would she?

He held up a hand to the cops, told them it was okay. Lambert babbled: "What is this? What's happening here? I don't understand—"

But Dan had no interest in him. He approached Meg, who stayed at the margins of the orchard, still toward the edge of the thicket where Earl Dawes

(*died earlier when I buried a spade in his side*)

had begun clearing out the undergrowth to make way for more trees. Dan said, "Meg, it's good to see you. What is this?"

She answered, "I don't know. I just felt something happening. I think we all did. So I came. The others did, too. We parked on the road and just . . . got out and started walking. I left so fast I forgot my mask."

Dan reached out and took her hand. "That's okay. This is beautiful." Her eyes shone with happy tears. She said nothing, just smiled and nodded. "Thank you," he told her.

With beauty in his heart and awe buoying his every step, Dan returned to Claude Lambert.

It was time for the reclamation, for the king bloom to show his petals.

HER FACE WAS SCRATCHED BY THORN. HER ARMS, RAKED BY THICKET and twig. But Calla didn't—*couldn't*—care. She moved forward, quiet and quick. And with every step, her mind flashed the image again and again of the dead man on the ground, the sound of the tabby cat chewing on him . . .

Stop that, she chided herself. But she couldn't get it out of her head. Like an obsessive-compulsive carousel of horrible visions. She had to make a plan.

When she was clear of the thicket, what would she do? She'd call—

Well, who?

Not her father.

Not Marco.

Probably Lucas or Esther. They were the only ones she had. The only ones who understood and believed in any of this.

What about the police? They were here. Right now. Were they in on it? Investigating it? She didn't know. Her head spun with the possibilities, none of them good, all of them a nightmare.

As she broke through the thicket, her feet hit gravel and she found herself by the line of cars, the dark shape of the cider house looming ahead.

She didn't see anybody—

But then, she *heard* something crashing through thicket. Moving fast. Right toward her. She tried to run, but the gravel beneath her foot skidded out, and the foot went with it, nearly dropping her to the ground. She managed to recover—

But she was too slow.

A dark shape slammed into her.

Hands pawed at her face. Calla smelled sweat and hot breath as she shoved her attacker backward—but her effort staggered her as much as it staggered them, and she tumbled backward onto her ass. As the shadow advanced upon her, all she could think to do was scoop up a handful of limestone gravel and pitch it hard at her assailant. It scattered against them in a clumsy shotgun blast of stone, and they cried out in pain.

She knew that cry.

"Marco?" she asked.

"Calla?" came his reply.

He sounded scared.

No. He sounded fucking *terrified*.

He grabbed her hand, pulling her up, but she fought him and yanked out of his grip. "Get away from me," she seethed.

"We need to go. We need to go *now*."

He tried to pull her again but she snarled at him and pulled away.

"I don't trust you! You fucking asshole!"

His face loomed into view, lit by the bright moon above. He looked haunted. Haggard. Like something had changed in him. *No*, she realized. *Like a spell had been broken.* Or, perhaps, had broken him.

"Please," he begged.

"Fine, I was leaving anyway," she said, and it sounded so insanely petty in this mad, dangerous moment, she almost wanted to laugh. It was enough to break the wall that had built between them. So she added, in a soft voice, "Let's go."

He nodded and together, they hurried up the driveway and to the road.

With human shapes ringing the orchard, their eyes watching Dan in his appleskin mask, he told the two officers to take Lambert to the first, nearest tree. The tree with one bloom.

He had them lean Lambert up against the trunk of the tree. Then he turned to Marco, telling him that Dan wanted him to see this—

But there was no Marco.

Dan looked around. Where had he gone?

He felt the pull of something inside of him. A distant, gossamer thread connecting him and the young man. *He ran away,* Dan knew, inexplicably.

Claude interrupted the reverie, looking up at him, and asking, grimly, "What are you going to do with me? Kill me? Then do it already. *Little Dan.*"

"I don't know what I'm going to do with you," Dan said, almost dreamily. And it was true, he didn't. He knelt down by Claude. "I'm following my instincts. And what they're telling me is that you tried to control this orchard. You killed people and put them in the ground here. The orchard showed me their bones. And I think your ego and your . . ." He searched for the word. "*Imperiousness* must be stopped. You must be humbled."

"Fuck you," Claude said.

Dan reached out and took Claude's injured hand. He did so gently, holding it up in the moonlight—not that he needed that light. It occurred to him now that not only was his eyesight improved, but he could see everything in the dark plain as if it were day. The darkness was no impediment to him. It was part of him, instead.

Almost lovingly, he took the hand and placed it back down, resting it on the ground—then pinning the wrist there. Lambert struggled—

Dan held his hand tighter.

The man's bones ground together in his grip.

Dan mashed the hand into the grass, flat against the ground.

Lambert bleated as something beneath the earth stirred. A gentle undulation of soil. Shimmering grass flicking like agitated cilia. Dan closed his eyes and he could hear it under the ground—a soft breaking sound, like the crust of home-baked bread pulverized in a slowly closing hand. And then that sound was lost beneath Claude Lambert's screams.

A single seeking root, black as the Devil's finger, sharp at the tip, eased its way up through the hole in Lambert's injured hand, blood smearing along its length as it urged its way up and out. It coiled in the air, knotting upon itself.

And at its tip, another small bloom formed.

This one, red as

(*blood, a beast's heart, meat*)

a Ruby Slipper apple.

Lambert wept, blubbering, trying to free his hand from the mooring root—or now, perhaps, it was not a root at all, but a small sapling. He moved his hand up its length, sliding his wound up a few inches and then down again before screaming louder. "That must be painful, Claude," Dan said. "Why don't you rest?"

The words that gushed out of Lambert were nonsense sounds, clearly angry, meant to be profane and hateful even though they were not fully formed. The man's eyes were wrenched so wide in fear and panic it was like they had no lids at all—they were just exposed white orbs.

Dan sighed and stood.

The first root was slow.

The next ones were not.

A second root stabbed through Lambert's other hand, punching through it with the force of a spear from a speargun. Blood sprayed. Another launched up through his kneecap, crunching through the bone, and the next came through the ankle of the opposite leg. And again the roots flexed at their tips, blooming like fireworks, each a new sapling, each part of the growing orchard. Lambert wept. Dan stepped back.

All his trees were blooming now.

And in the thicket he saw more pops of red—blossoms growing on saplings that hadn't been there moments ago. Those gathered fell to their knees, applauding. He turned to them and held his hands wide, the appleskin mask like a second face, fitting even tighter to his skull as if of its own free will. The orchard was alive. They would have apples soon.

57

RIDE OF THE VOMIT COMET

THE BACKROADS IN THIS PART OF BUCKS COUNTY WERE A ROLLER-coaster ride: hills with sharp bends, valleys across one-lane bridges and a series of potholes like the craters in the streets of war-torn cities. Esther didn't give a shit about any of it, and whipped her Honda Fit down all of them like she was a cat with eight of her nine lives left to live. It was common knowledge that she referred to her little hatchback as the Vomit Comet, and it was a moniker she accepted with no small pride. *Usually,* Calla told her to slow down, because this kind of driving was (a) terrifying and (b) a good way to yarf. But given everything, she was happy to be fleeing from

(*home*)

the orchard at high speeds.

Esther sat in the front with Lucas. In the back sat Calla and Marco.

Marco stared into his lap, babbling, a steady fount of horror: "Don't understand it. I can feel it even now. The, the, the guy, Lambert. Your dad, he—he put a corkscrew through his hand. The cops shot the other one, the one with the mustache—and he had this mask—"

"Who had a mask? The mustached guy?" Calla asked, trying to make sense of any of this.

"Your father." Marco licked spit from his lips and rocked back and forth. "He, he had this fucked-up-looking mask, Calla, and he put it on and he—the cops—dragged Lambert to the orchard and then they were just *there*—"

"They who?"

"People. People, ones who ate the apple, they just appeared out of nowhere, walking up like they had been called—" Suddenly Marco clamped his teeth down and growled behind his scowl, as if a migraine were rocking through him. "And I feel it, too. Jesus Christ, I feel it. I think he sees me. Fuck."

"Who?" Calla asked.

But Marco just made a low sound and put his head on his knees.

Lucas leaned back, glancing from Marco to Calla. "Girl, what the fuck is happening. What happened back there?"

"I—I don't know, Lucas. I found a dead man. A cat—" She tried to blink the image away but couldn't, so instead she just rode it out. "A cat was eating the dead man's face."

And at that Lucas freaked the fuck out. Recoiling, he said, "Holy fucking shit, Calla, what the fuck."

"I fucking know, okay? I know. And I don't know. I—I—shit." She clenched her hands into fists. "This is really messed up. I heard a gunshot, and now Marco is saying that the police shot a dude in the cider house?"

"The orchard is growing, the orchard is growing," Marco whispered again and again, faster and faster, the words running together, "*theorchardisgrowing orchardsgrowing orchisgrown*—"

"Guys, where the hell am I going?" Esther asked.

"Back to your place, your mom doesn't care if we're there," Lucas said. "We can hang on your back porch." Esther's parents were air-quotes "cool" in that they were totally negligent and didn't give a hot shit what their daughter did at all. They were too far up their own asses—Esther's father was a Cheaty McCheaterson pharma rep always traveling and (according to Esther) banging various medical office managers, and her mother was really, really, really into horses. They weren't even rich enough to *have* horses, so they, like, rented one or something at a stable nearby? Esther hated her parents. But in this case, that would serve them well.

Esther: "Like, okay but I can*not* get in trouble, my parents were pissed last month because I *maybe* 'lost' a bunch of my Adderall—"

"It's fine," Lucas snapped. "Shit's serious, Esther! We need to go somewhere and also you're going to make me puke up my toenails—"

Suddenly Marco screamed.

Panic throttled Calla. She screamed, "Stop the car!"

The Honda Fit slammed to a stop, skidding.

The car sat there, quiet on a dark backroad. Something in the engine went *tick, tick, tick, tick.* Marco stopped screaming and looked around, his skin gone gray and sweaty. Like he'd just broken a fever. He blinked.

"Are you okay?" Calla asked.

"I think . . . a little bit better."

Lucas made a face. "Well, you look like moist open ass, but you sound better."

"Thanks," Marco said, unironically.

"We good?" Esther asked.

Calla was about to say, *yeah,* but then, behind them, far down the road—

Lights. Strobing red and blue.

"We have to go now," Marco said. "It's them."

Esther gunned it. The Vomit Comet roared forth.

58

WHAT EMILY FINDS

It was around midnight that Emily realized Meg was gone. At first it was the simple discovery that her wife was not in bed with her, because that absence, that emptiness, was always keenly felt. A quick search of the house showed that the back door was open, a chill wind dancing through the open space.

Meg's shoes were still here.

So was her car.

Where, then, did she go?

Maybe it didn't matter.

Because it was at that moment Emily thought:

I'm free.

She could leave.

Meg was not here.

Noreen was not here.

She didn't have any of her things, though. And did she even want to leave? Well, okay, *yes,* she absolutely wanted to leave—but she'd seen a break in the clouds with Meg, hadn't she? If Meg was in withdrawal, that was an opportunity. That was a way to get her clear, to *save* her.

But at the very least, if Meg was gone, Emily could find her fucking phone.

Her feet raced as fast as her heart as she tore through the house, opening cabinets and drawers and looking anywhere and everywhere for her phone. Top of the fridge, under the couch, in the toilet tank—and still no phone. Despair set in. Emily realized: *She probably threw it in the fucking river.* Shit. Still, there was one last place she hadn't checked, in part because she *couldn't* check it—Meg's file cabinets. They contained files of her legal work, which meant the drawers in her office each were locked.

Emily did not have the keys.

Meg did. On her key ring.

"Which . . . she did not take," Emily said to herself, and quickly sprinted through the house to the key hooks by the door, and sure enough, there dangled the keys to the Audi, plus a set of house keys, and the small keys to the file cabinet.

She bolted back to the office, nearly crashing into the cabinets.

Emily held the first key above the lock, prayed it was the right one, and—

Yes.

It opened. Emily flipped through the files in the top drawer—nothing. *No!* She moved to the second drawer, threw it open.

Flies exited in a flurry. Little ones. Fruit flies. Emily batted at the air as they dispersed. She looked into the depths of the drawer—

Apple cores. A dozen of them. Wet, half rotten, chewed on, sucked upon. Like Meg was keeping them, savoring them. *What the fuck.*

But then: something else underneath those. Emily winced and pushed the moldering cores aside—

What she pulled out she didn't understand, at first.

It was almost like a swatch of chain-mail armor. A curtain of little metal things, hissing and jingling together. Then she saw what those little metal things were: the tips of fountain pens. What were they called? Nibs. Metal pen nibs. There was a strap, too, and a set of eyeholes. *Oh my god, it's a mask.*

A mask. But why? It called to mind something out of a slasher film. Hunting kids at a summer camp with, what, a mask made of silver pen tips? *Friday the 13th meets American Psycho,* Emily thought.

Beneath the mask, that's where Emily found the two ripped halves of her journal along with her phone. It was dead, but could be charged. She shoved it in her pocket and tucked the book under her arm—she went to stand up, and saw that the drawer contained one more curious surprise.

Emily pulled out a sheaf of loose papers. Not with words on them, but rather, drawings. Meg wasn't an artist, was she? Had she wanted to be one once upon a time? Emily wasn't aware of that, but at this point she wasn't sure who Meg even was anymore.

Did I ever really know her?

The drawings were . . .

Of Meg.

Self-portraits. One after the next. They got better and better as they went along, each drawn on a piece of stationery from her law office. Were they drawn there and brought home? Toward the front of the pack the self-portraits were crude, clumsy, if still identifiably Meg—the spikes of hair that looked chaotic but were actually quite well planned, the serious dark eyes, the mouth on the verge of a small smile but rarely making it. Further back the sketches got more detailed, more beautiful, with deeper shading and stronger lines, and then even further into the pile, they became almost . . . idealized. Beatific. Flawless, unblemished, so much so that it didn't look like Meg at all, not really, not in real life. But then the last few . . . the lines were heavy, messy. The face, scribbled more than drawn.

Emily regarded the sketches like they were an alien artifact. *Who are you?*

Emily hastily put the papers and the mask back in the drawer, on top of the rotting apple cores. As she relocked the drawer and moved to leave the office—

She heard the sliding door opening, then closing.

A voice. Meg's voice.

"Emily? Are you here?"

She sounded . . . different. Happy, almost. Like her voice was wind chimes. Light and airy, a murmur of hollow bells.

Emily looked down at her phone, the journal, and Meg's keys in her hand.

Quickly she darted out of the office and into the adjacent bathroom. Her pajamas were just pink track pants and a ratty black Joan Jett and the Blackhearts T-shirt.

"Emily?" Meg called again.

"Hey, uh!" Emily called back through the bathroom door. "Just using the little cowgirls' room, be out in a jiff." She winced. Under the sink was an awful hiding place because Meg had already found her journal there. But—*but.* A lot of her toiletries were messy, not in a proper kit or container but instead just zipped away in a moisturizer-greasy Ziploc bag. Emily pulled that out, chucked the phone, the book, the keys in there, and then—quiet as she could manage—pitched them in the back of the toilet, in the tank. *Hopefully that bag's waterproof.*

Then: a knock at the door.

"Emily?"

Her voice sounded wistful, distant, strange.

Emily opened the door.

"Hey," she said.

Meg *looked* different. Almost like the drawings she'd done, the ones where she seemed angelic, glowing. She wore a big, unreserved smile.

"Come on," Meg said. "I want to show you something *amazing*."

59

HOW DOES YOUR GARDEN GROW?

MEG LED EMILY BY THE HAND WITH A CARELESS KIND OF INNO-
cence, the feel of being shepherded through a sunlit meadow of wild-
flowers

(a lamb led to an altar)

as they left through the back door and went to the staircase that descended toward the river. Emily's breath held in her chest. Her skin
prickled. *The river.* An absurd thought: *She's going to drown me.* But was it
absurd? And if it wasn't, why was she still going? Why was she following
her down, down, down?

Because she's my wife.

Because I want to see.

Because I can still save her.

But as she thought those things, she worried that they were just delu-
sions. Indolence born of fear: It was easier to do nothing than something. It was easier to go along with the pain, to become part of the
madness, than to resist it.

(it is easier to drown in the river than to fight the current)

She expected them to continue their descent all the way to the water,
but they stopped halfway, on the landing. It was here that Meg bent
down, pulling out a little flashlight from her pocket and shining it on a
dark, twisting shape growing up through the wooden boards. It was a
small sapling. It had not been there yesterday, Emily knew. Yet here it
was, now, nearly a foot tall, and at its top:

A cluster of blooming flowers. Red at the edges, pink toward the center. Emily felt dizzy looking at them. They seemed to pulse in and out in
her vision.

"Meg—" Emily started to say, but Meg gently shushed her.

Meg knelt there with her eyes closed. Rocking back on her heels.

Like she was praying, almost. An ecstatic kind of praying.

"The orchard is growing," Meg said.

"This—this is an apple tree?"

"It is. A gift given to us tonight. But not just to us. To *so many*. You see that, don't you? It's growing, it's spreading. The roots pushing under the soft earth. Precious life, seeking egress. It's glorious."

"Meg, I—I don't think this is natural—"

"No, no, shh, come, come kneel by me. You can smell it, the flower. It has a perfume. It's intoxicating. Isn't it?"

Emily did not go to kneel. Though the smell was unavoidable, as it seemed to seek her out, to crawl up her nose like a serpent—it was a lingering floral scent, broken esters in the air that smelled of rose and elderflower, but beneath that, something else. Something bitter and foul. Rotten flesh in rancid lemon oil.

And Meg seemed taken by it. Emily had seen the look on her face before, seen it in every drug user who had fallen hard off the wagon and back into the ditch of renewed addiction. But there was something deeper, darker, too. The air of the cultist giving themselves to the cult wholly: mind, body, and spirit.

"This flower," Meg said, "will become an apple, a beautiful bright-red apple, and *that* apple will be the one you'll eat. Then you'll join me, and then you'll see. There won't be anything we can't do, Em. You want to help people? Shelter them? The apple will help them. It'll fix them. They won't *need* shelter. The apple will teach them to fix themselves. And you'll have done that. You'll have shown them how." She smiled a blissful smile. "You'll see how important you are, and how important I am, and how *necessary* we are to each other."

"I'm allergic, Meg—"

"Not to this. Not to this apple, Em. This one will be pure. This one will be clean."

"Meg, I'm not going to eat the apple. I already told you that."

And there, in the moonlight, Meg looked up at Emily, her face glowing with what Emily could only describe as a kind of bliss. But beyond the bliss was also something else: certainty.

"You will," Meg said quietly. "One way or another."

One way or another.

Emily felt sick. She recoiled, nearly tripping herself on the step behind her. Backpedaling, she reversed back up the staircase toward the house by a few stairs. Her wife did not follow; Meg remained captivated

(*captive*)

by the strange dark branch growing out of the landing, her hands moving around it the way someone would warm themselves at a campfire. It was as if she'd even forgotten Emily was there. Emily said to her:

"Meg, baby, please, you're scaring me. You were getting clear of it. I don't understand. You were doing better. We can do better again. Together. Okay? Just . . . come with me. Back up the stairs." Her voice trembled and shook. "Let's go somewhere. Anywhere. We can take a vacation. We can go to the city, or to the beach, or, or, to an island in the Caribbean like we always talked about."

But Meg didn't even seem to hear her. She instead dipped her head toward the sapling, letting the red flower brush her cheek. Was there a streak of blood in its wake? Yes, until no—just an illusion. Meg shuddered with pleasure. A small sound escaped her lips, something between a song and a moan.

Emily turned and bolted back up the staircase to the house.

IT WAS THERE THAT SHE WALKED IN FAST CIRCLES. SHE WAS TRYING to make sense of what had happened. Meg, leaving in the middle of the night. Returning hours later, and now they had their own little evil apple tree? What the fuck. *What the fuck.* None of this was okay. None of this was normal. And now Meg was down there on the landing, doing . . . what, exactly? Worshipping it? Praying to it?

She stopped walking and stood there in the grip of one single thought.

Meg's lost.

It was too late. Emily's chance to save her was now gone.

You have to leave now. Grab your phone charger and get out.

Fuck it, forget the charger.

Just go, Emily.

Go.

But Emily remained in that one spot. Feet fixed to the floor.

Another thought entered the room:

If someone is lost, they can be found again. The only way someone was really, truly lost was when you gave up the search. Right? A plane crashes, the survivors stay lost until someone looks for them, finds them, saves them.

One last chance.

Tonight. Right now.

But first, she had to do something.

Emily went into the kitchen and threw open the utensils drawer.

EMILY WAS NOT AN ACTOR, NOT REALLY. BUT FROM TIME TO TIME, at the shelter, she'd had to act a certain way—a youth in crisis needed to think you were an ally to them in that moment, and you were, absolutely, but they needed to think *not* that you were going to help them get sober, but that you didn't care they were high. You had to approach them like, *This is no big deal, everything is cool, I'm calm, you're calm, no judgment here.* They didn't need to see you as an ally who had their *best* interests at heart. They needed to see you as someone who had their *worst* interests at heart. Just for that one moment. Until you got close enough to take the knife away, or the drugs, or just hold them until they calmed.

And that was how Emily approached Meg.

She walked down the steps slowly.

One hand out, the other reserved at her side.

As she got closer, Emily told Meg, softly, sweetly, trying to keep the fear out of her words, working like hell to stop the adrenaline from breaking her voice: "I'd like to kneel with you. Can I be with you?"

And Meg never took her eyes off the sapling. "Of course, Em. Come on. It's okay. Come kneel with me."

So that was what Emily did. She crept closer, trying to mirror Meg's strange smile. Slowly she knelt down; again that smell of roses and rot reached her nose, making her feel dizzy. Making the world feel like it was a pulsing heart, throbbing to its own primeval beat. *Steady as she goes.* Emily moved closer to the sapling—

Meg met her eyes. She nodded. A moment of sweet solidarity. A joining of the two of them. Allies. Friends. Lovers. And something else, too, something beyond all that: a merging of souls, a surrender to uniformity, a great acquiescence *to* each other and *into* each other.

It was a lie.

Your best interests.

Not your worst.

I'm so sorry, Meg.

Emily slid the kitchen shears out, hidden as they were from behind her wrist. And with one swift movement—

She used the scissors to cut through the sapling.

Snip.

The sapling fell to the landing, a dead thing.

There was a moment. Meg stared, shocked. Grief-struck and horrified.

"Meg—" Emily started to say.

Meg's head wrenched back on her neck, her mouth open in a vicious scream that swiftly became a vengeful howl, an inhuman bellow that curdled Emily's blood. She tried to say her wife's name but couldn't even hear her own voice—

The hit was fast and jarring. The back of Meg's hand cracked across her face so hard she feared her jaw was broken and teeth were loose. Firebursts erupted behind her eyes and Meg reached out and grabbed her throat—

Grrk—

With little calculus, Emily thrust the blades of the scissors deep into the top of Meg's thigh. The blade stopped when it met bone.

Meg paused.

Her scream cut short.

She threw Emily down the steps. Emily's world went end over end. The back of her head snapped against wood. Everything was streaking light as a dull fist opened its fingers inside her skull—*have I stopped moving, am I falling or am I not falling.* She wasn't sure. Couldn't get her bearings in the dark. Her hands felt steps beneath her. Blinking, she realized—*I only went about halfway down.* The dock and the river were still below her. She tasted blood. Grunting, she reached up and pawed at the railing, trying to pull herself to standing.

And Meg was there, rushing at her, shoving her back again. Emily cried out, her feet juggling, trying to get up and stay up, but the push was hard and her ankles crossed—once more, she fell backward, sliding this time rather than tumbling. Emily ended up on the dock, rolling over onto her hands and knees and scrambling to stand, but already Meg was stalking toward her with a confident stride, looming over her as she grabbed a hank of Emily's hair and dragged her—

Toward the river.

Emily tried to get out of her grip, throwing an elbow behind her. It connected with Meg's chin, but Meg didn't care, and returned by pistoning a fist into Emily's kidneys. Pain bloomed there, big and bright—

And then the hand holding her hair pushed her chin over the edge of the dock, and into the cold water of the rushing river.

ANOTHER RECKONING WITH THE RIVER.

The black water felt like ice. It pushed into her ears. The world above was gone, just a pulsating *whoosh,* like the natal heartbeat of a great beast struggling to be born. She felt her chest and throat burning even as she struggled. But Meg was strong. Impossibly strong. Emily tried to use her own hands to prop herself up, to push, but another fist into her kidneys made her cry out underwater—more breath gone from her lungs, stolen by the swift water. Bubbles of her life. *Bye-bye.*

Somewhere she heard Noreen laughing, saying, *You're afraid of water, aren't you?* Then, replacing it, Emily's own voice. Her own thoughts.

Meg is going to kill me.

I tried to find her and save her.

But now I'm lost, too. Another body in the river.

Who would find her? Whose foot would step into her brittle skull? Would they try to find out who killed her? Would they be killed in return, a cycle of searching and drowning, the taste of apple, the ice of river water?

And then, suddenly, Meg's hand was gone.

Emily wasted no time in pushing herself up out of the water, gasping a great keening vacuum of breath—

For a moment, she could do nothing but lie there on her belly, chin resting on the outer edge of the dock, the water only inches beneath her. She panted. Gasping. Trying to cry, but unable. "Meg," she tried to say, but the word was a gabbled whisper lost to the sound of rushing water, yet another thing taken by the river. Someone knelt by her. She flinched. Tried to say no, but only a hoarse and ragged cry escaped her lips. She coughed. Spit. Someone's hand found hers. A big hand. Bony on the sides, knuckles like gambling dice. *John.*

"Come on," John said, helping her up. "You're okay. You're okay."

"John," she said, managing to squeak out his name. She threw her arms around him, lost herself in that embrace. But then she pulled away. "Wait—"

She was about to ask him about Meg.

But Emily didn't have to.

Meg was there, on the dock, on her back.

Eyes open. Mouth wide.

"Oh god, oh god, she's—"

Dead.

"No," John said, holding her back. "She's alive, Emily. Just knocked out. Tranquilized. We need to go." And then Emily saw the pair of darts sticking in her side like porcupine quills.

"John—"

He held her face and turned it gently, but firmly, toward his own. It was only now she realized: His face was painted in dark camo, and he was wearing a shaggy ragged jacket made to look like branches and leaves. *I died. I'm losing my mind.*

"We need to go," he said again.

"Not without her."

"We can't take her."

"John. Listen to me." She paused, racked by a coughing fit. "Whatever this is, whatever is happening to them, I've seen it weaken its hold on them. They can be saved. Okay? I'm not leaving her, so she needs to come with us."

John seemed to consider this. He bore his gaze through her.

"Okay," he said finally. "But my truck is a mile away—"

"We can take her Audi. I can get the keys."

He made a dire face. "This isn't a good idea."

"But it's the only idea."

"Fine. Let's go. I'll pull her up the stairs—"

"I can help."

"You're in no condition to help. I can do this. I'm strong."

Emily nodded. "John?"

"Yes, Emily?"

"Thank you."

"You're welcome, my friend."

60

MIDNIGHT IN THE ORCHARD OF MOSTLY EVIL

It was late now. That was fine. Dan needed some time to think.

He stood in the orchard. The others were gone—the cops left, going after Marco. The apple-eaters who appeared had since been called home, and Dan knew why: The orchard was growing. It wasn't just here, where saplings had grown up through the flesh of Claude Lambert, and beyond him, too, in the thicket, in the briar. The pops of red and pink out there in the understory were all around him, growing in the darkness like flowers out of tar. The orchard was here, but it was beyond here, too. The others, his people, the eaters of the apples, had gone home to see their own saplings, growing in their yards, out of broken walkways, from the old leafmulch in bent gutters. Which meant that for now, Dan was alone.

Except for Claude, who lay slumped against the closest tree, saplings spearing him to the ground. Sometimes he shifted, and when he did, a bleat of pain erupted from him before he fell silent and still once more.

Dan needed time, but not to wrestle with what just happened—there was no struggle, no battle anymore. Yes, some distant part of him knew that none of this was natural, that something about this was *wrong*. That little voice, warning him that he'd gone too far, too far to come back. But that little voice was easily countered by the truth of the bigger, bolder voice: Dan deserved this. When he had let Lambert take part of his orchard—he had ceased to deserve the gifts the apple accorded him. But when he took the orchard back? His power came back with him. And he knew these powers were not human. He did not feel human anymore. He felt better than that. Bolder, stronger, *beyond* human, and so if he was beyond human, why would he still anchor himself to any kind of human morality, any mortal sense of right and wrong? Things felt wrong to the *human* part of him. But that part was small now, and it was dying, and like any pest or vermin, it needed to die so it stopped weakening the whole. You found a Japanese beetle on a plant, you grabbed it, you crushed its brittle shell, watched its guts pop like a surprised worm, sticking it like glue to the green of the leaf. The human part of him needed to be pinched and crushed.

Pop would be proud, he thought to himself.

But then, also: *But Pop was weak.*

A surge of anger rose in Dan at his father. Big Dan *was* weak. He had been compromised by Claude Lambert. Not strong enough to push back against Lambert and the others, he fell prey to them instead. Suckered by rich white men and their talk of legacy and power, when really they were just using it as a lever against him. *Pathetic fool.*

The appleskin mask flexed around his face. This was Golden's mask. What that meant, he didn't know. Was Golden just another one of those rich white men making use of the poor saps beneath them? Or was he a man led by his cult, and not the other way around? Same way they tried to push Dan around, tried to control him, way they tried to steal his orchard and take away his apple?

Maybe he had more in common with Golden than he knew.

Or maybe he was better than Golden was. Because Dan wasn't some fancy explorer and inventor and artist. He was humble. Just a farmer, a grower. A man of the orchard, a man of the people.

Dan reached back, pulled the appleskin mask off his face.

Standing over Claude Lambert, he looked down at the beauty of what had been done to him. Claude wanted the orchard? Well, he got the orchard.

Something mixed into the apple blossom scent perfuming the air—

A smell of sweat. The bitter tang of urine. A whiff of infection.

Someone else was here.

"Come out," Dan said.

A shape emerged. Hunched over. Head cocked at a low angle. They were shirtless and pale. As they crept closer, their left arm dangling unused by their side like a strip of sick meat, Dan could see their face—

His face.

Prentiss Beckman.

"Have you come to join the orchard, too?" Dan asked. He gestured toward the other man on the ground. "Claude joined the orchard. It can still make something of you, if you're willing."

"I . . ." Beckman's voice trailed off. When he finally spoke again, his words were mushy, and Dan could see that his jaw hung at an odd angle. It had been broken, and remained so. *Good.* There was a wound, too, in his shoulder. A bullet had dug a trench out of him and it was swollen and sick with pus. Prentiss's tongue flopped over his lower teeth when he next spoke, giving his words a mushy gush, wet and wretched. "I'll be whatever you need. I want to be near you. I want to serve the orchard."

"You deserve your pain." Dan felt the roots beneath the ground shifting again. Searching and hungry. "You tried to hurt Joanie." It surprised Dan, his own feelings for her still. He wanted her. *I deserve her.*

"It was a mistake," Prentiss said, his voice weak and trembling. He sniffed a grume of snot back up into his nose. "It was a mistake, Dan. I'm sorry. I want to help you. I want to be whatever you need me to be. I felt it. I felt this place . . . wake up. And I want to serve."

"You're just a waste. A bug. Look at you." Dan shook his head. "You're a pest. An ugly, ruinous little pest. You don't deserve to be a part of this orchard."

Woe broke from Prentiss in a choking moan. The man threw himself at Dan's feet. His broken jaw glistened with saliva, snot, and tears. He bawled. "Please, I'll do anything. Anything at all. I don't wanna have to go, I don't want to be on the outside, I want to be in the garden, in the orchard, please please, oh fuck. Please, Dan. Please keep me. Don't throw me away. I want to belong, I want purpose for this miserable life of mine, please, gods, please. I can serve. I *need* to serve."

I can serve.

I need to serve.

What a revelation that was.

At the start of things, when Dan took his first bite of the apple off the

(*Harrowsblack*)

Ruby Slipper tree, he knew he felt different. Better. More himself than he'd ever been—like all this time he'd been walking through life with weights around his ankles, blinders at the sides of his eyes, and a heart slowed by the thick blood of regret. He felt lighter, faster, smarter. And when his eyes improved, when his body improved, he saw the same in all those who ate the apple—Claude Lambert ate the apple, didn't he? And Dan began to see him less as his enemy, and more as his equal. But did Lambert see it that way? No, he didn't. Lambert saw Dan as a head to step on only—like his father, he was simply an obstacle to knock over and use as debris in order to climb ever higher.

Dan took back his power.

It changed him. Changed Lambert, too. Hell, it changed them all, didn't it? And here, even Prentiss felt it. All he wanted to do was serve. He wasn't like Dan, not at all—wasn't even like Meg, or Lambert, or any of the Crossed Keys. Dan was better than them, and they were better than Prentiss—Prentiss was a gutter-fed fuck, just a slouching, pouch-bellied wretch. But—

He ate the apple.

He felt the call of the orchard growing.

And here he was, kneeling before Dan and the appleskin mask, begging to be better. To be *allowed* near him.

Dan understood a lot in that moment.

And so he reached out and placed his hand upon Prentiss's head—the man's hair was sweat-slick and oily, so Dan bore down, gripping the scalp harder. What came next was not difficult; in fact, it was easy as simply deciding for it to be so. There was a feeling radiating from his fingertips, and Prentiss sucked in a sharp intake of air, a whistling keening inhalation like the labored breathing of someone suffering some sleep apnea—

Inside the man's skull, Dan could feel something moving around. Little vibrations thrummed up through his fingertips. When he closed his eyes, he could almost see what was beyond the hair, the skin, the bone: long shapes shifting, like worms pushing aside dirt to make room for more of themselves. It was done. He let go of Prentiss's head.

Prentiss hugged his leg, weeping. For he could feel it, too.

He gabbled in a messy string of *thank you, thank you, thank you.* Dan kicked him gently back, the way you pushed away someone else's annoying, slobbering dog.

"You can serve," Dan told him dismissively. "You'll be better. I'll heal that bullet hole. But the broken jaw—that stays. A reminder of your mistake."

Prentiss smiled with his broken jaw, his tongue thrust out of the side, a pink-gray slug. "I'll do anything you ask of me, Dan. Anything at all."

"I know you will."

Contemptible, pitiable pest.

But Prentiss was *his* pest now. And maybe a pest could be useful.

61

ACAB

The cop was on them like a fly on a horse's ass. Esther cried out as she cut the wheel and whipped the Honda Fit down the serpentine backroads outside Coryell's Ferry, hard-charging the Vomit Comet toward River Road, the road that ran along the waters of the Delaware. The red-blue strobe did a dizzying dance behind and ahead of them. The cop hit the siren: a banshee's howl.

"Jesus Fucking Christ," Lucas yelled, arms straight out, hands mashed flat against the dashboard. "Lose him! Faster! Fuck!"

"Okayokay*okay*," Esther said, gritting her teeth. "Five Points! We're going to Five Points. *Ahhhhhh.*"

They hit the stop sign at River Road, but she didn't bother stopping. Instead, she cut the wheel, bounding past the stop sign and down the long ribbon of ruined asphalt that paralleled the river and canal. The car bucked as it hit every pothole—with the spring thaw, the roads expanded and contracted, leaving spectacular eruptions in the roadway surfaces. Some roads were worse than others. River Road was one of the worst of all, and they felt it. With every hit and bounce, Calla's teeth snapped together, and once her head nearly cracked into the back-seat window.

Marco's hand took hers and squeezed it tight.

He looked at her.

She met his eyes.

"I'm sorry for all this," he said. "I love you."

"I love you, too."

Ahead was Five Points—a completely bonkers intersection of five roads. Five Points comprised both ends of River Road, the entrance to one of the canal parks, Sugar Road, and Carverstown Road. This crossroads came with an unholy number of urban legends—a phantom hitchhiker would get in your car if you flashed your lights three times; a gravity hill up Sugar Road where the hands of dead ghost children would push your car up the hill; a spot where the Devil was supposed to wait at midnight during the new moon and there he'd challenge you to a footrace for your life and for your soul. They'd tried all the local rituals and none of that shit did shit, but at least they got high beforehand and it was still fun.

But Five Points wasn't fun now as the Vomit Comet barreled toward it.

The cop car raced behind them, a pursuing beast.

Esther screamed as they blasted through the stop sign at Five Points—the V that shot off to both Sugar Road and Carverstown was wide, and Calla understood suddenly what Esther was doing—she turned the car toward the farthest road, Sugar, but at the last minute pulled the wheel even tighter, bounding over a wild hedge and breaking onto Carverstown.

The cop fell for the bait. The police cruiser followed them onto Sugar, but wasn't ready for her juke move—and as they escaped, the cop car turned too slow, too wide, and clipped an old buttonwood tree, putting out one of its headlights.

The Vomit Comet accelerated toward its escape. Or so they hoped.

UP CARVERSTOWN, ACROSS LUMBERTOWN ROAD, BACK DOWN Fleecy Mill, and into the woods they went—there was a spot by the old abandoned quarry where they sometimes went to get high or drink shitty beer stolen from Lucas's diabetic uncle, Dave. Esther skidded the car to a halt and they all fell out of it, just trying to shake off the adrenaline that was surely coursing through them like an electrical storm. Lucas was the first one to laugh—a mad sound that bubbled up out of him. "Oh my fucking god, that was fucking crazy. Fucking fuck shit. Fuck."

Esther offered no such mirth, lunatic or otherwise. She just walked back and forth alongside her car, muttering, "He probably has my license plate, you guys. Like, seriously. That cop can find me. And I definitely broke the law by *driving away at dangerous speeds,* shit. Shit! Oh my god. Oh my god."

"Hey," Calla said, going to her and giving her a hug, rubbing her back. "It'll be okay. At least your dad isn't some kind of fucking monster."

"I . . . guess there's that. I'm sorry."

"I'm sorry, too."

They pulled the hug tighter.

As she did, Calla clocked Marco nearby, leaning up against a tree, rubbing his leg where it was once broken but had since

(*miraculously*)

healed.

Esther saw her looking, and told Calla, "It's okay, go on."

So that's what Calla did. She approached Marco, slowly, steadily.

"You okay?" she asked him.

"Super awesome," he said, thunking his head dully against the tree trunk.

"Are you . . . you?"

"What?"

She sighed. How to put this? "You weren't yourself for a long time, Marco. You were just, I dunno, different. It was like I recognized your face but not the person that was wearing it. Like it was just a mask."

Marco looked up. "Your dad. He wore a mask. A real one."

"What kind of mask?"

"I—I'm not sure. It looked like some kind of red leather."

"That's fucking weird." Calla had never seen him wear a mask like that or any mask at all. Her father used to be this sweet, goodhearted dork. And now? "That apple is poison. Like, personality-poison."

"Yeah, I think so. I'm sorry again."

"It's okay." She reached out and took his hand. Twined her pinkie with his. Her heart sang. "You look better. If that's any, you know, consolation. You seem clearer somehow."

"I feel a little clearer. I just—for a while I was really, I don't know, up my own ass. I felt unstoppable. I felt amazing. But the wrong kind of amazing. Like it was a lie, but I didn't care that it was a lie. I was drunk on the idea of me. And I didn't care about anyone else. I even started to think of other people as worth less than me, worth maybe nothing at all." He paused. "Like they weren't even people at all, Call. And then when there weren't any more apples to eat . . . I wanted one so bad, and I could feel my leg start to hurt. But it was only tonight, seeing your dad act like that—I really like your dad, Calla. Mister P gave me a lot of opportunity, gave me a chance, was nice to me in all the ways that mattered and I wanted to follow him . . . but he's not the same person now."

Calla took his other hand, now. "Maybe he can be brought back the way you were. Maybe he can be saved, too."

"Maybe, yeah."

But he didn't sound so sure.

"Hey," Lucas shouted. "Maybe you should get away from him, Calla. Maybe the apple is making him say that stuff to you. We should throw him to the cops. I bet they were after him. We give him up—"

"Lucas," Calla warned. But Lucas kept on—

"We give him up and maybe they leave us alone."

"No. *No.*"

Marco touched her arm. "Lucas might be right."

"Lucas is *not* right."

It was Esther who said, "How do we even go home? Calla, what about your father? And if the police know who I am because of my license plate . . ." They wrapped their arms around themselves. "We might be in real trouble. If Marco would give himself up to them . . ."

"No, no, *no*—" Calla raged. "I'm not even talking about this right now. We'll—we'll find somewhere to hide out. Somewhere safe."

"This is fucked," Lucas said.

Esther pulled out their vape pen and popped a cartridge in with shaking hands. "This is *crazy.*"

"Calla—" Marco started to say.

"They might kill you. Okay? You don't know. So we're not doing this. I just got you back and I'm not losing you again."

He opened his mouth to say something—

When they saw the distant wash of police lights. They heard the engine growling, the sound of tires breaking sticks on rough ground.

They couldn't go back. The drive back to the road was far too narrow—they'd run headfirst into the cop. And from here, where they parked, the paths to the quarry were just that: paths. No car could fit.

"What do we do, what do we do?" Esther asked.

"We run!" Lucas said, and so that's what they did—

They ran. They scattered into the trees just as the police cruiser eased into the forest like a wolf stalking its prey. Marco didn't want to go, but Calla wasn't going to have this discussion. She grabbed his hand and dragged him toward one of the quarry trails. Already she realized—he wasn't running fast. Marco's leg was still injured. Was it because he was away from the apple? Her father had been wearing his eyeglasses again, hadn't he? No time to worry about that now. Only thing they could do was run as fast as they could.

THE QUARRY WAS A DEEP, CANKEROUS HOLE IN THE EARTH. AT night, it was a great black void ringed by the dark woods, with a mirror-shine of water at the bottom. They came here in the summers some-times to jump down off the edge and into the man-made lake below, formed from when the construction company had dug too deep and struck the water table, flooding the quarry and making it useless for the company's purposes. They jumped and swam even though they'd long been told that the bottom contained the jagged sharp shapes of rusted mining equipment, and that the area was infested with both venomous water snakes and copperheads. It was not summer now—the air was cold and the water below would only be colder. Maybe dangerously so. But even so, they hurried through the woods, threading through the trees, slowly realizing their only recourse might in fact be to reach the edge—

And jump.

Then:

Light and loud sound. Like fireworks going off—

Not fireworks. Gunfire.

Calla was a girl of the modern age. She'd been through those fucking school shooter drills, the ones where they had to hide in classrooms, lock the doors, be ready to throw books and staplers and rulers at whoever was trying to murder them all with a bullet-chattering black rifle. It made the kids feel like, *Maybe we can do this, maybe we can survive,* but now that there were real bullets, a real gun, her whole self lit up like a strobe light of panic. She shrieked, ducking her head low, keeping an eye on Marco just ahead of her—

Pop. Pop. Pop. Her ears rang. Something sped past her head like an angry wasp. Still she ran, one foot following fast after the other, and she pictured the quarry ahead of her, and now she *knew* there was only one way out, and that way was jumping off the edge and into the dark cold waters below, and she could almost feel the ground gone beneath her, could feel the air rushing up around her—

When a bullet chipped a tree next to her.

A cough of splinters peppered her face—

She screamed, moving sideways, losing her footing—

A shoulder clipped a pine tree—

And the air was clapped out of her lungs as she fell to the ground.

Gasping, she struggled to get up, the pine needles underneath her forming a slippery conveyor belt—every effort to get up was taken away as the ground seemed to go the other way. She tried to call out for Marco, but her voice was gone, replaced with a squeaking wheeze. Marco was nowhere to be found.

Footsteps rushed up on her.

The cop.

Rough hands flipped her over.

It was him. The cop from the farmers market. Pale, red hair buzzed short, eyes like cigarette burns.

"Where is he?" the cop asked.

"I don't—" she tried to say, but could barely form the words.

The cop, gun out, swatted her with the weapon—the pistol's sights dug a furrow into her forehead and she felt blood already bubbling up and trickling down to her ear. She cried out in pain and shock.

"Get the fuck off her!"

Marco. He was here. Calla reached out and grabbed the pine tree, pulling herself closer to it as the cop pointed his pistol at the slowly advancing Marco.

"Marco, run," Calla said, her voice weak.

"Marco, *stay,*" the cop warned. Then he pointed the gun at the girl's head. "Stay, or I pop her. You're coming with me. You're going back to the orchard."

"Don't hurt her."

"That's up to you."

Marco looked from her to the cop and back again. Calla felt the blood from her head running into her eyes, down past her nose, onto her lips.

"You hurt her already," Marco said, shocked.

"And I'll do worse."

"You don't know who that is, do you?"

"Fuck you. I don't care."

Marco shook his head. "That's her. That's Dan's daughter."

A pause.

A cold breeze slithered past.

"What?" the cop asked.

"That's Dan Paxson's daughter. You hurt her. She's bleeding. Dan won't be happy."

"I . . ." Panicked, the cop looked to her and recoiled. "I didn't—I didn't know. I didn't mean to."

"But you did," Marco said.

The cop went slack. He stood there, in horror.

"I did," he said softly. "You're right."

Then he tucked the gun barrel under his chin and *bang,* fired his brains through the top of his skull. Calla screamed.

WHAT HAPPENED NEXT EXISTED IN AN INTERSTITIAL PART OF THE memory, some liminal hallway in Calla's brain—a place of blinking, buzzing lights and a line of locked doors. Memory can be impacted by brain injury, but trauma, real trauma, can be an injury all its own, and the mind will go to great lengths to protect the persona it contains. Calla remembered being back in Esther's car. Driving fast again, the dark forests and hills of Bucks County whipping past in a nauseating blur. She knew that Marco was not with her. He said he had to get away from her because he was putting her in danger—and then once he had her in the car, he ran. She remembered the cop—memory out of order, out of sequence, but there he was, not the moment of him dying but the afterward, the part where he just fell like a stack of books, where his leg kicked out and the heel juddered against the hard ground, dead leaves and dry pine needles whispering underneath. She remembered Lucas and Esther talking in the front seat. Them asking if she was listening, if she was all right, asking each other if Calla was comatose. They didn't know where to go. Lucas said maybe he and Esther could go home, maybe the cop was the only one looking for them, and now that he was dead, the chase was over. The cop, dead again. Dead again, dead again, dead again, the sound of a gunshot making Calla jump in the back seat, so sure was she that it was happening again, that someone in the car had a gun. *Are you all right? Jesus, Esther, I think she's really fucked up.* Calla couldn't go home. Couldn't go anywhere. Esther said she could stay over, but Calla didn't answer, couldn't answer, even though in her own head she was thinking, *That could just put you in danger, if you're not already.* Dad would come looking. Dad. He was there. At home. *Can't go home.* Maybe never again. That bridge was burned. Dad had burned so many bridges and Calla had been standing on them. Burning bridges, burning bridges. But that told her where she needed to go. She needed to go to one of those burned bridges and stand in the ashes.

62

THE LIGHT OF A BURNING BRIDGE

MORNING, EARLY. SIX A.M. JOANIE WAS IN THE KITCHEN CLEANING her .380 when her smartwatch pinged her with an alert—

Someone was approaching the front door.

Since Graham's death and Prentiss Beckman's escape, she'd had a whole smart system installed: doorbell camera, cameras at every corner of the house, in every room, plus connected thermostat, lights, smart speakers, and smoke-slash-carbon-monoxide detectors. Every bit of it tied to her phone, her tablet, her watch, and controllable too via voice command.

And now, just days later, someone was coming up.

They had a black hoodie on. Hood up. Hunched over.

Her heart quickened. Joanie willed it to calm. This was no time for anxiety. Whatever fucking PTSD she had or was going to have, this was not the time for it. That went into the box. Now: She took the pistol, clicked off the safety, and walked to the door just as someone rang her doorbell. Joanie, gun in one hand, approached the door, pulling out her phone with the other hand and swiping across the screen. The live footage from the doorbell camera appeared.

She saw bangs over eyes.

That's not Prentiss.

Joanie put the gun to the door, then opened it a mere six inches, the hidden pistol pointing right at the head of the person on the other side of it.

"What?" she asked.

A teen girl looked up from under the lip of the hood.

"Are you Joanie . . ." She seemed to be trying to remember the last name. "Moreau?" She tried to pronounce it too fancy—*Mor-ee-ohh.*

"It's Moreau. Who are you and what do you want?"

The girl pulled back the hood, and it was then that Joanie saw how badly the girl had been beaten up. Gash across her forehead, red and raw. Scratches across her cheeks, too, like swipes from a rosebush.

"I'm Calla Paxson."

Paxson. Jesus.

"Dan's kid."

The girl nodded. "Yeah. I—my Dad isn't the same anymore and—" Her lips were sticky, her eyes full. And it was like watching a summer storm crash down upon a quiet forest: next thing Joanie knew, the girl was full-on *sobbing,* her knees softening like sand touched by the sea.

Joanie put the safety back on the pistol and tucked it in her waistband before she got her arms around the girl, helping her inside.

"Okay. Mm-hm. Yeah. Come on in. Let's get you warm, get you cleaned up, then you can tell me what's going on. Sound good, kid?" The girl made a wordless reply, just a snorfling, sob-fed nod. Joanie sighed. "Okay, sure. Here we go."

63

JOHN COMPASS IS TIRED

THE ROAD TO OLD AGE WAS MARKED BY MANY SIGNPOSTS AND BILL-boards, but none more dramatic than the one that warned you that the bridge was out ahead, and yet you kept driving toward it, because what else could you do? The road was the road and you couldn't stop now. The bridge was out for everyone, and one day every car met the end of the line in a fashion that for some was dramatic—car on fire pitching over the edge!—and for others was softer, sadder, slower, as the car eased off the lip of the cliff, teeter-tottering on an old rock before rolling down the incline toward the river of oblivion.

John didn't know how close he was to the gone bridge, the oblivion river, but he knew that right now, he was passing one big signpost:

His body hurt.

His *everything* hurt.

No part of him escaped the misery of bone-deep pain.

It was bad enough waiting for days across the street from Emily's house. Once he suspected something was wrong in there, he went home to the Lehigh Valley, fetched an old ghillie suit out of his storage unit, and came back with some food and water and a pair of good binocs. That meant lying there in the tangle of ivy and dead leaves under the cover of trees, day in, night out. It wasn't his first rodeo, though this time he blessedly didn't have a rifle in his hand. But he did have a pistol loaded with tranquilizers, just in case. Once upon a time, he'd stayed on sits across various TAORs (Tactical Areas of Responsibility) watching for a target, waiting either to take the shot or for the orders *to* take the shot. Some of them were two, three hours. Others? Two, three days. A few had been more than a week on a sit. Like a hawk on a telephone pole, waiting for the rabbit.

Problem was, back then he could hop back up, do some stretches, be limber like a twist-tie in ten minutes. He knew all the ways to get the blood back in his limbs. But even those ways didn't work anymore. Once he heard screaming and yelling, the adrenaline let him move fast—and there was just enough in the tank to help Emily carry Meg to her Audi and then into his own vehicle, parked a mile off under cover of some big-shouldered spruces.

Now, though, next morning, his body was cursing him. Every inch in rebellion. Emily had to wake him up, too, which was an additional indignity for which he was not prepared.

You need to be better at this, John, he told himself. *Things are going to get a whole lot darker.* And soon, he feared.

"I'M NOT COMFORTABLE WITH THIS," JOHN SAID TO EMILY.

The two of them stood in the middle of his rented cabin. The cabin had only one room separate from the rest: the bathroom. Everything else—the bed, the couch, the meager kitchen setup, a tiny washer and dryer—was out here in the main room. Everything except Meg—

Who was chained up in the bathroom.

Which was the thing that made John uncomfortable.

"At least she stopped screaming," Emily said, folding her arms tightly inward—the cabin was cold this morning. She looked rough—her eyes deep set, her mouth in a tired frown. "I don't know how you slept last night."

"I'm old. That's how." As if to demonstrate, he shifted his stance and half the bones in his body crackled like logs popping in a hot fire.

While Meg lay tranquilized last night, John went to the toolbox in his Jeep and got some nylon rope, and they tied her up in one helluva tangle—hands bound in the front, then further to her tied ankles, and all of it fed back up to her torso, under her armpits, and tied the whole human package around the safety grab bar in the shower. He was an Army man a long time ago, and that meant he knew his knots. Thankfully, somebody had taken installing the grab bar seriously and had bolted it to the wall, not just to the shell of the shower interior.

He said, though, "We have kidnapped a human being, Emily. I understand that we both believe something bad is going on here—"

"We don't believe it. We know it."

John sighed. "Yeah, I suppose we do. But I don't like this. We should take her out of here. Let her go somewhere. She was knocked out when we came here. Meg doesn't know where we are."

Wasn't hard to see that Emily was distraught. A war played out on her face, one of indecision and fear. But then it was like something snapped into place. Her mouth formed a straight line. A decision had been made.

"We'll keep her for a few days. Just to see, okay? She was getting better, John. She really was. It wasn't long without the apple that she started to change—like she was going through withdrawal. And she hasn't had an apple yet, I don't think. Maybe—maybe she'll get back to normal quicker this time."

"Emily—"

"I know. Okay? I *know.* We're—we're basically torturing her. But she's not herself. I don't know if something is in her now, or if that apple just stripped away all her compassion, her empathy. But she's not the same. She has strength that she shouldn't have. She heals injuries like—" Emily snapped her fingers. "Like *that.* She tried to kill me, John. And would've had you not shown up." She sighed. "I've thought about it. This is the way. For now. For a few days, just to see if whatever it is in her loosens its grip."

"A few days," he said. "That's it."

"Yeah." She nodded. "Yeah, absolutely. And John?"

"Yes, Emily?"

"This isn't just Meg."

"I know."

"Do others know what's happening?"

"There have to be others who see it. We can find them. It's good to have friends when the world has gone mad." He thought, *I've been in war, been through hell, and the only thing that ever saved me was having friends to help one another get through it all.* "As to what we do . . . I think we have to kill the trees. Girdle the trunks, or maybe just burn the whole orchard."

"If that thing growing at our house was an apple tree, though, like Meg said . . . then there could be others. And if there are others . . ."

"Then it's going to be a lot harder to burn the orchard."

"A *lot* harder."

He nodded. "Our task is large. The darkness is strong. So we will just have to bring a very big light, Emily. A *very* big light."

INTERLUDE

—

THE APPLE HUNTER'S TALE

A LITTLE OVER FIVE YEARS AGO.

"HERE, I BROUGHT YOU SOME THINGS," WALT PURVIN SAID TO HIS daughter, Belinda, who met him at the door of her little condo in Telford but didn't let him in further. He jostled the box at her—a cardboard box full of random stuff. A light fixture for her downstairs hallway, some old paperback books (horror, thriller, mystery), some arrowheads, and of course, a bag of different kinds of apples. Everything (but the apples) came from flea markets and yard sales.

"I don't want this shit, Daddy," she said, arms crossed, staring down at the box like it was a bedpan full and dripping.

"No, hold on now, this is good shit. You said you needed a light, that you just had wires dangling, so here's one—" He pulled it out, showed it to her.

"It looks like a glass tit, I don't want that."

"You don't have a job right now so I just figured—"

"No, jeez. Come on, take it away."

"Look. Some good books here. Arrowheads. Apples. The apples are special—there's a Golden Russet in there, an Esopus Spitzenburg, and a few really rare ones, local, too, like these Haycock Mountain Limbertwigs—"

"Daddy, I don't want your weird-ass apples. You need a better hobby. And you need to stop bringing me your garbage."

"It's not garbage." Walt understood a vital truth of fatherhood: You brought things and stuff to demonstrate how much you cared about someone. Things and stuff were literal tokens of love and affection. "You need these."

"I *need* a father who has better things to do than bother my ass on a Saturday morning in September. Go home. You still not talking to John?"

Walt made a face. "No."

"Jesus. Just go talk to *him* and quit bothering *me*."

At that, Belinda closed the door on him, literally using the door to push him back onto the stoop.

To her credit, at least she didn't slam it. This time.

WALT PULLED INTO THE DRIVEWAY AT HIS HOUSE IN DINGMAN'S Falls, found a strange fellow on his front porch. Man in a white suit, hair so blond it was the color of staring into the sun. Teeth the same way: shiny and big.

He was dropping something off on the porch. Mail or some such.

"Help you?" Walt asked him, stepping out of his Chevy.

"Oh. Hello. Are you Walter Purvin?"

"Depends on who's asking." Collections had been sniffing around, though they never seemed to show up at his door. It was all threatening phone calls and emails. Easy enough to push them off, but maybe he'd pushed them off too long.

"Mister Purvin, I'm just here fulfilling a request."

Walt cocked an eyebrow. "Request?"

"FOIA. Freedom of Information Act."

Oh.

Oh!

Walt's big round chest shook with relief and laughter. "Hot damn. I sent that out so long ago, I'd forgotten. Here, lemme see." He jogged up onto the porch, and the man bent down and picked up the envelope he'd set down.

"Government moves very slow, Mister Purvin. It's really very . . . un- dignified, if you ask me."

"You got that right. And please, it's just Walt." The man, still smiling big as a billboard, handed over the envelope. "Is it something good? The information."

"Gosh, I can't say. They don't tell me what's in it, I just make sure that the person gets what they need is all." The man winked. "Have a great one, Walt. I hope I've restored a little of your dignity today."

Walt stared down at the envelope, started to unwind the thread that kept it shut. "I bet you have, Mister, ahh—"

But the man was already gone. Now, how the hell'd he do that?

PAY DIRT.

See, Walt had this theory—he'd been chasing this lost apple for years now, this Vinot's Allegresse. Came over here from France via Dutch traders and maybe, just maybe, one of Vinot's descendents—or stranger still, someone calling himself Vinot. Whatever the case, he brought the apple to America. An apple he said tasted like a blessing, like nothing he'd ever eaten. Paradise on earth.

Thing was, people didn't keep good records of anything back then. Everything was left to the luck of finding primary sources like journals and whatnot. Everywhere Walt turned, he met another dead end. John thought he was being obsessive about it, and Walt admitted, yes, he could get a little obsessed from time to time, but he viewed that trait as a damn good one to have. He told John, "People give up too easy, John. They fold like a cheap map. You say I'm obsessed? I say I'm stubborn and steadfast. Like a dog with a bone."

John had said, "If you're not careful, you'll choke on that bone."

Walt waved him off because, what did John know? He loved that bastard like he was a brother, but damn he could sure rub Walt the wrong way sometimes. Self-righteous know-it-all, always so cautious, so cowardly. Which wasn't a fair assessment given the hell he'd been through in the Gulf, but still. C'mon now.

On a lark, Walt thought to call him. Tell him what he'd found in that envelope. A little voice told Walt, *You're both getting older now, you dumb fool. Best to mend those fences before they fall all the way down.* But then he thought about John bailing on him with those bikers, and just being his stoic, overly ethical self, with all that Quaker light shining out his ass.

Whatever. So, Walt had hit dead end after dead end, but he knew the apple had to have been around after it came to America—hell, the whole reason he was looking for this apple in the first place was that old recipe card he'd found.

It was a Depression-era recipe. And that made him think to look back to that time and just before it, and what came just before that? Prohibition. Walt knew that apple orchards were in the crosshairs back then because orchards made apples not for eating but for *drinking*—cider apples. An American tradition, cider. Was probably the most common beverage found in this country before and after the Revolutionary War—hell, colonial *children* drank the damn stuff.

But with the government suddenly siding with the Temperance movement, they moved to cut down or burn all the cider-making orchards, which of course was what made way for the apple to become the eating apple it became for Americans—no longer a fruit producing a beverage of sin, it was now a pure Christian fruit for a pure Christian country, perfect enough to be eaten out of hand or baked into a pie cooling on a sill. (Walt didn't care for such moral rigors and had no truck with any church these days, though he had been raised Catholic. But he had to admit that Prohibition was a double-edged sword—so many heirloom varieties lost, true, but it also changed the American palate for apples, and a snacking or dessert apple was just what Walt liked. A fresh apple eaten off the tree was as close to Heaven as he could get. He hoped he got to die one day with an apple in his hand.)

Point was, Walt theorized that maybe, just maybe, Vinot's Allegresse apple was buried somewhere in Prohibition records. If there was an orchard out there? A secret orchard? Maybe one of the prohi agents of the Bureau of Prohibition would have found it. And if the apple was such a wonderful eating apple, then it wouldn't be no spitter, no sir—spitters were for cider.

Maybe it was out there, and maybe it would be saved.

And inside the envelope, he had his answer.

Stanley Thistle.

THISTLE, AN AGENT OF WHAT BEGAN AS THE PROHIBITION UNIT and ended as the Bureau of Prohibition under the FBI, didn't last long as a prohi. He got into trouble, though doing what, Walt couldn't tell. Most of the report was redacted, not with the usual black bars but rather white stickers that had been placed on the original and then photocopied over. So wasn't any way to remove the stickers because the stickers were on the originals only and Walt had just the copies.

Thistle, from Philly, had done a lot of work in his short six months on the job—a dozen-plus reports of orchards he burned across Pennsylvania and into both New Jersey and New York. As Walt read page after page he got this sick feeling in his stomach; he figured he'd see soon enough that overzealous teetotaler crusader Thistle found Vinot's apple and burned it like he burned all the others. And finding that meant Walt's road—or rabbit hole, if you talked to John, which Walt didn't— was at an end.

But then? Buried in one report? Walt found it. It was tucked away in the middle, a moment of editorialization from a real nutbag:

AND SO IT WAS THAT SLACK'S APPLE FILLED ME WITH THE GRAVEST DISAPPOINTMENT, A BITTER FOUL WORMS-PARADE OF AN APPLE GROWN BY A WORMS-PARADE OF A MAN. HIS PATH WAS SIN LIKE ALL THE OTHERS BUT STILL I CRAVE THE TASTE OF THAT FIRST APPLE, THE ONE THE MAN SHOWED ME FROM THAT SMALL ISLAND IN THE RIVER. I STILL CAN TASTE IT IN THE BACK OF MY MOUTH BEHIND MY FARTHEST TEETH. THE HANGMAN'S APPLE. HARROWSBLACK. I CAN FEEL IT, TOO. THE WAY IT PUT ME FORWARD. I WAS POWERFUL AND UNENDING.

Walt almost had to laugh. Boy howdy, that was some crazy talk.
But just the same—
Thistle was talking about Vinot's apple.
He had to be. Vinot had called it paradise, godlike, had suggested he was compelled by it. And here, this whackadoo prohi had found it—
On an island in a river.
Maybe, like Walt had figured, around Bucks County.

WALT HAD A MAP LISTING ALL THE ISLANDS. KNEW THERE WAS ONE out there they said was used for hanging folks back in the Revolutionary

War—a berm of land on the river that each side, the loyalists and the colonists, would use to hang their captors as a vicious taunt. Up and down Walt drove along the river, scouting island after island after island, but none of them seemed right, and none of them seemed to have a single apple tree on them, shit, goddamnit, shit.

FALL TUMBLED ITS WAY INTO WINTER AND WALT STOOD AT THE gateway to the season—Christmas—and looked around his little house. Belinda wasn't spending the holiday with him, she was back with her on-off boyfriend Derek, who for Walt's mileage was a real skeevy piece of work, probably a druggie. The two-a-them were blowing all their cash on a trip to the Florida Keys, and Walt told her, "You can't do that, you have to start saving for your future," and she just laughed and told him, "I'll just wait for you to die and take what's yours." Walt wondered when exactly he'd filled her with such venom. Maybe he just wasn't there enough for her when she was a kid. Certainly he and her mother fought all the time. But he didn't beat her, wasn't mean to her, hell, he never said a cross word to the girl.

And usually on Christmas he'd spend some time with John, too. Walt would have a tipple of something—maybe more than one something, like some blackberry schnapps and blended Scotch (together or separate or hell, why not both). John of course was sober as a stone wall, which wasn't new for him.

But this year there was none of that, and so Walt fried up a couple of hot dogs in his cast iron, tossed them with a bit of lard like his own mother used to do, and went hogwild with the relish and the mustard. *Christmas dinner ain't what it used to be,* he thought. Then he went out and looked at the orchard he'd started in his backyard. Wasn't really that much to look at. It was all right. He'd done some good work, searching up these trees and giving them life again, and he'd made a few online sales of scionwood, and once in a while he managed to get apples out to the road to sell in a little wooden farmstand he'd built. But half the time the yellowjackets got to the apples first. Autumn made the yellowjackets real hangry, since they knew a deep freeze was coming to kill them.

"The hell am I doing?" Walt asked himself.

Stupid trees, stupid apples, stupid John, stupid Belinda, stupid hot dogs, stupid Christmas, stupid Walt. Stupid, stupid, stupid.

"I'm giving all this shit up," Walt declared to the leafless trees.

Then he went inside and got drunk and fell asleep on the recliner, which screwed up his back for a good two weeks after.

IT WAS A COLD, HARD, STUPID WINTER.

Then, in early March, a phone call.

"I'M REAL GLAD YOU CALLED ME," WALT TOLD DAN PAXSON. HE wanted to add, *Because honestly I missed this, and I could talk about apples all damn day.* The two of them sat down at a little café at Pleasant Point. For some reason, Dan didn't want to meet at his house, not at first, but that was fine by Walt, because it meant Dan was buying lunch. And lunch for Walt was going to be waffles and a lot of syrup, which he knew would give his doctor the shivering shits, but too bad, Doc.

Dan said, "My pop wanted to have an orchard and—" Here Dan hesitated, and Walt could sense there was more to the story that the other man wasn't comfortable telling. "Well, let's just say it didn't work out. But I have a daughter, and she's a real whipcord of a girl, and I want to show her—okay, this sounds goofy as hell, don't sue me, but I want to show her you should follow your dreams."

Walt formed a big goofy grin. "I don't disagree, Dan. I don't disagree at all."

And so he laid out a plan for Dan's orchard. Said they'd plant some dwarf and semi-dwarf rootstock and graft some scionwood and budwood from Walt's own orchard, a cascading variety that would provide apples through the whole season, late summer through all of fall. Plus some good keeper varieties too, apples that would do well through winter storage. "Now, it's not a heritage variety, but the GoldRush is a real late-bloomer and to be honest, it tastes like juice-soaked cardboard when you pick it off the tree—but let it rest for a couple-few weeks, Dan, and it becomes the Swiss Army Apple. Good for eating out of hand, for pies, for sauce, for whatever you need."

"I . . ." Again, Dan hesitated. "I want something really special. I *need* it to be special. I feel like I've been given a chance and I want to do it right."

"All apples are special." Walt forked a hunk of waffle into his mouth and winked.

"Right, of course. But . . . I want something nobody's ever seen before. It—it has to be. There are other orchards around here, and even more down in Chester County, and I don't have the money or resources— or god, the time—to try to start a breeding program. But if I could find an apple that was really unique—"

"I have a few varieties I've rescued from obscurity. Like the Benscoter's Pippin, or the Tom Brown, or the Molasses Winesap—"

"Are they good?"

"They're real good, sure."

"I need great. Are they great?"

Walt chewed on that. On the one hand, they *were* great apples. But on the other, he understood what Dan was looking for. It wasn't just a good apple or a great one. Like he said, he wanted something *special.*

The power of hunting apples for Walt—or collecting anything, really—was chasing the lost joy of apples he'd eaten and that were now gone. When he was a younger man, Walt took a trip out to the Western Slope of Colorado to do some hunting—elk, mulies, whitetail—and while out there, he passed through a town called Fruita, and had a Northern Spy apple there bought from a roadside stand that blew him away. Before then he'd never even thought of an apple as anything other than a punishment. But it was so sweet, so fresh, so perfect. It changed him.

Dan was looking for one of *those* apples.

The kind of apple you eat and can forever taste in your mouth.

An apple that tastes like paradise on earth.

That's when Walt shrugged and said, "There's an old apple supposed to be around here that's said to be something truly special—heaven on your tongue. Only problem is, I haven't found it yet."

A spark danced in Dan's eyes.

"Tell me more."

So, Walt told him more. Told him all about Vinot's apple. Walt laid it out snout-to-tail, the whole damn quest. A failed quest, at present.

He expected at some point for the spark in Dan's eyes to die. It should've, after all—the difficulty, the dead ends, the whole *wild goose chase* quality of it.

But the opposite happened. The spark only grew.

Dan, in fact, smiled like someone who knew something.

And know something, he did.

"I think I know where the apple is," Dan said.

TURNED OUT, HE WAS RIGHT.

THE EVENING HE WAS SET TO DRIVE BACK DOWN TO BUCKS, WALT wrote a note to John. The note said,

> John—
>
> Found something
> If it's what I think it is we should meet
> My place tomorrow 3PM
>
> —Walt

But he paused. Wondered why the hell he was writing it. And he just didn't know. Part of him thought it was to share the joy—John, after all, was the man with whom he shared a great deal of excitement over the years, especially when it came to apples and apple-hunting. John was his buddy. His best buddy. But then, he also thought, *I'm doing it to gloat.* To shove it in the other man's face. To say *I told you so.* To get John to admit he was wrong about this, that it wasn't just some fool's crusade, that Walt had been right to look for Vinot's apple.

He couldn't figure out what he felt.

Maybe both things.

Whatever it was, Walt shoved it in an envelope, hastily put John's address on it, licked and smashed a stamp on it, and put it in the box with the flag up. A little part of him was scared for John to get it and see it. But another part of him hoped he saw it, gave him a call, and maybe they could put all this stupid shit behind them. Blood under the bridge and all that.

And in the meantime? The apple awaited.

THE TREE WAS LESS A TREE AND MORE A TALL, DENSE BRAKE OF branches. In the dueling beams of their flashlights, it looked to Walt like a black-barked fossil, a gnarled beast weighed down by time—like something ancient that struggled to live, that wanted to die, but that remained just the same. And remain, it did, living on: Dark leaves were popping off some of the branches, and off some of the shoots that sprung up out of the rough-and-tumble ground of the hangman's island—the island known as Harrowsblack. The river gurgled and splashed—out of sight, but nearby, below them. Beyond the tree, the ground fell in a sharp shelf of mud, with roots thrust out of the dirt like the fingers of buried skeletons trying to crawl free of their earthen prison.

They came here at night because it wasn't clear who owned this land, if anyone. Didn't need anyone poking around—the police did enough trips up and down River Road during the day.

Walt moved the flashlight beam up and along the length of a singular branch that thrust up and out from the tree.

"I think they used to hang people from that branch," Walt said.

"Uh-huh," Dan said, but he said it all dreamy-like, as if he heard Walt, but wasn't really *listening*. He smelled the air. "You smell that?"

Walt sniffed. He did.

"An apple."

Which couldn't be true. It was March. No apples grew in March. June was the earliest for apples, and even then, not likely. But maybe a blossom was popping off somewhere—he didn't see any flowers, assuming this tree was past fruiting, so he looked deep into the tangle of branches—

He was sure for a moment that the branches were moving. Gently easing together like a tightening bundle of rat snakes. Or maybe they were easing apart. He heard the wood creaking. The ground, too, seemed to shift beneath his feet. Like roots moving under the soles of his boots. His vision blurred—

"There," Dan said. The flashlight beam danced through the dark branches.

Walt blinked, shook from his reverie.

He saw it, too.

An apple.

Its blister-red skin seemed to drink in the light.

"That's not possible," Walt said.

"And yet, there it is."

They shared a look.

"We need to taste it."

"We sure do. I've got the longest arms—" Dan started to say, but paused and apologized, as if it was an insult. "I didn't mean anything."

"It's all right, I'm an old, fat, short-armed sonofagun. I'll gladly concede."

Dan licked his lips and moved his flashlight to his left hand and reached into the depths of the tree, straining as his fingers danced along the skin of the apple, unable to get a grip—

At that moment, Walt swore he saw the branches *ease,* just a little, like the tree itself was letting out a breath. Dan lurched forward, farther into the tree, his fingers wrapping around the apple like spider legs around a caught fly.

A grunt, a twist, and a pluck, and the apple was theirs.

Walt tucked his flashlight under his armpit, then pulled out a lockback knife. Dan handed him the apple and he cut it in half.

"Cheers," Dan said.

The two men toasted their apple halves, tapping them together.

Then they each took a bite.

The crunch was loud and pronounced. Juice flooded Walt's tongue. A feeling washed over him—a feeling of what could only be described as bliss. He felt young again. The sun was on his face. He was by that roadside stand in Colorado, biting into the Northern Spy. He was finding the hidden tree of the Tom Brown apple, holding its russeted skin in his palm. His daughter was holding him tight—she was young, she was happy to see him home from work, she was older now, still holding him, still proud of him for once, forever, taking that cardboard box out of his hands, telling him thanks, Dad, for the things and for the stuff, I love you

(something moved in his mouth, slithering past his teeth)

and there was John, too, and he and John were friends again, and John was telling him he was right, after all these years, *You were right, Walt, I was wrong, and I'm sorry I didn't help you when you asked me to, I made a mistake,* and Walt told him, *You're damn right,* and the moment felt good, and the gloating felt good, and it felt good, too, to realize that he was better than John this whole time, because what the hell did John have anyway besides a body count from a war and some bullshit cult religion and some old Indians who don't know him and don't care about him and

(larvae swimming around his spit, spiders making webs in the back of his throat, lantern flies lining his throat and drinking so much of his nectar they burst on his vocal cords)

he wanted to tell John, *You have blood on your hands and no dreams to call your own,* and for John to nod and smile and say, *You were always better than me, Walt, always a better man and a better friend,* and at that, Walt took a rock from the ground, a rock the shape and size of an apple, and bashed John's head in, stove in the forehead, skin ripping like the pleather of a cheap couch, the bone caving in like cracked tile, all the blood foaming up, bubbling out with a trickle of wet, weak brains, too—

Walt startled, spitting out a wad of apple onto the ground.

A crushing weight fell upon his soul.

He blinked. The flashlight under his armpit shone on Dan Paxson, who had already rolled out a tarp and gotten out some polyethelene bags to store scionwood—in his grip was a set of good-sized loppers, the kind that needed two hands to use, and he had the curved-moon blades gathering around a length of last year's growth—

"The tree's obviously not dormant," Dan was saying, "but it's still chill enough out that I'm gonna try to grab some scions—"

"Wait," Walt said, thrusting out his hand, grabbing the branch just underneath the lopper blades.

"Walt—"

"Something's wrong. My friend was right. This wasn't a good idea." He swallowed a hard knot, tasted the sweetness of the apple—but also something worse, something stranger, an oily foul slickness. He blinked back tears. It took everything he had to get to this moment—it was everything he'd been trying to find. Walt had been searching for this apple for years—*years!* And to get here only to realize . . . that something was very, very wrong. "Dan, you don't want this. You can taste it, can't you? Something's . . . off. Something's wrong with it."

He locked eyes with Dan.

He could see that the other man understood.

And so he was damn surprised when Dan closed the lopper handles hard, bringing the blades closed on not just the branch—

But on Walt's fingers.

His fingers fell to the ground, hitting the tarp with a scattered tumble. Walt cried out, holding up his ruined mitt. Blood pumped, red-black like the apple.

"It—it was an accident," Dan stammered, eyes wide as moons.

"My fingers. You—you cut off my damn fingers!"

"You tried to stop me."

Walt made a sound—a despairing bleat—before turning and going back the way they came, down through the trail, across the steep muddy mess toward the boat, and though part of him knew he should go back and get his fingers, his whole brain screamed with alarm, klaxons of panic going off in his head that told him to *run, run, something isn't right here, get the hell out of here, Walt,* but then something hit him from behind, hit him right in the head, and the toe of his boot hit a patch of rough ground—

The world went upside down. A rock cracked into his head or his head cracked into a rock

(*which came first, the rock or the skull*)

and then he pitched forward, the fingerstumps of his hand crushing hard against the earth as he failed to stop his tumble.

And then—

The cold embrace of the river.

The flashlight splashed into the water next to him. Its beam whirled about, a slow, dizzying pirouette of light—until the light flickered and went dark.

AS THE RIVER TOOK HIM, AS COLD WATER PUMPED INTO HIS throat and his lungs, he thought about John one last time. He missed him. He'd made a mistake. John had been right. Always the better man, the wiser man, the best of all the people Walt knew. In the deep dark of the Delaware, Walt said sorry to his friend. And as the last of who he was went away, the cold river never quite managed to rob him of the taste of Vinot's apple.

Walt felt both victorious and defeated. His body moved downriver, snagged on the bottom under an old I-beam. His flesh was chewed by fish, eyes eaten by turtles, all his empty spaces clogged with mosquito larvae and dragonfly larvae and the eggs of frogs and toads, the bones set loose and captured by the tangle of an old dead tree—

Until the day that Emily Bergmann fell out of her boat and onto his broken skull.

Rest in peace, Walt Purvin.

MAY

—

But apple trees are very patient. It's nothing for them to wait a hundred years, even two hundred. There is a bent old Black Oxford tree in Hallowell, Maine, that is 215 years old and still gives a crop of midnight-purple apples each fall.

—Rowan Jacobsen,
Apples of Uncommon Character

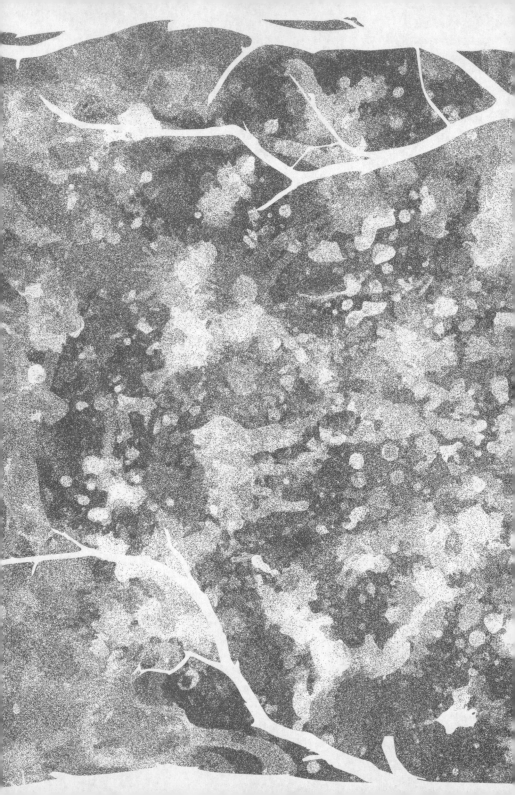

64

ALL COMES CRASHING

MIDNIGHT, AND CALLA WAS HALFWAY OUT THE DOOR WHEN JOANIE caught her. She thought the older woman would be asleep by now, but apparently? She wasn't.

"Going somewhere, kid?" Joanie asked.

Calla blinked back tears. "I'm—yeah, I'm gonna leave." She already had her phone in her hand, ready to text Esther to pick her up. She'd tried to keep communicating with Esther and Lucas to a minimum.

"That's your call and if you wanna make it, make it. I won't stop you. But you came here for a reason. Why leave now?"

"I just—I just can't. I can't stay. Okay?"

But still she stood there. Feet rooted. Hands shaking.

"Come back inside. Talk to me. What's going on?"

Calla didn't move. She just stood there in the springtime midnight, feeling the humid air sliding around her. The words were there, *right there*, on the back of her throat and it was like when you have a stomach bug and you know you need to throw up but also you don't want to throw up, but then there comes a point when you can't stop it—and she couldn't stop this, either. The words came out of her in a crash and tangle, and with them, tears.

"Today is Decision Day, Joanie, and I need to pay the school some money if I'm going to go there, and I don't have that money for the fucking deposit, my *father* would have that and, and—and I don't have any clothes, and I don't have my stuff, my hair looks like a fucking bird's nest, and—and! And I'm going to have to go to school tomorrow. I've been here for too many days. I can't take any more absences. I can only send so many fake excuses in through my father's email address, they're going to want a doctor's note, and if I don't go to school and I don't graduate then I can't go to Princeton at all, I can't get away from here, I'll be trapped—*trapped* in this place with whatever this crazy bullshit is, and my

Dad is definitely going to come looking for me and he's tried texting and calling but I blocked his number and—"

"Kid—"

But Calla kept going, the flood of her words rising and roaring. "And *you*—you're being super-nice to me but Jesus, Joanie, your husband just died and I hear you on the phone dealing with like, life insurance and being the executor of a will and holy fucking shit that's so sad and here I am being a burden on you, *god,* you don't need this right now, you don't need *me* right now, you don't—" And at that the words surged together, a mudslide of meaninglessness. Joanie winced and reached for her and Calla fell into the awkward hug, surrendering to it.

Inside they sat on the couch and, when Calla stopped her hitching breaths, Joanie said, "I thought maybe you were creeped out by the sex house thing."

Calla's softening sobs broke with a snorting laugh. "No. That's cool. I mean it's weird and whatever but that's my problem not yours."

"You're not a burden," Joanie said. "You're fine. It's honestly nice having someone here. This is a big house and it's empty without Graham. Having you to worry about gives me a little . . . I dunno. Purpose, let's call it."

"But I'm fucked. This is fucked. *Everything* is fucked."

"I'll pay for your deposit. For school. I'll sort it out today."

Calla recoiled in shock. Happy, disbelieving shock. "What? Joanie. No. You can't—I'm not—it's not—"

"I'm rich. *Ish.* Graham had money. I have money. I can handle the deposit. You don't even need to pay me back."

"Joanie. Thank you." But Calla needed to know. "Why?"

"Kid, I had a rough go of it when I was your age. My parents did not have money. I was a . . . I dunno, smart but certainly not wise. My family wasn't from this area and the people around here were not nice to us. Said I was poor and called me a whore and it just made me act out more and more. And I think—" Here Joanie paused, almost like she was holding back her own tears. "I think I could've gone down some bad roads if there weren't people to help me. I think I'd be dead, honestly. Some teachers were good to me, helped me apply to community college. I had a neighbor who took me in when my mother was drinking. And eventually I got out of here and found a life for myself. Been all over the country, did all sorts of things. Had a glassblowing studio for a while in a small Colorado town, made glass sex toys, if you'll believe it—sold the whole thing for a tidy profit, met Graham, who was an engineer, and he took a job back here working with the river, and I came with. I came home to spit in their eyes and show off how good I had it, how I'd survived and thrived. But the only reason I got to do that was because I had people to help. So maybe I can be that for you."

"Thanks. I'm sorry about . . . all that."

"Is what it is, kiddo."

"You know, if I stay here, Dad could maybe make life hard for you. He has . . . people now. The police."

"Let him try. Besides, he always had a soft spot for me. When I talk about how people helped me, Calla? He was one of them. He was always good to me. Even when I wasn't good to him. He believed in me. So—maybe despite all this shitty mess, your father is still in there somewhere. You said Marco was doing better, now. Maybe Dan Paxson can be fixed, too."

"I don't know. Maybe." She shrugged. "He's texted me a few times. Tried calling. Said he hopes I'm safe. Wants me to come home. You didn't tell him where I was?"

"I didn't. But it's possible he knows."

"Yeah."

Calla wondered. Could he be brought back? From that? From murder? *Maybe he's not a murderer,* she cautioned herself. Marco said Dad didn't kill anyone in that room. Maybe he didn't kill that guy Dawes, either. Maybe he didn't even *know* about that. Maybe his outbursts were due to whatever was in that apple. She flinched as the memory again hit her from when she was a kid: a bundle of apple sticks and, nestled among the cut branches, someone's severed fingers.

65

A DREAM OF BONES AND TEETH

IT WAS THE FIRST OF MAY AND MARCO'S LEG HURT SO BAD IT FELT like it was rebreaking itself. He could almost feel the bones shifting in the place where the fracture once was—the skin where a shard of fibula once emerged grew hot, and though he saw no bulge and couldn't feel one with his fingers he was *sure* it was there, like a finger pushing from the inside of a tent. It was agony. Only good thing about it was it let him stay home from school for the last few days.

His parents were attentive and kind, but they always were. He loved them and they loved him. His father didn't even offer any of that machismo bullshit of *are you sure it's really broken* or *go run it off, huh.* They didn't make him work, didn't make him go to school, and didn't rub in the fact that today was May 1, the unofficial National College Decision Day. Which didn't apply to him because, well, he didn't even apply. His brain had been clouded and now his future was in jeopardy. All for what? A damn apple?

His mother wanted to call the doctor, because she said, "What if it's an infection?" and he said it wasn't, it was fine, he just hurt it running. But he couldn't stop shaking. Aches throttled his joints. His brow was sweat-slick and he had the chills. Wasn't running a temperature, though. At least there was that.

Still. He knew different. This *was* an infection. Just not the kind his mother was talking about. No, this one was something deeper, something darker. He could feel it crawling around in him. Urgent and needy.

He texted Calla just once, the day after the cop shot himself. The exchange was short:

Marco: I want to know if you're okay but DO NOT TELL ME where you are, okay, just tell me you're safe or not

Calla: I'm safe

Calla: Are you?

Marco: I'm home

Marco: Everythjnt seems fine

Marco: EveryTHING

Calla: 😀

Calla: Glad you're back to being you

Calla: I'll see you when this is all over

Calla: I love you, M

Marco: I love you, C

Then he went back to bed. Sleep found him, and with it, dreams. And in those dreams, he was being chased, endlessly, by cops wearing red masks, and he couldn't run because his leg was broken and bleeding, the bone spearing through the meat, and though they hadn't caught him yet, he knew they would. That was what made it a nightmare. Not the chase. Not the running. But the realization that there was no escape.

MARCO WOKE IN A PUDDLE OF HIS OWN SWEAT. HIS HAIR WAS soaked, stuck to his forehead. He gasped for air and rubbed his eyes.

"Hey, kiddo," came a voice from the end of his bed.

It was Calla's dad.

Sitting there, by his feet.

Marco reeled in his legs—despite the pain it caused him to do so— and pressed himself against the backboard. He saw his mother, too, standing in the doorway, looking in, his father behind her. Peering over her shoulder.

"Get out of my room," Marco said.

"Your mother called me. Said your leg wasn't doing so hot."

"Mom?" Marco asked, his voice a ragged moan.

"I'm sorry, pechocho."

"Hey, hey," Dan Paxson said, "it's all right that she called me. We're all family here. I still want you to be part of my team. Part of the orchard. I think we maybe had a misunderstanding the other night and it's one I want to correct."

"There's nothing to correct. You need to go."

Dan nodded and sighed, then turned to Marco's parents. "Would you two give us a minute?"

They nodded in unison, and were gone.

Moments passed. Dan stared at Marco from the end of the bed. Looking down over his nose at the bedridden young man.

"Where's my daughter?" Dan asked, finally. His voice darker, sterner.

"I don't know."

"I think you do."

"We aren't in touch. We—we broke up. You know that."

"Well." Dan shrugged, picking up Marco's phone off the nightstand—which made his heart jump in his chest. Dan waggled the phone. "I would track her phone, but she turned all that off, and our provider has made it clear that they don't do that sort of thing. Privacy and all that. What if I was an abuser? A molester? It makes sense, I guess." He sighed, then tossed the phone on the bed near Marco. "Unlock that. Show me your texts."

"You need to get out of here."

"Or what? You'll call the police?"

Marco remained silent. The police hadn't been his ally before all of this—and they certainly weren't now. Not after that night in the cider house and in the woods after. He could still hear the gunshots. One into that man, Cabot. Another under the cop's chin.

"You know," Dan said, "there will be apples again soon. They're already growing. I think we'll have them by the end of the month, maybe sooner. You remember how they taste, don't you?"

Marco did. He could feel the memory of it on his tongue, in the back of his throat. A frisson of something greater—and worse—than hunger ran through him. Just the memory of eating an apple made his pain subside for half a moment.

Dan placed a hand on Marco's ankle. The grip was cold as ice. Fresh pain rose in the spot where his hand rested—and Marco could feel something stirring beneath the skin. The bones shifting both into and out of place, back and forth, a sawing feeling. He heard sharp cracks, like branches breaking off a tree in an ice storm. He cried out behind clenched teeth. Tears wet the bottom of his eyes as he tried to pull away—but Dan held firm.

"I can feel the injury in there. It wants to come back. But what healed you is still in there, too. My gift to you. It hasn't gone. Not yet."

Marco continued to struggle. The pain was a blinding white wave. "Let my leg go. Please."

"Open your phone. I want to know where my daughter is, Marco."

Marco told himself, *No.* He wouldn't. *Couldn't.* He wanted Calla to be safe wherever she was, but even as he was thinking it, his hand had already curled around the phone as the pain crawled into his foot and up the rest of his leg.

"That's my boy," Dan said. "Now unlock it."

Marco, trying not to sob, unlocked the phone.

Dan eased his hand off the young man's ankle. He put that same hand in front of Marco, palm up. "Now give me the phone."

That's when Marco took the phone and smashed it into the corner of the nightstand. The screen shattered. The whole thing glitched out. It was still powered on, but everything on it was an unreadable spray of mutant pixels.

He expected Dan to lose his shit, to grab his ankle, to twist, to urge the bone to push up and out. And for a moment that's certainly what it seemed would happen. Calla's father breathed loudly, his chest rising and falling as the rage rose within him. He shook with visible anger. But then—

"You know, Marco," he said, taking a breath. "I really cared about you once upon a time. Still do, honestly. You're a good kid. Now, I eventually realized you weren't good enough for my daughter—I mean, of course, who is? But you're not like her. Not a go-getter. Not smart enough.

Though please note I do appreciate that you're standing up for her, here—your little phone trick there? That's admirable. You care about her. And that makes me still like you. So, I'm going to do the right thing. I'm going to let your leg heal."

"I don't want it to heal. I don't want your help, your apple, your anything."

Dan leaned in. "You only want my daughter, hm? Well. That's not an option, so this will have to be the consolation prize."

A thrumming vibration arose in Marco's leg—with it, a wasp-nest buzz of pain followed by a wave of sudden numbness. He clutched at his calf muscle, afraid to feel any lower—

"Welcome back, Marco. I'll see you soon, I think."

Marco screamed.

And blacked out.

WHEN HE WOKE AGAIN, IT WAS MORNING.

Whatever fever he had was now broken—his bedding was soaked even further, but his color had returned and he didn't feel super-hot or awfully cold. Marco got out of bed and stretched his legs—

And there was no pain.

He didn't know whether to laugh or cry. Because the lack of pain was so good he wanted to get up and literally dance around the room. But the visit from last night haunted him, and stopped him from seizing that moment.

Dan had touched the ankle that had broken.

Told Marco that he was going to *let* it heal.

And Marco didn't want a damn thing from that man. Not anymore.

Still—no pain *did* feel good. And if that meant he could be stronger, faster, could run if he had to, could help Calla if necessary? Then that was a good thing.

Wasn't it?

From downstairs, his mother called: "Pechocho—I have breakfast for you. Ready and waiting. Adobo arequipeño and corn pudding. Okay? Come down."

"Okay," he said. His voice sounded strong. Not rough like rasped wood. "Be down in a few."

"You feel good?" she yelled up to him.

"I do," he said. And he did.

Just gotta brush my teeth first, he thought.

Down the hall and into the bathroom he went, rubbing sleep out of his eyes with the heel of his hand while still marveling at how *good* his leg felt. Idly, he ran water over the toothbrush and slid some paste on it, thinking about how Dan's visit last night maybe didn't even happen— maybe it was just a hallucination. Toothbrush hanging out of his mouth, he went back into his bedroom—

And saw his phone on the nightstand.

Screen shattered.

Okay, not a hallucination.

Marco scrubbed his teeth, went back into the bathroom—

And felt something go *click* in his mouth. Like the feel of something small snapping—and with it came a tugging sensation, like what you felt when you ran a length of floss through your teeth and it got stuck before it popped free.

He tasted blood. *Ugh.* Did he brush too hard? Marco stood at the sink, set the toothbrush down, and cupped water into his mouth—

Ptoo. He spat—

And something *ticka-tacked* into the sink, almost down the drain.

Marco stared at it for a second before hastily shutting off the water. A tiny trail of blood spiraled the drain, coming from—

A tooth.

One of *his* teeth.

He could feel the gap with his tongue. It was a tooth just past the canine on the right side of his face. "The hell," he said, running the back of his hand along his lips—and seeing a streak of spit-thinned blood there. With trembling fingers he peeled back his upper lip and looked in the mirror.

Sure enough, the tooth just past the canine was now gone.

But the lights in the bathroom were above the mirror, and didn't il-luminate anything. Again he probed the vacant space with his tongue—

And there, he felt something else. Something poking out. Sharp and smooth.

Like a new tooth.

Panic set in. Dan had visited. His leg was healed. He had no idea how a lost tooth was connected to any of this, but if a new one was already growing in? Maybe it made sense. Maybe the tooth he lost had a— a what? A cavity in it? Now it was healing. Like his leg.

He picked up the lost tooth to regard it. Saw nothing unusual.

"Crap," he said, and hurried back to his room to get his phone to use the flashlight—but of course, he'd broken the phone. "*Crap.*" He needed a light. Marco threw open his nightstand drawer, found an old Maglite flashlight . . . that of course was out of battery and had battery acid crusted at the bottom, *crap crap crap.* Wait, there. He had a backup battery for his phone and, for some reason, it had a little flashlight at the far side of it. He snatched it up and raced back into the bathroom.

Click. Light on. With one hand he lifted his lip and with the other, he held the backup battery and pointed its blue light into his mouth.

The gap was jarring. He looked like he'd been in a fight.

Craning his neck back further, he tried to see the tooth that was coming in—

He froze.

That's—

That's not a tooth.

His tongue tickled the edge of something that was long and dark, with a tapered sharp end. Marco snapped his mouth shut. He didn't want to believe. Couldn't believe. *This is a nightmare. I'm having a dream. I'm losing my mind, not my teeth.* Somehow that was preferable, that it was his mind that was gone, and not that tooth. A tooth gone. A tooth being replaced with—

He opened his mouth again—

An apple seed.

Marco vomited.

66

SCION

MEG WAS NOT GETTING BETTER.

This wasn't like before, Emily realized. She didn't seem healthier. Sure didn't seem happier. Meg looked leaner, meaner, her bones like hard corners under tight, graying skin. Her eyes, wide, rarely blinking. Hair snarled into a wild thicket.

And she watched Emily from the tub with a predator's gaze.

"I have food," Emily said. A bowl of instant ramen, chicken flavor.

"Don't need it," Meg said, chin low, eyes up. Like she was ready to pounce—even though she couldn't, not the way she remained bound. Her strength seemed to have waned. She didn't even pull at her bonds anymore.

John said it was torture, that they were torturing her, that he couldn't abide this anymore—but Emily told him, *Just look at her.* Meg hadn't eaten in the week they kept her here. Hadn't slept. She'd certainly diminished, but was still hissing and screaming and thrashing about at night. At no point did she adopt a demure attitude, nor did she fall into despair. And though she rubbed her wrists raw, they were never bloody, no matter how violently she writhed about. John feared they were hurting her, but Emily said no, she was still sharp as a knife. "We untie her now, who knows what she'll do to us."

She told John, *It feels like an exorcism.*

As if they were trying to wait out whatever was in her, till it emerged starving and mad, a tapeworm desperate for food.

EMILY ENTERED THE BATHROOM, SAT DOWN ON THE TOILET SEAT.

"Are you going to use it?" Meg jeered. "I'm tired of watching you both expel your body's garbage in here."

"Yeah, I know. You've told us already. And reminded us you don't have that problem."

"We're just better than you in all the ways that matter." Meg regarded her warily. "I even smell better than you. Of course, you're using a whore's bath to clean yourselves every day instead of using the shower. If only the tub weren't occupied with your poor, tortured, kidnapped victim." She suddenly affected a terror-struck face, crying out. "*Please. No. I just want to be free. I'm going to die in here, Emily. Why are you doing this? When did you become this monster?*"

And even though Emily knew it was a lie, even though she could hear the mockery ladled over the words, it still stuck a knife in her side. Because it wasn't wrong. They brought Meg here hoping to get her clean— but she wasn't getting clean. It was whittling her down, but not to splinters: a stick, cut into a spear.

All to what end? And where did they go from here?

"Stop," Emily said in a small voice. "Nobody believes you."

Meg chuckled. "It bothers you, though. And I like that. I like you bothered, Emily. I like you off your game. Desperate and reeling. If you weren't so *unclean* right now, I'd say you should lift your skirt, show me your wetness, and come visit me in the tub—I bet my tongue still knows how to dance, how to slither deep—"

"I want to ask you something."

Pouting, Meg said, "Fine."

"Did you want to be an artist? When you were a kid."

A flinch. "What?"

"I found your art. Alongside a creepy mask. Self-portraits, and . . . they were really good. You could've been an artist. If you wanted to be."

Meg paused. Considered this, almost as if it was a trap. She said, finally, "My mother always told me, art wasn't going to pay the bills. Art wasn't anything to her or my father. So I put that aspiration inside a drawer inside my head and I locked it like I locked that file cabinet you apparently opened. You little betrayer. Opening my drawers. Killing my *tree*. I still hate you for that, you know. For cutting up my little sapling. I hope it comes back. I hope it grows an apple I can force you to eat."

"You could still be an artist, if you want to."

"I know." Meg showed her teeth in a grin. "The apple lets me do anything I want. It tells me I can be what I want to be. It's a marvel you hate it so much."

"What is it? What *is* the apple?"

"An apple is a fruit, dear Emily, of *Malus domestica,* the common apple tree, with thousands of cultivars—"

"No. You know that's not what I'm asking. This one is different and you know it is, because you adore it, you need it, and it's changed you. So what is it, really? A parasite? A demon? Some . . . invasive species from beyond space and time?"

Meg smiled. "You really want to know?"

"I really do."

"It is special. I do adore it. It's unlike anything I've ever tasted— unlike even you." Meg winked. "But you ask if it's something unnatural or something evil and to that I say it is just an apple, but the taste of it, the glorious *taste* of it, tells me that I'm special, too. I'm special just like the apple. When I take a bite of it I taste all that went into it—I can taste the winter chill that cracks the seeds, the warming sun that feeds the leaves, I can taste the rich coppery loam of the earth, I can taste the blood that has soaked that dirt, the blood of a dead mouse, the blood of a dead fawn, the blood of a colonist whose throat was slit by a British bayonet, the blood of a child shot dead by another child who found a gun in his father's drawer, the blood of a dead baby that fell free from the mother's womb as she staggered out into a field having taken a tea of bitter and vengeful herbs—I taste life and I taste death and I taste potential, *American* potential, I taste the truly *exceptional*—"

As Meg spoke, her eyes closed and her head swayed back and forth, like she was imagining it, caught in some rapturous moment.

But then, she stopped suddenly.

Her eyes wrenched open.

Her chin lifted, and her chest rose and fell in fast, but shallow bursts. It was like her face was held firm by invisible hands.

Meg's mouth opened as if she were trying to say more—

But couldn't.

"Meg?" Emily asked in a rising panic.

"*Hkkkk.*"

She's choking.

But on what?

Emily eased closer—but not too close. Just in case.

"Meg, what is it?"

"*Hyyyyrrrrkkkk—*"

Meg suddenly lurched forward. The rope tugged hard against the shower bar—*wham*. It was in no danger of pulling out, as it was bolted deep into the wall, and Meg had been trying to yank it out for the last week to no avail. But even still, the wall shuddered with the force of her movement. She started gagging like she was about to throw up. Dry-heaving. "*Gaaaak. Hnnnngh. Hhhggkk.*"

"John!" Emily called. Fear paralyzed her. She didn't want Meg to hurt herself. But she didn't want to get too close, either. Emily stood up but stayed moored to the middle of the bathroom, uncertain what to do next.

Meg's mouth hung open. Her tongue thrust out—a grayish pink slug dying on the step of her lower lip. Her skin started to turn red, mouth blue.

Jesus, she's dying—

It was as if a cork popped. Whatever it was inside her suddenly wrenched free and she gagged, her throat bulging as she coughed something up and out—

A black, knotty shape—hard but slick with bubbled mucus—tumbled into the bottom of the tub. Meg gasped for air and sat there, catching her breath.

Emily looked at what had come out of her.

It was a small knob of something woody, thin filament-like roots wound around it. Bits of soft, rich dirt lay nearby, trapped in the spreading mucus, turning to mud. Flecks of blood dotted the white porcelain around it.

"Meg—"

The thing in the tub twitched. It crackled as it did.

What the fuck is that?

It popped again, rolling itself like a six-sided die.

Emily realized:

This is what was in Meg.

And now it's out.

Meg sat there, still heaving, gasping for breath, sweat-soaked hair plastered to her brow—the goo-slick root ball again took another hop, this time toward Meg As it tumbled, its roots began to unwind and unfurl, like invisible fingers untangling a hairball, and it used this to gain motion, end over end—

"Jesus Christ," Emily said, grabbing the bowl of ramen she brought in, hastily dumping it in the sink, and then pouncing into the tub and trapping the thing under the overturned bowl. Emily put both hands on it to hold the bowl firmly in place. She could feel the *ticks* and *taps* as it bounced against the ceramic. A beetle in a jar trying to get free.

"Meg," she said, breathless. "Meg, are you all right? Are you okay now?"

Dazed, Meg lifted her face. Spit swung from her chin like an oozing hammock. Her eyes lost and regained focus a few times before she looked down and saw Emily and the bowl.

"You . . . trapped it," Meg said, her voice hoarse.

"You're safe now. It's okay." She craned her head back and called again for John. "John! *John!*" Where the hell was he?

"The orchard sent me a gift and you *trapped* it."

"Yeah. I said I—"

Meg launched her head forward and slammed it into Emily's. It was like getting hit by a wrecking ball right above the bridge of her nose. Everything was one big lightning strike of white behind her eyes and she toppled backward, her bell rung, the back of her head hitting the edge of the tub—

Oh god she didn't like that I trapped it—

She wants it free—

Her ears rang, and Emily drunkenly lifted herself up, the world split in two halves that were far too slow to merge back together, and when they finally did, when she could see once more, what her eyes showed her was Meg sitting there, still bound, cackling and weeping with such laughter as the crawling, tumbling spider of root-and-twig found the drain, and skittered down into it.

67

THE DARKNESS AND THE LIGHT

JOHN NEEDED TO GET AWAY FROM THE SOUNDS IN THE CABIN, SO HE took a walk in the old Quaker cemetery—Slate Hill—across the street. While there, he paced between the modest graves of long-dead Quakers and talked to Cherie. Small talk. How was her dog, her cousin, so forth, but then she said, "You already asked me about the dog," and he realized he'd repeated himself.

"What's wrong? You're distracted."

"Sorry. I am. Quakers are pacifists, right? So how do we fight evil?"

"Why are you asking me about evil again, John? What is it that you're worried about? This seems to be a thorn in your paw."

He hesitated. "I am confronted by something that I believe is evil."

"You were a sniper for the Army."

"Okay . . ."

"Sorry, I realize that's blunt. But it's true, yes?"

"Yes. I was a sniper."

"Was that evil?"

Without hesitation, he answered yes.

"It was," he said. "I took lives. Not because I knew they needed to be taken but because I was told they needed to be taken. Maybe they would've taken lives themselves or maybe not. I don't even know who they were, half the time. I pointed the gun, I looked through the scope, I checked the wind, I fired. And I killed. Fifty-seven confirmed kills." He felt his hands shaking. "Fifty-seven *people*. Human beings. Mostly men. One woman. One teen boy, no other children."

"So that act was evil."

"I believe it was."

"And are you evil for having committed the act?"

"I—" This was one of the questions that literally kept him up some nights. A question chasing him like a pack of wolves. "I suspect I must be."

"And yet, evil men don't usually worry about whether or not they're evil, or what to do about evil. They just . . . be evil. So perhaps what you did was evil. You worked for the military-industrial complex as a state-sanctioned killer. That's not good and I won't say that it is. But Quakers tend to recognize nuance here, John, in that we are rarely one thing or the other. We are not all good or all bad. We're a mix of those things, and all we can try to do is to banish the darkness inside us with the light of justice. It's clichéd, but sometimes we need the darkness to see the light. Some understand that darkness as a natural process. One of your beloved apple trees begins its life deep down in the darkness of the dirt, doesn't it? And it has to rise up out of that darkness to reach the light and bring us its sweetness."

"But what if something truly evil grows down there?"

"I don't know, John. For me, the light is always the answer, and that's vague, I know, but it's meant to be. Because the light comes in a lot of forms."

Like fire, he thought.

"Where is this coming from?" she asked him. "What are you facing?"

"I don't exactly know." He didn't know how much to tell her. If any of it at all. What they were facing didn't seem possible. She'd think him deranged. "But I think I have to help banish this darkness."

"John, you're not thinking of doing something rash, are you? Are you okay? Are you safe? All this business with your friend's death and the mystery around it—you moving down there into that cabin. I worry about you."

"I'm okay, Cherie. I just want to do the right thing."

"If I know you, you will. But be careful. Keep on the path."

"I will. Thanks, Cherie."

At that, he hung up and said goodbye to the graves, then walked back down to cross the street. The day was warming up already. A little white butterfly flitted about. Squirrels chased each other across the asphalt as he crossed. He pondered the world around him, and if what they were facing was a part of it or separate from it. Was the darkness natural and necessary, or was it invasive? And in the end, did it matter? Was it still his job to bring the light? He suspected it was. He owed Walt that. He owed it, too, to the people he'd shot. And maybe he owed it to—

Emily.

Whose voice he heard—a scream, a panic. Calling his name.

John broke into a run.

HE LISTENED AS SHE TOLD HIM EVERYTHING, HOLDING A BAG OF frozen vegetables to her face. A few crumpled-up paper towel boulders sat on the edge of the cabin's porch railing, their tops red with blood from her nose. Inside, Meg continued cackling—a cascade of mad laughter that chewed past John's eardrums and into his brain, boring into him like termites.

"You need to go," John told her.

"What?" Emily said, pulling the bag of veggies from between her eyes. The top of her nose was already darkening with a sickly bruise, and was swelling.

"This is too much. You're already too far into this and I'm sorry."

"You talk like this is your fault."

He shrugged. "Maybe it is. We don't know what ripples we make when we commit acts in this world. Clap your hands here, an earthquake happens there."

"You're talking nonsense."

"Maybe." John sighed. "I just mean, I came here to find out what happened to Walt, and this is where it took me, and I got you wrapped up in it. You should go and get safe somewhere, Emily. You've already been hurt so much. I'll give you some money. You can go to the city—or you can go to my place in Bethlehem. I'll keep Meg here while I go kill the orchard, then I'll let her go. After that, whatever happens, happens, but you'll be safe elsewhere."

"No," she said, shaking the bag of veggie mix at him. "We're not doing this. You're not jumping on a grenade. I found Walt. It's my wife in that bathroom. I don't know what that was that came out of her, but it was fucked up. It wasn't natural. It was something ugly and impossible. And I—I want to be involved in this. From start to finish. Whatever the finish is. I want to be a part of something good. I want to help stop whatever this is. Okay?"

John leaned against one of the posts holding up the porch.

Finally, he nodded. "Okay. If you're sure."

"Sure as anything."

"Then I think we need to do this tonight."

"Tonight," she said, "we burn the orchard."

68

SUMMONINGS

BY THE TIME HE WAS A MILE DOWN THE ROAD ON HIS BIKE, MARCO had lost three more teeth. Each felt soft and loose behind the urgent probing of his tongue, and they popped free with little fanfare—clumsily, he spit them into his hand, trying not to tank his bike in a pothole, before shoving them in his pocket. His tongue found other sharp seeds, apple seeds, poking through the puckered holes in his gums. Marco screamed as his feet pumped the pedals faster, faster.

HIS PARENTS DIDN'T EVEN SEEM TO BE UPSET. HIS MIND RETURNED to that again and again. Marco had stumbled downstairs, weeping, holding the first tooth in his palm and already feeling the second one start to wiggle—and his parents looked upon him not with horror, but with a crazy fucked-up kind of pride. His mother nodded, tears in her eyes, and she smiled. *She smiled.* His father said, "It's okay. Go." Because they already knew where Marco was headed. They knew and they didn't care what was happening to him. Or what had already happened.

THE BIKE SKIDDED OUT FROM UNDERNEATH HIM AS HE KICKED IT away and broke into a run down Dan Paxson's driveway, not toward the house but toward where he knew the man would be—the orchard. As he ran, another tooth, a molar in the back, dropped onto the soft meat of his tongue and reflexively, he swallowed it.

Marco bolted down the gravel path, then off it, past the cider house, toward the thicket, toward the trees in the clearing.

He could *feel* Dan out there. Even before he saw him, or heard him, or *smelled* the crisp apple scent of him, he could sense Dan's presence.

And then, there he stood. Amid the apple trees.

The seven original trees had fully leafed out, and already had small red apples growing on their branches—not hanging heavy, not yet, but they would be soon enough. But these trees were not alone. The thicket all around was peppered with tall, reedy saplings, each with an apple of its own, hanging like the ornaments on a sad, strange Christmas tree.

Dan turned, smiling, and by stepping forward, he revealed a body on the ground behind him. It was Claude Lambert. Saplings grew up and out of him, each also carrying their own new apples. His skin stretched around them. He was alive. Somehow. The old man moaned and writhed against the trees that grew through his flesh, and Marco couldn't tell if the moans were sounds of pain—or pleasure. Something that wasn't quite blood—it was too thick, too brown—slicked the little trees as Claude struggled in their grasp.

"I knew you'd come," Dan said warmly. "I'm glad to see you, Marco."

"What is happening to me. Mister P?" Marco cried out, and even as he did so, another tooth fell out of its place and rolled off his lower lip onto the ground. He dropped to his knees, pawing through the dewy grass trying to find it. He looked up and bleated: "Tell me! *Tell me.*"

"You're changing, Marco, that's all it is."

His voice sounded so close, yet so far away. Everywhere and nowhere.

As Dan orbited Marco, something else was moving around them, too. Hunched over, moving through the underbrush. Through thorn and sapling.

A strange shape. Scuttling.

"I don't *want* to change," Marco said, already his words sounding different as they slid past a mouth of

(*appleseeds*)

failing, falling teeth. He spoke like he'd just gotten braces.

Words, wet and whistling.

"It's okay," Dan said, and when he said it, it almost made sense. Like it *was* okay now. Like this was how it was supposed to be. How it *had* to be.

Claude Lambert's perforated body stiffened, and a breathy moan leaked from him like air from a blown tire. A small voice threaded through that escaping sound, again something that might have been a cry of misery, or a cry of release. The saplings that shot through his body shuddered, the leaves hissing in a susurrus, *tch-tch-tch-tch*.

Marco's hand found the tooth, just as another fell out.

I'm falling apart.

Literally falling apart.

Oh god oh god oh god.

And he thought then of Calla. What she would think of him. What this would do to her. He knew then that he loved her. And he was sorry for whatever he'd put her through—and may put her through still. Because all this, he realized, wasn't over, not at all. Even as Dan spoke to him, the man's voice winding in his ear like a climbing vine, he felt his whole body react. His gums itched suddenly. His tongue found the appleseeds poking through the puffy meat, and worse, found more of them there—seeds behind seeds, like teeth behind teeth, like shark teeth, their sharp little thumbtack tips poking through the roof of his mouth. All his skin itched, too, and when he looked at the back of his left hand, he saw a patch of his skin had toughened, turned waxen and shiny, growing blister-red and thick.

Something continued to roam the thicket around them. Sticks breaking. Leaves hushing and shushing.

Scuttle, scuttle.

"You're not falling apart," Dan said to Marco, echoing the thought running through his mind. "You're transforming into something better. Something more useful. I had thought, falsely I admit, that you were going to be my second, that you would be here and help me run this place, but things have changed, Marco. You ran away. It hurt me deeply that you fled. I hate to brag, you missed a helluva sermon. But I still care for you, as you know. I still want you healthy. And I still want you to work for me."

"Please," Marco said, spit bubbling from his lips. Spit that tasted like blood and apple juice. Sweet and bitter. Copper-slick tang and tart sugars. "No."

"Here, look, you're not alone."

Dan held a hand up.

The thing from the thicket slipped free from the briar's tangle.

It hurried forward, bent over, its vertebrae forming a bony ridge beneath a foul T-shirt soaked in mud and blood—its neck was long, too long, and its jaw hung uneven from its misshapen skull, like a swing on a swing set with one rope longer than the other. From a ragged hole in shirt and skin front and back grew a fierce tangle of branches, like skeletal fingers reaching out of the grave. As the shape loped, Marco could see other details—patches of reddish, shining skin overtaking spots on its face, neck, and arms, skin like the skin of an apple, skin like what was growing on Marco, and this person, this *thing*, it had no human teeth, just rows and rows of gleaming black appleseeds shining black ticklike seeds forming fences upon fences, spiraling into the back of the mouth, a pale-green tongue licking at them, as if to savor their taste.

"Get it away from me!" Marco screamed, falling backward onto his ass and pushing himself backward with kicking feet. He swiped at the air with his hands.

As if in response, Claude Lambert moaned, writhing against the spearlike saplings that pushed through him—his form rising up and down upon them in a rhythmic motion. Rust-colored fluid slipped from his lips to his chin. The human-thing that came from the thicket bounded over to him and began scooping up the liquid with fat fingers, pushing the stuff messily into its broken mouth.

It made hungry, hungry noises.

"No, shh, no," Dan said, smiling and slowly walking forward. "Don't you see, Marco? Prentiss here has been blessed by the orchard, through me. He is an embodiment of it, as true a creature of the apple as any. He's pure in a way that even I'm not, and in that purity he serves me, and through me he serves the orchard as its guardian. It's a beautiful thing. This is the relationship we have to the land, to what grows from it. The orchard gives and Prentiss gives back. Just as you will give back. I don't want you to think of it as becoming lesser, but becoming greater— a being in service to something truly sublime."

Marco's words were a gush, barely comprehensible, but he said them again and again, like a mantra: "You're insane, you're insane, you're insane."

"Not insane. Just finally grabbing hold of the power I have been denied for so long."

The thing called Prentiss fed on the fluids leaking out of the old man, singing and giggling as it ate and drank.

Dan continued to walk forward as Marco backpedaled.

Marco wept.

Calla's father outpaced him handily, walking forward with long and easy strides, and in moments Dan stood over Marco, shushing him, *shhh, shhhh.* He placed a hand on Marco's warm brow—the hand was cool, the skin of his palm soft like unworked dough, and Marco instantly felt calmer.

"Marco," Dan said, his voice echoing all around and also inside Marco's head—*Marco, Marco, MARCO, MARCO, maaaarco-o-o-o*—and as it did, it was like a rope encircling him, a lasso of sound and words, a leash on his neck tugging him slowly to the ground and holding him fast to the damp grass. "Marco, before we go any further, there's something I need to know."

"Anything." It came out wrong, ruined, *ennythinnnh.*

"I need to know where my daughter is."

A pause.

"No."

That word. A moment of sharp and sudden defiance. Unexpected. Because Marco wanted above all else to give up and give in—it felt *good* to be here, it felt *right* to be in this place with this man standing in front of him. But Calla—Calla was a bright and shining light. A lantern hung in a dark forest. He had to get back to her. Had to help her. She was hiding and he could help her stay hidden, he told himself, but then Dan clucked his tongue in fatherly disappointment. And pressed his fingers hard into Marco's scalp—

Everything shifted suddenly inside Marco. It was as if something, a colony of choking vines and tightening worms, were coiling around his bones. It felt like his organs were being pushed aside, like his bones were hollow logs filled with things scuttling about inside, and whatever it was pushed up his throat and into his mouth and into his brain and it began to *squeeze.* And all he felt was white-hot pain and all he tasted was sweetness so sweet, the sweetness of overripe fruit, the sweetness of bursting apples rotting in the sun while lying in rough grass, the sweetness of roadkill. These things, these tendrils, he knew they were both worm and root, but more so, they were *searching* fingers, they were *things-that-seek,* and they found what they were looking for—the answers that Marco had, the only answers he had. They seized upon them and pulled them out of his brain and pushed them into his throat and urged them out upon his tongue:

"I don't know where she is but I know who knows, Esther knows, her friend Esther, Esther dropped her off somewhere, oh god, please stop."

And Dan did stop.

He moved his hand away from Marco's brow. And it was like what Marco imagined it felt like to have breathing tubes withdrawn from your nose and throat—the release of something that slid out of you, taking some of who you were with it. He collapsed into the damp grass, panting. Marco saw a strip on the underside of his right arm—a strip of raw, red appleskin. Tough and smooth. It hadn't been there before, had it? He was changing so fast now.

He whispered small apologies to Calla, softly babbled again and again, before darkness fell and he sank down deep into the earth, where the dirt took him.

SCUTTLE, *SCUTTLE.*

Marco woke in the orchard. Apple scent perfumed the air. Afternoon had started to give way to evening, the sun sinking beyond the thicket.

The thing called Prentiss hunkered down nearby.

Dan was nowhere to be found.

Marco sat up—he was not in the earth, but rather, sitting upon it.

Prentiss was sucking on something, like a hard candy. His eyes, yellow with liversick, stared out from the hollow sockets of his raw, red, shining face—he showed his foamy green tongue, and as the foam crackled and dissolved, Marco saw what he'd been sucking on: a tooth. *One of my teeth,* he thought. Anxiety spiked in his chest, but the apple scent calmed him.

"You're like me now," Prentiss whispered, juggling the tooth on his tongue.

"I'm nothing like you."

"Whimper, whimper, little baby. You are. You are. You don't *think* you are but you'll get it soon enough. How many teeth are left in your head?"

Marco checked with tongue-and-finger. Only five teeth left. He stifled a cry. The apple scent crawled up his nose.

"Yeah, not many," Prentiss said, then opened his mouth to show off
rows and rows of black appleseeds. He clicked them together and back
and forth like the tines of two black combs brushing together. "Mine are
all gone. See? And now this one of yours is gone, too." He showed off
Marco's tooth again and swallowed it back like a pill. Gulp.

"Leave me alone."

Prentiss waggled his fingers—they were fat, had no fingernails. Small
branch-tips, wooden and crooked and sharp, pushed through the tips of
those raw, red fingers. "Got these. You'll get them, too, I bet. Skin already
turning, huh," he said, looking over Marco with a leering gaze. "That's
good. That's real good. Everything is changing now. You and me. These
people. This country. Everyone. Dan has seen to that. Something's out of
its cage. Those who don't wanna eat the apple, they'll pay for that choice,
won't they? And the rest of us will laugh at them and hold them down
and *stick them* with broken branches and bite them with our *new teeth*
and—" Prentiss shuddered, and laughed a little, almost like he was embarrassed. "Oh hey. You hungry? Come here, come on."

Prentiss dropped to all fours and loped over to the body of Claude
Lambert, whose eyes wrenched wide open as the monster bent over the
old man and licked at his chin again and again, like Prentiss was a bee at
a closed flower trying to get the petals to open up. Not satisfied, Prentiss
snarled before thrusting his sharp branch-tipped fingers into the sagging
meat of the man's thigh and Claude made a small, pained cry—before
thick dark syrup oozed out from his mouth. "Come on. Come on, kid.
Look, look, it's happening—"

But Marco wouldn't move. He was rooted to the spot. Closed his
eyes. Even as the apple scent grew stronger and stronger, filling his head
with warmth and comfort and a strange buzzing noise. Prentiss made a
frustrated grunt and scooped up a pile of blood syrup before gamboling
back over to Marco and pressing his greasy, messy fingers into Marco's
mouth—

Marco tried to get away, but Prentiss held the back of his head. The
urgent fingers pushed the rust-red fluid past Marco's lips and his first

instinct was to use his new teeth to *bite, bite, bite,* to take off Prentiss's foul fingers at the knuckles.

But then the taste of the sap hit his tongue. It filled his mouth with a sourness, a rancidity, and then after that, unending sweetness. Waves of it crawling down his throat, into his stomach. He shut his eyes and submitted to the fingers feeding him more of it, but before he knew what his own body was doing, Marco was shoving the other man-thing aside and scurrying over to Lambert's mouth. Marco drank from what was pouring out, and he did so greedily and with great joy.

EVENING. THE SUN BLEEDING ON THE HORIZON.

A gagging sound woke Marco. He looked up, found Prentiss had gone, but Dan had returned. Someone else was here, too. A woman. She looked like that actress—the one from the Iron Man movies. Iron Man's girlfriend. But older.

Her head was bent forward. Her mouth, open. It was her gagging, and she did so over Dan's cupped hands. The woman made a wet sound and something bulged up out of her throat and pushed out of her mouth—like a fat spider, but harder, more rigid. Dark threads unfurled from it as it fell into Dan's hands.

It flailed and hopped around his palms.

Dan ate it.

Held it over his open mouth, dropped it in. It wriggled its way down his esophagus, his throat swelling with the shape of it as it passed.

He smiled.

"Do you see?" the woman asked. "Do you see where she is?"

"I do," he said. "Wonderful, thank you, Noreen. You're a valuable member of our community. And a good mother."

"I am. Yes. I am." She smiled big, as if she had been blessed. Stammering, she added, "I thought it best to bring it to you first—but I want to get her, Dan. I want to help her. I need to. We don't know what kind of danger she's in from these *extremists*—"

"We will."

"When?" she asked, desperate.

"Now." At that, he whistled. "Prentiss. Come." The thicket shook, and the Prentiss-thing crawled free, covered in leaves and twigs. He grinned, worms crawling over his teeth before he sucked them in, deep. Marco's stomach turned—not with disgust but, to his own surprise, with hunger. "And you."

Dan pointed to him.

"Me?" Marco asked. He heard the desperation in his own voice. *I want him to need me. I want him to love me.* Marco knew how awful that was. How *wrong.* But it's what he wanted. More than anything, he wanted to be *necessary.*

"Are you ready?"

"I am."

"Good. Then you two, get in the truck. In the back. Noreen, let's take a ride. We need to find Meg before it's too late."

69

FINDING OUT

NIGHT FELL, AND VIOLENCE WEIGHED HEAVILY ON JOHN'S MIND.

It always did, of course—he had committed it many times, and was the victim of it many times. Some theorized that violence and trauma marked you in ways that went deeper than the wounds suffered and the wounds given. That it changed you deep down inside, that it altered brain cells, even your DNA. Violence was like a parasite, John knew. It sat within you, curled up like a worm in the meat. Waiting to lay its eggs, its brood born.

As they loaded the Jeep up with supplies his ghillie suit, two gas cans full of gasoline, a machete, the tranquilizer pistol, a small case of tranq darts—he ruminated on this and how to square it with what they were about to do tonight.

He looked over at Emily, who was sheathing the machete.

"I became a Quaker because they, above most others, understood that violence always made more violence. You cannot do good by doing evil."

"Okay," she said, giving him a puzzled look.

He sighed. "I say this only because we have to be careful tonight. I don't want to bring harm to anybody. It's bad enough what we're doing to Meg."

"Meg is—she's fine."

"She's not fine, not at all. But that isn't our fault."

"Which is why we're going to the orchard," she said.

"Yes," he said, resigned. He knew that burning down an orchard was itself an act of violence—but not one against people. Done at night it might keep others safe. And the trees—well, John could not abide violence against trees, especially apple trees, but there was no denying that something evil was growing there.

"You doing okay, John?" she asked.

But he did not answer, because he saw headlights coming down the road.

And turning in to the long driveway that led to the cabin behind them.

"Back into the cabin," he said, snatching up the tranquilizer pistol. *"Back into the cabin*—go!"

Emily cursed under her breath and the two of them bolted for the cabin, only fifty feet away, threw themselves through the front door, and slammed it shut. John raced around, turning off all the lights as three vehicles pulled in behind his Jeep—and, in turn, blocking the Jeep from making an easy exit.

Two of the cars lit up red and blue. Police cars. Lights strobing over the cabin and the forest.

From the bathroom, Meg called out:

"They're *heeeeeere,*" she said, dissolving into mad laughter, laughter so broken it sounded like weeping.

"The fuck are we going to do?" Emily asked, crouching by the front window next to John.

John surveyed their options, which were few. They could go out the front, which would lead to certain confrontation, requiring them to surrender or something worse. Going out the back was best. Out behind the cabin was just a short expanse of mowed meadow. Beyond that, a tract of forest before you hit the canal path. From there, they had an easy path north or south.

He was about to say as much, when spotlights came on outside. One from each police car, pointing left and right, converging on a single person:

Dan Paxson.

His face clad in a strange mask.

"Hello in there," he called out, his voice genial, his arms spread wide. "I come looking for a friend. One who I am assured is in there with you. Meg Price. Wife of Emily Bergmann—who, I believe, is in there too, right? Hello, Emily. Been a while. And someone else, I believe. Someone who I met briefly already. John. John Compass. I hope I have that right. Listen, I'm willing to chalk whatever all this is up to a simple misunderstanding, long as I get my friend back. So, why don't you come on out, bring her with you, and we can be on our way."

Emily looked to John. "They're not serious, right? Gotta be a trap."

He nodded. It was. It had to be. "One doesn't wear a mask like that with the intent of just sitting and talking it out." The man looked like some kind of monster, some killer out of a horror movie. Then: movement. "Look!"

Just past the spotlights, behind Dan, two shapes scattered from the truck. One went one direction, and the other went the opposite way. Hunched over, loping on all fours.

"The hell?" Emily asked.

"I don't know," John said, but fear filled him like cold water. "We need to go and we need to go now. Out back. I'll lead the way. You follow behind. We hit the tree line, then the canal, then if it's clear, we head north from there."

Emily nodded. "What about Meg? What about the orchard?"

"Emily, they're going to take Meg. And I fear we are not going to the orchard tonight." He put a steadying hand on her arm. "This may be too big for us."

Another nod, this one, hesitant, sad.

Outside, Dan broadcast again: "I know you're in there. Your vehicle is out here. I don't want to have to come in there. If we have to come in there, it's going to get messy. So, let's keep it clean and aboveboard, and just come on out. We don't have to be enemies."

Then, someone else stepped out behind Dan—a woman.

John recognized her. By the look of it, so did Emily.

"I'm Noreen, Meg's mother. I just want my daughter back. I want my daughter safe. I know she's in there. In that tub. Tied up like an animal."

How do they know that? John wondered.

No time to figure that out now.

"Let's go," John said.

They headed to the back door—

But Emily stopped by the bathroom door.

He watched as she looked in and said to her wife, out of sight:

"Meg, I'm sorry I didn't help you. I wanted to."

Meg's voice answered, singsongy—

"It's okay, Em! *I'll make you eat the apple yet, my dear wife.*"

"Come on," John said, gently pulling at her elbow.

And out the back door they went.

SHE STOOD LOOKING AT MEG SITTING IN THE TUB, HER CHEEK-bones sharp, eyes set deep, skin sallow. And grinning like the cat that got the canary. *I'll make you eat the apple yet, my dear wife.*

Uttered with such glee. A proclamation and a threat.

Emily wanted to die. She had failed Meg.

She had failed herself.

She had failed everything.

And now they were running away. Because what choice did they have?

Out into the late-spring night they went—John darting ahead. They left the cabin behind, and somewhere beyond that, Dan Paxson bellowed again: "I guess we're going to have to come in after you . . ."

Which meant they wouldn't be far behind. Suddenly her heels itched with urgency—like she could feel something pursuing her in the dark.

Ahead, John moved into the tree line, and Emily followed after, keeping low.

Then, only ten feet into the trees, John halted suddenly, taking a step back—Emily nearly ran into him.

Someone stood ahead of them, between two oaks. Tall, lean, athletic. Moonlight shining on patches of strange, blood-red flesh. Like cancer keloids of oxblood leather.

"John," she said in a low voice.

"Y-y-y—" the person ahead of them stammered. "You n—need to—*you*—"

John took another step back, moving himself in front of Emily. The person stepped forward, and now she could see shining black teeth—

"Need to *runnnnn,*" the kid said, that last word drawn out, as if it was a difficult word to utter.

Then he looked sharply to his left—

Something crashed through the brush and into John. Hard enough to knock him down. *An animal,* Emily thought—it moved like one, for sure. She cried out—kicking at whatever it was that thrashed about atop of her friend—

John growled in pain behind clamped teeth—

Emily kicked out *hard* this time, connecting with something that could've been its head—and as it staggered back, hissing, John shoved it. It tumbled backward, and Emily saw a wet, greasy mouth and sickly yellow eyes—

As the thing fell, John rose, the tranq pistol in his hand—

Piff.

A dart stuck in the thing's cheek.

And the half-man thing fell to the ground.

That's when Emily saw the blood.

IT'S NOT HUMAN. THAT THOUGHT BOUNCED AROUND JOHN'S HEAD like a ricocheting bullet, *It's not human, not human, not human,* but as he stood up, he looked at the thing on the ground—

It *was* human.

Wasn't it?

Yellow eyes rotated in swollen sockets, and those were not human teeth, and the skin was thick with patches and striations of bulging, shining red . . .

"John—you're bleeding."

Emily. Her words jarred him from his trance of staring at the human-shaped thing at his feet. He looked briefly for the other person who had been standing nearby—a young man, he thought—but whoever it was, was gone.

His shirt was torn at the shoulder. Blood welled up, oozed down the length of his arm, to his elbow and beyond. The pain came, now. Not a normal pain, but a deep itching burn, crawling through him like it was working its way to the bone.

What had happened?

Whatever that thing was—

It had bitten him.

No time to worry about that now.

"Come on," he said.

"But you're hurt—"

"I'm fine," he assured her. "*We have to go.*"

Emily gave a curt nod, and once again they resumed their escape through the woods. Somewhere ahead, the canal awaited. He only hoped they made it.

70

LINGERING NIGHTMARES

To be chased once is to be chased forever, Emily feared—because though they heard no sounds and caught no signs of their pursuers, the act of being pursued stayed with her. She felt the shadows behind them, felt them pushing at the middle of her back like the nose of a starving beast. She felt harried, like prey. And she wondered if that feeling would ever go away.

They fled through the trees and, sure enough, reached the towpath that traveled up and down the Delaware River canal the length of the entire county. They kept going, heading north until they sighted an old white water tower and the Lutheran church beyond it. Canal Rock Road crossed here, and it would take them off the path if they wanted, to Main Street in New Yardley.

It was here they stopped to reassess.

Emily, panting, took her phone and flicked on the flashlight, shining it across John's wounds. The shirt, torn. The skin, ragged. As if . . .

"You were bitten," Emily said.

"Yes, I think so."

Red blood

(*like a Ruby Slipper apple*)

gleamed.

"The hell was all that, John?"

"I don't know."

"That . . . thing. Both of them. There were two. They didn't look all the way human. You saw that, right? I'm not crazy."

"At this point we can stop asking that question because we are most certainly not the crazy ones." He sighed. "It's reality that has lost its damn mind."

"One of those . . . things warned us."

"Or distracted us."

"Maybe." She chewed a lip. "That was fucked up. How did they know we were there? How did Noreen know Meg was there, tied up in the bathroom?"

"I don't know."

"And—and that was Dan Paxson in that mask. What was that mask, John? What is fucking happening? I already thought everything was really fucked up but I don't think we knew, I don't think we *really* knew, just how fucked up it is."

"You're right. This is much worse and much stranger and it is far larger than we can handle." At that, John winced. He was trying not to show his pain, Emily suspected. But he wasn't doing a good job of hiding it—

Which meant it was pretty bad.

"We need to get somewhere safe so we can clean your wound."

"I'm all right."

"You were bitten. You get bit by a cat, you need antibiotics—you get bit by a half-human thing like that, you probably need a flamethrower."

Grunting, he said, "Either way, you're right, we do need to go somewhere. We need a plan. But I'm lost. I don't know what to do." He sounded sad and desperate. John was her rock. John knew what to do. He felt like the thing you held on to in a storm so it didn't sweep you away— and if *he* was getting swept away and she was holding on to him? Emily felt sudden fear like she'd never felt before. Not just fear, but a kind of hopelessness, too. And all of it robed in raw paranoia: the certainty that no one could be trusted, that nothing was safe, that there was truly nowhere to go. Once again, the feel of a nightmare breaching the walls of its containment and slipping into reality and taking over.

"I don't know, either," she said in a small voice.

"You have your phone. Maybe . . . one of those rideshare services. I've never used one. But we can go to my place in Bethlehem—"

"If those were real police, then they will end up there, too."

He grunted and nodded. "Shit. Okay. So where?"

Emily turned off her flashlight, pulled up the Lyft app. "I worry that . . . maybe they can track me if I use that. Is that paranoid? Maybe I should just call a cab." She briefly thought of the last time she used the app—

That's when it hit her.

"Okay. I know someone who I'm pretty sure hasn't eaten any of those apples. A quote-unquote friend of mine."

Emily opened her contact list and hit the number.

71

WELL, THIS IS AWKWARD

THE PORSCHE MACAN WAS A COMPACT SUV, MORE A SEXY SEDAN than a proper sport utility vehicle. It was sleek and curvaceous, like its driver. The exterior was cherry red. The interior, the color of milk chocolate. It smelled of leather and lavender.

Four people rode inside:

Emily and John in the back.

Up front, Joanie Moreau driving, and Calla Paxson in the passenger seat.

They sat in silence as the car silently whipped down Bucks County backroads. Emily and John shared a look.

Emily leaned forward. "So, again, you're Dan Paxson's daughter?"

The girl nodded. "Yeah."

"Do you know your father is into some really hinky shit?"

"She knows," Joanie said firmly—with a hint of what might've been anger in there, Emily thought. More like she had her hackles up. Like she was defending Calla. A Mama Bear reaction, even though—as far as Emily knew, anyway—she was not actually the girl's mother.

"Why is she here?" Emily asked Joanie. "I mean, is this safe? We're trying to get away from Dan Paxson, not get closer to him. Is this a trick? If I open that glove compartment, will a bunch of apple cores tumble out?"

"I told you. She came to me for help. She knows her father is . . . different now, and she wanted a place to stay that felt safe—"

"Different," Emily said with a scoff. "That's one way to put it."

"It's fine," Calla said, though to Emily's ear it was more than a little mopey-sounding, her tone pulling an April Ludgate, vacillating somewhere between *venomously depressed* and *just slightly but also gleefully sociopathic.*

(Emily remembered being a teenage girl, and remembered hearing—and having—that tone well.)

Calla went on: "My dad isn't really my dad anymore. Okay? I don't know what he is or what happened. But I know it's the apple. Maybe it's like, a disease or just mass hysteria or fucking Satan, I honestly don't know, but I'm scared, and Joanie helped me out, and *no,* I'm not going to narc on any of you." She turned back around in a huff. "So you can stop worrying."

It occurred to Emily then—

This had to be hard for the girl.

There came a moment in every kid's life when they realized their parents were, at best, completely inadequate and unprepared, and at worst, they were narcissistic abusers who had wrapped their children in a tangled skein of trauma and anxiety like spiders securing food in a web. Calla had that, but a hundred times worse: Her father was a for-real monster in an appleskin mask. Worse, everyone in this car knew he was bad news, and she was the—well, the apple that fell from that tree. Emily leaned forward again.

"Hey, that sucks and I'm sorry."

Calla gave her a softened, sad look. "Thanks. It does suck."

"And Joanie, thanks for picking us up. You didn't have to and it means a lot. We're just . . . rattled and tired and John is—"

She was about to say, *injured,* but before she could, John lurched forward, groaning in the back seat. "It's burning," he said through clenched teeth.

Emily felt his head.

His brow felt like a red-hot skillet.

John screamed and Joanie pressed the accelerator.

72

THE VISITOR

"Got yourself in a pickle, huh," Walt said.

John woke up, a flash flood of sweat rolling off him. His shoulder throbbed like a beating heart. They were in Walt's orchard, the one out back of his house. The trees were still there, and in the middle of it all, a white leather couch on which John sat. Blood dripped off the cushions, and he tried wiping the puddle off, but whatever he pushed away just appeared again.

"I'm not really here," John said. "I'm somewhere else."

"Maybe. Probably." Walt snorted. "You always were a bit of a know-it-all pain in the ass, you know that? Always had to be right about everything."

"Always *was* right about everything, you mean."

Walt stared bullets at him.

But then he broke up laughing, and came over and hugged John, even being careful around his shoulder.

"It's good to see you," John said, "even if this isn't real."

Walt let go of the hug and chuckled. "Who said it's not real? Not really being here and not really real are two different things. I'm Walt. And I'm dead."

For a moment, when John blinked, he saw Walt with gray, dead flesh hanging on his bones, one of his eyes gone, a sunfish staring out of the socket. The sound of a river rushing roared loud in John's ears, but then Walt was Walt again, healthy and smiling. And as that happened, his shoulder began burning more—he felt the pain rise there, the pulse-throb grow in both frequency and intensity, so hard now it was like someone was punching him there, digging their fingers in, rooting around; his knees nearly buckled. But there Walt was. Holding him up.

"I need you to stay with me for a minute," Walt said. "Just stay here, stay standing, keep talking. Okay?"

John accepted the support from his friend and forced a nod as more sweat poured off him.

"John, listen," Walt said. "I forgive you and I know you forgive me, and the real story is, neither one has anything to forgive the other about except the crime of being two stubborn old sonsabitches who should've dropped their grudges a whole lot sooner than they did. I love you, buddy."

"I love you too, Walt, and I'm glad you're here with me as I—" John blinked. "Die," he said, finally, because that's what this was, wasn't it? He was dying. This was death, or the crossing over to it. Walt was here, and Walt was dead. Whatever happened to him tonight had led here, to this moment, in Walt's orchard. *Into the light, I go.* "I'm dying."

Walt laughed.

"Buddy, you aren't dying." He looked deep into John's eyes. "But you're going to feel like you are. So just hold on tight, because it's about to—"

The pain hit him like a freight train, a black iron locomotive on fire, flames kissing the night as it slammed into him, crashed through him—

Rifle going off, kicking hard into his shoulder—

Jiggle of an Iraqi's head as a bullet peeled his scalp—

Boom, as an IED pops the wheel off a Humvee ahead like it's just a toy—

Shotgun taking a bite of an apple tree—

John screamed. The pain radiated white hot, sun hot, sun bright, from his shoulder, and he craned his neck to look—and he saw the shoulder ripped open, something being pulled *out* of it, long jagged black threads like crooked lightning bolts, and he thought, *No, they're not threads, they're roots, little roots,* and those little roots tried so hard to grab hold of him, to cling to his bones and clutch the meat. They were slick with blood and bits of muscle tissue and his scream matched the pain, just an unending sound, an unending wave—

With a fast hand, Walt patted John's cheek and forced his face to turn away from the thing being pulled from his shoulder. Walt said, "Look at me. Stay with me. Look at the orchard behind me. Nice trees, good trees, happy apples. You're going to be all right. I'm with you. It's like that thing you always say, that Quaker thing. I'm holding you in the light, John. Holding you in the brightest light."

———

THE LIGHT WASHED OVER EVERYTHING. BIG, SCOURING, CLEANSING light.

It went supernova, then started to shrink, started to fade.

He heard Emily's voice. "John? You okay? Say something." He saw her now as the light washed past her, a wave of white going back out to a sea of darkness. Her cheeks were dotted with blood. Someone was putting pressure on his shoulder. He gave Emily a nod. Offered her a clumsy thumbs-up, too, though he wasn't sure he actually managed to get the thumb part of the thumbs-up up.

John passed out.

73

GROUP THERAPY, OPEN ALL NIGHT

It was two in the morning by the time Emily got cleaned up. She took a shower in one of Joanie's (many) bathrooms. Her hands still shook. John slept nearby on the couch, his shoulder wrapped in gauze, a towel underneath him just in case. He slept like the dead, in that he literally looked dead. Ashen, glossy. If it weren't for his chest rising and falling, she would've thought he had crossed over.

She walked over to the sink in the kitchen and looked down into the stainless-steel mixing bowl that sat there.

In it were bundles of tangled roots, black as night, most of them as thin as thread, or thinner. They sat in several dense clusters, each still damp with blood—blood that now pooled beneath them, too. At the apex of each root cluster was a black apple seed, broken open, birthing the roots that burst from them.

These roots had climbed through John's shoulder like his meat was dirt. They had pushed through his flesh, crawled deep, almost to the bone. Threading through muscle, winding around capillaries.

By the time they got here, John had already started to pass out—looking at the wound, seeing the black apple seeds buried in the wound nearly paralyzed Emily. And that horror only deepened once they tried to get those seeds out, and found they had already anchored themselves within him.

What would have happened if they let them go? It was an infection—of sorts. But not a natural one. Would they have ripped him apart? Climbed into his heart and stuffed it full of vine, closed his lungs with mulch and leaves? Or would the roots have corkscrewed their way to his brain—where they took him over?

"You're standing where my husband died," Joanie said.

Emily blinked. "What? Jesus. I'm—" Quickly she moved to leave the kitchen, but Joanie stopped her. "Shit, Joanie, I had no idea."

"It's fine, sorry. I shouldn't—I shouldn't have said anything."

"God, with everything that happened, I didn't even—fuck, Joanie, I am so sorry."

Joanie held it all back behind a monster-sized dam; it was easy to see her biting back her grief. But something she didn't—or couldn't—hold back was the anger. It danced in her eyes like a forest fire.

"You remember the fucko who gave me shit at the Goldenrod dinner? Called me a whore and whatever? Prentiss Beckman. He's the one who did it. Who shot Gr—" Her voice nearly broke. "Who shot Graham."

"It makes people horrible," said Calla, walking up from the other room, her phone in her hand, its screen on and glowing bright in the dim room. "The apple. I watched it change my dad. You don't think it's making them horrible because it seems to be bettering them—his eyesight improved, he got more confident, he seemed happier. But it also made him meaner. And more selfish. You don't even see it when they stop being who they were entirely."

Emily nodded. "My wife got like that. We . . . were having problems beforehand. But when she ate the apple—and eventually, Jesus, that's all she ate—she became manipulative, love-bombing me, gaslighting me. She was abusive, but not in a way you necessarily realized? And holy hell did she get *strong*. It wasn't natural. It felt like she could break me without a second thought." Emily felt herself tearing up. *No. Don't do that. Not now.*

"When Prentiss killed Graham—and tried to kill me, too—I shot him." She tapped her back, around her shoulder blade. "Right here. Hit him as he left the door. He didn't even stop. I thought at the time he was messed up on, I don't know, meth or bath salts. But then back in the house, I saw them: a little pile of apple cores. He'd been eating those fucking apples here in my house. Maybe before he killed Graham, maybe after, maybe both. I don't know. The real twist, though, is that when the cops were gone, they cleaned up those apples. I asked about them, they said they didn't see anything. That I must've been hallucinating."

"There were cops at the cabin tonight," Emily said. "They're . . . compromised. God, that sounds so fucking weird to say. *Compromised.* Like they're Russian spies or body snatchers."

"A cop shot himself in front of me," Calla said.

For a moment, nobody spoke.

Emily stared, speechless.

Joanie, too, looked shocked by this news.

"Yeah. Because of the apple, I guess. I—I told you shit went down at the orchard, but when the rest of us ran, a cop followed. This prick—he was a prick before the apple, okay? Officer Boyland. He came after us. He hurt me, that's how I got the cut on my head—" She pointed to what was now a mostly healed gash across her forehead. "And I guess he didn't know whose kid I was, because when Marco told him that I was Dan's daughter, he shot himself. Didn't even stop to think about it. Immediately, without thinking—" She mimed putting a gun under her chin. "So the cops are in on it, for sure. And they're *all* the way in. They'll die for my Dad. For the apple."

Emily realized that this whole thing was way, way worse than even she knew. And the looks on the others' faces said they were thinking the same thing.

"Did you get in touch with your friends?" Joanie asked.

Calla shook her head. "Lucas answered. Nothing from Marco or Esther."

"I'm sure they're fine. It's just late."

"Yeah." But she didn't sound like she was so sure.

"We can't handle this on our own," Emily said. "This is too big. Too fucked up. I don't even know what this is—I only know there's some kind of awful apple people eat, and it turns them into abusive monsters, and god, my wife coughed up something that looked like what we just pulled out of John tonight, but this thing? It *moved*. It moved like a somersaulting tarantula and—we should all leave. Let someone else handle this."

"No one else will handle this."

Everyone startled.

It was John. He stood there, stock-still, like the living dead. Pale, gray, his left shoulder drooping, the arm hanging low.

"John, you should go lie down—"

"No one else will know how to handle this and no one will believe us. There is no one to call. Local law enforcement is complicit. And I wouldn't trust police anywhere to handle this kind of nightmare. Whoever eats the apple changes. And not for the better. The parasite is spreading, soul to soul to soul. It's local, mostly. Still here, in the county. But soon the apples will grow again, and this time, they might travel. And just as Dan must've grown his orchard from scions, so, too, may others. Which means we don't have long before this is something far greater and far worse than it already is, and by then, it will be far too late to stop it. If it is to be stopped at all, it must be stopped soon. By us."

"Maybe not alone, though," Calla said.

Again, they all turned and looked to her.

She walked over, pulling out her phone, already popping open Instagram and showing them her video about the apples at school. "This was last month. Look at all the comments." She scrolled through them as they gathered around. Emily saw people threatening her, laughing at her, trolling her—but she also saw people who believed. Better yet, people who had seen just what they'd all been seeing.

"Others are seeing what's happening," Emily said. It was a strange sensation, to feel not so alone all of a sudden. It was already nice to be around Joanie and Calla, people who hadn't eaten the apple and who believed in—and had seen—the horrors wrought under the influence of Dan's orchard. But now? To see there were dozens of others who maybe understood?

She wanted to cry.

And then—

She *did* cry.

Broke down then and there. John told her it'd be all right, that he was all right, and he thanked her and the others for saving him. Calla awkwardly patted her on the arm—a kind gesture for a teenager. And Joanie? She said, "Well, I don't know about any of you, but I'm not sleeping a wink tonight, so I'm making some fucking pancakes."

Nobody disagreed. Pancakes it was.

74

PANCAKES: THE GREAT PANACEA

THREE A.M.

They all sat around Joanie's dining room eating pancakes and drinking coffee. The sounds of forks scraping plates and coffee slurping ensued.

At one point, Emily said, "You know, we all have something in common."

"The apple," Joanie said, her tone conveying a *yeah, duh* attitude.

"That, but we've all lost people because of it. Important people to us. Your husband. For me, Meg. For Calla, her dad. And John—"

"I lost Walt."

"Who's Walt?" Joanie asked.

"A friend. My best friend," John corrected. "I believe he'd been trying to find this apple for a long time—first as Vinot's Allegresse, then as the Harrowsblack apple. The Lenape called it the pkwësu. But now it's just—"

"The Ruby Slipper," Calla said. She dropped her fork with a clatter and sat back in the chair. "I named it that. Me. My dad wanted a name and I thought it sounded good. No place like home, that sort of thing. So stupid."

"None of this is your fault," Emily told her.

"Yeah, no, I know, but—" Whatever she was about to say, she gave up on it. She looked intensely at John. "I think I remember your friend. Walt. He maybe came around once or twice. He did help my father. Did my—" She seemed unsure if she wanted to ask this, but she pressed on. "Did my father kill him?"

John looked sadly upon her when he answered, "I think so."

"That would've happened before the apple."

"Again, I believe that is correct."

Calla looked defeated. "That means he was a monster already. Before this all started. The apple didn't make him that way. It just made him more of himself."

"We don't *know* that," Emily said. "There's a lot that's unclear—"

"Marco, my boyfriend, he ate the apple. And he was ... messed up for a while. It was like he was dead to me—or I was dead to him, like he didn't even see me or remember that he ever cared about me. But what he saw at the orchard broke him. It, like, snapped him out of it? I don't know. But he got better. He got free. I think maybe we can save some of them."

Emily nodded. "Meg was getting better, too, for a while. Though ... something changed. And now she seems lost."

"Maybe she can be brought back. We don't know. We have to try." But then Calla sat forward. "But my father, he can't be fixed. He's gone. He killed your friend before any of this started, which means—it means he can't be forgiven. It means he just has to be stopped. I don't care about him anymore. *Fuck* him."

They all shared looks with one another as Calla stared into the depths of her syrup-smeared plate.

"I have to go to school tomorrow," she said. "Can someone drive me?"

"School?" Emily asked, incredulous. How the hell was that even supposed to work? "Is that—is that a good idea?"

"Yeah, they still make kids go to school, who knew," Calla said, suddenly irritated.

"I'm just saying, that seems dangerous. And stupid."

"Yeah, no shit. But if I don't go, I don't graduate, and if I don't graduate, I don't go to Princeton. And if I don't go to Princeton? I stay *here*. In all of this fucking mess." She sighed. "Besides, maybe if I go, I can learn something. I'll see Lucas, hopefully Esther and Marco. I can do, I dunno. Recon."

They all looked at one another with acquiescing stares.

"Cool," Emily said, letting it go.

Joanie told Calla, "I can drive you."

"Congrats on Princeton, that's quite the achievement," John said to the girl.

She just shrugged, like it was a hollow victory. "Thanks," Calla answered.

THEY ALL TRIED TO SLEEP. OR NAP, OR WHATEVER SLUMBER THEY could manage in the scant hours between three in the morning and sunup. Only John managed. Emily guessed he was pretty wrecked.

She knew she should feel pretty wrecked, too—though she hadn't been bitten, she'd certainly run the gauntlet, what with them running from the cabin, getting chased, and her having to rip *invasive plant life* from John's shoulder. But even still, she couldn't catch anything resembling sleep. Anytime she started to doze off, she felt the pressure of something chasing her, or heard a sound that didn't exist, or was sure that Meg was there in the darkness, staring at her through the window. And then she'd startle awake with a hitch and a gasp followed by a wave of frustration and disappointment.

She soon found herself milling around downstairs, watching the distant horizon out the window burning with the firebreak of day.

Calla walked behind her, bare feet slapping on the marble floor. Towel over her head, vigorously using it to dry her hair. She looked lost in thought.

"Hey I'm sorry," Emily said, abruptly. She felt like a raw nerve herself and it probably wasn't a great idea to go jumping into the girl's business, but—her own mental state was like a cloud of agitated flies looking for a place to land.

"It's fine," Calla said, giving her a weird look.

"You don't even know what I'm apologizing for."

"Well. Whatever it is, it's fine."

"I'm just sorry I gave you crap earlier. I know this is awful for you."

"Everyone's going through it, whatever."

"Right, but I think it's worse for you. With school and college on the horizon. Boyfriends, friends, and god—prom? Isn't that coming up?"

"Yeah. Doesn't matter. Don't worry, not going. Obviously." She rolled her eyes.

"Can I ask you something?"

"I'm guessing you're going to regardless of what I say, so go for it."

"How . . . did Marco come back? What snapped him out of it?"

That question seemed to give Calla some pause. "I don't know for sure. He . . . saw my father put on a strange mask, and then Dad hurt a man named Claude Lambert. And the police killed someone else, a friend of Lambert's or something—they're all part of this group, the—"

"Crossed Keys."

"Yeah."

"So, I guess it just freaked Marco out and it broke him out of whatever hold the apple had on him."

"Seems like. Here, look," Calla took out her phone, and then showed Emily a video. "I was there that night. I didn't see what Marco saw, but I found this."

The girl used her finger to speed through certain parts—a lot of it was just her in the dark, moving through the shadows. With maybe other shapes out there, too. People in the night.

Cultists, Emily thought.

But then came the dead body.

A gardening spade stuck in his side.

A cat eating his face.

Emily looked away, tried not to retch.

"You . . . you *saw* this?"

"Yeah."

"Jesus, Calla. We—we need to show this to somebody. The FBI or—"

"I dunno. What good would it do?"

"I just mean, it's one thing to tell them there's an evil apple parasite cult, please come investigate—and there's a whole other thing when there are actual murders happening. The FBI, or, or—the media."

"What about social media."

"That . . . could work. It would definitely get attention. Why haven't you posted it already?"

Calla hesitated. "I just . . . I know if I post it, it changes everything. Like, I can't just go to Princeton and pretend I didn't upload some high-key creepypasta shit to my socials, you know? I can't not be the girl whose father killed someone, maybe several someones, in the name of, what? A piece of fucking fruit? He's legit running a cult, I mean, fuck. If I put this out there, I can't put it back."

"I understand. I guess think about it. If you need to talk it through…"

"Thanks," Calla said. It sounded sincere. "I gotta keep getting ready."

"School."

The girl rolled her eyes. "Yeah. *School.* Still. Ugh."

75

SCHOOL, STILL, UGH

Exhaustion and anxiety dueled inside Calla's body, up and down the length of her, in every bone, in every organ, in every cell. Every part of her felt so tired she wanted to lie down and so wired that she worried she might never ever get to sleep again. The paranoia didn't help. Walking up from the parking lot—Joanie having dropped her off—she felt eyes on her. *Maybe they all ate the apple. They're just waiting for another taste and they're fucking pissed at me because I posted that video trying to ruin their fun.* But that was crazy, right? Couldn't be all of them. Maybe they were just looking at her because it was high school and everybody looked at everybody. They wanted to be you. They wanted *you* to be *them.* They hated you, loved you, feared you, wished you were their friend, worried you were their enemy, wondered where you got that lipstick, those shoes, thought that embroidered drop-shoulder jacket was dope or ugly or cringe or cheugy AF wait oh shit does anyone even say cheugy anymore, they thought you were vibes, goals, hotness, thotness, whatfuckingever. High school was judgy and narcissistic enough without throwing the Chaos Apple into the mix.

"You're not wrong, they're watching you," Lucas said, sidling up next to her, tucking his arm into hers as he ushered her faster toward the school.

"You fucking scared me," she said, heart racing. "Jesus, Lucas."

"Good. Be scared. It's weird here now."

"It was weird here before."

"Yeah, *well,* things have changed."

"Where's Esther?"

Lucas made a face.

"Dude. What?" she pressed.

"Your father showed up at her house. She hid and didn't answer the door. Scared her pretty bad, so she went to live with her dad."

That was a lot to take in. "Wait, her parents aren't divorced."

"They're separated now. I guess they have been for a while and she didn't tell us."

"Why didn't she text me?"

Lucas shrugged. "You told her not to. Remember?"

"Fuck. Right. Okay. Fuck."

"Is . . . has Marco been here?"

"Uh-uh. Haven't seen him. And we're not like, *texting friends*."

"I haven't heard from him, either." *And I'm getting worried.* Acid pooled in her stomach and climbed into her throat. She hoped he was okay. She hoped Esther was okay. Shit!

They popped open the double doors, entered the west hallway near the Math Quad. The hall ahead sat lined with blue and yellow lockers, and hanging above it all, rubbing salt in the wound: a huge prom banner. Painted next to it in acrylics were a pair of dice and the words CASINO NIGHT. Prom was in a few weeks—early June, the week before graduation.

Not that I'm going, she thought. She flashed to an image of all the kids standing around to music, not dancing, just swaying like grass in a soft wind, staring at one another with dead eyes, eating their apples.

The first bell rang.

Shit. Homeroom. She wasn't ready for this.

"Remember," Lucas said. "After school. Meet me in the English lab. Solzman's room. Good?"

She nodded.

"We're not alone!" he called after her.

HOMEROOM.

Mr. Koltnow's class. Also her calc teacher. Owlish, round-headed, body-like-a-drinking-straw pseudo-hipster. Loved to talk about his *vinyls,* as if it wasn't some weird old-person shit.

Calla sat there. Toes tapping as the morning announcements came on-screen. Koltnow's gaze fixed on her like a pair of thumbtacks.

"Hey," came a voice behind her.

It was Taylor Pelton. He'd been sitting behind her in every homeroom since middle school. He was the swim-team captain. Lean arms, long neck, firm jaw. And dark, deep-set shark eyes. Swam like a torpedo.

"What?" she asked, irritated.

"Saw your post on social," he said, leering.

"So what. I don't care."

"You *should* care. Can't just put anything up online you know. It's irresponsible, Calla Lily."

Ants crawled in her veins. Calla Lily. That was her father's nickname for her. Just his. No one else knew it or used it.

Mr. Koltnow was still staring at her from the front of the class. And now she saw, from two rows over and two seats forward, someone else watching her. Barton Reese. One of Taylor Pelton's lackeys. Smaller, leaner, like an eel.

He showed his teeth in a big grin.

"Fuck you," she told Taylor, keeping her eyes forward.

"Fuck me? Fuck you. You little fucking bitch. Listen good. If you post anything else? Anything about the orchard, the apple, your father—?" He leaned farther over the front of his desk, his shoulder nearly on her chin. Ahead of her, Barton Reese snapped at the air with his teeth. "We might have to stick a knife in you. Open you up like a burlap sack. Fill you with a bushel of Ruby Slippers, no cap—"

She jerked up out of her seat. Pulse pounding in her neck like a drum.

"Calla," Mr. Koltnow started, but she couldn't deal with him—with *this*—right now. She instead just blurted something about having to use the bathroom, but Koltnow told her to sit, so she gritted her teeth and sat. Taylor chuckled in her ear. And when the announcements were over and the bell finally rang, as they filtered out of the room she was sure she saw Barton Reese lift his shirt and show her the serrated steak knife he had tucked into his khakis.

JUST BEFORE THIRD-PERIOD AP BIO SHE SAW THEM AGAIN. TAYLOR and Barton. They weren't in any of her classes besides homeroom, but there they were today, in the hallways, where she'd never seen them before. They were in the crowds. Close enough to watch, but not close enough to touch her. She saw no knife. *I must've imagined it.* But she couldn't help but wonder. What if they did have a knife? Or a gun? Fuck. *Should I go to the principal? Should I just leave?*

Can't make a scene.

Keep it together.

She felt like she wanted to scream.

Calla had to make it to the end of the day. Then to the end of the week, then the end of the school year, then to the end of the summer . . .

It felt impossible. Her skin crawled. Was she sweating? She was sweating. Gross. Fuck.

BEFORE FOURTH PERIOD. EUROPEAN HISTORY WITH MRS. RANCIT. She hadn't done her essay on the Hapsburgs and she was only just remembering that. Whatever. *I got into Princeton. None of this matters but graduating.*

As she headed to class, she didn't see Taylor or Barton anywhere.

Good. They'd given up.

But then—

There they waited. Outside the classroom door. One on one side, the other on the other side. Grinning like the cats that ate the canary. (Or the dead man's face.) Her middle cinched up. Her legs tightened, calves cramping with new fear as she imagined walking through that door, and as she did, Barton would slide that knife between her ribs and slit her open. Pop her lung. Air whistling as the lung collapsed, blood going down her leg, Mrs. Rancit telling her to take her seat as she sucked on a wet apple core—*fuck fuck fuck,* Calla thought. She couldn't do it. She turned heel and walked the opposite way. That meant skipping class. She didn't know where she was going to go or how she'd play it off. Maybe she'd pop in late. Tell Mrs. Rancit she was in the bathroom. *Fuck fuck fuck.* Down the hall she went as the final bell rang and the halls emptied. Leaving her alone.

Her feet echoing on the linoleum.

She stopped. Turned to look behind her.

All the way down the hall, there was Taylor striding toward her. Slow and steady. Head forward, shoulders back, like he was in the water.

And there, ahead of her, emerged Barton.

Steak knife in hand. He gave it a deft little twirl.

Between her and him was an intersection of the hallway that took you back toward the English quad. *Fuck this,* she thought, and bolted toward it.

Barton broke into a run, too. His knife out, slashing the air ahead of him.

He was fast. Like a torpedo.

But she was closer. She hurried around the bend, nearly losing her shit into a rack of lockers, but she righted herself and hurried forward—

Slamming into someone head-on.

Someone who caught her arms with unerring strength.

Mr. Koltnow. He was a slight man, narrow in all ways, and though she wasn't a big girl she should've knocked him on his ass—a bowling ball powering through the pins. But he didn't budge. Didn't even flinch.

And his grip on her arms burned as he squeezed.

"Let me go," she hissed, struggling. "I'm being chased—*stalked.* They wanna hurt me. Let me *go.*"

Barton and Taylor rounded the bend, no longer running.

"Thanks, Mr. K," Taylor said, "for catchin' that little fishy."

"Yeah. We might wanna gut her still."

"Stop," Koltnow said, his normally mousy voice taking on a surprising authority. The two boys stopped. To Calla, he said, still gripping her by the arms: "Your father would like to pass along a message."

"Please," she said, trying to escape his grasp.

"He'd like you to know the apple is waiting when you are ready to eat it. Meanwhile, you are to continue going here. Show up. Do your work. Make him proud. Above all else, graduate with high marks. Do not shame him with any of your nonsense. No more of this *posting videos* business. You are to be done with that."

"Or we'll peel your skin," Taylor called, cackling.

"Mister Reese and Mister Pelton," Koltnow said, baring his teeth. "I will remind you that her father has made it very clear that she is to be left alone for the time being, even though she's a *foul little thing* who *refuses* to eat the apple."

"Fine," they both said in glum unison.

"And you, you're late for class," the teacher told Calla. He relinquished his grip. Her muscles throbbed and numbness bloomed there. She turned around and headed back the way she came, the two boys leering at her. Barton tucked the knife back in the waistband of his pants.

"I hope you cut your dick off," she growled at him. But they just laughed and laughed, a donkey bray that followed her all the way to class.

END OF THE DAY NOW. AT LUNCH, SHE TOLD LUCAS WHAT HAPpened with Barton and Taylor, and he said, "Listen, Call, out there it feels like we're all alone. Like it's everybody staring at us, waiting to—what'd he say? Skin us like apples. But it's not. It's not even half of them. It's a lot but it's not as many as you think. And there are others who know something's wrong. They've vibed it. They've seen things. A lot of them saw your video. They're gonna meet us after school."

English. Solzman's room. Calla headed that way, against the crowd, swimming upstream. She kept waiting for Taylor or Barton to pop out, bury a knife in her stomach. But she didn't see them at all.

As she headed upstairs, her phone dinged.

It was Marco.

ONE TEXT FROM MARCO. IT JUST SAID:

Marco: Hi.

This was just too much emotional whiplash, so she had to still her trembling fingers just to type:

Calla: dude are you ok??

Marco: I'm fine, sorry for not texting. I broke my phone!

Calla: what's up where are you?

Marco: In the city. My leg got bad again and I needed to see a specialist. Here for a few days.

Calla: I love you I miss you

Marco: I love you and I miss you, too.

Marco: Are we still on for prom?

At that, Calla paused.

They weren't seriously going to still try to go to prom?

Did he really think that was a good idea? Like, okay, she did really want to go. They'd been talking about it for a year now. But . . .

With everything going on . . .

Calla: I dunno lemme think about it, k

Marco: Of course.

Calla: I have class

Marco: Okay, I love you!!

Calla started to type *I love you back* but instead typed *I love tou back* and considered leaving it and saying, *classic Marco move—*

She froze.

Typos.

Marco always made typos.

Always, *always* made typos, and then autocorrect always clowned him by turning those typos or the fixed words into something even stupider and it was never not hilarious.

But here he typed perfectly.

Flawless punctuation.

No wrong words, no missed words, nothing.

It's not him typing.

She knew it, deep down. But then who? His parents? Her *father?*

"Shit," she said out loud. Kids looked at her as they streamed toward the stairwell.

Her phone felt scorching hot in her hand. She wanted to throw it in the trash.

Instead, she pocketed it, just as the second bell rang, reminding her that she was now late for class, fuck fuck fuck.

MARCO SAT IN THE PASSENGER SEAT OF THE TRUCK. A BORROWED black hoodie was pulled low over his face so that no one could look in and see who he was or what he looked like. Dan Paxson sat in the driver's side, tapping away at a phone—Marco's new phone, one that his own parents ordered at the behest of Dan.

"There," Dan said, leaning across and popping open the glove compartment before tossing the phone inside. "She might know it's not you. She's a smart girl."

Marco turned away from Dan, looking out the passenger-side window at a place that felt so familiar but so far away: the parking lot at the high school. Beyond it, the big blocky building that had always looked to him like a prison—but right now, he'd give anything to be in there. With Calla.

"She hates you," Marco said, his voice small.

"Mm," Dan said, lazily waving a hand over Marco's body—and the pain lit up in him like a fire inside his body. He went to grit his teeth but had none left—just rows of black appleseed teeth, spiraling out of his swollen gums and down his throat, and they clicked like cricket legs, a song of anguish and misery, and so instead he pushed his head down between his knees until the pain stopped.

No—

Until *Dan* stopped causing him pain.

A blessing, Marco told himself. A necessary blessing.

"She doesn't *hate* me," Dan said, plainly, in a friendly, corrective tone. "She thinks she does. But all kids go through that. Parents, like yours, have to push their children sometimes in uncomfortable directions. It's like exercise. It's only working when it's hard. Only when there's pain." Dan smiled. "Isn't that right?"

"Mm-hmm," Marco agreed. Because he wanted to agree. Because he needed to agree. Because Dan was good, Dan was right, and because he did not want any more pain. He breathed through his nose, but the skin around his nostrils was stiffened with tough, ruby-red flesh. His finger-tips itched, too—his branch-tips were coming in. His own fingernails had already fallen off, leaving behind puckered pink craters. "We could get her," Marco said through lips so rigid that when he spoke, the skin split, spilling sweet thin blood, golden blood, apple blood. "We could be with her now." Even as he said the words he hated himself for that. The war in him was real: He loved Calla.

But he worshipped Dan.

"You're wondering why I don't just go in there and scoop her up? Well. I could. I'm her father. They wouldn't stop me." He smiled, obvi-ously satisfied with himself—the cab of the truck filled with the perfume of cut fruit. A narcotic miasma. "A number of them have eaten the apple. They follow me and wouldn't dare stand in my way, isn't that right?"

Marco nodded, clasping his hands together in an awkward gesture of prayer.

"No, I want Calla to stay in school. I'm her father. School is impor-tant, if only for what comes at the end of it. If she's going to carry my name into the world, she is going to do it with a high school diploma, and to a good school like Princeton. I won't rob her of that. She's earned it. I'd just as soon break a mirror I was looking into. To what end? To no end. Plus . . ." He chuckled. "She's helping me without knowing it. Isn't she, Marco?"

"She is, Father."

"Father," Dan said, repeating that word. "Marco, that's beautiful."

Marco hadn't called him that before. It just . . . came out of him. And it felt right. So right. Dan—no, *Father*—obviously agreed, too. The man beamed with warmth and Marco felt that warmth like standing in the summer sun after a cold rain. He wept with joy.

"Thank you, Marco, I appreciate that. I do. You may call me Father. I think that feels right. I will be father of this place, these people. Maybe all people, but I'm getting ahead of myself. First—" He cracked his knuckles before wrapping them around the steering wheel. "We have to keep an eye on our enemies to see what they are planning. Another thing I owe to my precious Calla Lily."

Marco nodded. This morning, they watched Calla get out of a cherry SUV that pulled up to the curb—a tall redhead driving it. Dan seemed to know who she was. He wasn't angry about it. Just intensely curious—and sad, too. And that sadness pained Marco as much as any of the pain that Father delivered unto him. It was the sadness of betrayal. But Father would make it right.

He'd make *everything* right.

Wouldn't he?

76

APOSTASY BLOSSOMS

After Joanie drove Calla home late that afternoon, she told them everything. How those two boys from the swim team confronted her. How the teacher backed them up. How Marco had texted her and didn't seem like himself.

And they all listened, worried. John with his shoulder wrapped in gauze. Joanie, anger lacing her tighter and tighter until she looked like she was ready to go back to that school and kill someone. Emily, who looked sad and anxious, more with every word, like she was on a raft drifting out to sea, lost to the spray, to the fog. But Calla felt the power in what she told them next:

"But we aren't alone."

They all perked up at that.

Calla explained that after school, Lucas and she met with a bunch of kids in the art room. "Thirteen of them, not including me and Lucas," she explained. Kids from every social stratum of the school—they'd all seen what the apples were doing. To their friends, their teachers, in some cases their parents. They were worried, too, and they were mad, but just being together and seeing one another—and seeing that they weren't alone—seemed to help. They said they knew of others, too. Other kids. Some adults.

"We can do this," Calla said. "We can stop my dad."

Those in the room shared looks. Finally, it was John who said:

"Okay. We are the insurgency. If everyone is in."

Emily nodded. "I'm here and not going anywhere."

"We need a plan," Joanie said.

That's when Calla grinned. "I think I have one. And it starts with me posting my last video from the orchard."

OUTSIDE THE HOUSE, THE SUN DIED, BURIED IN THE DIRT OF DARK-ness. And in that darkness, something crawled free. Its teeth clicked. Its skin glistened. It did not want to wait, but it was told to wait, and so it waited, and it watched the house, hungering for a day yet to come

(soon, soon, please let it be soon!)

when it could bury its branchfingers in the flesh of those inside, and drag them to the orchard so that they could be planted there like trees.

——

THE GOLDEN MAN'S TALE, PART THREE

1903, THE GOLDENROD ESTATE, BUCKS COUNTY,
PENNSYLVANIA.

IT WAS NOT THE INDISCRETION OF LUST AND CONTROL THAT UNDID
him, Henry decided, but rather, the indiscretion of toying with his prey.
The day he brought Oswald to the garden was the first pulled stitch. An
act of ego, of callow frivolity, just to see the look on a man's face.

(But it was something, that face.)

He remembered it well, even now. After their conversation at the
pool, Henry took Oswald to the basement—few knew that Henry had
built a basement beneath the Goldenrod. Hidden behind—cliché as it
might have been—a bookshelf in the Western Collections Room, a
bookshelf containing agricultural and botanical books. Pull an old book,
a children's book of all things—*A Is for Apple Pie,* by Christine White—
and the shelf slid silently away. Through which, a passageway awaited.

The basement itself was not beneath the Goldenrod proper, but at
the end of a long tunnel system. The tunnels were arched but narrow,
the walls white as bone but stained with great fingers of green algae and
black mold. The two of them went underneath the old fountain, then
the carriage house, then the front gates of the Goldenrod itself. In fact,
the fountain drained here, and the tunnels flooded a room, the slow-
draining water always up to your knees or so (though in a bad storm, it
would become unpassable). As you left the flooded room, you would
find a stairway, though the stairs still did not carry you to the surface. Up
the stairs, the tunnels widened and opened up into a large room. It
looked almost like a gallery—which was what he'd once intended it for.
A secret gallery of heretical things he'd collected over the years. All the
old books, the old bones, the parchments of ritual and recipe, the myste-

rious tools, the racks of strange spice and herb. But over time, it became something else. Not a gallery at all. But rather—

His garden.

He'd led Oswald to this space, the two of them carrying oil lamps lit with whale blubber, and it was there that he carefully watched the other man's face. The look upon Oswald's face as it transformed—the horror bloomed in a gloriously deranged way, like a fox rotting on your front step day after day, the sagging of the body, the rippling of the maggots under the carpet of fur, the eyes bursting and the fluids erupting. Henry adored it.

It was then that he turned to see what Oswald was seeing—

Something Henry had seen many times, because it was something Henry had himself chosen, had colonized, had *cultivated.*

But something Oswald was seeing for the first time.

Henry's garden of people.

The two young women, Beatrice and Victoria, stood at the fore, locked in an eternal embrace—Beatrice had been here longer, and had lost more of herself to the shears and the saw and the apple peeler. Both of her arms were gone, and Henry had painstakingly carved whip-and-tongue grooves through the rootstock of her bone and the scionwood of the tree branches, tying them together with the finest French silk so that the bone and branch would marry. And they did, as he knew they would (this was not, after all, his first garden).

More growth issued forth from her over time—a knot of wood pushing out her left eye, where sometimes a small fruit like a crab apple appeared. He would try to catch the fruit before it rotted. It tasted so much like her. It was regrettable that Beatrice had only another year in her here in the garden before she joined the others who had formed over time the rich loamy soil—dark like blood sausage—beneath her feet.

Victoria, however, was a newer prize. Her he had bedded first before he took her leg, replacing it with the scionwood branch—he had never done this before, curious how it would take. Would the branch grow downward and into the dirt? Or would the new growth instead curl upward as branches usually did, seeking the light? To his great delight, it did *both.* Roots sprouted like seeking tendrils, hungry for the earth. And the branch itself stretched gently outward and upward, budding and leafing and soon, blooming. Other roots and shoots crawled out of them like seeking fingers, winding around one another, braiding together, and pulling each young woman—their clothes already in rough tatters—tighter and tighter as time went on. They moaned in discordant song, a song of both pain and, to Henry's ear, desire.

It was just the two of them for now. The bodies of others were around in putrefying mounds—the smell coming off them was not the smell of rancidity and rot, however, but rather, the heady scent of fecundity and floral esters. Tangled little trees grew from those mounds, too. Sometimes, his apple—

His joy—

His delight—

His heavenly pleasure on earth—

—grew on them.

(And all around lay hundreds of apple cores. Some almost moldering into dirt, others still fresh and sweet-smelling. There were no flies down here, though. Any that dared appear . . . well, these beautiful trees took care of them.)

He went to Beatrice, her one good eye turned toward him, wrenched wide open by the branch's claw, and in that eye he saw so many things. Panic! Love! Abject terror and wanton need. Glory be. He kissed her brow, and then shoved two of his fingers into her mouth and around her lips, and when he withdrew those fingers, they were oozing with a tacky, coppery sap.

Fingers dripping, he stalked toward Oswald Lambert.

Frozen in place, the man wept and shook his head.

It was only at the last minute he tried to turn, tried to run. But Henry grabbed his hand and held it there with an unerring strength—he made it clear with a quick squeeze that it would be preciously easy to turn the man's wrist into gelée. And then with his other hand, he pushed his ooze-slick fingers past the man's lips, past his fake teeth, saucing his tongue. Oswald moaned, his knees nearly buckling.

"Tell no one, and I'll give you a taste now and again," Henry said. "But tell someone, and I will make you a part of my garden."

That, he hoped, would've ended it.

And it did, in a sense, bring an end.

He just failed to predict how.

Now, as he groaned, pulling his face up out of his own sticky blood, his head full of thick wool, he realized that was the moment that had undone him.

It was, after all, a bit of a pattern.

"It took me a while to pull that thread," Oswald said. He sat forward on a wooden chair at the base of Henry's bed, scraping his teeth with an ivory toothpick. The chair creaked under his weight. Four others sat around Henry's bed: Chalfont Butler, Harry Doyle, Edwin Cabot, and Lloyd Beckman. Their gazes flicked from Oswald to Harry and back again.

"I see you've brought your pigs, eager to knock over the trough," Henry said. His words oozed together. *I shee youf brut yourrr pigshh.* A little of his accent peeked out, too. Unintentionally. He'd been drugged, hadn't he? His hands, bound to the corners of his bed with taut rope. He should be able to rip these ropes apart but the drugs wouldn't let him. And his head throbbed—every time his heart beat, it felt like something was pulsing inside his skull, trying to get out. They hit him. He remembered that now. They'd pricked him as he stood up out of bed. A needle. Then someone had clubbed him in the face. He fell forward. He tried to pull himself up but they got him with another needle. Then another still.

Now he was here.

"Took a considerable amount of morphine to put you down," Oswald said. "In case you're wondering. But to finish what I was saying—no more interrupting, if you please, sir—it was quite an endeavor to figure out that 'Henry Hart Golden' is a fiction."

"Let me *go*, you *fools.*"

Harry Doyle stood up and drove a fist into Henry's mouth. He felt teeth come loose. (That was all right. He could grow new ones. Whatever happened to him here today, he would repair it. Long as he could taste his apple.)

"You left an effective puzzle box, hard to open, difficult to see that it was even a puzzle at all. Your parents: What's the story? Oh, father a humble woodworker, mother an herbalist, but woe, as both died in that bad hurricane of '69, mm, the one that washed those towns in Maine away. You were not born into wealth, and had little to your name, and *up you rose,* a self-made man, in the truest sense, making and remaking yourself, your story, as you went along. You worked here, worked there, a jack-of-all-trades—yet everyplace you worked, this schooner, that wharf, this factory, they're all no longer with us, with no one left to verify who you were. The schooner sank. Factory burned down. On and on. But we didn't bother looking, not then.

"Because you were a wonder, weren't you. A being as much myth as he was man, a voyager and explorer, your talents on display same as the artifacts you brought with you. I expect those were true, all your expeditions. But it's alarming how many of those trips ended in tragedy, don't you think?"

"Fuck you," Henry muttered through his bloodied mouth.

Harry Doyle, his hands like pulleys ready to drop, launched to his feet once more—but Oswald shook his head. "Leave him be. Let the snake spit venom to the sky. Fruitless as it is."

"So if I'm not Henry Golden," he said, coughing up red, "who the hell am I then, you plug? I can be only me."

Oswald chewed on that. "That's the trick, isn't it? Before last year, I would've assumed you were a charismatic con man, a modern day man-with-a-wagon, showing off his elixirs and his exotic wonders. But then you showed me your garden.

"So I took a page out of your book, so to speak, and I thought: Well, let's go backward in history. I started reaching out to folks, not just in the places you said you've been, but other places, too. Looking for missing girls. Young women, sometimes young men. I asked constables and Pinkertons, traveling merchants and bartenders, anybody who might have their ear to the ground to this sort of thing.

"But what I found couldn't have been connected. I found people missing long before you came around. Some before you were even alive. Or so I figured. Then I came upon the records—buried, if you'll believe it, down in the offices of the *Public Ledger* paper in Philadelphia. Newspapers have been absorbing each other for the last two hundred years, and the *Ledger* had bought up the *Press, Taggart's Sunday Times,* the *North American,* and so they had documents and journals and all manner of things. I ask you now, you know a bounty-hunter? Half-breed named Julius Silver."

"Nngh" was the sound Henry made as he shook his head.

"'Course you wouldn't. This was, what, a hundred years ago or so. Thing is, you know, the person Silver was paid to find? Story would've been too deranged, too *deluded,* to believe, had I not seen your garden. He was hunting a man who had been going up and down the Atlantic Coast, and he'd been, get this, cutting people into pieces and sticking tree parts onto them. And by the Devil's own might, those trees grew from those people same as if you grafted 'em to a real tree. Unbelievable. Except. *Except.*" Here, Lambert leaned in, and Henry could smell the tobacco rotting his breath. "Except I saw your godforsaken garden."

"We all did," Cabot muttered. The sound of his voice was hollow, like wind howling through an old log. Like he was haunted by what he saw. *Good,* Henry thought. Let him be disturbed. Let his mind be destroyed by it. A joy for Henry.

(A last joy, perhaps.)

"I kept looking," Oswald said, "often for the same fingerprint of demonic nightmare, the work of a madman that sounded invented by a madman—that bounty-hunter, Silver, he said you were like a, what was it, a reverse Johnny Appleseed. Not wandering around planting seeds, but wandering around, grafting those branches, branches onto cut limb, onto bone. So that's what I looked for. And I found it again in a town called Woodhull. Many miles north of here.

"There, records from a man named Finch say someone there killed a whole town, and from their carcasses grew an orchard of apple trees. What a detail. Apple trees. The Garden of Eden, as grown by Satan. The man they found there was a Frenchman, name of Vinot. Descendent of a famous chef's apprentice—or, perhaps, impossibly, the apprentice himself. Came here with the Dutch company. Story said they took that man out to sea to carry him to justice across the waves, but instead decided that justice had to come early. So they dropped him in the water. And yet.

"That boat never got to Europe. It turned around, came back. And a number of the men upon that vessel were missing. So maybe that man, Vinot, he survived. Maybe he was who Julius Silver found—sure, Silver said he killed him, but the body he brought in was unrecognizable, and after that, Silver was rich, far richer than the bounty he brought in, and later was killed in his own bed with a sharpened stick—a branch from an apple tree—to the neck. Quite a story."

"Quite," Henry said, smiling through broken, red teeth.

The men all stood as one.

They had been concealing their weapons—revolvers, each. Webleys and Colts. Long barrels. *So it's an assassination, then,* he thought, panic scrabbling inside his skull like rats trapped in a box on a burning ship.

"Any last words?" Doyle asked him.

"I have an offer," he said, licking blood from his own ruined lips.

"We want nothing you have for us."

"I have power, and I will grant it to you. Not merely wealth, but true power. I can heal the most grievous of injuries. I could crush a man's head with a clap of my hands." *And still would if I wasn't soggy with fucking morphine.* Maybe if he kept talking, kept dragging this on, he could come out of this fog. He could tear through these ropes. He could drive the bones of these men into one another. Or maybe use them in a new garden . . .

"I have been alive for centuries, gentlemen. I can give you the same. I have been keeping it secret, keeping it for myself, but I am no fool. I see that it is time to stop hoarding my gifts. I see it's time to empower you just as I have myself been empowered."

Of course, he knew that if he shared his apple with them, it would ruin them. Just as it had ruined others before them. Only he had the will to master it. Only he could manifest true glory.

But fine. Let them try. Maybe.

"We don't want your gifts, Frenchman," Cabot snarled.

"Against God is what it is," Doyle said. "Against the natural way of things."

"But it is natural," Henry said, and he could hear his words firming up. Could *feel* his thoughts tightening. The numbness through him started to recede. "It's something that grows out of the ground. Simple and beautiful, my friends of the Golden, something that isn't against God but *of* God." A lie. It was of no god. It was of something deeper, darker, and much older. Something that *made* gods. And killed them.

Thumbs drew back hammers.

"You cockless fools," Henry hissed, his French accent bleeding in now, thick as pine sap. His voice grew into a spittle-flecked cry. "They'll know what you did! The friends of the Goldenrod will not abide this treachery against their mentor, their savior—they will not accept a tarnishing of my myth!"

Lambert smiled, juggling the ivory toothpick. "We'll do no such thing. Your myth will remain intact. You are, despite your crimes, an inspiration. You've done so much for us, for this county. So we will keep your myth. What happens here today goes with you to your grave. You died of a wasting disease, such a shame. We will continue to speak of your ingenuity, your intrepidness, your innovative and indomitable spirit. Even if it makes liars out of us, we will not break this mirror, Vinot."

"You simpering, soft-fleshed betrayers!" At that, he found his power. It charged through him like lightning through an old birch, and he ripped his right arm forward, the rope snapping like a vine of frail ivy—his hand found the jaw of Chalfont Butler and he *closed* his fingers, mashing the bones and teeth into a pulp as the man's tongue popped free like a slug, his scream gargling through a throatful of new blood, and Vinot cackled as he wrenched his other arm free—

The sound of four revolvers going off was the last thing he heard.

And the last thing through his head—

Was four bullets.

And the taste of apple.

JUNE

—

Blight spreads quickly, and it's not always apparent on the fruit's surface. Even without the influence of invader or infection, an apple abets its own spoilage: its skin, minutely porous, exhales ethylene, a gaseous compound that induces ripening, and the fruit has no interest in stopping at the point where it serves our needs.

—Helen Rosner,
The New Yorker,
June 8, 2020

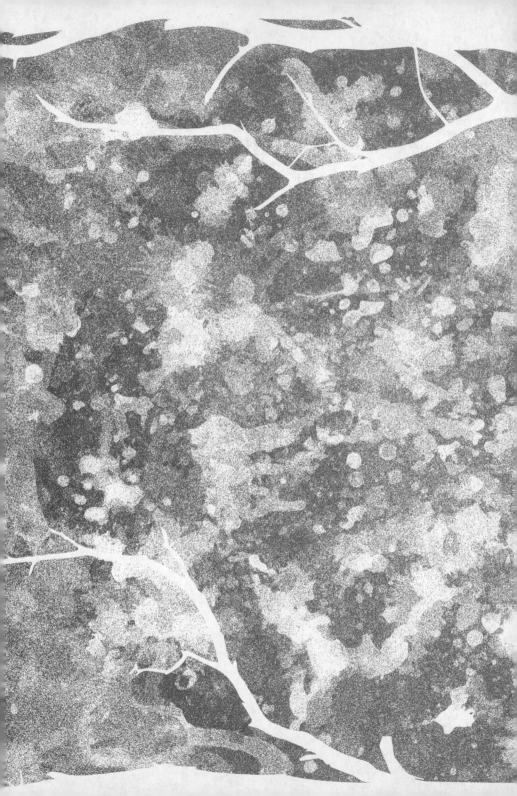

77

ACTS OF LUSTRATION

THE FIRST APPLE RIPENED ON THE LAST DAY OF MAY, AND BY THE next day, the first of June, others followed. Every apple hanging from every one of the Ruby Slipper trees hung full and dark like a bead of blood from a cut finger.

The seven trees of the orchard were bursting with the fruits, boughs bent and heavy. The saplings of the thicket, and those beyond, had only a few apples apiece, but that was all that would be required to feed those for whom the apples grew. The apples would grow bigger and taller in the years that followed, more apples swelling on those new branches, and more saplings would grow nearby, and more fruit would emerge upon those new trees, and in this way the orchard would swell, there would always be new apples, all the apples, and so many mouths hungry for those apples, tongues ready to taste, teeth ready to chew, hearts full of themselves and only themselves, until the day all the world was an orchard, and all its children were keepers and tenders of those black trees and red apples. One day. The last day.

But that day was not today.

Today was the first day, anew, renewed, amen.

IT WAS FATHER, OF COURSE, THAT FED FIRST. THOSE GATHERED—hundreds of them, from all around the county and even beyond it—watched as he picked that first apple, glistening and round and old-blood-black, gently unscrewing it from its mooring and then holding it aloft like treasure stolen from the gods. He brought it to his face. Pressed his nose against it, taking in its scent before dragging his lips along its skin. Deep breath in—

And a bite. Loud as his teeth punctured the skin and the flesh, juice popping from it, running down his chin, swatches of red-black apple in his teeth, on his mouth. Behind him Claude Lambert (now a flesh-kite of a man stretched wide, a syrup-slick patch of raggedy meat putty) cried out with a fervid, ecstatic moan—

Those gathered moaned with him, *ahhhh,* an exhalation of joy, an exhortation of pleasure-by-proxy—

Father Dan dug in, chewing faster, eating all the way around the apple, then snapping the core in half, then using both hands to shove the rest of it—from stem to stern—into his mouth before swallowing it. The crowd's sounds grew louder, faster, more insistent, a roller-coaster ride of rising euphoria.

And then the apple was gone.

He licked his fingers, held them up, the orchard-keeper's hands, hands of glory, hands of god. Then he reached behind him, revealing the appleskin mask. He held that aloft, too, before pulling it over his face. It seemed to tighten of its own volition—a creaking, a cracking, like teeth dragging across teeth.

"My children!" he called out. "It is time to *feast.*"

They responded, in unison, "*Yes, Father.*"

And feast, they did.

MARCO, THE ORCHARD-TENDER. NOT A KEEPER, NOT A KING, BUT A tender of the garden, a child of the trees, creature of the fruits. A guardian. He watched from the shadows of the thicket. Somewhere nearby, Prentiss skulked, too. They would not feed. Their teeth could not in fact bite into the apples—no, they could only feed on what was *exuded* from Claude Lambert. (And Lambert was almost dry.) It was the only thing that sustained them. So all Marco could do was watch, and wait, and bear witness.

As night fell, he watched them rise up as one. They mobbed the trees, clambering over one another to grab apples from the branches—they ate greedily, mashing the apples into their own mouths, smashing them against their teeth.

There were faces he knew: the police, the woman called Noreen, her daughter Meg, the other old men of the Crossed Keys, his teachers, even his own parents. It was young and middle-aged and old. Parents and retirees and teenagers. They surged together, like a tide. Some fell to the ground, writhing as they ate as others fell over them. They hissed and moaned and spat. Their clothes grew filthy with grass stains and swipes of mud; they tore at their garments, rending them in places as juice flowed from the fruits. They swarmed, gorging on everything they could shove into their mouths. They fed one another. They wept and laughed and babbled. The air sang with the scent of apples and sweat and spilled tears. And all the while, they *changed*. They radiated strength. They seemed to glow. Clean, bright skin. Wide, dark eyes. Vitality and lust flowered within, nectar and pollen and golden light. Soon they were no more than a human mound, rising like a pregnant belly of a mother breathing—in, out, in, out, one two three four five. Limbs lay entangled. Some spit apple flesh and strips of raw, red skin and sharp stems into each other's open mouths. Slick spit dribbled. Some were naked, their parts throbbing, swollen, sticky with the juice of the fruit.

Marco felt his own body stir in response: both pleasure and pain crackled through him like fractures across fragile glass.

And all the while, Father stood at the far end of the orchard.

Watching, as Marco was watching.

No. Father was lording over this. Marco was watching as a rat watches: from below, from a place of yearning, a place of weakness. But Father stood above it all. Looking down upon them. As a Father did. As a Father must.

Marco felt the hunger and thirst aching in all his hinges—all his empty places crying out for something, even as something else inside him, a small voice but a voice just the same, begged him to get up and run away. Like a little mouse the voice scurried around inside him, chased by a cat of shadows, pleading with him, *Marco, this is wrong, you can see how wrong this is, this isn't human, this isn't right—you can still escape, you can still break free, Calla needs you . . . Father does not matter, but it is the Daughter who calls your name.* But the smell of the orchard—the sweat, the juices, the crushed pulp, the kicked grass, the stirred earth—was truly narcotic, and the mouse with the tiny voice was slowed by it. So slowed that the shadow cat pounced and ate it up, yum. Marco wished he could eat it all up, too. That he could be with them in the orchard and not here in the thicket.

I could've been with them.

Like them.

An apple-eater instead of an eater of waste.

"*Look,*" said a voice hissing inside his ear. Prentiss. Back from the woman's house, it seemed. Prentiss was more evolved than him. Or more devolved. Did it matter? Transformation was transformation. Prentiss stood just behind Marco, Prentiss with his eyes like bulging cherries, his black seed teeth long and sharp, his fingers topped with vicious splinters, each the length of a carpentry nail. Most of him was raw, red flesh now. *Like armor,* Marco thought. He longed to have all his own skin replaced with it. A true child of the orchard. "See? They finish. And then we join them." But Marco didn't know what that meant or what came next. It wasn't long, though, before he found out.

The apples of the seven trees were gone. All of them. They stripped them clean, a flock of starlings, a plague of locusts. The eaters paused, lying upon one another, panting, sighing, softly gabbling a language that was not human, not of this time, not even of this place.

A moment of peace.

It did not last.

They all lurched up as one. Sniffing the air. Heads turning in simultaneity toward Father, who stepped into the orchard, his appleskin mask part of him now, fused to the flesh at the edges of his face—

"This is the true Ambarvalia," he said, his voice the loudest thing in the world even though he spoke at normal human volume—because the voice was outside of them but also inside of them, too, a deafening echo. "It's time to feed the orchard that fed us. We feed the trees, and we feed the orchard-tenders. Bring others into our garden, and they will eat the apple—or they will join the roots."

Marco felt something deep within him called to service.

And as the others moved, their heads low, tongues tasting the air—

So, too, did Marco move, and Prentiss alongside him.

Night was here.

It was time to hunt.

78

INVASIVE

A MAP OF THE COUNTY HUNG AFFIXED TO THE LARGE WHITE WALL with four crooked nails sticking out. The map took up the space where a flatscreen TV once did in Joanie's considerable living room. It definitely did not complement the space, and would not be in any photographs she'd use to publicize her house ever again.

In fact, once all this was over—assuming it ended, *and* that she was alive when it did—she intended to put all the sex gear and toys and décor into a storage unit, sell this house, and move far the fuck away from this goddamn county full of cult-minded apple-eaters. She was thinking Maine. Portland area. Somewhere that got cold, and where people wanted to get warm in whatever salacious ways gave them joy.

Besides, Graham still haunted this house. Not as a ghost—nothing so literal. But every part of it contained a memory of him in passing. Simple things: him cooking his famous scrambled eggs (cornstarch was key, he said, something he learned from someone named Kenji on YouTube, always talking about Kenji said this, Kenji did that, Kenji Kenji Kenji), him trying on hats in the upstairs mirror (none of them ever looked good, though she humored him just the same), him downstairs in the finished basement practicing his mixology (he was a wiz with the fancy cocktails, though she told him if he ever put cucumber in a drink again, she'd divorce him, because she was here to get pleasantly drunk, not eat a salad).

Or him upstairs, in the bed, bound facedown, ass up. Her approaching him, a latex cock bobbing between her legs, gleaming and ready. That, she would never tell anyone—not that she was ashamed of it, not at all, not in the slightest, but they'd never see it the way she did. She knew others would think her reminiscences of their kinky dalliances were shallow. But Joanie knew those acts were the furthest thing from shallow. They were no mere carnal explorations. To the contrary. They were acts of trust and intimacy of the highest order. Him being vulnerable with her in that way was extraordinary. It was Graham giving himself to her as a profound act.

It wasn't just sex. It was the truest kind of love:

Sacrifice.

That's not to say he didn't enjoy it; he did, and she did, and for a long time she viewed that as enough. But there remained a powerful acquiescence to it, a *giving in* that only enhanced the power of the act for the both of them.

It was a good sacrifice. A wonderful, pleasurable one.

But it was sacrifice just the same.

Because love was always a little about sacrifice, wasn't it? The offering of yourself—and getting enjoyment from that offering. She took far too long to understand that. For so much of their marriage, she viewed her and Graham's time together as if they were sharing space together, sharing air, sharing their lives, and it was without pressure—they could come and go as they pleased, do as they wanted, and neither would impact the other. She saw this as the highest form of love, but now she worried it was something else, something weaker—renting instead of buying, or worse, just a prolonged vacation you expected to end.

But Graham was her everything, and you don't get to have your everything without giving some part of yourself to that all-encompassing love. Graham knew it. She thought she did, but she only truly understood toward the end—

And especially when it was gone.

So, this place, this house: to hell with it. It was always just a receptacle for their work, for their sex, for their love, but like the bodies they inhabited until they didn't, this shit was just temporary. When it came time that John asked if he could put up a map of the county somewhere, she nodded, and had them help her rip the TV off the wall, pull off the mounting bars, and hastily nail up the map. John said she could've just used thumbtacks, but she said, "No, I want to hit something with a hammer."

Besides, they were going to need the thumbtacks.

———

THE THUMBTACKS MARKED SPOTS ON THE MAP. CURRENTLY, FIFTY-five spots.

It was Emily that figured it out first. She and John had been driving around through the suburban Bucks County towns, past the farms and fields and vineyards, when she spied something that looked familiar to her—

A sapling, growing up not just out of someone's front yard, but right out of their walkway. A stamped concrete walkway. As John idled the truck, Emily looked through binoculars and saw that the tree had pushed itself through a shattered patch of the cement—not popping up through a spot that had already been broken by time or by water or by some earlier impact. No, here the concrete around it lay scattered in broken, lifted shelves—

Like the tree had punched its way up and out.

This was a small rancher-style house. One floor. Sat southwest of Doyle's Tavern by about five miles, not far from the ag school. The yard was pristine. The flower beds, manicured by a steady hand. Wasn't a weedy patch in sight.

So it was strange that someone who paid such dramatic, precise, *insane* attention to their yard was also perfectly cool with a tree growing up out of their very nice stamped, stained concrete walkway.

Soon as Emily said as much to John—

The curtains in the front bay window of the house whipped open.

A woman stared out at them. Suburban Yoga Mom. Blond, casually messy, V-necked T-shirt. Not someone who would normally intimidate Emily, beyond their Karen-like heteronormativity and anti-vaxxer bullshit—but this woman? The way she stared? Hatred burned in her eyes. She bared her teeth like an animal—and then was gone from the window.

She's going to the door, Emily realized.

"Go," Emily said, and John sped away just as the woman came out of her front door—

With a gleaming chef's knife in hand.

Screaming at them: a howl of inchoate, wordless rage.

The tree that grew out of her own walkway—the one Meg whispered to, the one Emily cut down—wasn't the only such sapling. They were growing in other places. *They were growing near to those who had eaten the apple.*

The orchard really was spreading. But how far and wide was its—and it felt insane to think of it this way, but insanity was the order of the day—territory? Figure that out, and you figured out just how many people were in Dan's—what? Cult? Could you call it anything else?

Which meant they had a job to do:

Find all the trees they could find—

And cut 'em the fuck down.

SO, OVER THE LAST SEVERAL DAYS, THAT'S WHAT THEY'D BEEN DOING.

(The finding, not the cutting-the-fuck-down. That would come soon.)

Calla was right: They didn't need to do this alone. It was easy to get those who were wary of the apple-eaters on board. Calla got everyone she could find and trust onto a private Discord server online, so they had a place to coordinate their efforts. From there, she marshaled them to note down anything they could: if they thought someone was "altered" (the code word they used for the apple-eaters), if they saw anything strange, and most of all, if they found one of the strange apple tree saplings growing somewhere it shouldn't be.

"Welcome to the resistance," Lucas said after the first people started showing up in the Discord days ago. Their group got a boost from the video Calla posted, too—sadly, the boost was short-lived, because the video got reported *almost immediately*. They tried reposting it to other accounts, but those reposts got shut down, too, usually within an hour of posting. Still, it gave their numbers a goose, and at this point it was vital to take whatever, and whoever, they could get.

And now, they had the map.

That, from days of work—and they were still finding saplings.

Calla was trying to match the locations of the saplings with names and more formal addresses. Lucas was pacing the marble floor behind her, scrolling social for any other signs of the trees or the altered—or if Calla's video had managed to go viral and end up *anywhere* online. "Okay, I'm not seeing *shit*," he said.

"I feel like I'm doing homework," Calla said. "An office temp making a spreadsheet of cult members. Which is fucked, right? It feels super-fucked."

"I know we're doing the right thing, but it *is* a little fucked up putting people on a *list*. Putting people on lists has historically been kinda problematic."

"I know. We just need to know who is part of my dad's group so we can figure out if they have those trees. These people are dangerous—or in danger. Emily and John say that if we can find the trees, we can cut them down." Though how that was supposed to work, Calla had no idea. Already they'd found over fifty trees. Some were on private property. Others behind fences. And according to Emily, cutting the one down *really* upset her wife—like, she hulked out, turned into a rage machine psycho. So that meant trying to cut down a whole bunch in a single night. And that *still* left the trees back at the orchard. Calla knew her father would not let harm come to those easily.

Whatever. That wasn't her problem. That was for John and Emily to figure out—and they were still out there right now, scouting. Nighttime made it harder for them to see, but easier to not get seen.

She hazarded a glance at her phone.

"You keep looking at that thing," Lucas said, a note of accusation in the air.

"I'm a teenager. It's a phone. Of course I look at it."

"You're seeing if Marco will text."

"It's been a few days."

"It's not him. You know that, right?"

"I *know*," she seethed. "I know it's not him. Okay? I know it's my father but I keep waiting and hoping that maybe my phone will light up and it'll be a text from Marco, a *real* text from the *real* Marco, and he won't be in danger. Because I know he is. He hasn't been in school. His parents closed the restaurant for a few days but they're not in Philadelphia—I saw them in there, in the window. It makes me sick and I don't know what to do about it so I sit *here* and I type names onto a screen because they might be afflicted or infected or *altered* and, and—" She growled in tearful frustration and pushed the laptop away from her.

Lucas got up close to her, gave her a hug.

It felt good.

She leaned into it.

"We'll figure this out," he said.

"I hope you're right because I don't know if I believe that."

"We need to believe it or I will lose my fucking mind. Here, let's switch topics." Lucas got close and lowered his voice. "Like, we can talk about how this house is a McMansion full of sex rooms. I mean, girl."

"I told you, she rents it out or something—"

"I know, but ew—"

"Don't be so judgmental."

"It is my nature, and besides, I'm not judging, I'm just *fascinated*—"

His phone chimed. Then it chimed again. And again. *Ding, ding, ding.*

"Okayyyyy, well somebody's insistent," Lucas said, lifting the phone and tilting the screen toward his face. "Oh. *Oh.*"

"What?"

"Something's happening." A worried look crossed his face.

"Well what is it?"

"I—I dunno. Kyle Kobre says he just saw his parents—they were roaming the street with other people from his neighborhood. And April Tamburri said her brother left earlier in the afternoon suddenly—but now he's back, and he took her little brother away in his truck. Tried to get her, too, but she ran." Under his breath he muttered, "What the fuck."

Calla snatched his phone to see. It was the Discord server. Chatter was lighting up. She scrolled backward, then forward, to see all the messages—

ERIKAT: swear to god just saw my dad across the street but he's

eben gone for days

KARIM47: the little tree out front of our house has apples on it now

KARIM47: they weren't there this morning

LHETT-AND-RINK: I swear to god I just saw a bunch of barefoot people walking on the old covered bridge on Schnell's Grove Road, I think I saw my math teacher???

SUZYLUZ: OK this is weird but earlier my neighbor joined this rando group walking down the street and now they're back and I'm SCARED

She and Lucas shared a look.

"Joanie!" Calla called.

Meanwhile, she watched as the messages kept coming:

ERIKAT: oh FUCK my father just forced my mother into the trunk of our car

ERIKAT: there were other ppl in the car

ERIKAT: they all had masks on

ERIKAT: weird masks too, like Halloween masks or sumthin

CARDCAPTOR99: I hear screaming and crying in the woods WTAF

ERIKAT: 911 is busy nobody is answering FUCK

Joanie hurried over.

"What is it? Is it Emily and John?"

Calla turned the phone screen toward her. "I dunno what this is, but I don't think it's good. We need to call them. Now."

THE JEEP CRUISED DOWN RIVER ROAD AS NIGHT SETTLED IN. EMILY sat with a bajillion-candlepower spotlight in her lap as John drove. They'd added another couple of "sapling sightings" to their list—one north of here, outside the Regalsville Inn, and another five miles west, growing literally out of the roofline of a series of small row homes out on the edge of Perk Point.

John winced a little as he adjusted his position in the seat.

"You all right?" she asked him.

"Mmm." He grunted a little, shifting again.

"Shoulder?"

"Yeah. I'll be all right. I have been through worse."

Emily would put smart money that he was telling the truth. She knew not to pry. But John hid a lot beneath his surface. Murky waters could hide all kinds of strange things. He was a sniper in war. A successful sniper, by all indications. That told her all she needed to know.

"Hey, thanks for still being here," she said.

"Huh?"

"I mean, after getting your shoulder chewed on by a . . ." *Apple monster.* "Whatever that thing was. You don't have to still be here. You get a pass. Honestly, we all do. We should all just leave."

"We can do this. We have people. We're making progress. And we're all doing this for someone. You, for Meg. For me, it's Walt. And there are a lot of people who have been taken in by this man, Dan Paxson, and his orchard. Sometimes, a cult like that needs its back broken, its leader humiliated, its sacred tools thrown to the ground. It breaks the illusion."

"I think this is more than an illusion."

"It is, and it isn't. They're still under some kind of spell—you could see it with Meg. She was captivated by herself. She was in love with the torment she waged against you. Something seduced her, twisted her head around. Maybe together we can find a way to untwist it."

Now it was Emily's turn to shift uncomfortably in the seat. "And you think finding the trees will do it? Cutting them all down? That's a big task."

"Not so big it can't be done."

"Do they grow back? The trees."

He looked suddenly concerned. "I don't know."

"We cut the one down at Meg's. We could—"

"Emily," he cautioned.

"I'm just saying we could go take a look. We aren't far from there now, right?" She winced. "Do I have that right?"

"You're getting better with your area knowledge. Yes, I think we are just a few minutes from the house. Fine. We can go. I will take a look. You will stay in the vehicle, okay?"

"Scout's honor."

They sat quietly for a couple minutes.

Emily looked out at ribbons of glowing silver through the trees—the bright light of the moon trapped on the river water. She shuddered. Even this far from it, she could feel it calling to her. *I want to drown you, Emily.* She thought about Walt again. Down there in the dark, dragged along.

Then it hit her.

"What about the original tree?"

"What?"

She frowned. "At the start of this, we were looking for the same tree Walt was looking for. On the island in the river. We couldn't find it, but it seems like he did. Wouldn't we have to cut down *that* tree, too?"

John's jaw hung open as if he was searching for words but couldn't find them. Eventually, he found a word: "Shit."

Then: Emily's phone rang.

She got it out.

John gave it a quick look.

"Who is it?"

Emily was about to say the name she saw on the phone—Joanie—when she looked up, saw someone standing in the road directly ahead. She called out John's name, and he looked back just in time to grab the wheel, cut it sharply—

The Jeep skidded past the person—a person wearing a mask that glittered in the headlights.

The tire dipped into a mud-slick ditch, and Emily's head bounced one way then bounced back, cracking into the passenger-side window. Streaks of light tore across her vision and then whirled sideways as the back end of the Jeep slid one way, the front went the other—

And then her stomach pitched. The ground was suddenly outside her, beneath them, as the car rolled sideways toward the river.

"THEY'RE NOT ANSWERING," JOANIE TOLD THE TWO KIDS. SHE TRIED again; the phone rang and rang, going to Emily's voicemail every time.

Lucas sat glued to his phone, which had been returned to him. "Something's up, y'all. People on the chat are freaking the fuck out."

"I don't like this," Calla said to Joanie. She could feel the girl's tension—it was like a hum radiating from her. Calla buzzed with it.

"I'm sure it's all right. Emily and John can take care of themselves. Well. John can take care of himself *and* Emily, at least." She texted Emily. The text sat, undelivered, unread. "Shit."

"What do we do?"

"I dunno. We keep monitoring the feed, keep working to put a picture together of who is part of your father's group—"

"Cult. It's a fucking cult."

"Whatever it is, it's on us to keep our eye out. Maybe it's like John and Emily say, and we hit the trees. Maybe with enough information, we can get state police or FBI interested. We just keep trying, and hopefully at some point—"

The power went out.

"—we make a dent," Joanie finished, just as they were plunged into darkness, lit only by the garish glow from their battery-powered devices.

"Oh fuck," Lucas said. "Oh fuck oh fuck oh fuck."

"Joanie—"

"I know, Calla. I know. Stay close, I'll get some flashlights and some candles. I'm sure it's just a normal power surge." But Joanie feared it was no such thing.

JOHN STOOD BY THE RIVER, WATCHING THE MOONLIGHT BOB ON the water like a boat made of silver. He looked out over the current, seeing something out there in the darkness, in the middle of the river: a shape, a rise, like the back of a sleeping beast, Ya'kwahe the sleeping bear, Maxaxak the great snake, Mishibizhii the water panther. An island formed of a turtle back—its shell, a place to live, a place to dwell, a place to seek and to die. But he saw something else, too. Something moving beneath the current. Black roots, twisting and crawling. An efflorescence of darkness emerging, like oil, like disease.

"You're so damn close," Walt said, standing next to him.

Surprise jolted him, but comfort washed over John in its wake.

"Walt. I didn't think I'd see you again."

"You will, sometimes. I told you, I'm not gone. I'm real. I'm here."

"You're dead."

"I know that. Still." Walt took a flat skimmer stone, whipped it across the river. It hopped like a frog, skipping across the water, scattering moonlight. "You were close to figuring it out, but now's not that time. You have to wake up."

"I'm asleep. I can tell. Because I'm by the river and not the canal. The river should be farther out. The canal, here, just below me."

"Mind's a weird place, John. Besides. You took a tumble. Shook your cookie jar real good. But it's time to wake up, John. Emily needs you. C'mon now. Get up."

"Walt—"

Walt's face roared up into his own, detached from his head, a great screaming specter—mouth wide, teeth like stalactites, voice howling—

"GET UP."

JOHN GASPED AWAKE.

Blood throbbed in his head. His temples pounded. His eyeballs felt thick and full.

His hands dangled, knuckles brushing against the roof of his Jeep.

We're upside down.

He looked over, saw Emily in the passenger seat. Her head drooping.

"Em," he said, his voice a scattering of loose gravel. "Emily."

"Hnnh." Her head stirred. He saw a bruise, but no blood. In a small voice she said, "John?"

Out the driver's-side window, he saw that their descent to the canal had been caught by a tree—a big white pine tree. Past that, he saw the black shining waters of the river.

"You okay?" he asked Emily.

"Mmm," was all she answered, and he didn't know if that was a yes, a no, or if she didn't even understand the question. He needed to get her out of here, make sure she was okay. *Make sure I'm okay, too,* he thought.

He couldn't open his own door, so he popped his seatbelt, which had been holding him up—and he fell the few inches to the ceiling of the Jeep. Hit his shoulder, too, and that burned like hell, but he'd felt worse, so he bit back the pain like he was biting off the head of a snake, and kept going. John crawled into the back seat, slid across to the same side Emily was on, and tried opening that door—

But it wouldn't budge.

Well, hell.

All the way into the back he went, then, clambering over the sharp angles of an old rusted toolbox and all its spilled metal guts, and he realized—

The back was already popped open.

A pale shape moved through the trees, nearby.

Then he remembered:

Someone was in the road. I swerved not to hit them and—

He realized they were not alone.

AFTER GETTING FLASHLIGHTS AND CANDLES AND A BUNDLE OF long matches, Joanie went to the front window to peer out at the rest of her gated neighborhood and beyond. Weren't any lights on she could see, though she heard the growling sounds of distant generators starting to wake up and kick on. Graham never wanted one of the big whole-house ones, said they were noisy and wasteful—plus, this place never lost power for more than a day, usually just a couple hours, since they had a pretty cherry spot on the grid. Graham always said it was good to live near a major intersection or municipal buildings, because they made sure to get power to those first, and if you were on their grid, well, you got power back, too.

"It's not just us," she called over her shoulder to Calla and Lucas.

"That's good, right?" Calla asked.

"Yeah, means it's just a fluke or something." *Probably. Hopefully. Shit.*

But then—

Something out there moved across her lawn. From the cul-de-sac across.

A black shadow. Hunched over.

And it moved *fast.*

Just a deer, she thought. Not uncommon. That, or a stray dog—though it sure looked too big to be a dog, didn't it? She shivered. Couldn't suppress it. Because that shape—it moved on all fours, but not like an animal, not exactly.

"Fuck this," she muttered.

Joanie went and got the small fingerprint safe out from underneath her couch, opened it with her thumb, and extracted the .380 from inside. She grabbed the magazine, checked it for bullets, and slid it into the gun.

A match flare danced in the dark as Calla approached, lighting a candle. Lucas trailed her and they both looked at Joanie—at the gun in Joanie's hand—in shock and fear.

"What's wrong?" Calla asked. Lucas looked even more nervous, watching the gun in the glowing candlelight with wide, terrified eyes. Joanie realized that guns hit different for kids these days: With so many school shootings, they didn't see a gun and think hunting or self-defense or target shooting. Instead, it was the last thing they expected they'd ever see, pointed at them in the middle of third-period English. Joanie felt bad for triggering the poor kid, but that couldn't be helped now. She needed the gun to protect them.

"It's maybe nothing," Joanie said, trying to keep her voice calm. "This house is safe." *For the moment.* "But just in case, we need an escape plan. So listen to me carefully—"

"What the fuck," Lucas said, erupting. "No no wait what the fuck is happening, why are you getting out a *gun* and talking about *escape plans*—"

"*Hush,*" Joanie said, getting irrationally angry and knowing she shouldn't be. At least it quieted the kid. Again she tempered her voice. "Panic is bad. Okay? We don't like panic. But we do like preparedness. If anything happens, and I tell you to go, here's where you go—"

"Joanie—" Calla started.

But Joanie didn't let her speak. "*Here is where you go.* Listen to me. You go out the back patio doors. You go past the patio, across the yard, toward the hedgerow. On the other side are fields—part of a farm. Soybeans mostly. You go. You run. Fast as you can. Hide if you have to, there should be plenty of places to hide in the hedgerow, in the trees, in any of the farms past it."

"Bullshit," Calla said. "We can just stay here."

Lucas: "It's safer in here than out there."

"We can go to the basement. It'll be safe down there. Like in a—a tornado."

"It's not. The finished basement has a door to the outside." It had to, to be up to code. Otherwise, it was a fire hazard. "It's not a panic room or a bomb shelter."

Before they could continue the conversation—

Something hit the side of the house hard.

Whumpf.

Lucas gasped.

The sound was past the living room, on the other side of the guest bathroom.

"What was that?" Calla whispered.

Joanie shushed her.

She tried to tune her ears to hear—

There was—what? A muffled tapping. A scratching. And then—a series of whumps, like someone kicking the house itself. Except the sound went *up*.

Like someone was climbing up the exterior wall of the house.

"*Fine,*" Joanie hiss-whispered. "Down to the basement you go. *But—*" She stopped them before they went. "Like I said, there's a door out. If anything happens, you go out there, up the steps, out the Bilco, and you *run.*"

The two kids nodded.

And down to the basement they went.

Just as upstairs, a window shattered.

IN THE DARK, EMILY MADE A SOUND AS JOHN CRAWLED OUT OF THE back of his Jeep, his shoulder burning, his head dizzy. He got to his feet, hearing the passenger-side door open—*good, she's coming out on her own,* he thought, but when he planted his hand on the bumper to support coming around the other side—

He saw it was not Emily that had opened the door.

A woman stood there. Clothes bedraggled, ripped, and stuck through with twigs and thorns. On her face was a strange mask—a curtain of pen nibs in gold and silver. Moonlight crawled across them.

He knew who it was. Emily had told him about the mask.

Meg stood there, door open, peering down at her wife.

She reached in, undid Emily's seatbelt. *Click.*

John staggered forward—

Meg's head whipped toward him. Her eyes shined with pain and terror.

"You. *You.* You hurt her! I—I came to find her, to tell her I was okay, and you *hurt her, you monster.* You'll pay for this, John Compass." Her face twisted up in grief and rage. John didn't understand. Had she come to her senses? Swung far 'round the other side, now thinking John was Emily's enemy?

He let go of the bumper, held up his hands as if to placate the charging beast that was her accusation. "Meg. This was an accident. I think she's okay, we just need to get her out of there—"

"You groomed her. You led her astray. You led her to this. She's not *breathing* anymore, John. You were abusing her and now you killed her!"

That last sentence, she screamed. Her whole body clenched up.

He felt lost, spinning, out of control. He tried to tell her, *No, no, that's not it, she misunderstands,* but her howls drowned him out—

Howls that dissolved into hitching laughter.

Meg was laughing at him.

This was all a lie. A trick.

"Move," he said. "I need to get her out."

Her laughter died down, a balloon giving up its air. "I can handle that, John. She's my wife. I'm going to take her home now."

"Step away from her, Meg."

She reached behind her, pulled out the tranquilizer pistol.

"Remember this? I do."

"Meg—"

She pulled the trigger. He wanted to duck, run, get out of its way— but he was still rattled from the accident, his shoulder burned, his ears rang.

The dart hit him just below the ribs. It stuck. He swatted it to the ground—but it was too late.

The world went greasy. Like melting butter on a hot skillet. He blinked, saw Meg pull something else out—something shining and sharp.

A pair of scissors. Covered in dried blood but still gleaming.

Meg rushed at him, blades closed, the scissors now a knife.

John grabbed the bumper, hauled himself around the other side. Meg was already behind him, slashing with her weapon—the blades just missed him, kissing air. His hands fumbled for a pine branch and found its soft needles, and he pulled himself forward as Meg advanced toward him, scissors above him like a dagger—

His toe caught a root—

His knee tweaked to the side. He heard something crunch—

And then once more, everything turned upside down. His shoulder erupted in pain as he landed hard on it. He rolled through the brush and the trees, end over end, off a dirt wall and crashing down into brackish water, crying out in pain as the river—no, the canal—swallowed him up. He struggled against its cold, wet embrace. But he was weak, his body detaching from his mind even now.

The water dragged him down into the deepest dark.

JOANIE BLEW OUT THE CANDLE, TRIED TO LET HER EYES ADJUST TO the darkness. Her house was big, roomy, which made it feel like something could come at her from any angle. She tried to still her breathing and figure out where she should go—should she go find whatever broke the window upstairs? *No, that's what some idiot in a horror movie would do,* she decided. She had to find a tactical place to wait.

This wasn't a thing she was trained to do. She took firearms safety courses—both as a teenager and routinely throughout the years. And Joanie always flirted with the idea of doing some of those more tactical courses: stunt driving, CQB training, home and ranch defense. But time always got away from her and it felt silly, frivolous—until this exact moment.

But then, an ugly memory resurfaced—

Her, coming home. Finding her husband dead.

And Prentiss Beckman hiding there, standing in plain sight yet going unseen.

He stood by the tall lamp at the far side of the living room. Next to the chair.

A little cairn of apple cores on the ground.

That's where she would go.

Joanie slid through the darkness, gun up and out, sidling alongside the tall floor lamp, making herself part of its verticality. Just another long shadow.

It was there she waited. Working hard to calm her breath, her pulse, to clear her head, to stay open and focused. It was impossible. Her thoughts raced to the gallop of her pulse, which in turn paced her shallow, gasping breath, and with every heartbeat, every breath, every racing thought, she saw a flash of her husband on the kitchen floor, his head empty of its face.

She gritted her teeth. *Stop shaking. Calm down.*

Then—

Thump.

Thump.

Thump.

Something was coming down the staircase.

One slow step at a time.

Through the balusters, she saw the shadow pass—a satanic zoetrope of an ink-dark beast stalking on all fours, head low, shoulders high. She smelled something: a terrible mélange of scents. Blood. Piss. The perfume of flowers. The sour stink of cut fruit gone to rot.

Thump.

Thump.

Thump.

It wasn't human. She knew it. Against all her understanding and expectation, she knew this thing was not human. Nor was it an animal—no animal walked like that, moved like that, *smelled* like that. The air seemed to curdle around it.

Hand tight on the gun, she considered opening fire now—

But she didn't want any chance of missing. And with the bars of the balustrade in the way, she knew her shots wouldn't be clean.

Come on, motherfucker.

The thing reached the bottom of the stairs.

It sniffed the air. She gripped the pistol, keeping it at her side, waiting for a moment. *Come out. Just a little farther.*

Then it stood up.

On two legs.

Something gleamed. Slick, smooth skin. Shining. Light played off a wide maw of teeth, endless teeth, blacker than the dark. It spoke, its throat wet and clicking around the words that came sliding out:

"I smell you here, *whore.*"

MURK AND GLOOM. THE WATER, STILL AS A CORPSE, THICK WITH vegetation, fibrous and binding. A single spear of moonlight stabbed through the dark, impaling the space between pockets of algae. In that beam emerged a face, not swimming up so much as simply stepping forward. It was Walt.

"Before, you thought you were dying. This time? You really are. Or you're going to be. Drowning, just like me." In the deep of Walt's mouth, something moved. An eel. A fish. Then it was gone again.

John floated in the cold black void.

"Is this how it happened to you?" John asked.

Walt shrugged. Black tendrils—roots, like the ones he'd seen earlier—crawled around him in the gloomy river. A blush of poison. "Not quite, but close enough." He held up a hand that was now missing most of the lengths of each finger. He gave the stumps a little wiggle and wave. "Lost some digits, got knocked in the head, fell into the river."

"I should've been there with you."

"You should've been. But I also should've listened to you." Walt laughed a little. Oblong bubbles burst from his mouth and fled to the surface. "We've been over this. We're here now. You drown, you can't fix shit."

"Emily—"

"She's getting taken away, John. Just like I was taken away." Walt paused. Something warred on his face. "She's your friend." Said like a statement, but served like a question.

"She is."

"That's good. You need friends, John. Especially now that I'm just fish food." Another laugh, another scurrying of bubbles. Bubbles popped by the darting stabs of root tips. Pop, pop, pop. "But you only get her if you can keep her. You couldn't save me but maybe you can save her. It's all right there in front of you if you wanna find it, old buddy. You just gotta find what I found. Find the tree. Find the island. Follow the roots and save your friend." Walt walked his little stump fingers like they were a tiny stump-legged person.

"I can't help anyone. As you say, I'm drowning." He tried to remember what happened. "I was shot. Tranquilized. I'm out."

"Not all the way, old friend. You knocked the dart out, didn't give you a full dose. Just a little taste. So, you're down—but you're not out."

"I don't know how to wake up. To get out. To—" *To save Emily.* Around him, the roots began to gather. Like they'd just realized he was here. They began to reach for him. Closing in now. He imagined they'd soon be in his mouth. Pushing down through him. Like the ones from the seeds that had been stuck in his shoulder. Roots climbing through his veins, his heart, his bowels, his brain.

Using my body as dirt to grow more of itself.

But where do they come from?

Follow the roots . . .

"Welp, I don't know how to help you. If I knew that sort of thing I might not be dead! But what I do know is something about you: You've been through the mouth of Hell and shit out the other side. You've seen some monsters and, though I know you don't like to talk about it, been the monster yourself. You're pritner the toughest sonofabitch I know, John, a real piece of work. I figure if anybody is going to crawl his way out of this canal, it's going to be you."

"I don't know," John said. But if Walt believed in him, he could believe in himself. But the roots were coiling around his wrists now. He felt them tighten. They were crawling up his pant legs. Sliding around his neck.

"C'mon," Walt said. "Go on now. It's time."

"The roots—" John felt them, wet and sharp, probing at his lips. Scraping across his gums.

"You're stronger than those roots. Always have been."

I'm not.

Nobody is.

I SMELL YOU HERE, WHORE.

That voice.

Each word, spoken with the wet, crisp click of an apple slice broken between the fingers—it was inhuman, but also very human, and it was a voice Joanie knew.

Prentiss Beckman.

She raised the pistol and fired.

Her finger tugged the trigger again and again, the gun spasming in her grip, her left hand holding the wrist of the right to keep the pistol steady and stable, each bullet finding its mark in the center mass of the glistening shadow standing there at the bottom of her staircase. The shadow jerked with each hit, finally slumping against the wall as the hammer of the .380 fell on an empty chamber.

The air, now suffused with the eggy stink of gunfire.

Her ears, a shrill scream of tinnitus.

Joanie stood, shaking.

The shadow remained on its feet, leaning into the corner at the base of the stairs, unmoving.

"Fuck you," Joanie spat at the darkness.

With her thumb, she popped the magazine release and gravity snatched the magazine from the pistol, dropped it to the ground with a clatter. She reached for her pocket to find the second one—

Through the sulfur stench, she again smelled rotten fruit and apple blossoms.

The shadow shuddered and launched itself forward, fast, too fast, down like a wolf, leaping from the bottom of the staircase to the back of the couch, then to the coffee table, and then up over it toward her—

Joanie heard a sound coming from the back of her throat, a sound of both fear and rage, and she took the second magazine, jammed it toward the pistol—

Just as the Prentiss-thing slammed into her. The lamp crashed to the ground. She retained her grip on the pistol even as the magazine fell to the floor, spinning away as her foot danced out, kicking it. *Fuck!* Something sharp—*many* sharp somethings—pierced into her shoulders, lifting her up and pushing her into the wall by the window frame. It was the beast's fingers. His *claws.* She screamed as they pushed in deeper. For just a moment, the power in the room flared on, the lamp on the ground not broken, its shade tilted up so that the light that burst forth did so as a spotlight—

And that's when she saw what had become of Prentiss Beckman.

His face, lean at the bottom, bulging at the top like a ruined apple. His skin like appleskin, split in the middle as if from ripening rot, and in that ragged gash was a nest of black appleseed teeth, a winding spiral of them disappearing down the shuddering tube that was his throat. A moist leaf of a tongue flapped against those teeth as he spat invective upon her:

"You fucking bitch you nasty little sinner you think you can do whatever you want and run this brothel and spit on Father and spit on me!"

His mouth split wider, the flesh cracking at the corners of his maw, black syrup bursting from the cracks. The mouth, big enough to bite her head in half, moved toward her, hungry and eager to chew.

The lights flared up and went out again, plunging them into darkness.

Joanie had the gun.

It had no bullets.

But even without bullets, it could still be a weapon.

She gripped it on her hand, brought it up hard against the side of Prentiss's head. Once. Twice. A third time. She felt something give. The monster stepped back, its claws not all the way out but easing back. It gave her room.

Joanie splayed out a leg, planting her foot on the edge of the nearby chair, and used it to give herself leverage. She hit him one more time— and when she did, pushed up and out, wrenching herself free from his grip, the claws tearing ruts as she extracted herself and fell to the floor, the Prentiss-thing raging in the darkness above her, thrashing and howling.

IN THE BASEMENT, CALLA WAITED WITH LUCAS IN THE DARK. THEN: a series of gunshots dully echoing through the house, through the floor, and she cried out as they happened. Lucas did, too, clasping his hands over his ears. They held each other and sank to the floor.

More sounds above: a scuffle, a crash. Then the lights came back on for a few moments—*whoosh,* an eye-scalding wave of light in which the margins of the basement were revealed, exposing all the strange furniture that came part and parcel with this house, leather and vinyl furniture with purposes Calla could only guess at. As the lights lingered for a moment, Lucas looked at her, fear in his eyes.

"What do we do?" he asked, pleading with her.

"We run," she said.

So that's what they did. They ran to the Bilco door, flung it open, and ran out into the damp June night.

"YOU BITCH, YOU BITCH, YOU FUCKING BITCH," PRENTISS HOWLED, leaping back atop the coffee table on all fours. In the half darkness, she saw the gleam of his eyes, and the bone-white cracks in the raw crimson skin of his face, like the flesh of an apple. His voice suddenly became small and plaintive: "Joanie, why did you and your husband hate me, why didn't you both *see* me, why did you *mock* me and *treat me like refuse*—"

Joanie, bleeding from the claw-gashes in her shoulder, surveyed her escape routes. Prentiss was dead ahead of her, perched on the coffee table like a gargoyle—and behind her was their map, the one nailed into the wall.

Going left would take her back to where she came from, and the right path could circle her back around to the stairs. Or, if she was fast enough—to the front door. But Prentiss had proven himself fast. Too fast for her.

I can't escape him.

I have to kill him.

Or, maybe—maybe it was that she wanted

(*needed*)

to kill him.

Even if it killed her, too.

The Prentiss-thing gabbled at her: "You don't fucking *understand* how *hard* it was to be me, but now I'm so much *better,* so much *more,* and *you stupid fucking cunt I can make you just like me if you'll let me*—"

"Be like *you?*" she said, the words containing a cruel, mocking laugh.

"A small, shitty little man, a *bruised bad apple* not fit to feed a sick horse? No thank you, Prentiss Beckman. I'd rather be dead than be a squirming grub like you. Fucking worm. Your father always knew how weak and pathetic you are."

A noise came out of Prentiss, then. A sad bleat—the sound of deepest injury. "I have a different Father now. I am given to Father and to the orchard. Like you'll be. Taken in by the roots and the trees, the seeds inside you, germinating, sprouting. Pulling you apart, putting you back together again." Joanie tried to juke right, but Prentiss jerked in that direction. She tried left, too—the direction of the gun she'd dropped and, somewhere, the magazine—and he flinched that way, too. "Where will you go?" he asked, his turn to mock. "You can't go anywhere." He snapped his massive jaws open and closed, the black teeth clicking against one another, bending and twitching. Ruined gums mashing together, a moist, tacky sound. "Let me have a taste of you. And you can have a taste of me, too, *Joanie Maroney.*"

Prentiss leapt.

A GASP OF AIR IN A PATCH OF MOONLIGHT, AND JOHN COMPASS WAS awake.

He sat up in the darkness, his head feeling boggy, like all his brain was marshland and all his thoughts were travelers whose boots were mired in its mud. His clothes were soaked. Boots, too. He reached out to plant his hand on the trunk of a nearby oak—and he felt something take his hand. No. Some*one*. He smelled Old Spice—the *old* Old Spice, the aftershave, the one Walt always wore. And then the hand, a callused hand, a rough hand, was gone and he found the tree and pulled himself to standing.

The canal's edge was right in front of him. Here, it was about seven feet down from a berm of near-vertical earth. Other parts were walled with old stone.

It was a far drop down there.

And he spied no ladders, no good footholds.

Maybe he found some in his stupor.

But maybe, just maybe, he had

(*Walt*)

help.

John heard Walt's words echoing in his ear, too: *She's getting taken away, John.* Emily. He grunted, pulling himself back up the steep slope, using trees and their branches to help himself ascend, until finally he found the Jeep.

Car was still upside down. Trunk remained open. Both front doors, too.

And nobody sat inside.

He called out: "Emily."

His voice was hoarse, and his yell was barely above a whisper. He coughed and cleared his throat and gave it all he had: "*Emily!*"

No answer came.

Emily wasn't being taken. She'd already been taken.

He was too late.

Where had they gone?

Where would Meg take her?

But he already knew that answer. The orchard.

THE MOMENT CAME WITH A FLASH OF CERTAINTY THAT IT WAS over. Joanie's hopes of either escape or fighting back were gone. Prentiss had killed Graham, and now he was going to kill her—or, if the monster's threat was true, steal her away to the orchard, to whatever nightmarish fate awaited her there.

Prentiss leapt toward her, maw open wide, teeth flashing, claws out.

Her injuries bled and throbbed.

She did all she could do—

Joanie reached out, trying to hold him back, praying she could stop his claws from once more burying into the meat of her shoulders or arms.

Her hands caught him.

She recoiled, staggering not backward—

But to the side.

Prentiss, though, had momentum.

And as she held him back, pivoting—

He turned, and kept going.

As his thrashing body spun, it crashed into the drywall, the back of his bulging skull slamming hard against it—

Against one of the nails that affixed the map to the wall.

Thuck.

His legs and arms stiffened, seizing up. A gassy hiss blasted from his mouth, which snapped open and shut again and again. Prentiss hung on that nail, blinking, trying to form words, but only managing a wet gargle of gibberish.

Joanie's heart hammered so hard she was pretty sure it was gonna crack her sternum.

Prentiss tried to extract himself from the head of the nail, but couldn't seem to make his limbs work right. His feet were on the ground. His hands sat splayed out against the wall. But he seemed confused. Blinking as his protuberant eyes looked around the room, eventually settling on Joanie.

She stepped backward, frightened by his gaze.

Her foot nudged something.

The gun, she thought, hearing its scrape across the floor.

But it was too heavy.

Not taking her eyes off Prentiss, she knelt down and felt around the floor—until her hands wrapped around the handle of a hammer.

Same hammer she used to crudely pound those nails into the wall.

Joanie stood up.

And she stepped forward.

Prentiss reached for her. His fingers searched the air. She could see the tips of those fingers were burst open like bad meat, and from the peeled-back petal-like flesh were several inches of crooked, sharp branches. Glistening with her blood.

"Be with me," Prentiss said to her, the words a damp croak.

She buried the hammer into his forehead.

The tool broke through skin and bone with ease, going deep. Felt like hitting a rain-rotted pumpkin. Brown blood, thick like motor oil, welled up around the handle of the hammer—its head gone all the way into him—as his eyes went unfocused and his mouth opened wide and hung there.

Joanie bellowed, an act of rawboned rage.

Pain corkscrewed into her shoulders. She felt her shirt soaked through with blood. Blankly, she staggered around the room, finding the gun on the floor and its magazine about ten feet past it. Then she lit a candle and headed slowly, groggily, miserably down into her basement, each step an agony—only to find the Bilco doors wide open, and the two teenagers gone.

JOANIE'S INSTRUCTIONS RAN THROUGH CALLA'S HEAD LIKE A MAN-tra: *Out the back patio doors. Past the patio, across the yard, toward the hedgerow. Beyond that, the fields. Go, run, fast as you can. Hide if you have to.*

Go.

Run.

Hide.

So that's what Calla did. Her muscles burned like lit fuses as her legs carried her hard and fast out of the double Bilco doors, across the patio, toward the yard. Lucas was falling behind, and she called for him to catch up, and he told her he was running as fast as he could. Still, she heard his feet pounding across the patio pavers—*he'll make it, you'll both make it.*

The grass was damp, the ground soft, and she nearly tweaked her ankle from the moment she stepped off the patio, but she didn't care, *couldn't* care. All she could do was

Go

Run

Hide.

Calla bolted hard across the yard. She knew she wasn't ever going to run as fast as Marco could, but the absurd thought struck her, *I hope he'll be proud of me when he hears how hard I ran.* She never liked running, and would run with him only on rare occasions, and she totally complained about it when she did—but now, with escape on her mind, she couldn't wait to see him and tell him.

Ahead, the hedgerow loomed—tall trees separating this neighborhood from the fields beyond. Big, brushy pines, a few oaks, and undergrowth beneath it—*I can go there, hide in the brush,* she thought. Hunker down, keep an eye out, and wait. She called to Lucas, told him to hurry up.

No response.

She looked over her shoulder, slowing her pace—

And she didn't see him.

She skidded in the grass, stopping short of the hedgerow.

"Lucas?" she said, a loud hiss-whisper. "*Lucas.*"

In the distant mist, with no lights from the neighborhood to illumi-nate them, she thought she saw dark shapes. Shifting, moving. *Just a trick of the eye,* she thought. But then where had Lucas gone?

Maybe he'd made it to the fencerow already! *Duh.* She spun to look—

Only to find someone standing between her and the tree line.

"Hello, Calla Lily," her father said, smiling.

79

EVERYBODY HURTS

Every part of John hurt. It wasn't just the accident, or the tumble, or even the fall into the canal. It was something deeper than muscle pain. Misery dug its way into his very marrow, a kind of soul-weariness that burned of fear and failure. *I failed Walt,* he knew, and further, he had failed Emily as well.

But some failures, he prayed, could be undone.

Before they got worse.

He'd find her and he'd save her. No two ways about that. Even if it cost him everything.

John began to walk.

The walk to Meg and Emily's house was slow, but it was only a couple miles, and he managed even though his knee was tweaked bad enough he had to limp. He got there and found the house dark. He peered around the front and headed around the side to the back walkway and staircase that led to the river. That, too, was quiet. They weren't here.

Which meant they were likely at the orchard.

His hands burned for the throat of Dan Paxson, Meg Price, all of them who took a bite of that apple. He wanted to get his hands around those throats and *squeeze.* It was not a good feeling, nor was it kind, but that, he knew, was the nature of urges: They were uncaring things, thoughtless things, quick to snap like beaten dogs. The urge was in him to go to that place. To drag his broken, tired, limping ass to the orchard. To bring a gun, or something heavy, or something sharp, and cut down anybody who got in his way, cut them down like a sapling. He had killed before and it had never felt personal—someone always said, *That person in the distance, they did something, or hell, maybe they're gonna do something, and if you want to serve your country, you're going to pop 'em.* That person had never done anything to John. They were on a list, and he was following it, like a Santa Claus who cared about only who was naughty, and forget those who were nice.

This, though, was real personal.

Walt, dead.

Emily, taken.

If ever there was a time to burn that candle, it was now. And he knew it would feel good, too. Real good. Like breaking a long fast with the greasiest, nastiest hamburger and shake you could find. He'd so long committed to non-violence after a life of it that he felt like a cork about to burst out of its bottle.

But he also knew, that only went one way.

He'd die fast. And he'd likely find no succor for Walt, and gain no rescue for Emily.

Besides, he was too tired, too hurt. He needed some time.

He peered in through the window, seeing darkness plus the few little blips of light common to the modern home: microwave, oven, some kind of power strip, and, he hoped, a real phone. A landline phone, which seemed rarer and rarer these days. Well. Only one way to find out.

John searched for a rock in the landscaping.

HALF AN HOUR LATER, JOHN LIMPED BACK OUTSIDE, BOOTS crunching on broken glass, to meet Joanie at the mouth of the driveway.

JOANIE LOOKED LIKE SHE'D BEEN SUCKED UP INTO A TORNADO AND spit out the top. She must've seen the way John was looking at her, because she told him in a raw, blistered voice, "Don't get judgy, you look like stepped-on dog shit."

He said, "I feel the way that I look."

"Me too."

Joanie said she was wary taking these backroads—along the way, she thought she saw shapes running through the woods. *Wild like wolves,* was the way she put it. So instead she took a straight shot to Route 413, headed north from there.

They each shared their losses. Calla, gone. Lucas, too. Emily, taken. Joanie said she didn't know where Calla and Lucas were. The Bilco door was open, and she went out to try to find them—the lawn was matted down in spots, and she saw footprints there. Footprints that didn't seem to belong to her or Lucas.

John said, "It was Meg that came for Emily. Appeared out of no-where. Like she could . . . sense us. I don't know. But I suspect I know where she is. Maybe Calla, too."

"The orchard."

"Uh-huh." He extended his leg out, rubbed the spot just above his knee. Wasn't the first time he'd had pain here. Doctor said it was his MCL. Wasn't a tear. Probably a strain. *Hopefully* a strain. He looked over to Joanie and—

"You're bleeding," he said, trying to keep his voice calm.

Joanie dipped her chin and gave the two spots on her shoulders a look. Her T-shirt looked new, like she'd changed into it—but blood was now soaking through it. "Shit," she said.

"How badly are you hurt?"

"It's not good." She looked weary. Even a little dizzy.

"We need to get you some medical care."

"I'm fine," she said, stubborn as hell. Reminded him a little of

(*his own damn self*)

Walt.

"Besides," she added, "who even knows if the hospitals are safe? I go to the ER or something, they put me in a room, next thing I know, they stick me with a needle and I wake up surrounded by apple-skinned freaks." She shook her head. "I'm not doing that again. That thing that attacked us? It was Prentiss Beckman. But it also . . . wasn't. Some of these orchard cult creeps aren't people anymore, John." She nodded, as if to confirm for herself the truth: "They aren't people."

John nodded. He didn't know what she had seen or been through, but he guessed it was one of the same things that bit him. He had to ask: "You didn't get bitten, did you?"

She shook her head. "I made sure not to. Claws got me good, though."

"You need first aid."

"The Wegner's in Mercer Square is twenty-four hours."

"Then we better hop to it."

MIDNIGHT AT THE WEGNER'S GROCERY STORE. IT WAS A LOCAL chain—you found it only in the surrounding counties and just across the river in New Jersey. One just opened up where he lived in the Lehigh Valley, in Bethlehem. Mostly organic, a lot of local produce and meat, similar to Kimberton, and meant to compete with the likes of Whole Foods.

The two of them hobbled to the pharmacy aisle, each looking like a different flavor of shit.

The store didn't have many customers, but the few it had stared at them. Some with worry and concern. But John saw another kind of stare, too—cold disregard, suspicion, alienation. An almost-inhuman gaze that picked him apart. *The eaters of the apple,* he thought. They had to be. Fear nibbled at his brainstem like a starving rat.

Blearily, Joanie stared at the bounty of pharmaceutical options in the wound-care aisle. She said, "I'm not sure what to get, John. My first-aid care stops at BDSM recovery."

"I don't know what that means."

"Bondage, discipline. Impact play and ropes and stuff—you get abrasions and bruises sometimes. Honestly, first aid is part of aftercare. Aaaand for some people, just part of the play if they have a . . . nurse or doctor thing."

John still didn't really know what any of that meant. "Is that what sex is these days? Ropes and nurses?"

"It can be. Have you not had sex in a while, John?"

"It's been a while. Not something that really interests me. Now or ever."

"You ace? Asexual, I mean."

He shrugged as he gathered up items—gauze, Neosporin, alcohol, cotton balls, hydrogen peroxide. "If you say so."

They left the pharmacy section, heading toward the registers at the front of the store. More eyes regarded them warily, coldly. "You ever get the feeling you don't belong somewhere?" she asked.

"All the time, but now I'm really feeling it," he said.

But then, Joanie didn't respond. And he saw she stopped short behind him.

"John," she said.

"What is it?"

She pointed.

There, in the produce aisle: a big empty wooden table with a deep bin. A chalkboard sign above it, in cheerful hand-scrawled font, said:

COMING SOON, THE RUBY SLIPPER APPLE.
TASTES LIKE HOME!

And someone had drawn a little smiling apple with a worm coming out of its head. The worm, too, was happy. And it had sharp teeth.

"Let's get the fuck out of here," Joanie said.

John agreed.

BACK AT THE HOUSE, THE POWER WAS ON. JOANIE SAID IT HAD GONE out, but somewhere along the way, it had come back, illuminating a house that looked like a pack of angry elk had gone through it. John took a moment to regard the horrible thing stuck on one of the nails of the map—a map that now seemed foolish, part of a plan that never could've worked.

The map was splashed with dark, thick, oozing blood. And the once-human thing hanging there—a hammer embedded deep into the vegetal shell of its skull—was already deliquescing, like an apple turning brown. Its jaw hung loose, at an off-angle. Rows and rows of teeth—some broken off—nested in its mouth and throat.

This is the thing that attacked me, John realized.

A chill grappled up his spine.

He backed away and told Joanie, "Let's get you cleaned up."

———

THE TWO OF THEM WENT UPSTAIRS TO THE BATHROOM WHERE John tended to Joanie's wounds best as he could. They were bad enough he thought they needed stitches, which was not something he was qualified to do. The deepest part of the injuries thankfully had a narrow circumference—like she'd been stuck with the tip of a small branch. Which, according to her, was exactly what had happened, and it explained why he had to use tweezers to pull out some splinters. The claws must've dragged as she pulled away, though, leaving furrows a couple inches to the left of each wound. Those, at least, were shallow.

Joanie sat there, shirt off, bra on, as he cleaned the wounds, using butterfly bandages to cinch the cuts shut. To her credit, she took it without complaint. Occasional vacuum-hisses of surprise, and a few little grunted exhalations. But otherwise, she kept a lid on it. Joanie was a tough cookie. She'd seen some things, he guessed. She almost seemed like she'd been military once upon a time, but she said no, she was just "a tough bitch."

His own shoulder ached as he cleaned her up.

"John," she said, halfway through it all.

"Hm?"

"That store. They were going to sell his apples."

"Seems like."

She paused, as if considering this. He knew where her mind was going, because his went the same way: down, down, into the darkness of the truth of it. "The apples change people. And if those go in these stores, and soon in other stores, and then those trees keep on growing and growing and the orchard gets bigger and bigger—then everything is over."

"Yes."

Joanie turned to face him. Her face had gone near to bloodless. "Everything would be over, John. I mean it. These people, they've lost their minds. They're worse than a cult. They don't have empathy. They just want to make more of themselves, each as horrible as the next—and then you have others like whatever that thing is downstairs. Do they all end up like that? I mean, fuck, John. It would be the end of things. The end of society, civilization, the fucking apocalypse. All the world, a wretched orchard. And dancing among the trees, sycophants and monsters."

John sighed and nodded, because she was right. Of course she was right. He asked her to spin around so he could finish up, but she stayed facing him.

"What are we going to do?"

"We need to get our friends back. Emily, Calla, Lucas. Anyone who can be saved needs to be saved."

"Yes, but *what are we going to do?* How do we get them back?"

His finger itched to squeeze a trigger.

"I don't know," he said, forcing himself to relax.

"You're really a Quaker?"

"I am."

"Non-violent and everything, huh?"

He offered a hesitant nod.

"What would you have done against that thing that was Prentiss Beckman? Could you have killed it? Would you have had the stones to handle it? Or would you just have let it kill you? Because that's what non-violence is and means, John. It means getting killed. It means letting your loved ones get killed." She was speaking now through her teeth. Like they formed a dam to hold back a sudden river rush of emotion. "Like my husband."

"I don't know. The Quakers believe that love and light spread like fire. That peace between people is part of a vision for the world—a vision that transforms the world and the people in it. It's a process, making friends with enemies, finding the light within them, and making peace."

She was angry now. He could see that.

"How do you make peace with evil?"

"I don't know," he said, his voice breaking. Because he didn't.

She softened—a little, at least. "You were a soldier?"

"Army. Sniper."

"How do you get from there to here? From killer to . . ." Joanie seemed to be holding back a word. Like she wanted to dig in, say something nasty. "Quaker."

John turned so that he was next to her. He leaned against the sink—in part because he was tired, and everything hurt. "There's this thing they found in the soldiers who went to Vietnam. A lot of them, you know, it was hard being there, and they had access to drugs—nicotine, opium, heroin—and a lot of them got hooked. All really addictive drugs, right? You can't just turn that kind of thing on and off. But when they left that country, when they left the war that was lost for them, they came back here, back home, and . . . some of them never touched heroin again. Didn't want it. Didn't think about it. It was like the spell was broken. And you know, I guess science people think that something like that, addiction, you know, it has a—" He searched for the word. "Contextual component. They had none of the triggers for the addiction here. The smell of the other soldiers, the heat of the jungle, the trauma of the war. And I think that's what it was like for me, in a sense. Being over there, in the Gulf and beyond, I think of it as an Otherland. And the me that was there was Other Me. And over there, in the context of war, you kill because that's what you do, that's what they tell you to do, there's a chain of command and you're a link in it. I wasn't a person over there. I was my eyes, I was my trigger finger, I was my agreement to kill for my country." *I was blood and bloody patience and spent brass.* "But then . . . I left that place, and I came back here *to* my country and . . ." He rubbed his eyes. "And it was like leaving a fantasyland. This wasn't Otherland. This was reality, this was *this* land, Hereland, a land where we don't do things like that. Where we shouldn't just shoot people who get in our way. I was a killer there but what was I here? I never lost a night of sleep there, but back home damn, every night I lose hours thinking about the people I killed. I guess it's like I said: The spell was broken."

Joanie looked upon him with something John couldn't quite peg. To his eye it was somewhere between sympathy and scorn—maybe both, somehow, at once.

"I get it, John," she said. "I do. But truth is, we're up against something neither of us really understands, and if we let it go, if we're not willing to do what we need to do, then people we care about might get hurt, and the world will change for the worse. It'll be the worst version of the world because we didn't stand in the way of it. You can't shake hands with evil, John."

He nodded. "I understand."

"I hope you do."

She turned back around and he got back to work. But only a minute in, they heard someone pounding on the door downstairs.

Someone scared—or someone angry.

AT THE DOOR: *WHUMP WHUMP WHUMP.*

WHUMP WHUMP WHUMP.

John and Joanie shot looks to each other.

She grabbed the gun tucked in the back of her jeans—which, to his own dismay and disappointment, he'd missed—and racked the slide.

"You open the door," she whispered. "I'll be on the other side."

John winced, but nodded.

He unlocked the door, gently opened it—

And found a panicked teenager on the other side.

"Lucas," he said, steadying Joanie behind the door to get her to stand down. The young man came in, tormented and wide-eyed.

"Thank god you all are here," he said, on the verge of tears. He hugged them both and then whooshed past, babbling as he went: "Calla—she ran fast, she was ahead of me and then—then I saw him, I think it was her dad, and I heard other footsteps and I saw . . . shapes of people in the trees and I—" He nearly collapsed in on himself, like an imploding star. "I ran. I shouldn't have run. I should've stayed and helped her but shit, I didn't, I'm so sorry. Shit, shit, *shit.*"

"Hey, hey, it's okay," Joanie said, patting him on the arm.

"I lost Emily," John said.

Lucas sniffed and went to sit down, but then noticed that the room all around him was in dire shape, the craters in the wall, the broken lamp, the blood. His eyes drifted over the wreckage until they stopped at the room's unpleasant centerpiece: the oozing shape that was once Prentiss Beckman.

That's when Lucas threw up.

TWO A.M.

They sent him home, of course. It wasn't safe here, and it was already morally questionable having teenagers around all this in the first place.

On the way out, with his tears dry and his voice hoarse, he asked them: "What are you going to do?" And neither of them knew. They had no answers. Both John and Joanie searched for something to say, but there was nothing to say.

After that, Joanie drove Lucas home.

John should've gone with her but she told him to stay behind—*just in case* Calla got away and came back. So he sat, waiting, knowing he had to stay awake to make sure she got back okay. And he figured he might never sleep again. But whether it was just the horrors of the day, or the residual tranquilizer still creeping around his system, sleep found him whether he liked it or not. It stole him away into the dark, whispering in his ear that the darkness would soon steal everyone around him if he didn't figure out what to do next.

80

CLICK YOUR HEELS, DOROTHY

THE CELLAR IN THE OLD PAXSON HOUSE HAD WALLS OF ROCK AND A floor of broken concrete. The far side was a small room with an old coal furnace converted decades ago to fuel oil, but next to it was a long coal stall—wooden brace beams framing out the space, the broken cement stained eternally with black coal dust. The stall had no light and a cruel coal-dust stink; Calla always hated it as a child, always assuming it was haunted, making up stories in her head about how someone had died there, or killed people there, or killed themselves there—someone who was now buried under the fractured floor, beneath the silt, deep in the dirt. That or they came in through the old coal chute above it (a chute that had long been sealed up and offered her no chance for escape).

She stared at that space now from across the

(*prison*)

cellar.

This half of the cellar had been changed somewhat since last she was down here. There was still the old gun safe, the one that belonged to her grandfather. There were the wooden shelves bolted into the rock wall, each lined with a variety of long-forgotten and disused items: paint cans, stain cans, turpentine, an old tackle box, a set of lug nuts, the hubcap of some ancient Oldsmobile or Buick, an old metal Scooby-Doo lunch box. Some of it was Dad's stuff. Some of it belonged to her grandfather. All of it was grimy, rust-caked, and bound in the matrimony of cobwebs.

But the center of the space had been cleaned up—a little, at least. Swept out. Her bed had been brought down here. A nightstand, too, with her reading lamp next to it. A few stuffed animals from when she was a kid—stuffies that had long been in a Hefty bag in her closet upstairs—sat on the bed, propped up against the pillows. (Nigel, the bear. Snoobug, the corgi. And one of those hella fugly dolls with the human-looking teeth and the warped eyes and the nasty fur, a doll so ugly it actually came around the bend to cute again? What had she called him? Oh, right. Mick Jagger. Because her father loved the Rolling Stones and it made him fake-angry when she named the ugly stuffie that. That was one of their games they used to play that she loved—trying to make him fake-madder and fake-madder until she could imagine steam coming out of his bright-red ears.)

(Those days, Calla knew, were now just dead as coal dust.)

She sat on her bed now, Mick Jagger in her lap. Snoobug to her left, Nigel to her right. And she stared at that empty coal stall space, swearing she saw something or someone in there. It was like being a kid again. Certain there was a ghost haunting that long, dark stall. Stranger still, she smelled freshly cut apples. A whiff that was sometimes fragrant, sometimes foul.

Upstairs, she heard footsteps.

Then, the rattle of a key in a lock.

Her pulse raced. Hate and fear slithered through her as she tucked in her knees and pulled Mick Jagger closer. The door opened.

Her father descended.

He had in one hand, an empty plate. And in the other, a dark-red apple.

One of the

(*her*)

Ruby Slipper apples.

"Hey, Calla Lily," he said so softly and so sweetly it made her want to die, because it sounded like him—like her father, not the one standing here now but the one she grew up loving. The one who was once her best friend in the whole world.

"Die in a fire," she told him, and then flinched, because she was sure he would break suddenly. That he'd snap, descending upon her, smashing a plate over her head, cutting her with the shards of ceramic before shoving the apple so hard into her mouth her lips bled. But he didn't. His eye twitched a little, but then he just sighed sadly and sat on the end of her bed. He put the plate down between them.

Then he placed the apple in the center of the plate.

"You know, I've missed the hell out of you, kid," he said.

"You haven't. Maybe you think you did, or maybe you're just lying to me to make me feel good, but I don't think you're capable of caring about anyone anymore. I think you're dead inside."

"I'm more alive than I've ever been, sweetheart."

"Maybe on the outside. But your soul died. I can smell it in your breath. You're like that Halloween jack-o'-lantern sitting too long on the step. Still got the smile but inside you're all bugs and sludge."

He smiled. "You still have a way with words. You're still going to make a helluva—what do you call it?—influencer one day. Or whatever you want to be. You're going to be a force to behold in this world. A bearer of the Paxson name."

Calla tried like hell to show she wasn't scared, even as she inched backward toward the wall. "Great, so let me out of here and I'll go do that."

"Mm. Not quite yet." He seemed like he was going to say something but decided differently. He cocked his head and squinted—a move he used to do when he was going to, in his words, *drop some knowledge.* Once, that was quirky and dorky and she loved it. Now she feared the lecture to come. "You know, you say that I don't care about anyone, but that's not true, not true at all. I care about the people out there." He pointed toward the ceiling, toward the exposed pipes and floorboards and pirou-etting cellar spiders, but she knew he meant the people of the orchard. *His cult.* "I found something special. I found it, you named it, and now I'm changing lives. Calla, we humans are—we're a mess. A tangle of little ailments, a nest of anxieties, a series of failures from meager to calami-tous just tumbling our way to the end of life. But the Ruby Slipper changes that for them. For *me,* too. It makes us better. Stronger, faster, smarter—it clears the fog of fear and uncertainty and we know, *we know truly,* how good we are deep down, and how useful, and how essential we are."

"Drugs, Dad," she said through clenched teeth. "You sound like any idiot who found his older brother's Adderall."

He laughed at that—a sincere sound. "Yes, but it's just an apple, Calla Lily. It comes from nature, which means it's good for us."

"Maybe you should go eat a mushroom in the yard. They come from nature, too, which means they're good for us."

His laugh died, his smile went cold. "You're mocking me."

A frisson of fresh worry rippled through her. She knew not to push it. Knew not to say anything else. And yet, her mouth was opening, and words came out.

"Tell me about Walt Purvin," she said.

"Walt." His muscles tightened in his jaw.

"You say you found the apple. What would Walt say? Or, I guess he wouldn't say anything, because you killed him."

"Calla—"

"You think, *Oh wow, what a good person I am, I'm better now, I'm righteous and smart and an excellent leader,* but you had to kill someone to get here. And what about Earl Dawes? Wasn't that his name? The dead man in the orchard. I found him, Dad. I found his body."

"He was conspiring against me, Calla. He was part of Claude Lambert's plan. He would've hurt me—hurt *us,* hurt this *family,* and I couldn't allow that—"

"Where's Marco, Dad?"

He hesitated. His voice was cold when he said, "You don't want to ask that question, Calla, honey."

She leaned forward, emboldened and angry. "See, here's the thing, *Dad.* You're high on your own supply thinking what a wonderful person you've become, but the truth is, good people don't kill everyone who's in their way. They don't kill, they don't start cults, they don't kidnap their fucking *daughters* and lock them in *cellars* "

"I was going to let you live your life out there but then you became *trouble.* You started to *agitate* against what I'm building here."

"The words of a real hero, Dad. What a good person you are."

"You don't understand."

"Yeah, no, I fucking get it. I get the Ruby Slipper is a poison apple. I understand that poison got inside you and ate you up. And now you're— you're like any other piece-of-shit god-complex dickhead who got too full of himself to see the people around him as people. Some narcissistic monster, a shepherd leading his sheep over the edge of a cliff." She paused. "Except maybe it wasn't even the apple that made you that way. Maybe you were always like that, and you hid your true face. Maybe the apple just helped you take the mask off."

Dad was stunned into silence.

He sat there, his face softening. His chest rising up and down.

And in that moment she thought maybe she'd reached him.

The strike came fast. He backhanded her, *hard*. Knocked her head into her bedside lamp, almost sent it spinning off the table. She tasted blood.

And she tasted fresh anger.

Still bent to the side, she grabbed her reading lamp—

Holding it by the extender arm, she whipped it around, smashing the base into the side of her father's head. He toppled off the bed, crying out.

And something came from the coal stall.

It scrabbled forward on four legs, wide mouth snapping at the air, face pulled tight with raw, red appleskin—

Oh shit oh fuck, something had been there this whole time, she knew it, *she fucking knew it,* and now it was free, and coming for her—

But already her father was standing, extending an arm out, his hand flat. The thing, halfway across the cellar, swiftly slinked backward into the stall.

It sank into shadow and dust, invisible once more but for the faintest outline.

Panting, trying not to cry, Calla shrank backward hard into the wall as if she could sink into it. But the rock wall was sharp and unyielding.

Her father's head was bleeding. A flap of skin and hair peeled back— and below it, a fragment of black plastic embedded in his face.

Blood was running into his eye. Down his nose. Along his jaw.

He sniffed, putting the skin back in place, and using his fingers to comb his hair, too—which only smeared the blood around.

She watched the injury begin to heal.

The wound shuddered and shook, making a wet worm-crawl sound as the skin sealed back up. Dad plucked the plastic out, too—and the little cut opened for a moment like a small red mouth before closing again for good.

Somehow, through all of it, the apple and plate remained on the bed.

"You're not human," she said to him in a small, trembling voice.

He picked up the lamp slowly, regarding it with disdain. "Look at that. You ruined this lamp. No reading light for you now. I was going to bring some of your favorite books down—remember when you used to like reading?" He shrugged and sighed. "Not now. And no. I'm not human. Not anymore. Why would I want to be? Why do *you* want to be? It's disappointing you don't see it. The chance I'm offering you. The *opportunity*. You always wanted to be more than what you were—than what *we* were, as a family. It's one of the things I loved about you. You were ambitious. You got me, and I got you, and one day we knew we were going to rule the world from our humble little farmhouse, but—what, now you spit in my eye when I say it's time? I really did think I could leave you be out there. With Joanie—and really? Joanie? I'm going to have to talk to her, I guess. Show her the error of her ways. But I thought, fine, you can keep going to school. Go to prom if you want it. Long as you graduated, long as you went to school—maybe take some of our apples with you—then I could leave you to it. But you had to ruin it. Had to *spit in my eye*. So, you'll still graduate. I have people inside the school, they'll make sure of it. But I don't know if I can let you go off to Princeton like this. Like some rebellious thing. That's okay. We can fix you, still."

"I hate you."

"You hate me now. But you won't forever." He forced a smile. "Your breakfast is that apple. We've found that someone can't be forced to eat it. Choice in life, and in this, is everything, I guess. You have to want to eat it. You gotta want to be better than you are. And I know you do, baby." His smile widened, almost painfully so. "So I think you'll come around to it."

"That's the part you don't get," she said, her voice shaking.

"Oh? What's that?"

"I already did. I already tried your apple. I had to spit it out. There was a moment when I . . . knew it was wrong. I think you had that moment, too. But it made you feel so good you didn't care, so you kept on eating. Maybe that's the difference. Maybe some people know it's wrong, but they don't care, because it feels too good."

His face fell. This, of all the things she'd said, truly hurt him.

"You already tried it?"

"I did."

"You'll try it again," he demanded. "You will. And you'll change. Because if you don't . . ." He made an angry, bestial sound in the back of his throat. "You want to see what happens to those who upset me, Calla?

You want to know where Marco is? You already saw him. Just minutes ago."

No.

He reached up his hand toward the coal stall—

No!

And waved something forward.

The long-limbed shape emerged, again on all fours, from the shadows. She saw now the appleseed teeth, the shining crimson skin peppered with starburst lenticels. Marco's hair was there, but was patchy. His beautiful eyes were still his eyes, even as they distended and swelled in their sockets.

"Calla," he said, his voice a clotted, oatmeal mush.

"Marco," she said, barely managing to say his name before the tears started. *I'm so sorry I'm so sorry I'm so sorry.*

"I'll let you two become reacquainted. I'm sure you have a lot to catch up on. Maybe if you eat the apple, Calla, maybe I can do better for him. And if you don't eat the apple, maybe we plant Marco in the orchard instead."

And then Dad—no, not her father, just *Dan,* now, just some stupid, foolish, cruel, evil man—hung his head and walked back up the stairs, taking the apple with him. She heard the door close. And the lock engage.

Calla buried her head under her pillow as Marco, her love, slid back into the darkness of the coal stall.

81

THORN AND THICKET

THE SCREAMS, THE WEEPING, THE GABBLED LAUGHS—THE HORRORS of the night before were carved into Emily like initials on an old tree.

She'd been barely awake as Meg dragged her by the leg through an orchard lit by electric lanterns and firelight. She saw others being bound to trees, or chained to the earth with a stake, all of them brought in same as she was: dragged in, or pushed forward, or carried aloft upon the hands of the apple-eaters. Who they were, Emily couldn't say anymore, as they all wore strange masks: a mask of tree bark, a mask of brittle vines, a dollar-store Easter Bunny mask. And Meg, with her mask of pen nibs, fixed together with pinched rings of copper wire.

Emily herself was given a position of witnessing it all—that's how Meg put it. "I want you to see this," Meg whispered in her ear, the metal of her wife's mask tinging like wind chimes as Meg shoved her unmercifully into a metal cage sized for the biggest dog, closing the door and snapping it shut with a small padlock. All the while, the tranquilizer slowly fled her body, giving everything a greasy, oozing edge—she heard people begging to be let go, begging people who were their neighbors or their friends or even their closest family. All were offered the apple, and some took it, greedily and gladly devouring it like starving squirrels eating pilfered acorns—turning it over and over in their hands, sawing away at the fruit with gnashing teeth, their bodies slackening in ecstasy. Those who did not take the apple were afforded no such pleasure. Emily watched in horror as dark shapes like lashing ropes sprang from the ground, seizing the captives, pushing into them and through them— a wet sound, a breaking sound, like teeth through an apple. The victims screamed and sobbed as they were cinched tight to the earth, threaded through with what Emily soon realized were roots. Others were drawn to the trees themselves, speared through with sharp, thornlike branches from the bark. *Thuck. Thuck. Thhhhk.*

And all the while, the masked apple-eaters celebrated. They danced and clapped. They sang strange songs in unknown languages with lines that almost rhymed. They whirled about, arm in arm. Some of them ran like children, chasing each other, playful as if they were fully innocent— and those who had just eaten the apple tonight, those who made that choice, ran with them, like beasts freed from a zoo, the wildness within them, the *hunger,* allowed to resurface and become them completely. They ran through the orchard, but through the thorn and thicket, too, unbothered and untouched, as if the very undergrowth eased aside to let them pass. The air smelled of blood and apples. It sang of pain and joy.

Soon the tranquilizer won, and Emily slept.

SHE SLEPT UNTIL MORNING, WHEN THE SUNLIGHT PRIED APART her gummy eyes. Emily found herself curled up on her side in the cage. The wire bit into her and her body ached, half numb, half on fire. Her head throbbed from where she'd hit the Jeep window. She startled suddenly, then pushed and banged on the door, hoping somehow that it was so cheaply constructed it would simply fall apart—but it was too well made and would not open.

Blinking back sleep, she focused on the orchard itself. Her cage sat tucked into the thicket, the thorny understory surrounding her on all sides of the crate except its exit.

Out there, she saw the victims in the light of day.

Those who did not eat the apple numbered in the half dozen. She saw someone she thought she recognized—a waitress, wasn't she? From that bougie diner, Lumbertown Crossing.

She sat up against one of the trees.

A branch had pushed up and out through the meat of her shoulders, just under her collarbones. She was alive. Her mouth, working soundlessly. Black roots had pushed up out of the grass, binding her ankles to the ground.

The others were similar. Dark, woody tendrils pushing through their skin, lumps and furrows showing how they coiled around their bones.

They bled, but their blood was not red—

It was sticky and dark. Brown, like some kind of sap.

They moved against their bonds, even as the roots pushed them up and down, their bodies undulating as if on a gently bobbing tide.

One man, his belly round and fat, lay naked at the base of one of the trees—a whole sapling had grown up out of his mouth, three feet's worth, and he gagged around it, *kkkktt chhhhhk ghhaawwk.* The sapling was already blooming at the tip.

Then: movement.

Three shapes emerged from the thicket.

Things *shaped* like humans—

But not human, not really. They moved low—two on their legs, a third on all fours. They wore no masks, and their faces looked confused, partly in pain, partly eager—the look of a starving animal tempted by food. Patches of raw red skin, dark and crimson, stood slick at their necks, elbows, cheeks, midriffs. Their mouths were full of teeth both human and not, and the teeth that were not looked like—

Appleseeds.

Like those that she had pulled from John's wound.

The three of these shapes went first to the waitress at the tree—

No, gods, no—

She cried out, mewling in fear and pain as they descended upon her, lapping at the thick sap-blood that soaked her shirt and oozed from the branches stuck under her clavicles. Emily in turn cried out, too, banging on her cage door, yelling at them to stop, to get away from her, screaming for help in case someone somewhere could actually come and save them.

One of the three monsters—a woman, by the look of her, hair long and stringy and already falling out, her clothes just a tattered terry-cloth bathrobe—spun toward Emily, mouth open wide.

Emily heard a low whine from nearby, before realizing it was coming from within her—a dark aria in the back of her throat singing of a deep primeval horror.

Bathrobe Woman began to slink toward her. She seemed curious who was making this noise and yelling, but also angry at being interrupted. She crept closer, mumbling something that became clear only as she got within ten feet of the cage—

"—hungry, just hungry, who is this, *who is this,* why are they here, why are they *hollering at me*—"

"I'm sorry," Emily started to say—

Bathrobe Woman opened her mouth and shrieked, leaping for the cage—

A hard boot kicked out from the side, knocking her in the head. She tumbled to the side, and as this half-human woman got back up on her feet, she saw who had kicked her and became instantly deferential. Bowing her head like a chastened dog, slowly easing backward, mumbling, "Sorry, sorry, so sorry."

Meg stared down at the woman through the holes in her metal mask and spat at her. "Go back to your meal."

"Yes, *yes,* yes."

Bathrobe Woman scurried back to the other two. By now the waitress had gone quiet, her body racked with silent sobs as the apple-skinned monsters suckled at her wounds.

Meg squatted down by the cage door.

"Let me out," Emily said—she tried to make it sound demanding and angry but she couldn't keep the fear out of her voice. It sounded less like a threat, more like a plea. She hated herself for that. *I won't say please.*

"But I like the parity of this. You kept me tied up in a tub for days on end. I keep you in a dog cage." Meg smirked. "My dear wife, if I'd have known you were into this kind of play earlier, we might've had more fun in the bedroom. Turns out, I like control."

"Meg. Listen to me. This isn't okay. You've—you've fallen prey to something I can't understand but you have to let me out. We can get away from all this. You and me, together."

"Emily, this *is* me and you together. I am your wife and you are mine and here we are. Without your so-called friend, John, salting the earth of our relationship. We are here, we are home in the orchard."

"No—John *is* my friend. John cares."

Meg lifted her mask and made a sad face—a fake one, by the look of it. "Then I have bad news, Emily. John is dead. He drowned in the canal when I took you. I'm sorry you cared for him but if he cared about you, then maybe he would've fought harder."

A pit formed inside Emily. It was a great, sucking void of sudden grief—a black hole made of rage and sorrow. *John. No.* She killed him. Meg killed him.

"I hate you," Emily seethed.

"I thought that was true once, but then you tried to help me. You do love me. And you feel guilty because I was kind enough to bring you—this lost and wayward little thing, savage and undomesticated—into my life, my home, my heart, yet you were so unappreciative of that. You took my grace and pissed on it, cheating on me, acting out. But that's okay. Because *I* still love *you*. If I didn't, you'd be in the canal with your 'friend.' I wouldn't share the orchard with someone I didn't love."

"*Share the orchard,*" Emily said, repeating those words back to her. "Is that what this is? You make it sound like it's a gift."

"It is. The others were offered the apple and now it's my turn to make that offer to you. You can have the apple or I'll take you out there and let the orchard have you. It will take hold of you one way or another. You can celebrate it, or join the roots and the worms and the dirt. You are an eater, or you are eaten. And when you're an eater, Emily . . ." Meg's eyes closed. "Well. You already know how good it feels. The power it gives you. I've told you that. But now I'll present it a different way: If you eat the apple, you join me. You married me once and you can marry me again. If there is a part of you beyond that guilt that truly loves me, then I ask you to prove it. *Show* it. Ask for an apple and I will bring it to you. I will watch you eat it. Ask and you will experience a bliss like nothing you've ever felt. Ask and we will be truly together, and the world, the literal whole wide world, will be ours for the taking. Please, Emily. I am begging you to ask."

EMILY REMEMBERED THE DAY THEY DECIDED TO GET MARRIED. IT was April, and it was cold. The sky like chipped flint. Early spring flurries danced around them. They held hands and walked through Rittenhouse Square. And Meg said, with sudden forthrightness, "We should do this for real." Emily asked if she meant what it sounded like she meant, and Meg confirmed it. "Yeah. Let's get married." She explained that they'd been dating for six months, so why not? It seemed spontaneous. Odd, in a way, for Meg. That's what sold Emily on it. That rare glimpse of spontaneity.

The marriage that came after worked for a while. It felt like the two of them balanced each other out—like they each took something from the other, in the best way possible. Emily had taken away some of her wife's rigorous intensity, nibbling away at some of the stresses that seemed to form the core of Meg. And Meg had taken a bite from some of Emily's irresponsibleness, some of her chaos.

It was like a great leveling. But in her head, Emily always felt intimately that meeting in the middle meant one had to sink, and one had to rise—and that Emily was always the one to rise, with Meg forever forced to lower herself back down to earth in order to meet Emily. Meg was the one who flew higher, shone brighter. Up-and-coming lawyer, big at the firm, good family, lots of money. And Emily was the urchin brought in off the street. Dirt-cheeked with an empty gruel bowl held at the front. A contemptible thing, *lost and wayward,* as Meg had put it. Meg's interest in her felt like a gift to her at the time. A gift she had to appreciate. Had to love. Lest she be thankless and vulgar.

They acted as if they were equals, but they were no such thing. Meg was always better. Meg was always more. Because that's how Meg wanted it.

Maybe how she *needed* it.

"WE WERE A MISTAKE," EMILY SAID.

(The real Unspoken Thing, now summoned by the speaking.)

"What?"

"I did love you. I do love you. But our marriage was a mistake. You were always better than me. Or you thought you were and I bought into that myth. But I was a person before. I had a life and you acted like it was an inconvenience to you and a toy for me. You dismissed me. All of me."

"See? So unappreciative."

"I won't eat your apple. I won't ever eat your apple. I won't ever join you in whatever this horror show is. You're lost. You're gone. Maybe there was a chance before but that window has closed and now here we are. Throw me to the orchard. Give me to the trees. Go fuck yourself, Meg. *I want a divorce.*"

Meg pulled off her mask. Underneath, hate burned on her face. It rose in her like magma from broken earth. Her eyes burned with it, and her mouth twisted into a vengeful sneer. The mask dropped to the ground with a chain-mail *kshh*.

She leaned in, wrapping her fingers around the metal grate of the cage door. Teeth bared, she started to speak—

"I'll let you watch for a little while longer, to see if you change your m—"

Emily grabbed one of Meg's fingers and bent it sharply upward.

The finger broke as the bone snapped.

Meg yelled out in pain, withdrawing both hands and tumbling backward. She shook her hand like it was on fire, launching herself to her feet and pacing back and forth, hissing invective under her breath. She couldn't contain it anymore. The rage blasted forth and she stomped up and delivered a hard kick to the cage.

Emily pushed herself to the back of the crate—

As Meg's foot dented the crate door. The whole cage moved backward into the briar. Emily's wife leered down and said in a low voice:

"Sit there in your cage. You'll eat the apple yet."

Meg turned tail and stormed away.

But as she fled, Emily noticed something.

The cage door's hinges were now bent—and nearly broken.

82

ROOT SYSTEM

IT WAS LATE MORNING AND THE TWO OF THEM LOOKED LIKE THE living dead. John sat across from Joanie, both of them hovering over big mugs of coffee. For John, everything ached, from the deepest marrow to the topmost layer of skin cells. Joanie looked like hell, too, and earlier, John took a look at her injuries—they, thankfully, did not sprout roots and shoots in the middle of the night, nor did it look like an infection was gaining ground. But her wounds still looked like raw, red hell. Injuries aside, the long days and nights had taken their toll. Their eyes sat at the bottoms of pits and their faces seemed etched with lines cut with a crooked knife.

"I have an idea," John said.

"Is the idea we get guns and go down to the orchard to get our friends?"

John hesitated. "No."

"Still not willing to do what needs doing, huh, John? Okay. Let me guess: You want to call the authorities. Being a military man, you still trust somewhat in government and think they can come to the rescue."

"Being an *ex*-military man, if there is one group I do not trust, it is the government." He shook his head. "I want to cut down a tree."

Joanie blinked.

"A tree," she said.

"Yes."

"John, I think we're past the point where landscaping can save us."

"All along, Emily and I had been searching for the tree where these apples came from—and they are not the trees at the orchard. Walt was looking for the original tree of Vinot's apple—the pkwësu, the Harrowsblack, the Allegresse, or now, the Ruby Slipper. But we lost our way, got drawn into all of this—and we never found the tree that Walt and Dan

Paxson found, the one he must've used for scionwood to start his orchard."

"So, what's that even get us? You find the tree, cut it down, so what?" Irritation and impatience flashed in her eyes. "Kill one tree, the others die? I'm not a . . . a botanist or an arborist, but I don't think it works like that."

"Few years back, I had a problem with wisteria."

"And that's relevant how?"

"It wasn't native. It was invasive wisteria, and it kept popping up everywhere. You let it go for even a month, it'll climb trees, fences, everything. Walt always joked that if you sleep near wisteria it'll strangle you by morning. Let it go a couple seasons and you'll get a hundred feet of vine. It'll pull down gutters, smother a pine or cedar, choke out and break down whatever it reaches. I pulled it whenever it popped up, but it just kept coming back. I don't use Roundup, so I figured I had to find out where it was coming from. So, I dug a little, found some roots. Whole system. Kept going down. So I dug some more. Deeper and deeper, the roots getting thicker and thicker as I went, from thick as my thumb to thick as my wrist, and still I wasn't to the source. Turns out, these plants were coming from one single root system ten feet down. Main root was like a, a taproot from Hell, thick as my calf—and from here, all these shoots and runners, thick and thin, kept growing. I pulled that root out like Excalibur from the stone, and that was it. No more wisteria."

"You're saying the trees of the orchard are literally connected to the first tree? Kill it and you kill them?"

"All this while, we see the roots growing everywhere. Even in us." He shrugged. "I dunno."

"That's a pretty big *I dunno,* John." But a look did cross her face. "Still. Isn't that how vampires work? You kill the elder vampire, all its children die?"

Another shrug. "If you say so."

"No. You know what, it'll just be more direct if we go to the orchard, John, and you know it. Maybe you can do a distraction—"

"That's the other thing, Joanie. If I go after that first tree . . . I think that *is* the distraction."

She sipped from her coffee and leaned in. "How so?"

"When Emily cut down the sapling that was growing by their house, Meg *felt* it—like something inside her had been cut. Hell, I know how *I* feel when I see someone hurting a good tree—it pains me physically, but for these people, for this cult, I think it's a hundred times worse and more real than that."

Resolute, Joanie stood. "Fine, let's go cut down a tree. We'll know soon enough if it did anything at all."

But John didn't stand.

"Just one problem."

"What?" she asked.

"I don't know where the tree is."

"Then we're back to storming the orchard, just you and me."

"You're not in shape to do that and you know it. Listen, Walt was sure it was on the river somewhere. On one of the islands." He went on to explain to her what they knew about the island called Harrowsblack—that it was once used by both sides of the Revolutionary War to hang captives in order to taunt the enemy, and Walt's body presumably drifted downriver from that spot. "We—Emily and I—just couldn't figure out where it was." *It's what Walt's been trying to tell me. Walt's body, found on the river. Walt's ghost, telling me to follow the roots and look at the river. Message received, old friend.*

"The river? The Delaware?"

"Yes. There are islands there—"

"Yeah, I know." She laughed, like she couldn't believe it.

"What is it?"

"John, maybe there's a reason we found each other. Because my husband, Graham, was a civil engineer. And you know what his specialty was?" She didn't wait for him to answer, and instead blurted it out: "Artificial islands."

GRAHAM'S OFFICE, UPSTAIRS. JOANIE TRIED NOT TO LET THE GRIEF, the rage, the bad feelings drag her down as she pulled out some of his maps, unrolling them on the desk. Instead, she just said a silent thank-you to her husband. *I love you, Graham. I'm sorry you're gone, but maybe you're still here helping us in your own way.*

As she started to use various desk implements (stapler, pen cup, a book about local zoning laws) to pin down a map of the Delaware, she explained to John, who still wasn't entirely getting it:

"See, they build artificial islands for a variety of reasons. They might be used to modify the current, or clean up pollution, or, if it's big enough, host a nuclear power plant. Graham worked on one, let's see, let's see . . ." She stabbed a finger down on the map, at a spot just at the mouth of the Delaware River, between Marcus Hook, Pennsylvania, and Gloucester County, New Jersey, also at the very tip of Delaware, the state. "Here. They put in a wind port and wind farm. They'll build wind-powered turbines on that spot but also have a length of them down the river to generate power to itself."

"I don't think the tree is, or was, there."

"No, yeah, I know—but I bet it's *here*."

She tapped a spot far up the river, north of there.

There, John saw not one island, but rather, two. The easternmost island dwarfed, almost swallowed, by the western one.

"The bigger of the two," Joanie said, "is a man-made island. It was used to store dredged-up silt and sediment. Built in—" She leaned in, squinting at the map. "Looks like 1978. It's a big, ugly island."

John's face sank, like he was realizing what she was telling him.

And like he felt suddenly very, very stupid.

"We only looked from the Pennsylvania side of the river," he said. "The man-made island here is big, I bet. So big, it blocks the view of the other island. But if we had looked at it from the Jersey side . . ."

"A rare day when Jersey is the side you want to be on," she said.

He laughed, though it was not precisely a happy sound.

"Let's take a ride," he said.

"I'll be right down," she told him. He headed out as Joanie lingered in Graham's office for a minute longer. She blinked back tears and told him again that she missed him, and then she left the room, shutting the door behind her.

THEY PARKED HER PORSCHE JUST OFF RIVER ROAD ON THE JERSEY side (each side had its own River Road), and after climbing over a guardrail and forging a short walk through some brush, they got to the pebbled shoreline and—

Sure enough, there waited Harrowsblack Island.

It was a gnarled, craggy island, dwarfed by the mound of weeds and mess on the Pennsylvania side. Even from here, before he put the binoculars to his face, John could see the old apple tree at its apex. It was a thing bent over itself, twisted and hunched, wreathed in bramble.

For a moment, he smelled flowers—and then the wind turned, and brought the odor of rotting vegetation and the stink of dead fish.

"So, you have a plan?" Joanie asked.

John nodded. He did. "I need a boat. And some other things you ought not to know about. I'll go tonight. And while I'm there—you need to go to the orchard."

"How will I know it's time to go in?"

"You'll know."

Or so he hoped.

83

THE THING IN THE COAL STALL

CALLA HUDDLED IN THE BED, STARING AT THE COAL STALL AT THE far end of the cellar. She did this for an eternity, both wishing that Marco would emerge again from the dark, and wishing that she would never, ever, *ever* see him again.

But sometimes, as her eyes adjusted to the darkness, she thought she saw him, an outline darker than the shadows. Sometimes near the floor, sometimes near the ceiling. Sometimes skeletal. Sometimes wormlike. Maybe it was in her imagination. Maybe he wasn't here at all. Could it have been that it was just a trick? Something her father had rigged up to mess with her? She didn't know. All she could do was stare, and shiver, and try not to cry, and try not to scream.

And then, some unknown period of time later—

"I'm sorry, Calla."

Those three words, spoken from the shadows of the coal stall. No. Not spoken. *Uttered.* Grunted. Human but not human. Like the words first had to push through soft mud and deliquescing apple mush before they could be burped up to be born. Sticky and tacky and foul.

"Marco," she whispered. And now the tears came, but she quickly stifled them, wiping her eyes and nose on the sheets of her cellar bed.

Silence stretched between them again. Calla didn't want to ruin that silence. She wanted to keep it. She wanted to live in it forever. A snowglobe of quiet, where nothing changed. Things were bad now, awful even, but seeing Marco again would be so much worse.

And yet.

And yet.

She needed to see him.

So she forced the words out the way you forced yourself to jump off a high dive—pushing them to fall. "Marco, what happened?"

More silence. Then, a click on the ground. A scrape. Like sharp toe-nails.

A shape began to emerge into the meager light of the cellar.

He moved like a scared, hesitant dog. His fingers, topped with branch-tips, moved out first, and his bony shoulders rolled as his face pushed free from the dark. She could see Marco in there, but he had changed so much. All of his face was shiny red appleskin, and his eyes were like bulging white fruits—like those pale strawberries you could buy, bloodless as the vegetables that served as Bunnicula's prey in the old kids' book. Thin lips peeled back over black seed teeth. The rest of him was long and sinewy, lean and vinelike. He crawled forward, branches on fingers and his toes *clicka-click*ing on the cellar floor.

"Father blessed me," he gurgled.

"You're not blessed," she said, her voice cracking as she held back tears. *Keep it together, Calla.* She sniffed. "This isn't a blessing. And he's not your father." She felt the anger in her chest like thunder.

"He healed my leg. Put something . . . in me. I can f—" He drew that sound out. "*Fffffffeel* the orchard. It's like its heart is beating nearby. And all its . . . veins and capillaries are above us. Around us."

"Hearts and capillaries. Do you remember that you wanted to be a doctor?" She inched forward on the bed. Toward the end of it. Not quite ready to dangle her feet over the edge

(*in case he wants to bite off my feet like a monster under the bed*)

she instead crossed her legs underneath her, and wrapped her arms around herself tightly. "My genius doctor boyfriend."

"That's not going to happen now." He sounded sad when he said that.

"We had a lot we wanted to do. We had prom coming up. We would graduate. We were going to go to college together."

"Things have changed."

Marco eased forward a little bit, sat on his haunches.

"Don't stare at me," she said.

Marco looked away, at the floor, chastened.

"I don't understand how you're like this. Or why. This can't be real."

"I'm different. I'm better."

"This is not better."

"You can be better, too."

"Better like you?"

He shook his head slowly, sadly. "Better like Father."

"No." She scowled. "Not better like him. He won't let anyone be better like him. He'll always be at the top. They serve him. You all serve him."

And it was now she realized: It was always Dad's dream that mattered. His dream for the orchard, his dream for the farm's future—a dream inherited from her grandfather, which then metastasized like cancer. Even him wanting her to go to a good school wasn't about her. It was about him. About how it made him *look*. About how his ability to send her there constituted a success. For him.

"He loves us," Marco said, but she heard the uncertainty in there.

"He doesn't. He loves only himself." *And it wasn't the apple that did that.*

"You don't understand. It feels good to eat the apple. I . . ." Marco gagged, and some kind of thick spit dangled from his mouth—she smelled a stink like overturned compost, like hot mulch. "I went against him. And so I was given a different ch—" Another gagging cough. "Choice." He paused, still staring at the cellar floor. "I need to feed soon. I can feel the orchard. It's full of food now. I have new friends. I have to show them our ways."

He started to scrabble toward the cellar steps.

"Wait," she said.

Marco stopped. Chest rising and falling fast, like the breast of an agitated songbird. He tilted an ear toward her—an ear that was now little more than a puckered hole in the side of his gleaming, polished skin. A hole that was like the bottom of an apple. But still he kept his eyes pointed away from her.

"If I eat the apple, will you be made better?"

"I am better. Father has chosen my form."

"No. *No.* You know what I mean. Will you be—" *Normal.* "Will you be Marco again and not . . ." *Whatever you are now.* She couldn't finish her sentence. "That's what he said. He said maybe he could change you back. If I did that. If I ate the apple." *If I chose to.*

Marco said nothing. He just hunched there by the stairs, breathing.

"Tell him I'll eat it."

Now, *now* Marco looked at her. His eyes seemed to bulge further.

Cherry tomatoes squeezed between thumb and forefinger, ready to pop. In that stare she read a frequency of fear and warning.

"Are you sure?" he asked, his voice a mucky gargle.

All of her was tied to this apple, this orchard. Marco's life—his body, his mind. Her family's success. And her success, too. If she just went along with it, if she just gave in, she could pay for school. She could live the life she wanted. She could love her father again and he would love her once more, too. The fight was leaving her. Every part of her felt crushed, flattened to the ground like dead grass and fallen fruit.

I love you, Marco.

And I'm so tired.

"I am," she answered.

"Good. Glory be to Father."

At that, Marco bounded up the steps, like a hound eager to find its master.

84

EMILY CONSIDERS HER EXEUNT

THERE WOULD BE NO SLEEP, THERE WOULD BE NO REST. TERROR filled every part of her, every cell in her body a pulsing heart of anxious readiness. She had to get the fuck out of this cage and the fuck away from here. Then she had to get back to John and Joanie and Calla.

She could tell them what she had seen and heard in the orchard. That she'd heard what the apple-eaters were planning: another night of abductions. That the apple-eaters were also mobilizing in other, stranger, scarier ways: They were talking about putting all their money together and buying up land and businesses. And that they were putting together a list of the most influential people in the county: Politicians. Journalists. School principals. Restaurateurs. Millionaires and even a couple of billionaires. People who, she heard one woman say, *just needed a taste.*

Emily had to get out of here. Had to tell the others.

Earlier, Meg's anger had been the key.

The bent and busted crate door—damaged by Meg's kick—would be Emily's way out.

Emily lay on her belly and found the thick, woody stem of some plant—something blessedly without thorns. Something whose leaves smelled fragrant, almost like a whiff of sarsaparilla. She was careful not to pluck anything off any of the nearby apple saplings that were growing up out of the thicket, and doubly careful not to make any movements while the cultists were roaming the thicket, looking for apples. But when she was alone and had time—and when the appleskin freaks weren't patrolling the clearing—she broke off a stiff branch and got to work on the hinges. The hinges on the cage weren't proper hinges like on a door, they were just three loops of metal holding the crate door to the enamel wire mesh of the crate. And those loops were now bent and widened, thanks to Meg's door-denting kick earlier. So, Emily pushed the length of woody stem—about five inches' worth—in through one of the loops and used gentle leverage to open the loop wider. Like how you had to pry a keychain ring apart to get the key off, she just had to widen the gaps enough to loosen the door.

One hinge after the next.

Slowly.

Methodically.

Stealing moments when she could.

Spying when she couldn't.

The day passed into afternoon. Afternoon into evening.

The second hinge, now wide enough.

She hadn't seen Meg all day. Where was she? That felt worse than seeing her, somehow. Like she was right behind her. Or above her. Waiting.

As the moon rose, the third hinge was open.

Emily was exhausted. And starving. And trembling with fear and agitation.

But it was almost time. She plotted her course: Get the door off, then crawl out, and stay crawling along the thicket line. Into the thicket, if she could manage it, but that might slow her too badly—and already she felt a sudden bout of claustrophobia at getting stuck in the briar like a bleeding fawn with wolves advancing. No, she'd stay out of the bramble, and stay along the edge, and then—well, there had to be a way out. She didn't know the landscape, didn't know the topography, but somewhere, there would be a way, wouldn't there?

But what if there were fences? Gates? What if there were more patrols? What if she couldn't find her way out, like someone in a bad dream trying to get through a curtain but finding only more curtain, or being chased down a hallway full of locked doors? It didn't matter. She had to take the chance. She was outside. Not trapped in a room. She'd find a way.

The moon passed behind clouds.

The orchard was lit with fire and lantern light.

It was brighter than she liked, but this moment was the best chance she'd had.

But then: a commotion.

A dozen or so of the apple-eaters swarmed together, moving to the right as if to meet someone. There was a murmur, a gasp. Three of the apple-faced monsters loped forward, too, following—and then the crowd was pushed back like a tide as a tall figure emerged, arms spread wide. At first, Emily thought he was like the monsters, but she realized: That was Dan Paxson. He was wearing the mask, the appleskin mask, the one of dried flesh that cinched tight to his face.

"*Father,*" they called in unison, heads bowed low, staggering backward as he stepped forward.

"My daughter," he said, his voice booming. "She has chosen to eat the apple and join the orchard."

A great ecstatic moan rippled through them, their heads rolling around on their shoulders as if this brought them true pleasure and great pride.

He produced an apple and held it high.

"I picked this one for her even before I picked my own at the start of this harvest. Hers will be the first. She will join me at my side and you will call her Daughter, just as you call me Father."

They bowed and nodded, pawing at him—not touching him, no, but pawing at the air, as if just the proximity to him were enough to bless them.

"And here," Dan said. "One of the orchard-tenders has proven himself."

A fourth apple-faced monster nestled up to his side.

Dan reached down and stroked the thing's nearly hairless head. It nuzzled his hand like a dog. But Dan cupped the thing's chin and gently lifted—

And the apple-faced monster

(*the orchard-tender*)

stood tall, like a man.

No, Emily realized, like a young man. Almost a boy.

"Marco has done his job, carrying my message to my baby girl. And so he will be allowed to once more walk among us, if he so chooses."

Another moan rippled through them.

Marco—that was Calla's boyfriend, wasn't it? That meant Calla was here. Shit. *Shit!* Emily was going to run for it but now, could she? Should she? A selfish part of her was a coyote trying to chew its leg off to get out of a trap—*adjust your oxygen mask first,* she told herself madly, because if she got free, then she could come back for Calla. But if that poor girl was really about to eat the apple . . .

Could Emily just leave?

She had to save her, didn't she?

Shit shit shit!

"Follow me," Dan said. "Follow me, my friends, my family. When I come back out of my house again, you will know me a changed man. A family man once more. And you will know my Daughter."

He moved, the Pied Piper herding his children.

And that left the orchard empty but for the sighs, whimpers, and orgiastic cries of those who had been taken by it. The waitress, pinned to the tree. The round-bellied man, braided to the earth, a sapling spearing its way out of his mouth, his jaw working soundlessly.

Those, she could not free.

They were lost.

But Calla was not.

Emily was going to save her.

But first, she had to save herself.

With no one in sight, she got her hands around the door and lifted it slowly out of its hinges. It took some finagling—and as she finagled, the metal scraped on metal and one of the looped hinges groaned and she winced, pleading with the universe, *Please, please, please don't make any noise, please don't let anyone hear,* but no one did, no one showed, and then the door was off.

Gently, she set it down ahead of her, in the grass.

Emily started to crawl free—

And then, something walked right in front of her.

A cat.

An orange tabby.

Round-bellied, soft-furred. Its whiskers twitched.

Emily loved cats, and on any other day, she would regard a *surprise cat* with great, unbidden joy—but something was wrong with this animal. The fur around its mouth and neck was viscid with a glue of blood and spit. Its eyes seemed to shine unnaturally. She smelled the floral esters of chewed apple.

It refused to move. Instead, it sat right on the cage door. In her way.

Fine, she thought, swooping an arm out and moving to urge the cat off to the side—but the cat's paw moved faster and clawed the inside of her arm. It hissed at her as she whimpered in pain.

And then the cat *yowled.*

She hissed at it to shut up, and she pushed the animal aside—and this time it darted forward, swatting hard at her face. She flinched, and it just missed her eye. Blood wetted her cheek and jaw. Emily ducked her head low and crawled all the way free, even as the cat climbed onto her and bit down hard on the back of her neck. She shook it free and lurched to a standing position, her numb legs barely managing to keep her up. The cat continued to howl and hiss.

It's an alarm.

It's telling the others.

The cat has eaten the fucking apple.

And sure enough, as Emily finally got her bearings—

Meg came marching toward her.

And from the sides came others, too.

Two of the monsters—the so-called orchard-tenders—came loping up from the side. She spun around, looking for a way to run, seeing only the briar. She thought to jump up atop the cage she'd just escaped and leap into the thicket, trying to bolt her way through it. So that's what she did. Emily took a step even as Meg called her name

And the cat darted in front of her ankle.

She fell forward—

The fucking cat tripped me—

And her arm barely caught her as she collapsed hard against the cage.

Hands grabbed her by the throat. Meg hauled her up and dragged her kicking into the orchard. "Meg—" Emily choked.

"You're going to eat the apple," Meg said, firmly, as the others followed, as the orchard-tenders snapped at her hips and elbows with their long black teeth. "You're going to eat the apple or the trees will take you. They will pull you apart. They will make fruit from your flesh, and sap from your blood. It is time, Emily. It's time to join me one way or the other."

85

CHOICES MADE AND UNMADE

THE MOMENT FELT LIKE BOTH AN EXECUTION AND A BAPTISM, a religious conversion and a death sentence in equal measure.

Calla knelt on the dusty floor on the far side of the cellar, near the coal stall. The apple sat before her on a plate. The apple the purple of a fresh heart, the plate the color of blue veins.

Her father

(*The Father*)

stood there on the other side of the plate. He held the appleskin mask in his left hand. Its empty eyes stared at her.

Marco sat on his haunches to her left, occasionally nuzzling at her father's hip—a loyal animal hoping to be made a real boy again.

(But also, she knew, conveniently blocking her way to the stairs.)

(Would Marco hurt her if she tried to escape?)

(She wasn't sure, but she thought he might.)

Outside, she heard singing—or something like it. A wordless rise and fall of voices in one, *ahhhhh-AHHHhhhh-ahhhhh-AH-ah,* as persistent as wind rustling the trees, as steady as summer cicadas. The absurd thought struck her: *I'd love to be streaming this stuff live. The views I'd get. Instantly viral.*

But maybe it was like she had hoped would happen when she considered eating the apple before: Maybe if she took a bite of the Ruby Slipper, she would finally be what she wanted to be, which was a person with influence, a person with a massive audience, with clout, with *reach*. Not that she cared much about that anymore; it was hard to, after all, after all this. But maybe that, too, was another favor the apple could grant her. Maybe it would erase all of that. Maybe it would kill the part of her that was scared, the part of her that hated her father, the part of her that made her afraid of Marco. Maybe she could love her father again. Maybe they could be besties once more. Father and daughter, finding each other anew. And maybe Marco would change back to what he was before: a sweet, kind boyfriend, handsome and smart, dutiful and diligent, and she'd go to Princeton, and her father would let Marco join her, and they'd get married and have children and, and, and. *There's no place like home,* she told herself.

There's no place like home.

"My sweet Calla Lily," Dad said. "Let's go home."

There's no place like home.

There's no place like home.

She blinked back tears and nodded. "Okay, Dad."

The apple sat, waiting.

Her jaw felt tight. Saliva collected in her mouth. She anticipated the sweet taste but then remembered the flies. For a moment, she could hear them crawling around in the apple. She did her best not to gag.

Eat the apple, Calla.

There's no place like home.

She looked to Marco, who watched her eagerly. His bursting fruit eyes flicked from her to the apple and back to her again.

"I love you," she said.

"I love you, too, Calla Lily," her father said.

"I wasn't talking to you." Those words, she said bitterly. They were so acidic her father looked burned by them. His hands tensed into fists.

"Just eat the fucking apple and come home," he said.

But again she looked to Marco.

"You'll be okay soon," she told him. "I'll join you."

She reached for the apple.

Marco cried out, and in one fast motion brought two fists down on the apple. It smashed to nothing. The plate shattered. Calla screamed out, falling backward—as her father advanced on Marco with hatred in his eyes.

A FOOT KICKED THE SPOT BEHIND EMILY'S KNEE, AND HER LEGS buckled. She fell to the ground, even as hands pulled her back up so that she was kneeling in front of Meg. Behind her, the seven full trees of the orchard, one after the next, each the home of bodies bound to them by tangled root and spearing branch. Somewhere in the orchard, far away,

Emily heard more singing and chanting—a mad ballad of gibberish, a wordless and godless hymn. *Calla,* she thought.

Meg stepped forth, once again masked.

What have you become?

Behind the gleaming curtain of tarnished metal, Emily saw her shining, trembling eyes. Someone handed her an apple, and she presented it.

"Eat, and be free," Meg said.

"I'm *allergic,*" Emily said, two words ladled with spite. She grinned as she said it, drunk on her own defiance.

Something moved fast to her side. One of the orchard-tenders— a mouth of teeth both still human and appleseed—snapped shut on the meat of her left arm. It burned as they sank deep. She tried to pull away but hands kept her there. The thing wrenched away, taking some of her arm flesh with it. Already she felt seeds stuck in her skin. Already she could feel them burrowing.

It's time to join me one way or the other, Meg had said.

Emily clutched at her bleeding shoulder. Bodies pushed in on her. The apple danced in front of her, held fast in Meg's grip.

"Take it and eat it," Meg said. Then her voice softened: "Please."

"No."

Meg was more urgent, pushing the apple almost into Emily's nose. She sounded desperate, frantic, when she pleaded further: "Emily, I don't want to see what the orchard will do to you. I don't want that for you. I always wanted us to be together. You wanted to save me but now let me save you." Still, Emily didn't take the apple, and she turned her head away, like a child refusing its meal. Meg got down on her knees, level with Emily, and with both hands she cradled the apple and held it between them, the only thing separating them. "Marry me again. Join me again. Let's do this for real and you'll see the promise of the future. *Our* future."

"I've given too much to you already," Emily croaked.

Then she spit on the apple.

Meg failed to stifle a cry. She shot to her feet and said to those gathered: "Take her to the trees."

———

ON AN ISLAND IN A RIVER, A HAND HOLDING A HATCHET REARED
back—

And swung forward, the blade biting into black bark.

Thock.

MARCO WAILED AND SHRIEKED AS CALLA'S FATHER PICKED HIM UP
and slammed him into the rock wall of the cellar. Calla heard the sounds
of branches breaking inside Marco's body—crackling and snapping. She
scrambled to the floor, reaching for the apple mush to push some of it
into her mouth, but the piles squirmed with ticks and threadworms.
Fear ratcheted through her. Fear, then anger.

Calla picked up a shard of plate

And buried it in her father's back.

His elbow pistoned into her nose. She saw fireworks. She smelled her
own blood.

Blinking back tears, she tried to stay standing—and could barely
manage that even as Marco tried desperately to get away. But her father
was fast now in a way he never was before, fast like a nightmare. She
blinked and he was again on Marco, smashing him down into the stairs,
then up and into the shelves on the wall, her boyfriend's body looking
like a raggedy puppet with its strings cut. Calla moved toward them,
staggering forth, hand on the cold wall, hand on the railing, pulling
herself forward even though it felt like she was climbing up instead
of walking forward, a miserable slow pursuit that felt like it was slow
motion—all while her father dropped Marco onto the bed, hovering
above him.

She saw—

No

—Dad pull the plate shard from his back—

NO

—and raise it above his head—

"No!"

Dad began stabbing Marco. In the chest. In the head. Blood both
brown and black spattered up on the stone even as Marco's limbs flailed
around like the legs of a spider pinned under a burning match-tip. His

scream was a stormlike thing, the howl of hurricane winds through broken windows.

I'm too late I'm too late I'm too late, Calla thought as she reached her father, grabbing for him to pull him off Marco—

He whirled on her, pushing her back—

The plate shard again above his head, the ceramic dagger dripping, and he advanced on her this time—

But he stopped.

Frozen.

His jaw worked soundlessly.

He clutched at his chest.

That's when she heard the screaming outside.

THEY SLAMMED EMILY UP AGAINST THE TREE HARD ENOUGH THE breath clapped from her lungs and she was left keening for air. At her feet, the waitress lay just to the side, staring up with pleading, rheumy eyes even as black sap ran from her tear ducts like the blood of a crushed grasshopper. The crowd pushed in, holding her fast to the tree. Behind them, she saw Meg pacing back and forth, head down, apple pressed to her forehead. Babbling. As if she were praying.

Pain crawled at Emily's shoulder. She could feel the threads and tendrils running through the ragged meat. She hazarded a look and wished she hadn't—

One of the apple tree's branches was bent toward her.

And from her biceps and shoulder came squirming roots like thick hair, crawling through open air, reaching toward the tree—

Oh god oh god oh god

It fucking hurts

Please somebody help me

Faces pressed against hers, excited, hungry. One of the appleskinned orchard-tenders snapped at the open air in front of her. Hands pawed at her, eyes full of lust and glee looked to the seeking roots pushing free from her wound.

Then, it was as if they all took a collective gasp.

And a single step backward.

They clutched at the sides of their heads. Meg, too. As if a migraine had drilled into the center of their heads—

Their heads then craned backward on their necks.

They screamed in unison.

The tree behind Emily shuddered, as if in a quake.

Meg, too, was holding her head and baying in something that might have been pain, but might have been something stranger, something deeper. Some kind of horror, as if at their own existences.

Emily fell forward.

They streamed forward, suddenly, heading toward the house. Not all of them. Some remained behind. Emily crumpled into the grass, weeping.

Meg stood nearby, a trickle of blood coming from her nose.

"What have you done?" she asked.

PAPER WASPS

ONCE UPON A TIME, JOANIE THREW A STICK AT A WASP NEST HANG-ing in a tree out back of their house. She should've known better. Every kid worth his salt knew you didn't throw shit at a wasp nest, but there she was, looking at this papier-mâché, skull-looking thing dangling from a cedar out back, and she hadn't seen a wasp fly in or out of it in days.

So, she was feeling very *fuck around* without remembering the *find out* part, and as such, hunted up a stick—a short stick, but not rotten, one with enough heft—and she thought, well, let's just see. Joanie hauled back and let fly, and missed the nest entirely. The stick was clumsy; her aim was poor. But it still hit the branch, and it was like something out of an old 3-D movie—a lone paper wasp made a, well, a beeline *right for her face*. It popped her right in the forehead like a BB from a BB gun, and stung her, *zap*. She blinked, struck by the speed of it—and by the sudden pain.

And when she looked again, here they came, all the paper wasps in all the world and all of them knowing somehow, intimately and intuitively, that she was the motherfucker who threw that stick that disturbed their home. She ran like hell back to the house. Got stung about seventeen times— all over, too, head, neck, even under her shirt. (She wasn't allergic, thank god.) But she'd never forget how they'd streamed out of that nest, agitated as hell, single-minded on fucking her up because *she* had fucked with *them*.

And she was reminded of that very thing right now, as she watched— from the seat of her Porsche—cars stream out of Dan Paxson's driveway. She finished dry-swallowing a handful of Advil, watching car after car purge forth, tires bounding over the ditch, spraying gravel, burning lit-eral rubber as they bounded away. Going off to find the bitch that threw a stick at their nest.

She knew where they were going.

This was her chance.

Joanie got her gun, popped open the door, and ran.

HATCHET MAN

JOHN TOOK A BREAK FROM CHOPPING THE OLD APPLE TREE AND SAT at the base. He didn't turn away, for it felt restive and vengeful, like if you turned your back on it, it might reach down with one of those old, knotty branches and grab your head and twist it right off, like a cap on a soda bottle.

Sometimes when he looked askance—not at the tree, but not all the way away from it, either—he saw bodies hanging from its branches. Swaying in the river wind. Tattered uniforms from a long-ago war, the war that gave this nation its dark, bloody birth. A nation that had not done well by anybody that lived here before, then, or since, John figured. A nation that had made him kill for it. And sometimes, too, when he looked-but-didn't-look, he saw heads through scopes scalped by fast-moving bullets, he saw the man, the chef, Vinot, cutting off the arms and legs of men, women, and children, and sticking scionwood into the wounds, grafting tree onto bone as he laughed and laughed and laughed. He saw a fellow in a white suit, a white tie, white shoes, with teeth even whiter than all that, looking up into the tree and clapping like a little kid watching the town parade. And he saw Walt, his hand bleeding, his skull caved in, as he fell past the tree, through the undergrowth, and off this island into the hard, gray-churn current.

John's bag sat nearby, illuminated by an electric lantern. He set the hatchet—its blade still peppered with chips of applewood—on top of the rumpled fabric. He looked at his boots, with the shoelaces gone, those same laces tied together on the ground, leading into the undergrowth. He kept the boots on, though. For appearances. Then he grabbed a bit of pemmican out of his bag and chewed on that for a while, until eventually he heard the sound of engines. Headlights, distant, gleamed through mist and shadow. Then came brakes braking. Doors opening and closing. Voices. A chant, a call.

A splash, then.

Continued splashes.

Not a boat.

Then, nothing.

John stepped out over the edge of the small island, looking down through the tangle to the water. He swore he saw a shadow sliding through the dark water.

It was Dan, he knew. Moving through the river like the current didn't bother him. Like he didn't need air. Didn't need to swim. Like the river was part of this all—and maybe, John thought, it was. The apple had grown up and out of this island—a hangman's island, a place of broken necks and spilled blood—and it had set down roots, roots that surely went deep, that were river-fed. But maybe the river was itself fed by the roots. Maybe the tree was leaking its poison into the black waters. Drowning Walt. Trying to drown Emily, too. Even him.

Seeking roots, hungry river.

And now, Dan was coming.

John put half the pemmican back in his bag, thinking, *I'll get back to you later,* but then he laughed a little, because would he? Would he, really?

Eventually, he heard someone crashing through shallow water, stomping loud, then the crackle of brush, boots on dirt. Someone climbing.

He set the lantern a little way away from his bag. To the other side of him. Grunting as he did, because even such a small and simple movement hurt to do so—it was his shoulder. That deep ache wasn't going away.

As he set the lantern down, a shape came through the shadow. The lantern illuminated a man in an appleskin mask. Taut over his skin, like it belonged to him in a way far deeper than material ownership. Like it owned him as much as he owned it. Something went through John, then. A frisson of rage. His knuckles burned with their desire to close on the man's windpipe.

"You," Dan said through the slit in the mask. Words pared to a hiss by the knife-edge of skinned fruit.

"It's me."

Dan's gaze shifted to the apple tree. "I felt you . . . hurt it."

"I figured you might." What was interesting to John was that Dan *hadn't* figured on that. He'd forgotten about this tree. Built his own little orchard and never looked back. Maybe that was how the tree wanted it. Or needed it to be. "How'd you know this tree was here? Walt looked for it a long, long time."

A smile from Dan stretched behind that appleskin mask. "My father. Used to take me fishing on the river. Some of the best trout fishing around. He always said the tree on this island looked like an apple tree but we never thought anything of it. But when Walt showed up, said there was an apple tree on an island in the river, he just didn't know where, well. I knew where. Because of my father." Dan's smile lingered a little while, then died on his face. "You aim to kill me."

John sighed. "Bad apple spoils the bunch. That's the saying. Ben Franklin said it a little different: *The rotten apple spoils his companion.* Thing is, when it comes to apples, real apples, it's true. Isn't it? A rotting apple gives off a gas, accelerates the rot in every other apple near it. Rot compels rot."

"What's your point?"

Keep him talking. Let's play this out long as I can, John thought. To give Joanie time.

"I figured the apple from this tree—the one in your little orchard— was the bad apple, but that's not quite right. You were the bad apple, Dan. You're the one who had holes in his soul, who was pkwësu—the poison in this apple, the parasite, it needed a host, and you were a willing one. You were bad long before the apple got in you. Bad and broken and now you're breaking everything and everyone around you. I don't think you even see it."

"What I see is a sad old man who blames me for the better world I'm helping to make," Dan seethed. "What is this? You here to kill me?"

"You know, I want that, I really do, but I've made a choice with my life and that choice is walking a path of trying my damnedest not to hurt other people. Not on purpose, at least. Not directly."

"But you want revenge. I can smell it on you."

"Can you? What's it smell like?" John was, for real, curious.

Dan inhaled through his nose, then let it go. "Blood and roses."

"Mm. Okay then. Blood and roses it is, Dan. I want revenge. You're right. You killed Walt and I think you should be made to pay for that."

Dan hesitated. "I didn't kill Walt."

"Oh, but you did. Maybe you've talked yourself around it and out of it and you think, well, I don't know what you think. But somehow you're convinced of your own inherent goodness. Some of that is the apple lying to you. Most of it has always been you lying to yourself. However your head shakes out, the truth of it is that you killed him. Brought him here, betrayed him. Cut his fingers off, I think. Hit him with a rock, too. Or maybe the broadside of—what, the loppers?"

Dan stiffened.

"You can't know any of that."

"I must be close to death, because I can see some of it."

Again Dan looked to the tree. Then to the hatchet.

"You hurt the tree, but it'll heal. It's older than the both of us."

"Mm-hmm."

"You really thought you were going to bring down the tree with that little thing?" He was talking about the hatchet. "You're smarter than that."

"I am."

Again, Dan tensed up. He was starting to get it.

"You didn't want to bring down the tree. You were summoning me."

John shrugged. "Like a text message sent through those dark roots."

Down the dark roots, and along the river's current.

The other man stepped forward.

"You can't kill me with the hatchet, either, John. Just like you can't kill that tree. The tree will heal. I'll heal. Oh, but you won't. I'll break you in ways you can't mend. I'd give you a chance to take a taste of the apple but I don't think you deserve that." Another step forward. "And you wouldn't want it anyway."

Gently, John stood, grunting as he did. "No, I would not."

"For what purpose did you call me here then? You weren't cutting down the tree. You don't want to kill me. Why?"

"Oh no, we established that I want to kill you. I'm capable enough. I went to war after all, and was very good at it. Brought home a lot of souvenirs, Dan. Bullets, scars, couple land mines, not to mention an airplane's worth of baggage stuffed with all that guilt and grief. But I'm a Quaker now—"

Dan moved fast, grabbed John by the throat.

But he continued talking, even as Dan squeezed.

"—and we believe in holding, *grrk,* people in the light. And you know—*hkkkk*—what makes a very bright light?"

His hand wrapped tighter around the shoelace in his grip.

"Fire," John said.

Dan lifted John up high—

It was enough to do the trick. The shoelace pulled—

The land mine, a P-25 Italian anti-personnel mine, one John brought back from Iraq because the Iraqis used them, went off like a cork—the shoelace had been attached to a trip wire, and the trip wire to the mine that he tucked into the notch he carved out of the base of the apple tree. Tucked it in there tight, the big boom pointing right toward the trunk of the beast itself.

CHOOM.

The explosion detonated behind John, blowing that black tree into nothing more than a stump and splinters. The concussive wave blasted him and Dan Paxson through space and time, through Heaven and Hell. Everything was sound and noise and motion. The world whirling around him, breaking as his rag-doll body fired through it like a cannonball. He felt splinters tear him apart. Felt both of their bodies tumble as one through the brush. Head on pebbled shore. Body skipping like one of Walt's skimmer stones.

All John could hope for was that Joanie did her part. In those moments, fast and also slow, he said his goodbyes to Emily. Wished her well. Hoped he could see her one day soon, same way that Walt had found him. Then the cold water snatched him up, dragged him down and away. And the darkness finished the job.

PEACE WAS THE NOTHINGNESS, THE VOID OF EVERYTHING, THE GREAT empty. He just had to find that place. Dive into it like a black cave. You had to fall past despair and doubt to get there. But once you did, you gave yourself to it, found solace in the oblivion.

REST IN PEACE, JOHN COMPASS.

88

ECSTASY AND DESPAIR

A FREQUENCY WENT THROUGH THE ORCHARD—A STRANGE FEEL-
ing like the air had gone sick. Same way the air might feel before a bad
storm. Emily got to her feet, found Meg standing only ten feet away,
staring her down.

"Something's wrong," Meg said. In her voice was confusion and panic.
She pulled off her mask and her face was strained—the tendons in her
neck stood stiff like branches.

Emily felt the threadlike roots embedded in her shoulder squirming
in agitation. They weren't boring deeper, and they weren't reaching for
the apple trees any longer. But the way they twitched inside her felt electric, each one a hot wire. She clutched at that arm, gritting her teeth,
looking around the orchard.

In the lantern and firelight, Emily saw that those who remained
seemed to have the same vibe as Meg did: They were just standing there,
looking around, looking to one another, the same way she saw people
stand around after 9/11, or any disaster. Like they were trying to figure
out what had happened, what was happening, what might happen next.
The raw-skinned orchard-tender hunched low toward the thicket's
edge, staring out, paranoid, snapping at the air with teeth both human
and not. Firelight playing off its too-shiny, too-polished flesh.

"What did you do?" Meg asked her, stepping forward.

"I—I didn't do anything."

"You hurt me. You hurt this place."

"Fuck off, Meg." Emily thought she heard commotion somewhere—
not here, not in the clearing, not in the thicket. But up a way.

She took a step in that direction—

But Meg circled around.

"I should break you," Meg said.

"You already did. Again and again. You broke me."

Meg laughed—but it was a sad, wretched laugh. "I didn't, though. I almost did. But here you are. Still Emily. Still defiant. Still unabashedly *you*. I wanted you different. I wanted you like *me*."

"That was always your problem, wasn't it?"

The way Meg moved—fast. Too fast. Impossibly so. The back of her hand met Emily's jaw, and it was like getting hit by the side mirror of a speeding truck. It knocked her off her feet, and she moved her mouth, trying to figure out if it was broken. She tasted blood. Her lip was split. Her ears shrieked. *Concussion.*

Meg, sobbing now, grabbed her and pulled her back up.

She held Emily by the jaw, as if threatening to crush it. And she could, too. Emily felt the strength in her hand. It wouldn't take much to turn her jawbone to chalk, to crush her tongue like a slug. She felt her own bones grinding, crackling.

Then: The commotion Emily heard grew louder. It had entered the orchard. A gunshot rang out, *bang*. Meg wheeled toward it, and Emily looked, too.

Joanie stood there, gun up in the air.

Then she leveled it at the orchard-tender and moved forward into the clearing, her gun arm on a swivel as she pointed it at anyone who got close.

"Back the fuck up," Joanie called out. "Anyone comes at me, they get shot. *Back the fuck up*, I said."

They were vulnerable. Confused. They gave her ingress. The orchard-tender circled around, hissing, gabbling words that were not words. Soft, urgent mumbles.

Joanie barked to Meg: "You too, sister. Let her go. *Let her go.*"

Emily felt Meg's grip relax. She lurched backward to escape her reach just as Joanie came up alongside her.

"You're hurt," Joanie said to Emily.

"I'm okay." It wasn't a lie. But she wasn't sure it was the truth, either.

The two of them backed up toward the trees of the orchard. The cultists moved on them slowly, led by Meg. The orchard-tender slipped among the advancing horde like a restless cur. The barrel of Joanie's gun moved from person to person as she pointed, threatening for them to step back or she'd start firing. But Emily knew if that happened, they'd be dead. These people had power. Unnatural strength. And they could move with alarming speed. One shot and they'd have the gun out of Joanie's hand, the arm out of her socket. Emily would be torn to pieces. They were starting to get their bearings again. The confusion she'd seen on their faces just minutes before was fading.

"Where's Calla?" Joanie asked in a low voice.

"I don't know. The house, maybe."

"Then that's where we go."

"You're not going anywhere," Meg seethed.

And they tensed up—as if they were collectively going to pounce.

They started to move—

Joanie pointed the gun at Meg—

But another strange frequency ran through the air. A tremble, like an ill wind. Somewhere, Emily swore she heard a short, muffled pop—like a firework going off one town over.

The cultists braced suddenly, their limbs gone stiff.

They lifted their heads and moaned as one:

"No."

Then the ground trembled, as if in an earthquake. A rifle-shot crack snapped the air at their backs, and Emily tumbled forward, almost losing her footing as she looked back and saw one of the trees had split in half, as if lightning came from above and cleaved it in two—but there was no storm, no lightning at all, and then the same thing happened to the next trees in the line, one after the next. *Crack, crack, crack,* each tree splitting down the middle, broken by a jagged, splintered line. Leaves began to fall off as the cultists dropped to the ground, screaming as if they were on fire. Thrashing about. Clawing at themselves. Their masks pulled off and cast into the grass.

"Come on," Joanie said, tugging on Emily's arm. "Let's get Calla."

But Emily stood there, staring. The orchard-tender lifted branch-tip fingers and drew them down over his own face, rending ragged vents in the appleskin before reaching into his own mouth and widening it further and further until she heard bones grinding and cracking. Tongue lashing the air as it shrieked.

The others, too, were clawing at themselves, biting at their own bodies. One took a hunk of meat out of her forearm. Another bit hard through his own thumb, hard enough to dismember it—and he swallowed it back and began to gag and choke on it.

Meg, too, was self-destructing. Her hands were in fists and she was pounding them into her temples harder and harder.

She'd crush her own head like a stone fruit. A pulped peach.

Meg.

"Come *on,*" Joanie said.

Emily told her: "You go."

"Emily—"

"I'll catch up. Go!"

Joanie cursed—but she relented, and ran.

Emily went to Meg.

JOANIE MOVED THROUGH THE GARDEN OF WRITHING BODIES, blood spilling and spraying in the flickering lantern light. Faces she knew, the maskless ones at least, stared up at her, exposed: the cashier down at the Genuardi's, the woman who owned the horse farm down the road, and people she remembered seeing at the Crossed Keys dinner that night at the Goldenrod. One of the old Keys, Fritzy Letts, staggered out in front of her, howling and screaming, hands cupped around his cheekbones, pushing the flats of his fingers deep enough into his eyes to draw blood. Chase Hardiaken was nearby on the ground, knees on his father's chest, choking the old man.

They deserve it, Joanie thought, bitterly. *Die, you old dinosaurs.*

Emily, though, she didn't deserve this. Joanie thought to stop, to go back and get her—but no, Emily had made her choice.

But Calla still needed help. So Joanie kept on through the orchard, gun in hand, fleeing to the gravel driveway where she hurried toward the house. Screams echoed through the thicket south of her. Screams and sobs. Joanie made it to the front porch and threw open the front door, her gun at the ready—

And there, she found only Calla Paxson, standing in the living room. There was blood on her. Red and gleaming. Blood, but something else, too. Something sticky and wet, dark sap, red sap. The room smelled sickly-sweet of apples, and it made Joanie want to vomit. But instead, she slammed the door shut behind her, locked it, and set the gun on a side table nearby—that, before she swept the girl up in an embrace. Calla cried, and said that Marco was gone.

Joanie just held her, telling her it was going to be okay now.

Even though she knew it was a lie.

IT WAS LIKE WAITING OUT A STORM. EMILY CRAWLED ON TOP OF Meg and held her fast and firm, holding down her arms, pressing her cheek to Meg's cheek. Meg thrashed and nearly bucked her but Emily shushed her, soothed her, even as she heard the brutal sounds of the apple-eaters around her. The throat-rending screams. The broomstick snap of bones breaking. The wet sounds of eating (*themselves, they're eating themselves*) and chewing and biting. Crying around mouthfuls of (*flesh*) whatever it was they could not help but eat. And all the while Emily told Meg she was sorry, she loved her, she just had to hold on. *I'm sorry, I love you, hold on.* She told her, *I saw your art, I loved your art, you can be an artist if you want to, you're free now, it's okay, it's going to be okay, just hold on, just hold on.* And Meg did hold on. She held on to Emily as Emily held on to her. She shook and her teeth clacked against one another. She was dying. Emily knew that, then. She had to be dying. Seizing up, something inside her failing, some crucial short circuit where just like the trees had shattered, so, too, was she shattering. They all were. All who ate the apple were breaking.

CALLA WASN'T SURE HOW LONG IT TOOK, OR WHAT WAS HAPPEN-ing. She was in shock. Every time she closed her eyes, she saw a snapshot of Marco on her bed in the cellar. The bloody plate shards. Her father, gone. Calla left alone, all alone, forever alone. But then she went upstairs and Joanie came, and though Joanie's visits made her felt less alone, she still felt no longer a part of this world. She had no family, no love, no friends. She felt like a balloon cut from its string.

What she knew was: Outside, the apple-eaters were in pain. That much was clear. They howled in a discordant chorus. Before, they had sung their songs as one; now their anguish was theirs alone. Just as Calla's was hers alone, too.

Joanie tried to talk to her, tried to soothe her. She said she could go down into the cellar and help Marco, but Calla told her not to. It was too late. "Don't go, just stay with me," Calla begged. And Joanie listened.

Calla asked where Emily and John were?

Joanie told her, "John is—he's the one who made this all happen. And Emily . . ." Her voice trailed off. "She's out there."

"I hope she's okay," Calla said.

"I hope she's okay, too, kiddo."

"Where is my father?"

To that, Joanie had no answer.

WHEN IT WAS ALL QUIET, WHEN THE FIRST LIGHT OF MORNING started to brighten the windowsills in the old Paxson family farmhouse, Joanie asked Calla if she wanted to leave this place.

Calla said, yes, she did.

Together, they left the house to find the light.

EMILY LOOKED UP. THE SUN WAS COMING UP, JUST NOW KISSING the tops of the thicket. She didn't know how long it had been. Meg had gone quiet long ago. And the others in the orchard, too, had quieted down—their screams shifted to soft cries and eventually only to murmurs before falling silent. She sat up, rocking back on her haunches. Meg's body lay still in front of her, curled up in a fetal ball.

Meg.

"I'm so sorry," Emily said.

Then—

"Em," Meg said, her voice a small, miserable sound.

She's alive.

"Meg, Meg, oh my god, Meg." Emily got arms underneath her, tried to help her sit up. Meg had bitten her left arm in multiple places. But the wounds weren't too bad, and she hadn't bitten anything off, or out. Her eyes seemed clear. If sad.

"Emily," she said in a faraway voice. "I'd like to go home now."

"Sure. Yes. Of course. Come on, I'll—I'll help you up."

Which is what she did. Emily stood and helped Meg stand, too.

They started to shuffle through the orchard, one slow awful step at a time. The slow walk of a patient leaving a hospital. Around them waited a nightmare. Bodies sprawled about. The end of Jonestown. They were bloody, bent at off-angles. One man had pulled the skin of his own cheek free from inside his mouth—it hung loose like the paper of a torn-open envelope. Another woman had eaten most of her hand. A third person, gender no longer clear, had beaten their own face into a bruised, swollen mess.

It shocked Emily to realize: *They're not all dead.*

Some moved, shifting in unconsciousness. Some mumbled as Emily and Meg passed. A few hands reached for them, fingers searching.

"I could've been like them," Meg said in a hushed, horrified whisper.

"Shh. Keep walking. Don't look at them, Meg. Let's keep going."

So that's what they did.

Step by step through the bloody orchard. Toward the clearing's edge. Past the cider house. Toward the driveway that would take them to the house, to the road. But as they walked out onto the gravel with an un-steady step—

They saw him.

Dan Paxson.

His appleskin mask hung loose in the grip of his left hand.

He looked bloodied but uninjured. Like many of the others, he had the zombie shamble and lost gaze of someone who had been through a disaster but didn't yet understand the scope of it. He looked up at them and stopped.

Behind him, two more people emerged.

Joanie and Calla.

Dan turned to see them.

Moments passed in silence. All stood, staring, waiting. Unsure about Dan, what he had become.

He opened his mouth to speak, reaching toward his daughter—

"Calla Lily—"

Bang.

His head snapped back. A spray of red and gray caught on the morning light. He fell to the ground, a house of cards flattened to the table.

Steam rose from the hole in the center of his forehead and from the crater at the back of his skull.

JOANIE DIDN'T KNOW CALLA HAD HER GUN. SHE MUST'VE TAKEN IT off the side table where Joanie had left it. The girl held it in an unsteady grip. She said nothing. Their ears all rang from the shot. The air smelled like blood and roses.

ONE YEAR LATER, JUNE

—

When first we saw the apple tree
The boughs were dark and straight,
But never grief to give had we,
Though Spring delayed so late.

When last I came away from there
The boughs were heavy hung,
But little grief had I to spare
For Summer, perished young.

—Dorothy Parker,
"The Apple Tree"

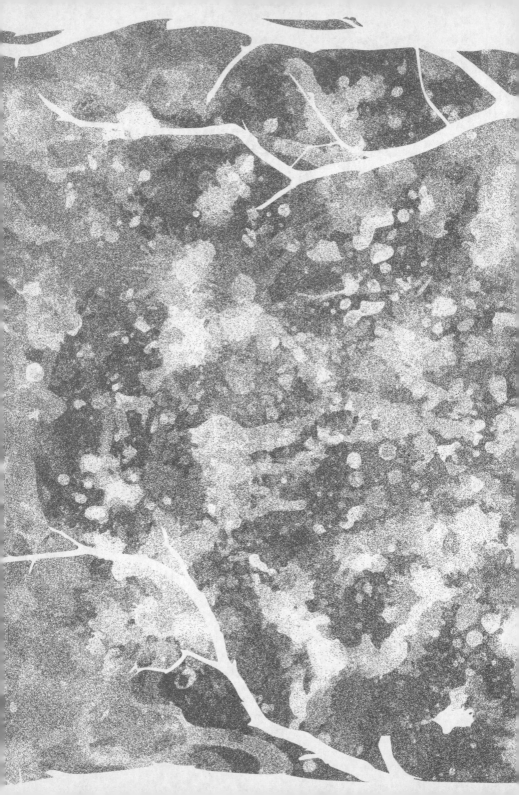

89

WHAT GROWS FROM BROKEN EARTH

ONE YEAR LATER.

AS ALWAYS, AN AFTERMATH.

Life to death to life again. Spring to summer, to fall to winter, and back again. The apple grows, the apple falls, maybe it's eaten, maybe it's not. In the end, the apple rots. But the seeds work their way into the soil again, and from them comes a little green shoot, up through the hard earth, maybe even through the crust of a late-spring snow. The shoot to a sapling, the sapling to a tree. Green leaves and pink blooms and apples once more, until fall rusts the leaves and winter knocks them dead again. Life carried forward. Decay and rejuvenation. Pain and grace locked in a whirling dance, the blur of red and green. Beauty and horror. Fuck around, find out. Everything cut down to nothing. But nothing becomes everything, too, on a long enough timeline, because that's the way of things.

THEY DIDN'T TALK MUCH ABOUT WHAT HAPPENED. NOT ANYMORE. They were like a family, now, one not bonded by blood or ancestry, but lashed together by the rough cords of trauma and terror. But those, as it turned out, were ropes not easily cut, and those bonds kept them together time and again. Calla had set up for them a texting chain through an encrypted app called Signal, too, where they kept up with one another even when they weren't *around* one another.

What happened that day lived with them all.

But it was what happened after that they talked about.

Mostly.

JOANIE

Joanie stands at the grave plot, freshly dug. Graham didn't want one and she didn't want one, either, but that was in part because she never felt like she truly belonged to this area, even though they lived here, even though she grew up here. But now it's different and so here she is, atop Buckman's Mountain, in the little cemetery upon that hill. She hasn't talked to Graham since it all went down. But now it all falls out of her. How insane it all was. How the cops said it was a cult, and only a cult, and how it was a member of that cult who murdered Graham. But she tells him that she got justice. She got Prentiss Beckman. He died pinned to their wall, she said, and it wasn't long after that he rotted there like a smear of old fruit, and the stain was so bad (and the smell was worse) that they had to just tear that wall down and replace it. But she said she was doing okay now. Because though she didn't have Graham anymore, she wasn't entirely alone.

"HEY, KIDDO," JOANIE SAID. CALLA NEARLY FELL OVER HER SUITCASE as she leapt into a rib-crushing hug. They stayed like that for a while; it had been a few months since they'd seen each other, though they talked often enough.

Calla babbled about Princeton, how great it was, how beautiful the campus looked, what pricks some of the rich kids were. Joanie reminded her that she was a rich kid now, too, what with the sale of the house and property. (Sold to some private equity firm. They seemed to be buying houses these days, and though it was gross, Calla needed to be rid of that house once and for all. "It's a graveyard now," she said on the day of closing. "And I don't want to be responsible for any part of it.") Not accepting the *rich kid* moniker, Calla told Joanie to shut her mouth, that she was still a poor farmer's kid in her heart. (But at that, she got quiet, and quickly changed the subject.)

Calla stayed here at Joanie's place, of course. This was her home when she wasn't at school, which delighted Joanie—and that delight *surprised* Joanie, too, because she never wanted kids, didn't like kids, would've been content to remain alone now that Graham was gone. But Calla wasn't a *kid*-kid. She was an adult child, and for Joanie, that was the best-case scenario. She got to fast-forward past all the diaper changing and middle school bullshit and now leapt forth into having a college-aged daughter. Or niece. Or sister. Or whatever the hell Calla was. All three rolled up into one. Sometimes Lucas and Esther came by, too. It was nice, though she would be hard-pressed to admit that out loud.

"I have a surprise," Joanie said, and revealed to Calla a bountiful spread of her favorite foods: fancy-ass donuts from that new joint off 263, the cheesesteak from the Carvers Inn (they used Cooper cheese, which was the best possible cheese to melt on top of meat), and pints of various ice creams from both Nina's *and* Owowcow, since Calla had always said they were both *differently amazing* in their own special ways and she would not pick a favorite so go fuck yourself.

Another hug, and Calla said, "I just need to clean up a little bit. I still have that Uber-stink on me. The guy used, like, a thousand air fresheners and now I smell like a cherry-vanilla chemical bomb."

"I told you I could've picked you up. It's barely a forty-minute drive."

"I'm fine, it's fine, I'm a big girl now."

And away she went to get cleaned up.

Unaware that more surprises were to come.

EMILY

At coffee in the city, Meg looks like weak tea. Not her impeccable self these days, Emily notices. She tries to cut her some slack. It's been only three months. They bond over the horror of that day, but not too often, because it would kill them both. (You can only pick a scab so many times. The paradox of the scab is, you have to let it heal halfway before you get a scab to pick, dontcha know.) Emily didn't go to any of the funerals. Certainly not to Noreen's. Meg handled the funeral and all the estate administration stuff, but not with the same aplomb as she would've, usually. Her father's still around, but broken by it all. Just like Meg is. They all are. Broken, that is. But again, trauma does that. Shakes you up, puts cracks in you. Over coffee, they talk about life. Meg's not at the firm anymore, obviously. She's painting more, which is good. She dances around it, a new Unspoken Thing, until the end, when they're leaving—then it becomes the Spoken Thing. "You ever think we might get back together?" Meg asks. Emily smiles and feels sad at the question—because it means she's going to have to answer it, and answer it truthfully. "No," she says. "We won't." Then

Meg asks her an even harder question: "Are you happy?" And Emily doesn't know if it's the truth or a lie when she says, "I am."

EMILY WENT TO RING THE DOORBELL—

"Hold up," came a voice behind her.

She knew that voice, and wheeled around to find John, hobbling his way toward the house, his leg stiff at his side, wincing with every step. Emily wanted to be the Hobbes to his Calvin, pouncing on him and knocking him to the ground—but they had a style of embrace that didn't, using his words, knock his old ass over. They met each other face-to-face, and he leaned on his cane with his right hand and pulled her close with his left. She, too, went in for the one-armed embrace.

"Thanks for being gentle with my old broken body," he said. His voice was a soft growl, now. Like parts of his insides were loose, rattling around in there.

"You're not old."

"I sure *feel* old."

She didn't want to say it, but he *looked* old. The events of that day last year had taken a lot out of him. His leg was still bad. He was on dialysis, too—splinters of that apple tree had gone all through him like shrapnel. Poor guy spent three weeks in a coma. They didn't think he'd make it. But somehow, he did. (Emily knew how: He was tougher than that pemmican stuff he liked to eat.)

Old or not, he was alive. Which was all that mattered at this point.

"Shall we?" he asked her.

"We shall."

And so they went inside.

JOHN

"So is it all over now?" Cherie asks him. It's been only a few weeks since he got out of the hospital—there for months, lost in a coma on a sea of dreams he barely remembers—but she's come damn near every day to see him, bring him soup and tea and pastries that they

enjoy while they play cards. "What was it that happened down there, John?" It's the first time she's asked him about it like this. Cherie looks worried. She should. "Are you in trouble?" she asks when he doesn't answer her right away. He tells her he's not in trouble. The cops think this was all the work of some kind of whackadoo cult, which, in a sense, it was. But it means none of it is washing up on his beach, so to speak. Cherie asks if John met true evil there. If he saw the face of it. He says to her, "I did, I think. True evil is real. But it's still a human evil. Even if it comes from outside of us, I think at the end of the day, it only wins when we let it in." Cherie nods and smiles. "Like a vampire," she answers. "Like a vampire," he says. Then they eat pastries together. It hurts to chew. But that's all right. She tells him she knows he'll be better real soon, and to show her faith in him, she buys him a gift card to a nearby laser tag place. He laughs at that, and laughing hurts, too. She says, "Don't laugh. I'm gonna smoke your ass, John." And he believes her.

CALLA CAME DOWNSTAIRS JUST AS EMILY AND JOHN CAME through the door, and the eruption that followed was Pompeiian: a lot of happy screaming and selfies and then they sat and descended upon the food with the voraciousness of wasps at the end of summer. John was hungry for the first time in a while, and he thought maybe it was the company that did it to him. They felt like family, now, in a way. Same way Walt did. Something sideways to friendship. Something more, but something stranger, too. Like you were who you were because of these people—but maybe they were who they were because of you.

When they asked, he told them that he was doing okay. He didn't want to weigh them down with the details of his suffering, though it had been . . . considerable. The pain in his leg was like lightning. His middle always felt empty, like pieces had been taken out. (And, in a way, they had. They took near to twelve inches of bowel out of him.) His dreams were bad most nights, though sometimes Walt was in them, and then they were good.

The subject came around to apples, which was curious, because nobody seemed to want to mention them before. It was Calla who asked him, "Are you still out there hunting apples?"

"No," he told her. "I think I've had my fill of that."

"Do you miss it, though?"

"I do. I think. Walt loved the hunt, but I just loved being out there.

Seeing the world, meeting people. I loved the birds, the bugs. That good quiet." He sighed. "And I do miss the apples some days. I still have a list of them I haven't found. But I think I'm a little too old and too beaten up to go back out there. I'd need a babysitter—I fall down in some field, I'll never get back up. Some farmer will mow over me, turn my ass into hay."

They laughed at that. Joanie didn't laugh, though.

Staring over a pint of ice cream, hand still on the spoon, she said, "I'll go with you. Make sure nobody turns you into mulch."

"You sure? It's not very exciting."

"John, I think I could stand a little less excitement in my life."

At that, he offered a true grin. "You and me both, Joanie."

CALLA

One thing she never tells anybody, not the kids at school, not Joanie or Emily or John, not even her own damn therapist, is that she can still feel the gun in her hand. It's always there, like a phantom limb. Calla wakes up screaming and crying a lot. She takes antidepressants, anti-anxiety meds. How could she not? Everything feels fucked up. She killed her own father. Shot him in the head. Even now she wonders if it's because of who he was or what he became. She didn't give him a chance to be better. To be a person again. But then she tells herself, he was who he was—a monster. And that wasn't going to change. He killed Marco. But he also killed Walt. So she couldn't have him hurting the people she loved anymore. She tells herself that killing him was an act of mercy and not of revenge—and hey, some nights, she even believes it.

"TELL ME FUCKING *EVERYTHING,*" CALLA SAID, SO EAGER WAS SHE TO hear about everyone else that her voice did this kind of Cookie Monster thing. "I want all the hot goss, all the nummy bits, the *who* and the *what* and the *whatever you got.* Emily, you start. Did you go to Meg's show?"

Emily quickly swallowed a wad of cheesesteak. "Mm. Mmph. Yes. I did." Meg had a show down in Coryell's Ferry last week and Emily hadn't been sure she was going to go. "You know, it was pretty interesting stuff.

I think she's still . . . processing. She doesn't remember everything, but some of that—it's in there. In her sketches. She's doing fine otherwise. Still technically a lawyer, but I guess the art thing has really taken over."

"And how's—oh god I'm sorry, what's her name?"

"Francine," Emily said, except she said it *Fran-seeeeeen*. She tickled the air with her fingers and fluttered her eyelashes. "She runs a food insecurity charity called Feeding Fishtown and she's got the longest legs I've ever seen and she's somehow always tan and she has too many cats and I don't really like cats anymore but it's okay because we're in *loooooove*." Emily wrinkled up her nose. "I mean, whatever. Not love. Shut up. She's pretty and we're having fun and that's good enough for me."

Calla knew this was, like, what, Emily's third girlfriend now since Meg? She loved them all. Let her have fun. She deserved it.

"Francine smells like patchouli," Joanie said with a little bitterness. "I mean, who wears that anymore? I didn't think that was even a thing. God, that smell *clings* to things like a needy lover."

"Yeaaaah," Emily said. Joanie had taken to living here in the house full-time, and turned the Rittenhouse Square apartment into the sex rental. Emily managed it, kept it clean, helped the guests get in and out of the space. "Sorry, she does have a heavy hand with the hippie-shit scents." To Calla, Emily asked, "What about you? Boyfriend? Girlfriend? Anyfriend?"

"No," Calla said, her stomach suddenly falling fifty feet. *Marco . . .* "No, nah, I'm like, cool and whatever. Just focusing on my *studies*."

The conversation kept going, with Calla pretending she was listening, and she was, a little. They asked how John was doing and he, often a man of few words, grunted that things were good. They had to pry the info out of him that he had done the plantings this year for his new orchard, an heirloom orchard of indigenous apples. The night went on and they ate themselves sick and eventually Emily said goodbye and headed back to Philly, and John said goodbye and went back home to Bethlehem, and Joanie asked Calla if she was all right, and she said she was.

She didn't tell Joanie her grades weren't too good, and she especially wouldn't tell her why: that when it came time to do an inventory of the nightmare that was the orchard, they never found a body in the cellar. And so she spent nights looking for him. She found a Reddit thread of something that might've been a sighting of him—that, under the Harrow Crossing Bridge not far from Frenchtown. A blurry photo looked like him. So she went, but found no sign, so she kept looking, night after night, driving around with Esther and Lucas. And one night she thought she saw him—eyes reflecting red in the trees as her spotlight found a Marco-shaped thing. She could've sworn some of his skin, his human skin, had returned. And that in his mouth were white teeth, not those black oily rows of appleseed. But then he was gone, hurrying away like a startled deer.

She hoped she could find him again. She thought about telling the others. About him. About the nightmares that kept her from sleep— nightmares of her father as a tree, looming over her, red fruits bursting on his branches and raining blood upon her. His face looming from a crack in that tree, worms slowly circumnavigating the bullet hole in the center of his forehead. But she didn't want to do that to them.

These dark seeds were planted in her and her alone. Everyone had their own orchard to tend, she decided. This one was hers.

THE RESTORER OF LOST DIGNITY

IT WAS A CURIOUS THING, SUCCESS. ON THE ONE HAND, SUCCESS was success was success. You did it. Good job! Bully for you, applause! Parade! Cake for everyone! But on the other hand, success was never truly totally a success all the way, was it? Never quite 100 percent. It always fell short of perfection, which was exactly the point, and so Edward Naberius, the demon, felt hoisted by his own petard.

Because it was this *falling short of perfection* thing he always used against others, counting on their imperfections and failures to worm his way into people's lives. He so often found success not with people who had truly lost everything, but who *thought* they had—who felt aggrieved by what they lost or by what they deserved but did not have. *You're so close, it's undignified not to go all the way,* he'd explain, grinning like the fox with chicken feathers still in his mouth. But now here he was, feeling the exact same way.

He'd almost had it. They spoke about the massacre at the orchard as if it were Jonestown, as if it were the Koresh compound, or NXIVM, or some QAnon thing—a cult grown and destroyed by itself. A charismatic leader. His sacred orchard. His precious acolytes self-harming and self-destructing both at the farm and along the river. A daughter imprisoned. A crusade of vengeance against those who wronged him. It made all the news. The internet was all over it. There were rumors of a Netflix documentary, if only those foolish survivors would relinquish the rights to their story (and so far, they would not). It was a grisly mess, all of it, good for them. It made an excellent true-crime story, what with the girl killing her father, the rehabbed cultists, and the *whiff* of the supernatural—apple trees cracked in half, bodies that seemed mutilated in some way, plus all the creepy stuff out of history. You had good characters, too: the woman who rented sex houses, the apple-hunting man, the high school influencer, the sparky lesbian. Alas.

Though he wanted the story told, it didn't matter much to him. Chaos unfolded. Blood was shed. A nightmare had darkened this county and it had a long, long shadow. That was his job, was it not? To sow the seeds of madness and horror in the guise of offering a hand to those who felt aggrieved? To those whose lost dignity left a ragged hole yearning to be filled?

But still.

Still.

He'd gotten so close to the real prize.

If this had just been allowed to go further . . .

Yes, yes, of course, it never did, and maybe it wasn't meant to. But he just wanted that 100 percent. He wanted the gold star, he wanted that sweet perfection. He wanted *completion.* He wanted a fire that didn't burn just the forest but all the world. If that apple orchard had grown and grown and grown . . . if the apples had found their way into stores . . . if more trees could be grafted . . . he just needed to find another Dan Paxson.

So, he bought the property. The orchard, the farmhouse. No one else would touch it—not anyone with real money. That suited him fine.

It took him a long time to scour the property, to find what he needed.

But find it, he did.

Thanks to an orange tabby cat.

The cat would not leave him alone. Rubbing up against him. Hissing. Purring. Scratching and biting and then seeking to be petted. (As cats did.) It knew what he was, he wagered. Cats were good at understanding things. At *seeing* things as they really were.

Finally, he acquiesced. He told the cat plainly as he followed it down into the cellar, "I could kill you. I could kill you with a touch. Sometimes I have to release what's in me. I have to pay that price." Staying here in this place, this place of *humans,* was hard. It cost him. Well. It cost *them,* really. But the cat, he decided, would remain. As the last guardian.

It was down in the cellar he found what he was looking for. It waited in a little bundle of ratty cloth, like a baby blanket—probably belonged to that girl, the lily girl. It wasn't much, it just looked like a long, crooked finger. A demon's finger. Which, in a way, it was. At some point, Dan Paxson must've clipped a bit of scionwood from one of his own trees.

Thinking to graft another somewhere. But perhaps once the orchard took off, he forgot about it. He didn't need it, after all.

But now he was gone.

And so was the orchard.

But this little branch—

This demon's finger—

Remained.

Edward took it.

It throbbed with power. More to the point, with *potential*. He'd gifted the seeds to a man long ago in a garden in Normandy, France. And the seeds grew into a tree, and the man grew into Vinot, and Vinot grew into Henry Hart Golden—all failures, too, in their way. All imperfect, all incomplete. But they were roots, pushed deep, growing out like shoots and runners, and from them came Dan Paxson. Gone, now. But the roots pushed a little bit deeper.

Naberius turned the branch over and over in his hand. It was like a little magic wand. He flourished it in the air, a childish act of pretend. It felt nice.

But this wand had a different kind of magic, he knew.

He just had to find someone who would graft it.

To a tree.

Or to themselves.

He could begin it again. He could restore their lost dignity.

And with that act, maybe this time, he could end the world.

ACKNOWLEDGMENTS,
OR HOW I ATE THE APPLE

———

STORIES ARE FUCKING WEIRD.

And the writers who write them are fucking weird.

It's all weird.

Let's rewind and talk about ideas.

IDEAS ARE MOSTLY BULLSHIT. WHICH IS TO SAY, WRITERS IDOLIZE ideas unnecessarily. We treat them like precious gems, but ideas are costume jewelry: It's all in how you wear them. We doubly expect that our ideas must be original, that the stories we tell around those ideas must also in turn be original, and we further idolize originality and, ultimately, originality is bullshit, too. Stories are stories are stories, told again and again throughout time, the bones of them the same even when their shape looks different.

What *are* original, however, are the authors themselves. Not to lean too hard on the whole *writers are special snowflakes* thing, but we are, in a way, special snowflakes. (Sometimes prone to melting.) Each of us has no repeat. We are a unique culmination of our anxieties, our fears, our experiences, our traumas, our joys, and of course, our obsessions. And it is the combination of those things, and how we apply them to stories, that is ostensibly timeless—*that's* the narrative alchemy that matters. But that only matters if we let it.

This book is me letting that matter, for better or for worse.

FIRST THING IS THIS:

In my couch I found a note.

The couch is orange. It's in my shed, and, yes, I write in a shed. (Writers' sheds are awesome.) When I moved this orange couch into my shed, it puked up a little slip of paper written in handwriting that is decidedly not my own.

This paper said:

> *ADRAMELECH*
>   *MEPHISTOPHELES*
> *BAPHOMET*
>   *!*

I did not write this.

I do not know who wrote this.

My couch is not a previously owned couch. It was new when I bought it. I had it for a couple years before I ever found this note.

Nobody ever really sits on my couch except me, because nobody ever really visits my writer's shed.

And yet, somehow, the couch contained that note, which had that list of three demons on it, and the letters *M* and *E* underlined in each.

ME. As in, me.

Well, that's fucking weird, I thought. So I pinned it on my corkboard.

(Where it remains to this day.)

SECOND THING:

I once didn't care much for apples.

Apples, generally speaking, were not very good, I thought. I mean, they were *fine.* That word, *fine,* said with an aggressive wince. I did not pursue them. I did not buy them. They were hard-skinned, bitter-on-the-outside, too-sweet-on-the-inside shiny red baseballs. Good for throwing. Less so for eating. My only interest in apples was their usage in the form of *pie.* Apple pie is one of the ten foods given to us by the gods (included in this non-exhaustive list: tacos, Pop-Tarts, gin and tonics). But apples themselves? Ennh.

Fast-forward to my adult years, where we discover, unsurprisingly, that I am the kind of person who goes to farmers markets. I fucking love farmers markets. Gimme those grass-fed meats, those duck eggs, those goat soaps.

Came a point when our farmers market of choice was the Emmaus Farmers' Market (shout-out to a favorite bookstore, Let's Play Books, which is in town there), and in the middle of our first summer attending, a new vendor showed up: North Star Orchard.

And I thought, *Well, it can't hurt to look. Apples, meh, whatever, but maybe I'll try one.*

I walked over there, and looked at the bounty of bins, each heaped with apples of every color, shape, and texture.

I read the names of these apples.

I did not recognize a single one of them.

They sounded like they had crawled out of a fantasy novel. *Limbertwig.* (A hobbit, obviously.) *Lord Lambourne.* (Vampire, for sure.) *Husk Spice.* (Magical reagent, obvs.) *Red Berlepsch.* (Obviously the stage name of a goblin doing a stand-up act—*And now, the comedy stylings of Red Berlepsch!*) *Ashmead's Kernel, Tompkins King, Cob's Quince, Razor Russet,* all of which I'm sure I read about in a George R. R. Martin novel. Didn't Cob's Quince get killed in the dragon brothel by Razzor Russet during the funeral of King Tompkins?

So, I knew I was being punked. None of these were real apples. This was bullshit.

Just to make sure, I bought a bunch and brought them home, and figured, okay, let's try these out. Here I thought I knew what apples tasted like. They were apples. They tasted like *apples.* Same way oranges taste like oranges. The thing defines the thing.

I was wildly incorrect.

I ate all of those apples.

(Head's up: Apples contain a lot of fiber, do not eat a shitload of them in one go. Because *shitload* becomes literal, not metaphorical.)

In those apples I tasted a panoply of flavors I'd never before tasted in an apple, or, really, in any other fruit. I tasted spices you'd normally add to applesauce or pie, somehow present in the flesh itself: cinnamon, ginger, anise. I tasted other fruits: pineapple, banana, kiwi, melon. Sometimes you'd taste rose, or elderflower, or other mysterious floral esters. Some were crunchy, others soft. Some snapped when you broke them, others bent. One would be sweet as bubblegum, another so tart it tasted like licking a lime dipped in battery acid. A juicy apple might give way to an apple that seemed like it vacuumed the moisture from your mouth.

It was wild.

And I thought, *Wow, we really fucked up apples, didn't we?* The apples I'd just eaten were forgotten apples. We'd lost the best and kept the most mediocre. We all know that the Red Delicious is neither red nor delicious. It's purple and bitter: a liar apple, a Judas fruit. (Though, confession: It's not as bad as you think. There are far worse apples on grocery store shelves.) It's similar to eating an heirloom tomato: The flavors present are so much better, brighter, more interesting than what you buy at the local grocery store. Except with apples, the deviation swings wider. While we find maybe, *maybe* a dozen varieties on our store shelves, there are literally thousands of apple varieties you won't ever find unless you land at an orchard growing them.

Apples as they are to us in the grocery store represent a monoculture—apples grown for hardiness and, generally speaking, their sugar, but there is such wild diversity in deviation across all the fruits that it saddened me that most people will never know that, never experience those apples, never have that weird moment of tasting something they've never tasted before (and may never taste again).

You dive a little deeper, too, and you find that there are varieties remembered but lost, discovered in old journals or talked about around town—and there are people out there, like OG apple hunter Tom Brown, who do their best to find rare trees of these apples in order to rescue them from obscurity by grafting. Then you read about Johnny Appleseed and how he was a Swedenborgian who believed grafting was against God's plan. Or how, as in the book, colonists brought apples to America, giving the fruit to the Indigenous Americans only to ultimately kill their orchards in order to run them off their land so they could steal it. Or how the apple itself may originate in Kazakhstan? Look to folklore or mythology and you find the apple of Eris, the apple of Eden, or the old wassailing songs.

Needless to say, I got real interested in apples.

Obsessed, even.

WHY AM I TELLING YOU THIS?

Because I think there's not much point to writing and telling stories if you're not going to just be the weird that you are. We are weird. Stories are weird. We shouldn't resist that. The things that made this a story I want to tell were my obsession with apples and that weird little note about demons I found in my couch, the one that maybe indicates the thing that binds these demons together is . . . the self? Selfishness? I don't know.

I think it's very easy to fall into a trap where we avoid our own voices, our own obsessions, our own anxieties and wonders, in the hopes of finding something more universal. But the reality is, our own weirdnesses may not be universal, but they are, at the same time, something someone else can understand. Storytelling is a cry in the dark. We just want someone else to hear us. We each have jagged edges cut out of us, and we hope that others have complementary cuts taken out of them, so that we'll fit together like puzzle pieces. Authors want to fit with their readers, too, and while it might be tempting to try to file down as many of our edges as possible in order to fit with more readers more easily, that's also what makes stories boring. Boring to readers, but boring for us to tell, too.

Point is, this story is a culmination of all that fucking weirdness inside of me. It's apples and demons and the area in which I live here in Pennsylvania, and it's some of who I was growing up and some of what I saw with my own family and other families. I just went with it. And I hope if you're a writer, you go with the weirdness, too. And if you're only a reader, then I hope you like the weirdness, because it's all here. Glory be.

Of course, I don't get to display my weirdness without a lot of other people. It takes a village to raise an orchard, and this is that village:

Thanks to Lisa and Ike Kerschner of North Star Orchard—Ike calls what he does being part of an "apple cult," which I love so much. (Also, I apologize to both of them for any apple-related information I get wrong.) Their orchard is in Cochranville, PA, and you should go visit them immediately if you can.

Thanks, too, to Scott Farm in Vermont, where I also procure weird, wonderful apples. And, local to me, Manoff Market Gardens & Cidery and Solebury Orchards, too.

Good books to read on the apple subject: *Apples of Uncommon Character,* Rowan Jacobsen; *The Ghost Orchard,* Helen Humphreys; *Apples of North America,* Tom Burford; and of course, *The Illustrated History of Apples in the United States and Canada,* a seven-volume, roughly 3,500-page encyclopedia about apples (!) by Daniel J. Bussey.

Thanks to everybody who lives here in Bucks County and has so far resisted emailing me about all the stuff I got wrong. (Hopefully some of you realize this takes place in a very alternate-universey version of Bucks County.)

Thanks to Basil Wright for the invaluable early read of the book.

Thanks to Margo Price and Jeremy Ivey. If you're not listening to Margo Price's music, who even are you?

Thanks to my editor, Tricia Narwani, and my agent, Stacia Decker. Thanks, too, to Scott Shannon, Bree Gary, Alex Larned, Keith Clayton, Greg Kubie, David Moench, Ashleigh Heaton, and the whole wonderful publishing team at Del Rey.

It's also worth noting that right now, horror is in a particularly excellent place—horrific in the best way. It's really having a moment, and so it's worth noting those horror authors who are currently very inspiring to me: Paul Tremblay, Christopher Golden, Hailey Piper, Eric LaRocca, Cina Pelayo, V. Castro, Alma Katsu, Erika Wurth, Stephen Graham Jones, Gabino Iglesias, Kiersten White, Clay McLeod Chapman, Nat Cassidy, Catriona Ward, and—well, that list goes on and on and on. And also thanks to the authors who are both talented and keep me sane, folks like Kevin Hearne, Delilah Dawson, Aaron Mahnke, Adam Christopher, Lin-Manuel Miranda, Matt Wallace, Erin Morgenstern, Stephen Blackmoore, and—well, that list goes on and on as well. Thanks especially to Sadie Hartmann who, as Mother Horror, really carries the torch for the genre and the writers who write it. It's a huge help.

Thanks to booksellers, librarians, and most of all, the readers.

And finally, thanks to Michelle and B-Dub, who are the reason I do this whole thing, and at the end of the day, are very kind to put up with Daddy as he wanders the dark orchards and black rivers in his mind when he should be, like, cooking dinner.

PHOTO: MICHELLE WENDIG

CHUCK WENDIG is the *New York Times* bestselling author of *Wanderers, The Book of Accidents, Wayward,* and over two dozen other books for adults and young adults. A finalist for the Astounding Award and an alum of the Sundance Screenwriters Lab, he has also written comics, games, and for film and television. He is known for his popular blog, terribleminds, and books about writing such as *Damn Fine Story.* He lives in Bucks County, Pennsylvania, with his family.

terribleminds.com

Instagram: @chuck_wendig

ABOUT THE TYPE

———

This book was set in Requiem, a typeface designed by the Hoefler Type Foundry. It is a modern typeface inspired by inscriptional capitals in Ludovico Vicentino degli Arrighi's 1523 writing manual, *Il modo de temperare le penne*. An original lowercase, a set of figures, and an italic in the chancery style that Arrighi (fl. 1522) helped popularize were created to make this adaptation of a classical design into a complete font family.